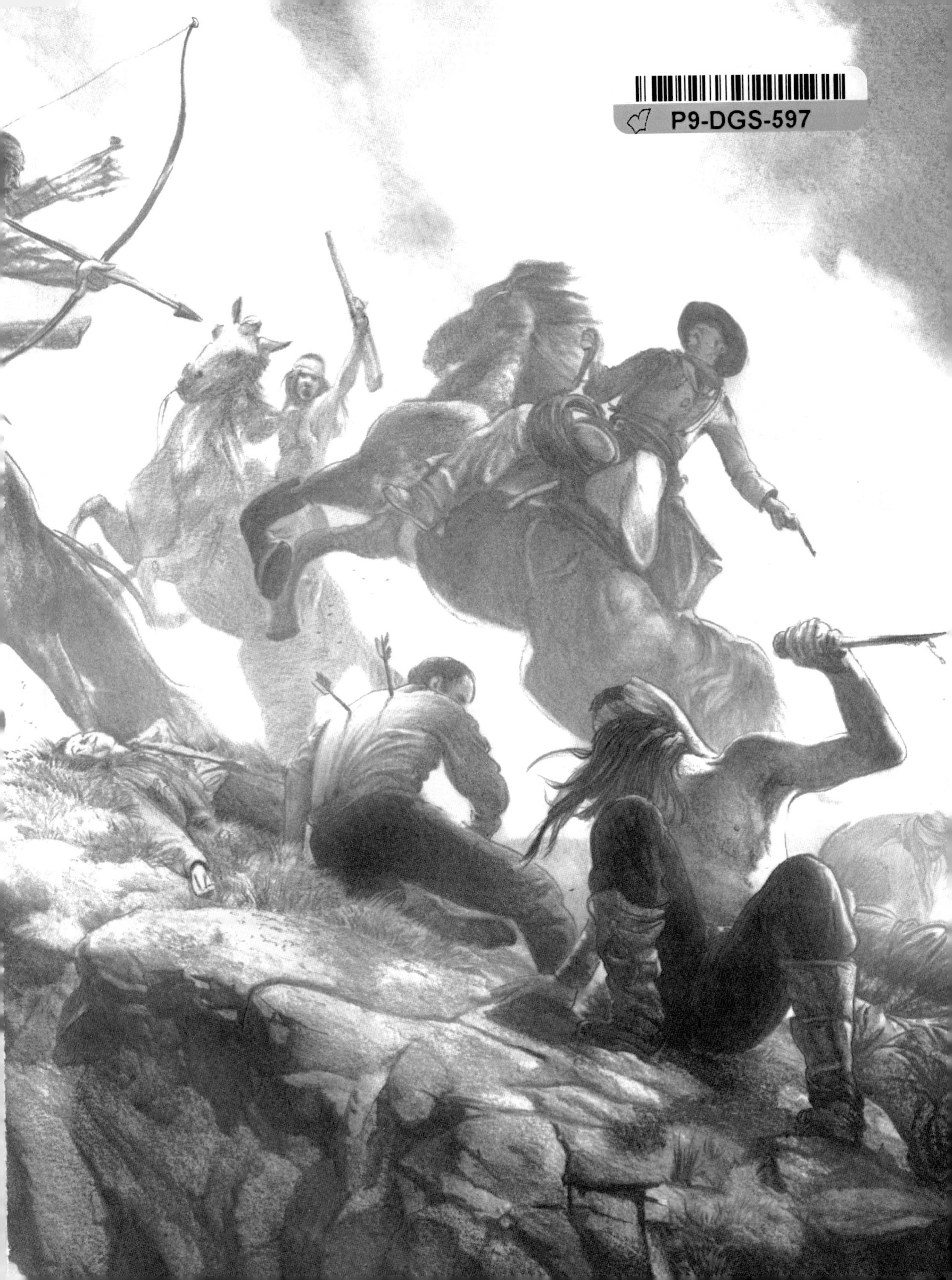

INDEH

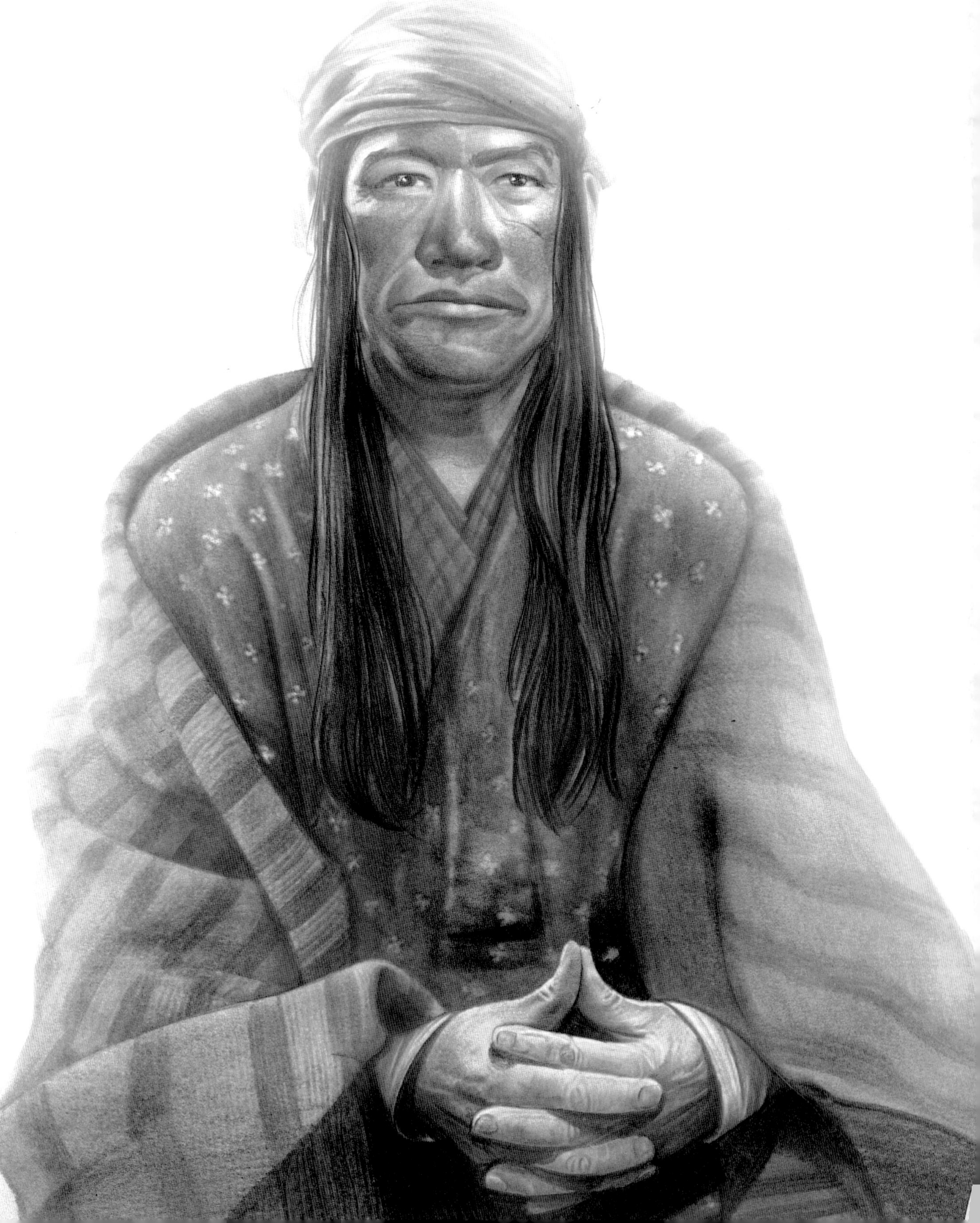

A STORY OF THE APACHE WARS

ETHAN HAWKE
GREG RUTH

GRAND CENTRAL
PUBLISHING

NEW YORK   BOSTON

This book is a work of historical fiction. Certain real locations, public figures, and general historical events have been included in the book. However, the authors have taken literary license, and all other characters, dialogue, and events described are totally imaginary. Any resemblance of such non-historical persons or events to actual ones is purely coincidental.

Cover design and art by Greg Ruth

Grand Central Publishing
Hachette Book Group
1290 Avenue of the Americas
New York, NY 10104
grandcentralpublishing.com
twitter.com/grandcentralpub

First Edition: June 2016

Grand Central Publishing is a division of Hachette Book Group, Inc.
The Grand Central Publishing name and logo is a trademark of Hachette Book Group, Inc.

The publisher is not responsible for websites (or their content) that are not owned by the publisher.

Excerpt from *Neither Wolf nor Dog: On Forgotten Roads with an Indian Elder* by Kent Nerburn. Published by New World Library, Novato, California.

Library of Congress Control Number: 2015960375

ISBNs: 978-1-4013-1099-8 (hardcover), 978-1-4555-6410-1 (ebook), 978-1-4555-4178-2 (signed ed.), 978-1-4555-4177-5 (Barnes & Noble signed ed.)

Printed in the United States of America

WOR

10 9 8 7 6 5 4 3 2 1

AN APACHE FOREWORD

Apache culture is very complex. It is a deep blend of belief, ceremony, insight, survival strategy, and social mores that benefit the whole tribe continuously.

For decades American popular culture has attempted to speak for us (Apache) via films, books, and television. Often these stories converge on a road to stereotype, tragedy, pity, savagery, or exploitation. In this book, researched and created by Ethan Hawke and Greg Ruth, the story of the Chiricahua Apache fighting for independence is told again, but from a rare Apache point of view, making this book unique in its creation and purpose.

From the murder of Geronimo's family to the capture of Cochise under truce to the beheading of Mangas Coloradas for sport and "science," *Indeh* pulls no punches, providing readers with an honest account of the desperate and bloody history experienced by the Apache from the 1860s until the surrender of Geronimo.

Indeh comes to life in the fluid brushstrokes that capture the immediacy of the Apache plight, painting a vivid portrait of a people upended and forced to be bold, driven, and wholly at war, yet still remaining very human.

What motivates people to battle the most technically advanced and powerful nation in the world? People assume it is savage violence for its own sake, as so many Hollywood films have interpreted it. Popular culture would have you believe our own innate tribal nobility prompted us on paths to violence. In reality, any time a culture around the world has its way of life threatened, it has fought fiercely to preserve it.

Apache tribes and bands were no different. Apache people were not senseless marauders nor rambling nomads, as anthropology would have us believe, but a people pushed to the brink of violence time and time again due to greed, deception, and the cold blatant racism of the times. *Indeh* provides a rare sympathetic look into the harsh circumstances the Apache people faced during a tumultuous era. What Ethan and Greg have done here is present this to us all in a new and unique way in hopes of bringing a broader understanding of those times, and our own today.

Today xenophobia is at an all-time high. I hope this true story of the Apache Wars serves not only to educate and bring understanding of diverse cultures and human rights, but also to bring about a greater sense of the historical responsibility we all must face for the decisions we make, now and into the future.

Douglas Miles

www.apacheskateboards.com

Douglas Miles Sr. lives and works on the San Carlos Apache Nation. His father, David Miles, was born on the White Mountain Apache Nation and his mother was born on the San Carlos Apache Nation in Arizona. In addition to creating Apache Skateboards, the premier Native-owned skateboard company, Douglas has cast a spotlight on the Apache ethos as a painter, filmmaker, and public speaker, sharing his experiences as a Native artist in America. He's also a fine artist, muralist, filmmaker, and public speaker, and manages the Apache Skate Team.

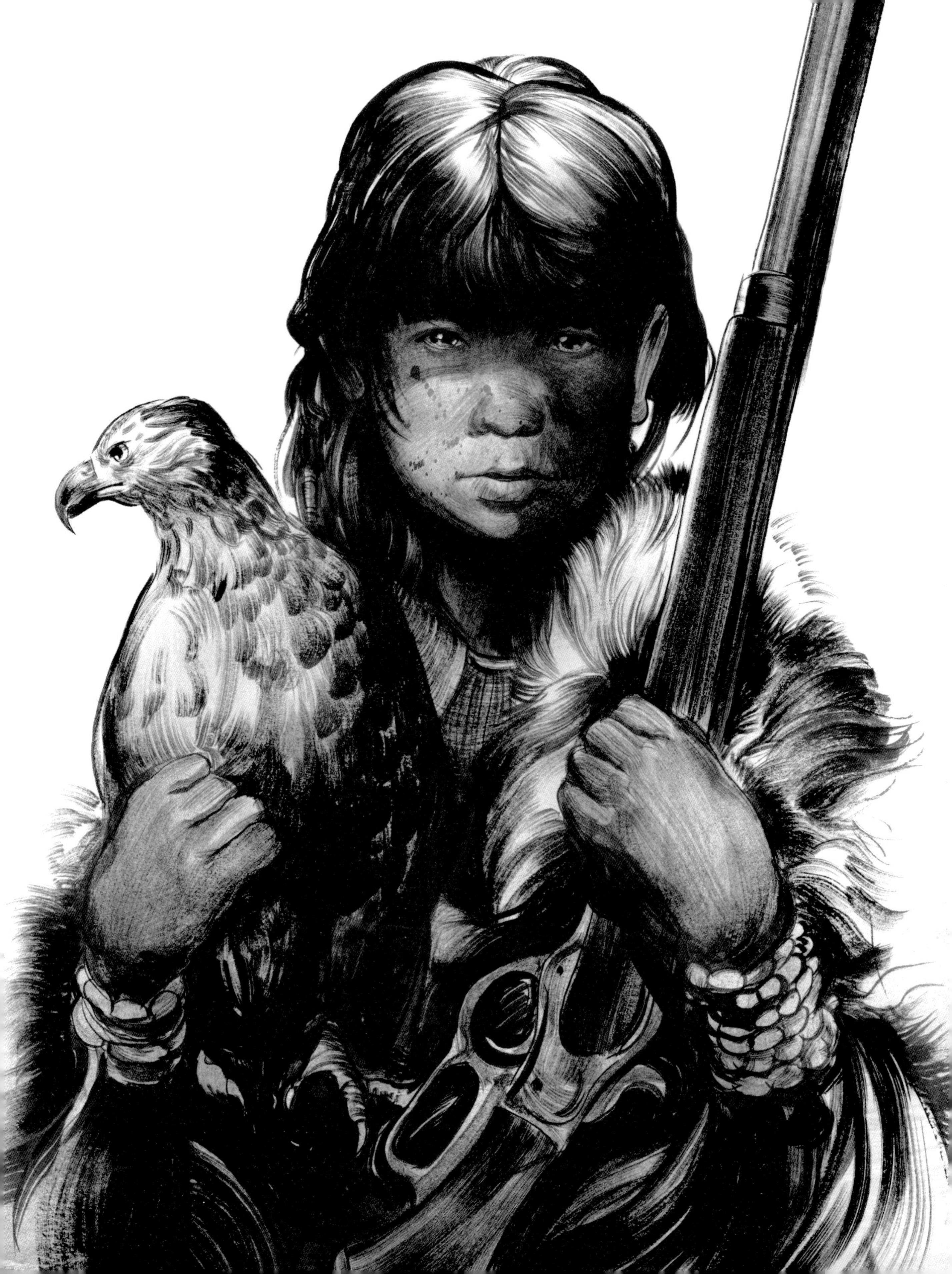

· PART ONE ·
A BLESSING AND A CURSE

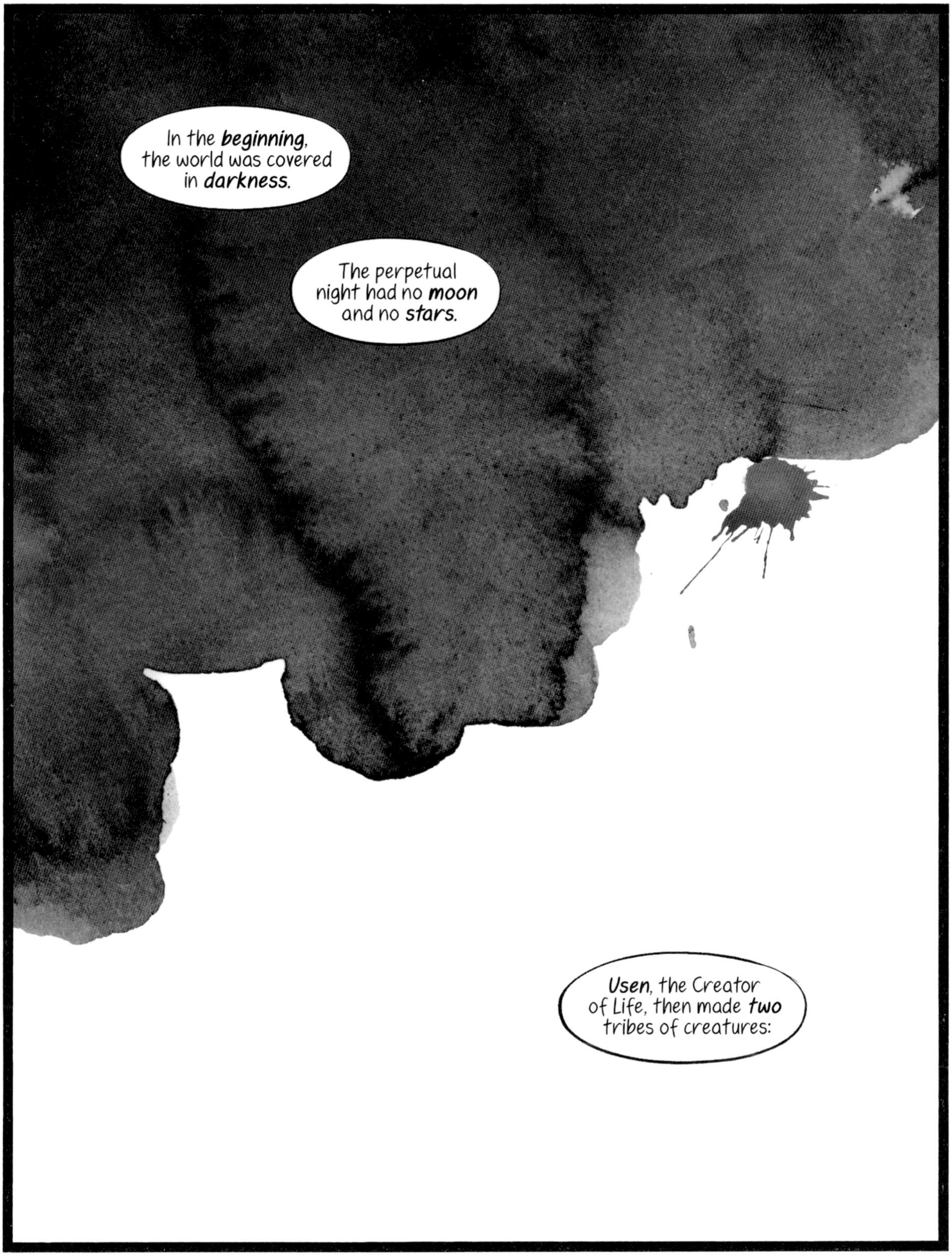
In the **beginning**, the world was covered in **darkness**.
The perpetual night had no **moon** and no **stars**.
Usen, the Creator of Life, then made **two** tribes of creatures:

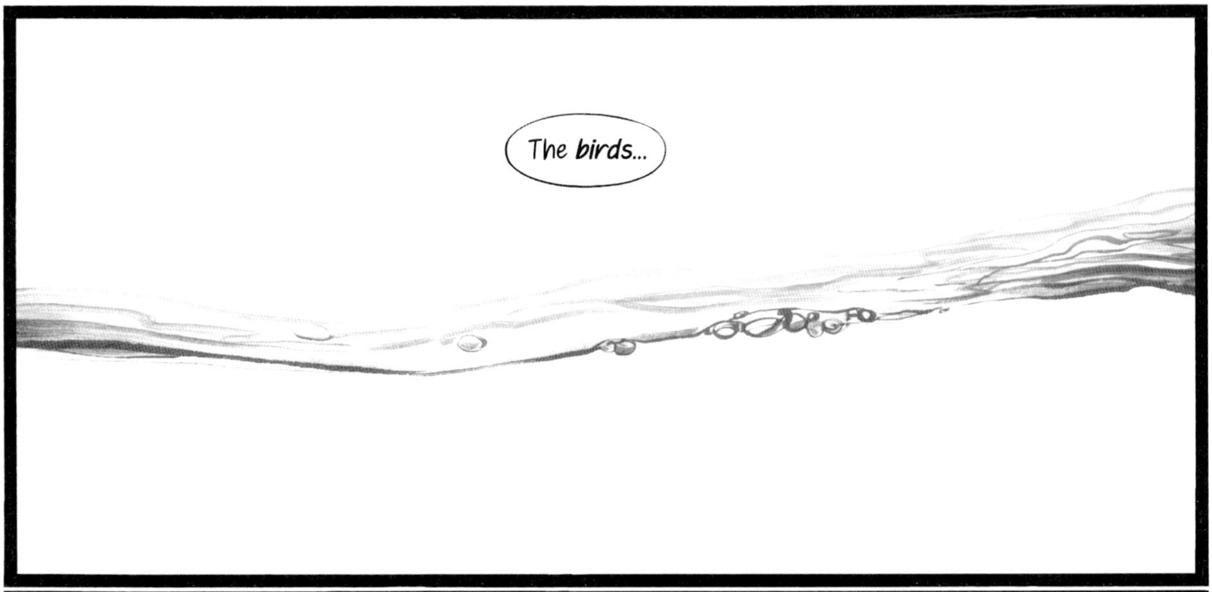
The *birds*...

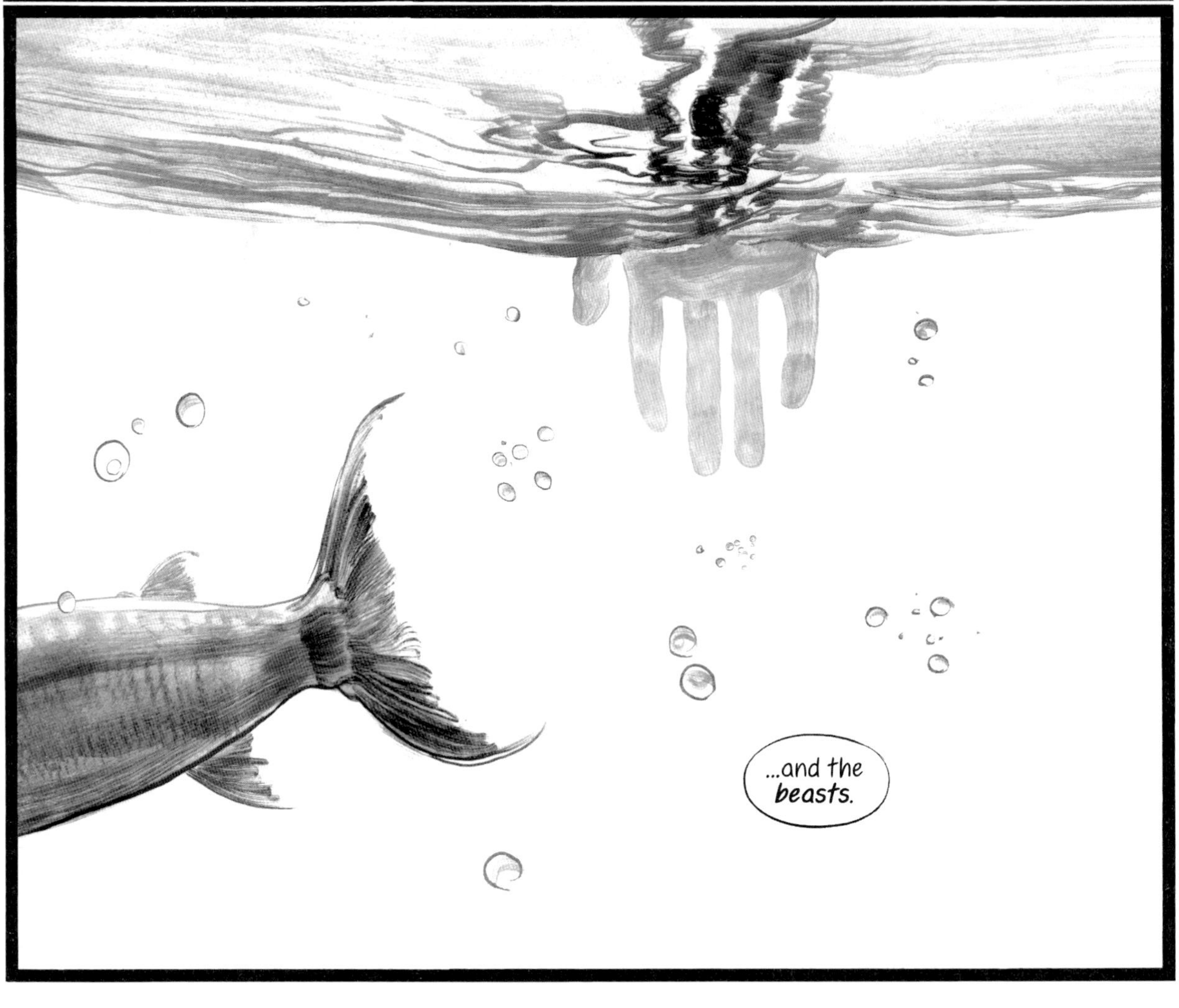
...and the *beasts*.

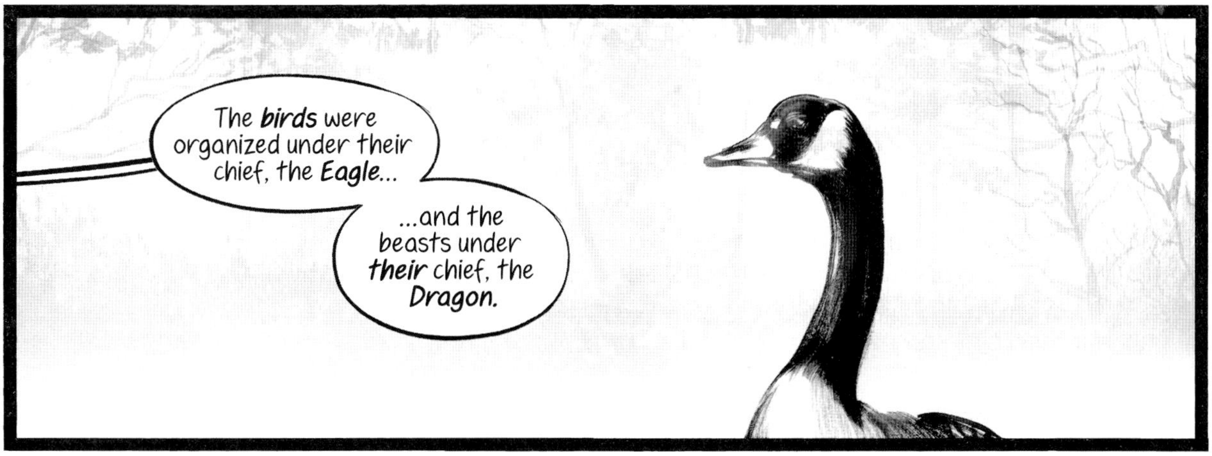
The *birds* were organized under their chief, the *Eagle*...
...and the beasts under *their* chief, the *Dragon.*

COCHISE IN OJO CALIENTE • SPRING

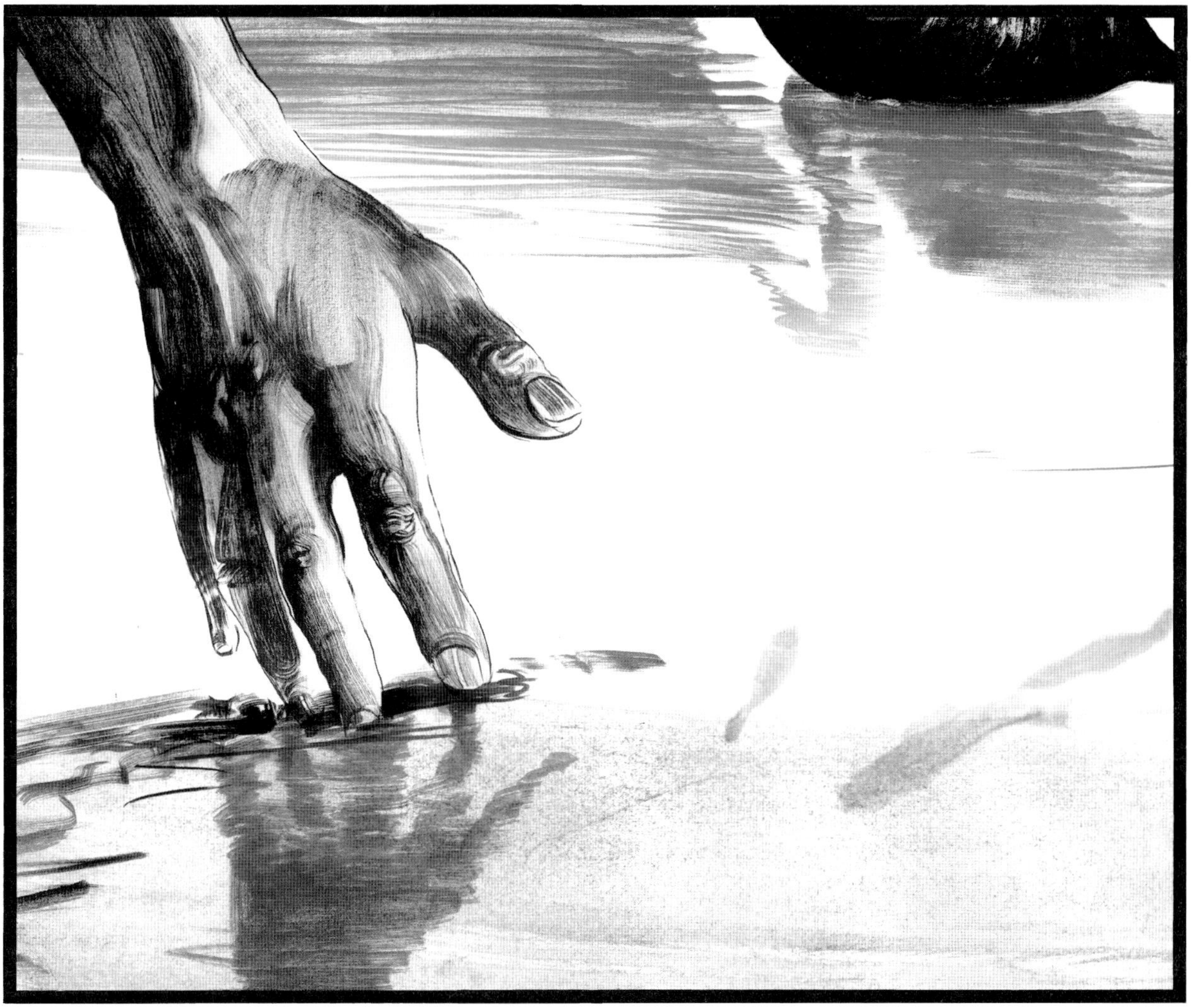

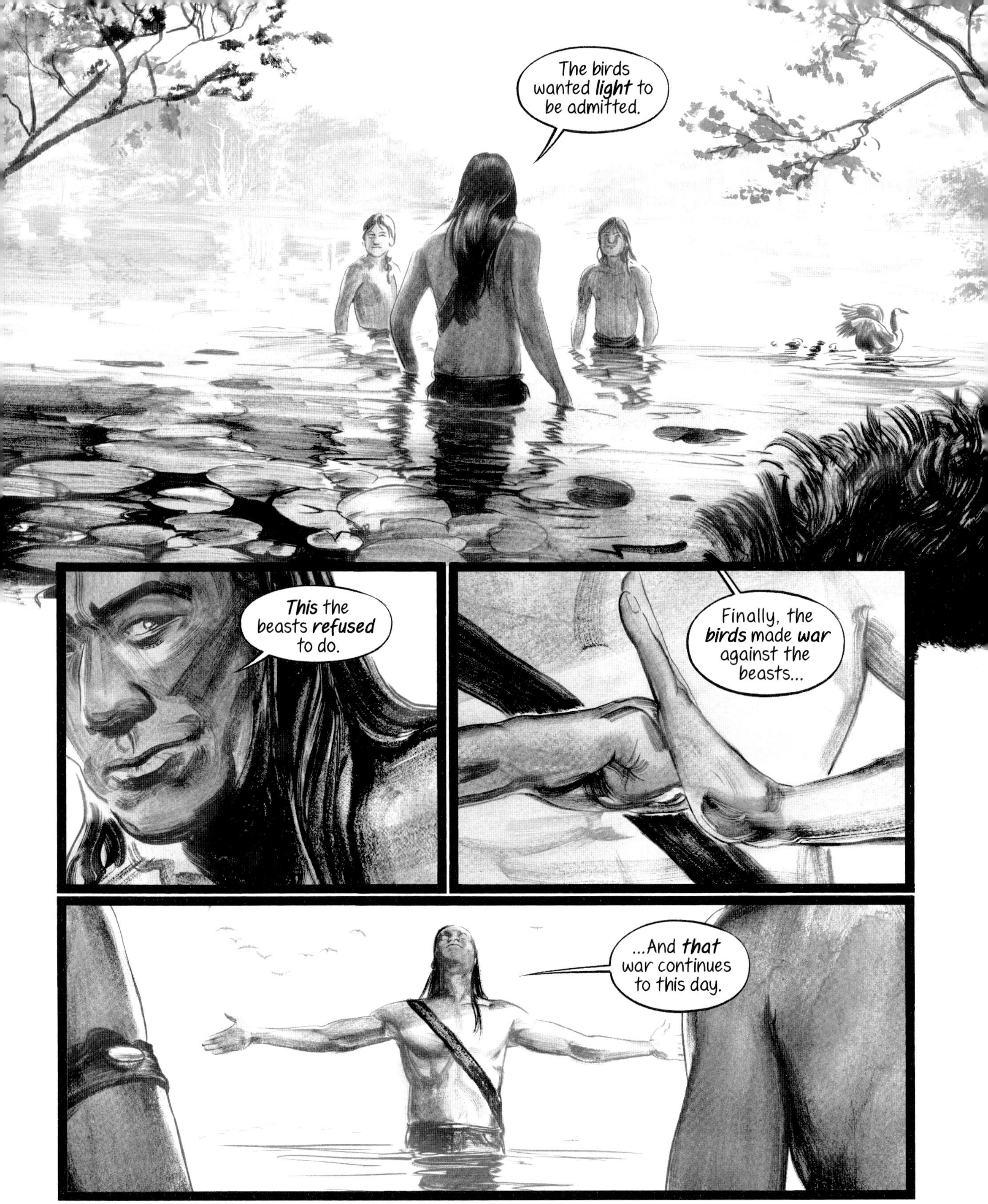
The birds wanted **light** to be admitted.
This the beasts ***refused*** to do.
Finally, the ***birds*** made ***war*** against the beasts...
...And ***that*** war continues to this day.

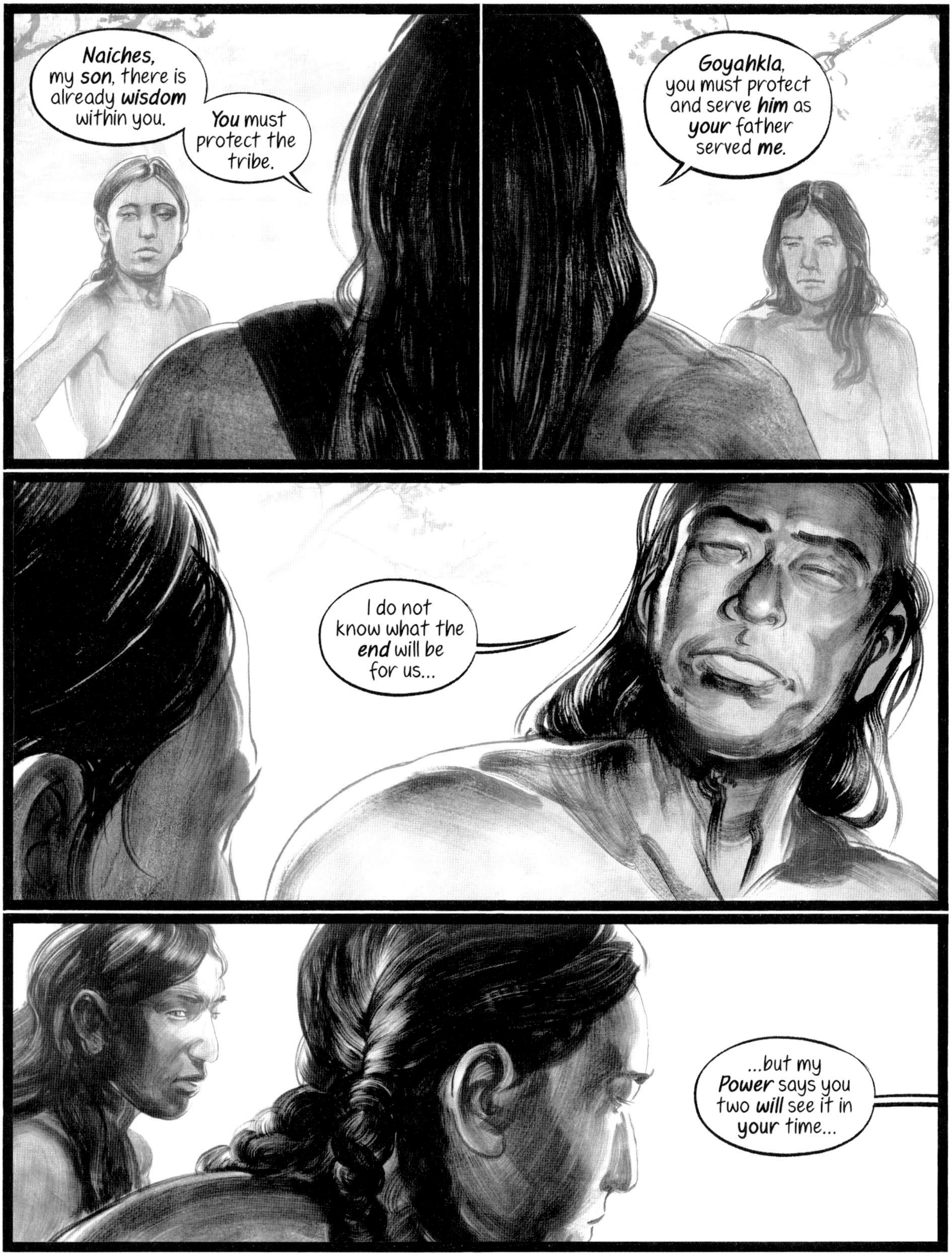
Naiches, my son, there is already wisdom within you.
You must protect the tribe.
Goyahkla, you must protect and serve him as your father served me.
I do not know what the end will be for us...
...but my Power says you two will see it in your time...

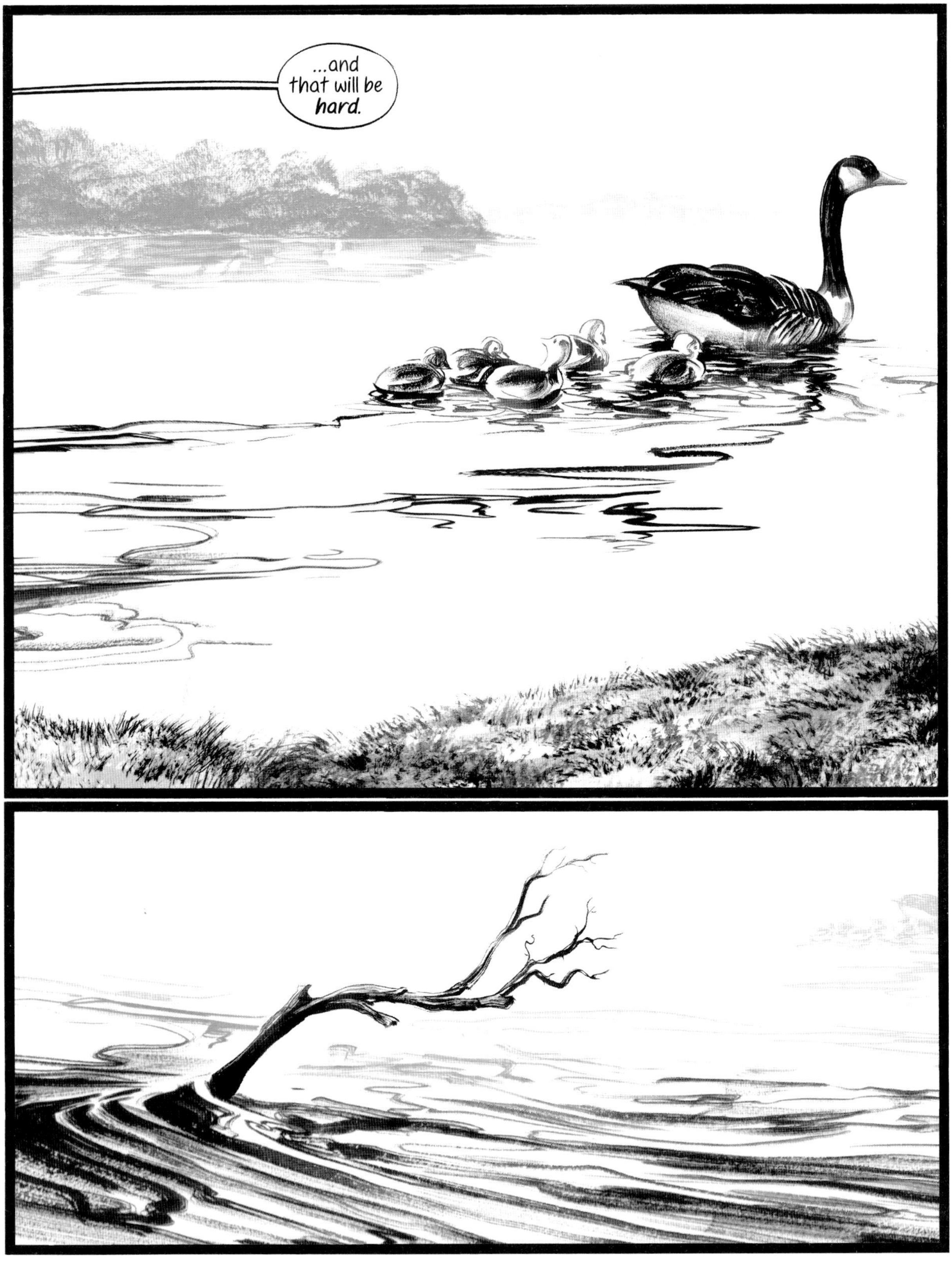
...and
that will be
hard.

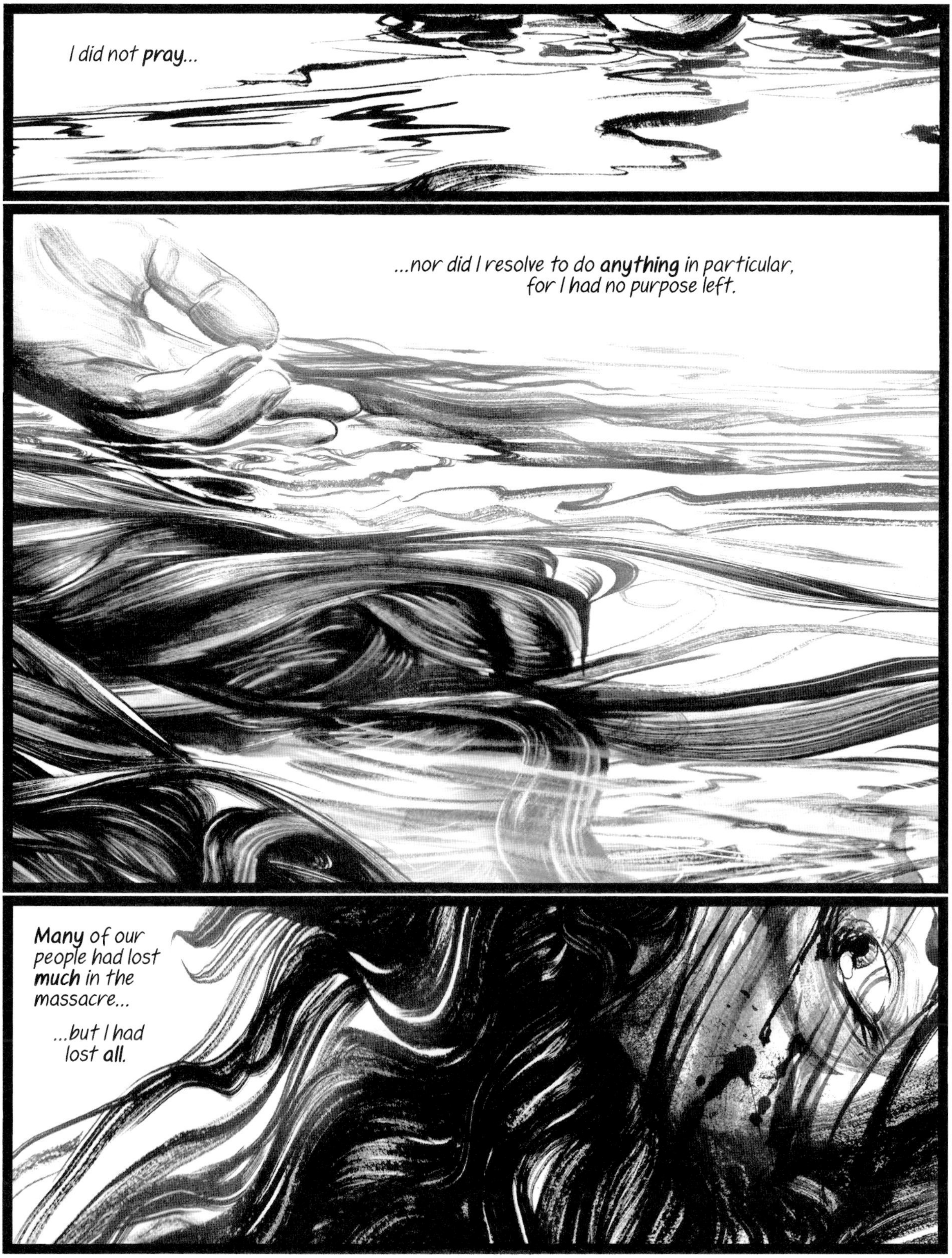
I did not pray...
...nor did I resolve to do anything in particular, for I had no purpose left.
Many of our people had lost much in the massacre...
...but I had lost all.

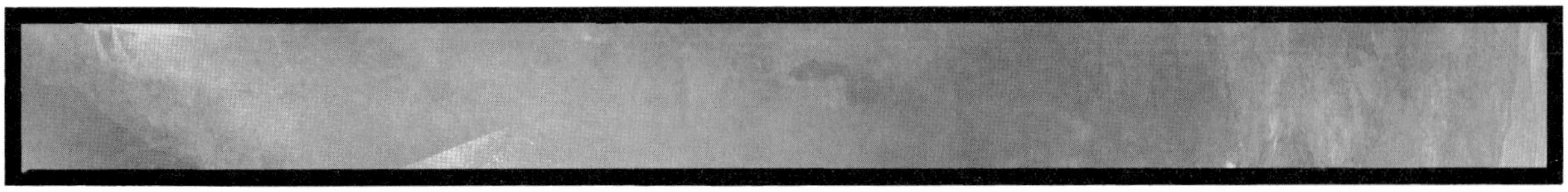

SEVENTEEN YEARS LATER • MEXICO

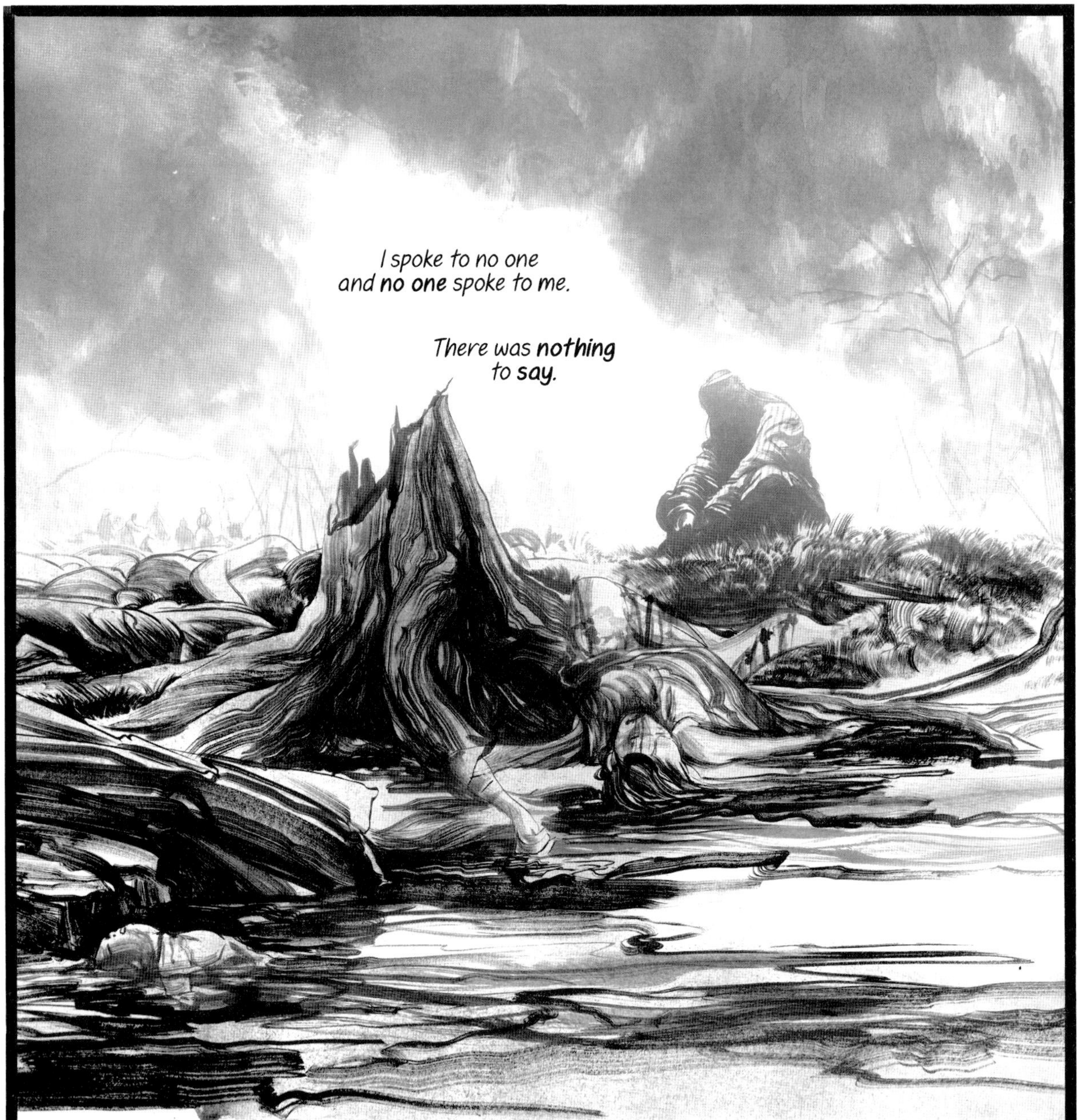
I spoke to no one
and **no one** spoke to me.
There was **nothing**
to **say.**

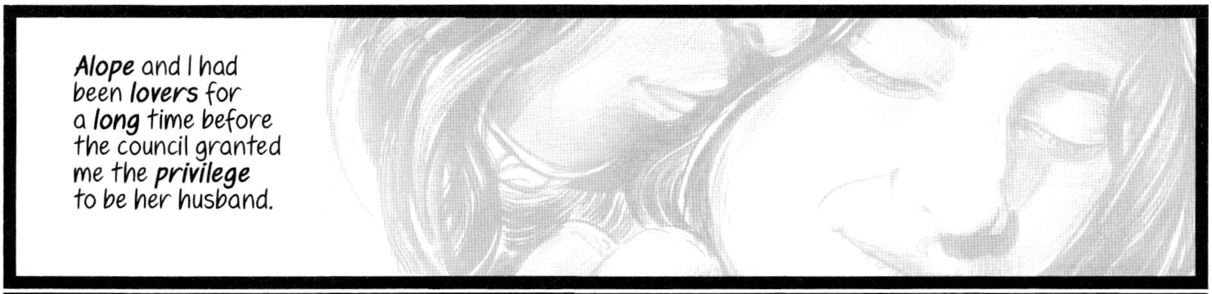
Alope and I had been lovers for a long time before the council granted me the privilege to be her husband.

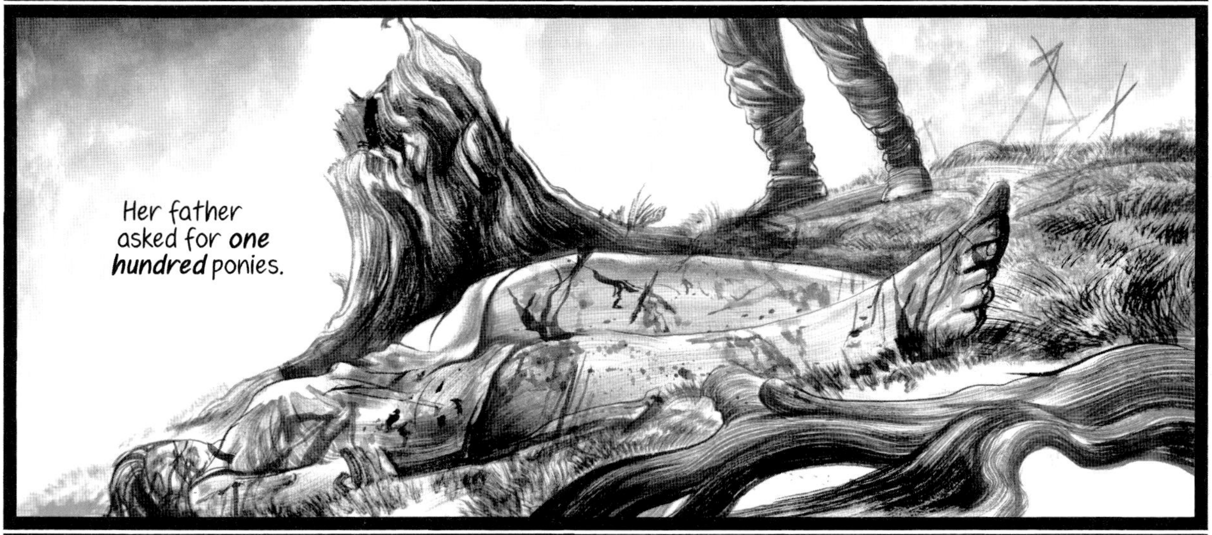
Her father asked for one hundred ponies.

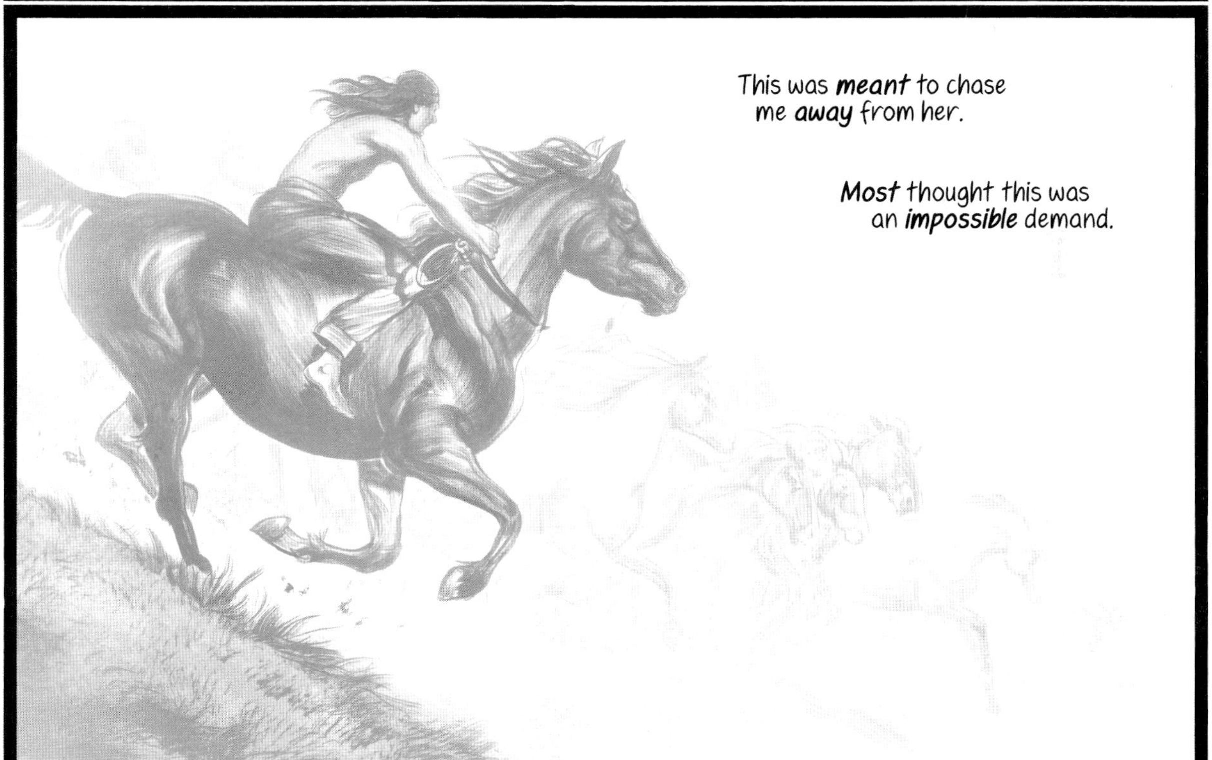
This was meant to chase me away from her.
Most thought this was an impossible demand.

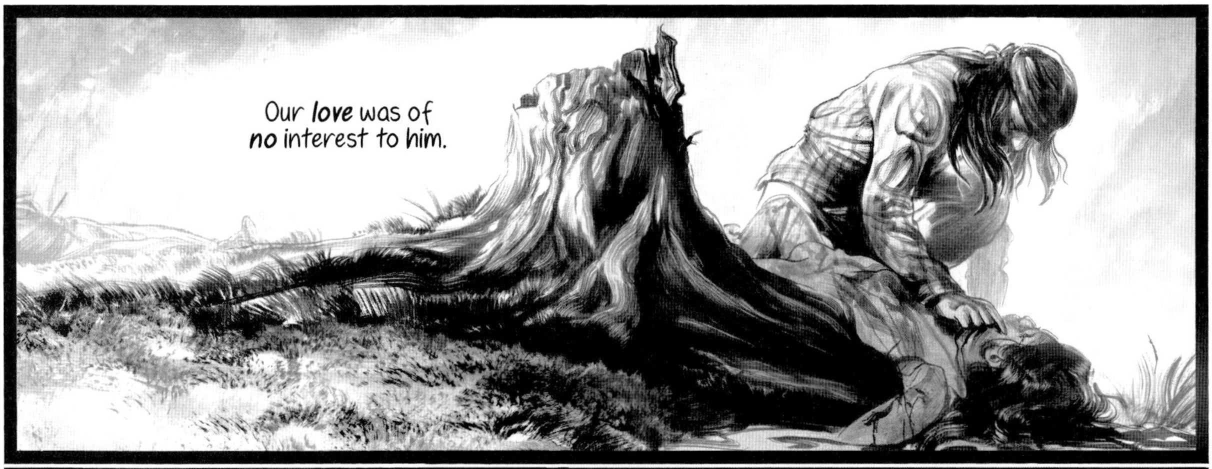
Our love was of no interest to him.

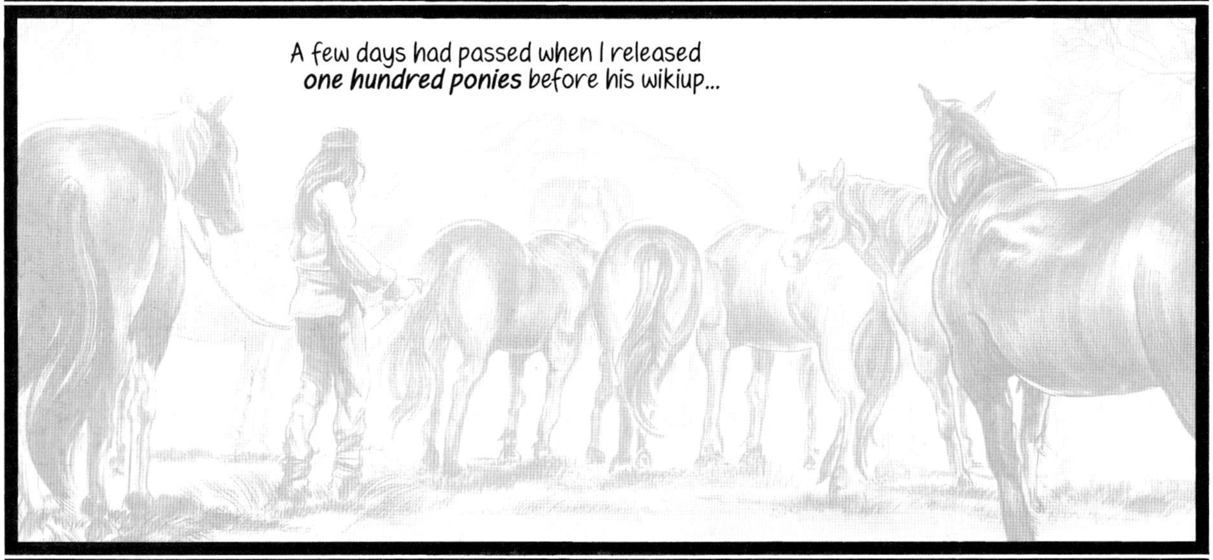
A few days had passed when I released one hundred ponies before his wikiup...

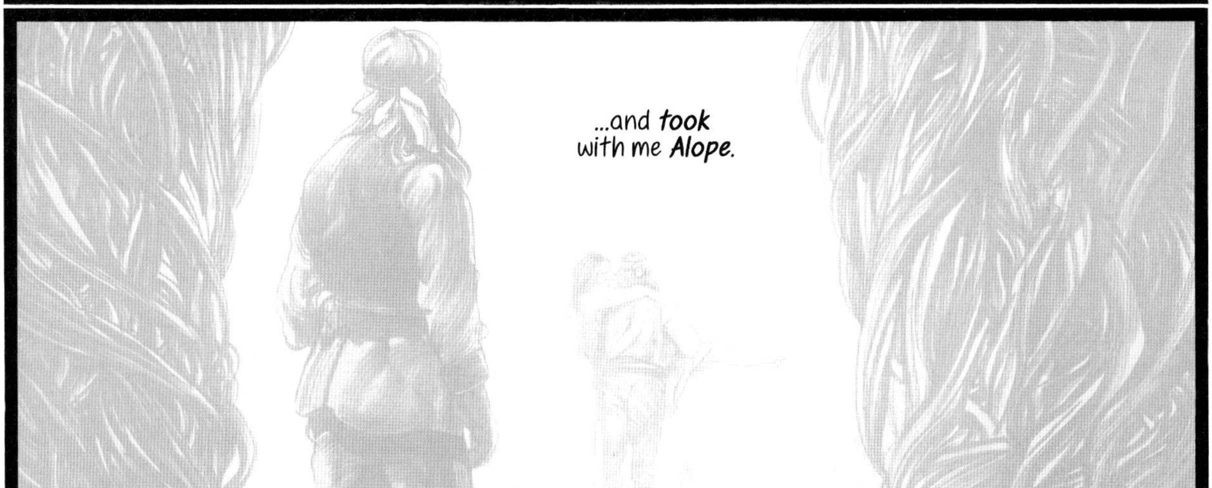
...and took with me Alope.

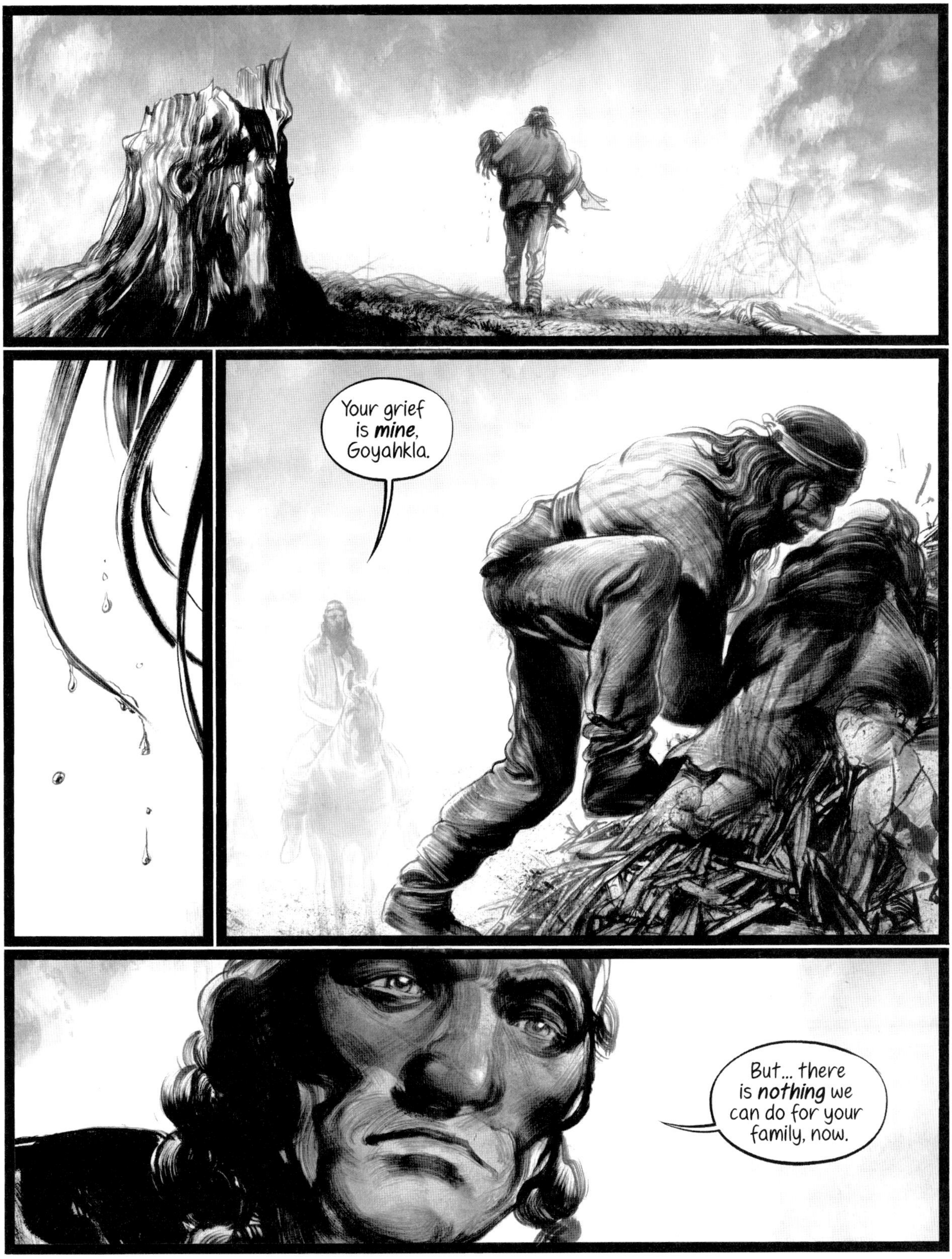
Your grief is **mine**, Goyahkla.
But... there is **nothing** we can do for your family, now.

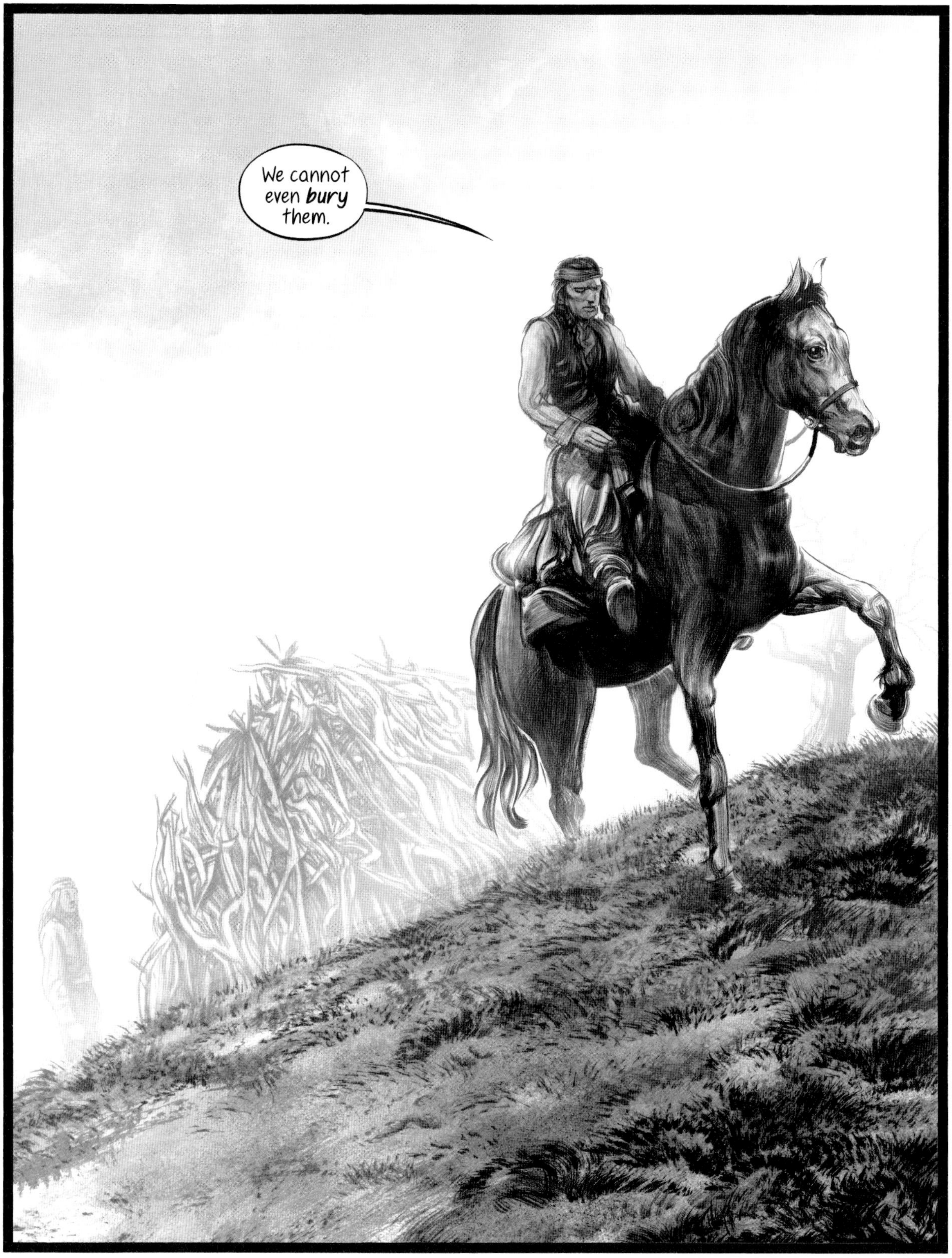
We cannot even **bury** them.

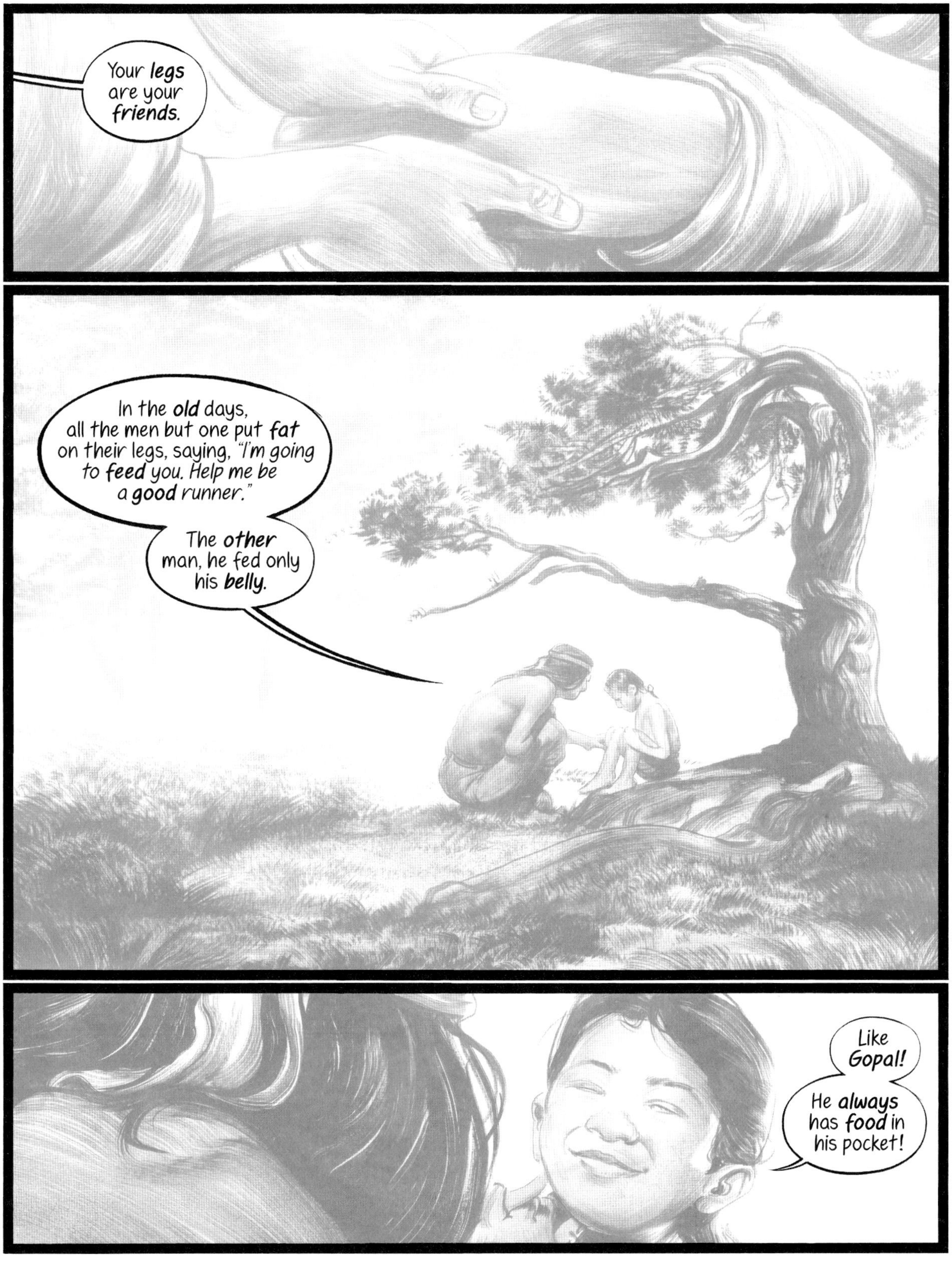
Your legs are your friends.
In the old days, all the men but one put fat on their legs, saying, "I'm going to feed you. Help me be a good runner."
The other man, he fed only his belly.
Like Gopal!
He always has food in his pocket!

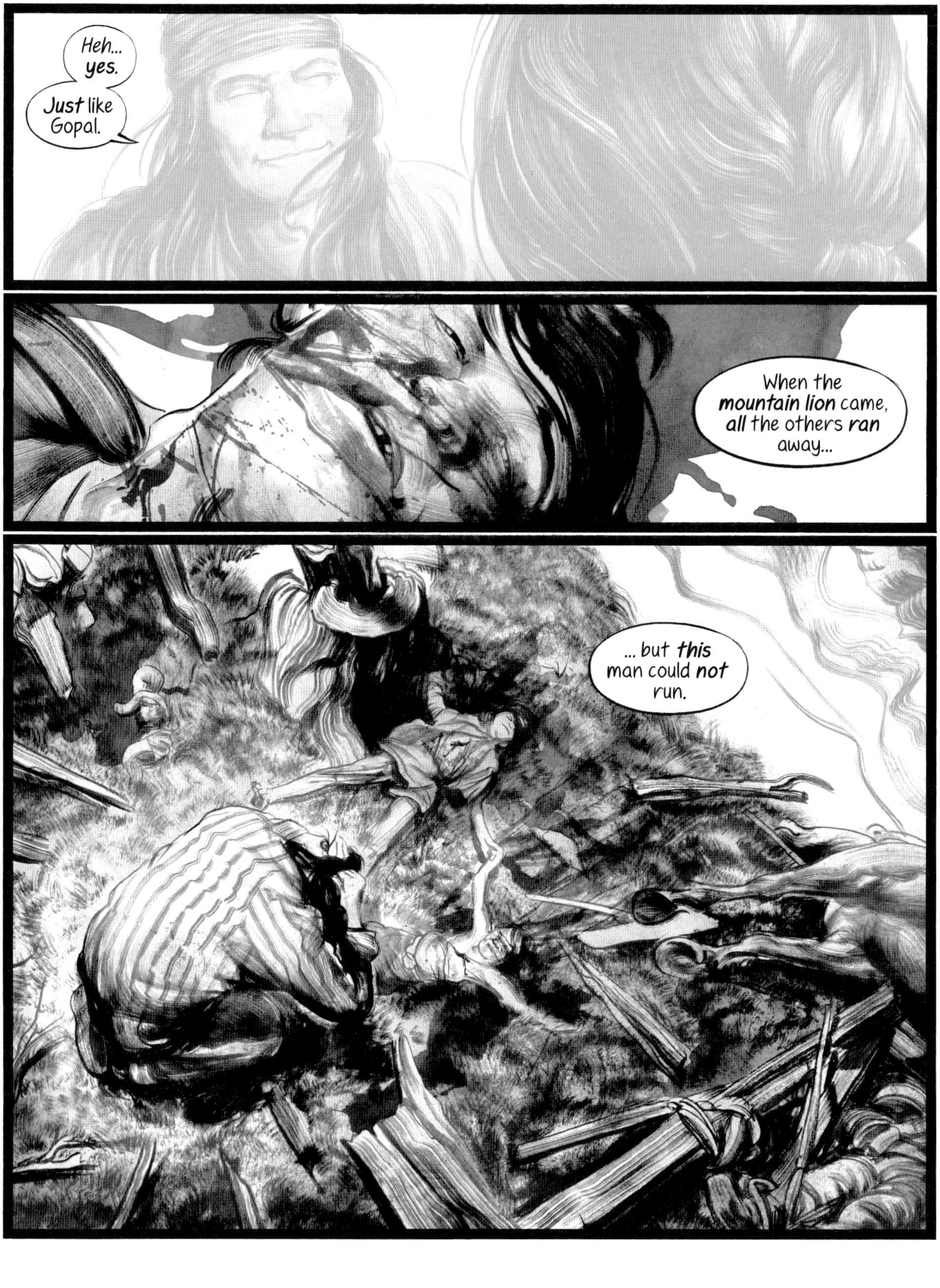
Heh... yes.
Just like Gopal.
When the mountain lion came, all the others ran away...
... but this man could not run.

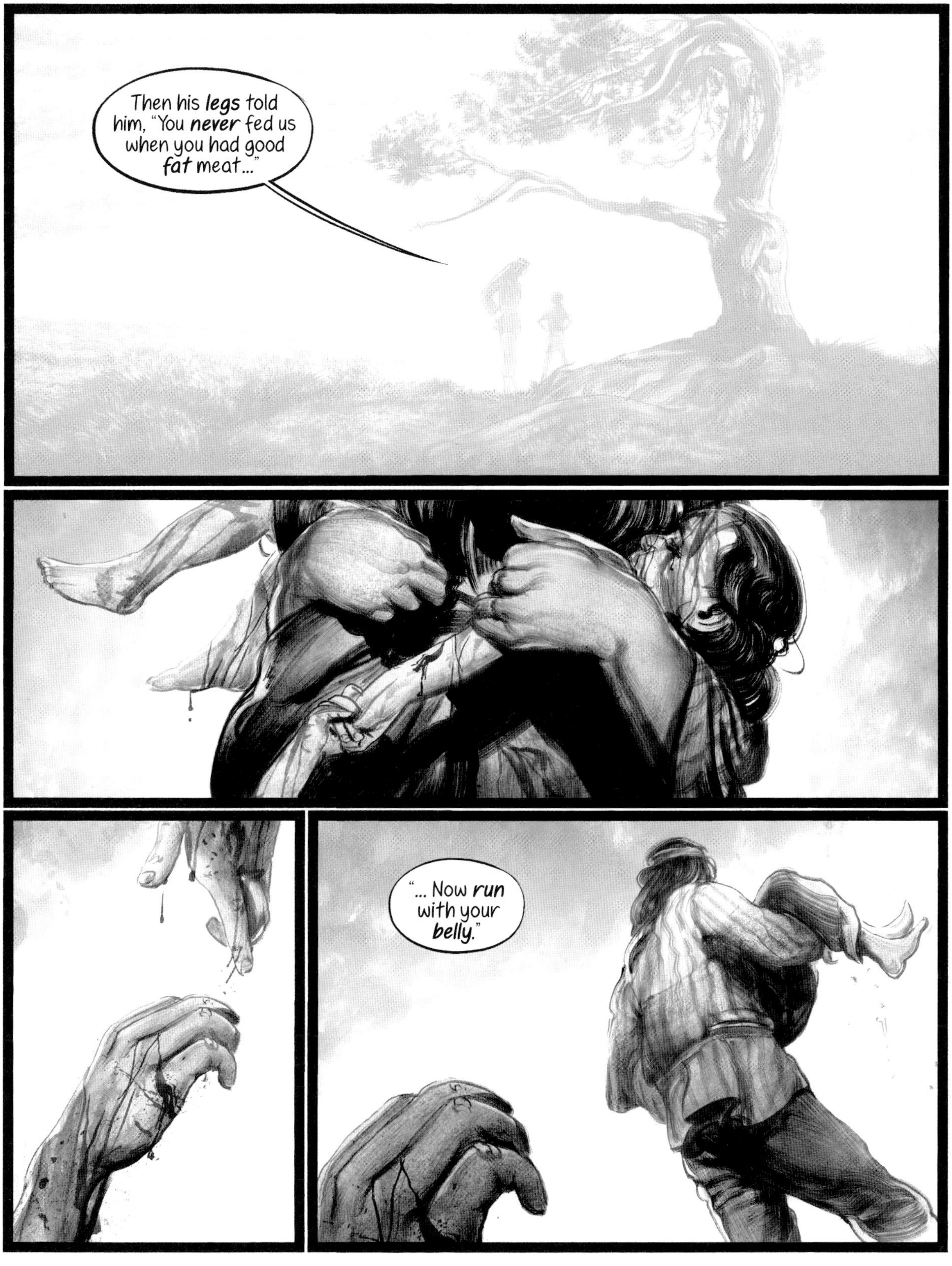
Then his **legs** told him, "You **never** fed us when you had good **fat** meat..."
"... Now **run** with your **belly**."

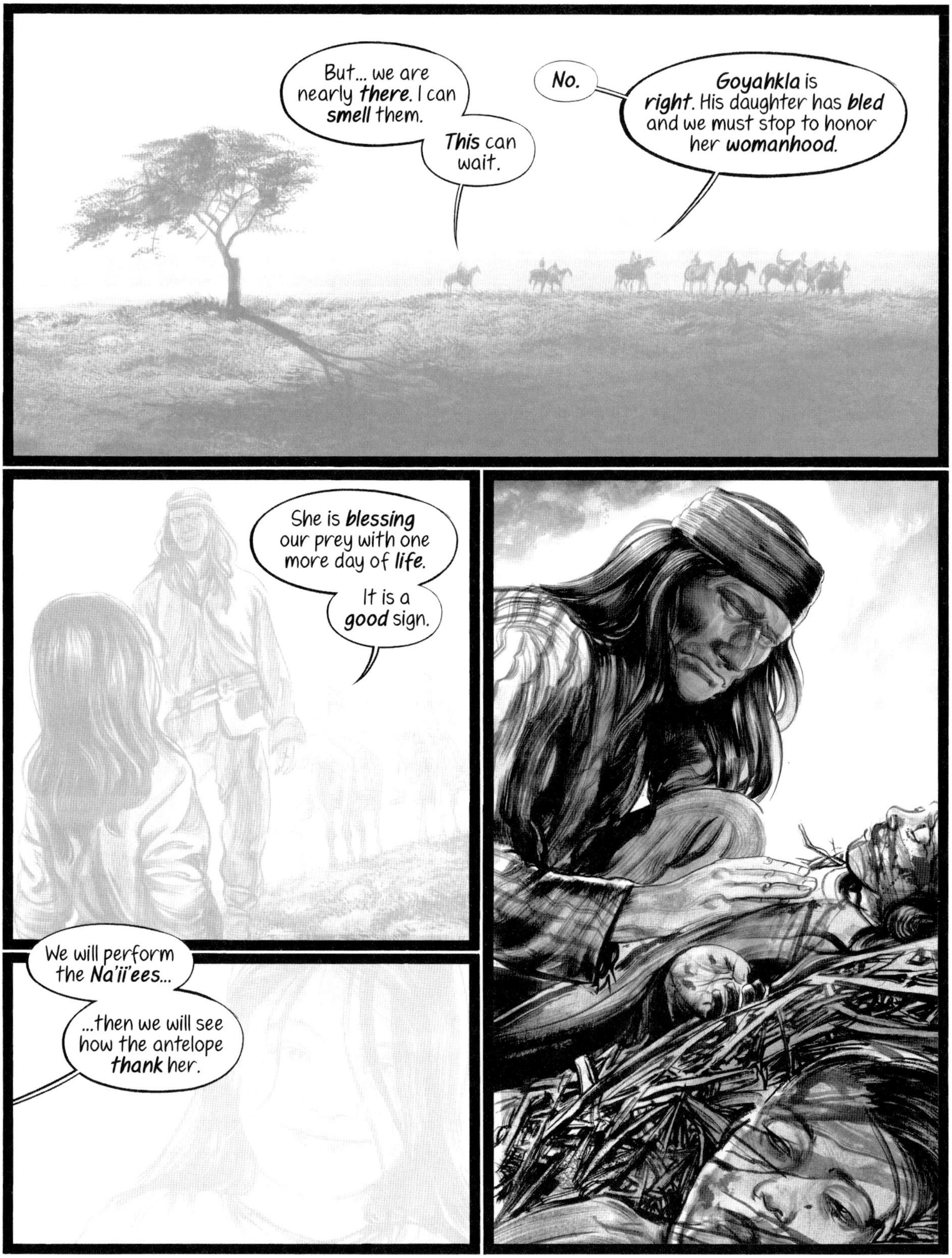

But... we are nearly there. I can smell them.
This can wait.
No.
Goyahkla is right. His daughter has bled and we must stop to honor her womanhood.
She is blessing our prey with one more day of life.
It is a good sign.
We will perform the Na'ii'ees...
...then we will see how the antelope thank her.

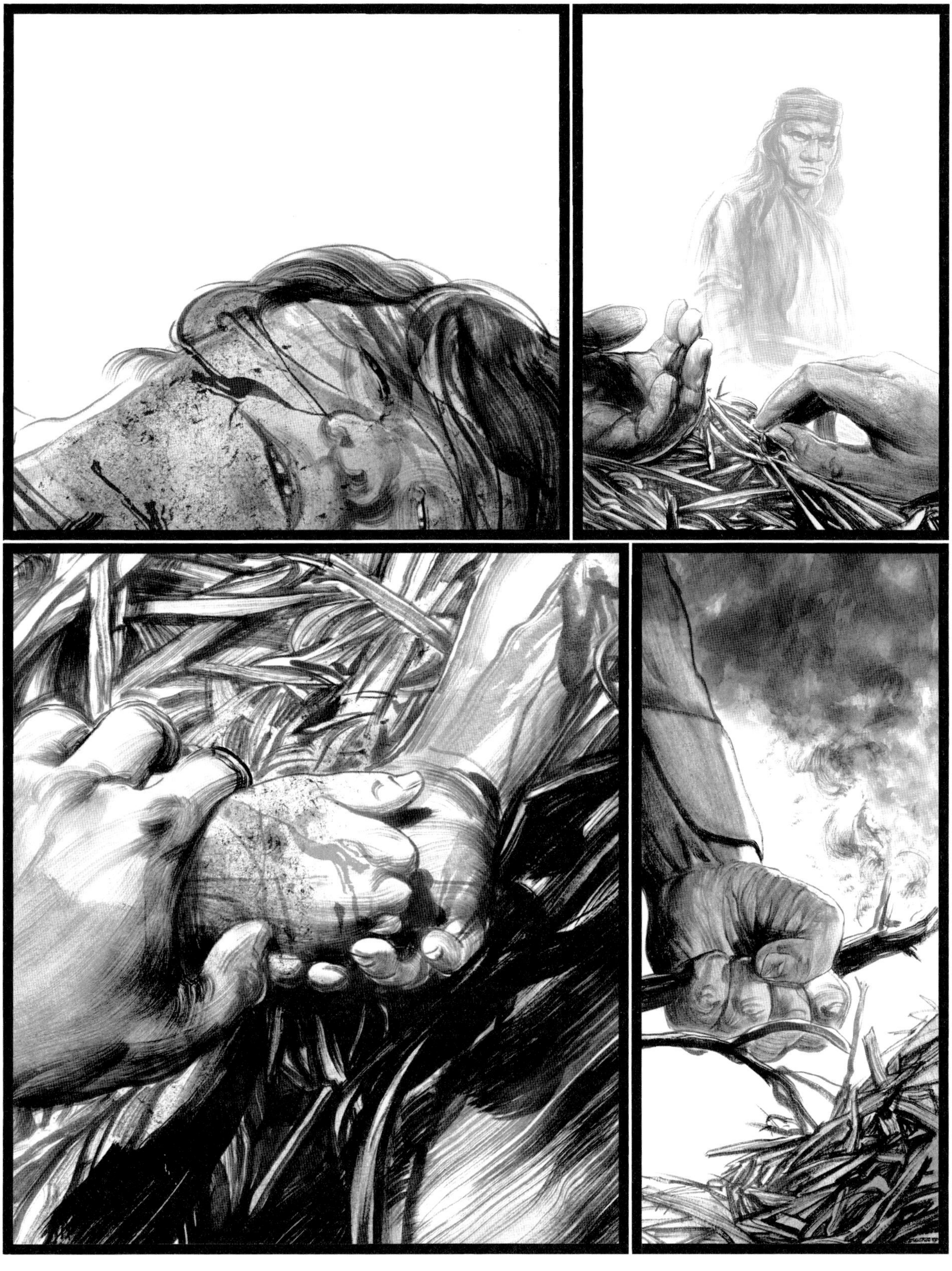

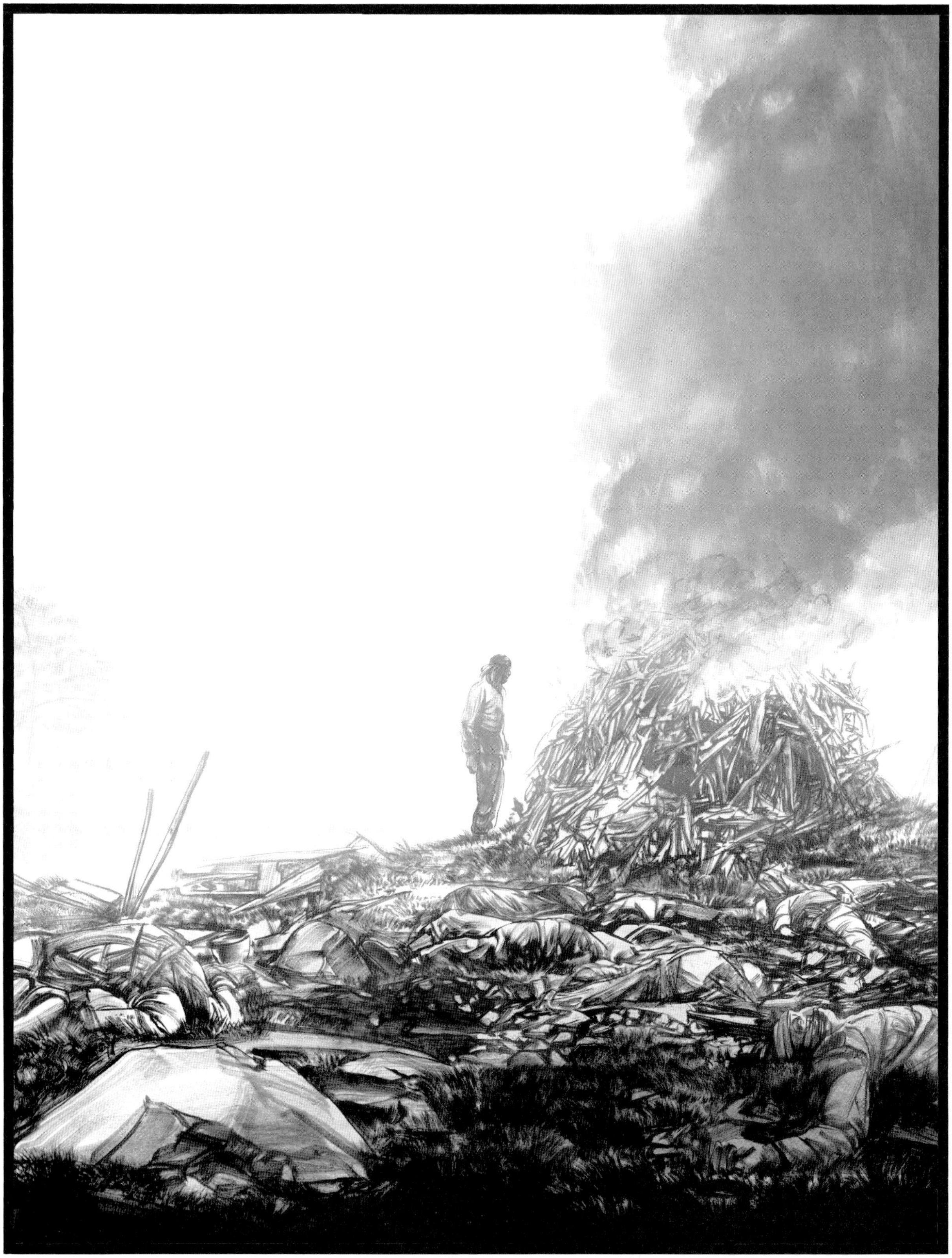

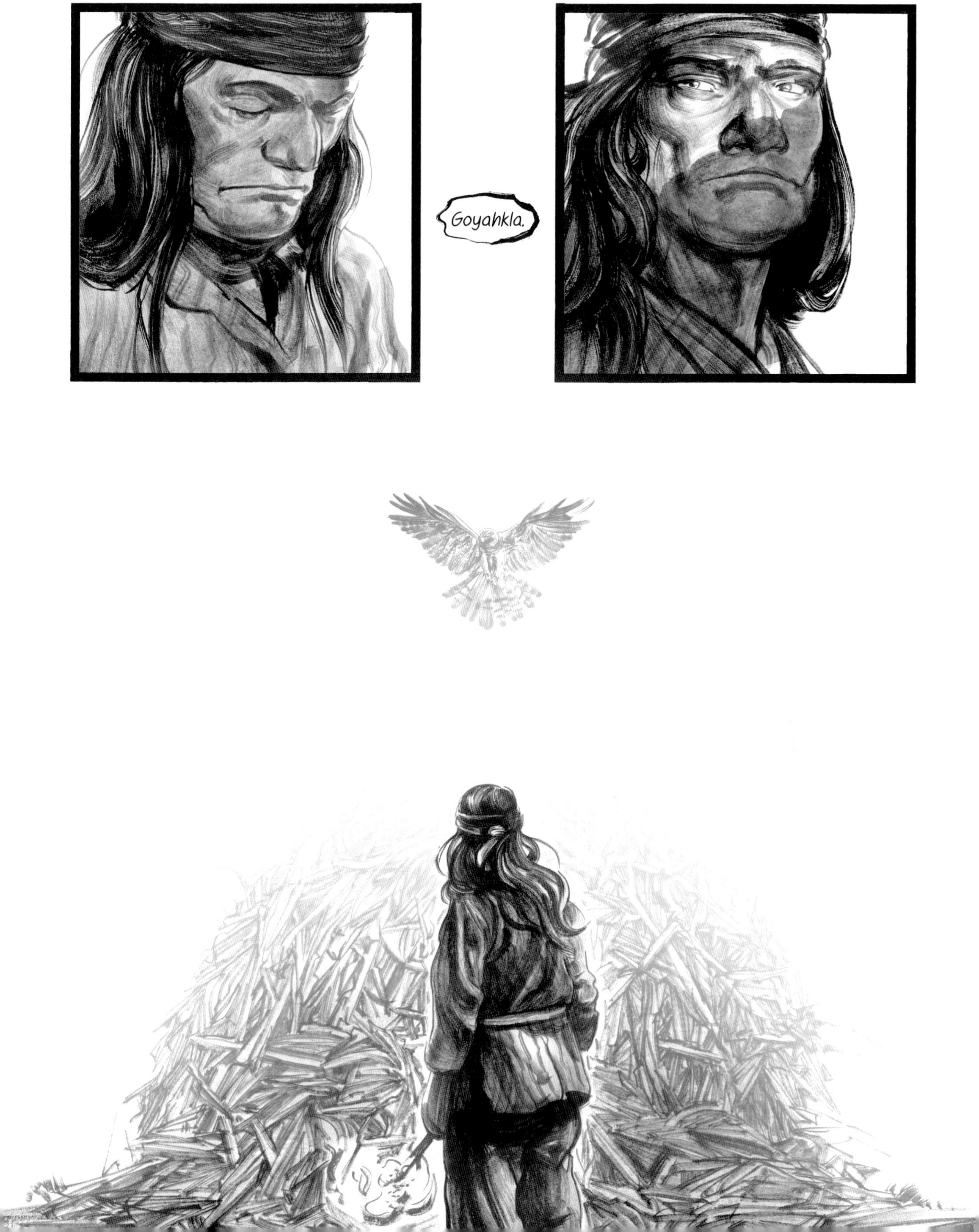
Goyahkla.

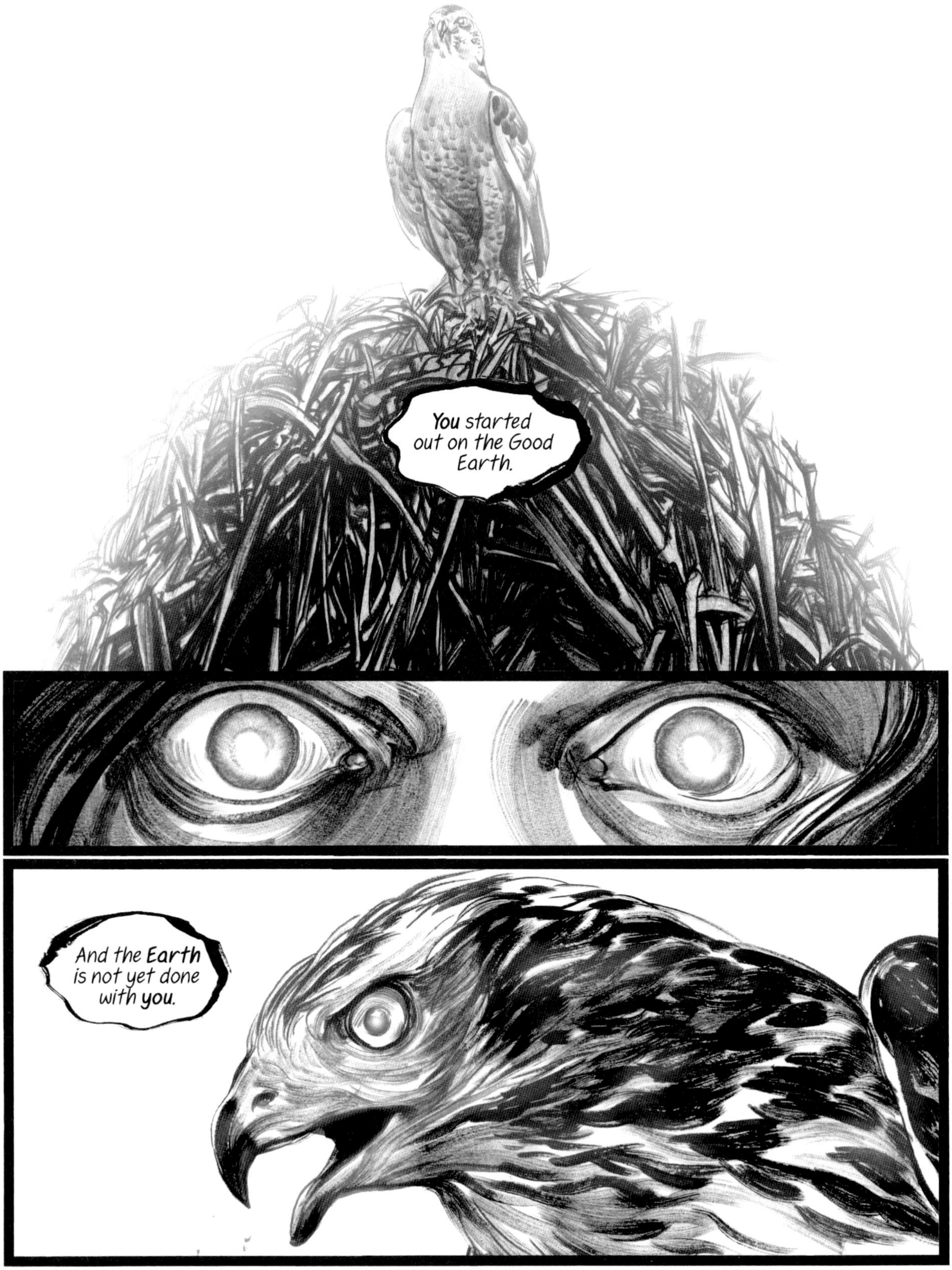
You started out on the Good Earth.
And the Earth is not yet done with you.

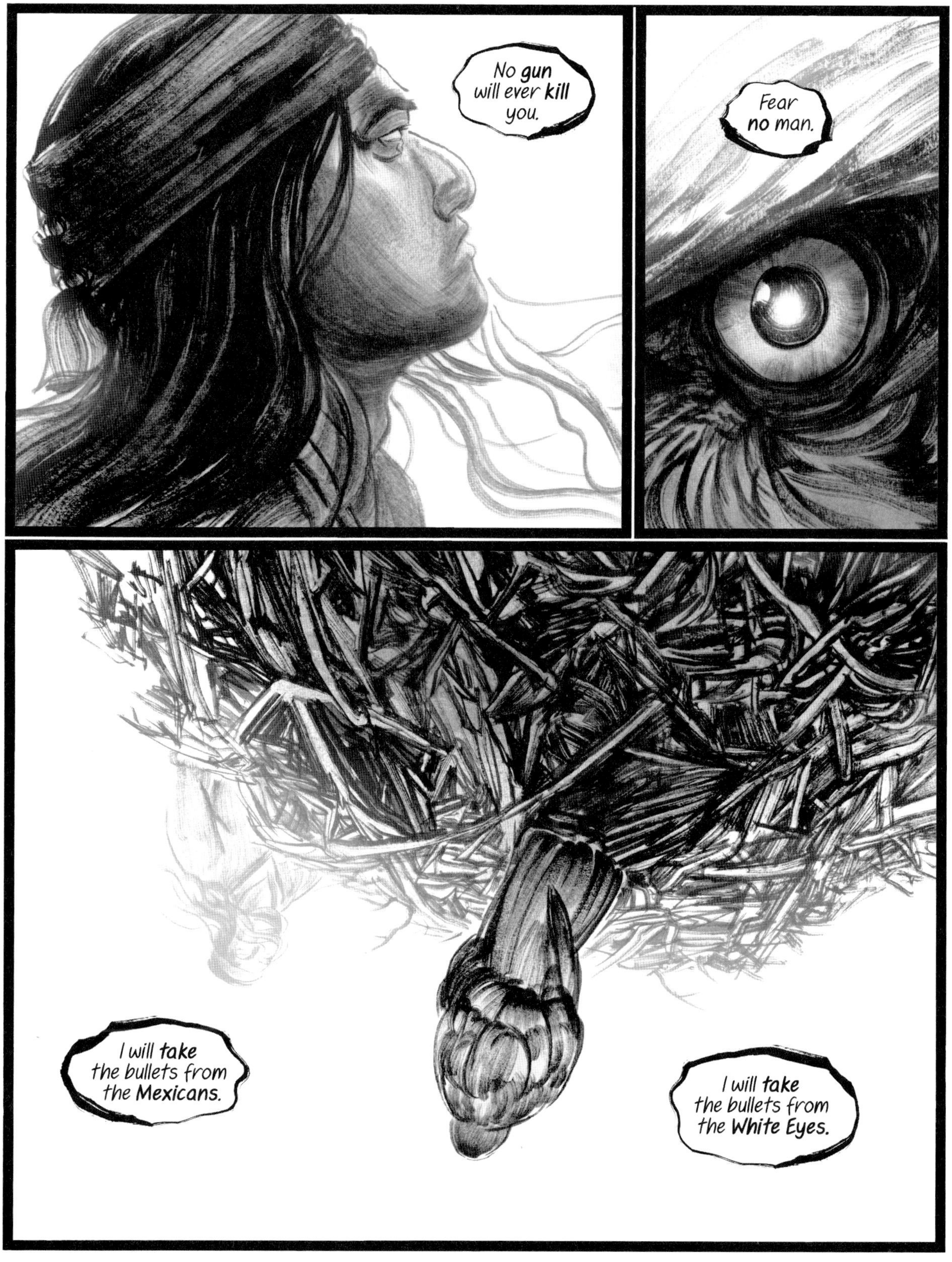
No gun will ever kill you.
Fear no man.
I will take the bullets from the Mexicans.
I will take the bullets from the White Eyes.

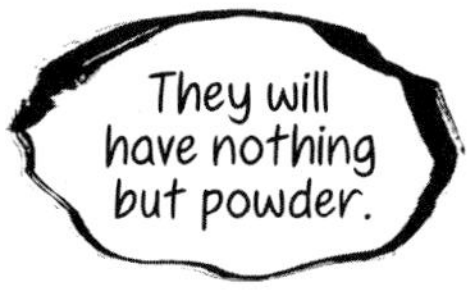
They will have nothing but powder.

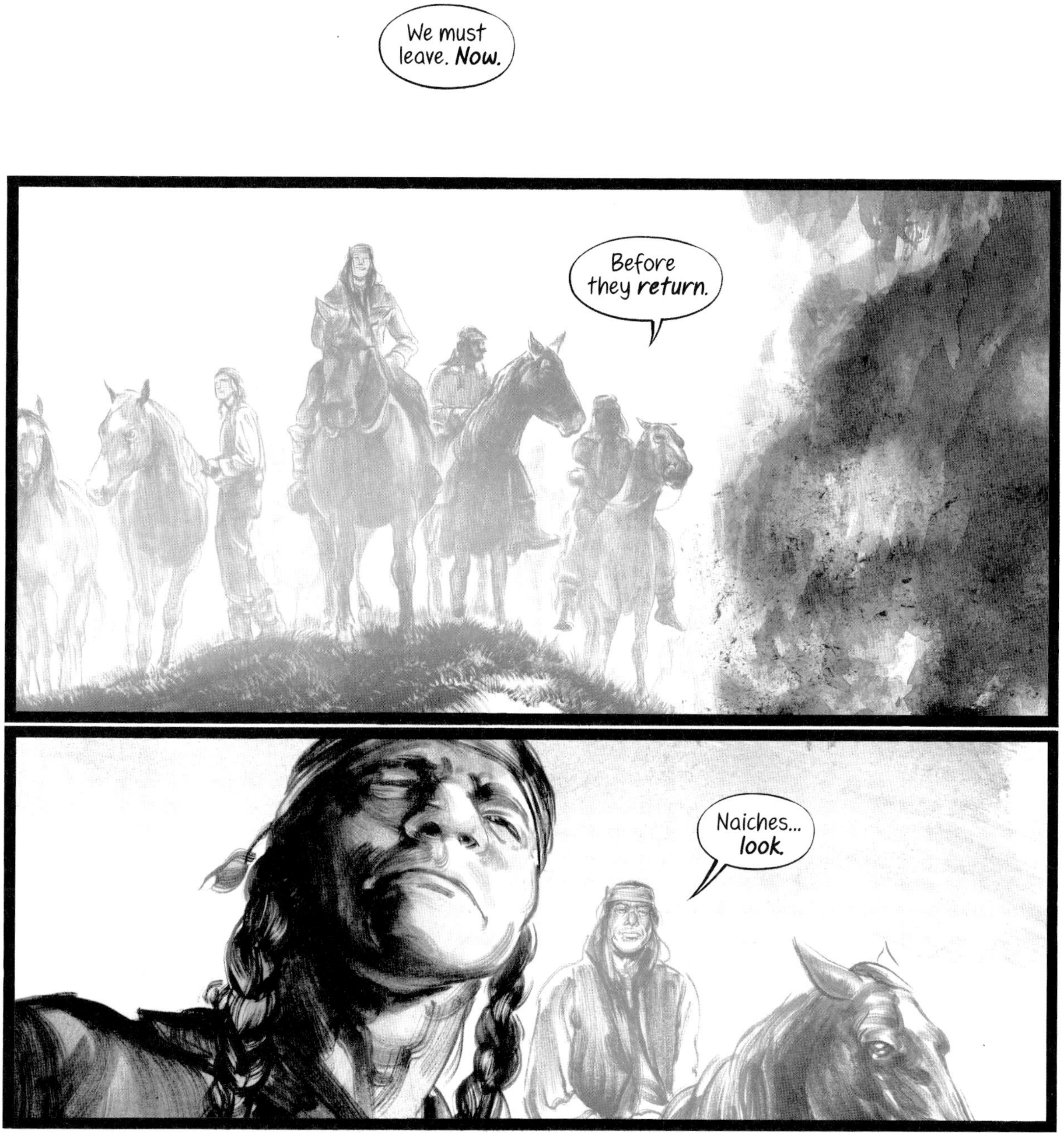
We must leave. **Now.**
Before they **return.**
Naiches... **look.**

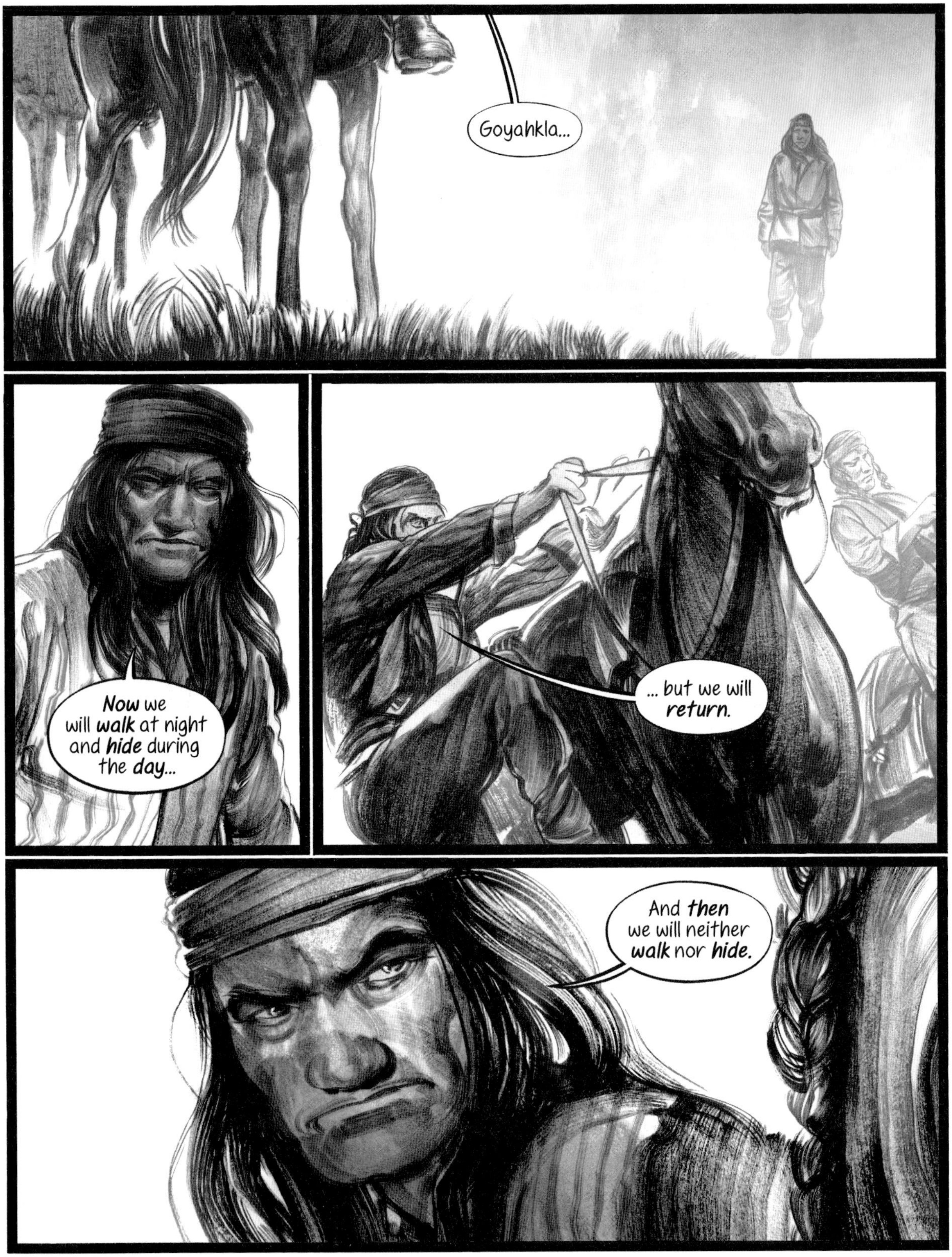
Goyahkla...
Now we will walk at night and hide during the day...
... but we will return.
And then we will neither walk nor hide.

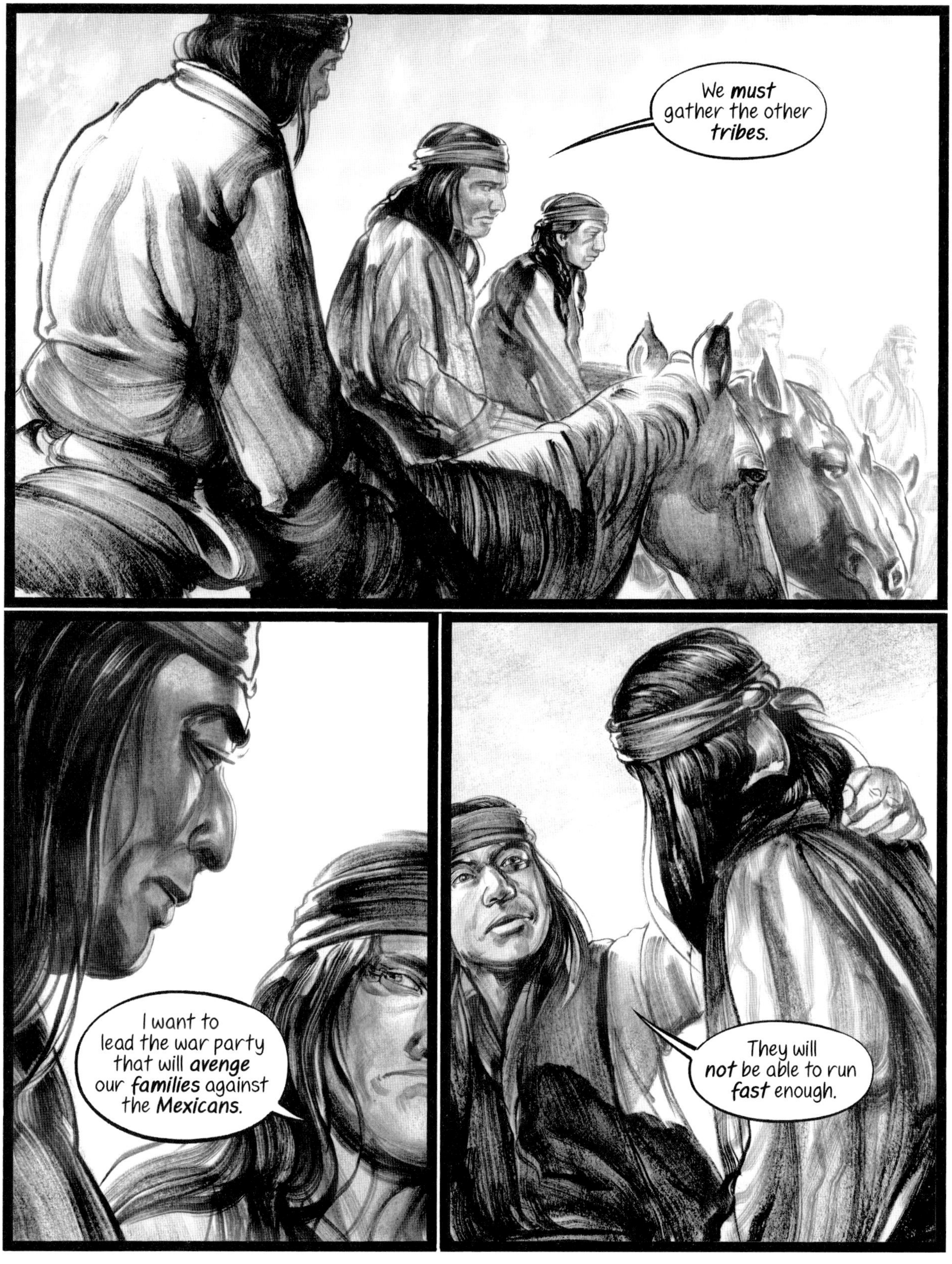
We must gather the other tribes.
I want to lead the war party that will avenge our families against the Mexicans.
They will not be able to run fast enough.

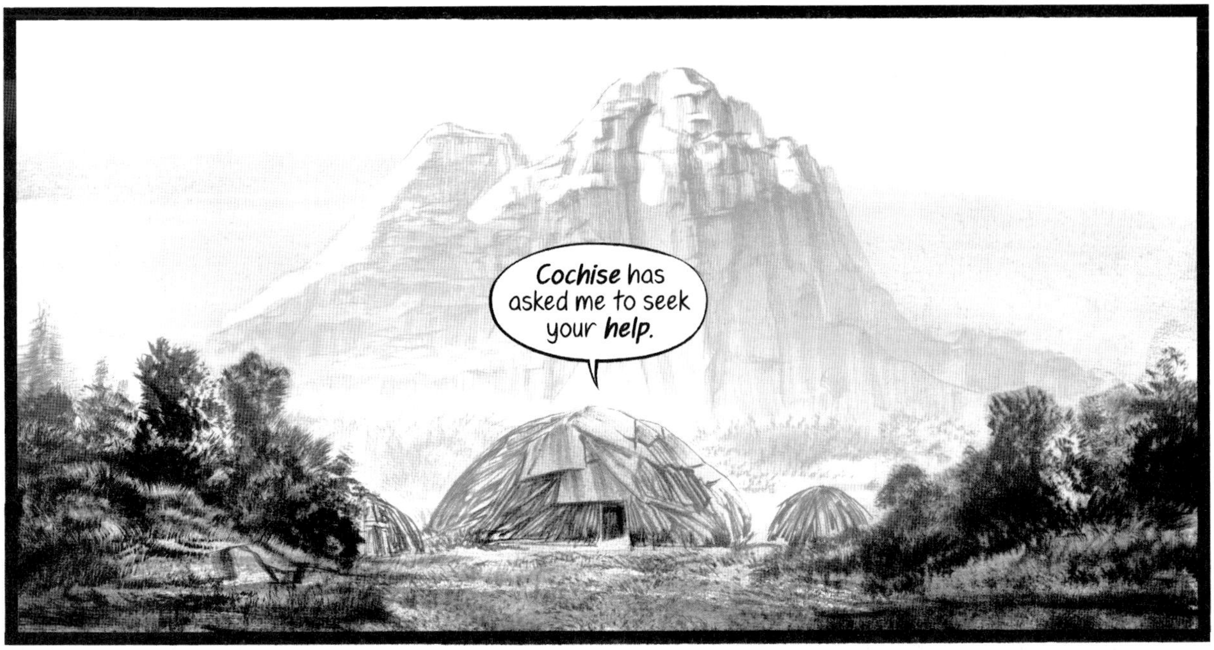
Cochise has asked me to seek your help.

THE CHIRICAHUA APACHE OF CHIEF MANGAS

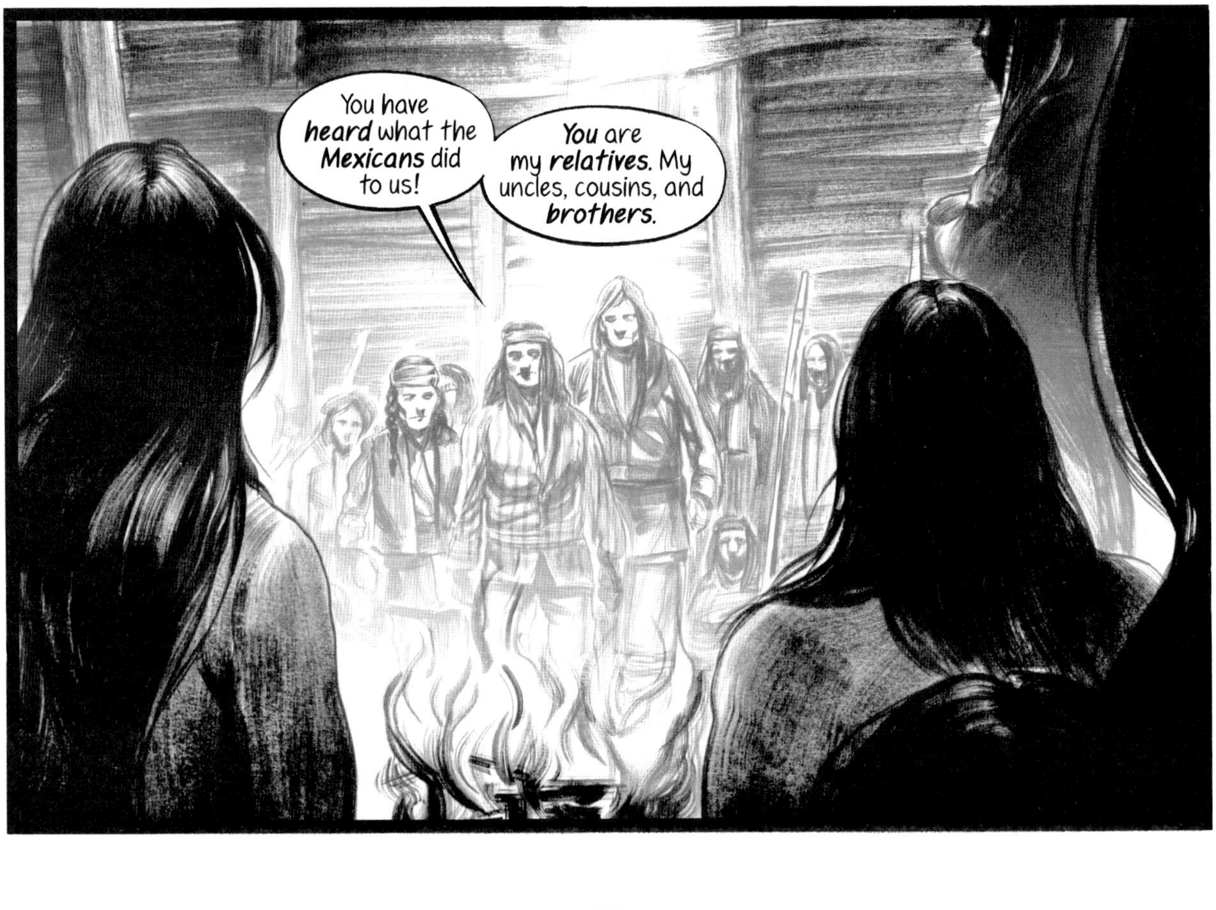
You have heard what the Mexicans did to us!
You are my relatives. My uncles, cousins, and brothers.

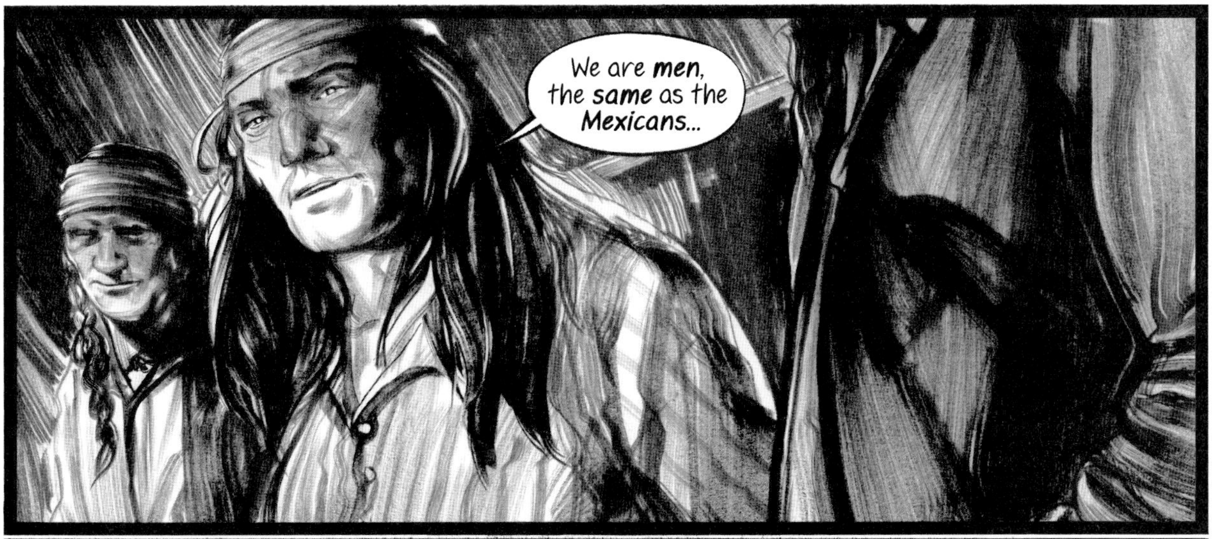
We are **men**, the **same** as the **Mexicans**...

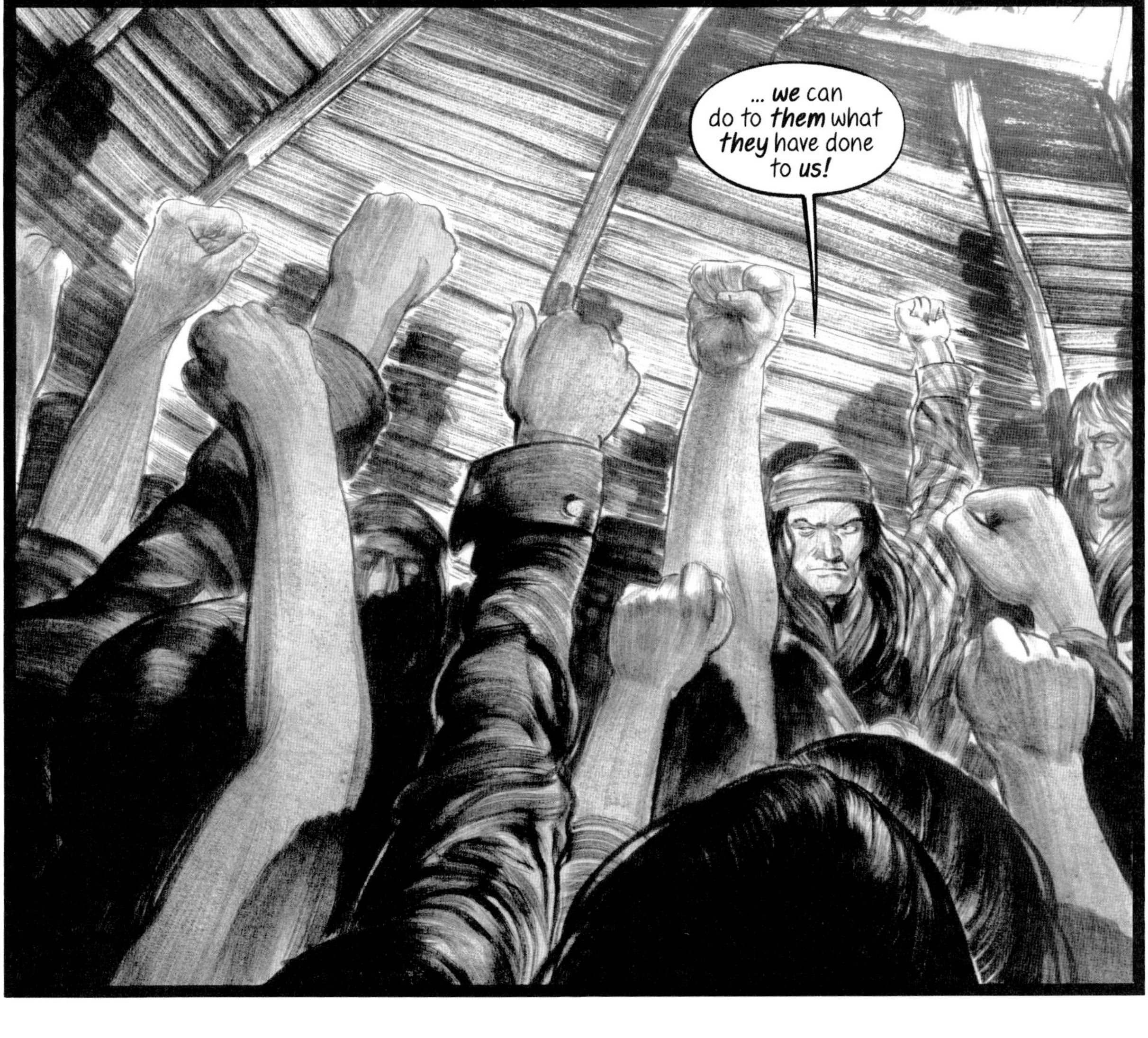
... **we** can do to **them** what **they** have done to **us!**

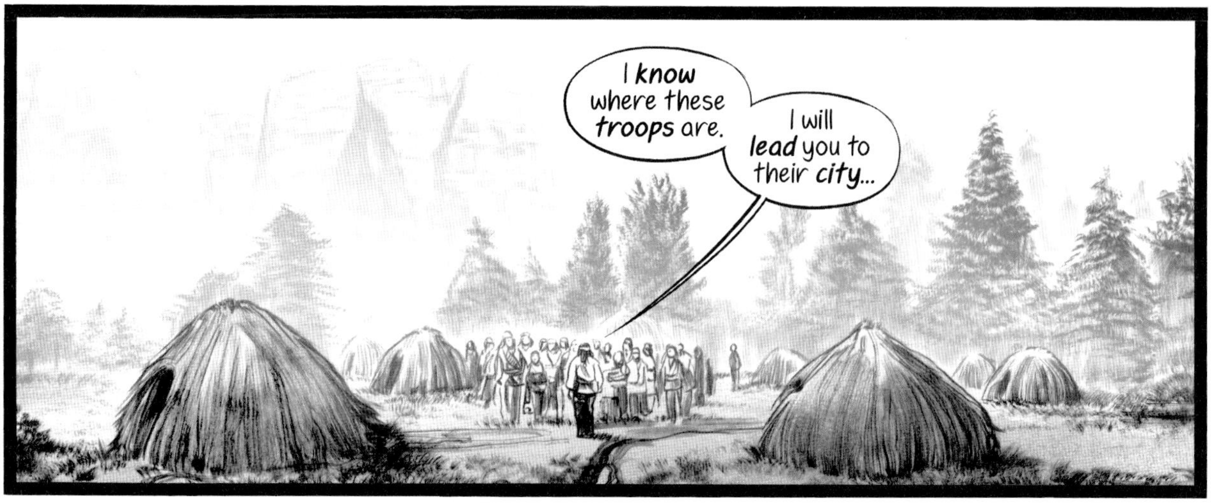
I know where these troops are.
I will lead you to their city...

THE CHIHENNE APACHE OF CHIEF VICTORIO

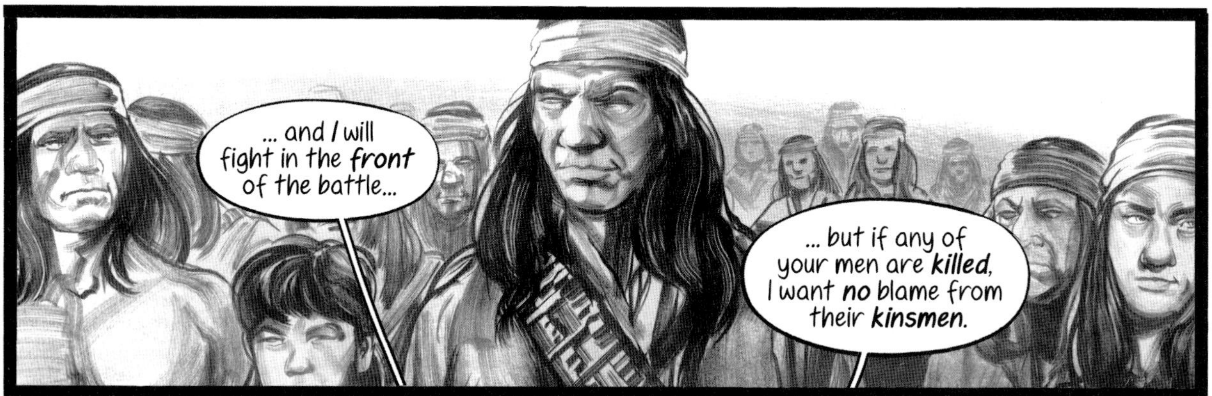
... and I will fight in the front of the battle...
... but if any of your men are killed, I want no blame from their kinsmen.

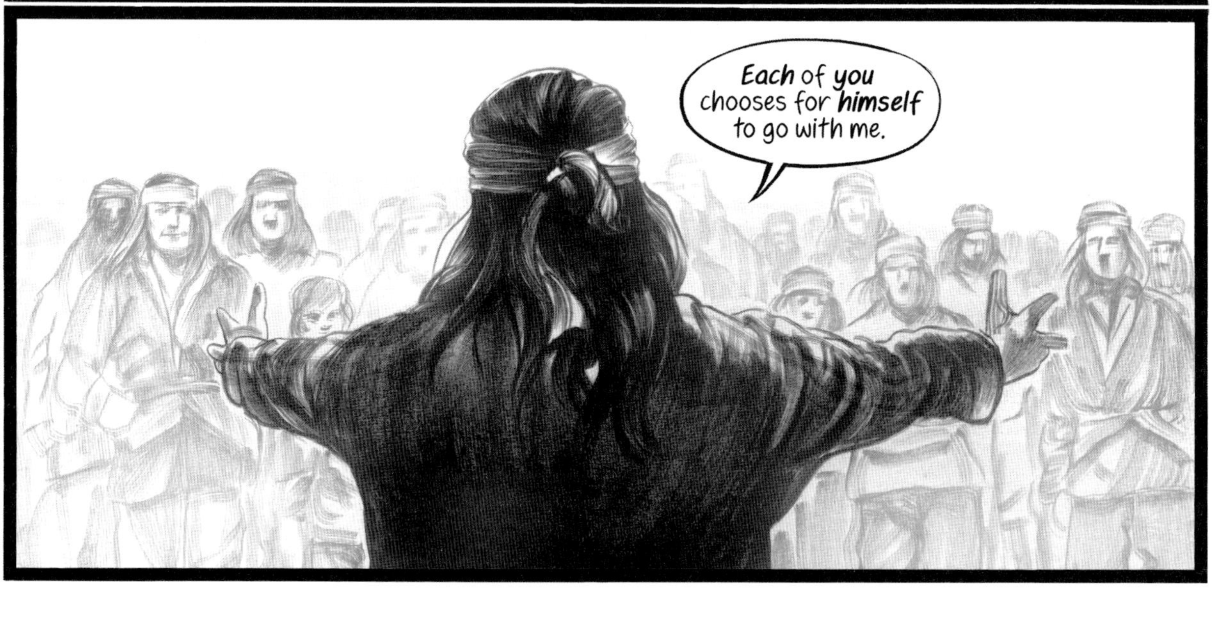
Each of you chooses for himself to go with me.

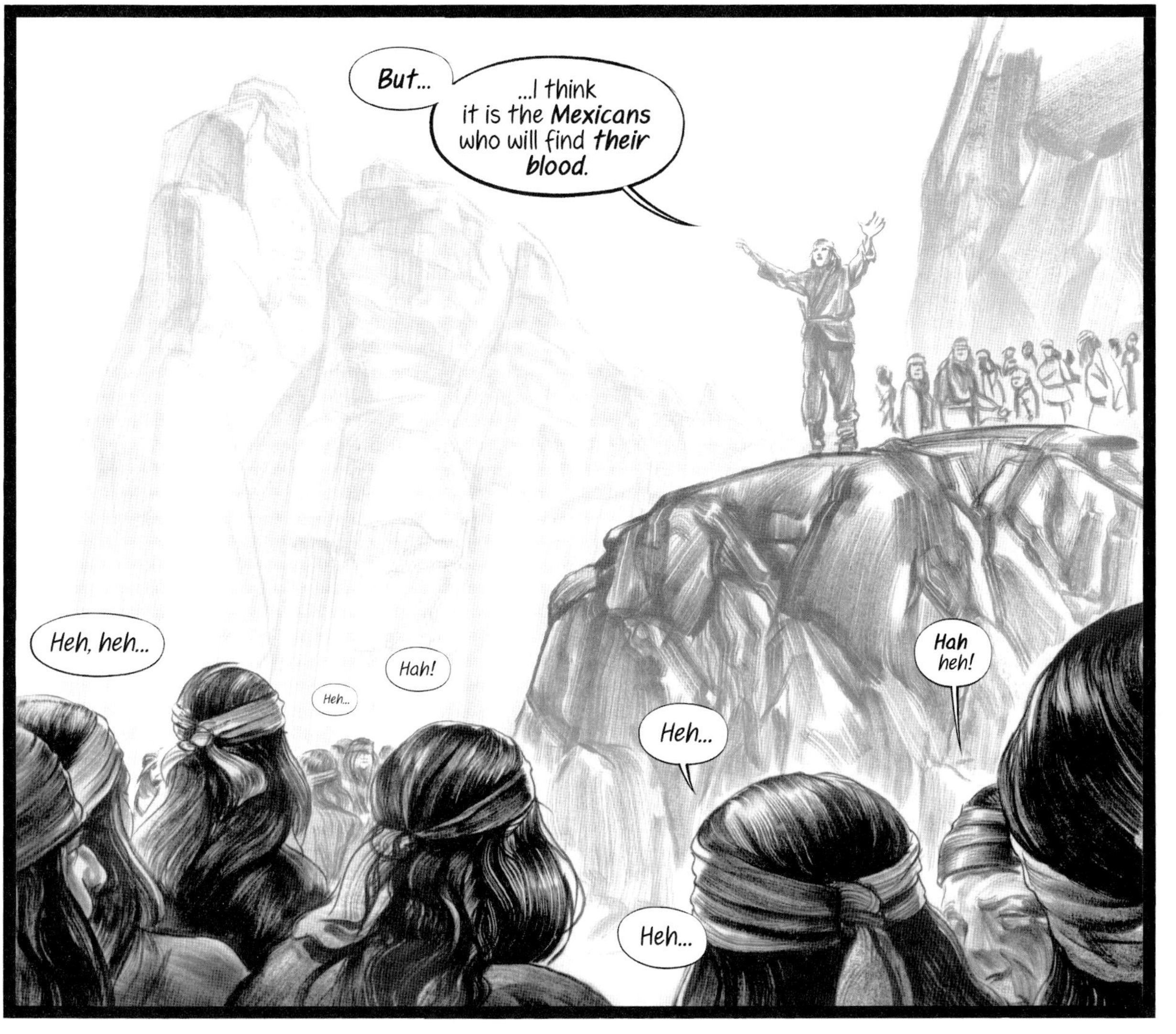
But...
...I think it is the Mexicans who will find their blood.
Heh, heh...
Heh...
Hah!
Heh...
Hah heh!
Heh...

THE NEDNI APACHE OF CHIEF LOCO

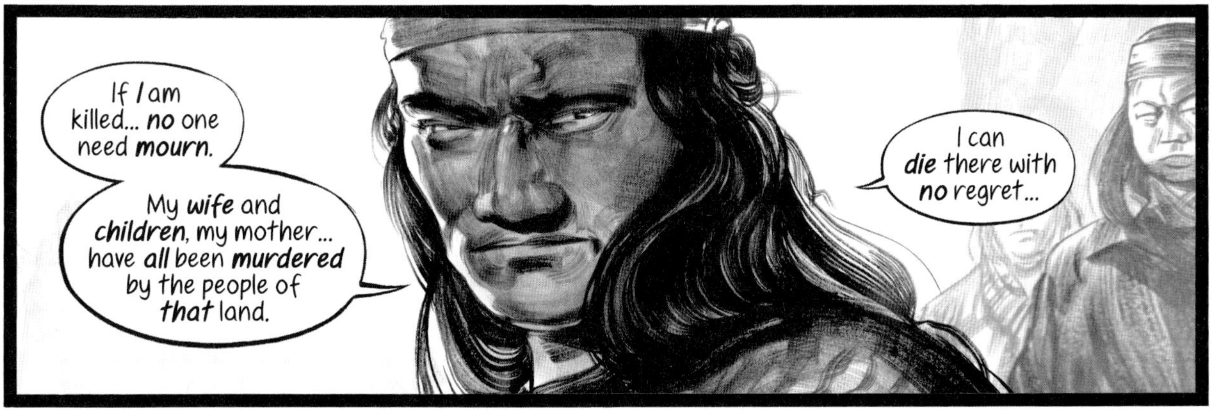
If I am killed... no one need mourn.
My wife and children, my mother... have all been murdered by the people of that land.
I can die there with no regret...

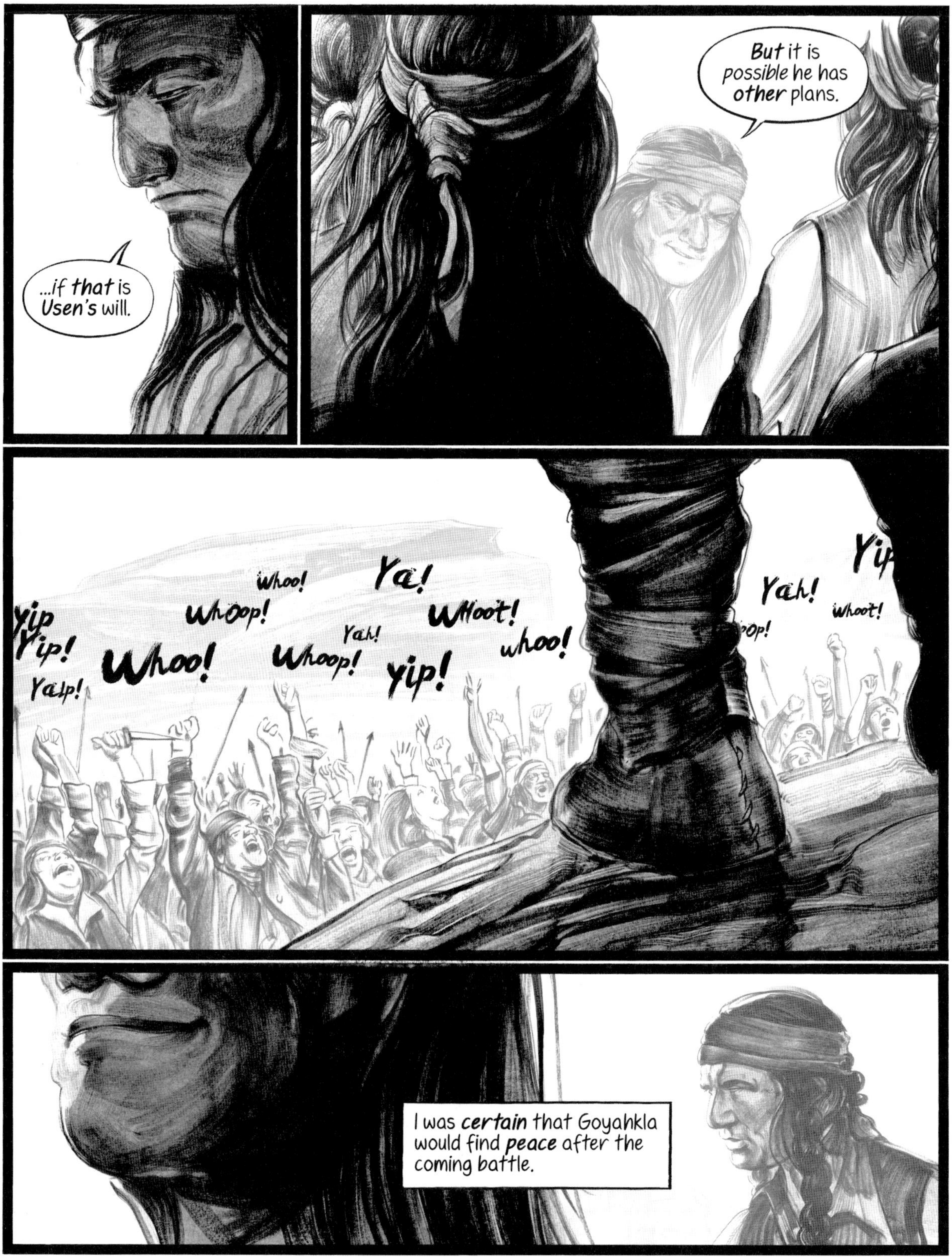
...if that is Usen's will.
But it is possible he has other plans.
Yip Yip! Yalp! Whoo! Whoop! Whoo! Ya! Whoot! Whoop! Yah! yip! whoo! Yah! Yip Whoot! Whoop!
I was certain that Goyahkla would find peace after the coming battle.

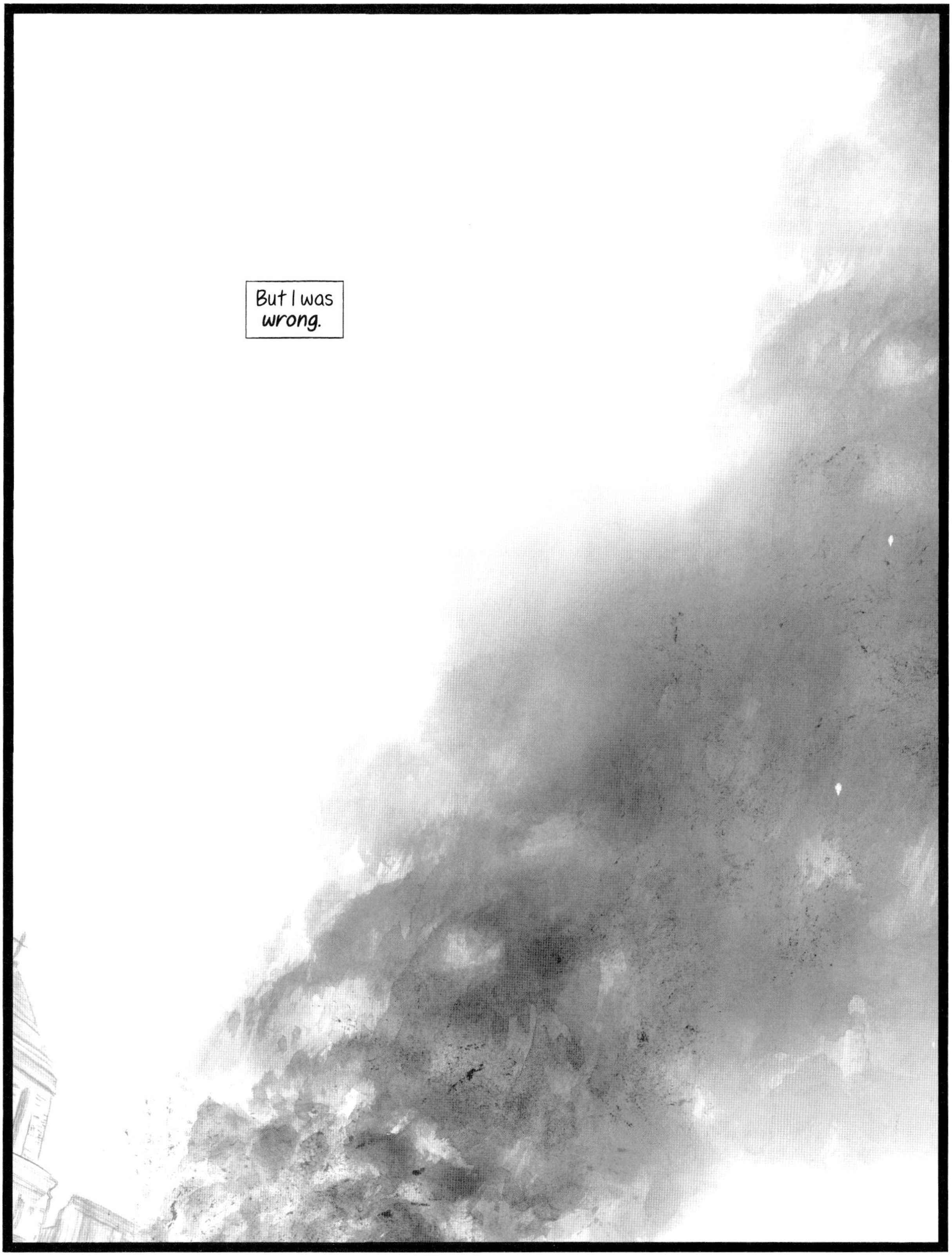
But I was wrong.

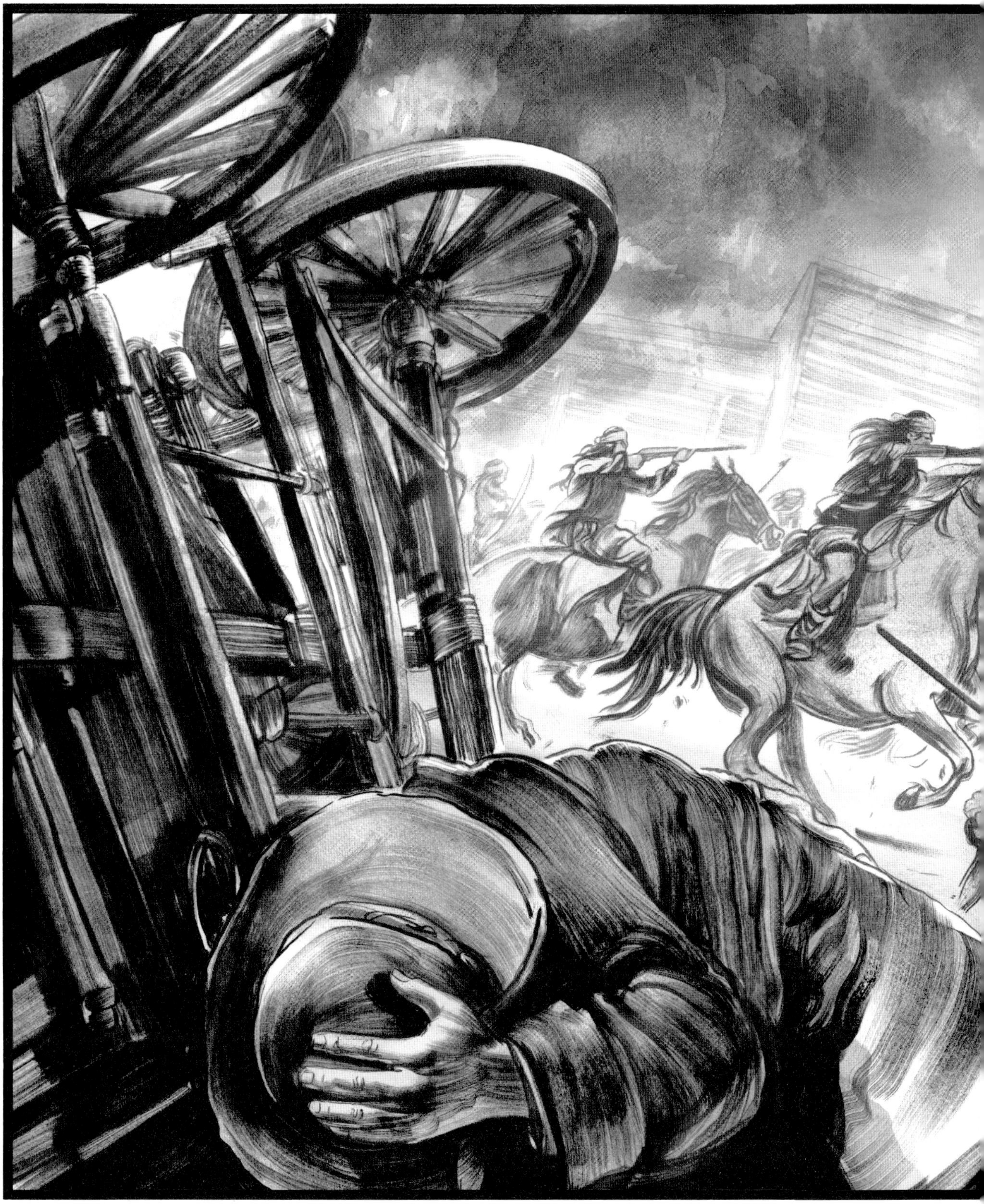

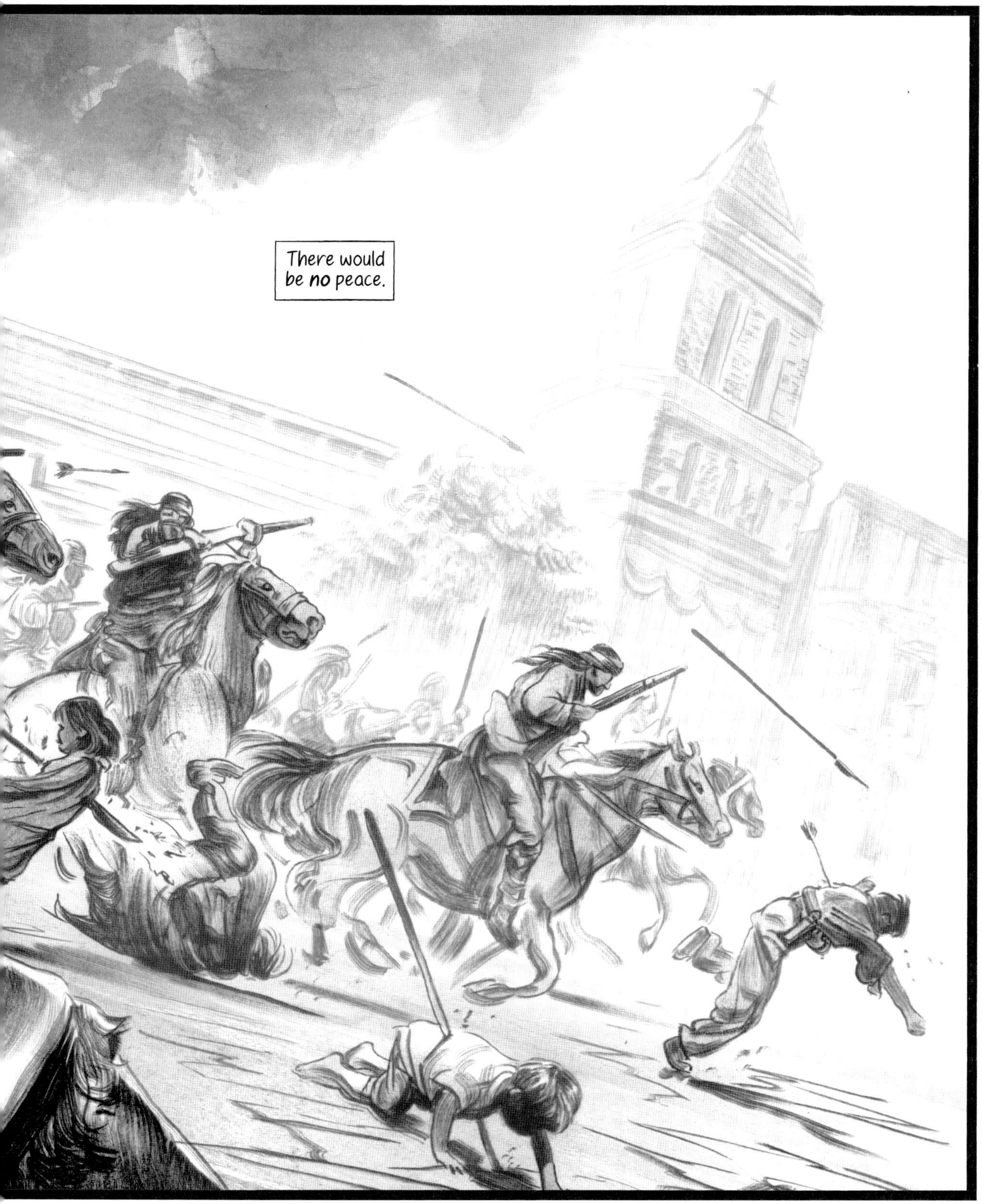
There would be **no** peace.

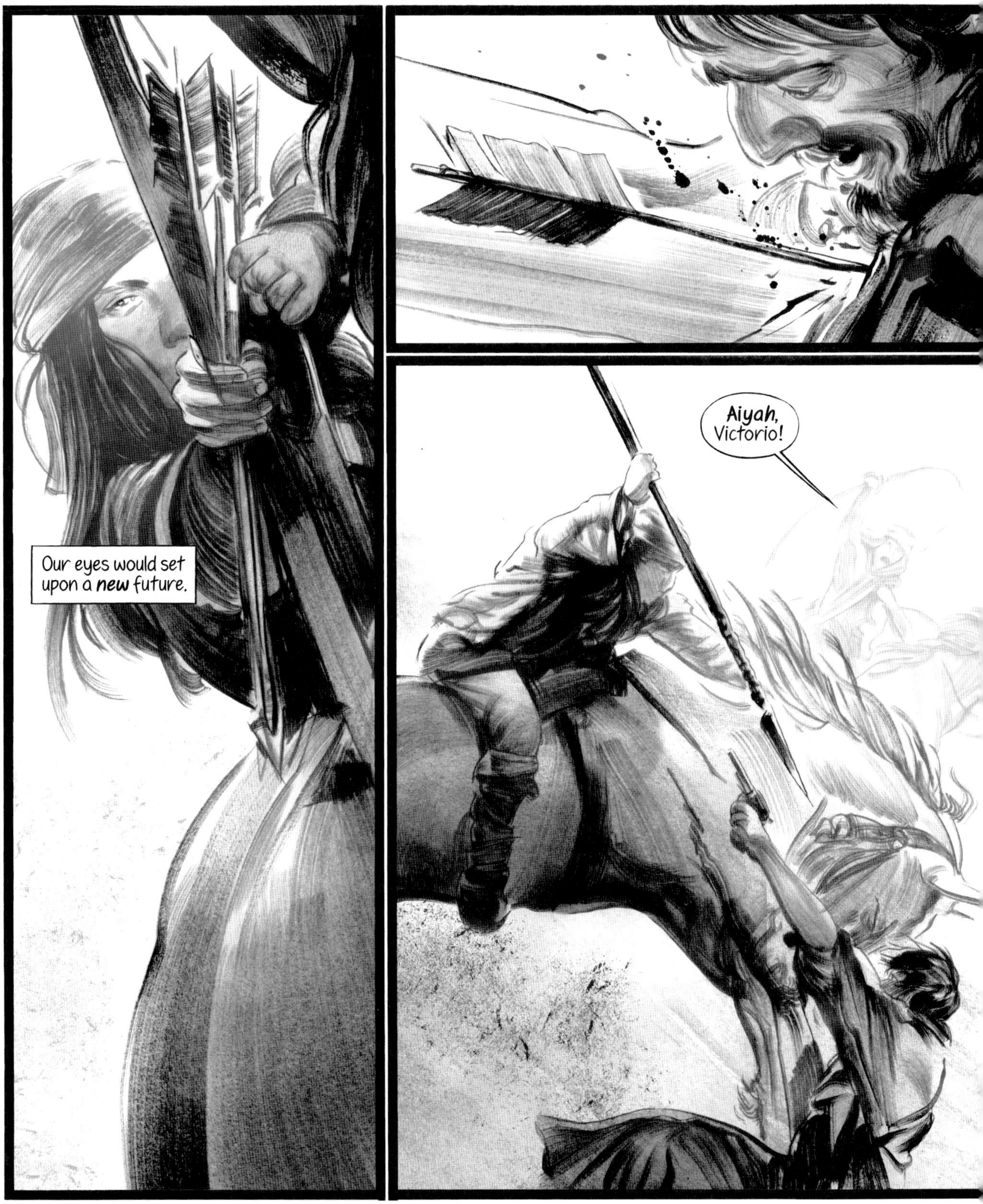
Our eyes would set upon a **new** future.
Aiyah, Victorio!

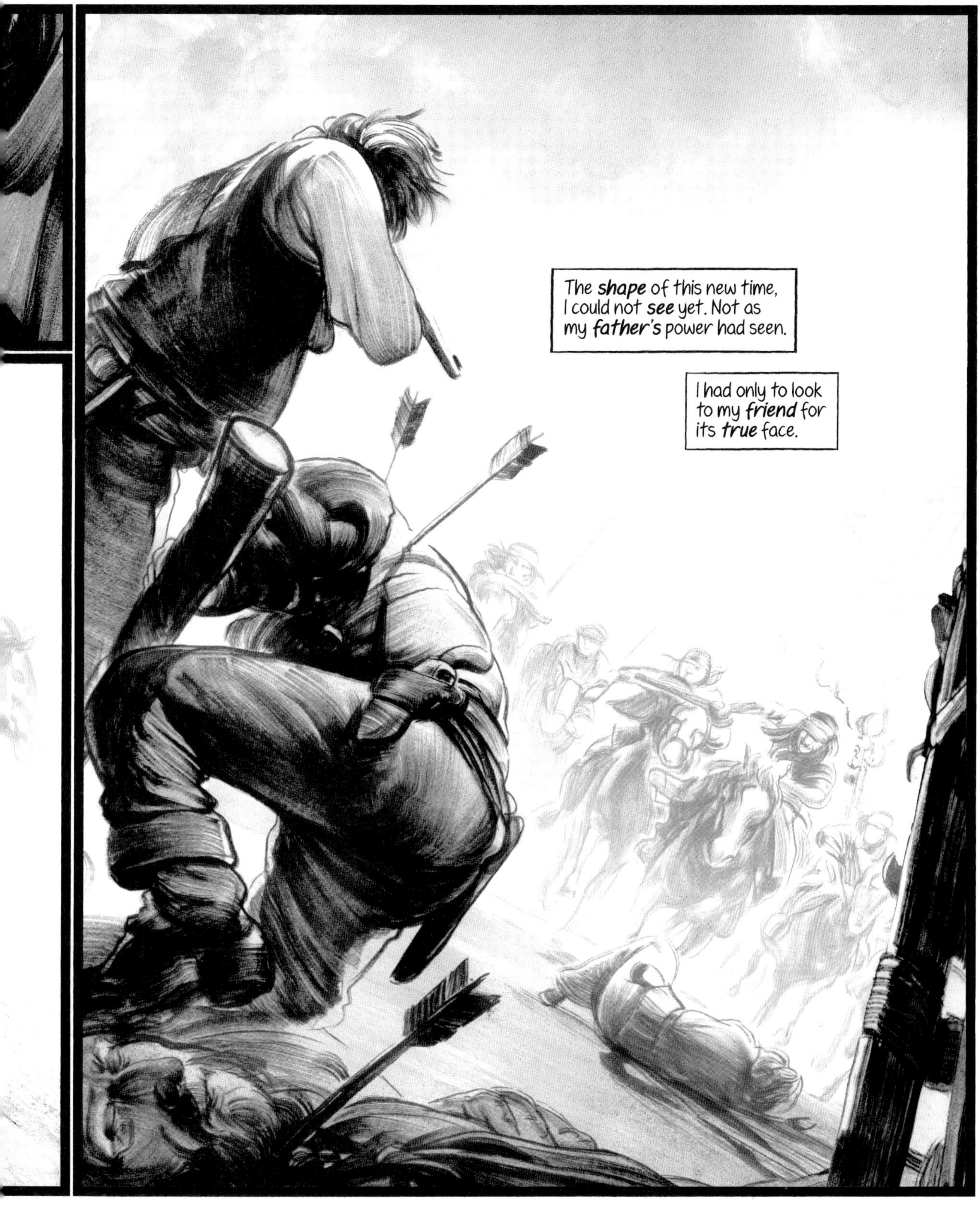
The shape of this new time, I could not see yet. Not as my father's power had seen.
I had only to look to my friend for its true face.

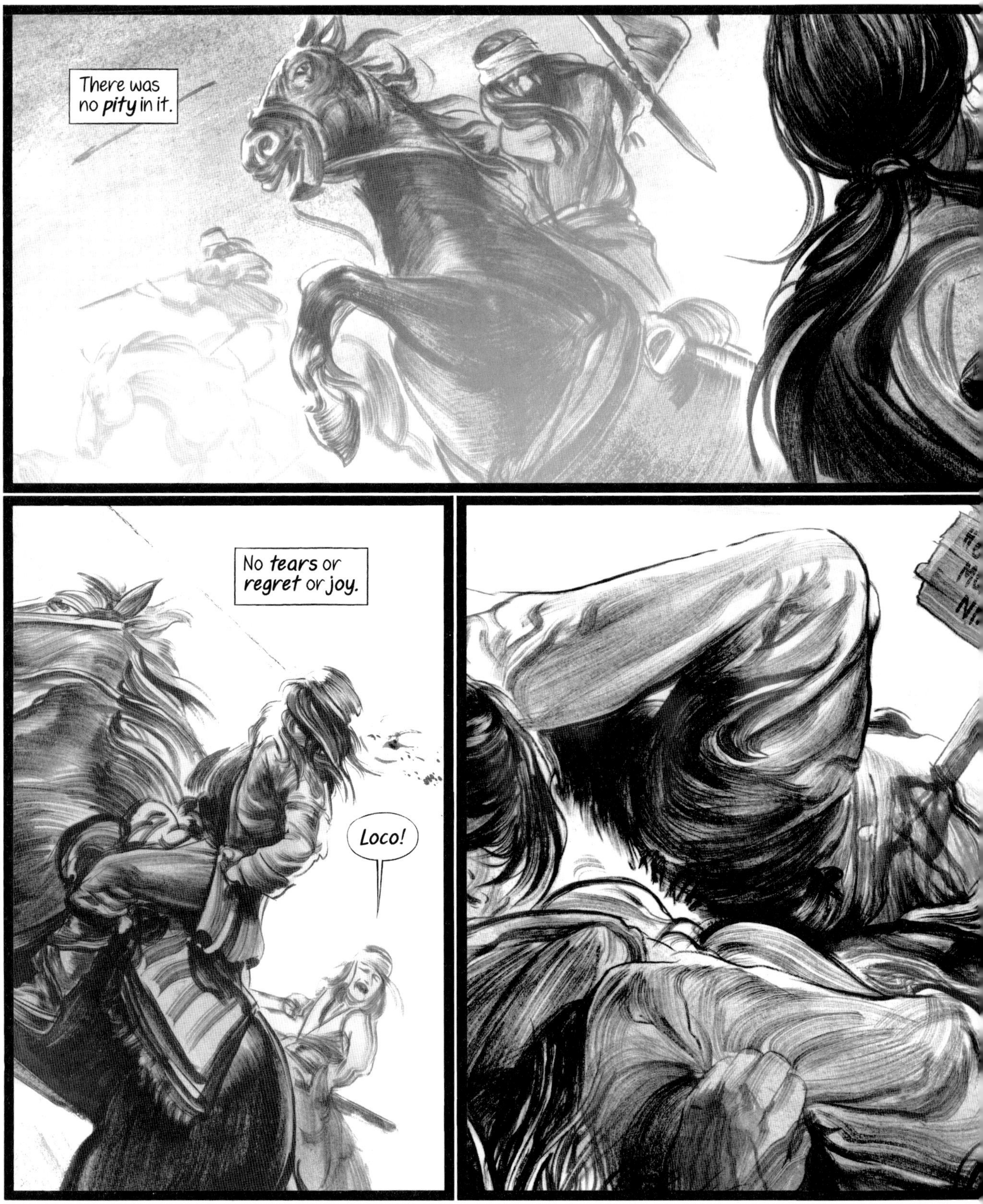
There was no *pity* in it.
No *tears* or *regret* or *joy.*
Loco!

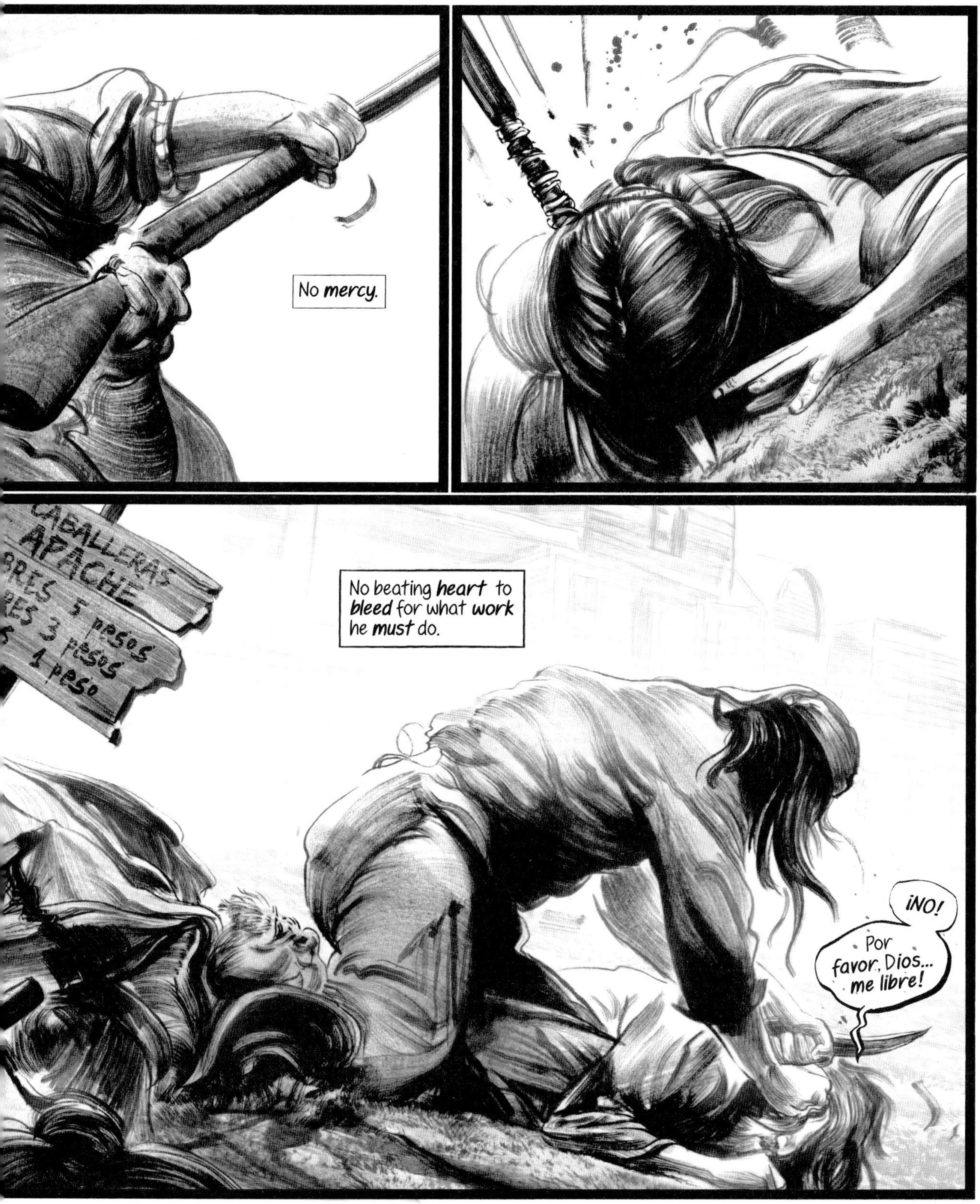
No mercy.
No beating heart to bleed for what work he must do.
CABALLERAS
APACHE
5 pesos
3 pesos
1 peso
¡NO!
Por favor, Dios... me libre!

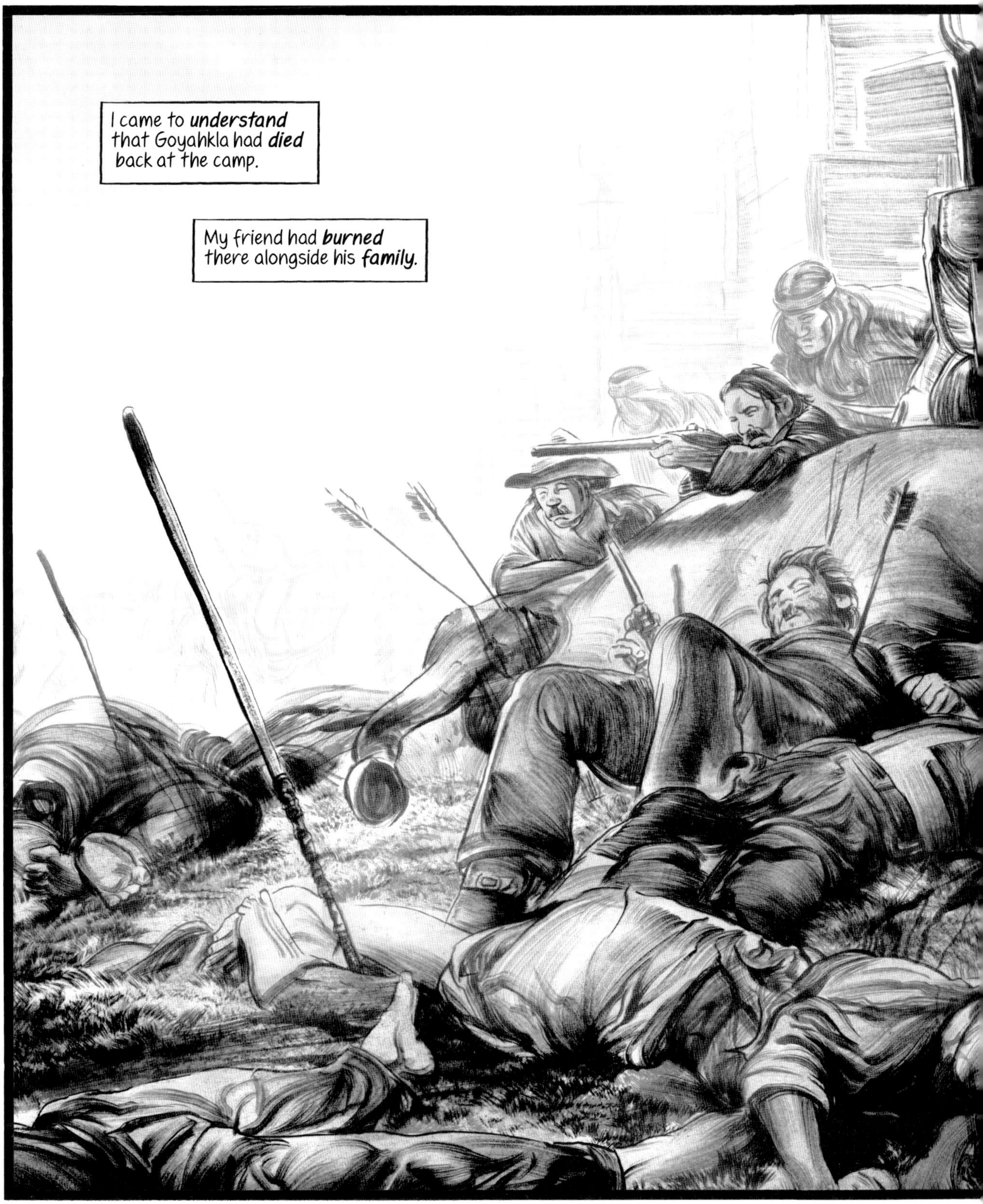
I came to understand that Goyahkla had died back at the camp.
My friend had burned there alongside his family.

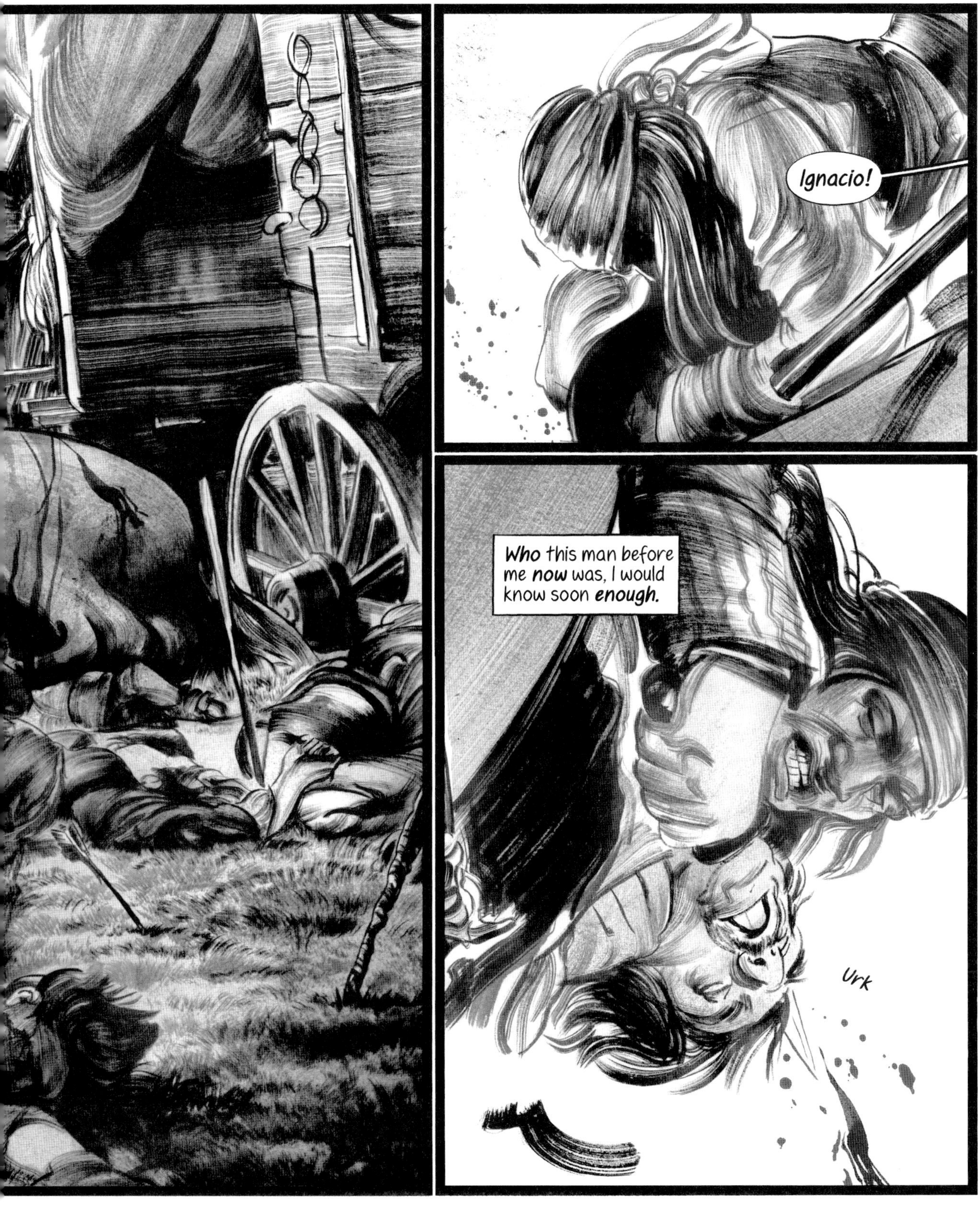
Ignacio!
Who this man before me now was, I would know soon enough.
Urk

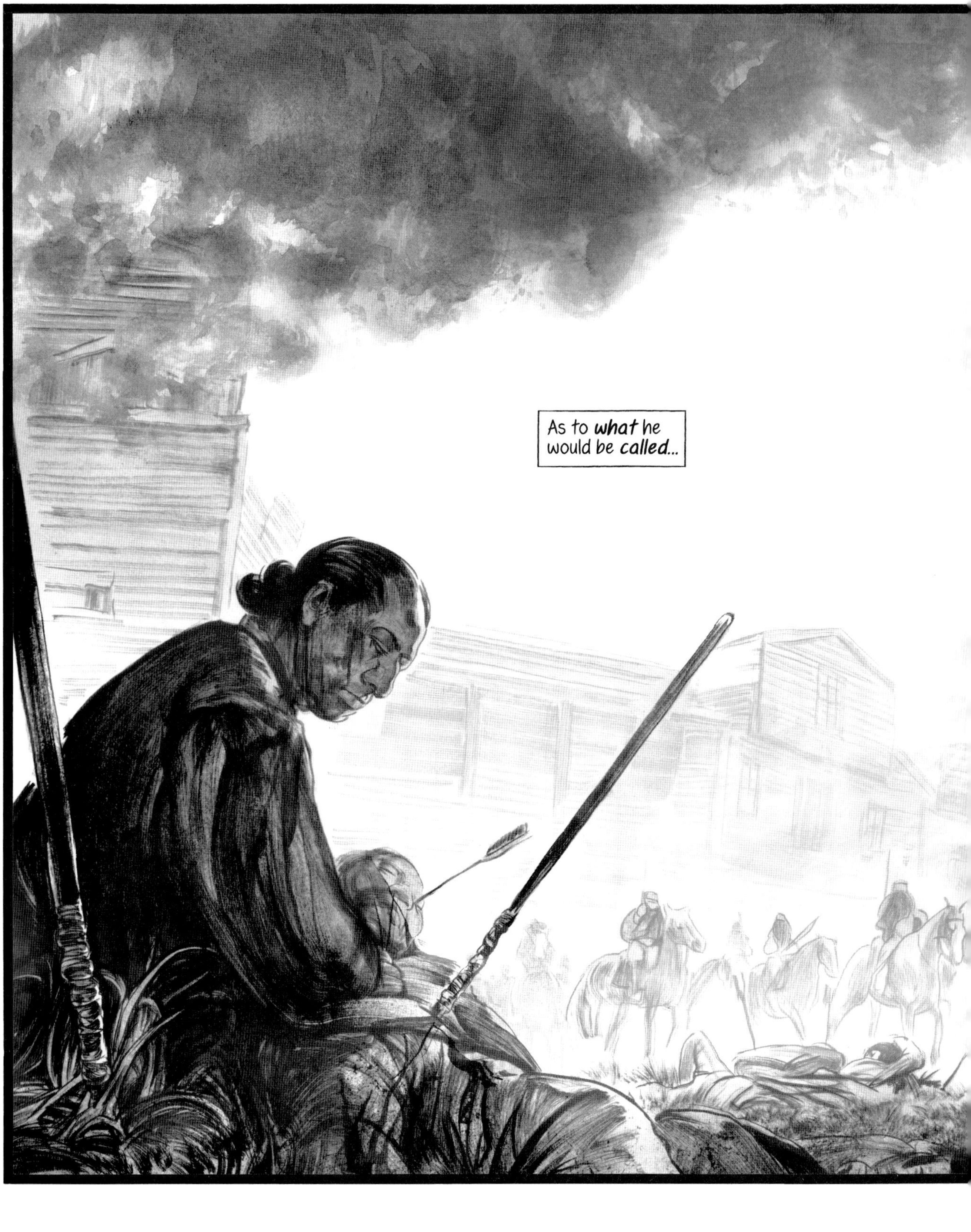
As to **what** he would be **called**...

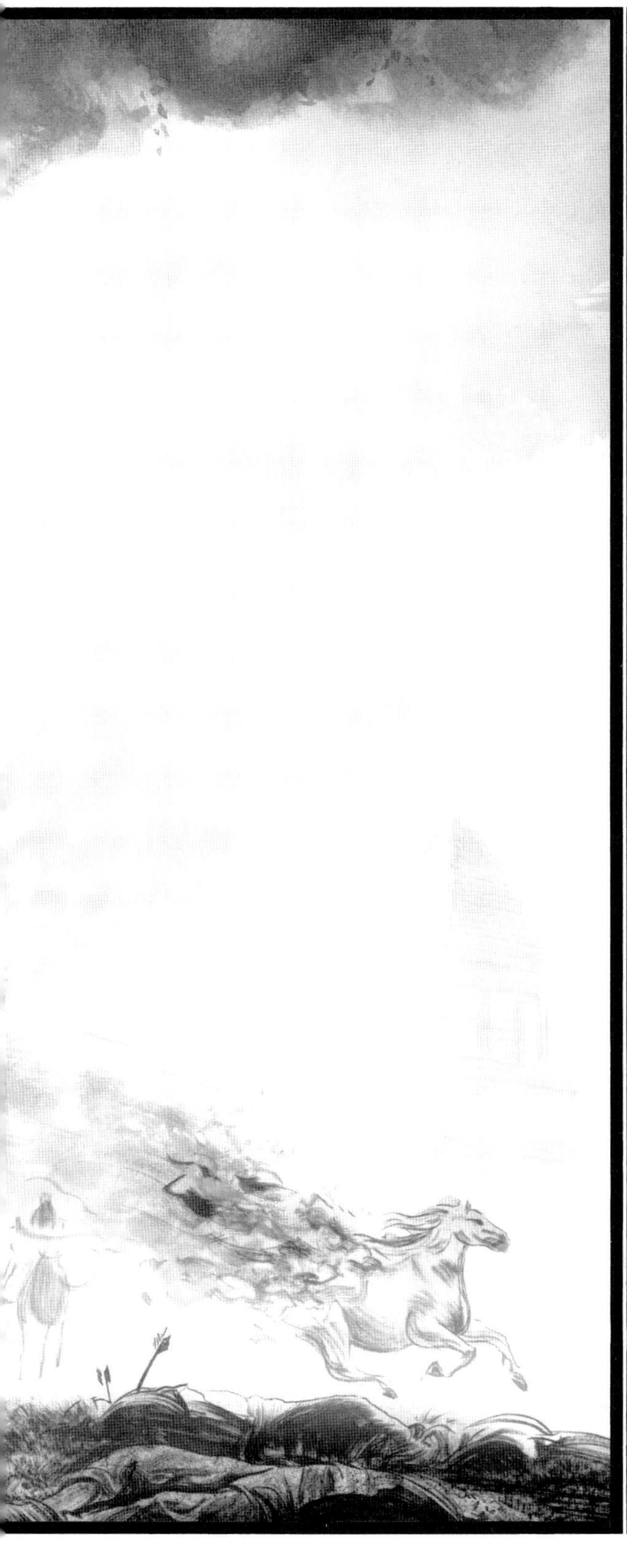

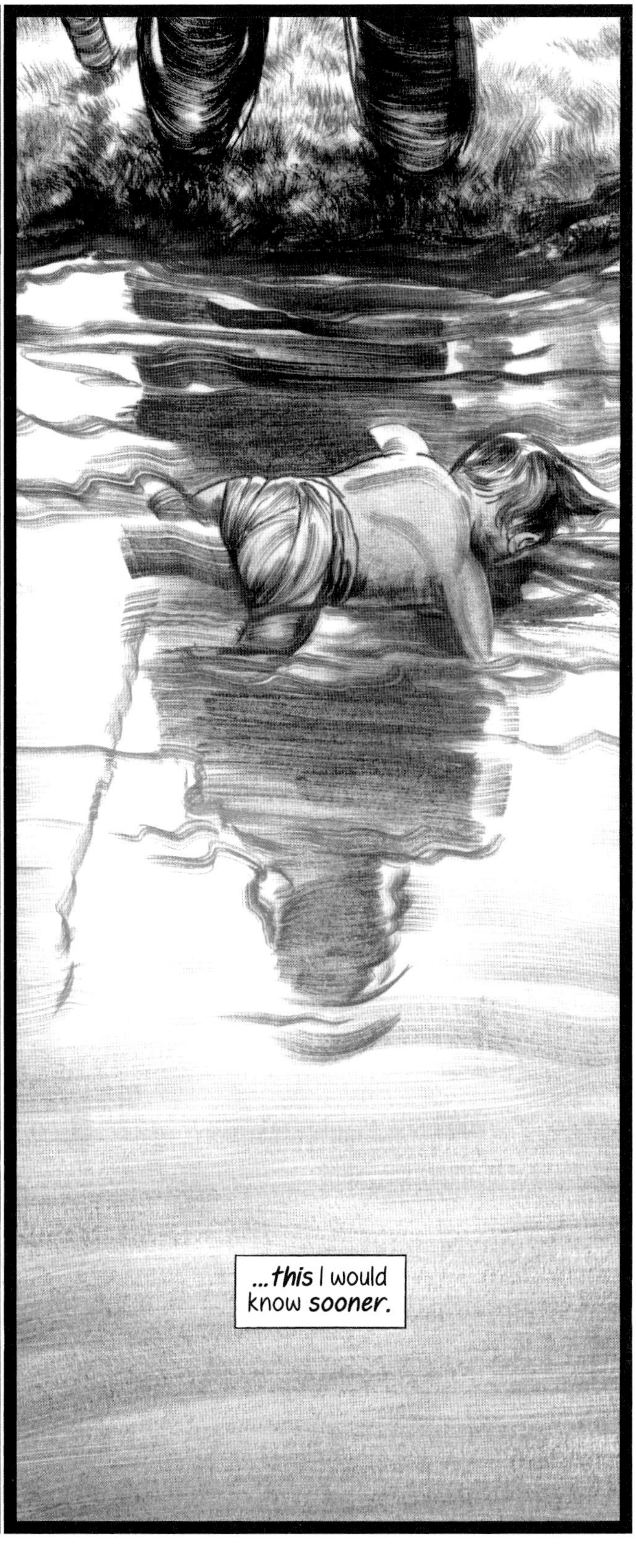
...this I would know sooner.

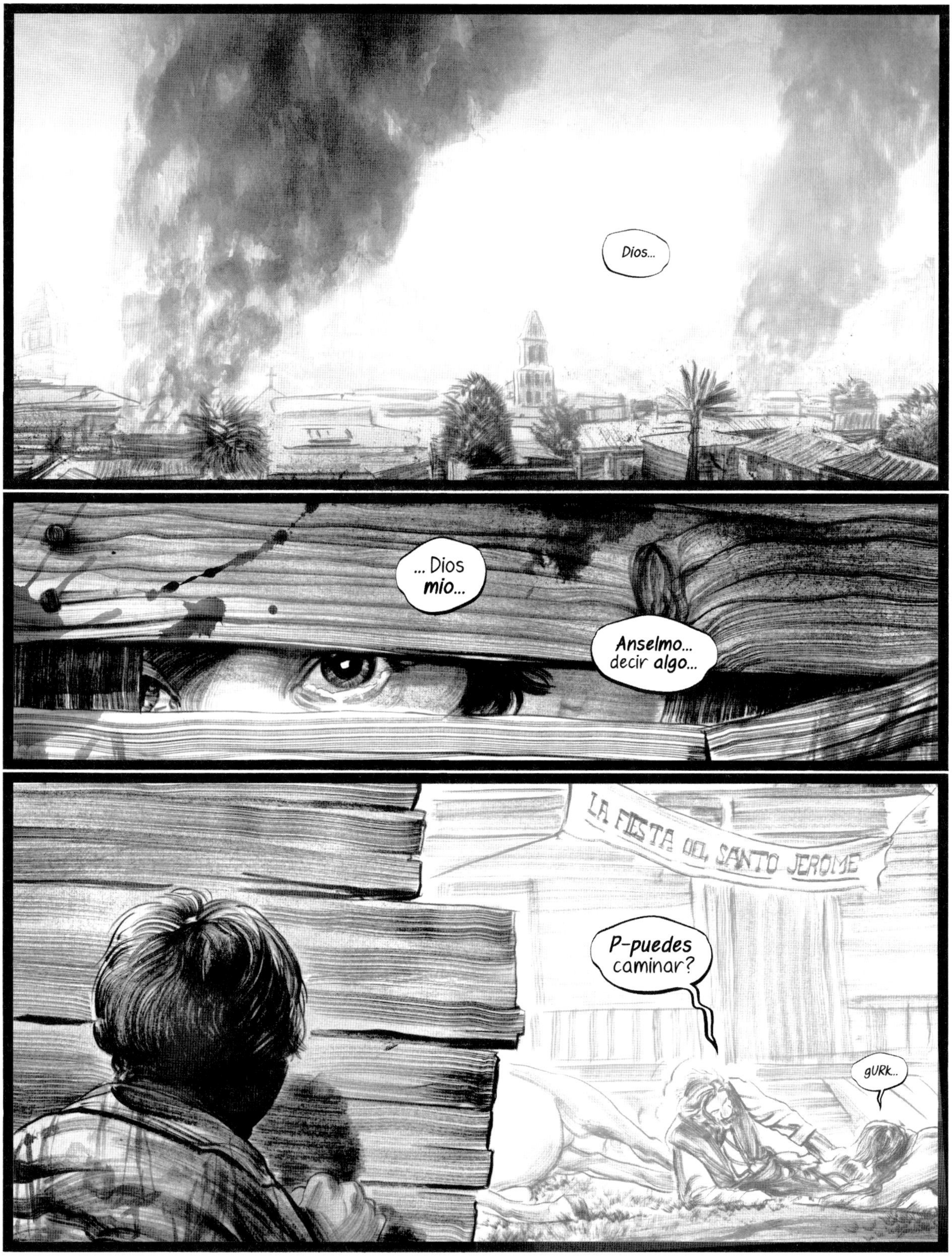
Dios...
... Dios mio...
Anselmo... decir algo...
LA FIESTA DEL SANTO JEROME
P-puedes caminar?
gURK...

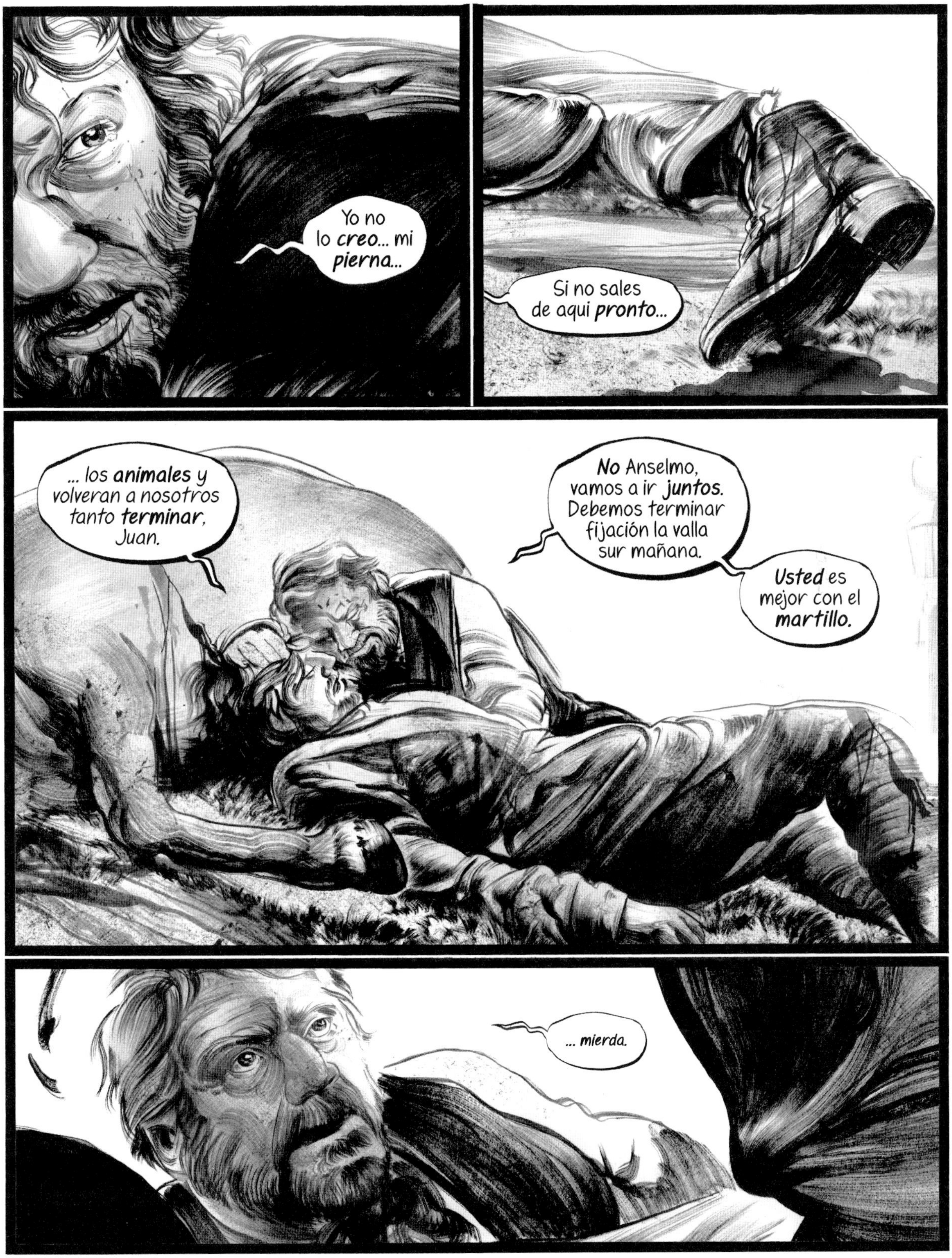
Yo no lo creo... mi pierna...
Si no sales de aqui pronto...
... los animales y volveran a nosotros tanto terminar, Juan.
No Anselmo, vamos a ir juntos. Debemos terminar fijación la valla sur mañana.
Usted es mejor con el martillo.
... mierda.

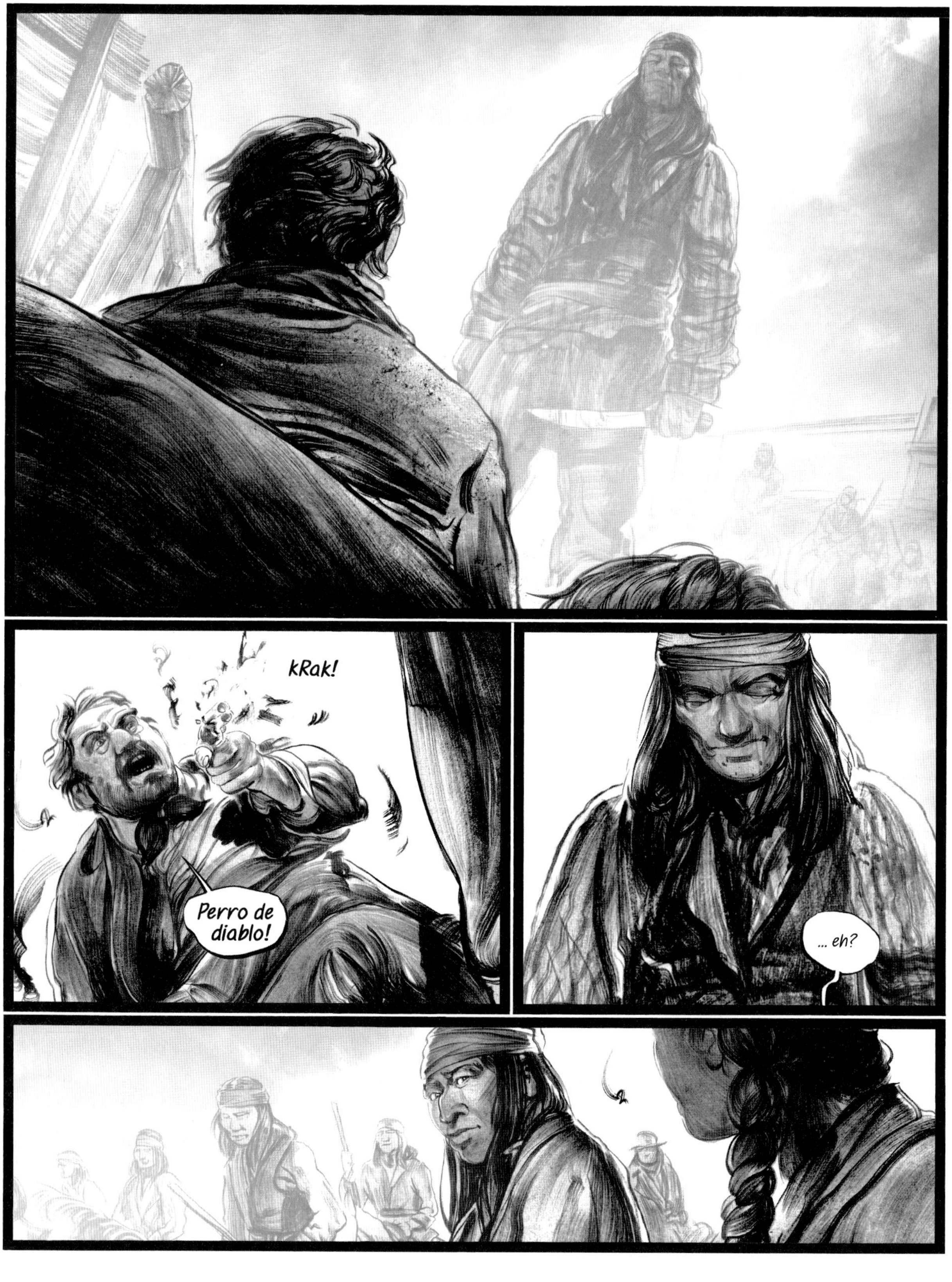
kRak!
Perro de diablo!
... eh?

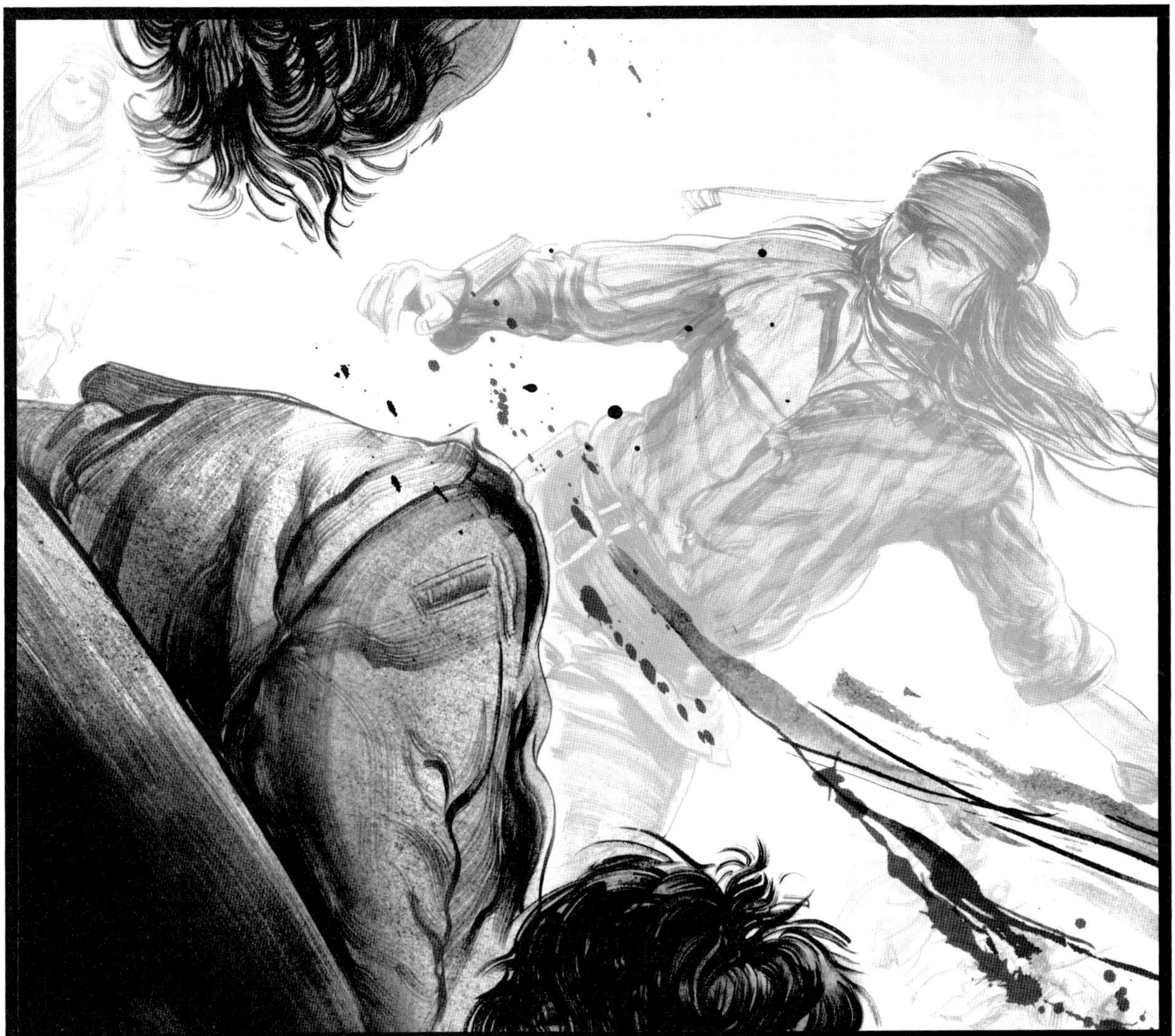

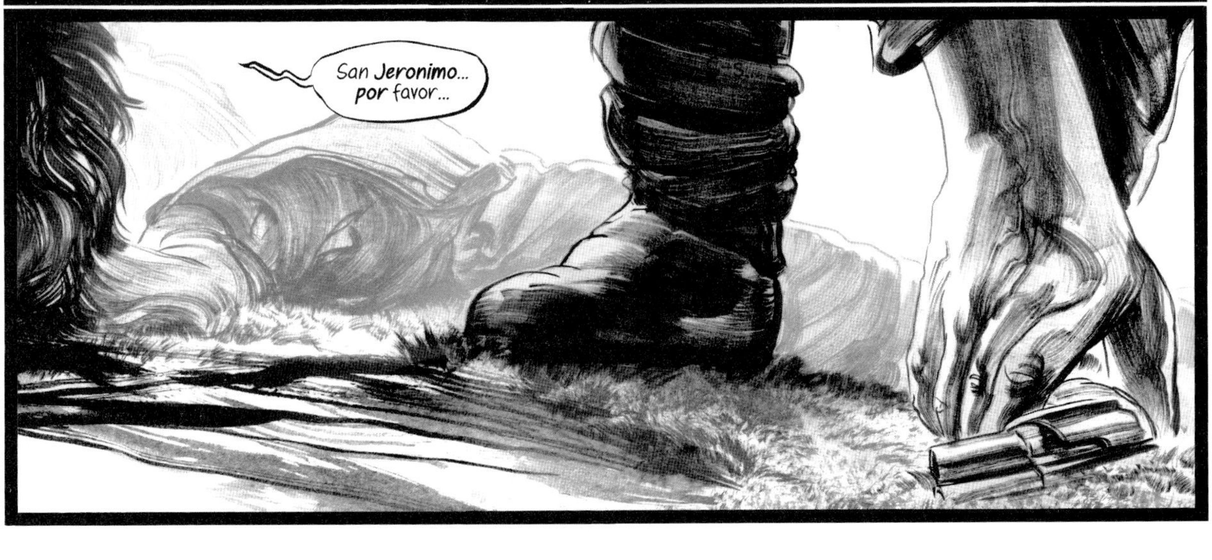
San **Jeronimo**...
por favor...

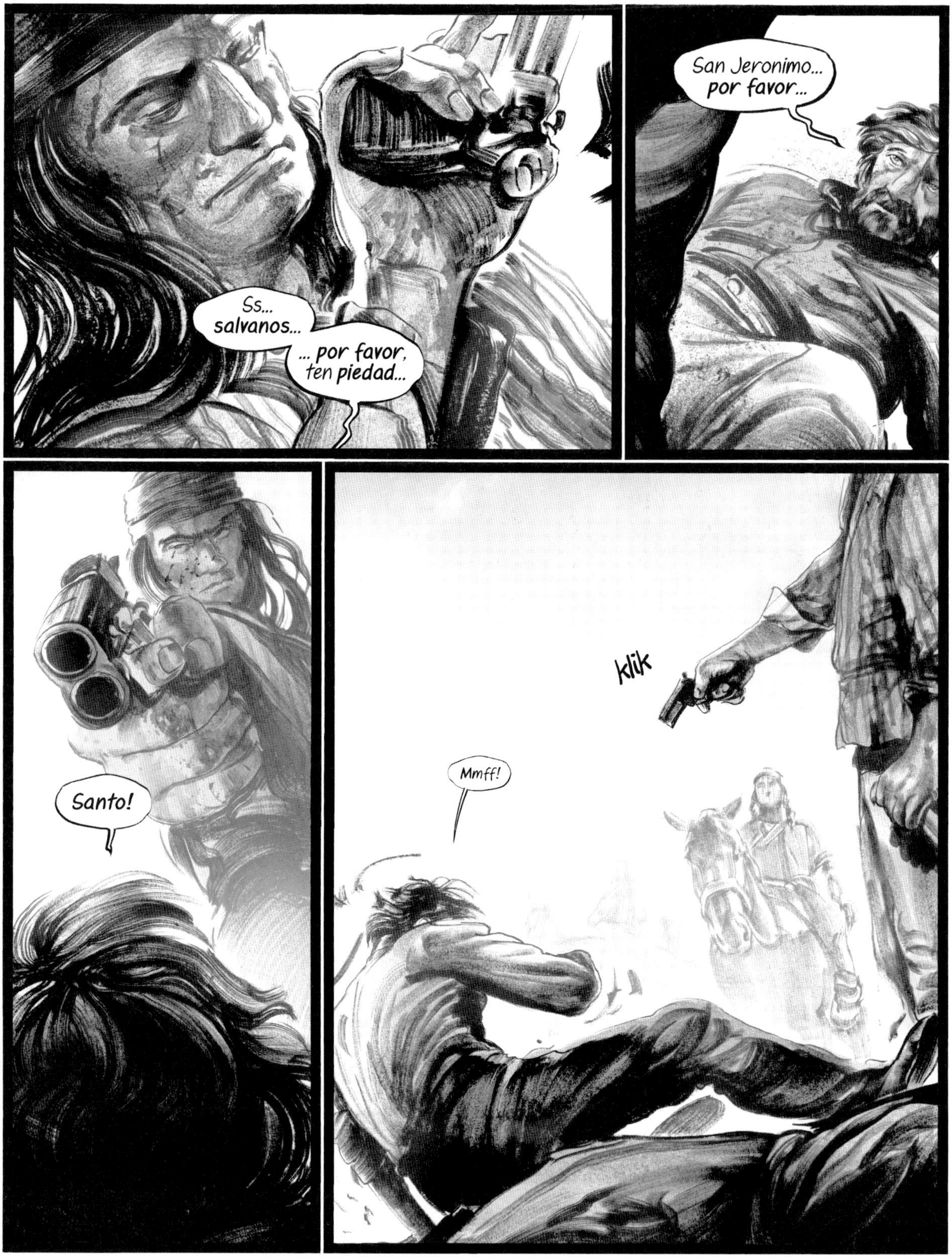
Ss...
salvanos...
... por favor,
ten piedad...
San Jeronimo...
por favor...
Santo!
klik
Mmff!

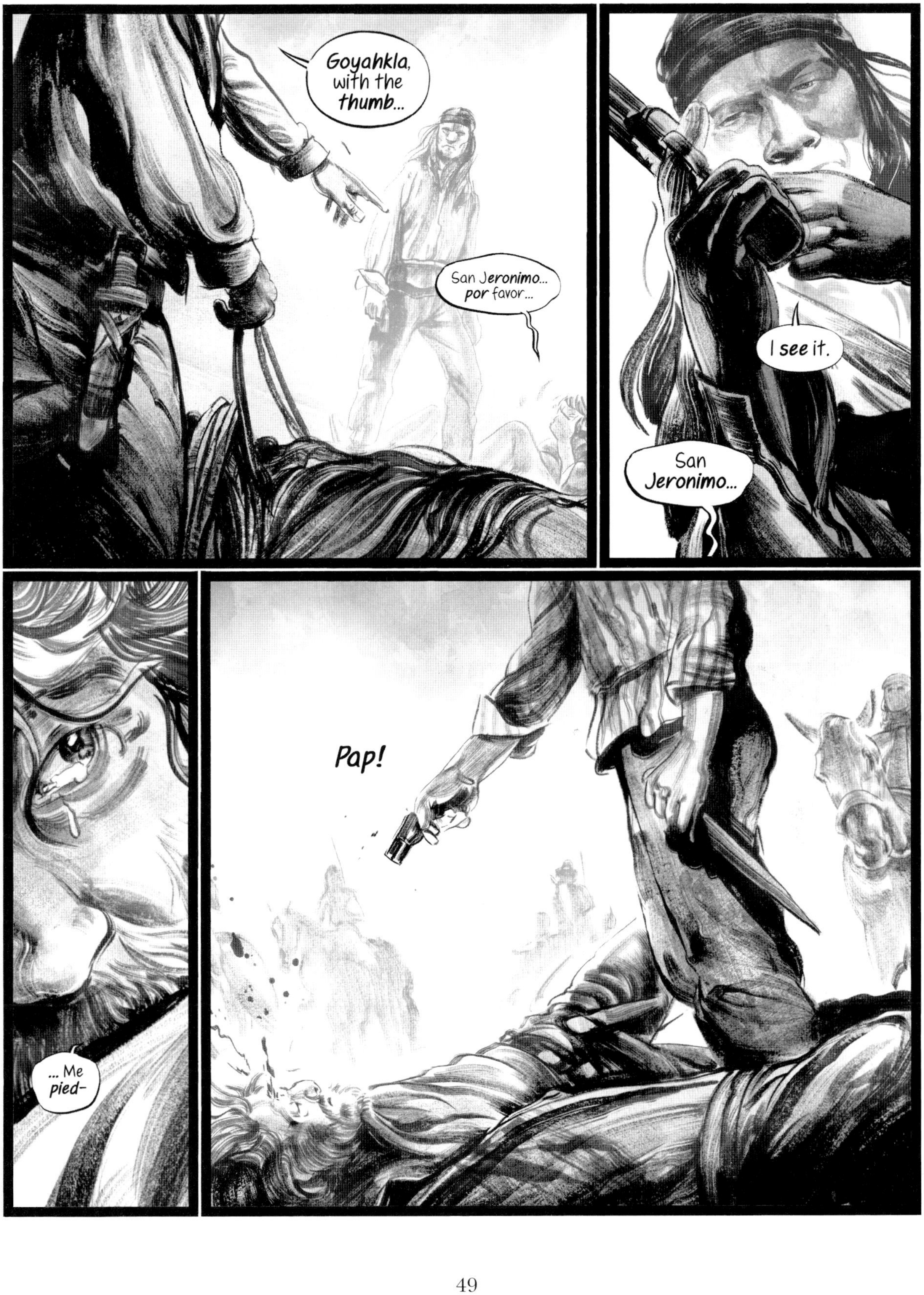
Goyahkla, with the thumb...
San Jeronimo... por favor...
I see it.
San Jeronimo...
... Me pied-
Pap!

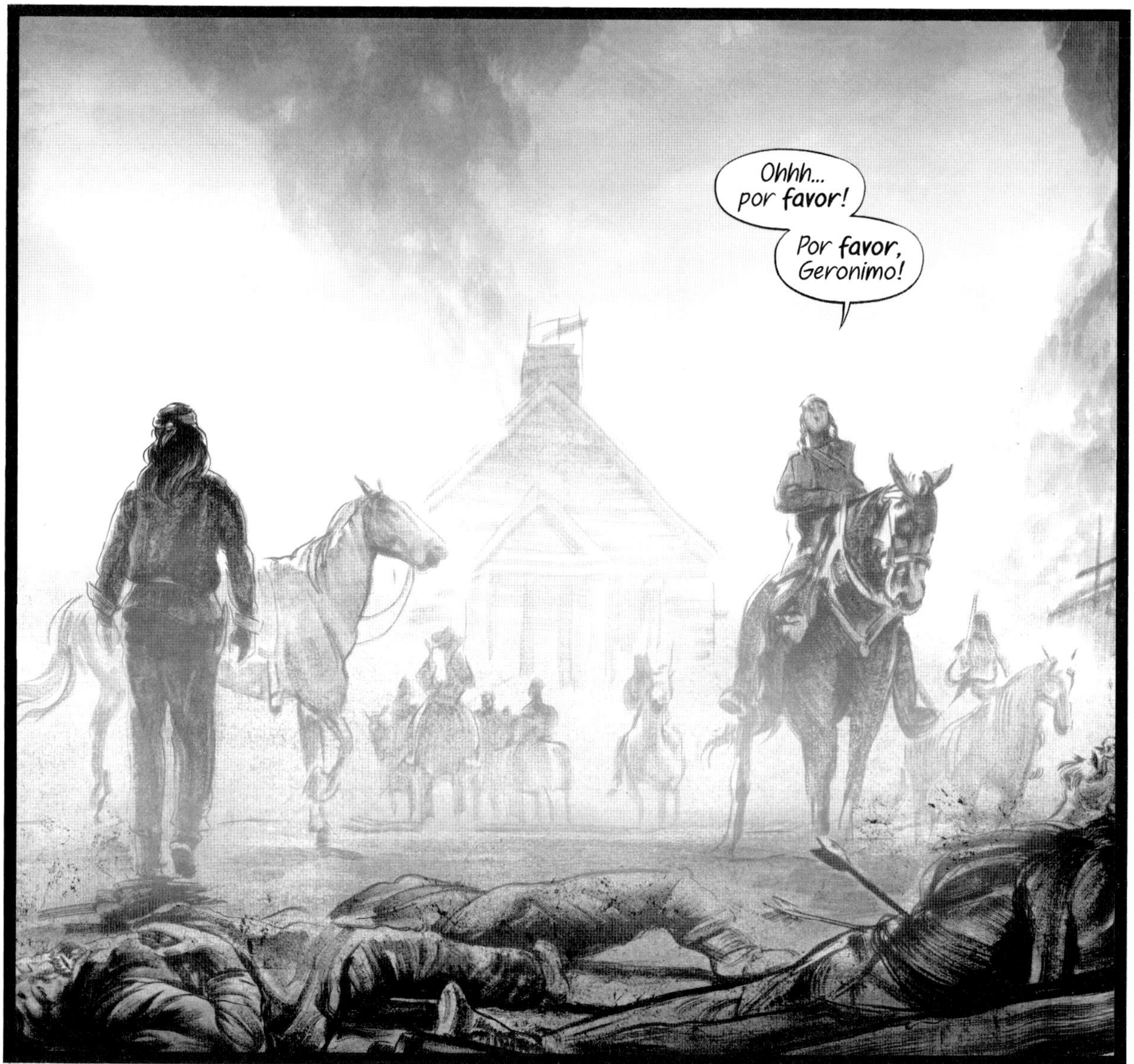
Ohhh... por favor!
Por favor, Geronimo!

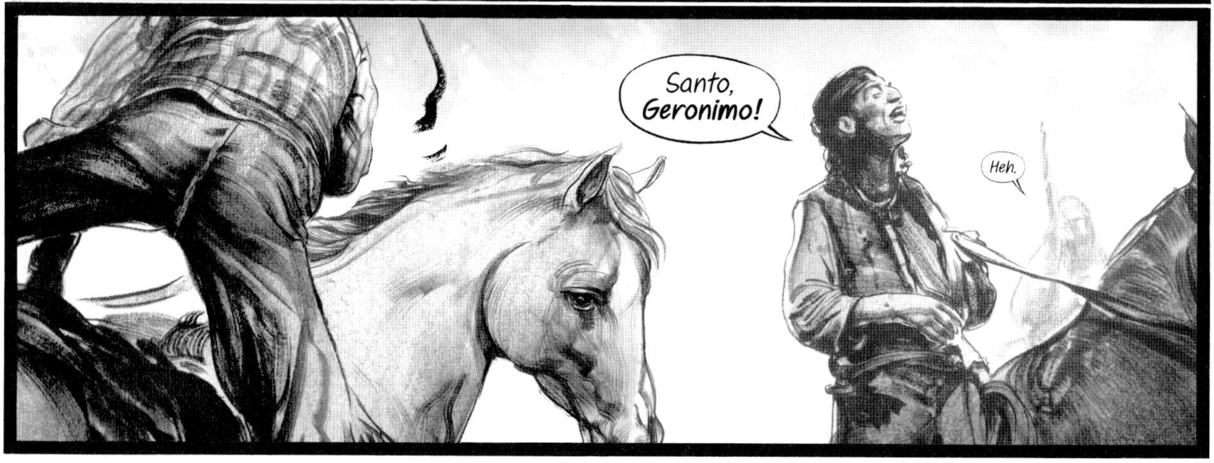
Santo, Geronimo!
Heh.

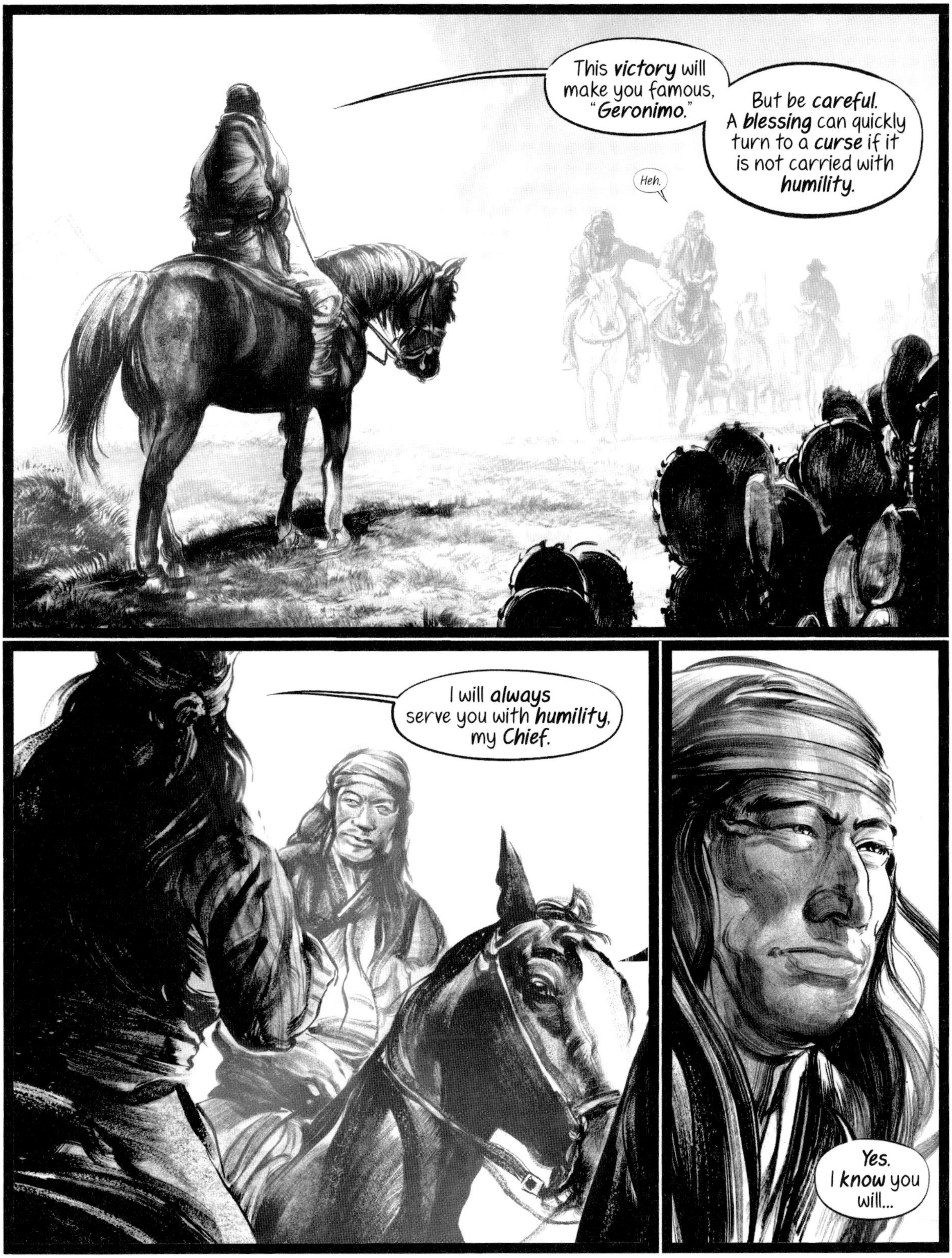
This victory will make you famous, "Geronimo."
But be careful. A blessing can quickly turn to a curse if it is not carried with humility.
Heh.
I will always serve you with humility, my Chief.
Yes. I know you will...

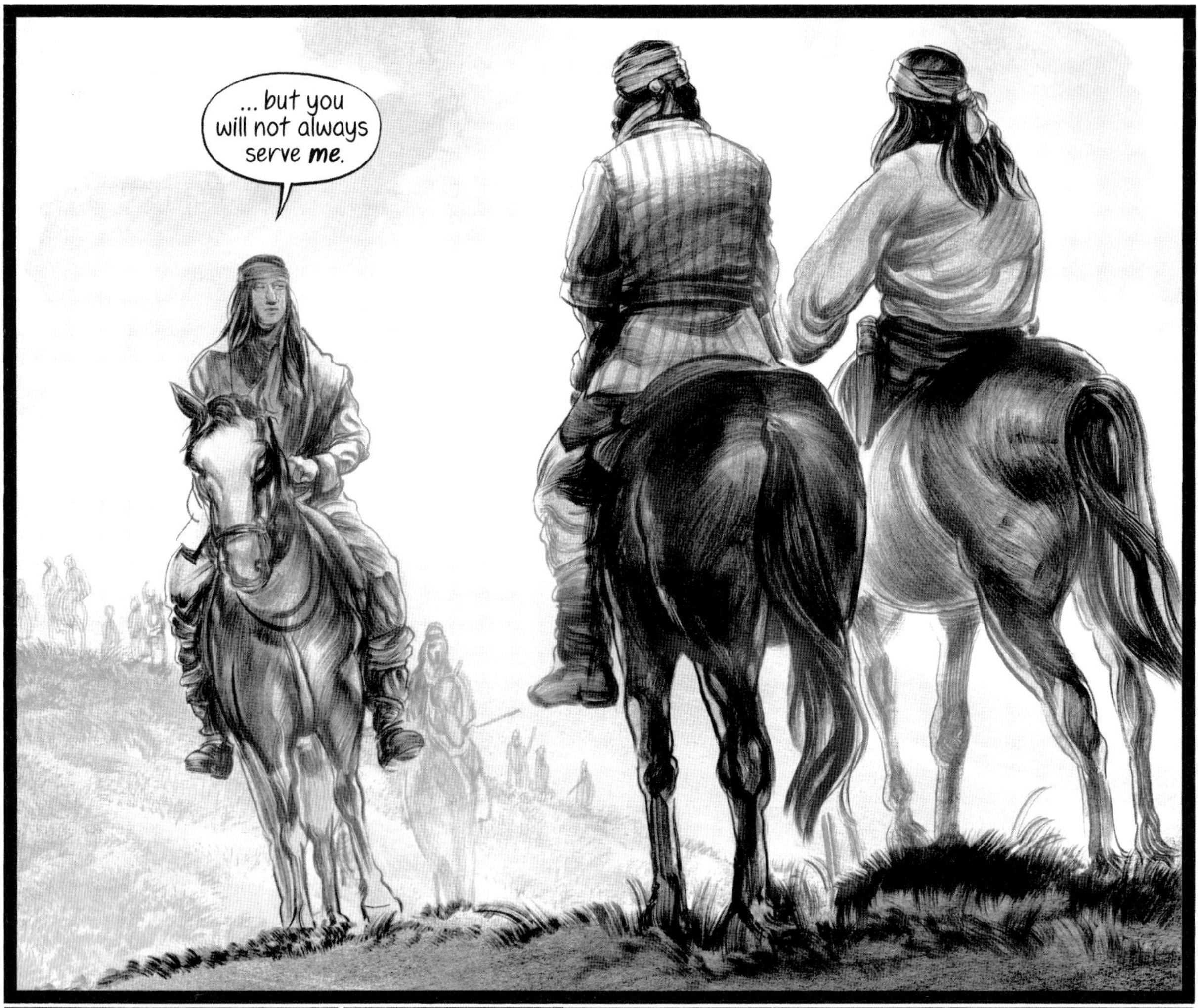
... but you will not always serve **me**.

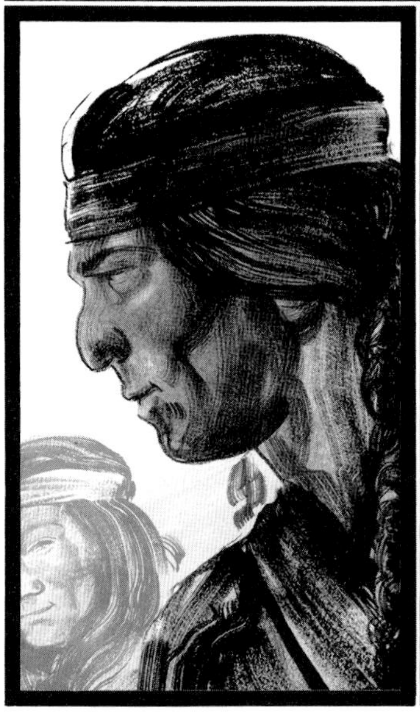

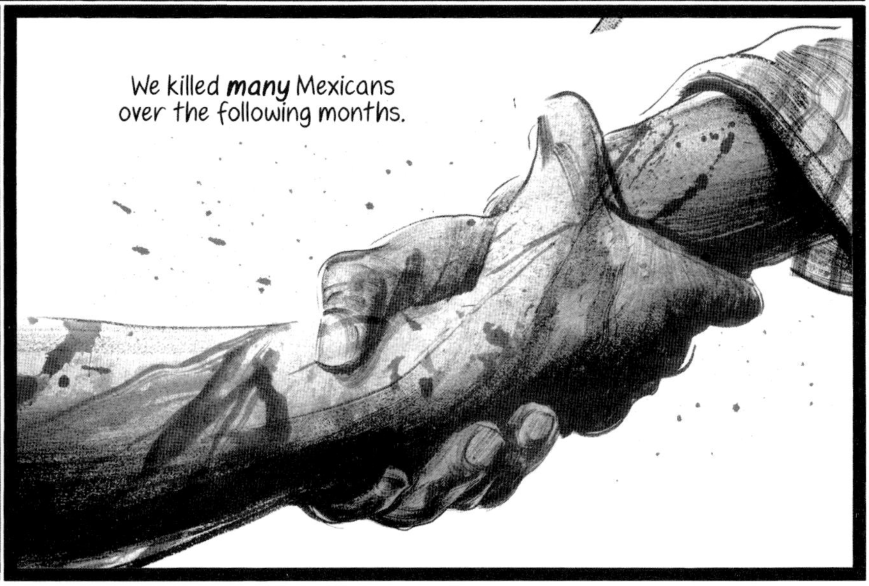
We killed **many** Mexicans over the following months.

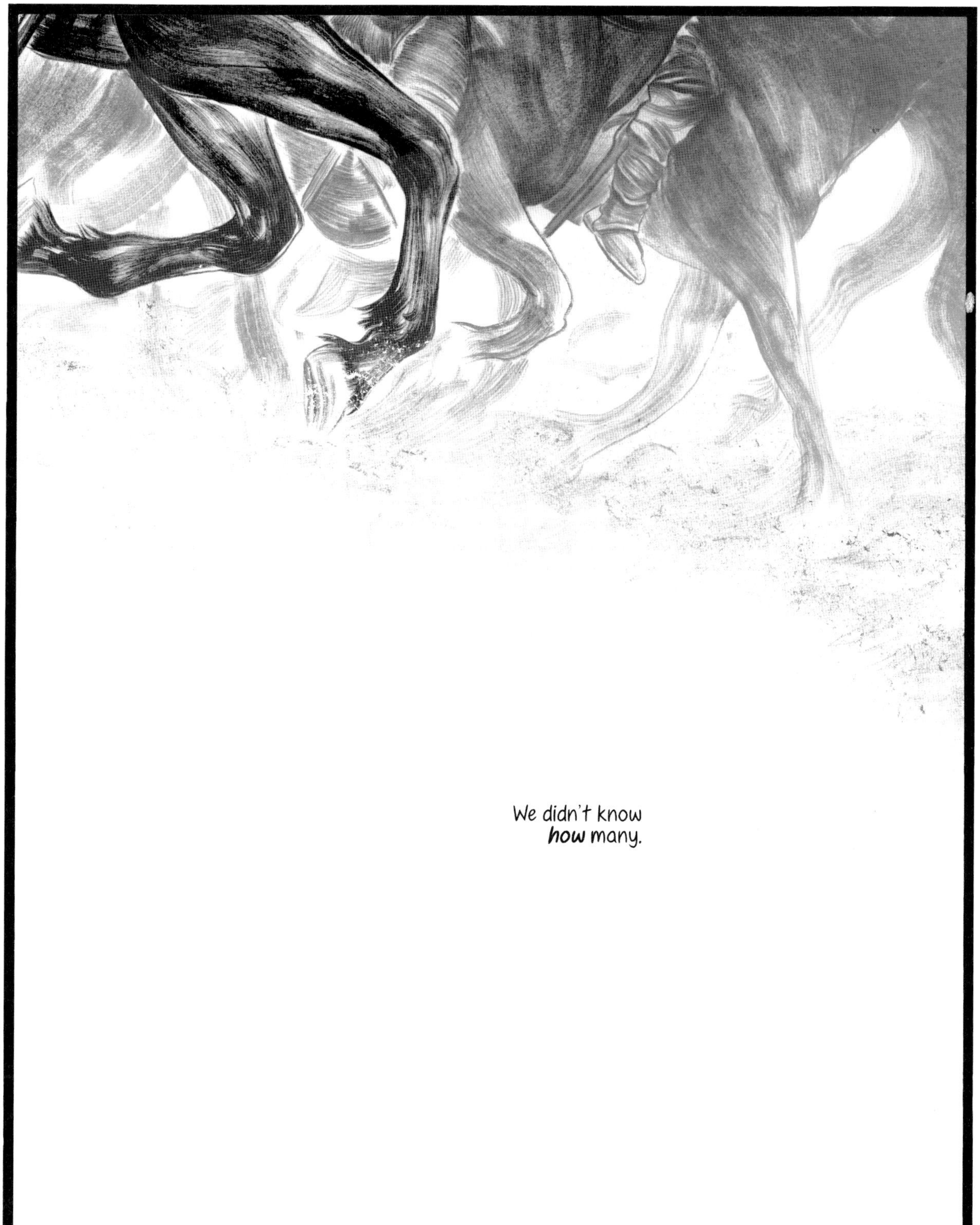
We didn't know **how** many.

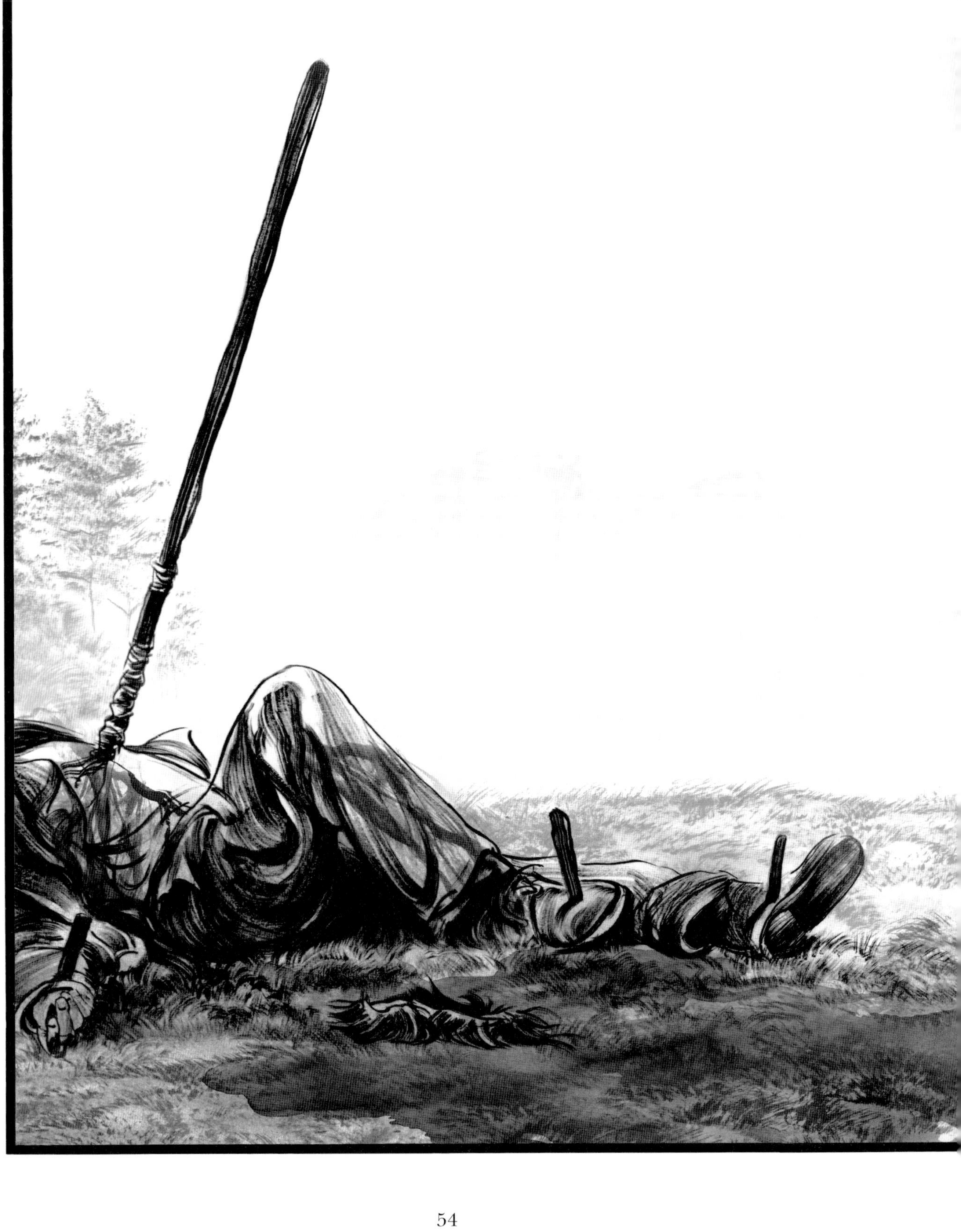

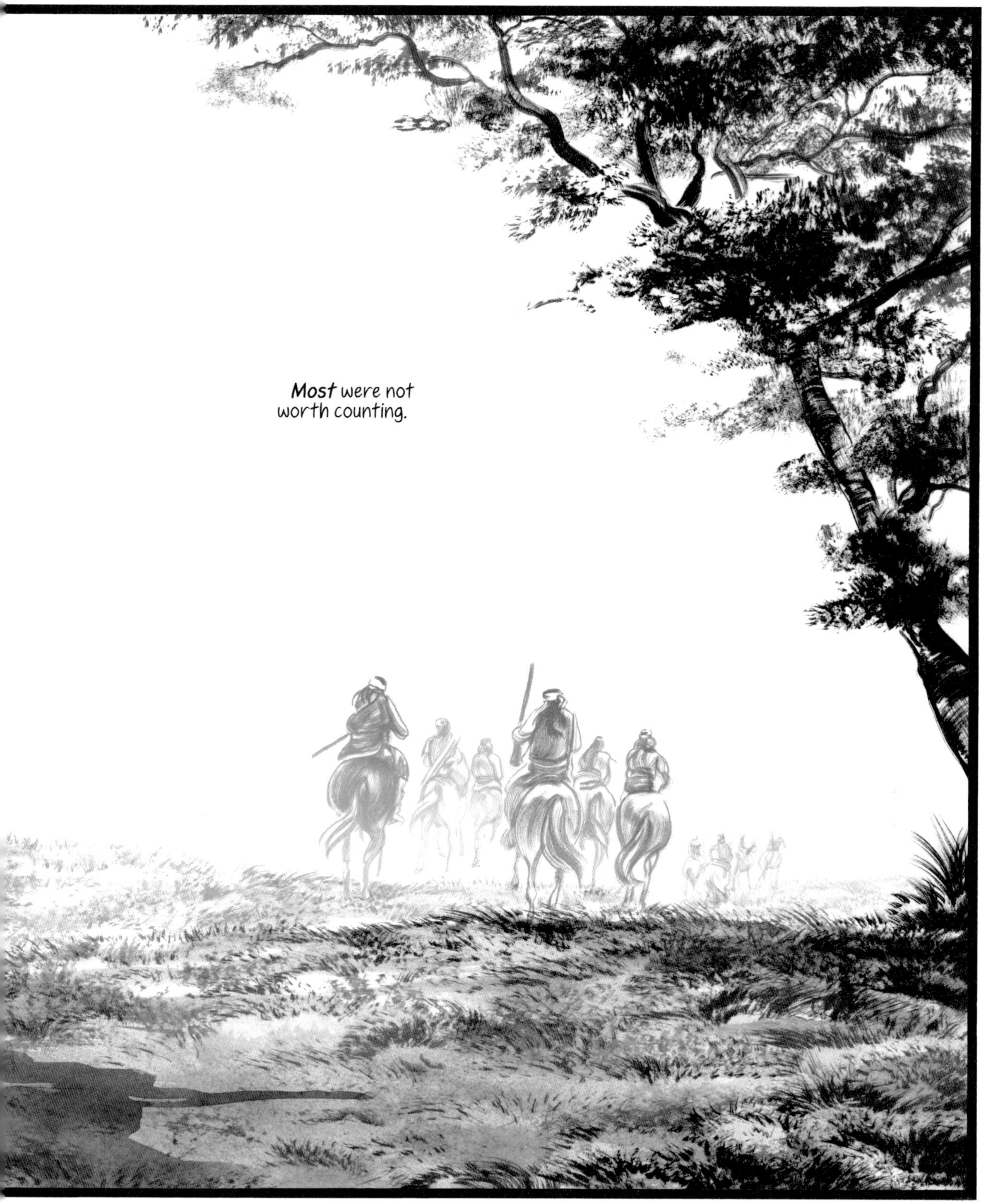
Most were not worth counting.

· PART TWO ·
LOCUSTS

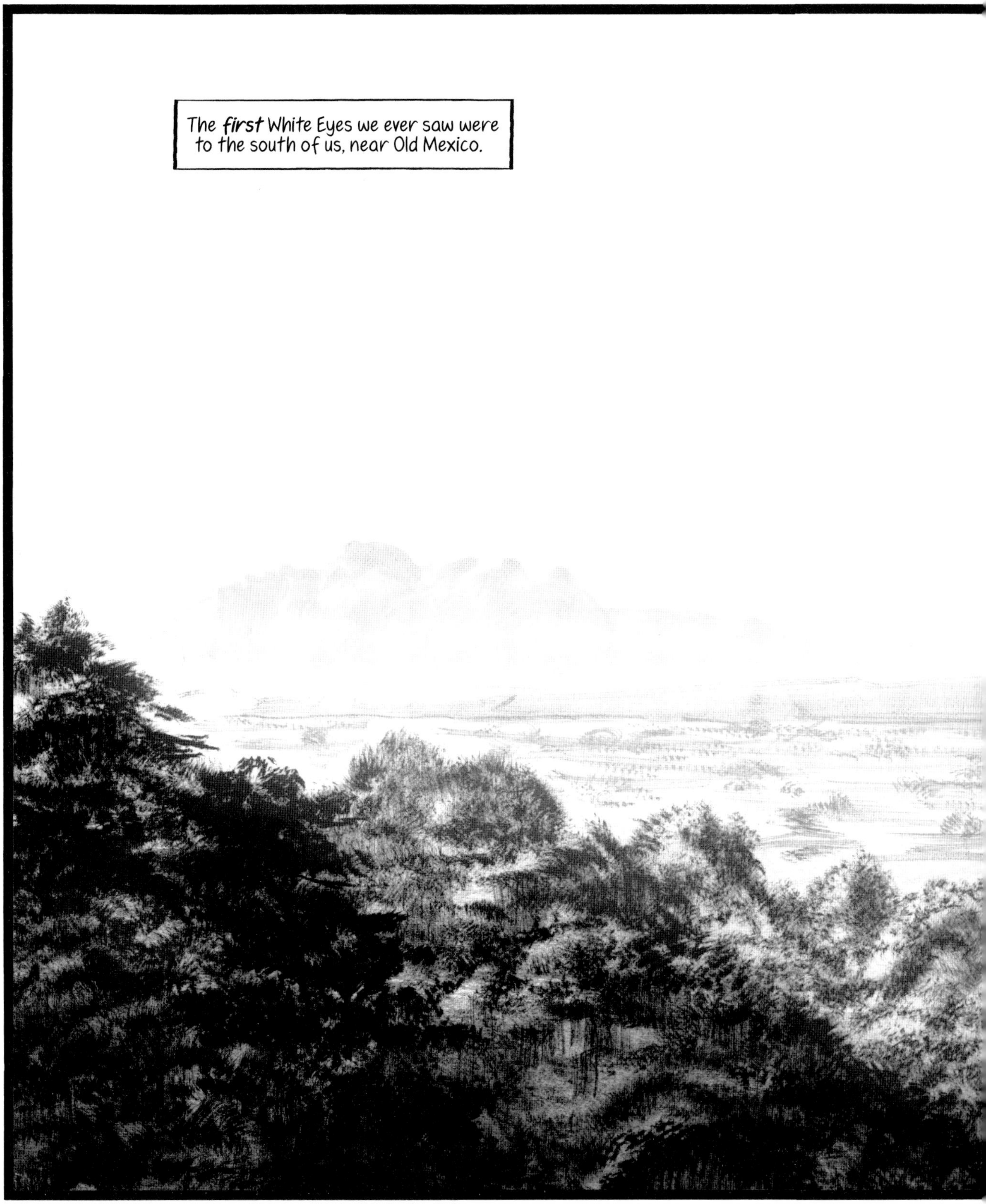
The *first* White Eyes we ever saw were to the south of us, near Old Mexico.

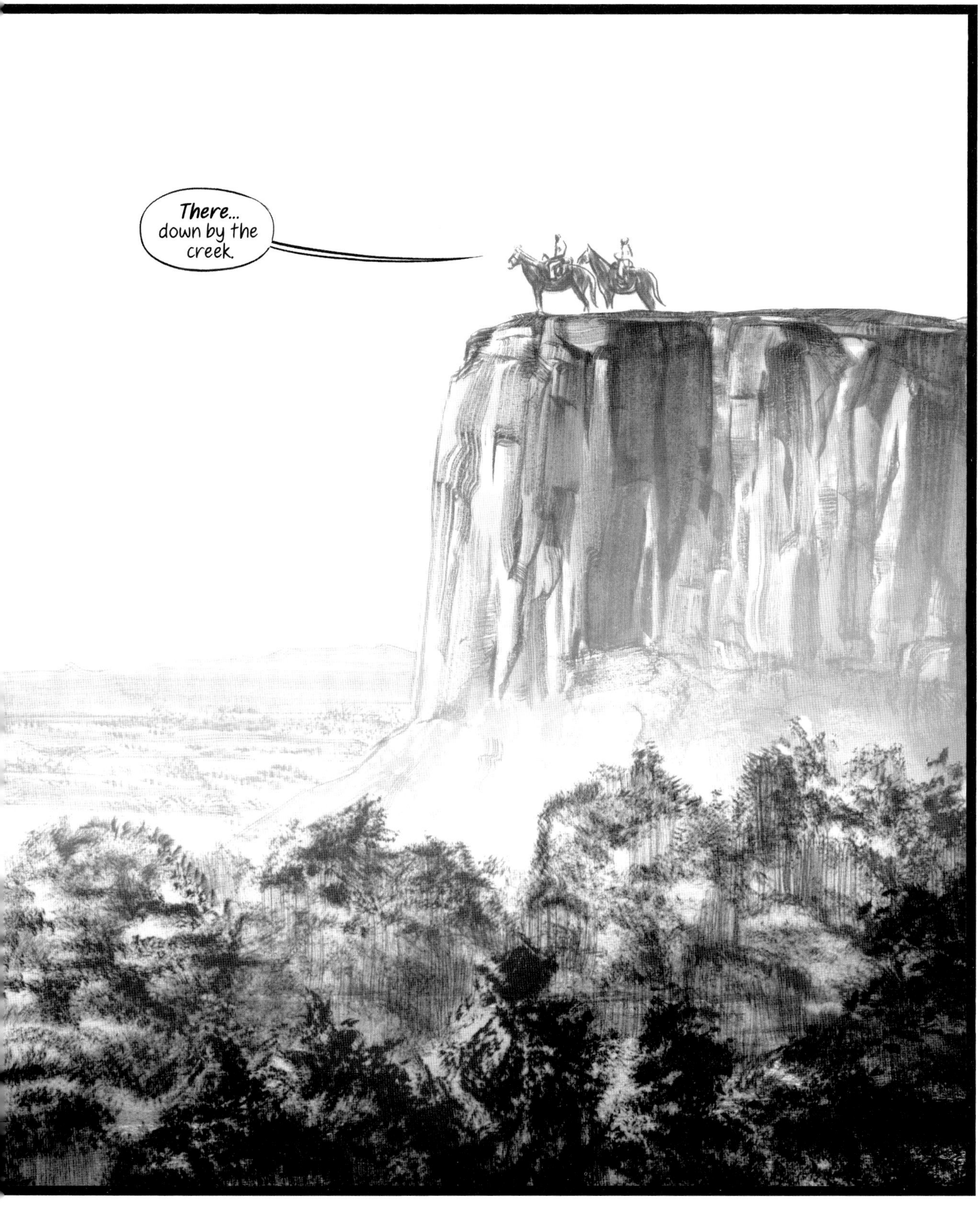
There... down by the creek.

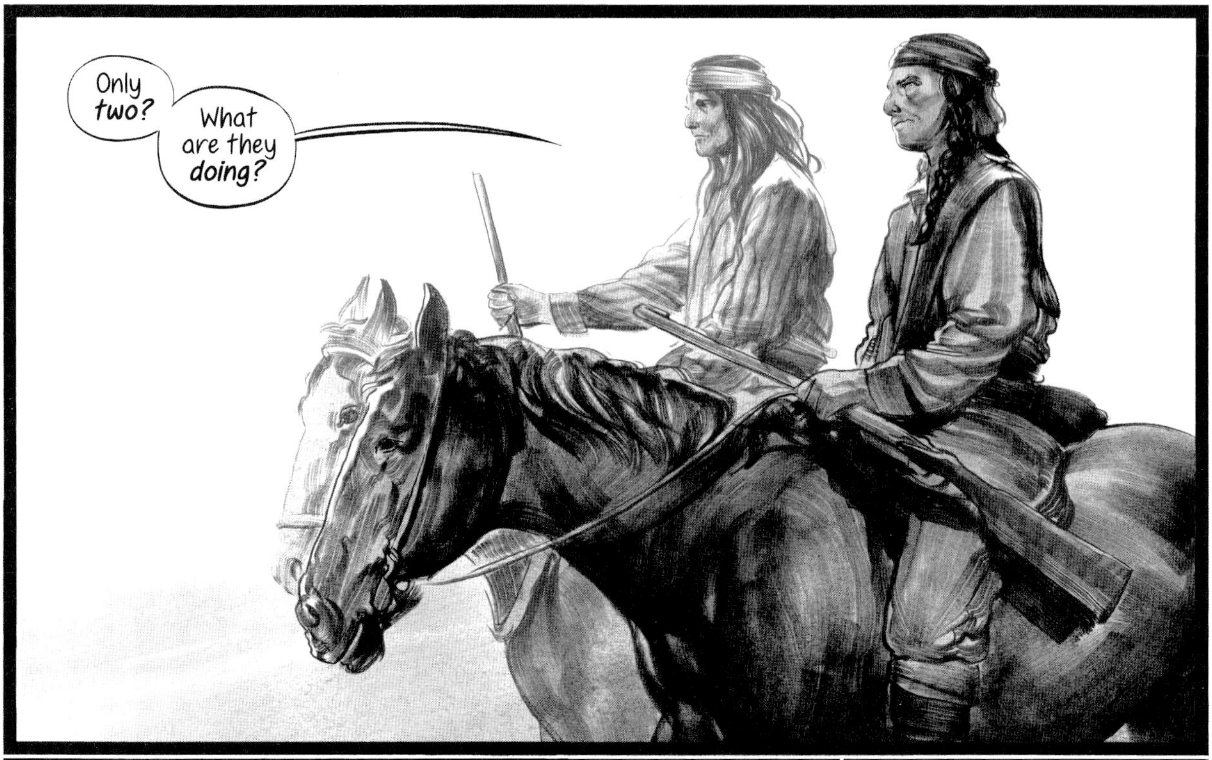
Only *two?*
What are they *doing?*

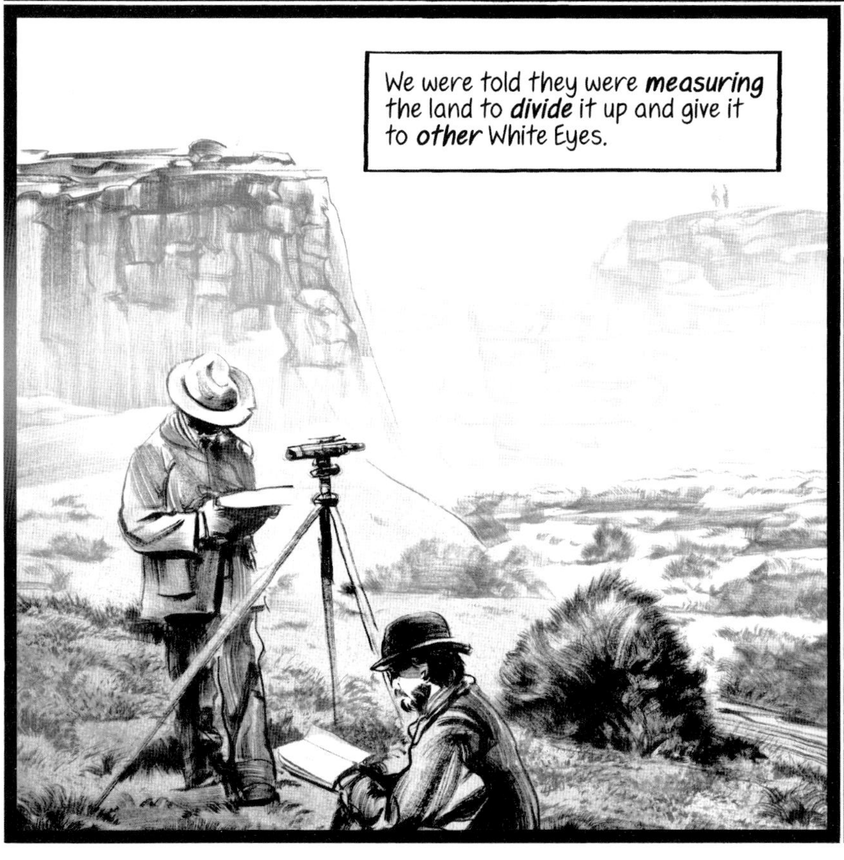
We were told they were **measuring** the land to ***divide*** it up and give it to ***other*** White Eyes.

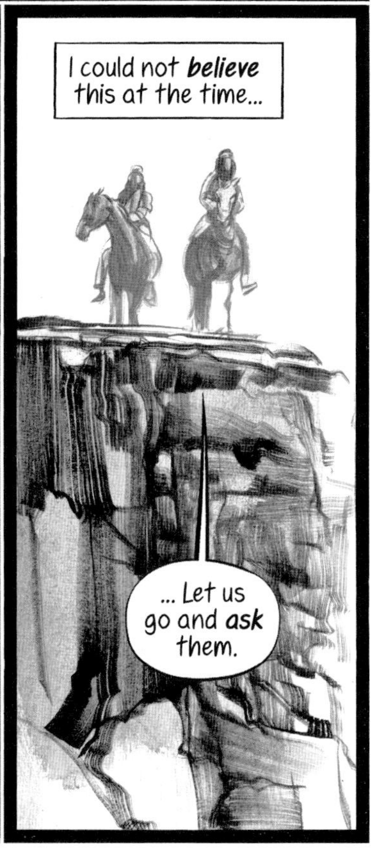
I could not ***believe*** this at the time...
... Let us go and **ask** them.

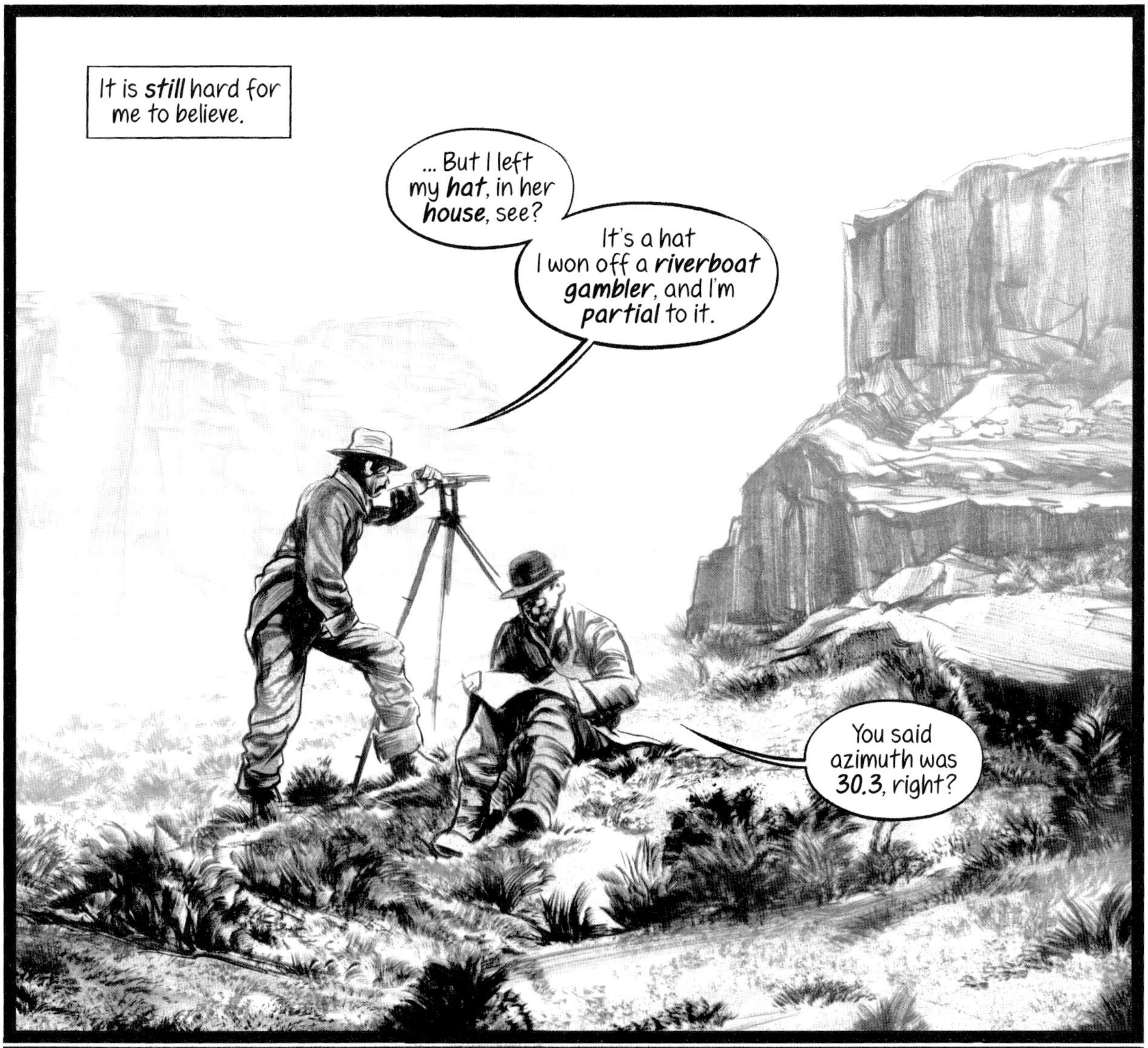
It is still hard for me to believe.
... But I left my hat, in her house, see?
It's a hat I won off a riverboat gambler, and I'm partial to it.
You said azimuth was 30.3, right?

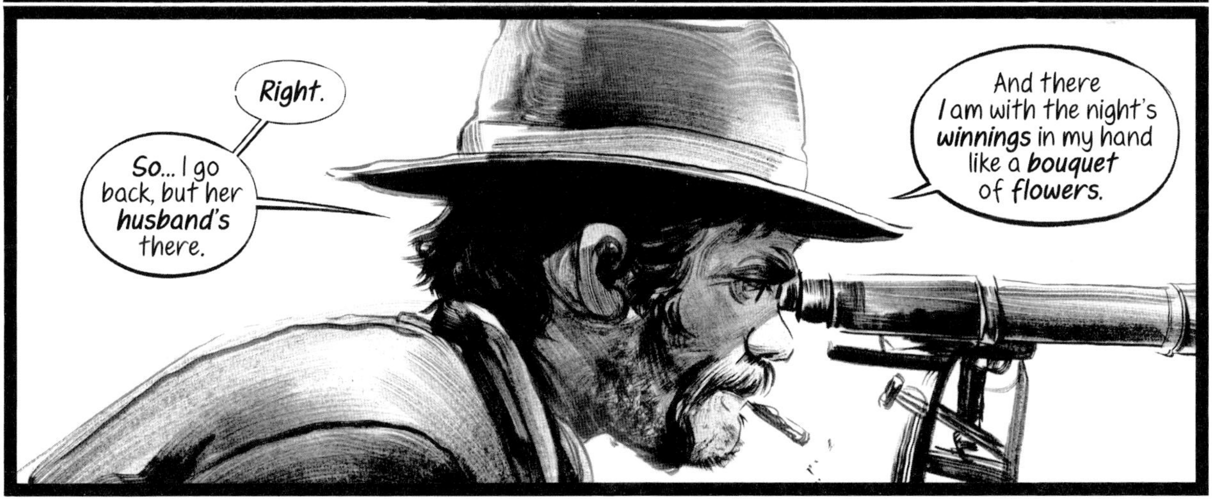
Right.
So... I go back, but her husband's there.
And there I am with the night's winnings in my hand like a bouquet of flowers.

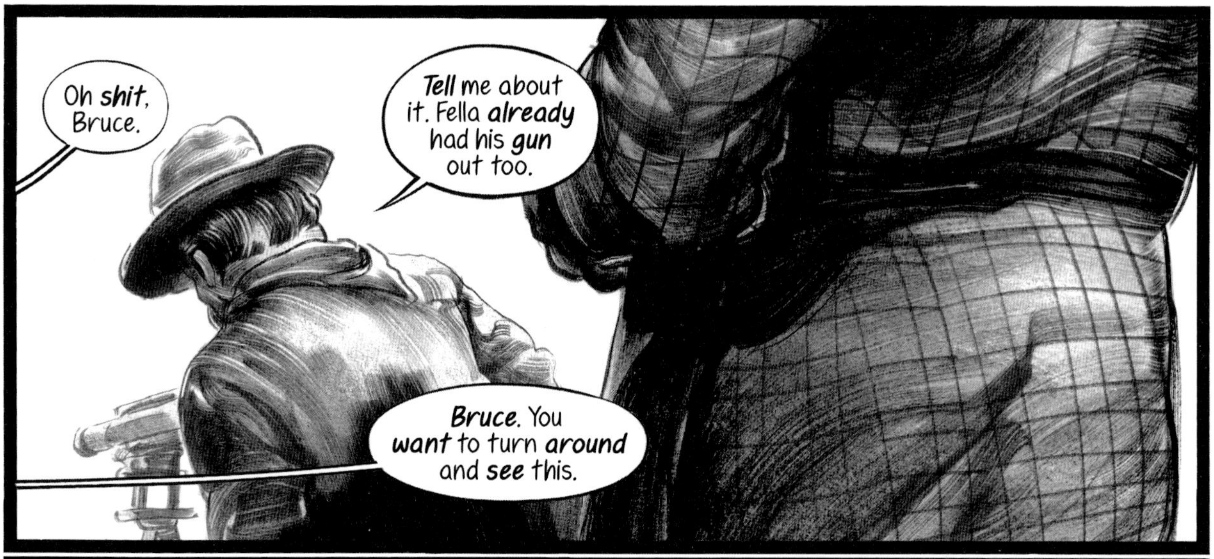
Oh shit, Bruce.
Tell me about it. Fella already had his gun out too.
Bruce. You want to turn around and see this.

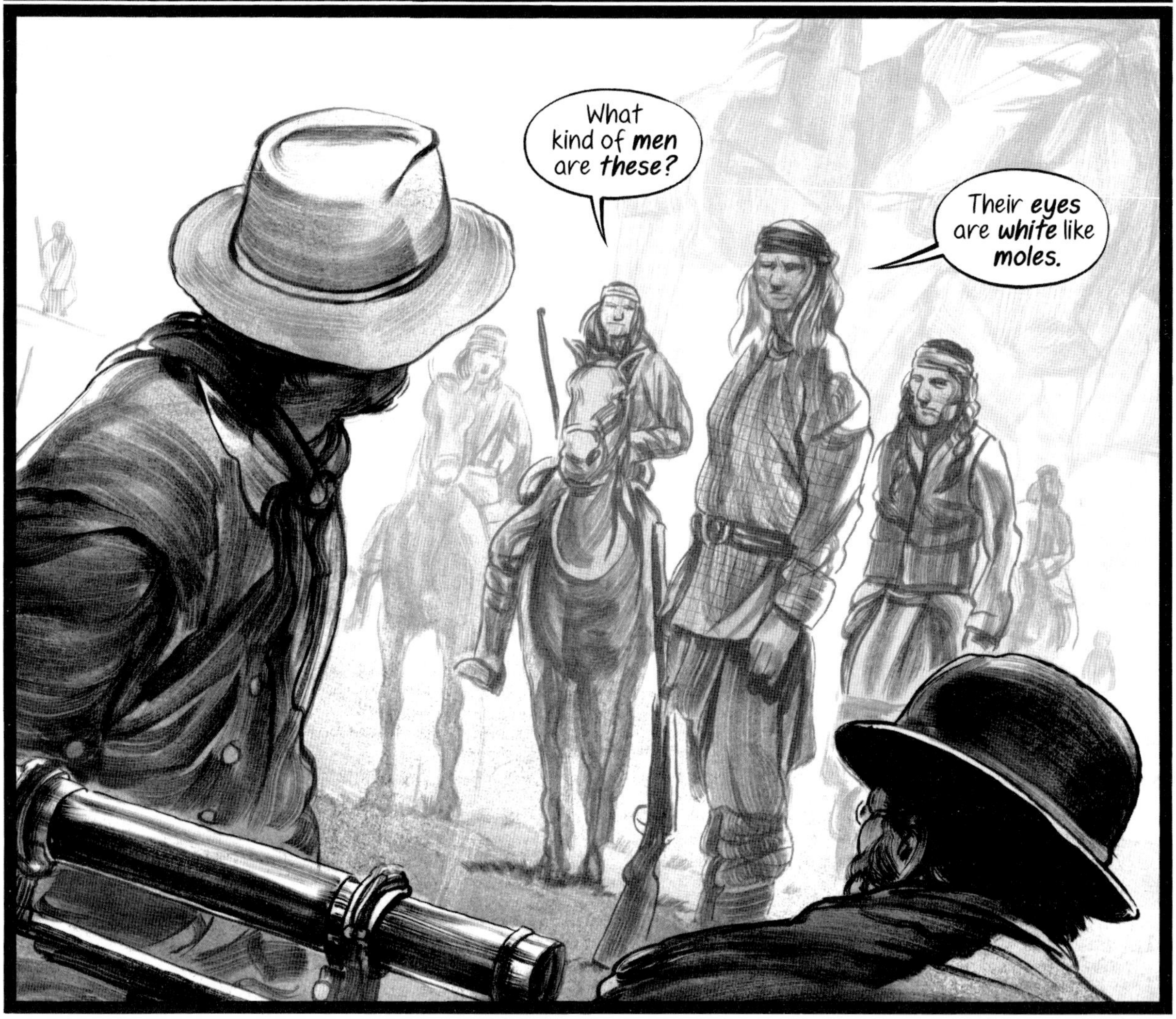
What kind of men are these?
Their eyes are white like moles.

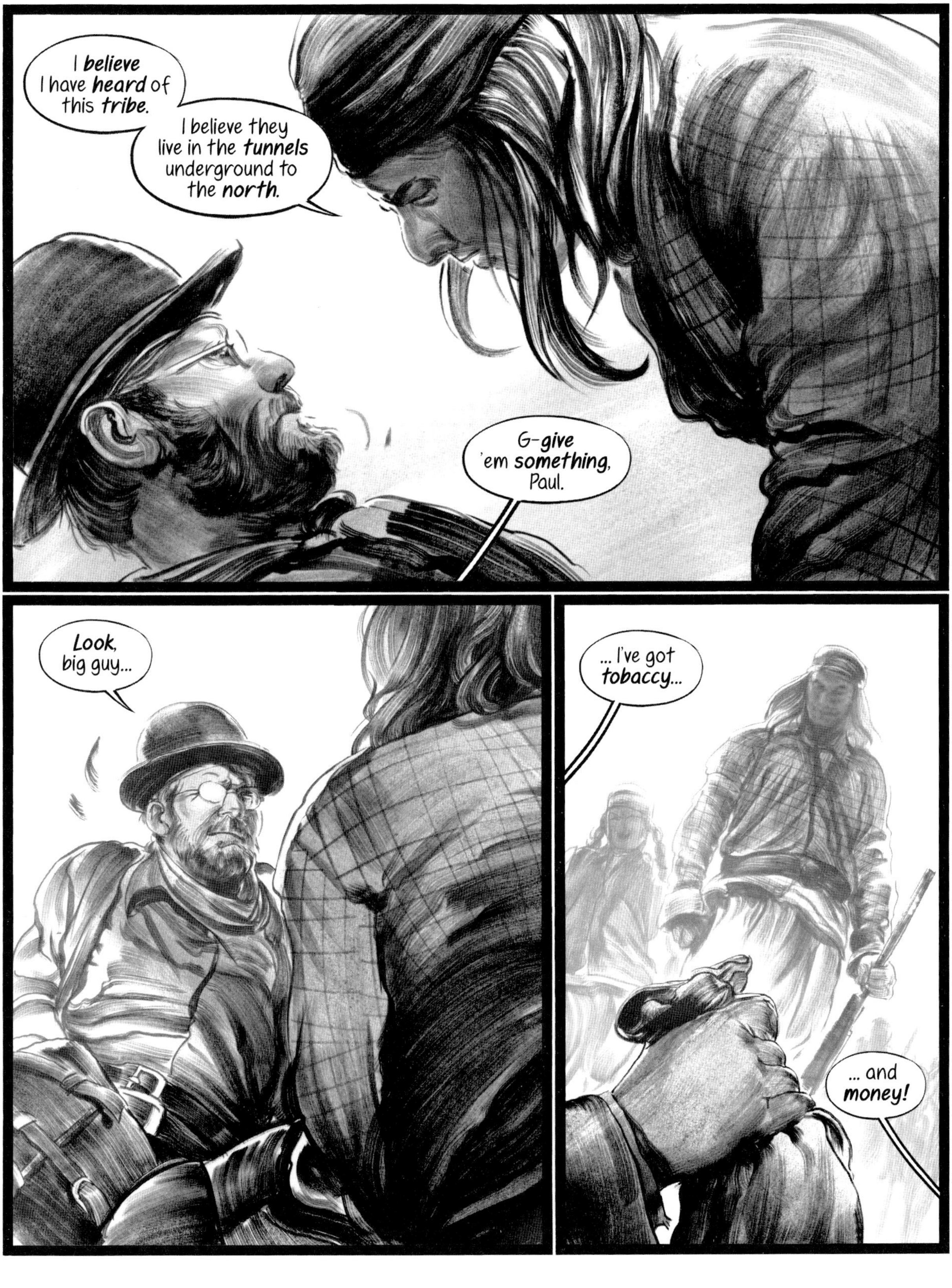
I **believe** I have **heard** of this **tribe**.
I believe they live in the **tunnels** underground to the **north**.
G-**give** 'em **something**, Paul.
Look, big guy...
... I've got **tobaccy**...
... and **money**!

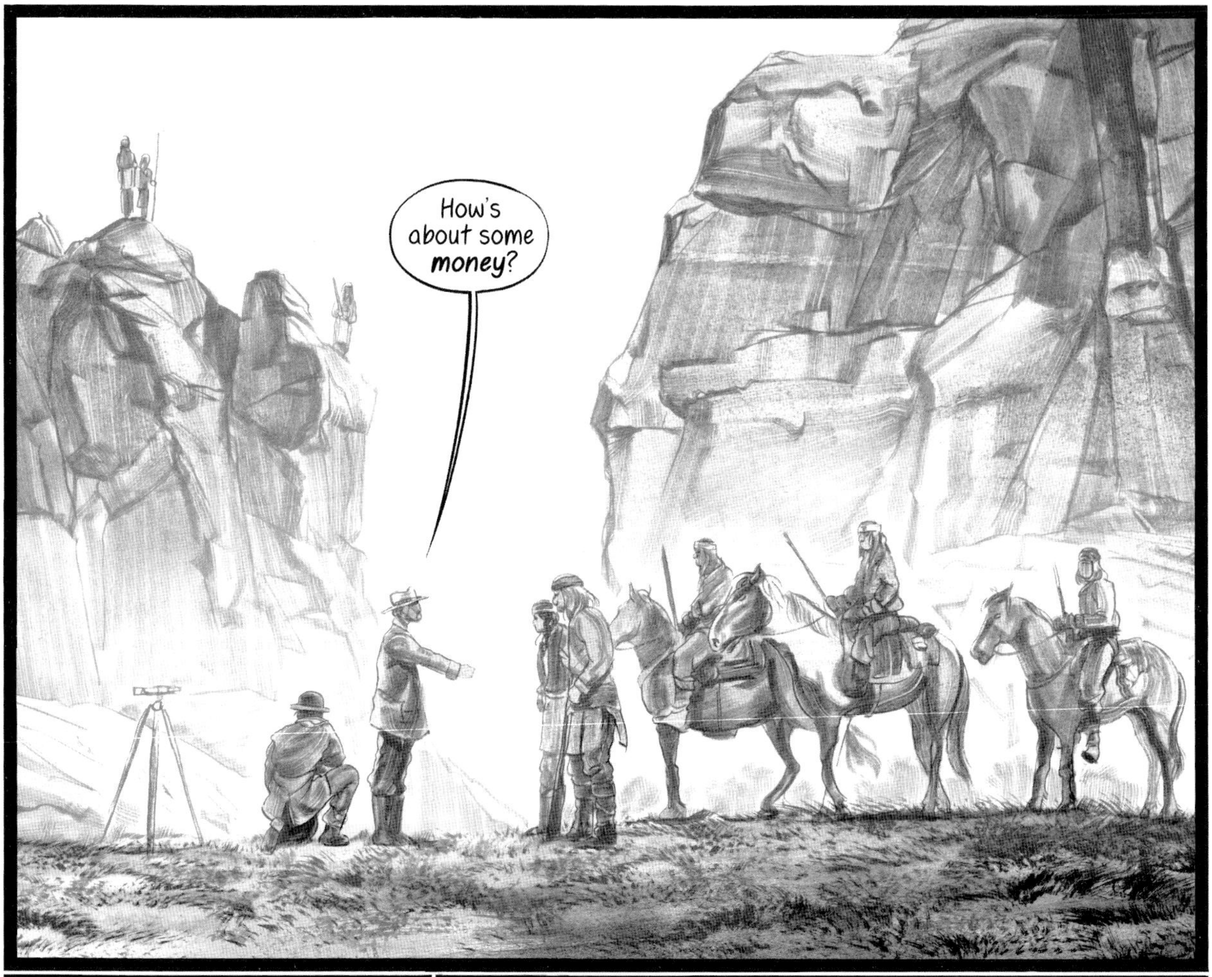
How's about some money?

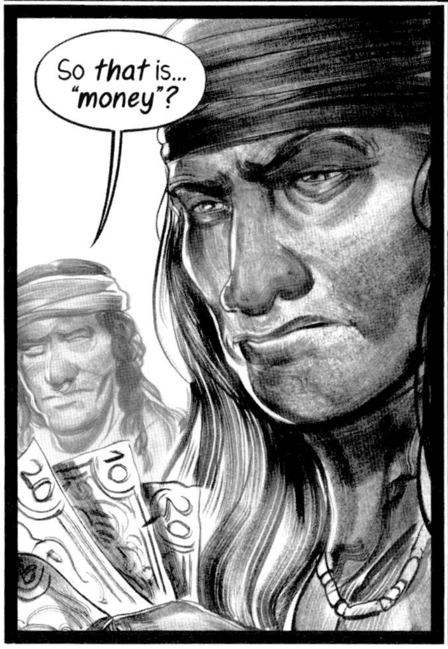
So that is... "money"?

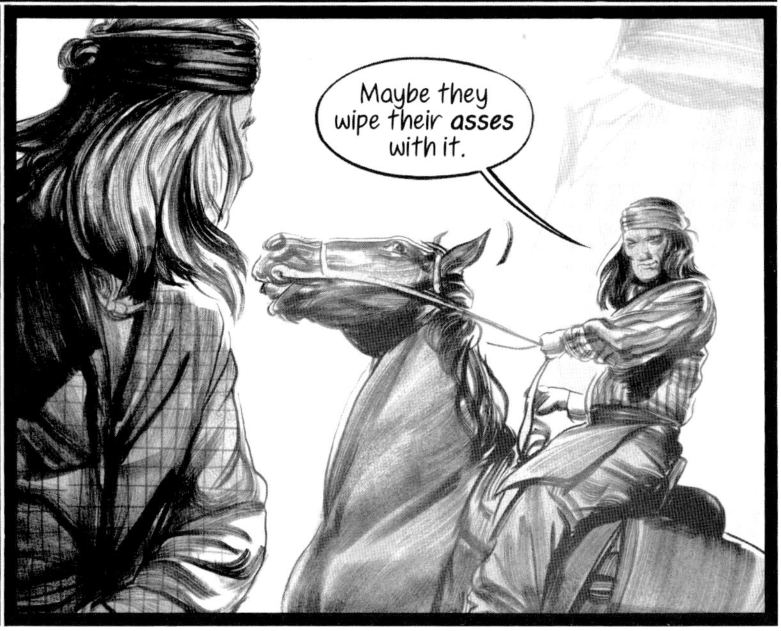
Maybe they wipe their asses with it.

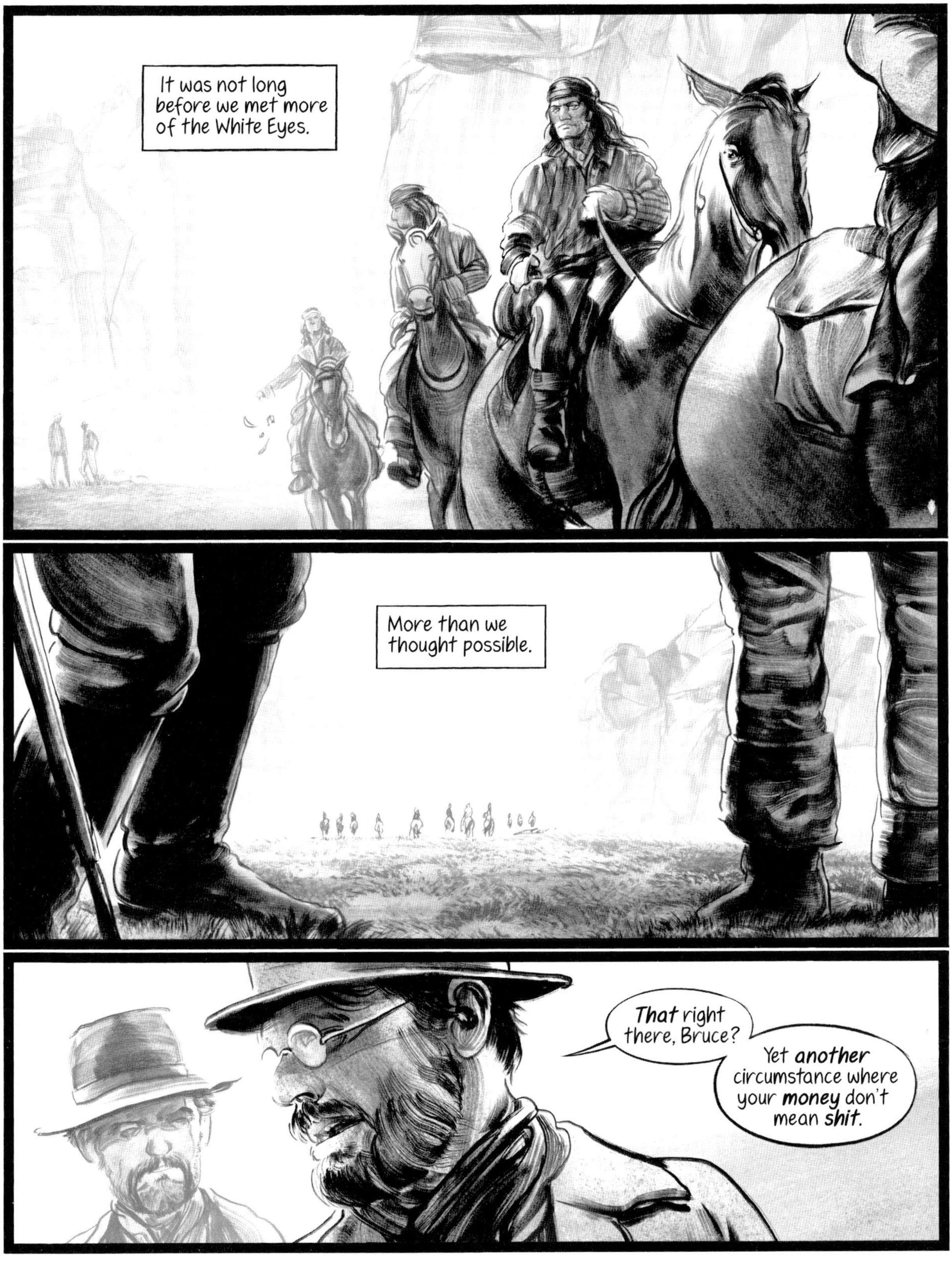
It was not long before we met more of the White Eyes.
More than we thought possible.
That right there, Bruce?
Yet another circumstance where your money don't mean shit.

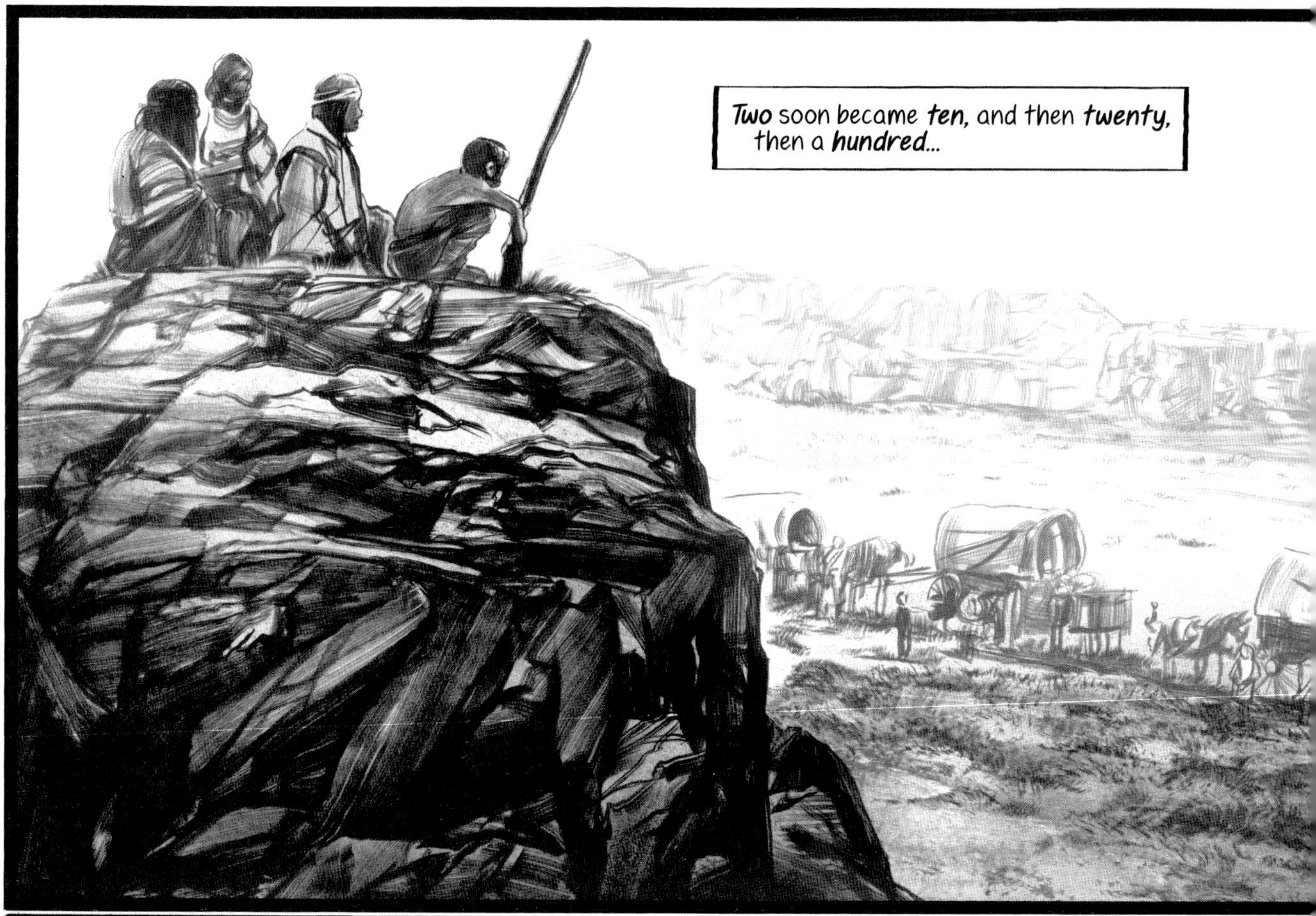
Two soon became ten, and then twenty, then a hundred...

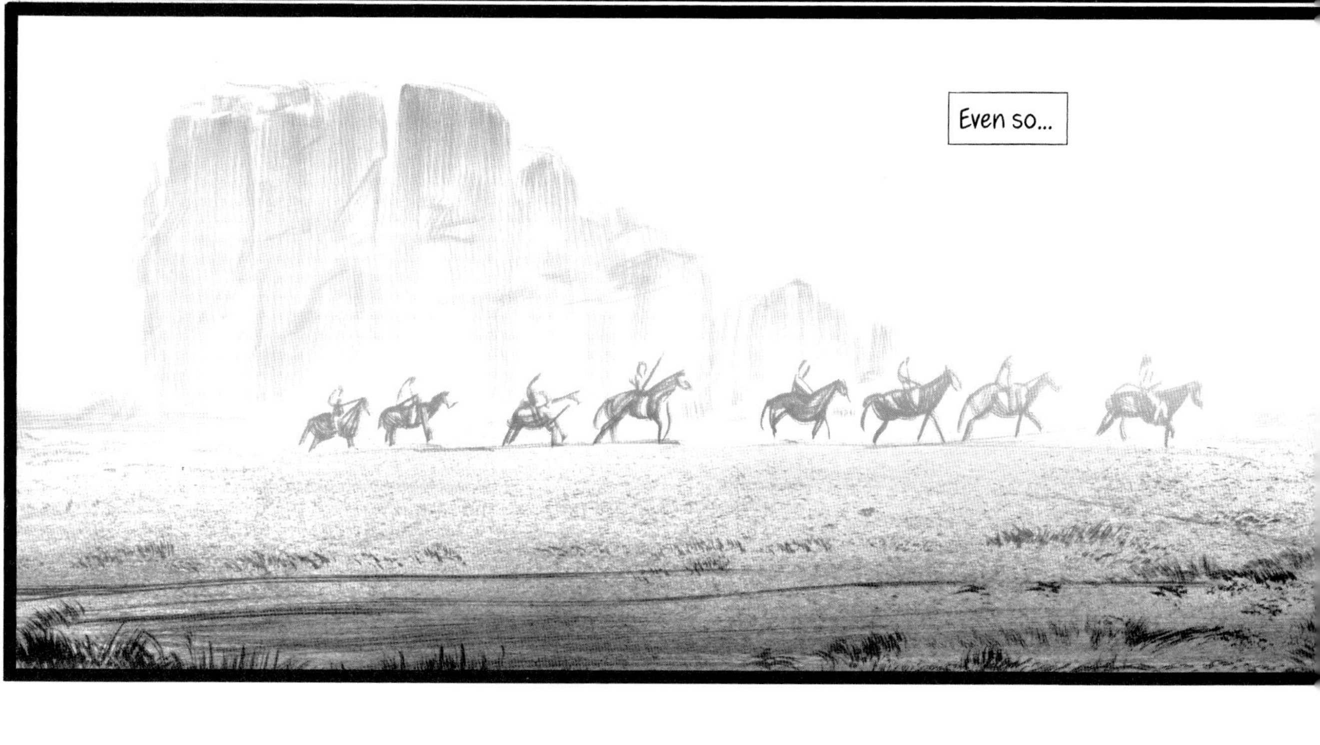
Even so...

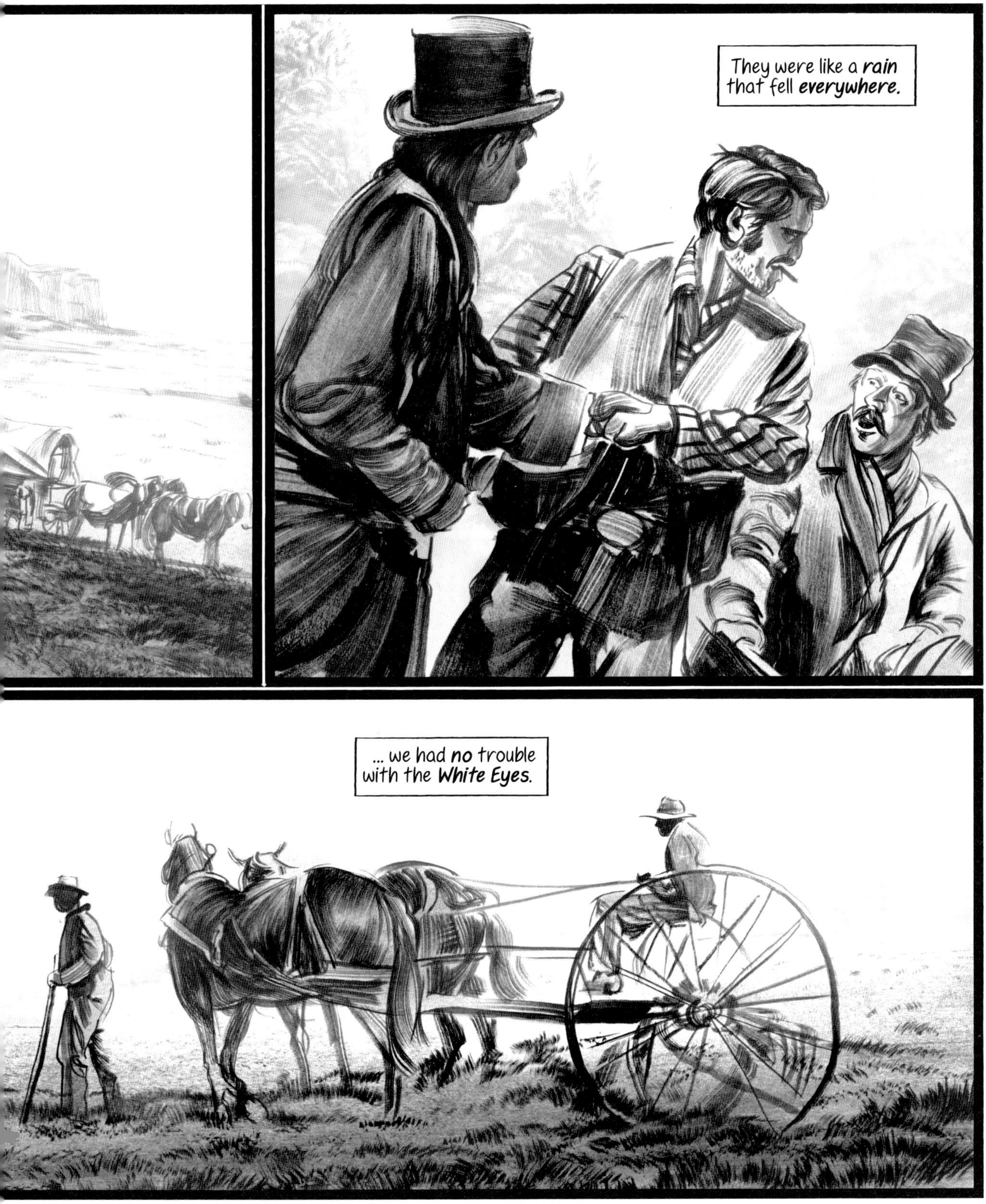
They were like a rain that fell everywhere.
... we had no trouble with the White Eyes.

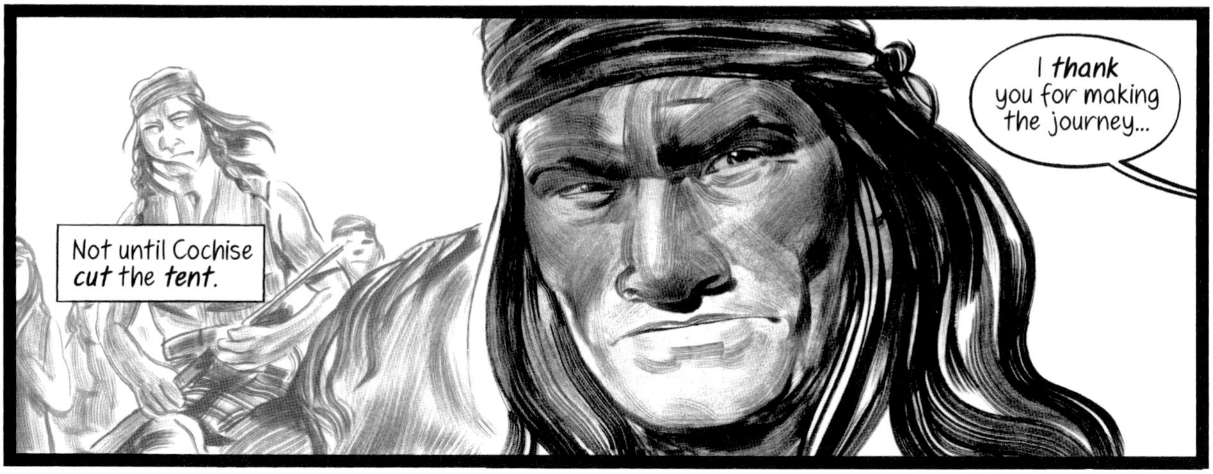
Not until Cochise cut the tent.
I thank you for making the journey...

TWO YEARS LATER · FORT BOWIE

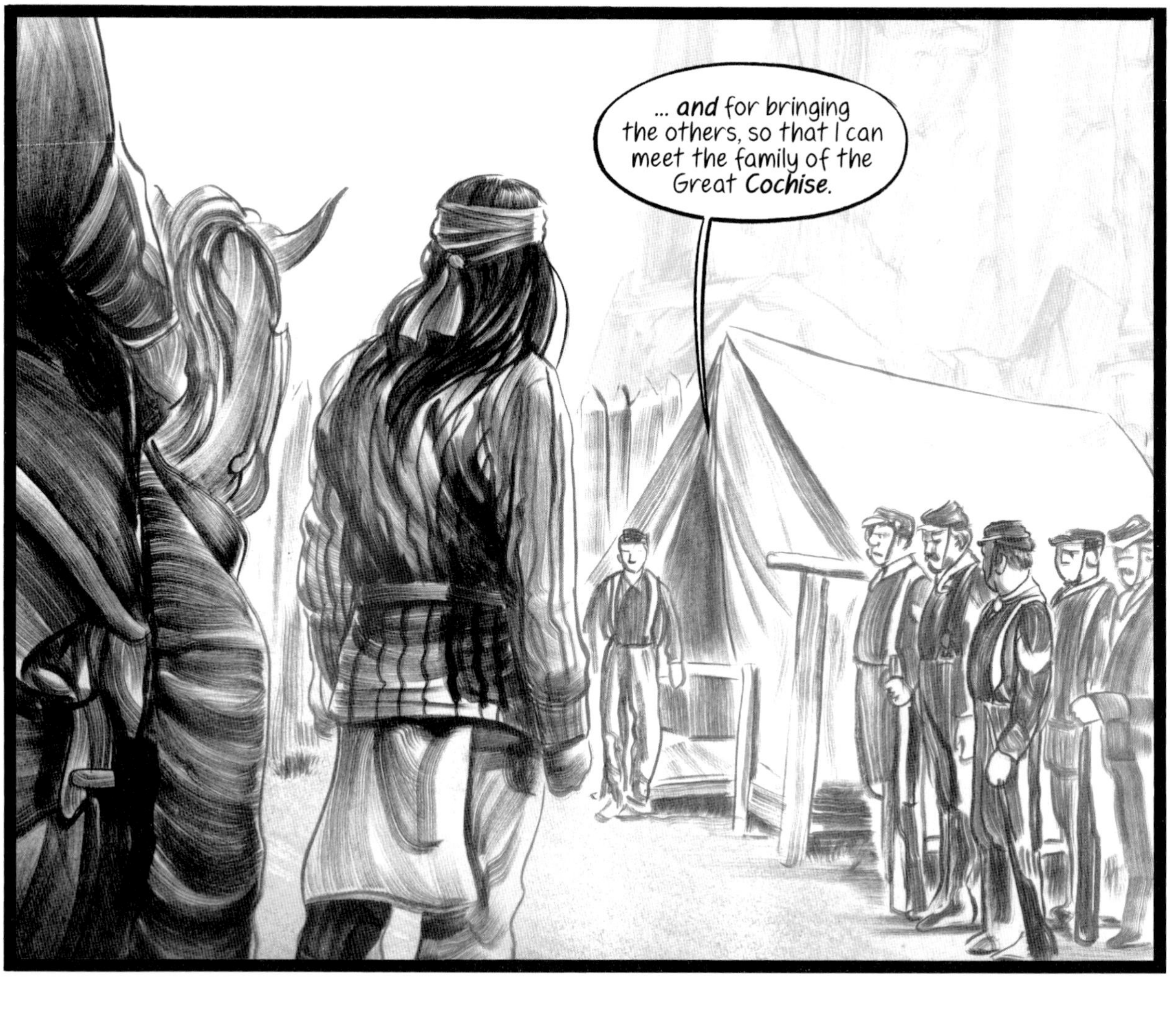
... and for bringing the others, so that I can meet the family of the Great Cochise.

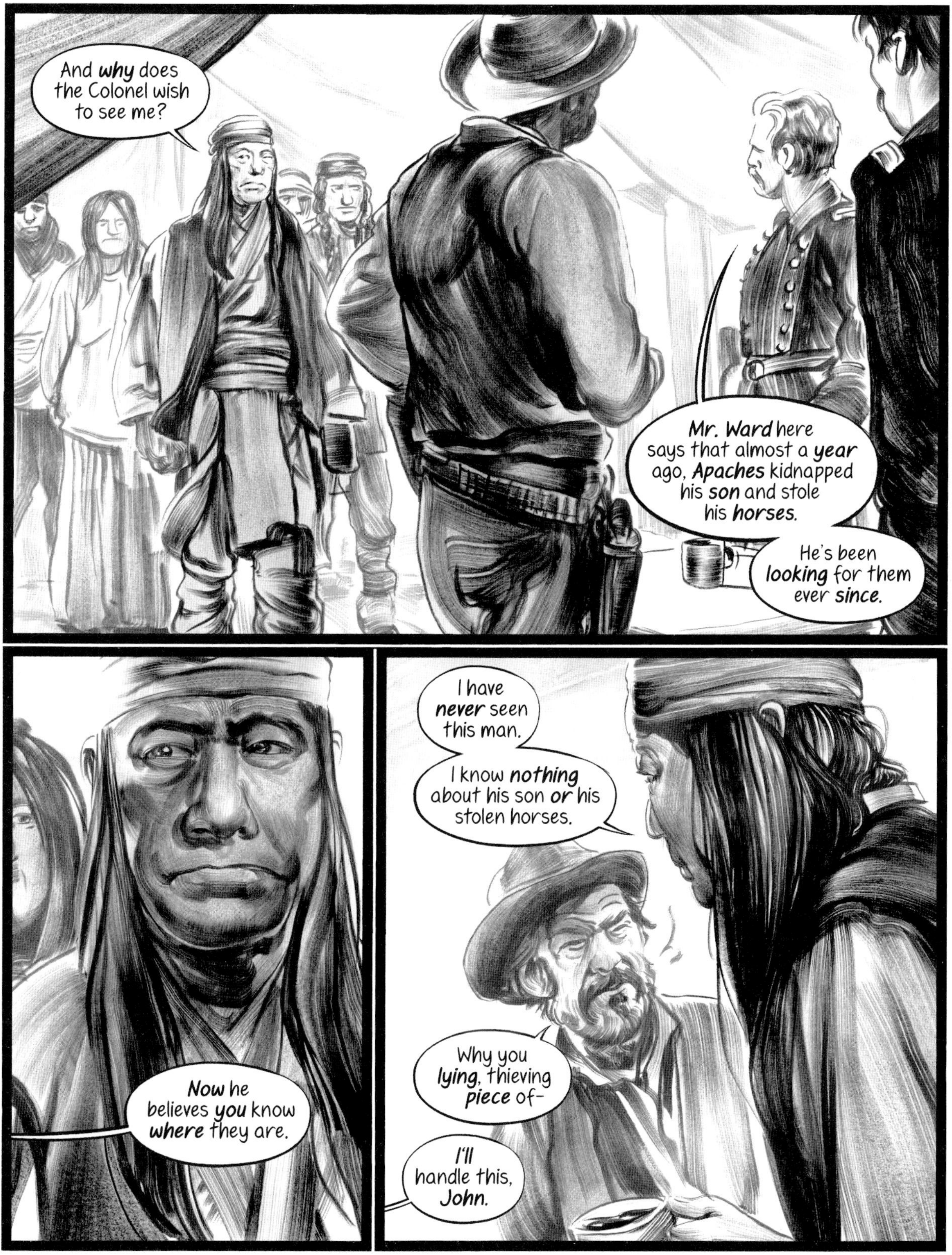
And why does the Colonel wish to see me?
Mr. Ward here says that almost a year ago, Apaches kidnapped his son and stole his horses.
He's been looking for them ever since.
Now he believes you know where they are.
I have never seen this man.
I know nothing about his son or his stolen horses.
Why you lying, thieving piece of-
I'll handle this, John.

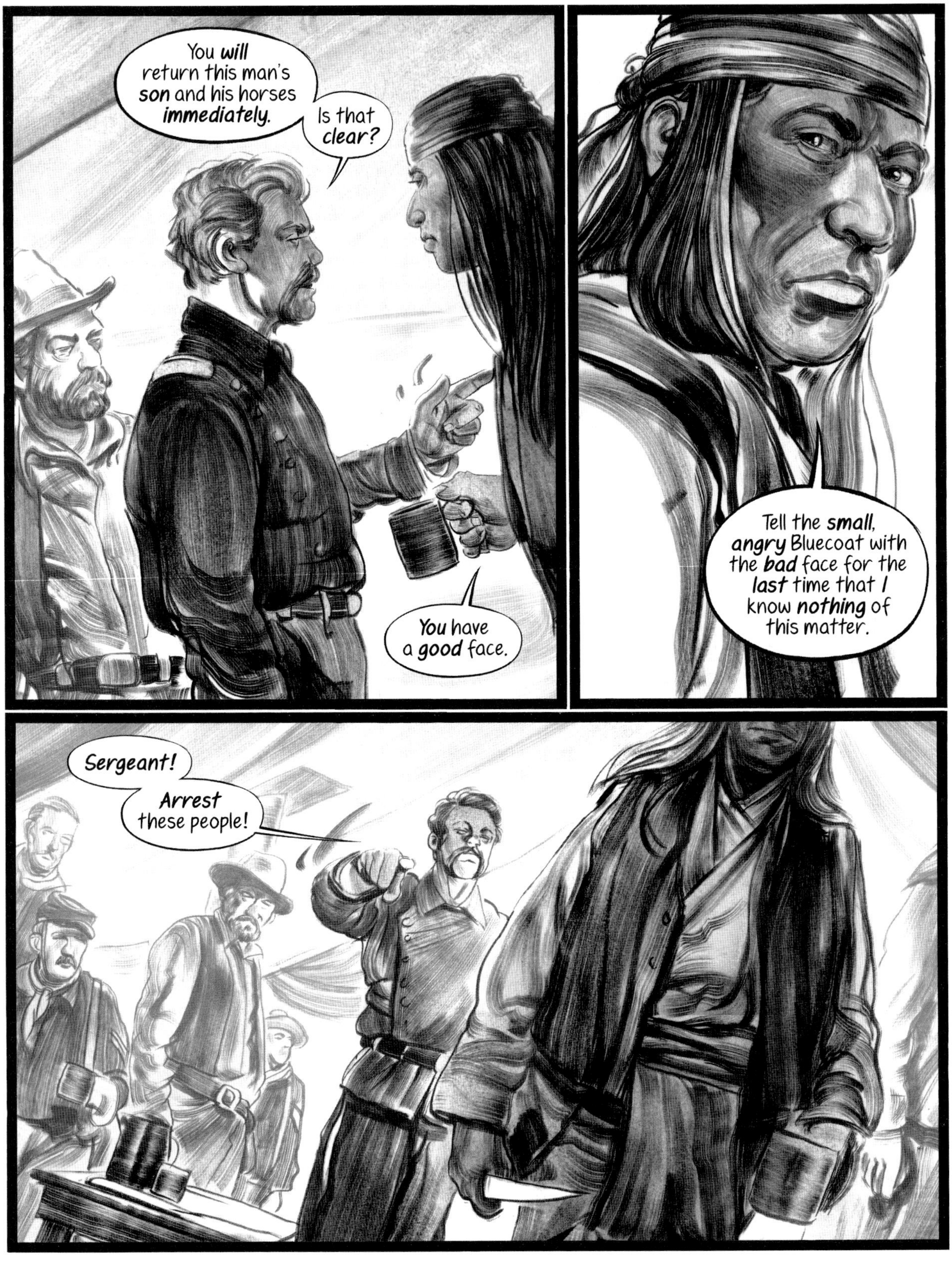

You will return this man's son and his horses immediately.
Is that clear?
You have a good face.
Tell the small, angry Bluecoat with the bad face for the last time that I know nothing of this matter.
Sergeant!
Arrest these people!

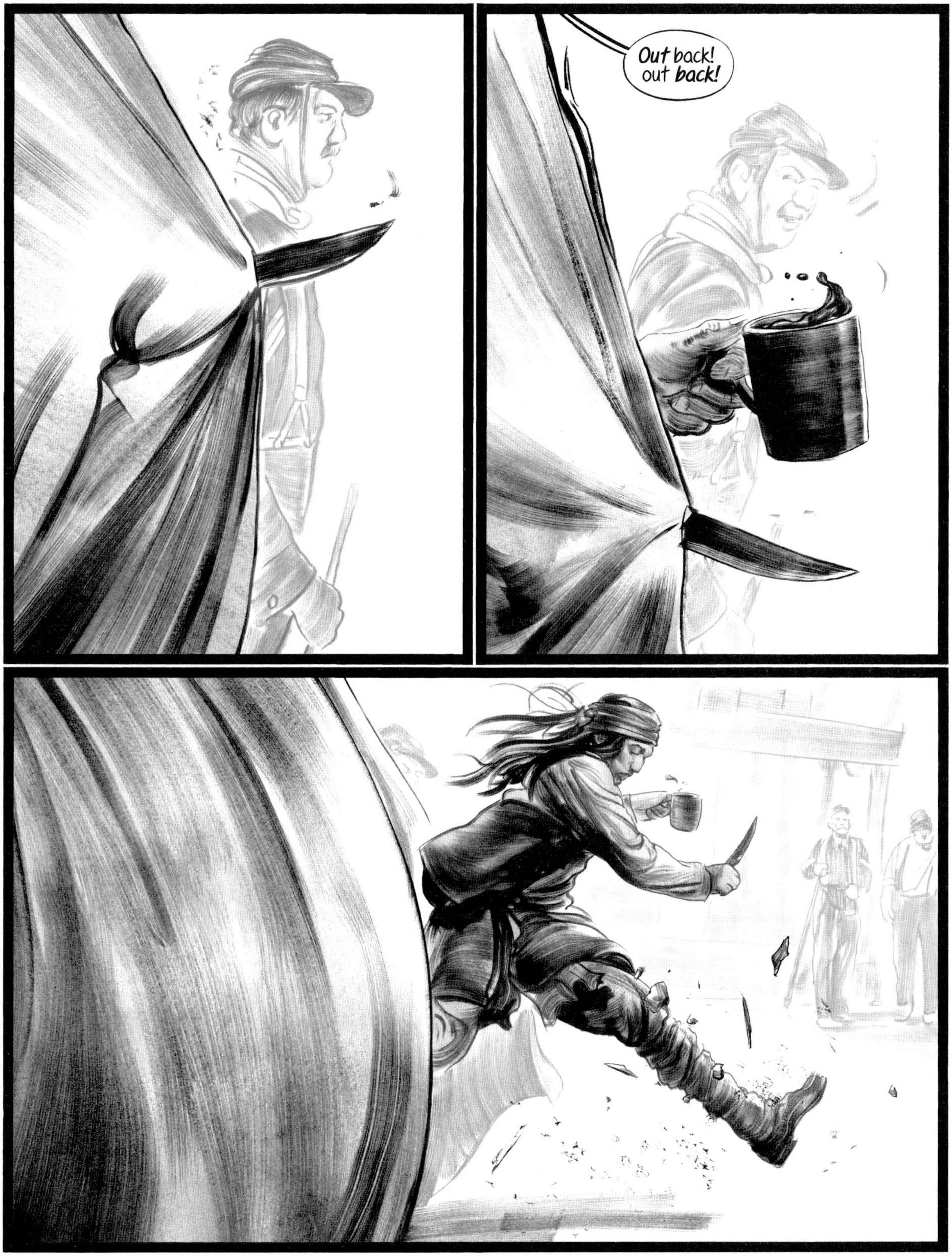
Out back!
out back!

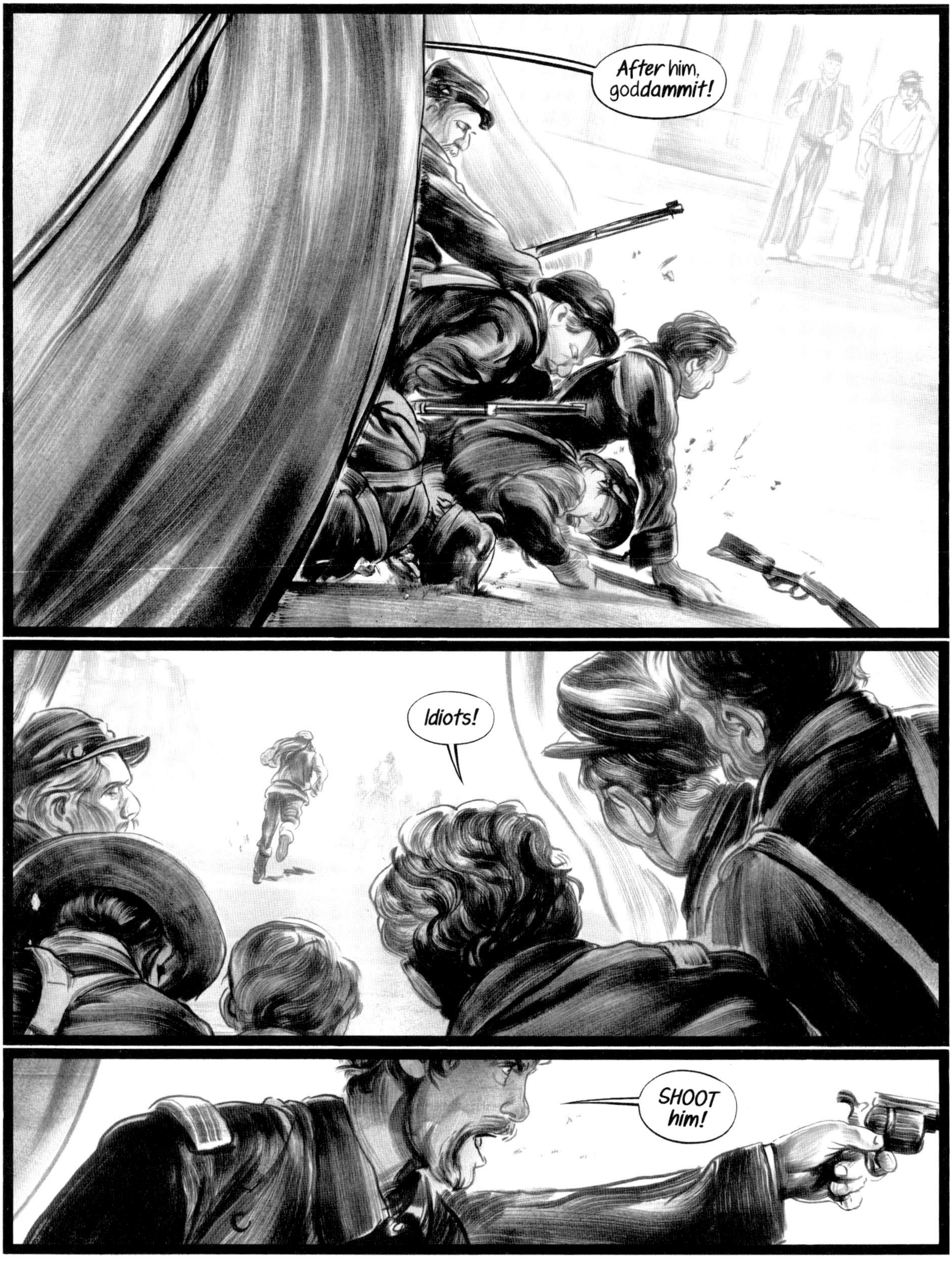
After him, goddammit!
Idiots!
SHOOT him!

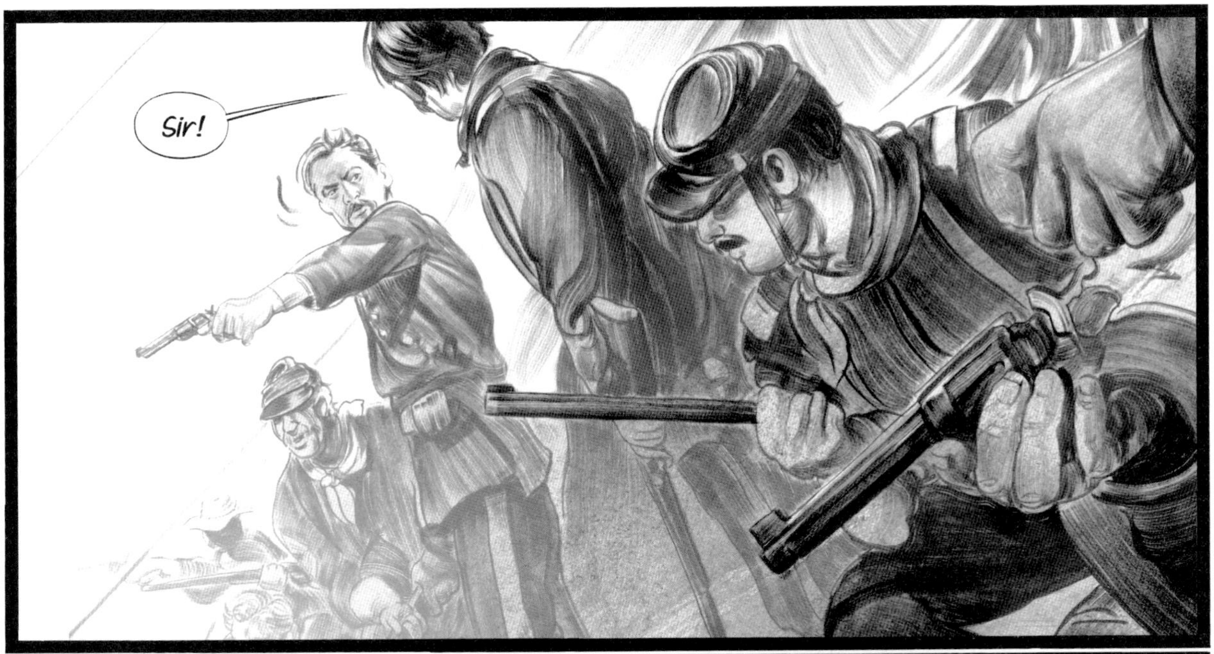
Sir!

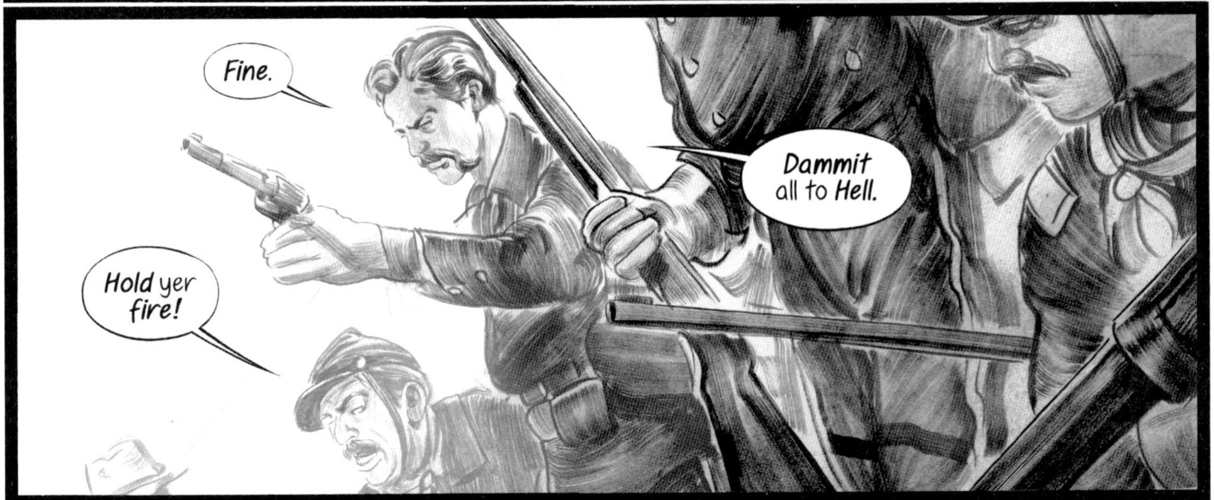
Fine.
Dammit all to Hell.
Hold yer fire!

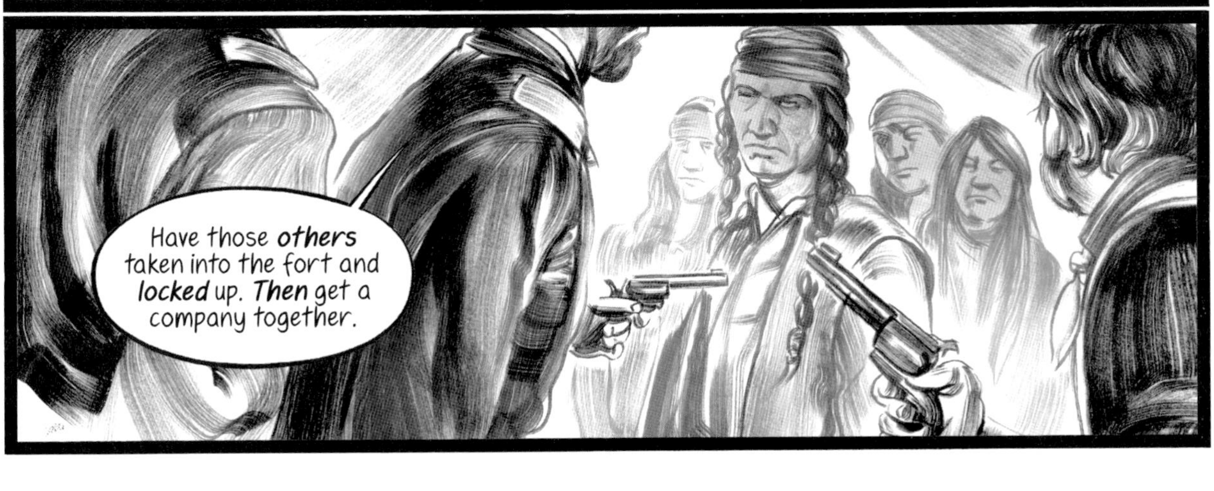
Have those others taken into the fort and locked up. Then get a company together.

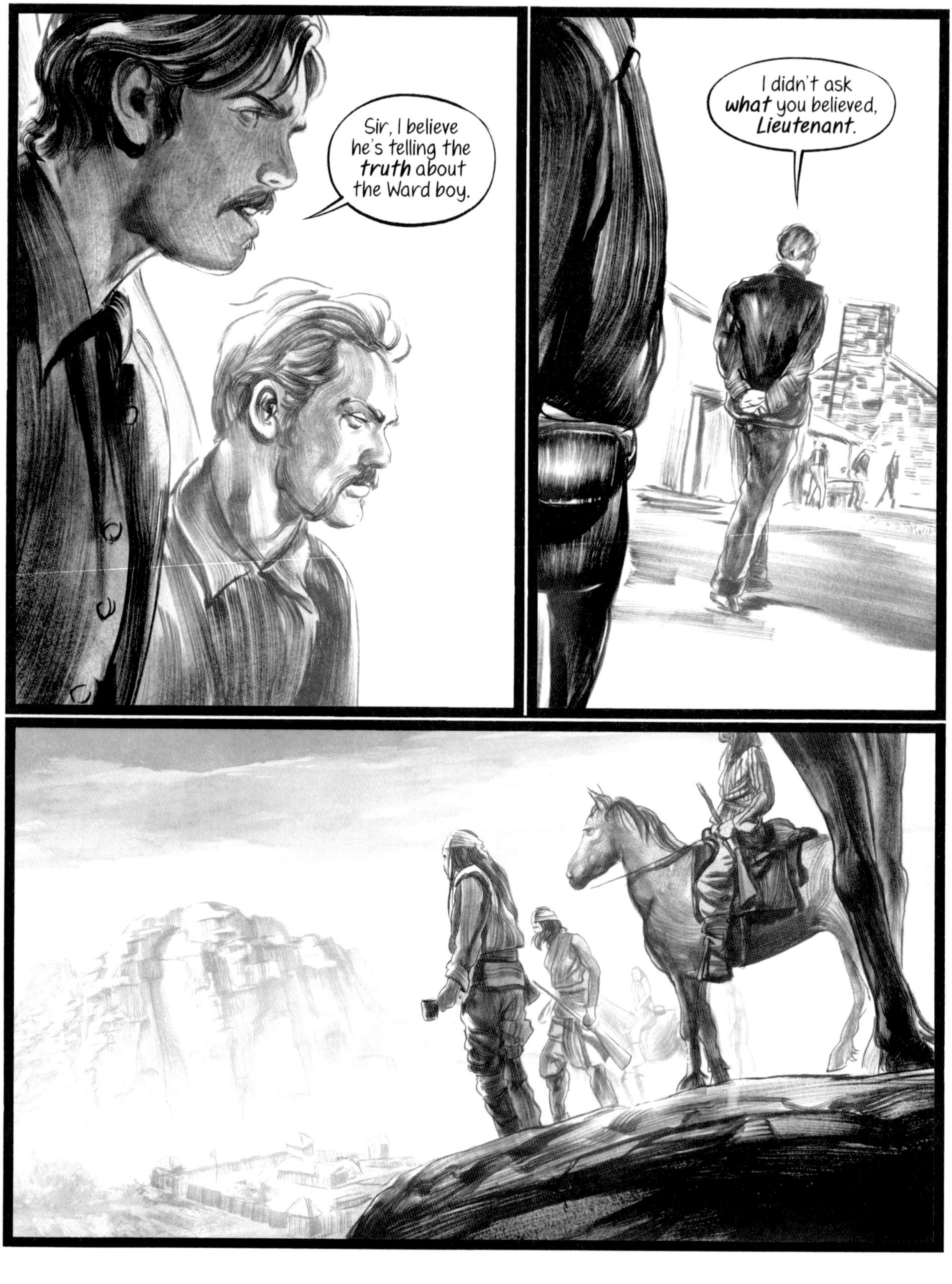
Sir, I believe he's telling the **truth** about the Ward boy.
I didn't ask **what** you believed, **Lieutenant**.

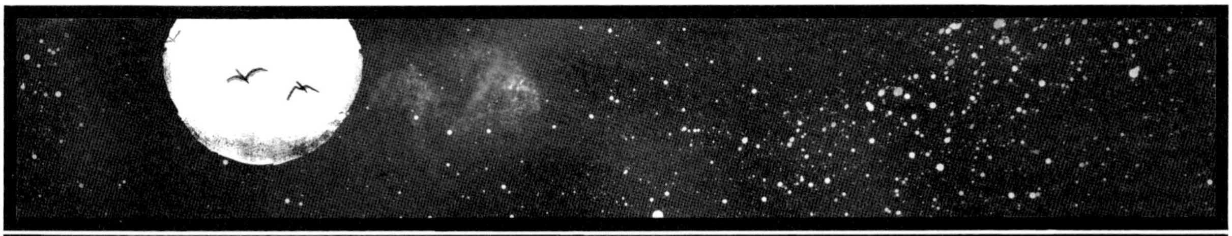

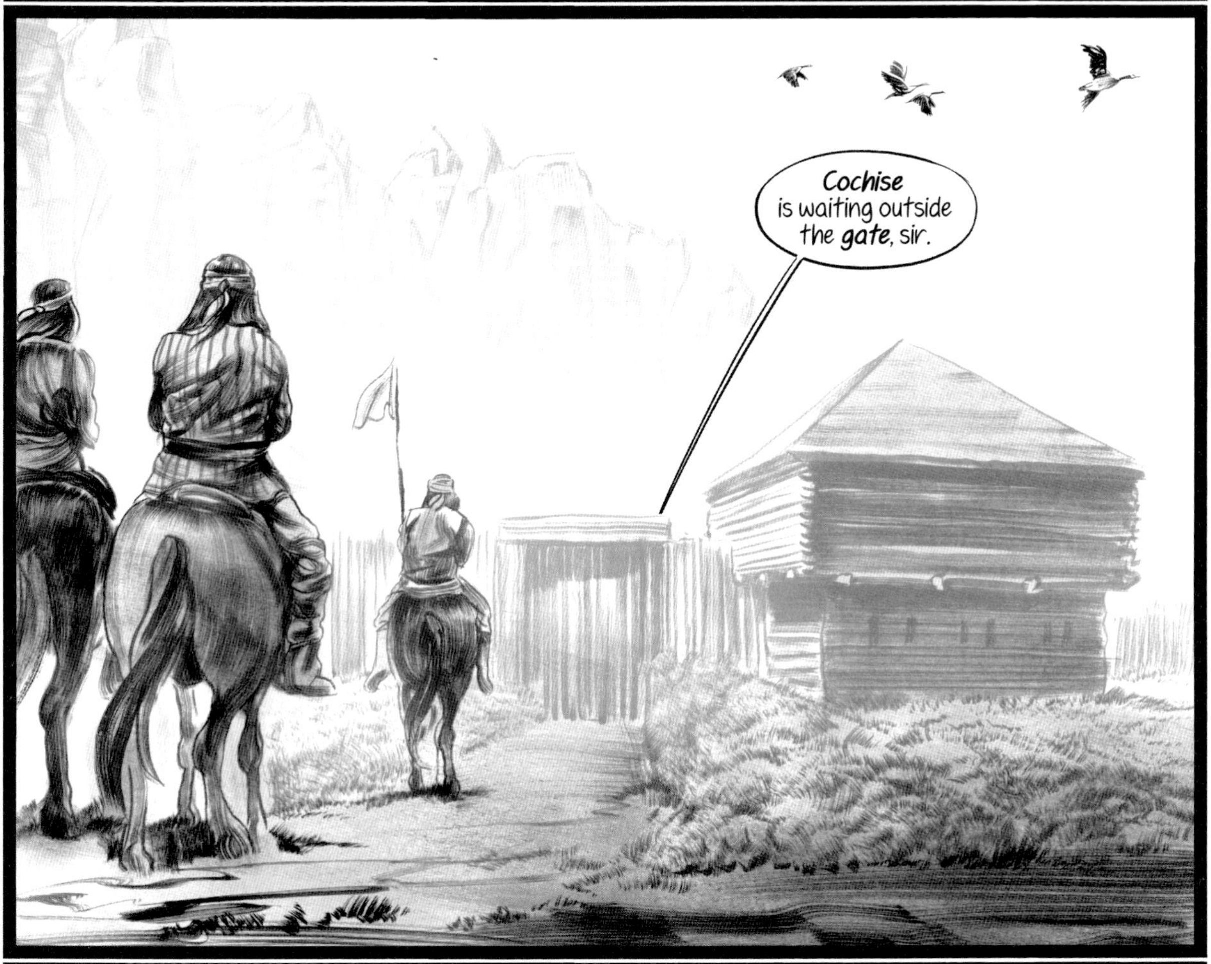
Cochise is waiting outside the gate, sir.

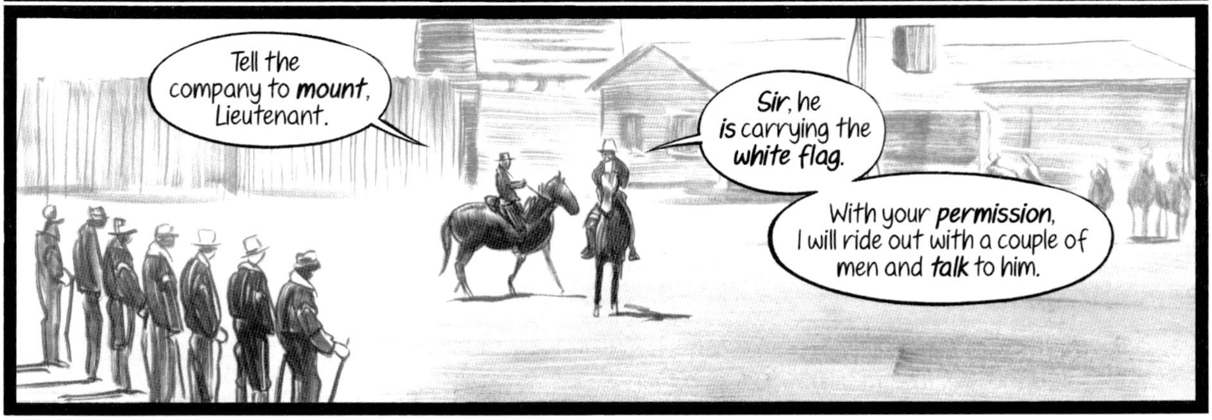
Tell the company to mount, Lieutenant.
Sir, he is carrying the white flag.
With your permission, I will ride out with a couple of men and talk to him.

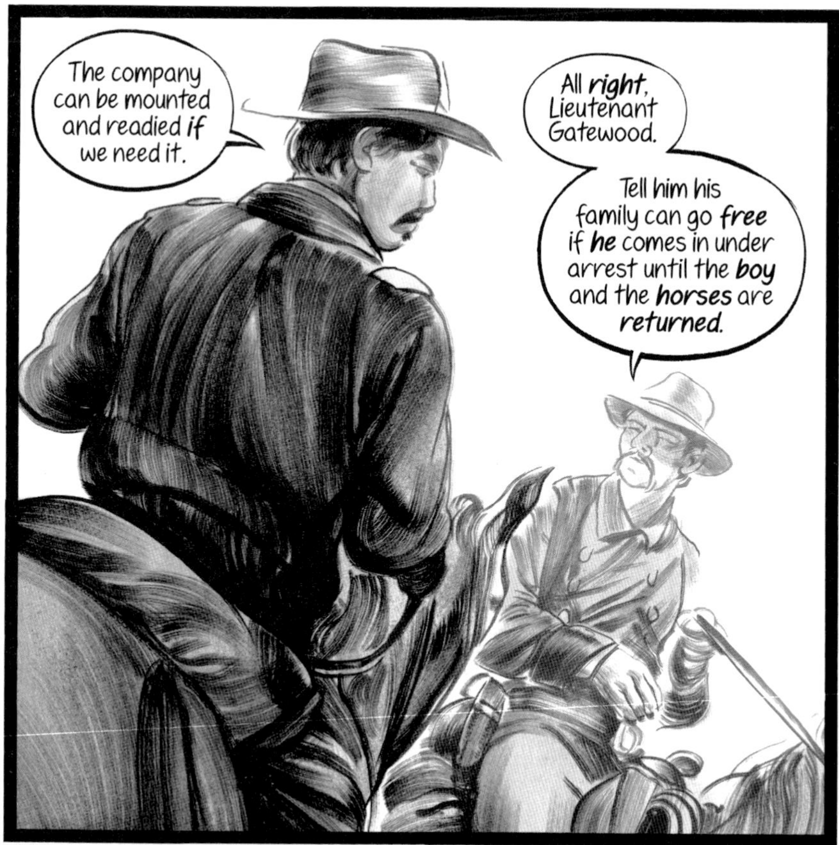
The company can be mounted and readied *if* we need it.
All ***right***, Lieutenant Gatewood.
Tell him his family can go ***free*** if ***he*** comes in under arrest until the ***boy*** and the ***horses*** are ***returned.***

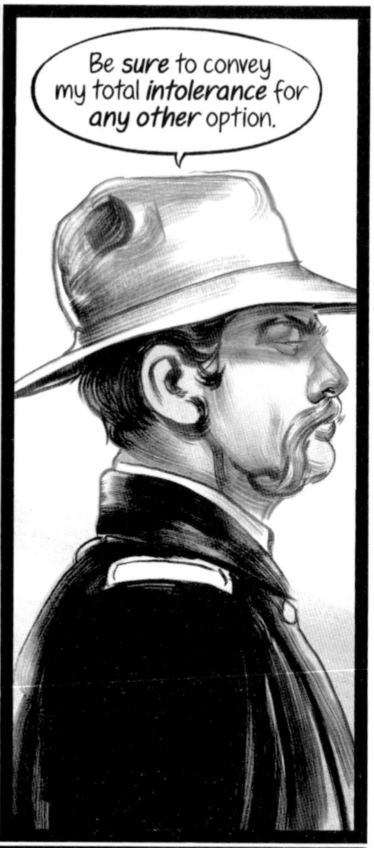
Be ***sure*** to convey my total ***intolerance*** for ***any other*** option.

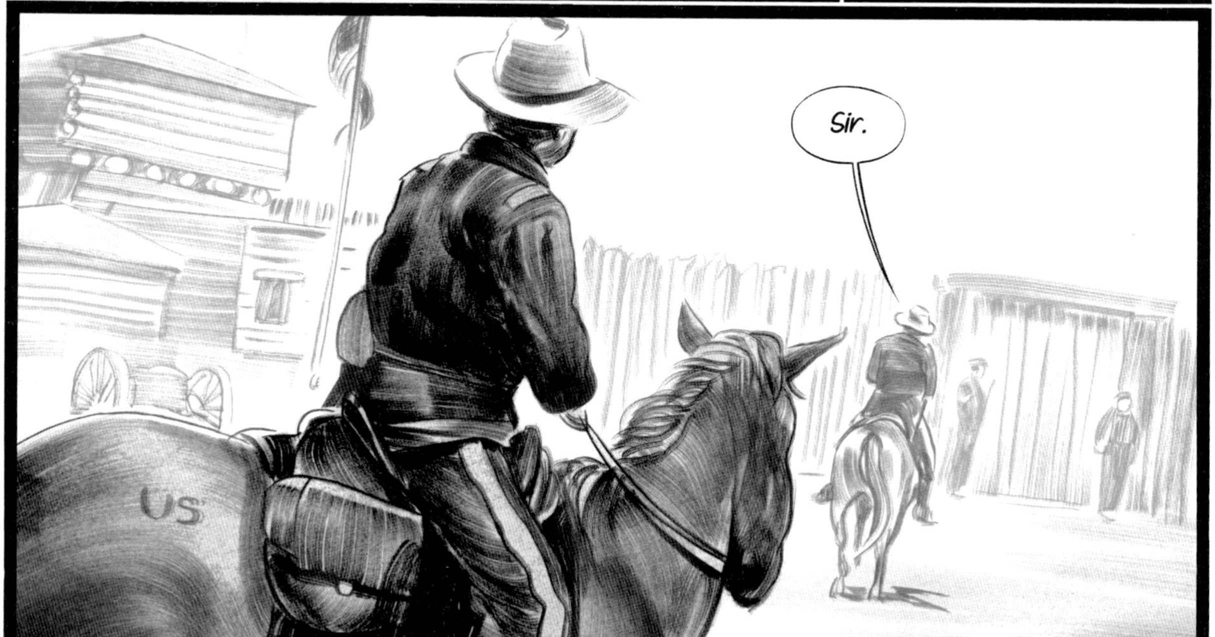
US
Sir.

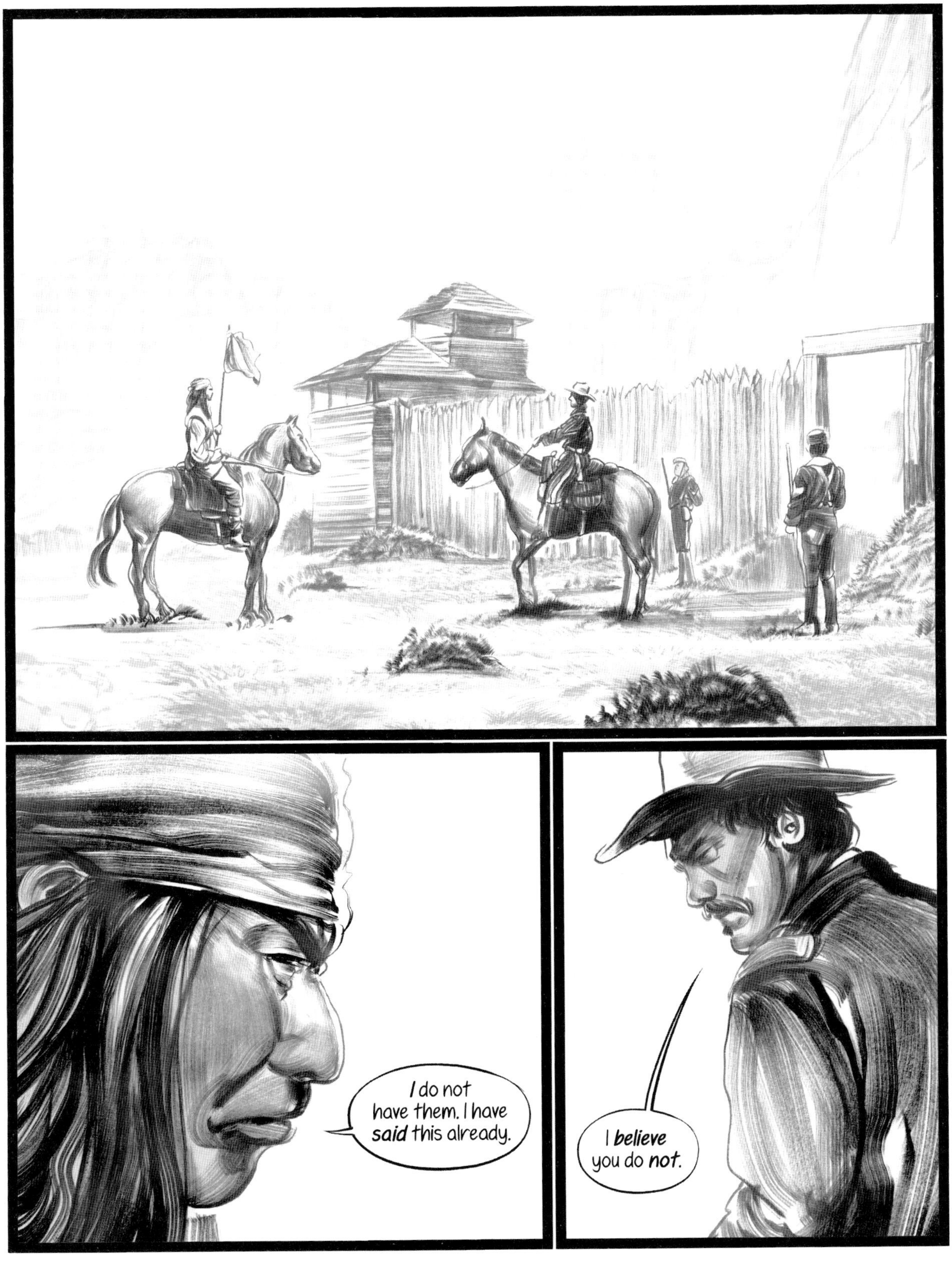
I do not have them. I have *said* this already.
I *believe* you do *not*.

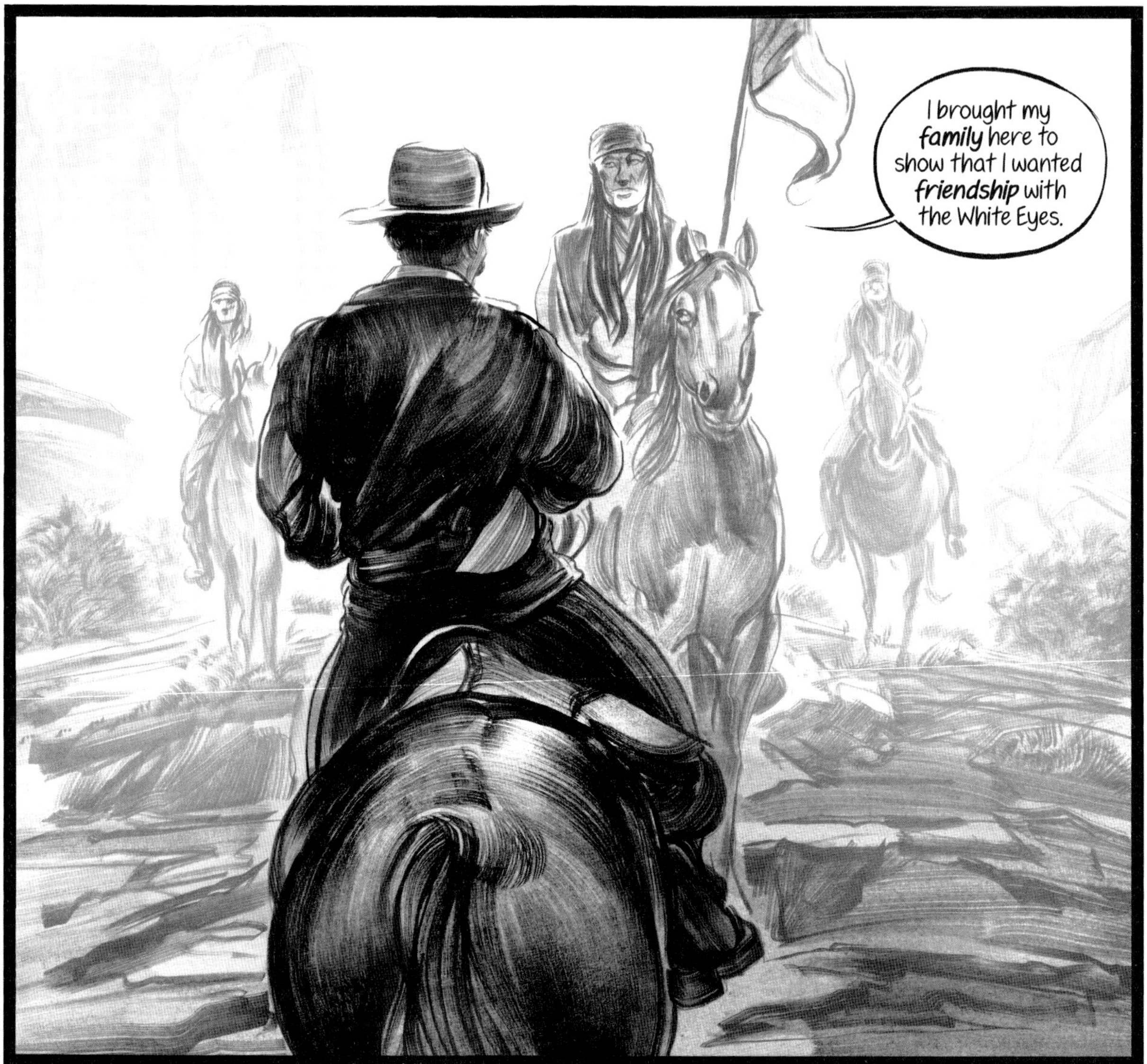
I brought my **family** here to show that I wanted **friendship** with the White Eyes.

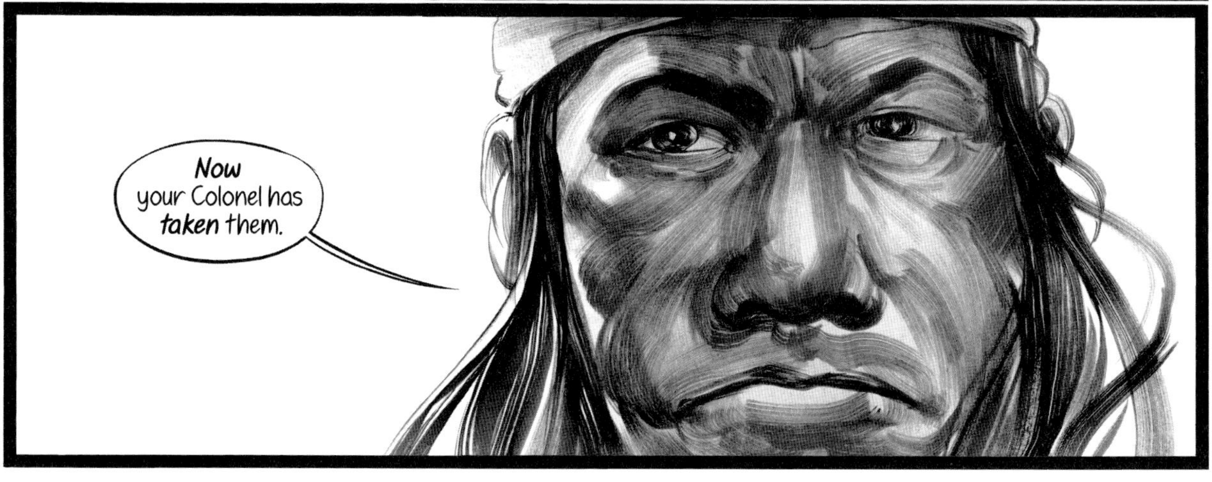
Now your Colonel has **taken** them.

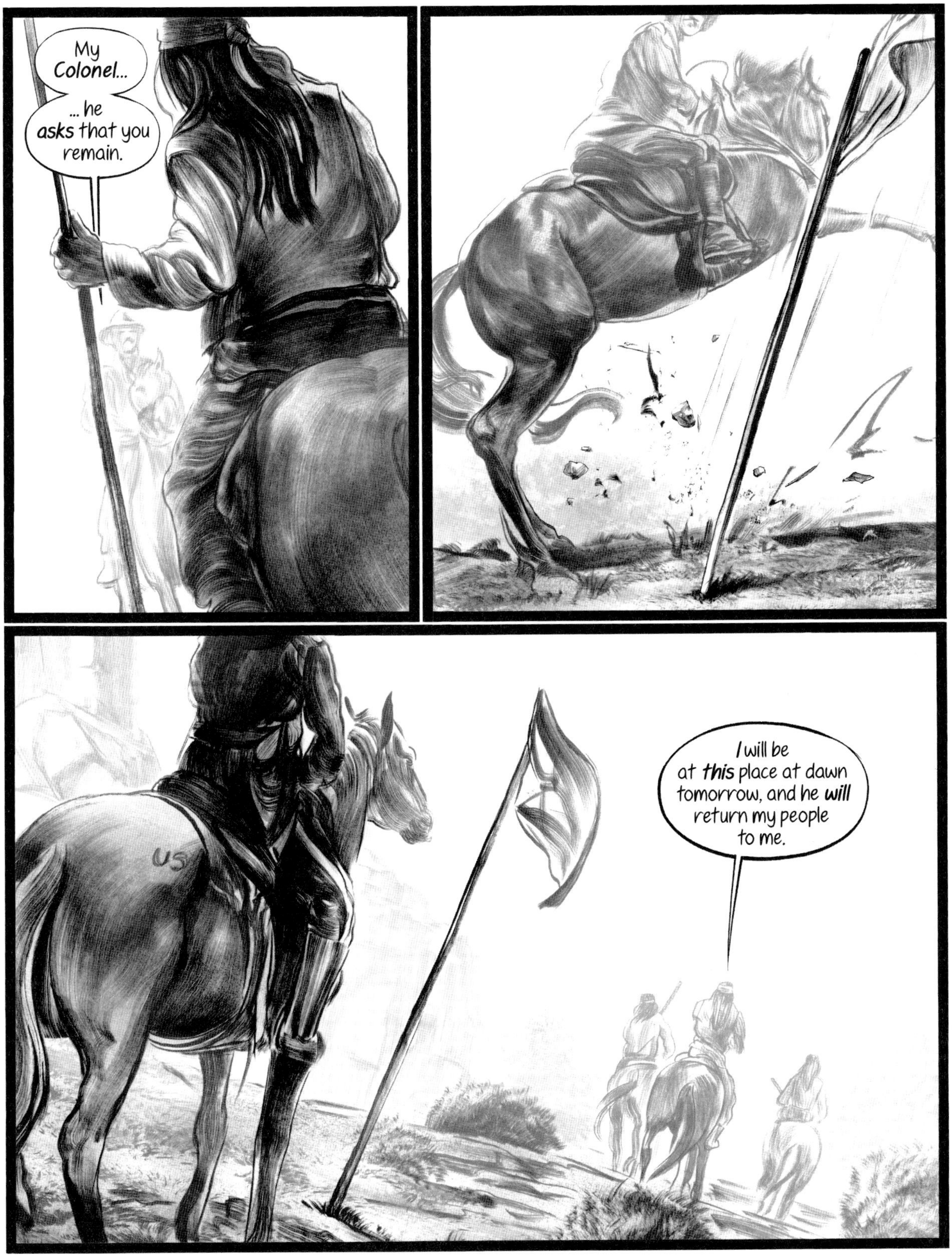
My Colonel...
... he asks that you remain.
I will be at this place at dawn tomorrow, and he will return my people to me.

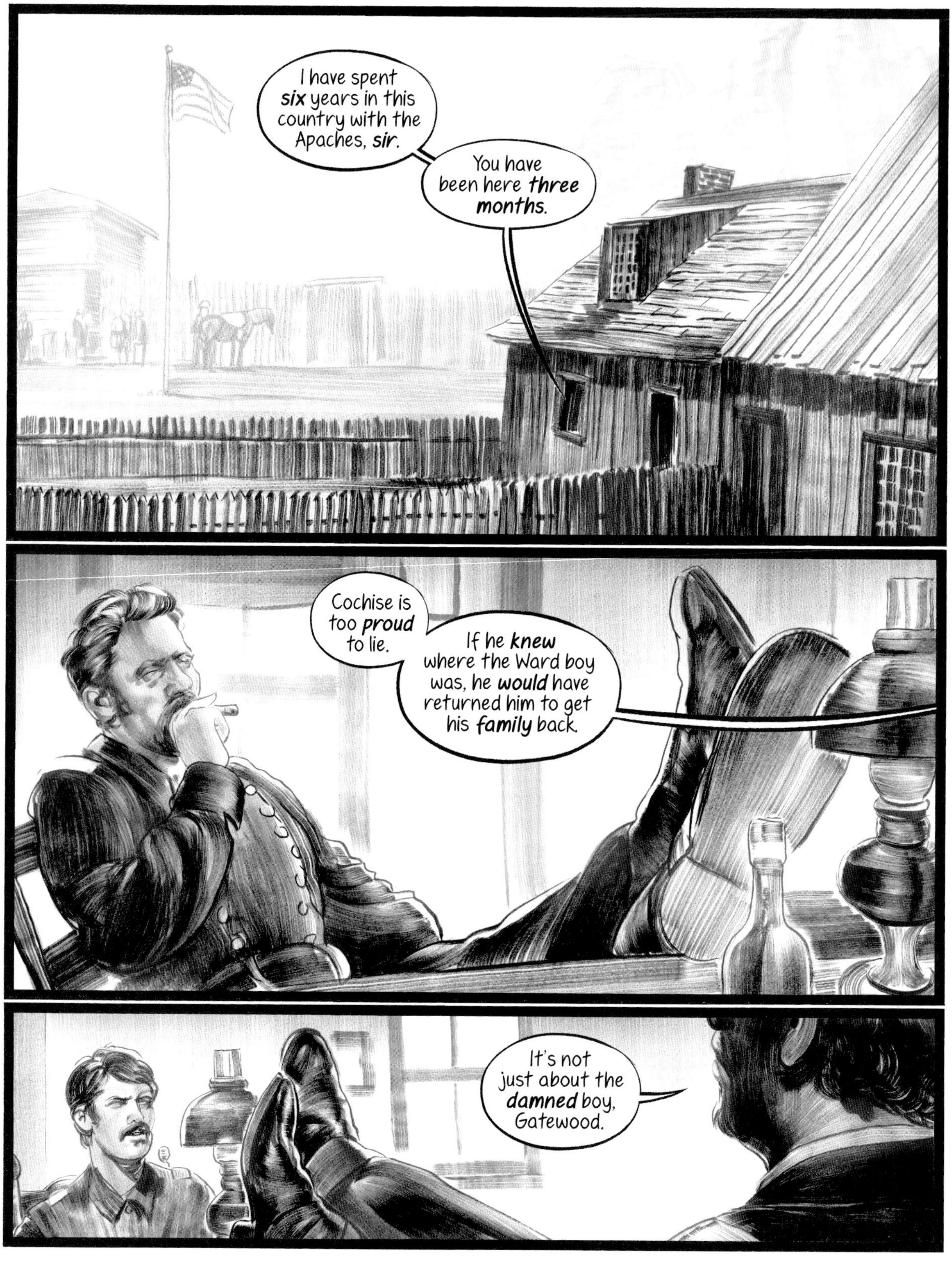
I have spent six years in this country with the Apaches, sir.
You have been here three months.
Cochise is too proud to lie.
If he knew where the Ward boy was, he would have returned him to get his family back.
It's not just about the damned boy, Gatewood.

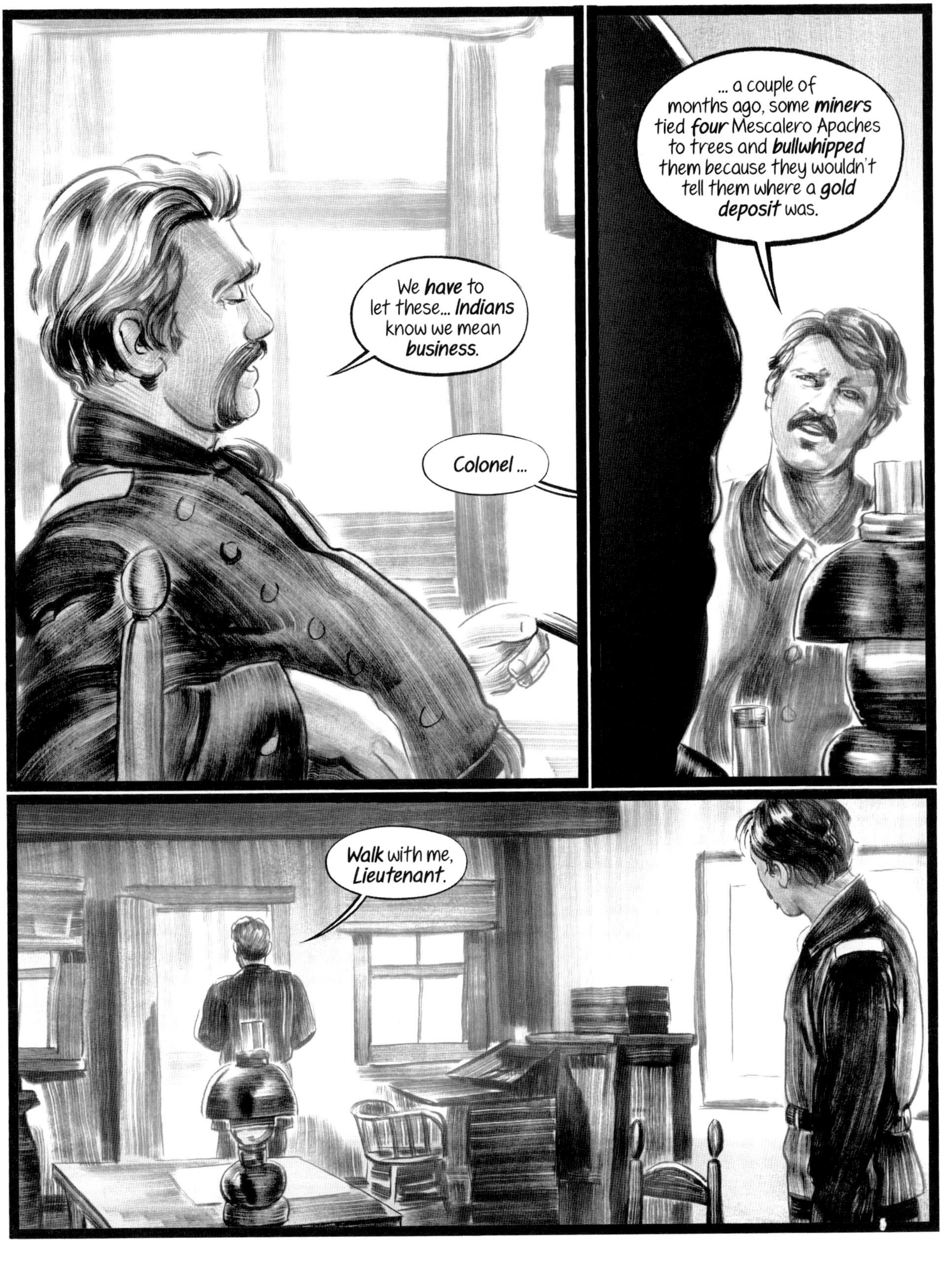
We have to let these... Indians know we mean business.
Colonel ...
... a couple of months ago, some miners tied four Mescalero Apaches to trees and bullwhipped them because they wouldn't tell them where a gold deposit was.
Walk with me, Lieutenant.

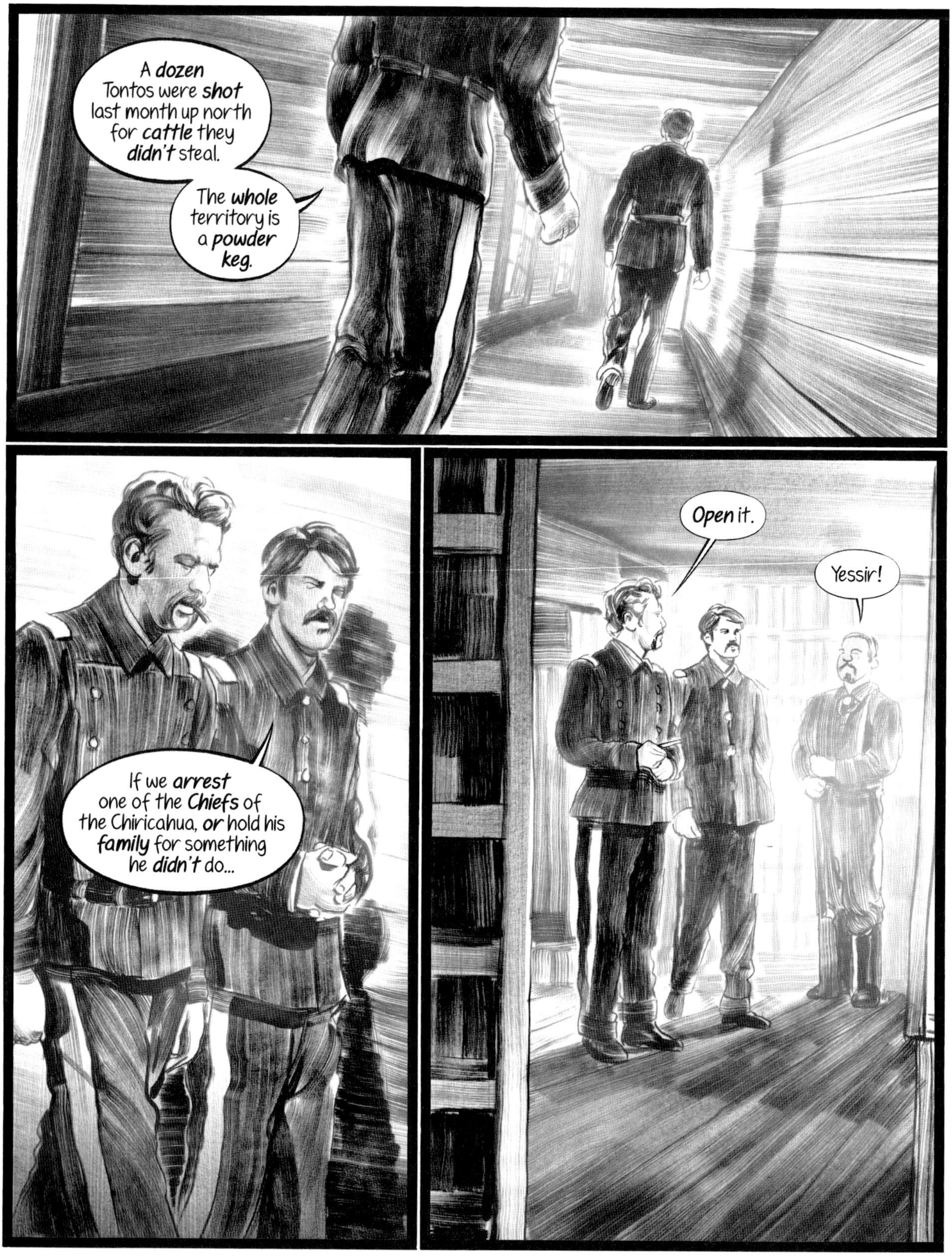
A dozen Tontos were shot last month up north for cattle they didn't steal.
The whole territory is a powder keg.
If we arrest one of the Chiefs of the Chiricahua, or hold his family for something he didn't do...
Open it.
Yessir!

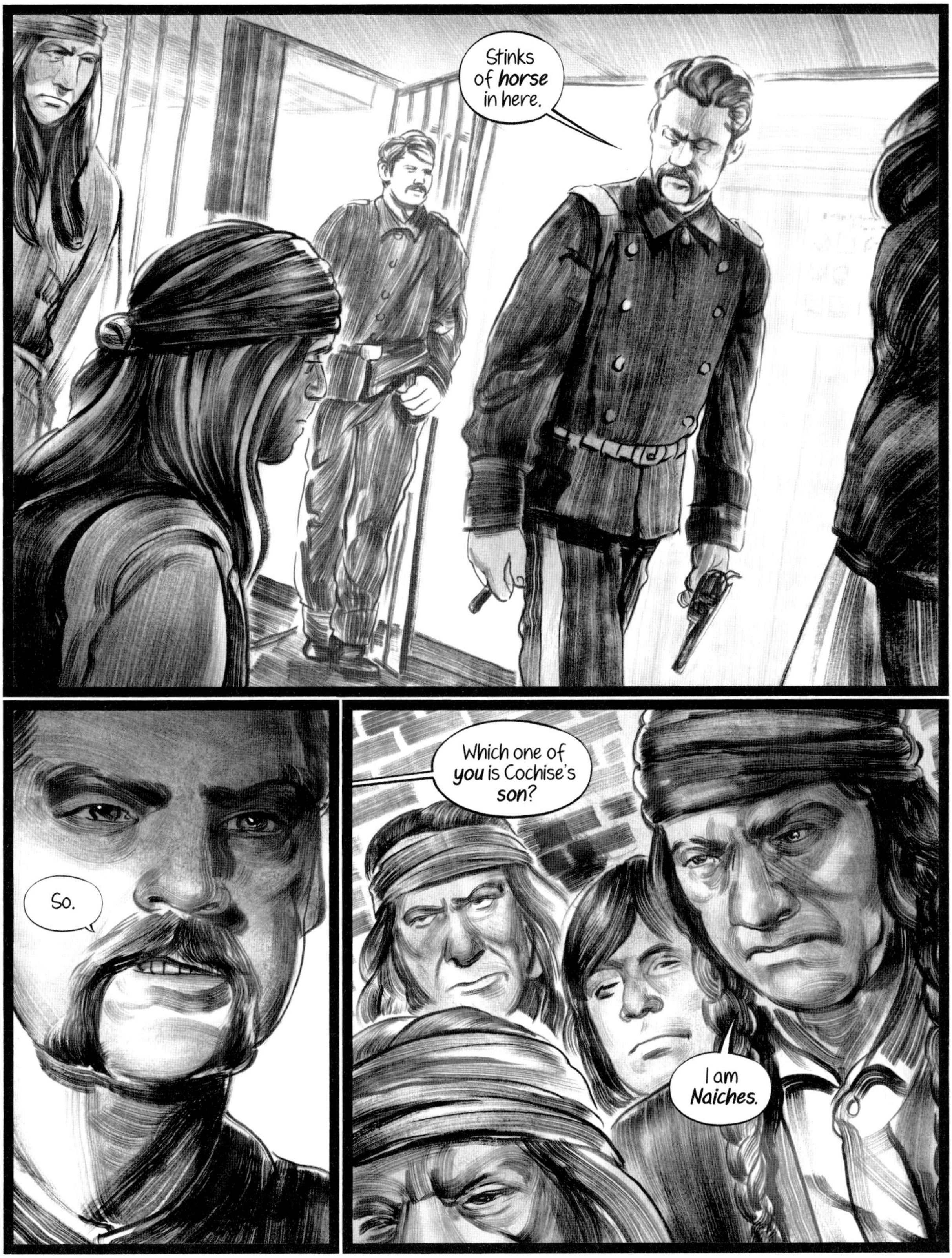
Stinks of **horse** in here.
So.
Which one of **you** is Cochise's **son**?
I am **Naiches**.

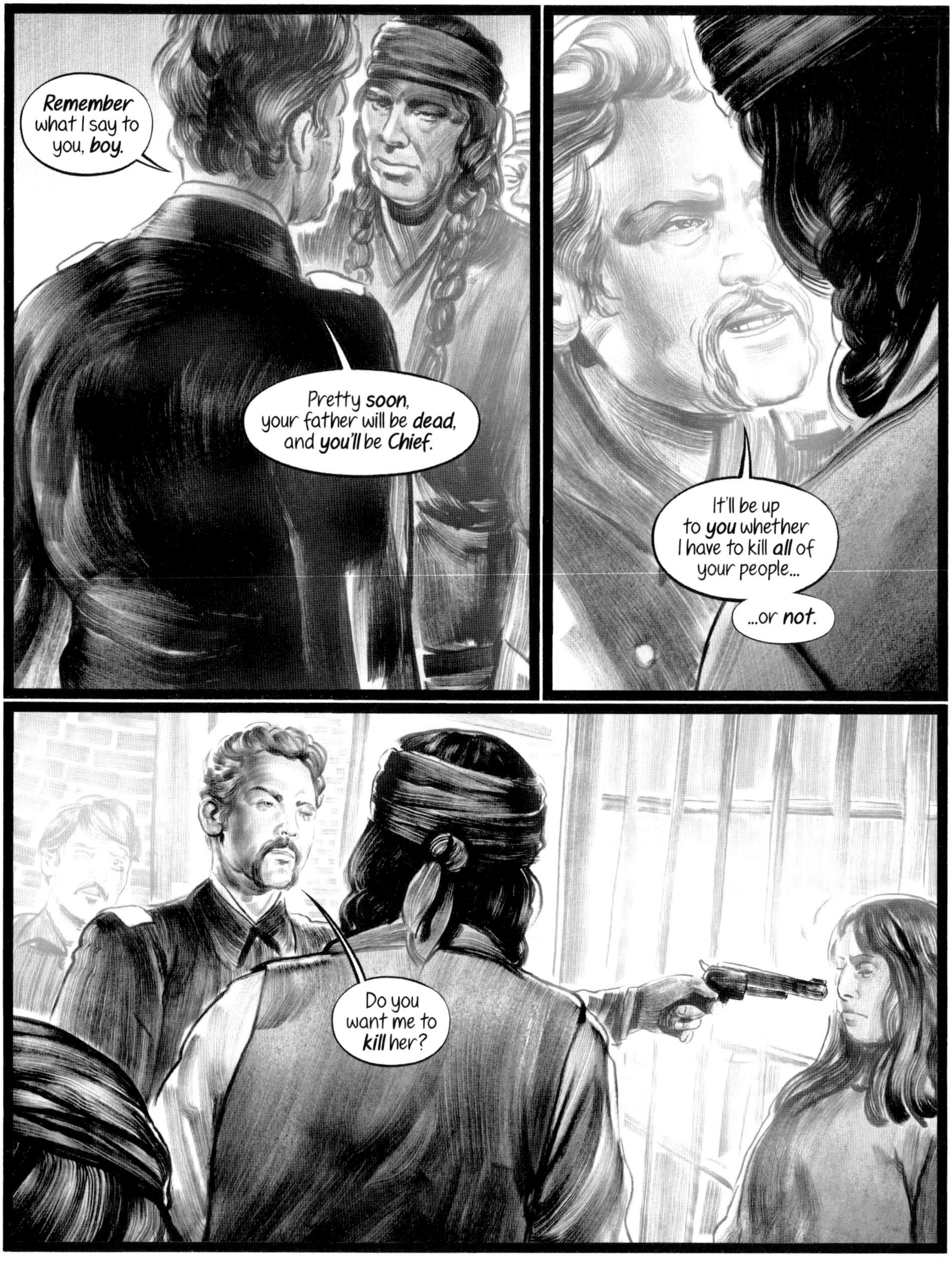
Remember what I say to you, **boy.**
Pretty **soon**, your father will be **dead**, and **you'll** be **Chief**.
It'll be up to **you** whether I have to kill **all** of your people...
...or **not**.
Do you want me to **kill** her?

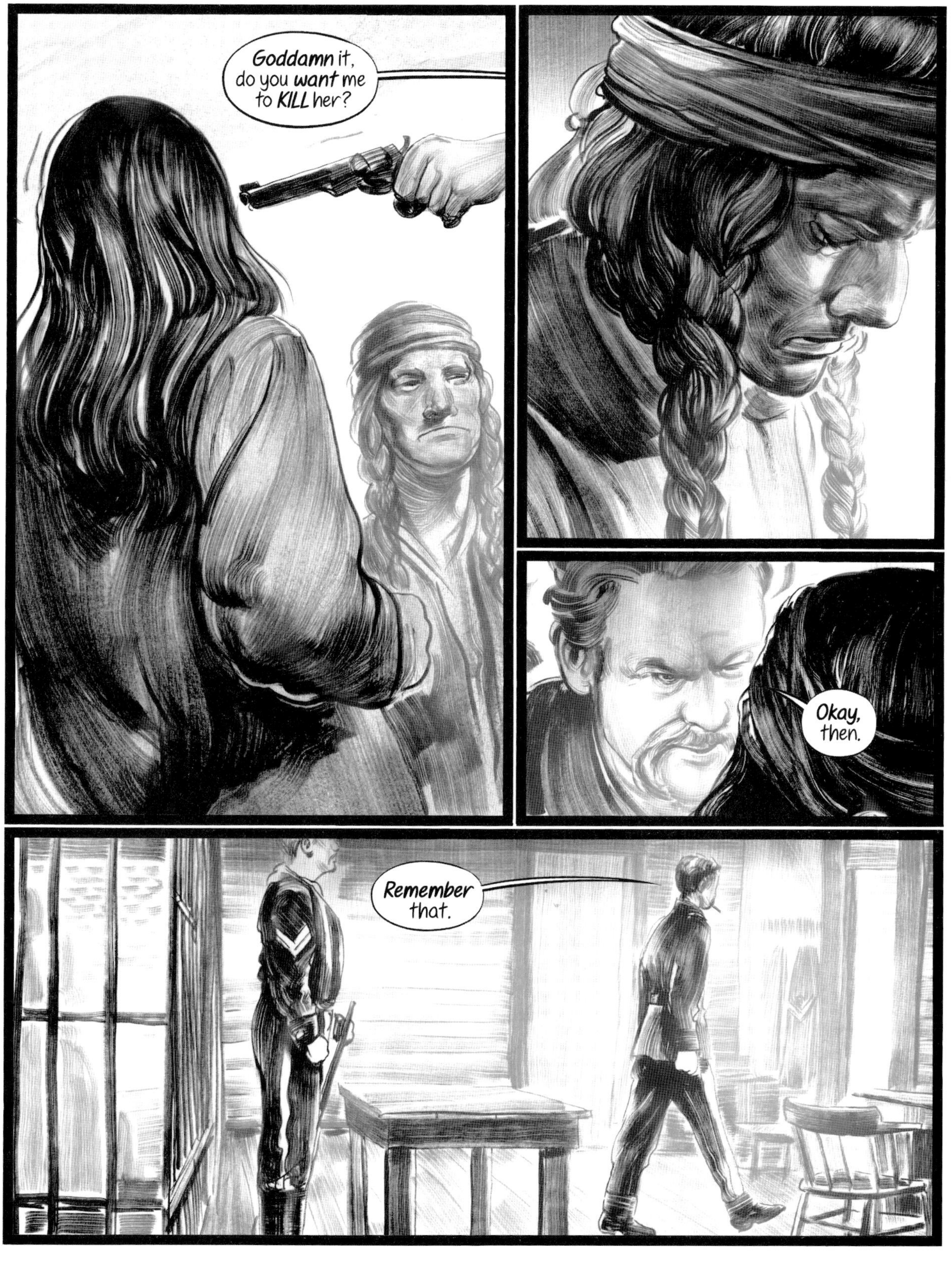
Goddamn it, do you want me to KILL her?
Okay, then.
Remember that.

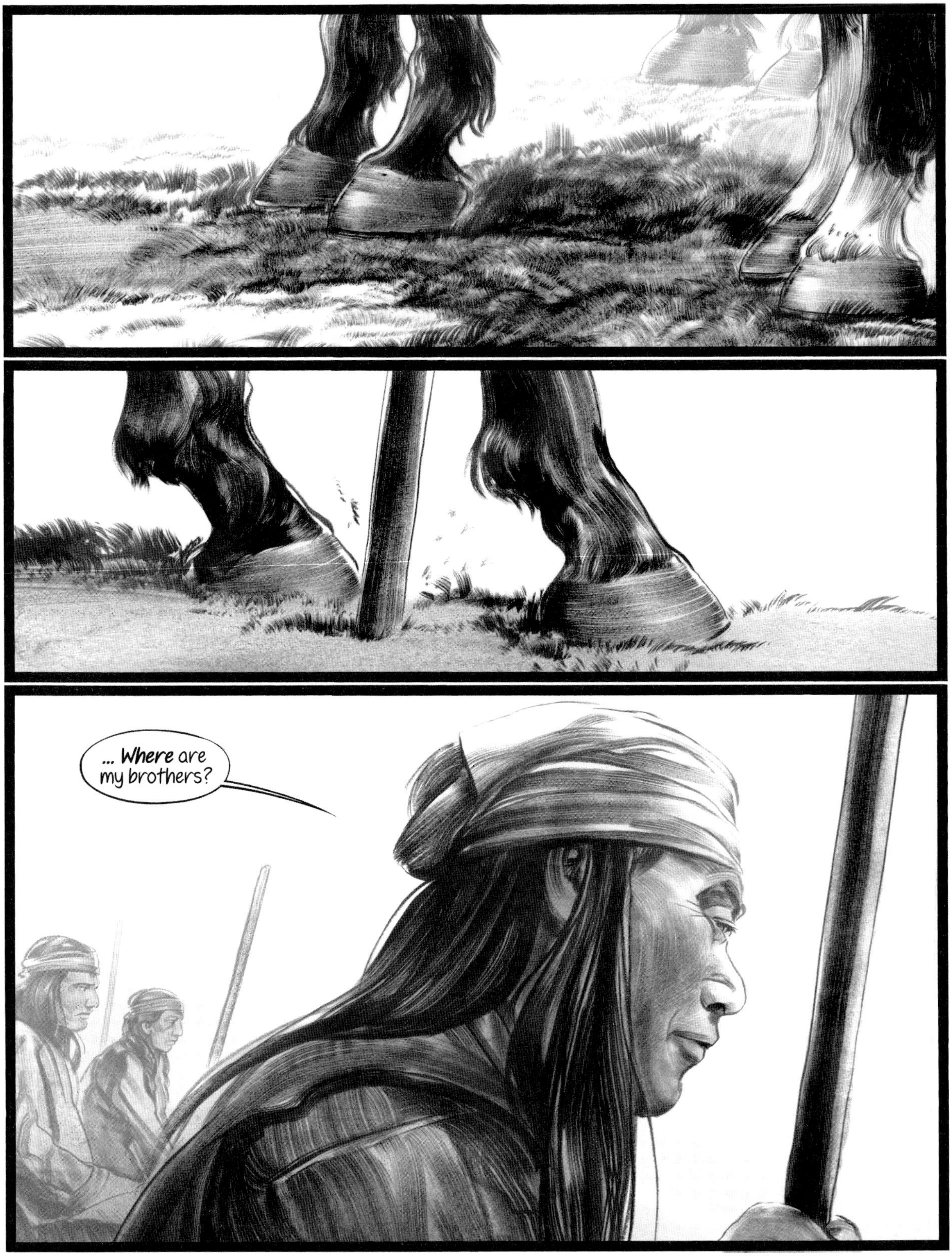
... Where are my brothers?

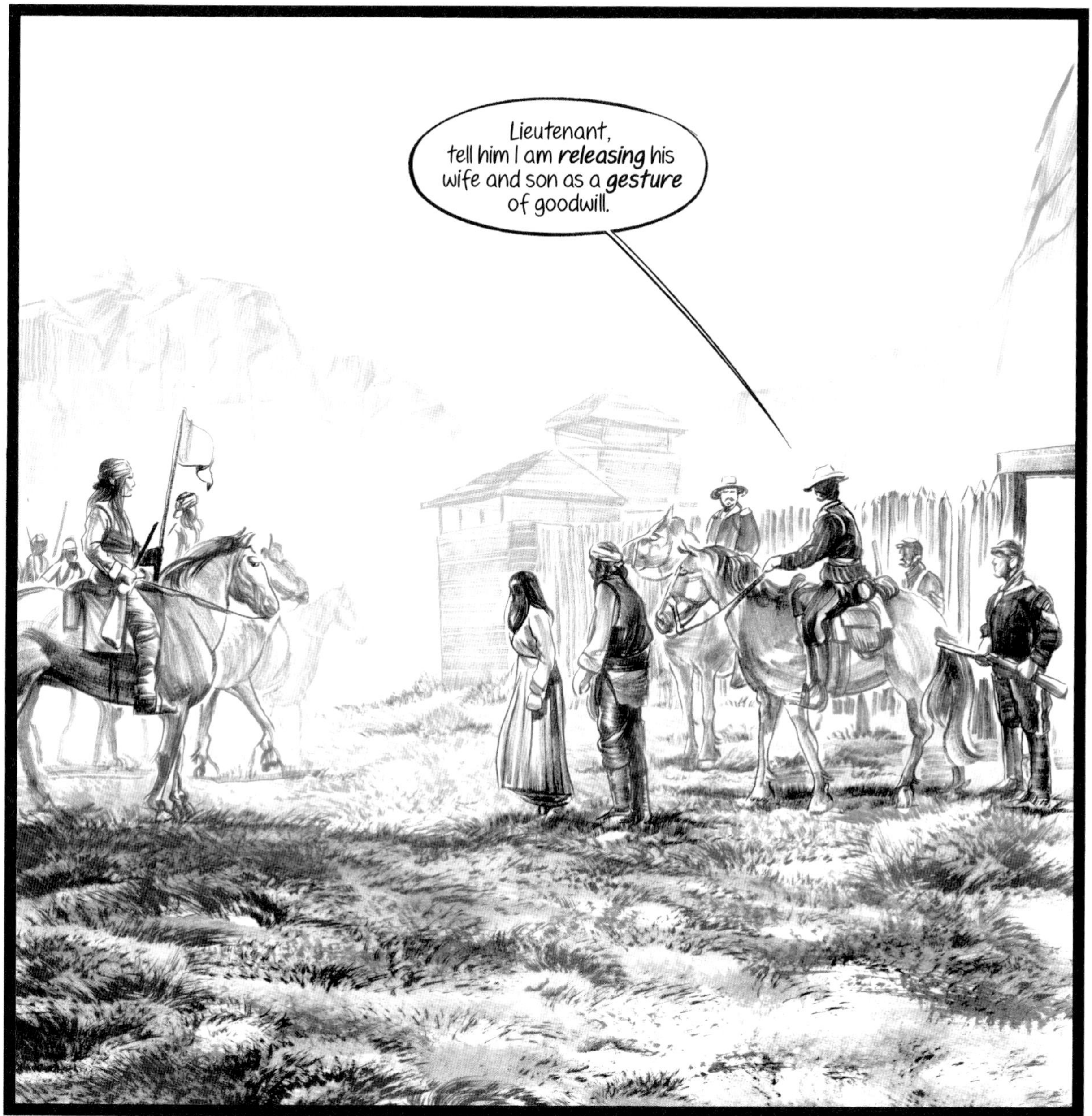
Lieutenant, tell him I am releasing his wife and son as a gesture of goodwill.

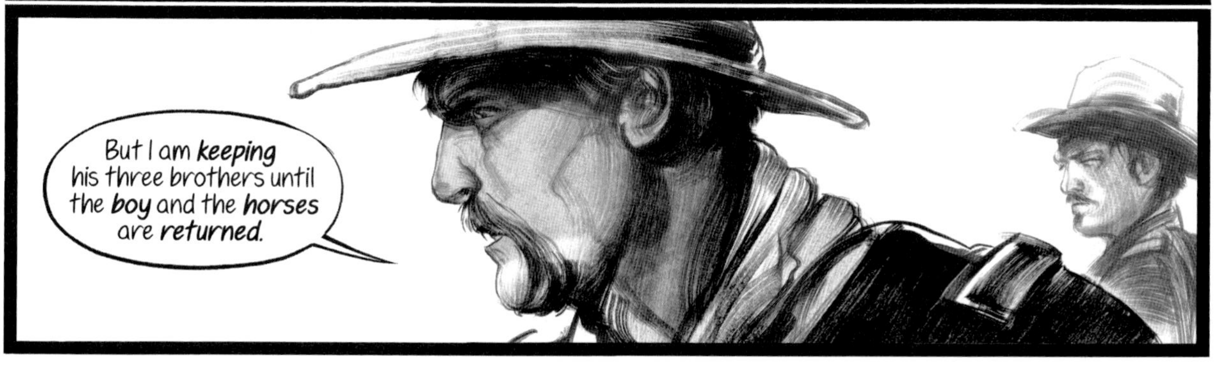
But I am keeping his three brothers until the boy and the horses are returned.

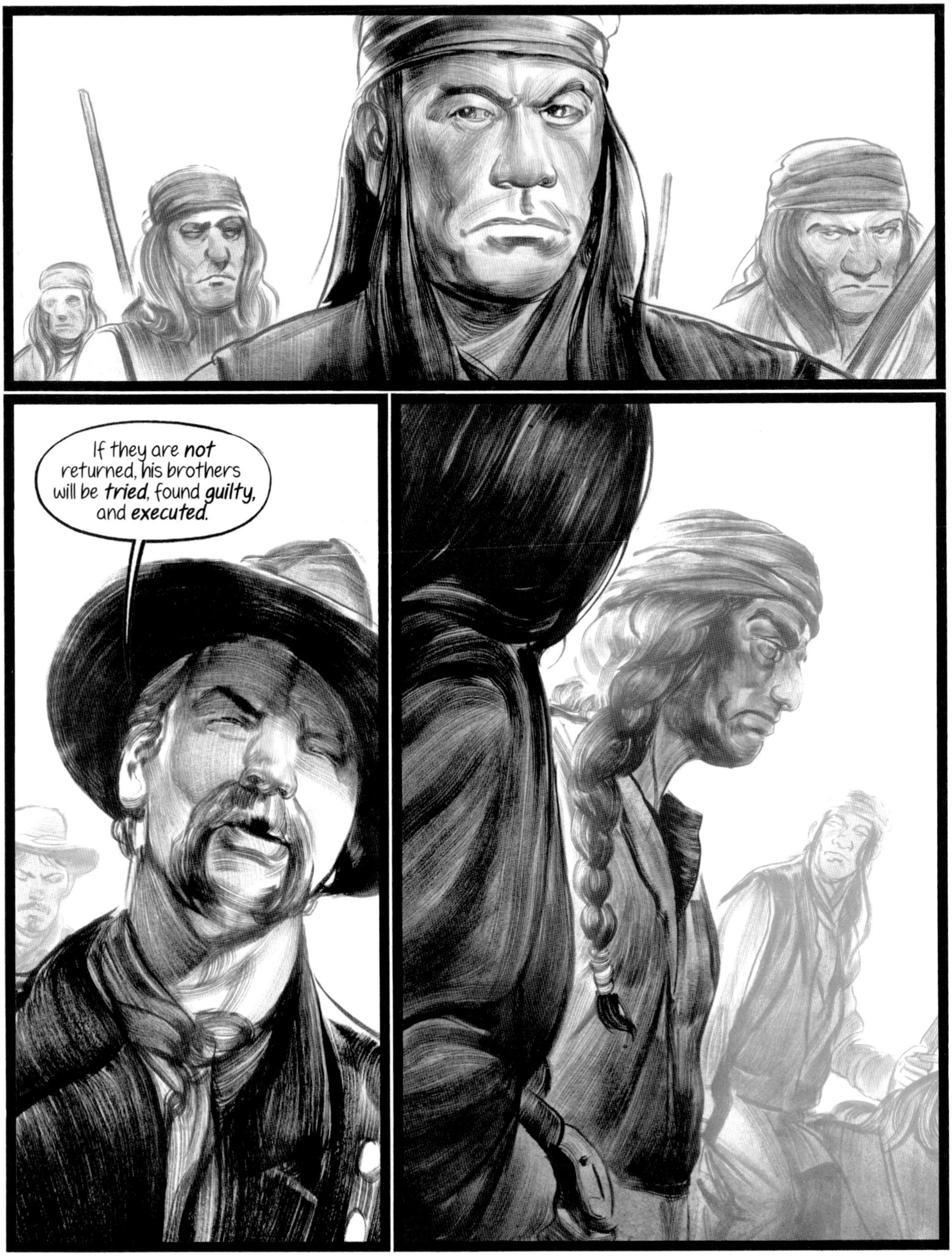
If they are **not** returned, his brothers will be **tried**, found **guilty**, and **executed**.

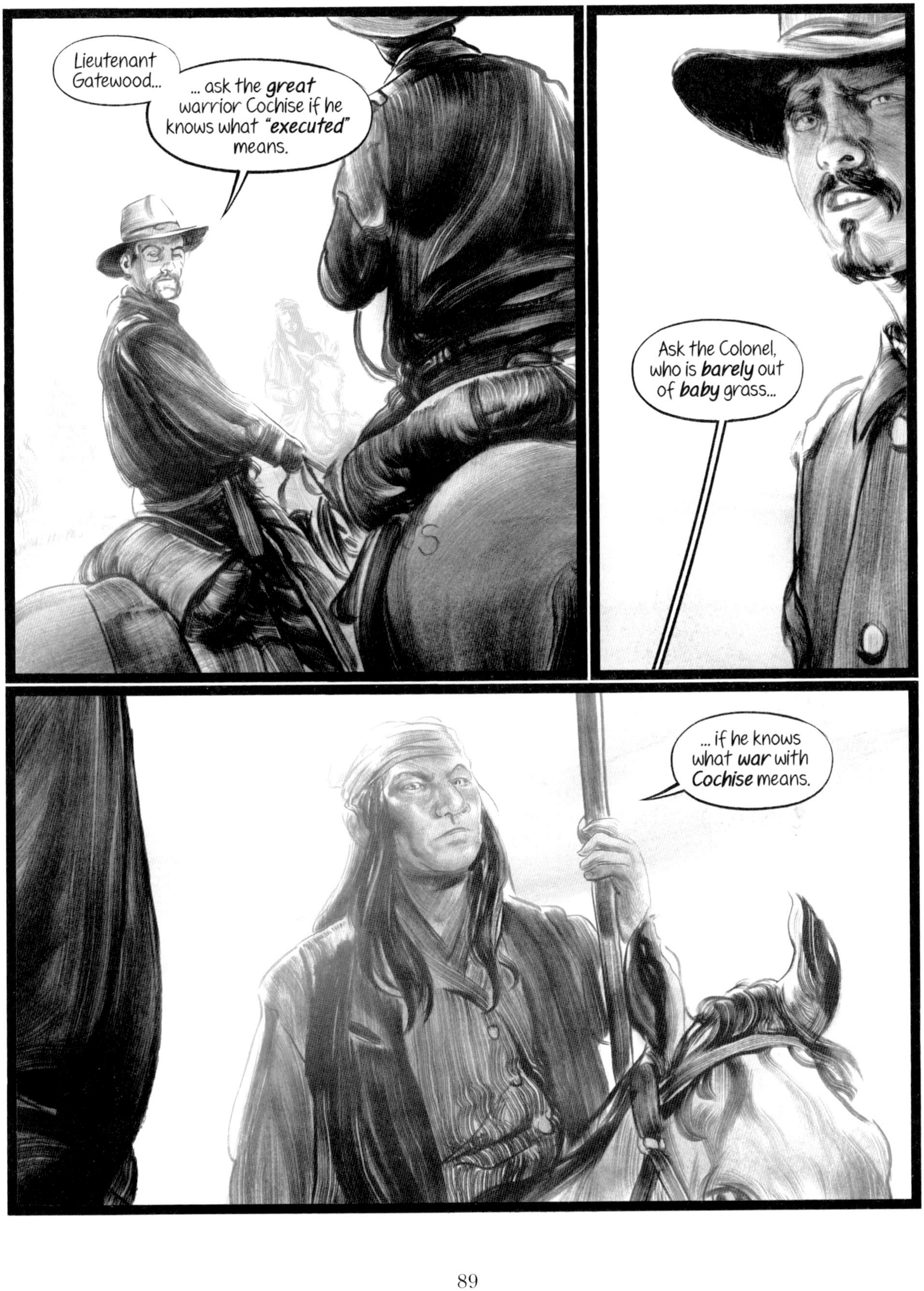
Lieutenant Gatewood...
... ask the great warrior Cochise if he knows what "executed" means.
Ask the Colonel, who is barely out of baby grass...
... if he knows what war with Cochise means.

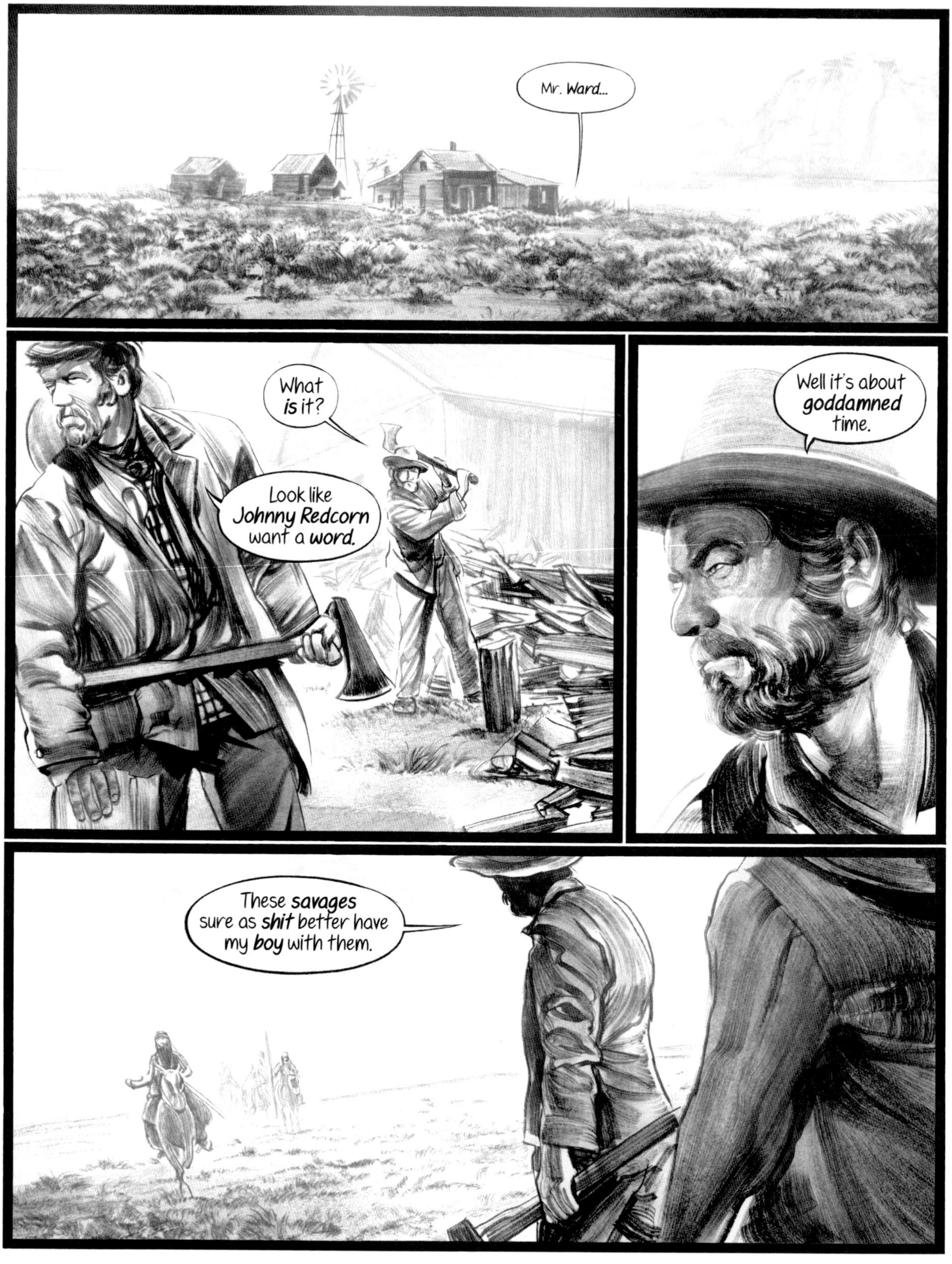
Mr. Ward...
What is it?
Look like Johnny Redcorn want a word.
Well it's about goddamned time.
These savages sure as shit better have my boy with them.

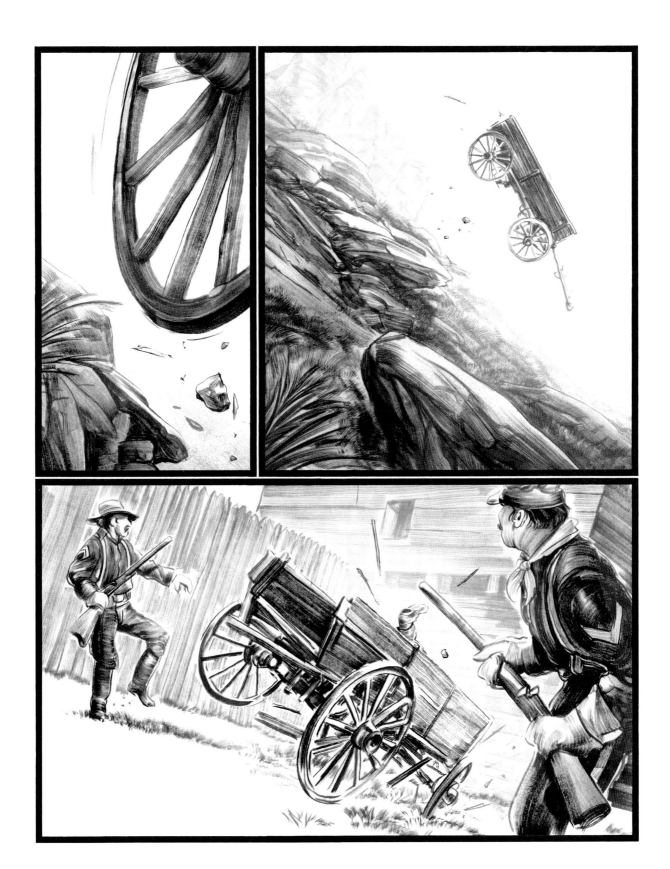

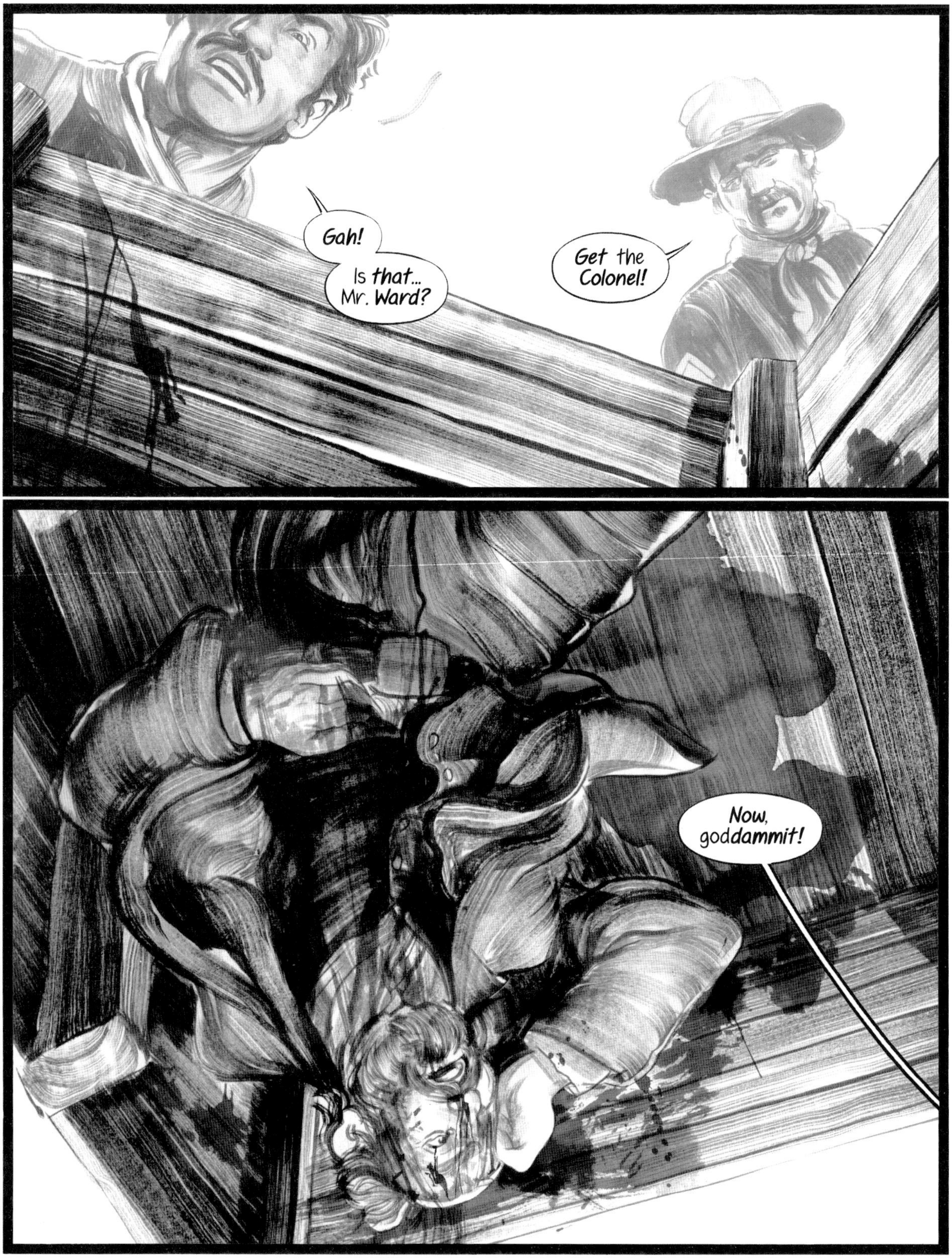
Gah!
Is that... Mr. Ward?
Get the Colonel!
Now, goddammit!

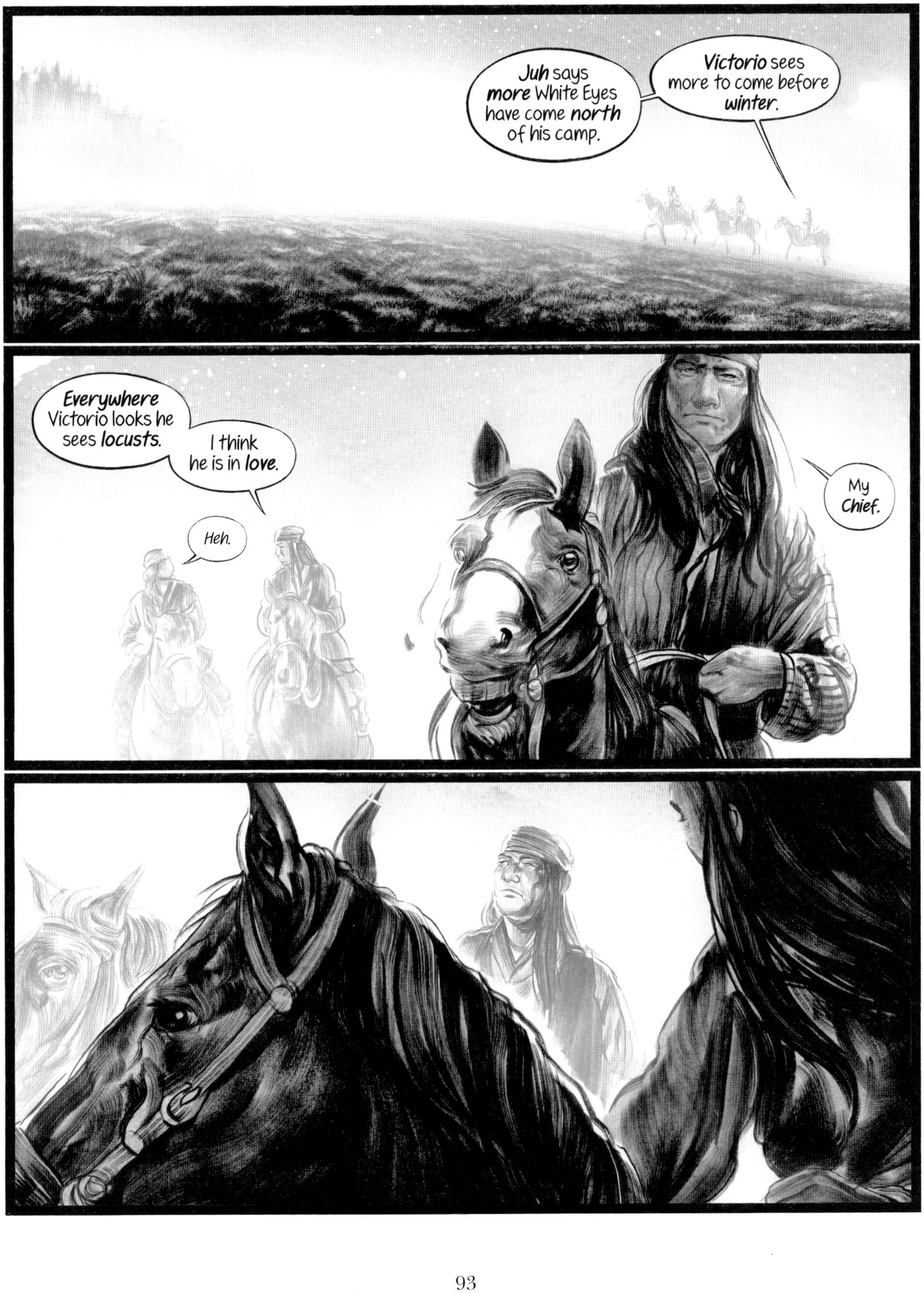
Juh says more White Eyes have come north of his camp.
Victorio sees more to come before winter.
Everywhere Victorio looks he sees locusts.
I think he is in love.
Heh.
My Chief.

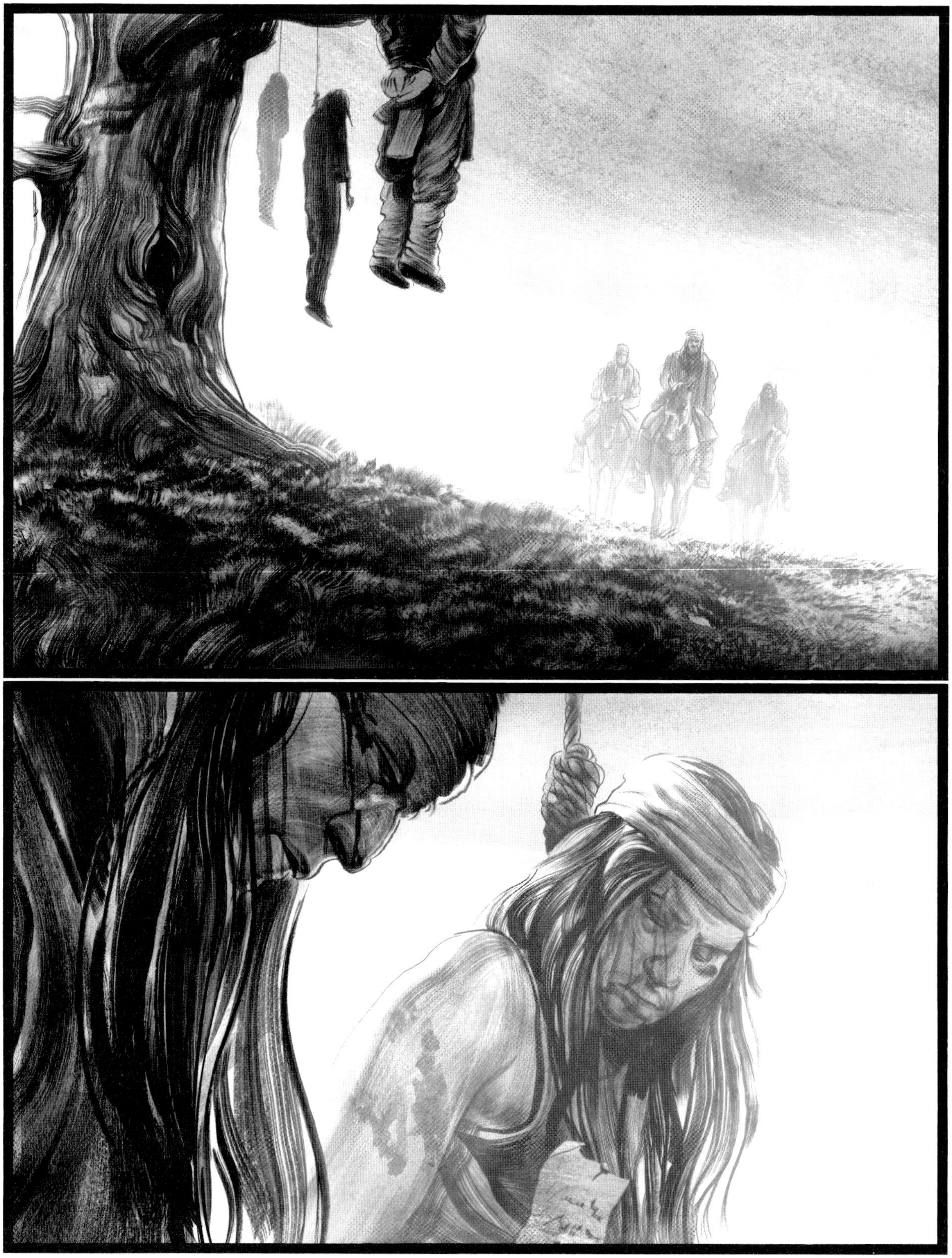

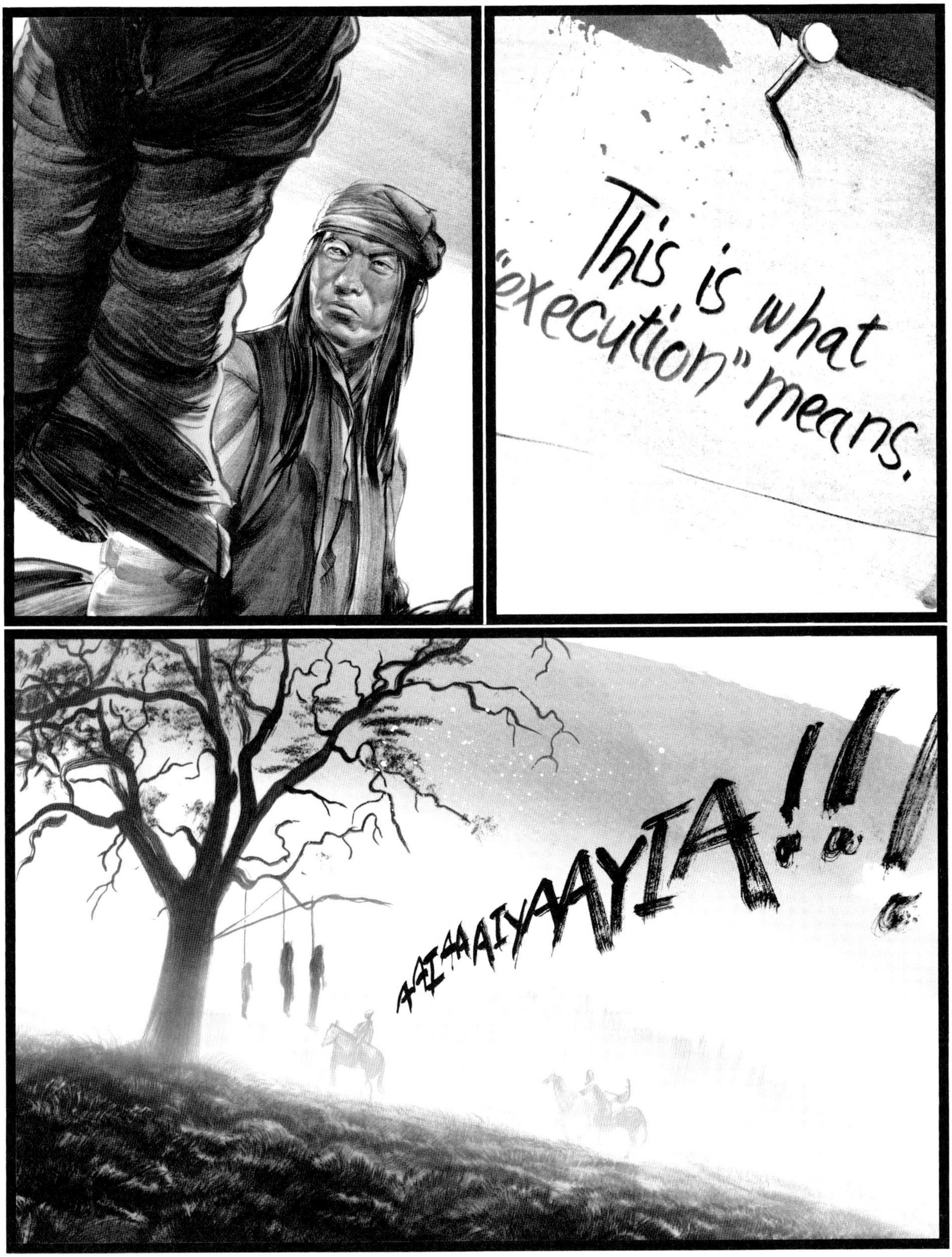
This is what "execution" means.
AAIAAAIYAAYIA!!!

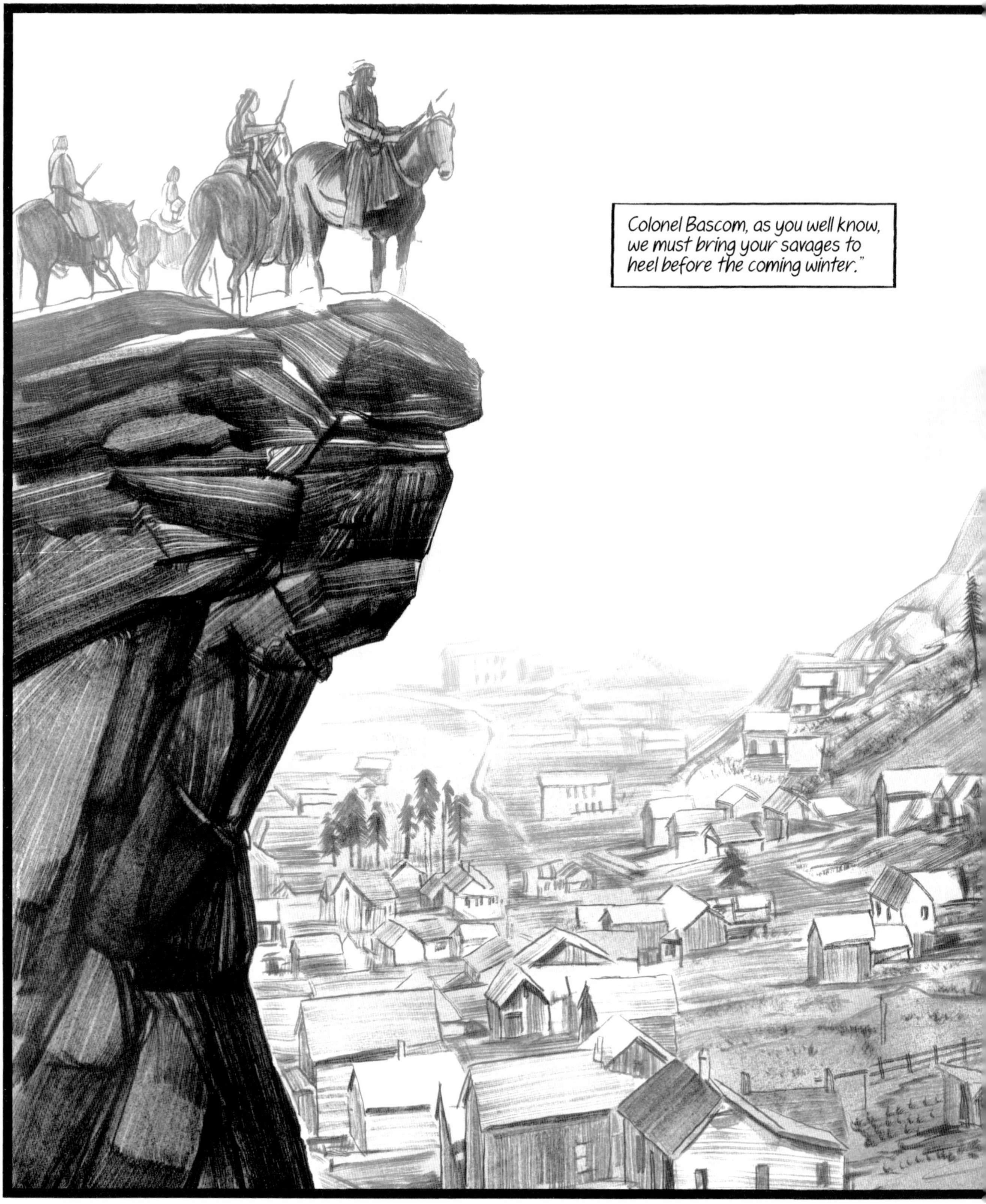
Colonel Bascom, as you well know, we must bring your savages to heel before the coming winter."

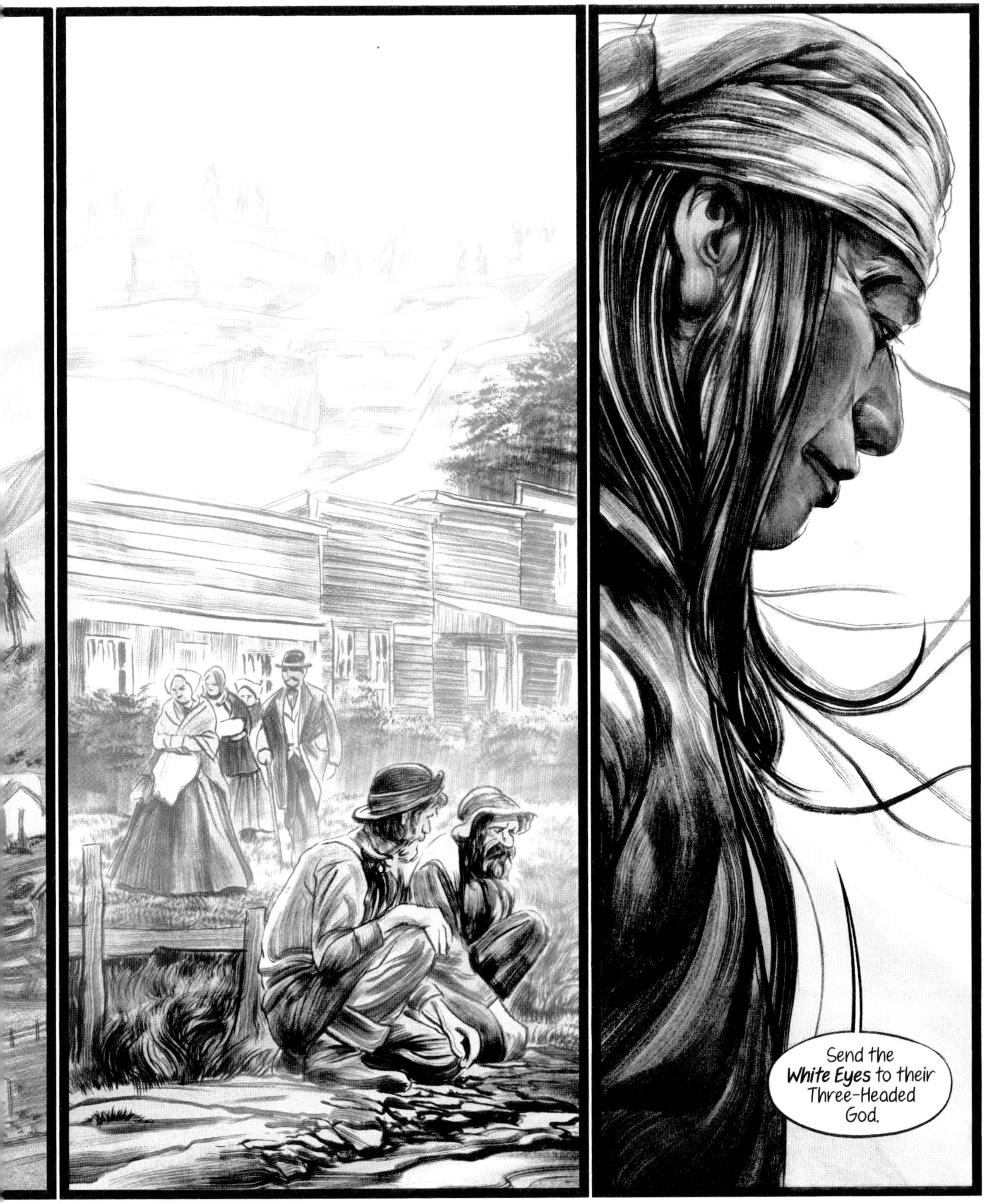
Send the **White Eyes** to their Three-Headed God.

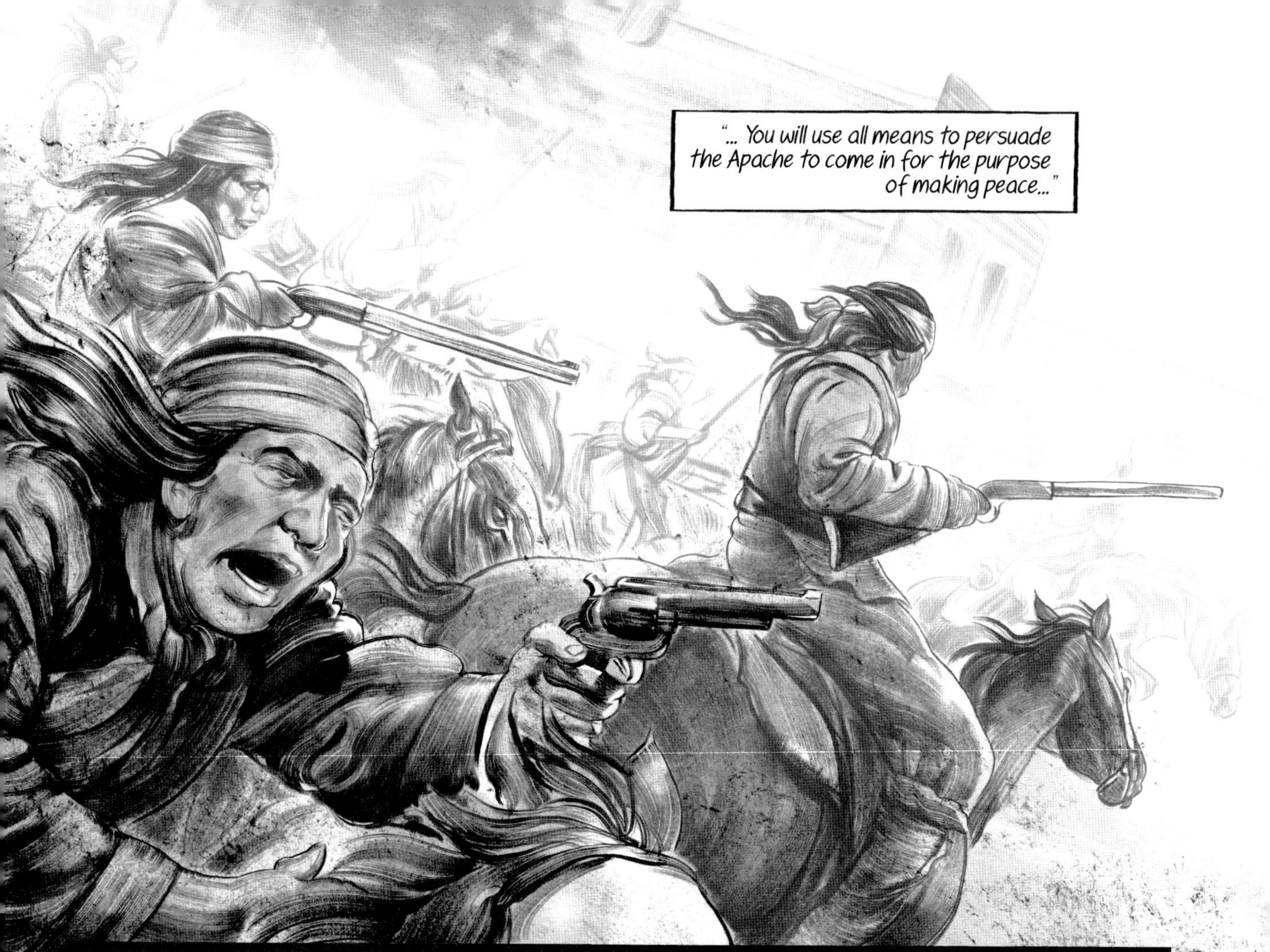
"... You will use all means to persuade the Apache to come in for the purpose of making peace..."

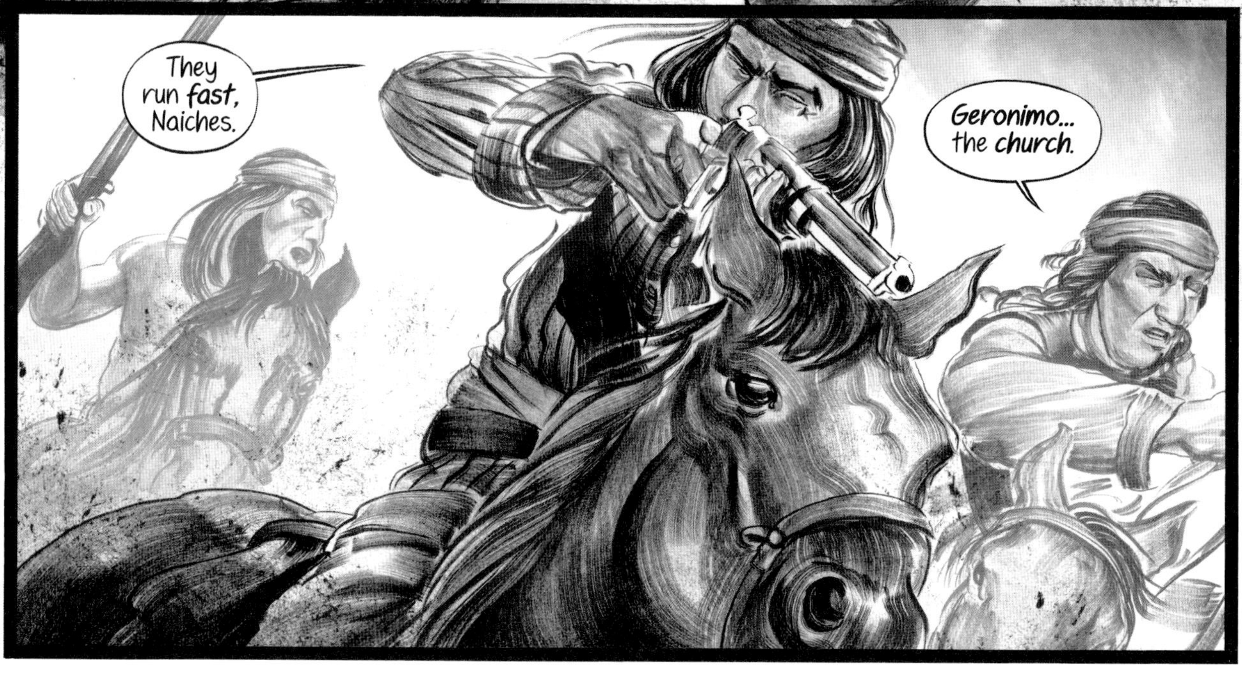
They run fast, Naiches.
Geronimo... the church.

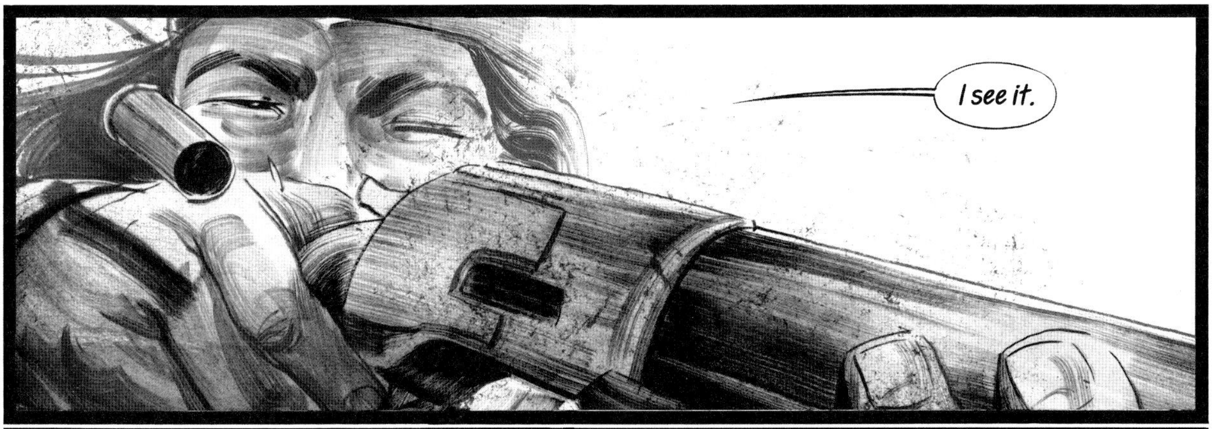
I see it.

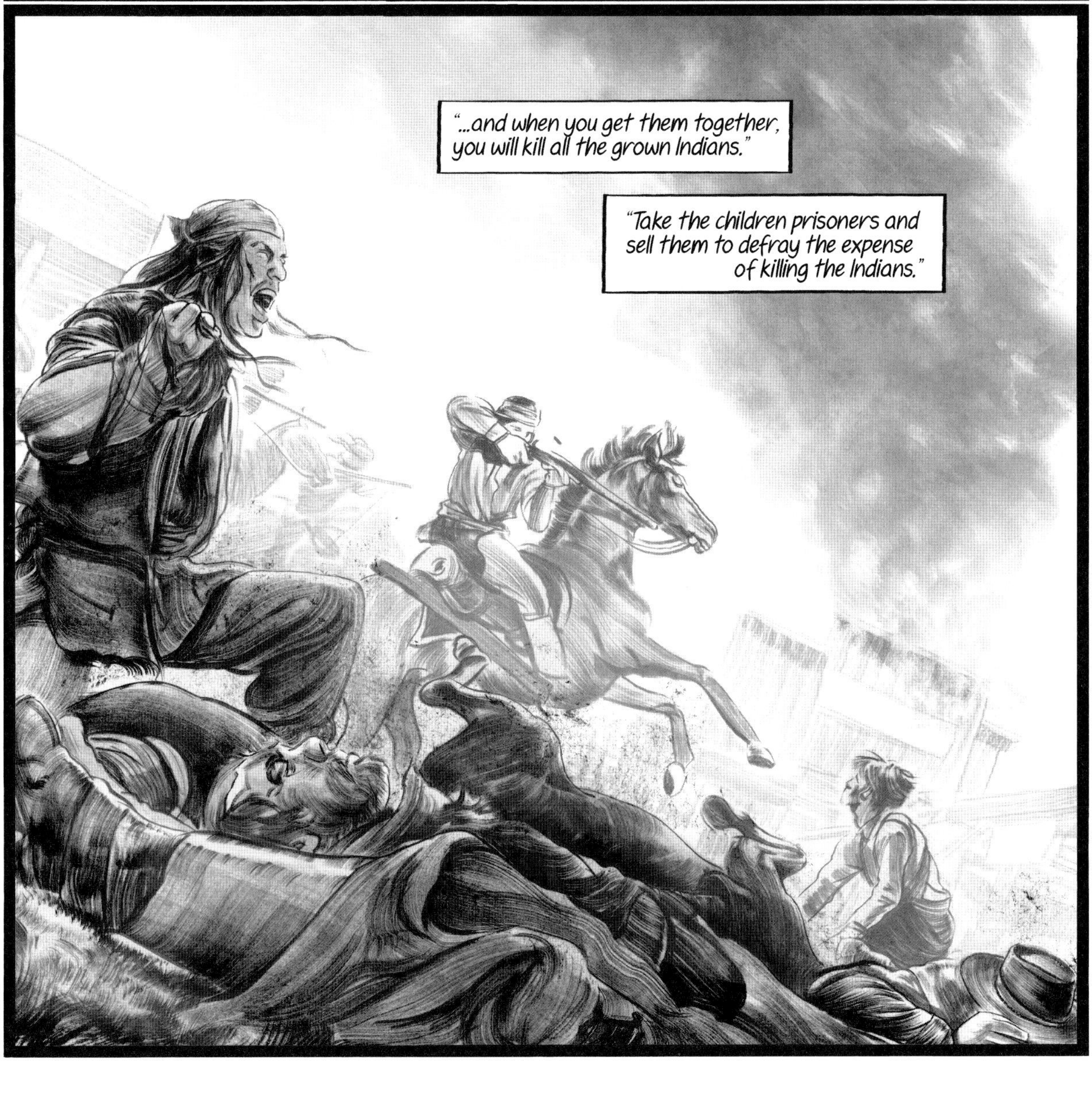
"...and when you get them together, you will kill all the grown Indians."
"Take the children prisoners and sell them to defray the expense of killing the Indians."

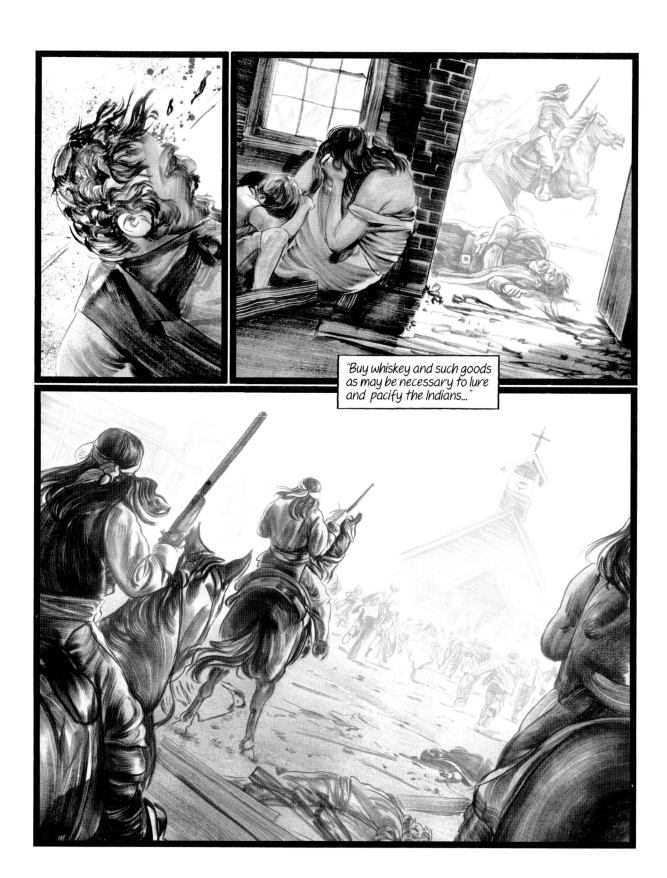

"Buy whiskey and such goods as may be necessary to lure and pacify the Indians..."

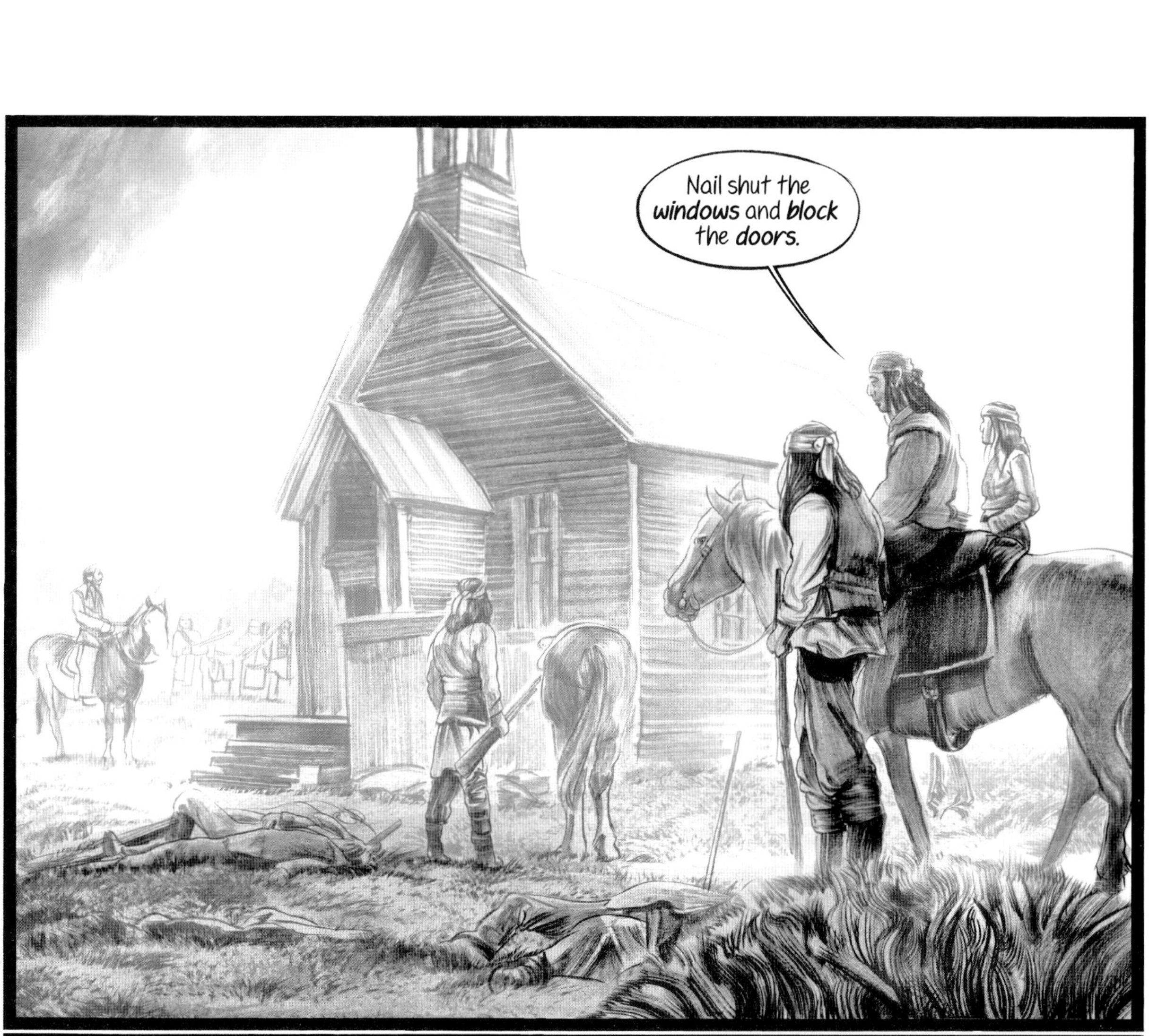
Nail shut the **windows** and **block** the **doors.**

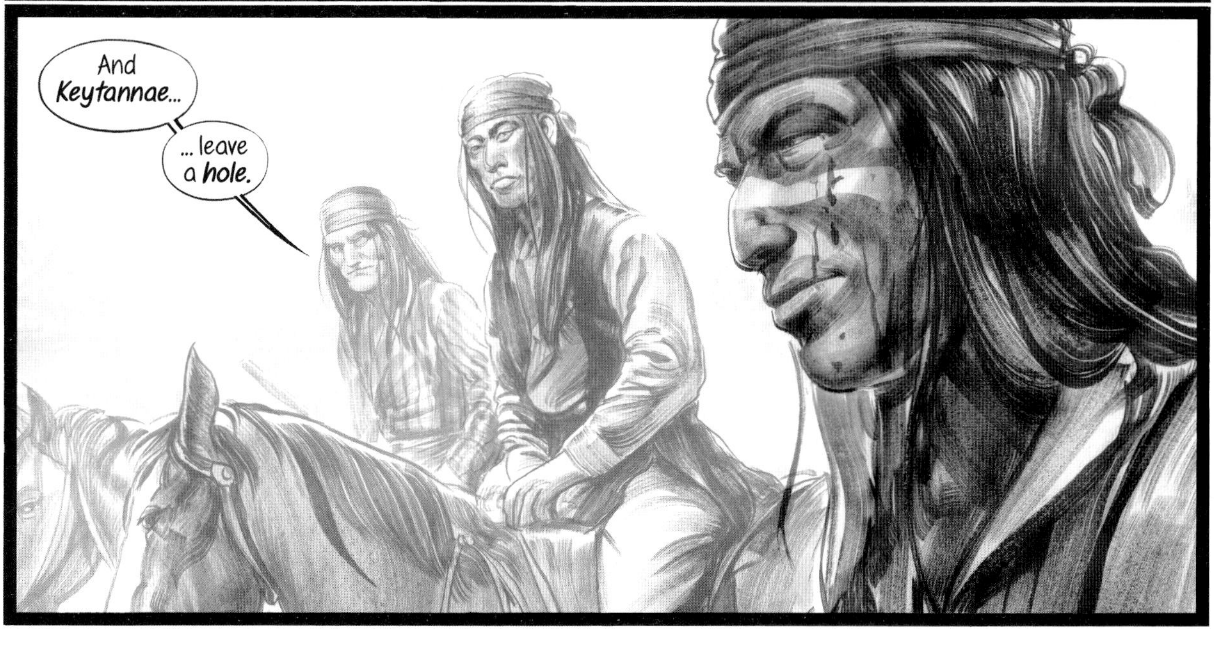
And **Keytannae...**
... leave a **hole.**

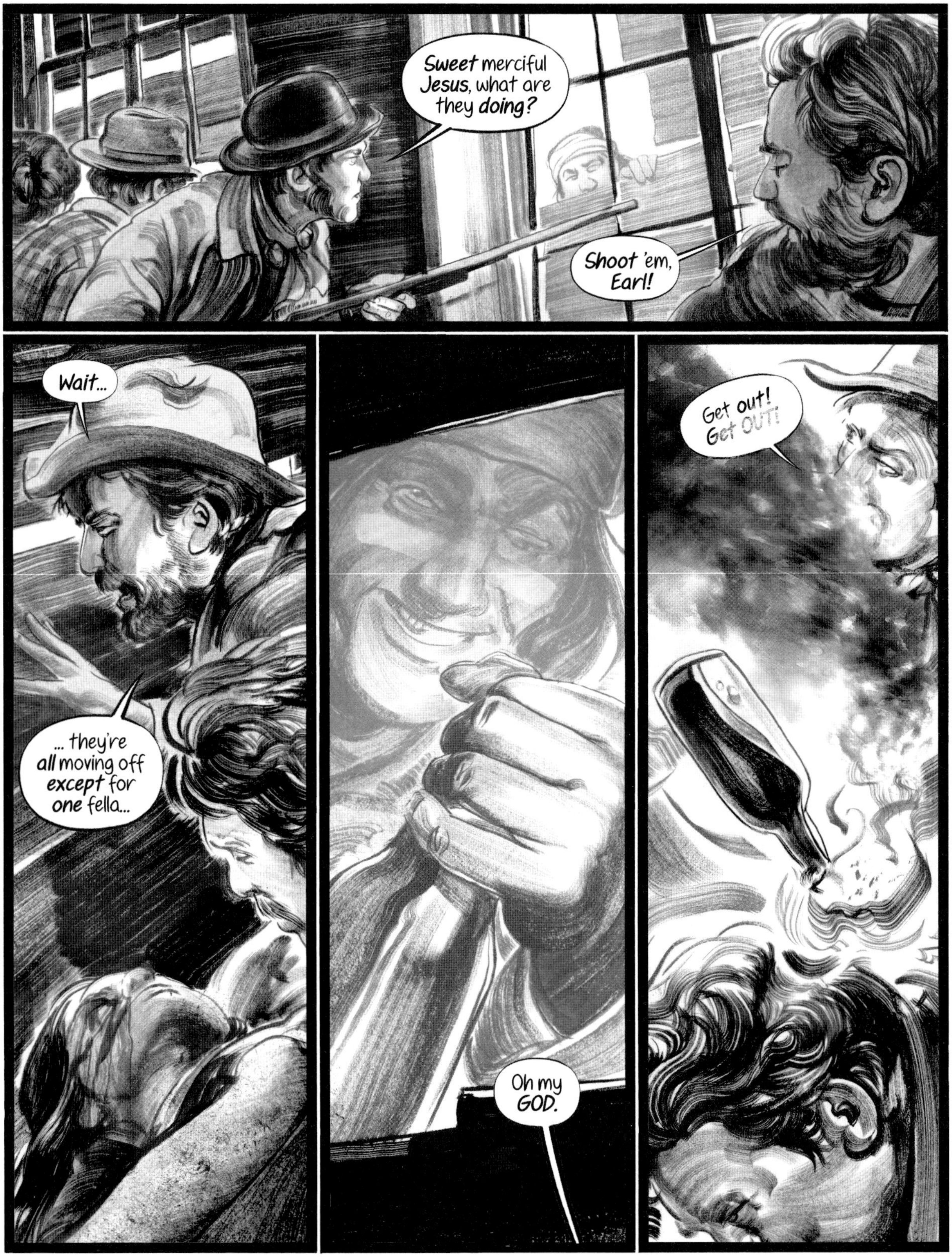
Sweet merciful Jesus, what are they doing?
Shoot 'em, Earl!
Wait...
... they're all moving off except for one fella...
Oh my GOD.
Get out! Get OUT!

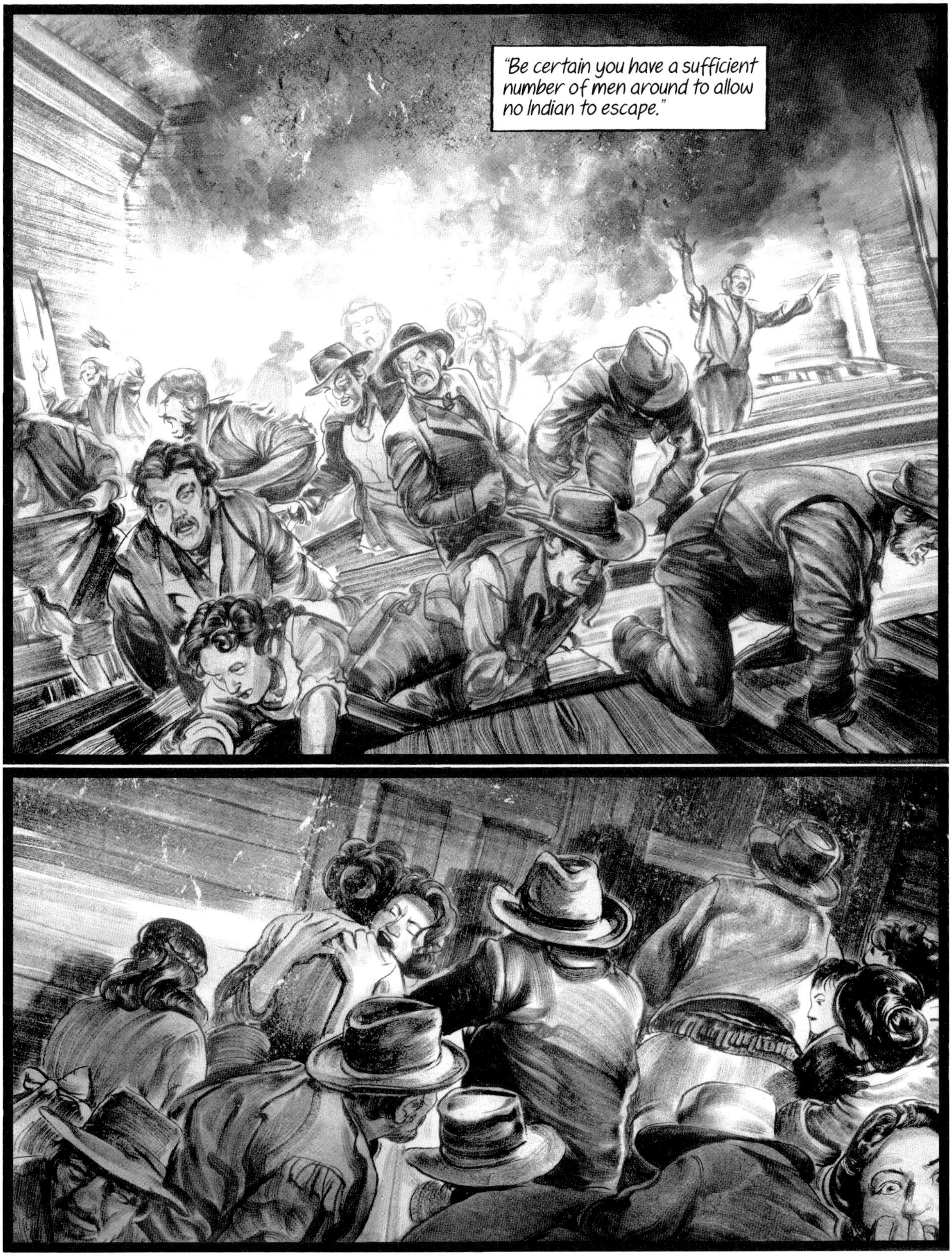
"Be certain you have a sufficient number of men around to allow no Indian to escape."

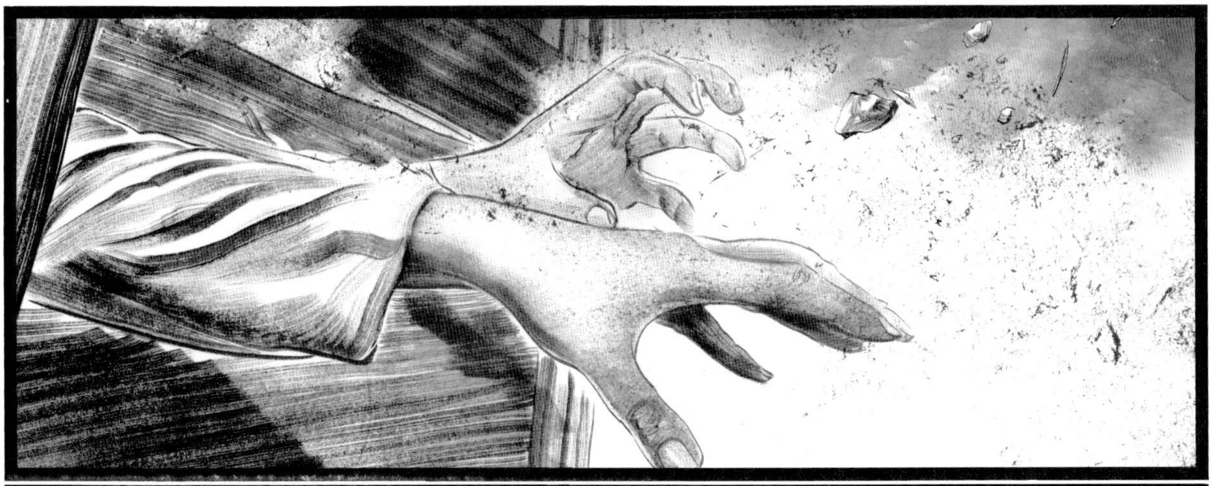

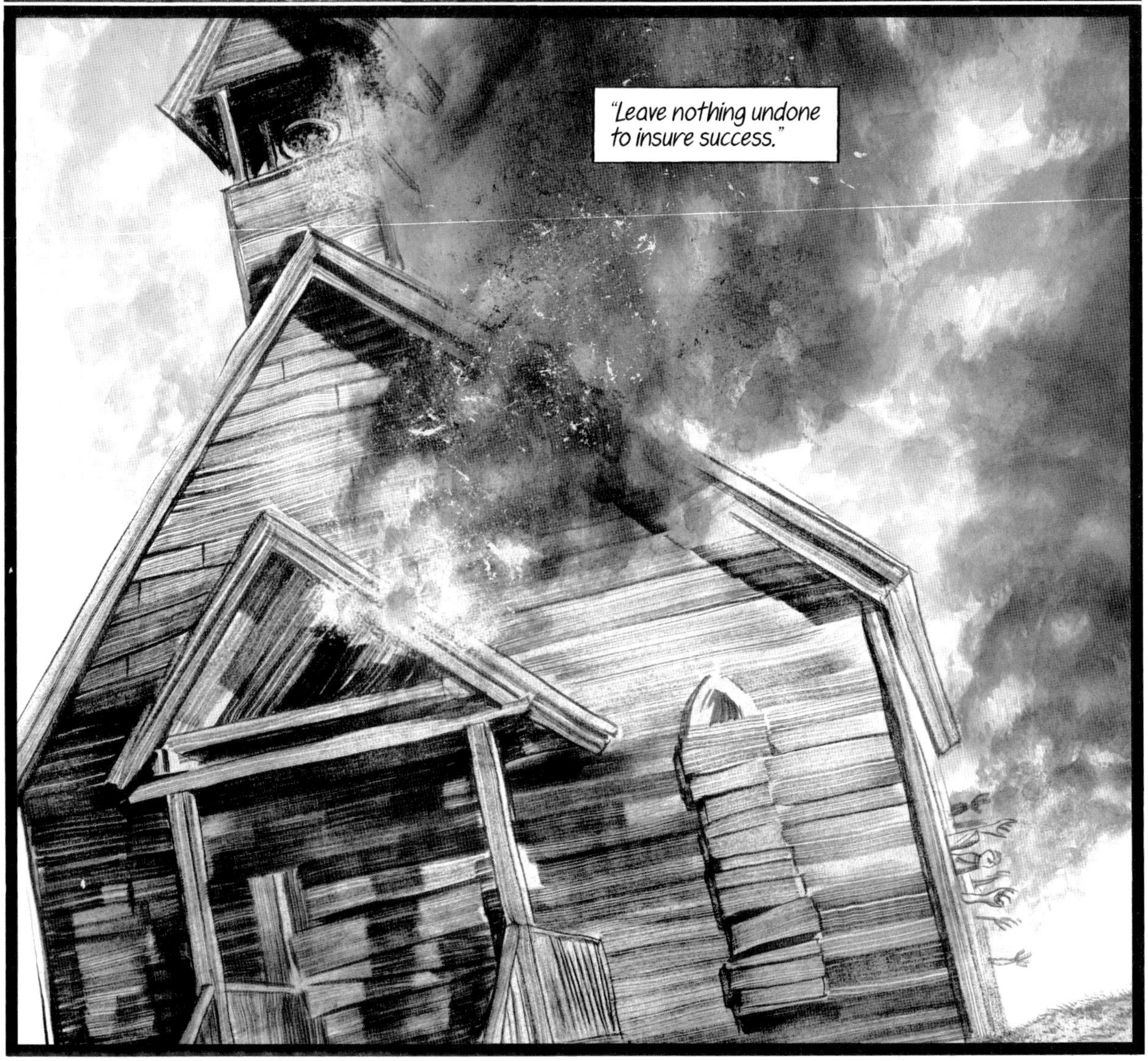
"Leave nothing undone to insure success."

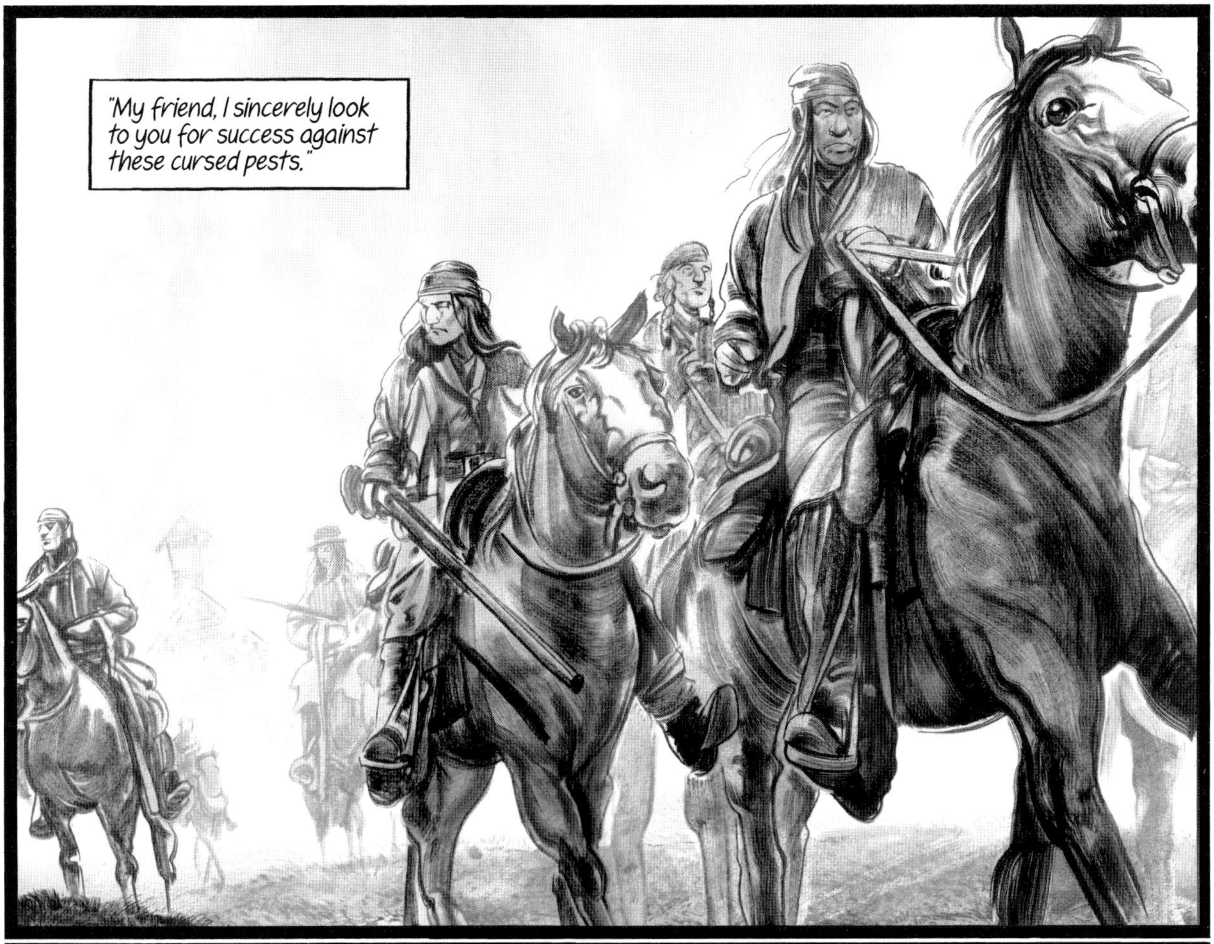
"My friend, I sincerely look to you for success against these cursed pests."

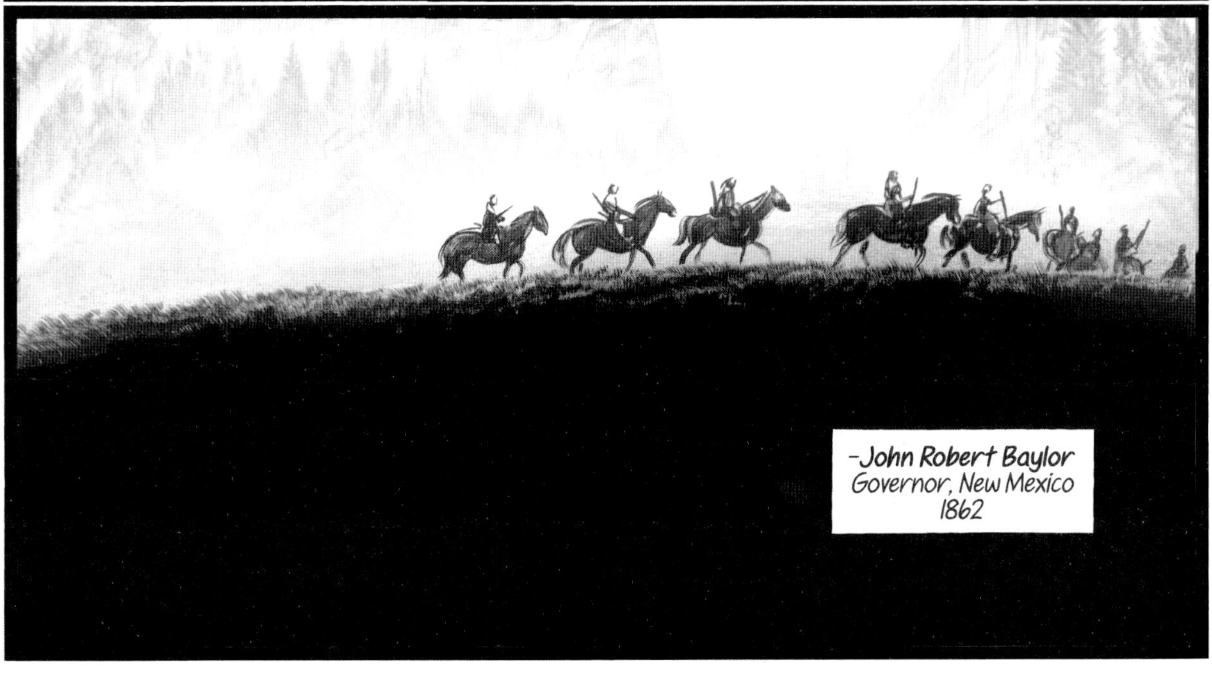
-John Robert Baylor
Governor, New Mexico
1862

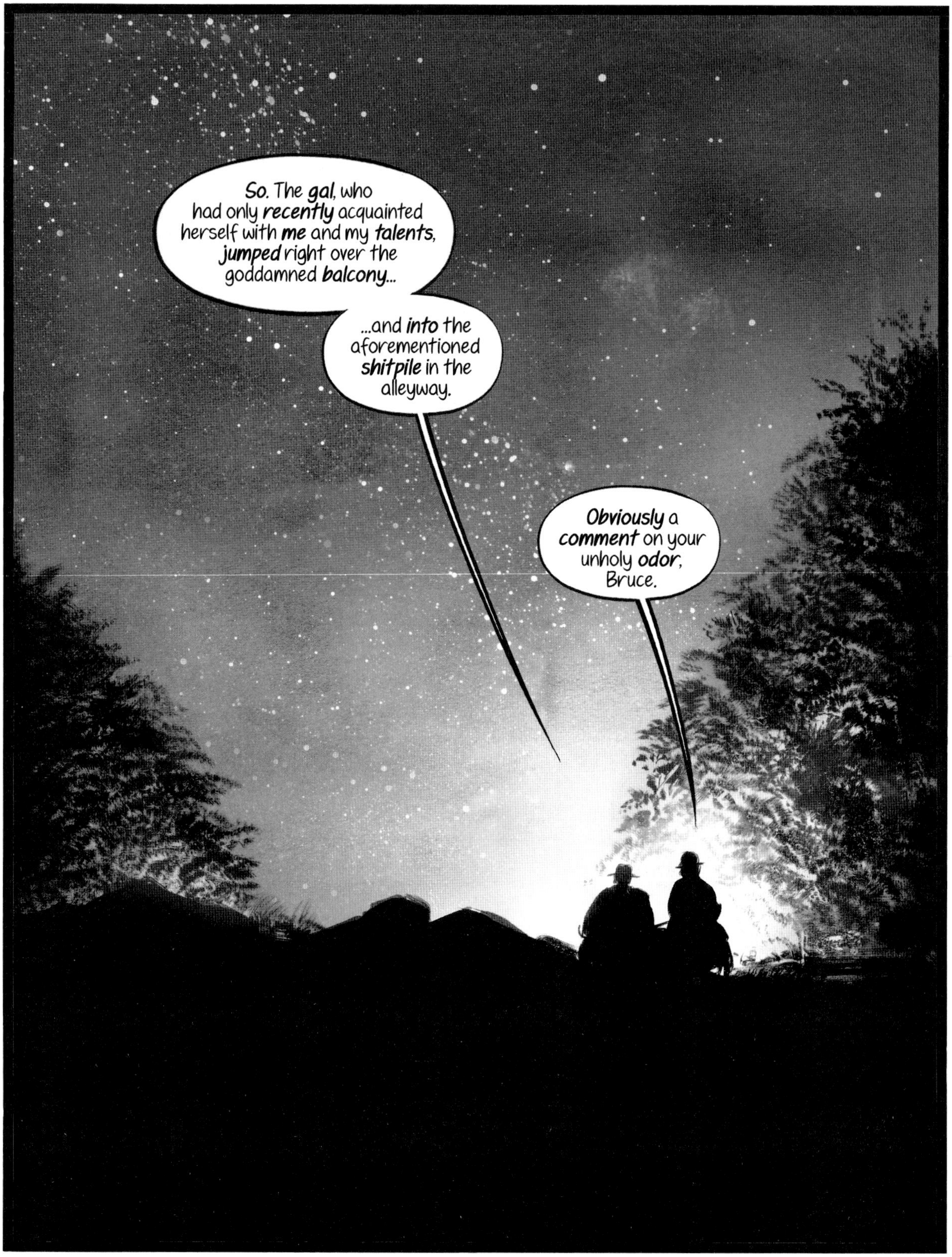
So. The gal, who had only recently acquainted herself with me and my talents, jumped right over the goddamned balcony...
...and into the aforementioned shitpile in the alleyway.
Obviously a comment on your unholy odor, Bruce.

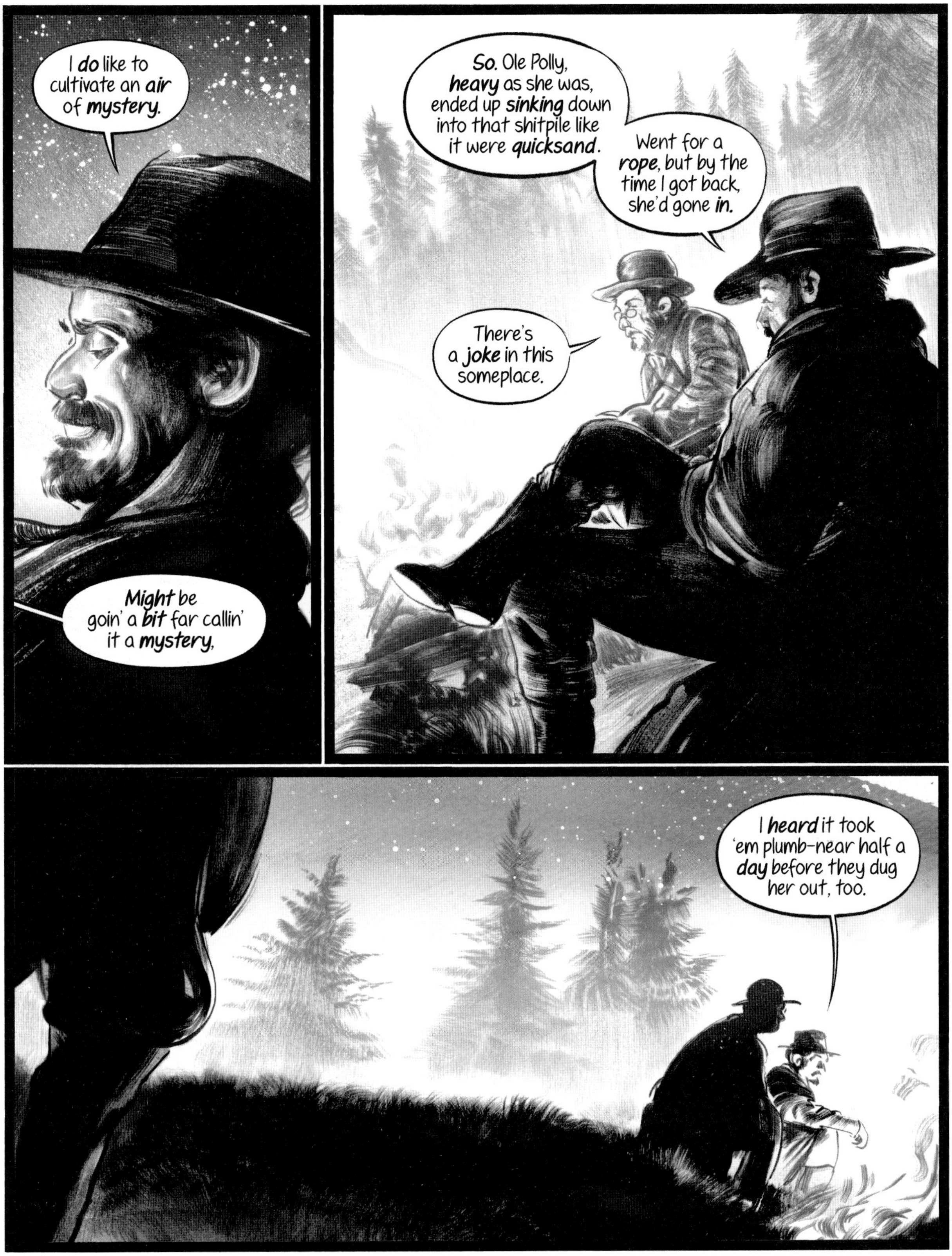

I **do** like to cultivate an **air** of **mystery**.
Might be goin' a **bit** far callin' it a **mystery**,
So. Ole Polly, **heavy** as she was, ended up **sinking** down into that shitpile like it were **quicksand**.
Went for a **rope**, but by the time I got back, she'd gone **in.**
There's a **joke** in this someplace.
I **heard** it took 'em plumb-near half a **day** before they dug her out, too.

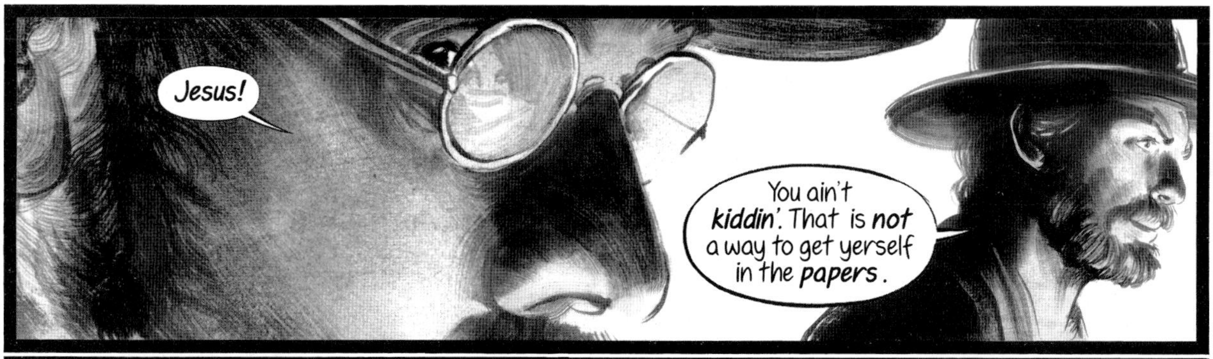
Jesus!
You ain't kiddin'. That is not a way to get yerself in the papers.

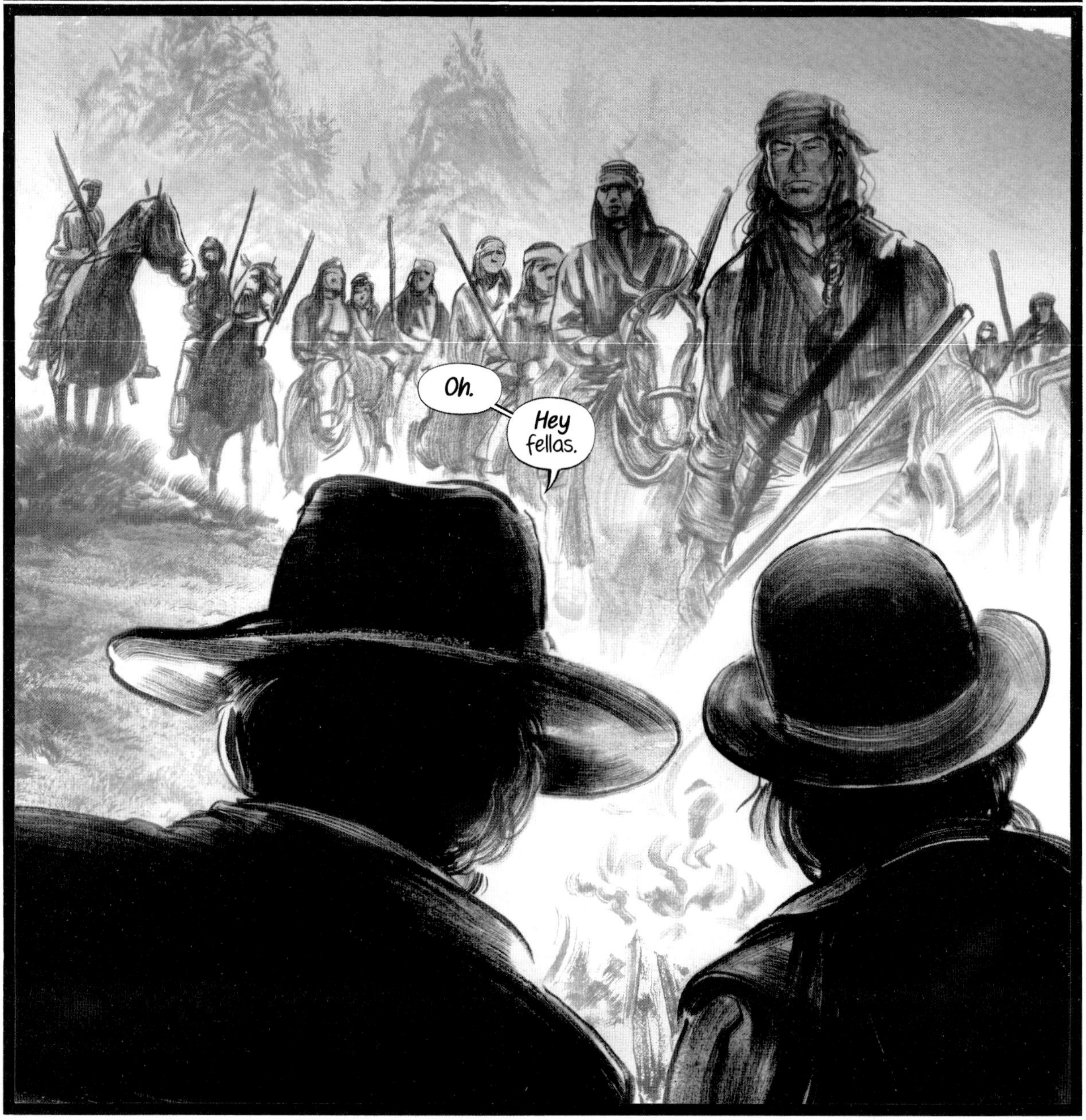
Oh.
Hey fellas.

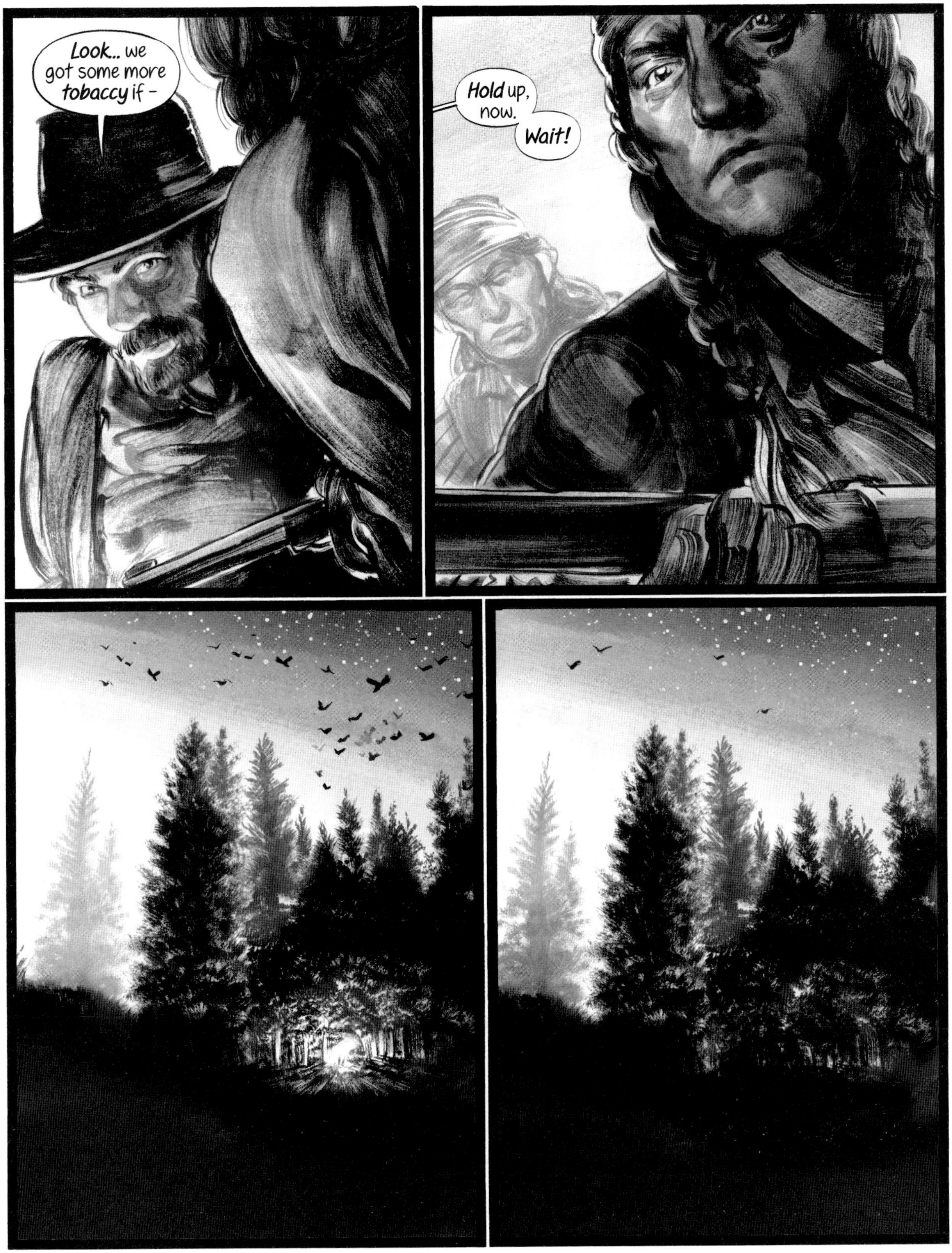
Look.. we got some more tobaccy if -
Hold up, now. Wait!

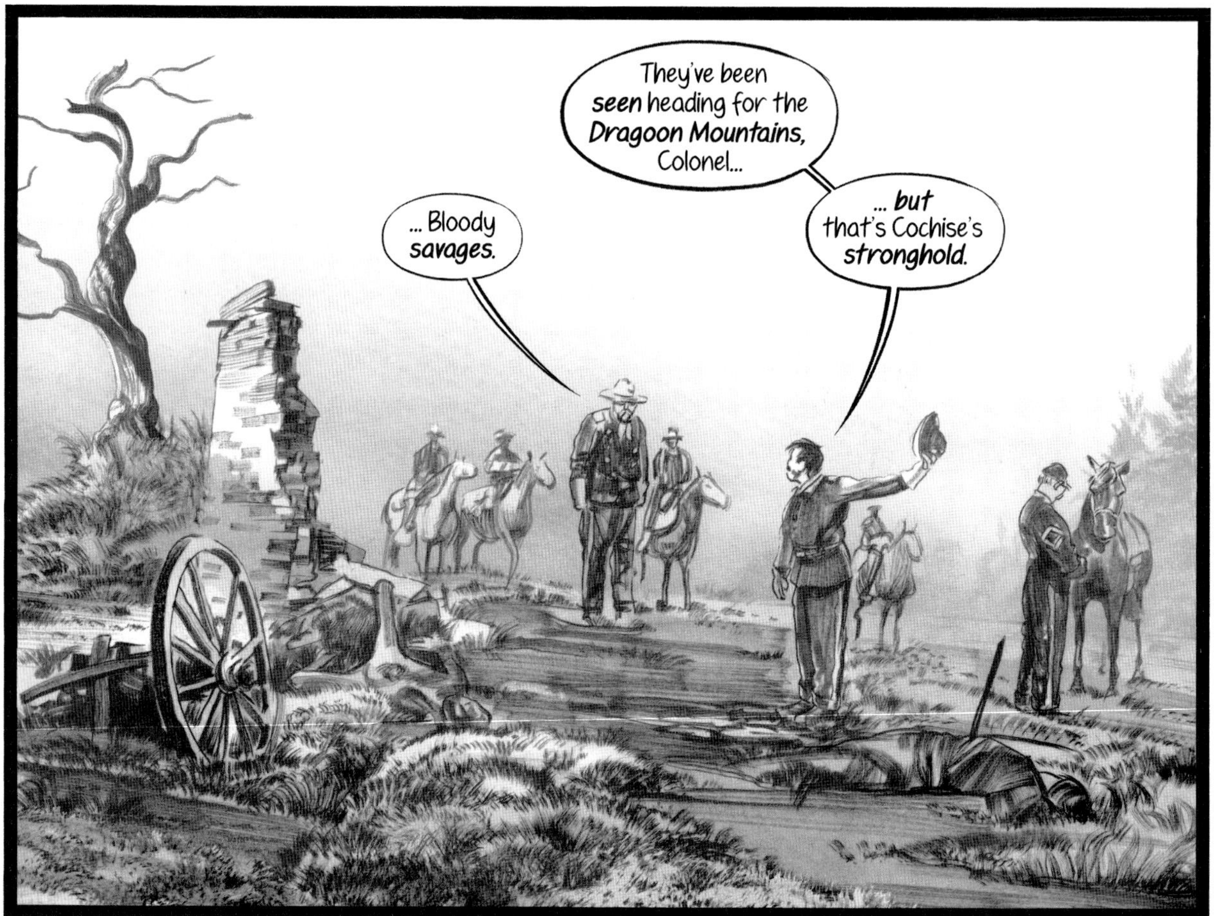
They've been seen heading for the Dragoon Mountains, Colonel...
... but that's Cochise's stronghold.
... Bloody savages.

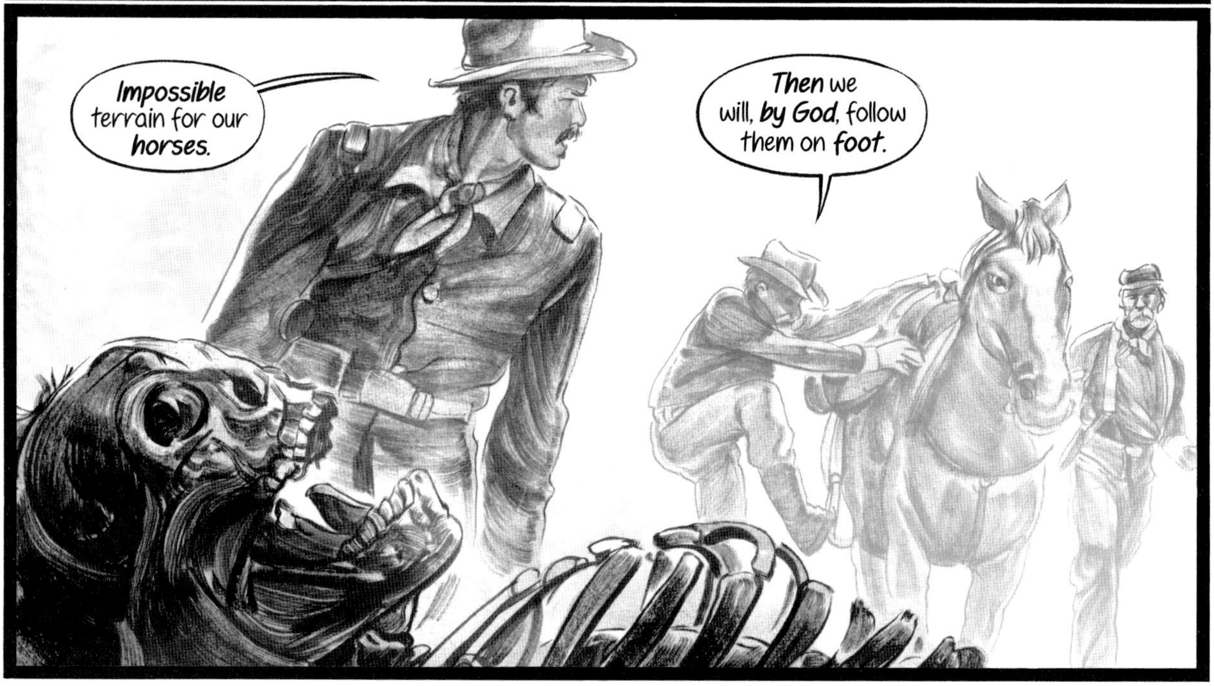
Impossible terrain for our horses.
Then we will, by God, follow them on foot.

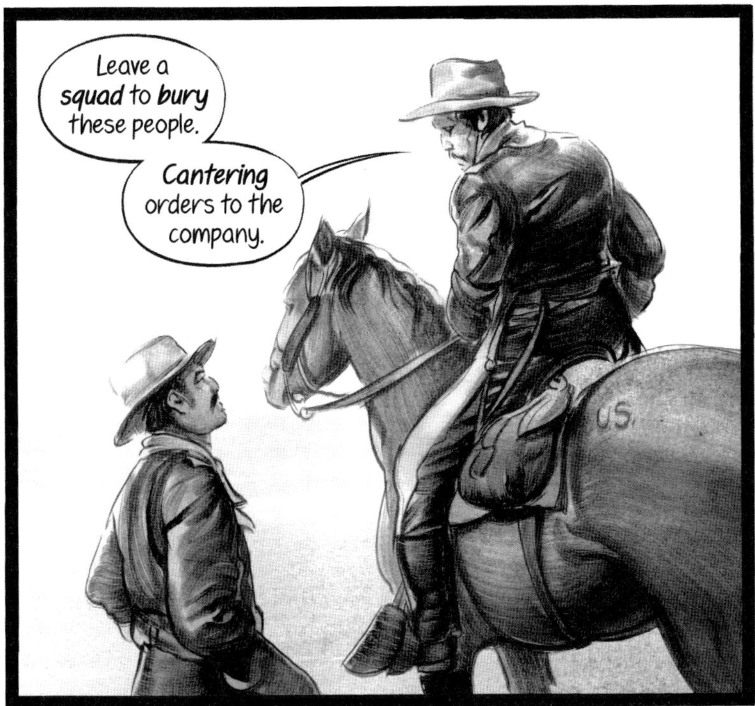
Leave a squad to bury these people.
Cantering orders to the company.

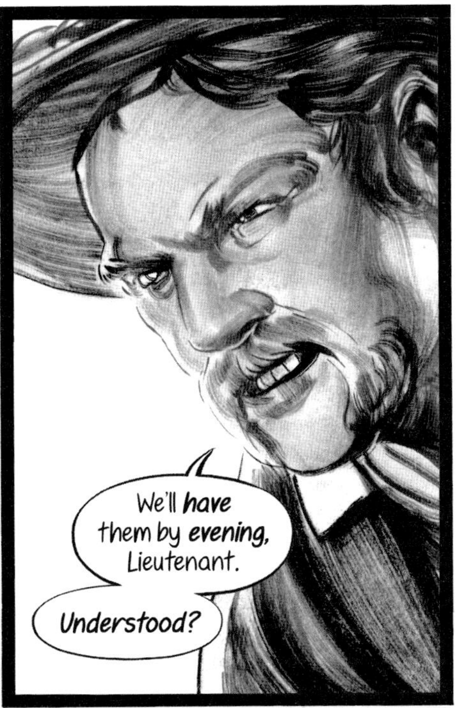
We'll have them by evening, Lieutenant.
Understood?

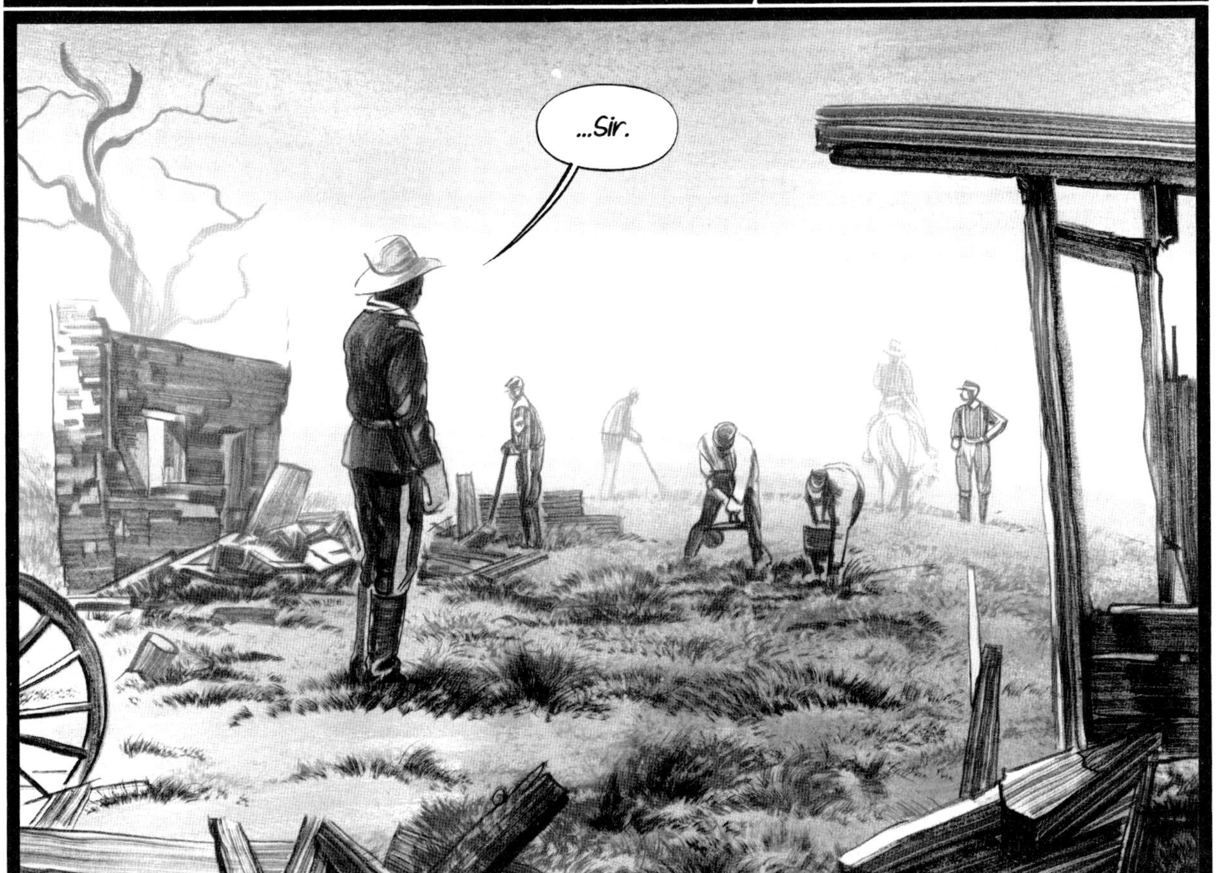
...Sir.

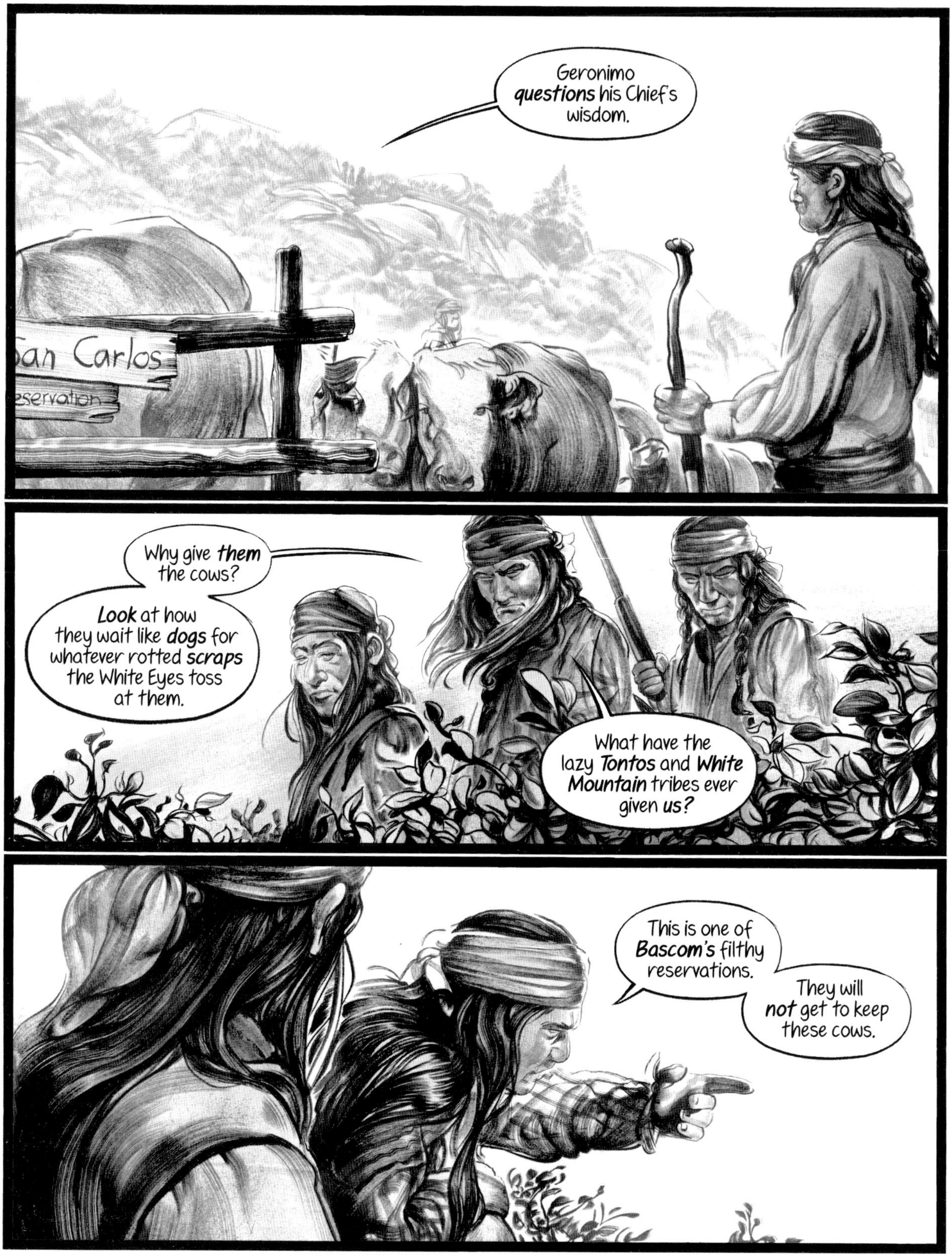
Geronimo questions his Chief's wisdom.
San Carlos
eservation
Why give them the cows?
Look at how they wait like dogs for whatever rotted scraps the White Eyes toss at them.
What have the lazy Tontos and White Mountain tribes ever given us?
This is one of Bascom's filthy reservations.
They will not get to keep these cows.

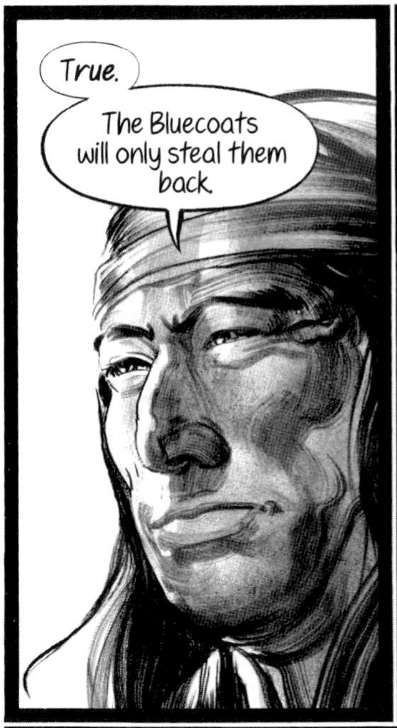
True.
The Bluecoats will only steal them back.

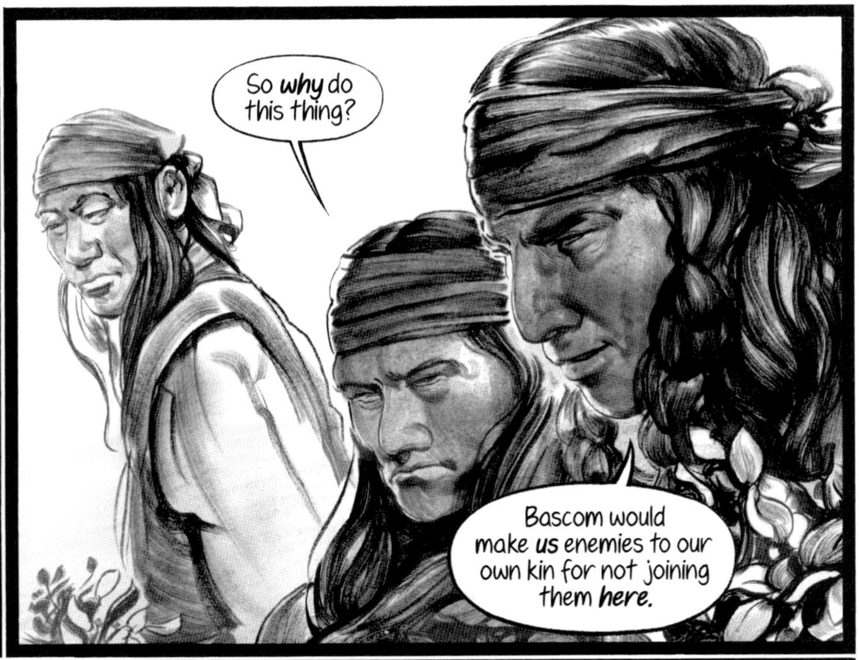
So why do this thing?
Bascom would make us enemies to our own kin for not joining them here.

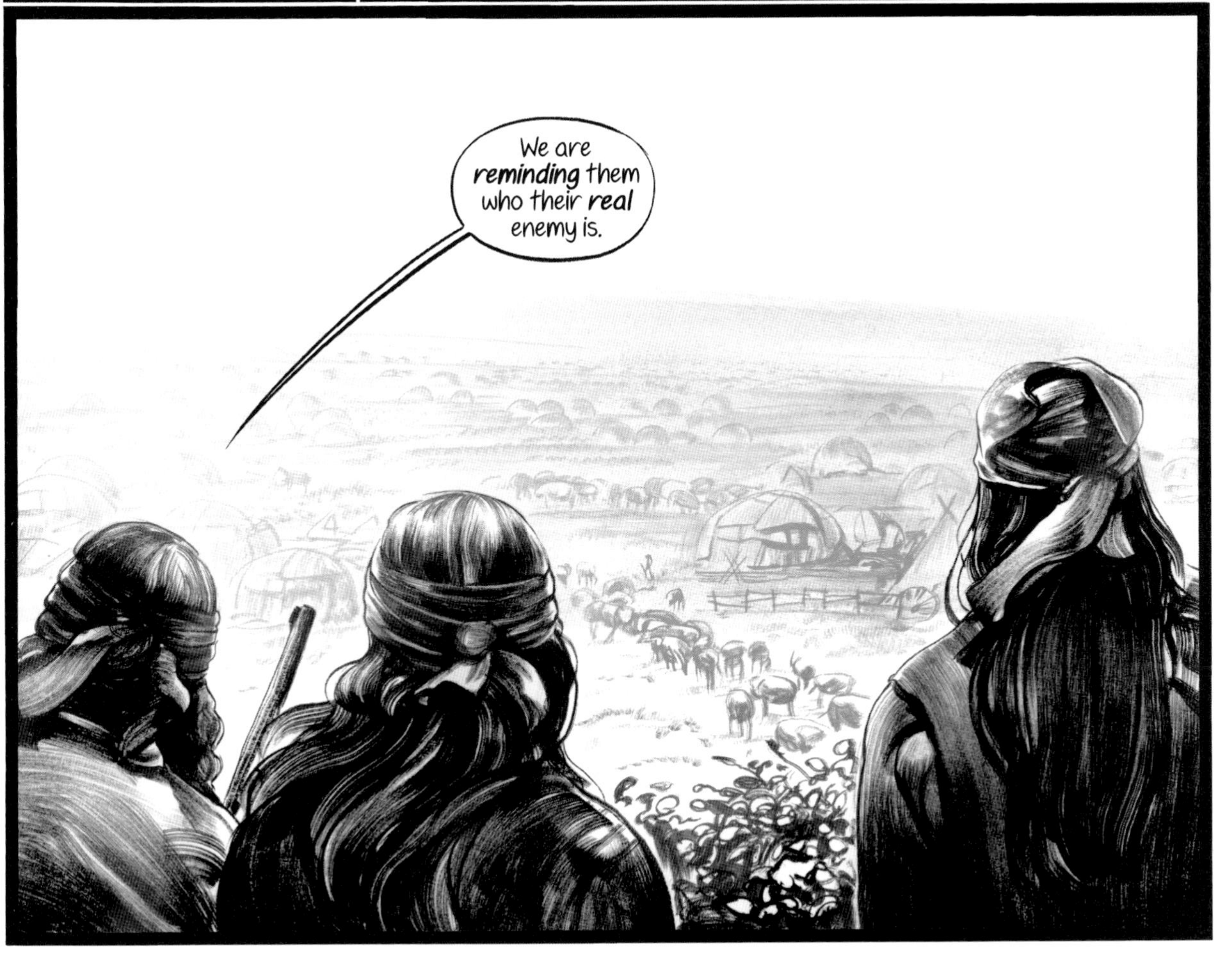
We are reminding them who their real enemy is.

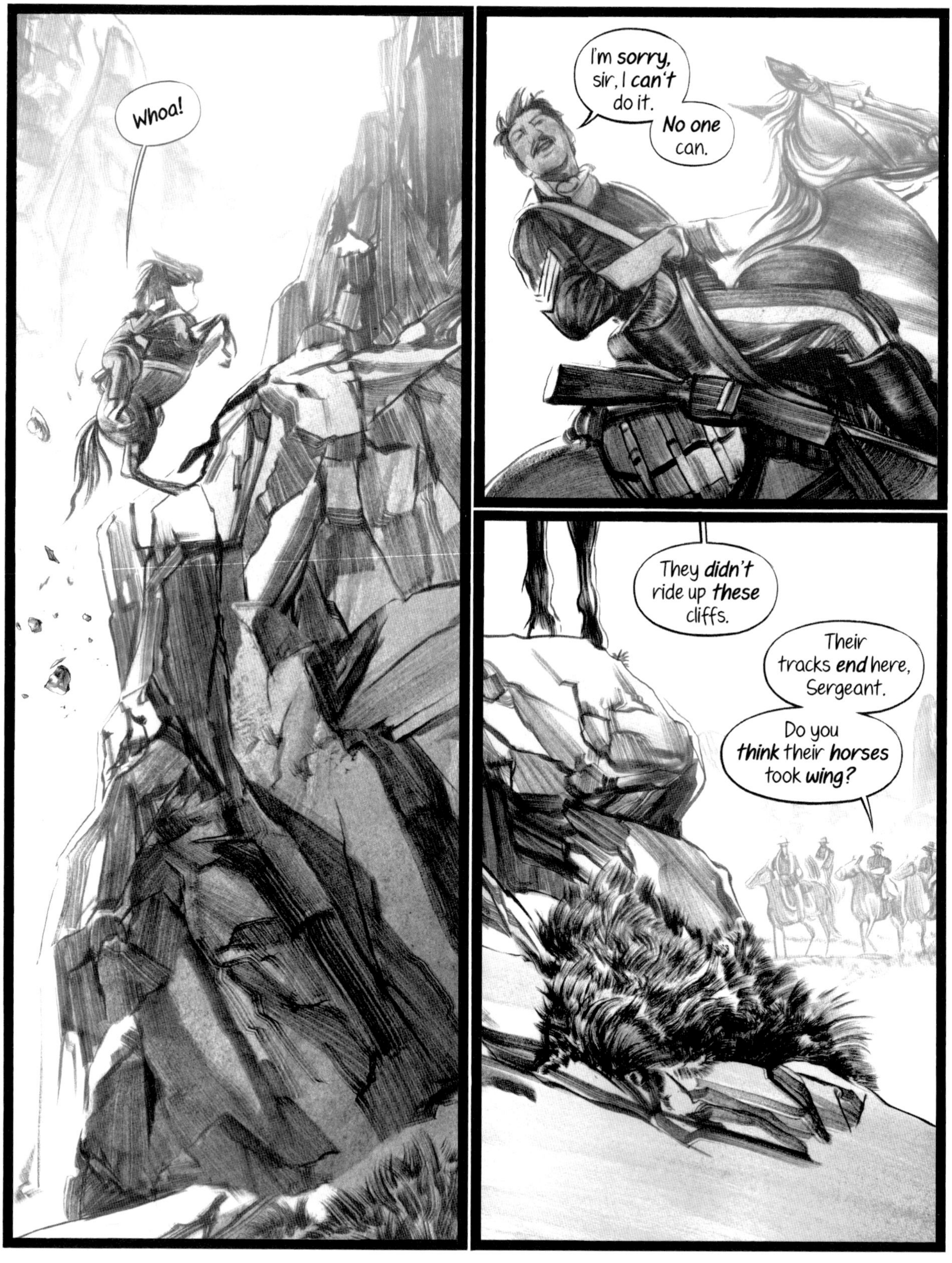
Whoa!
I'm sorry, sir, I can't do it.
No one can.
They didn't ride up these cliffs.
Their tracks end here, Sergeant.
Do you think their horses took wing?

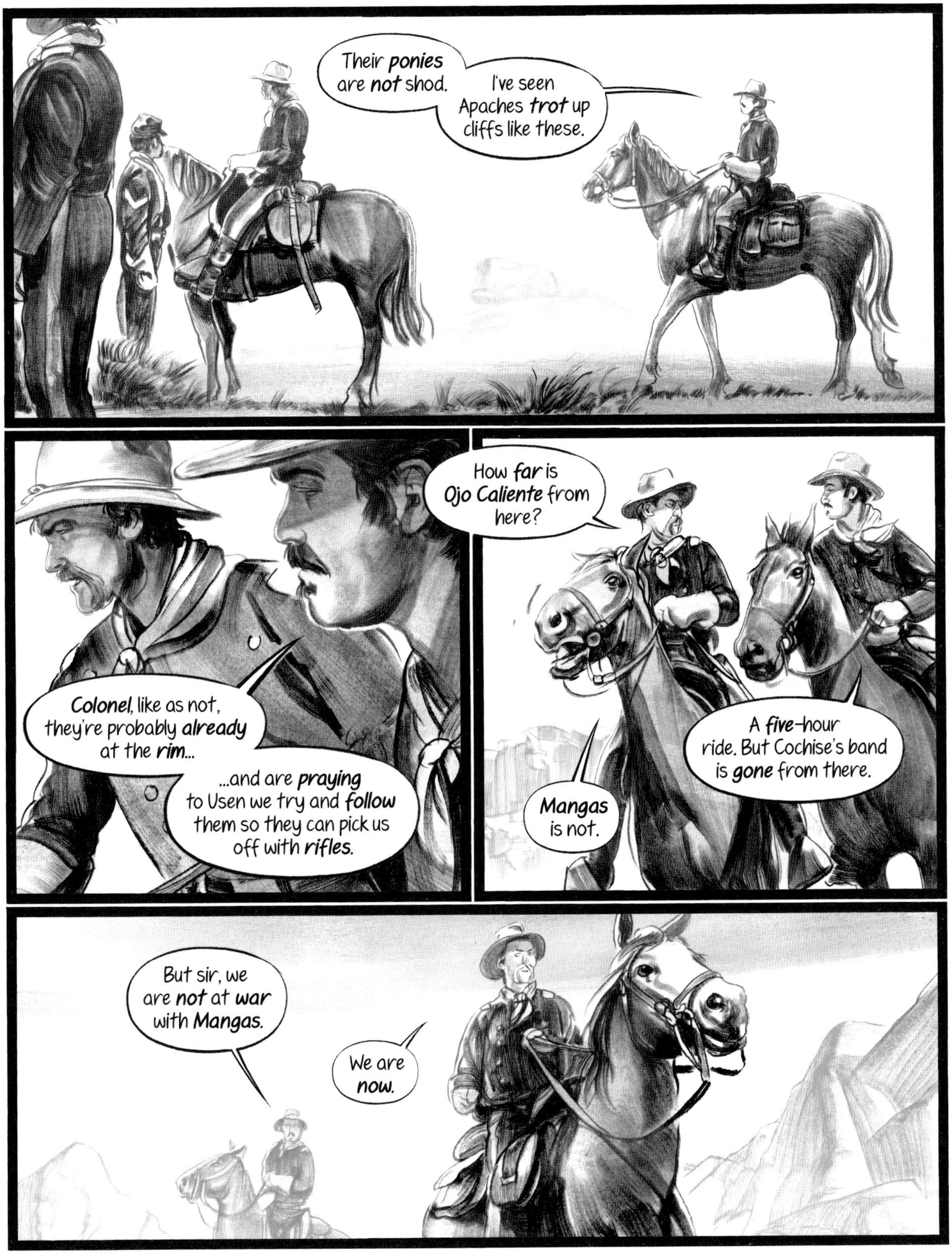

Their **ponies** are **not** shod.
I've seen Apaches **trot** up cliffs like these.
Colonel, like as not, they're probably **already** at the **rim**...
...and are **praying** to Usen we try and **follow** them so they can pick us off with **rifles**.
How **far** is **Ojo Caliente** from here?
A **five**-hour ride. But Cochise's band is **gone** from there.
Mangas is not.
But sir, we are **not** at **war** with **Mangas**.
We are **now**.

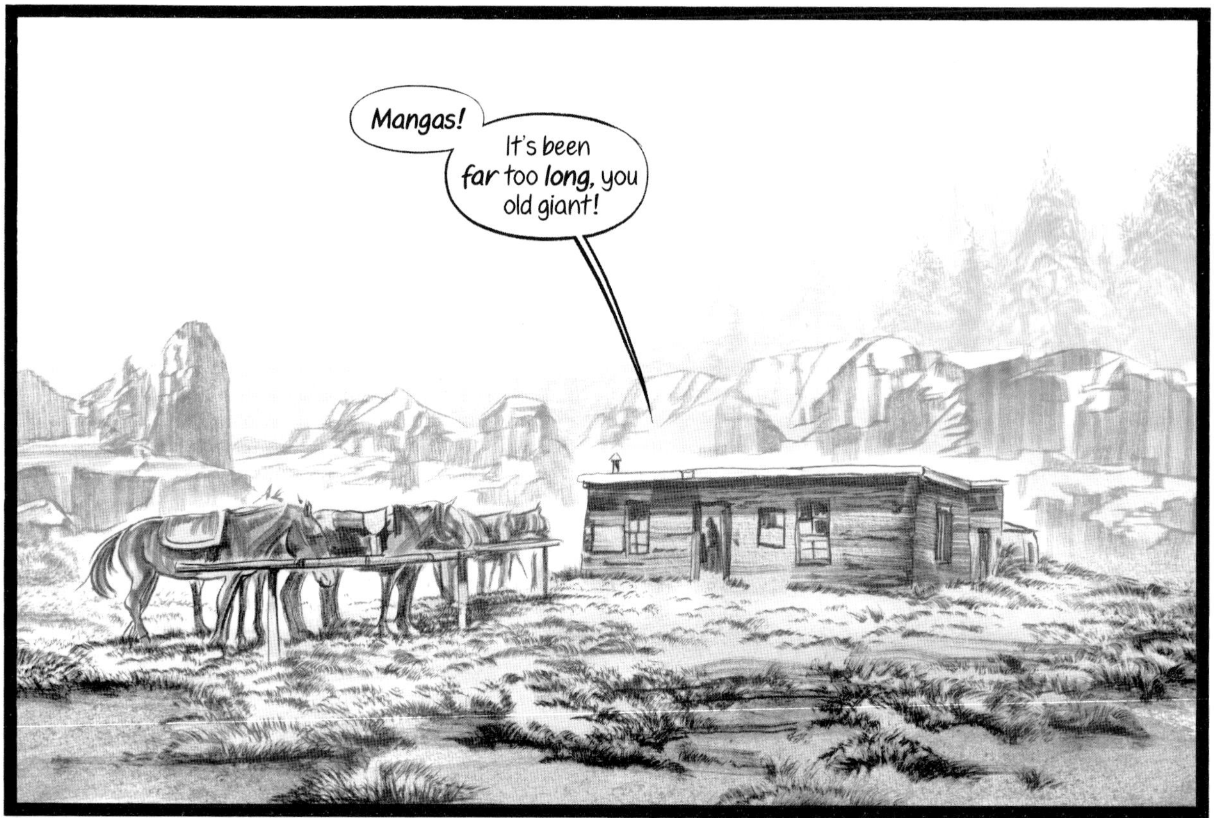
Mangas!
It's been far too long, you old giant!

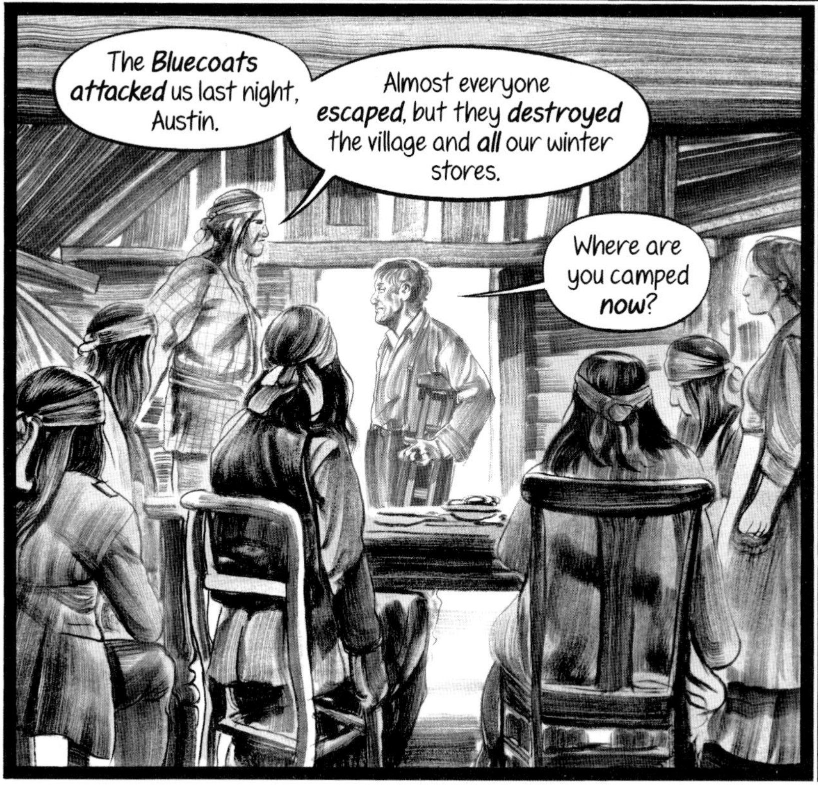
The Bluecoats attacked us last night, Austin.
Almost everyone escaped, but they destroyed the village and all our winter stores.
Where are you camped now?

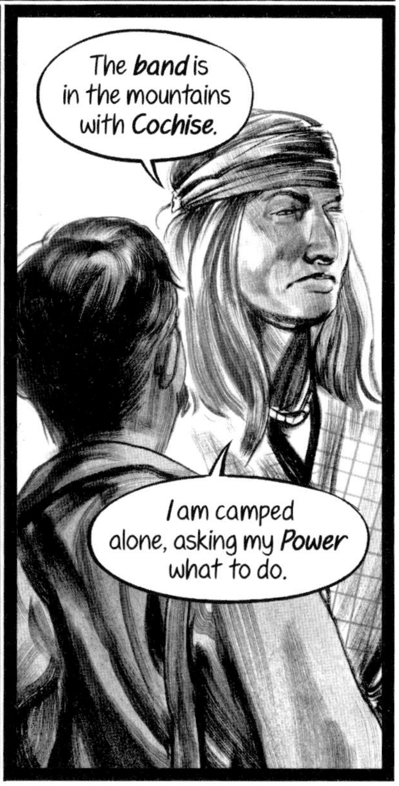
The band is in the mountains with Cochise.
I am camped alone, asking my Power what to do.

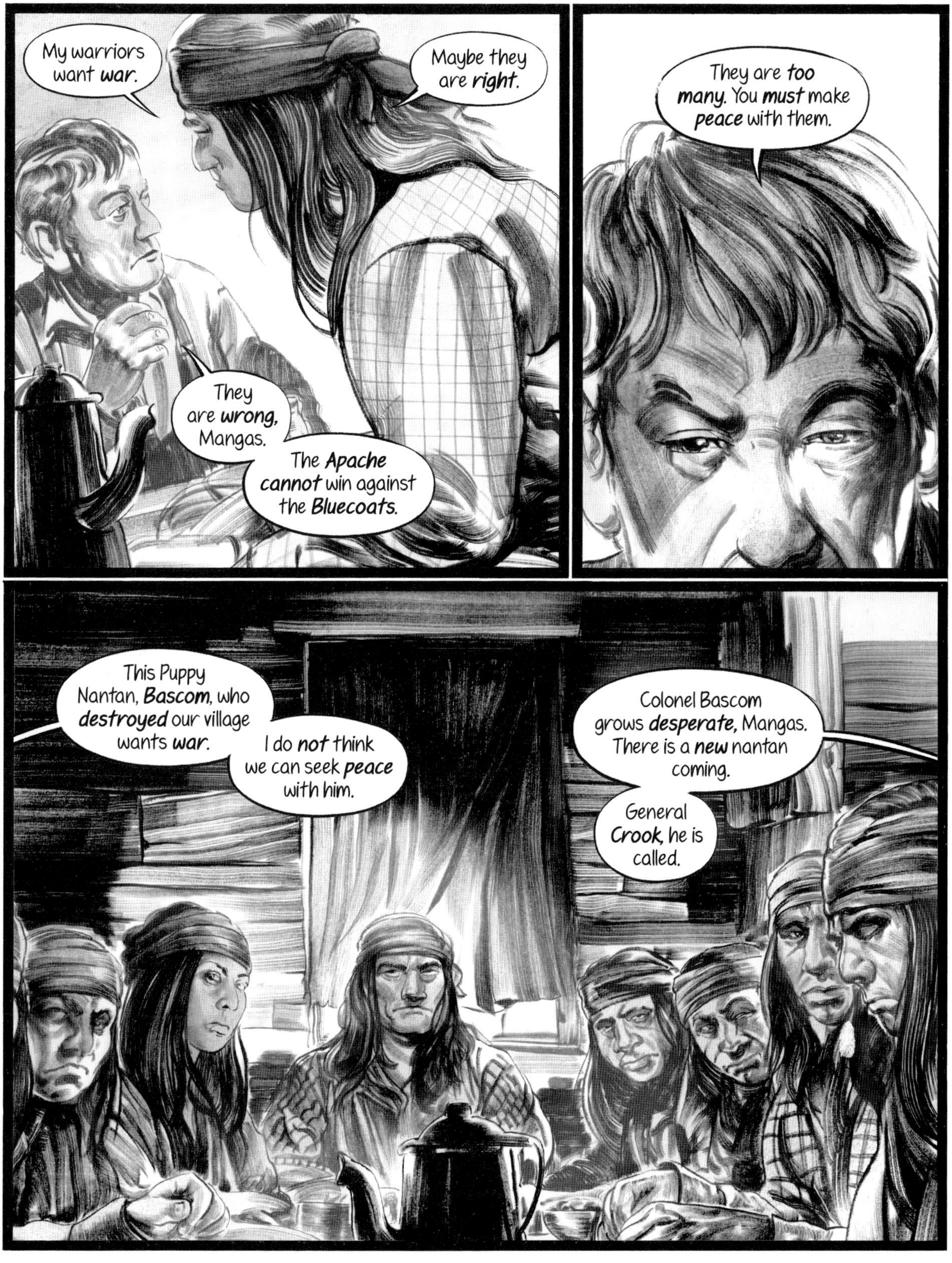
My warriors want **war**.
Maybe they are **right**.
They are **wrong**, Mangas.
The **Apache cannot** win against the **Bluecoats**.
They are **too many**. You **must** make **peace** with them.
This Puppy Nantan, **Bascom**, who **destroyed** our village wants **war**.
I do **not** think we can seek **peace** with him.
Colonel Bascom grows **desperate**, Mangas. There is a **new** nantan coming.
General **Crook**, he is called.

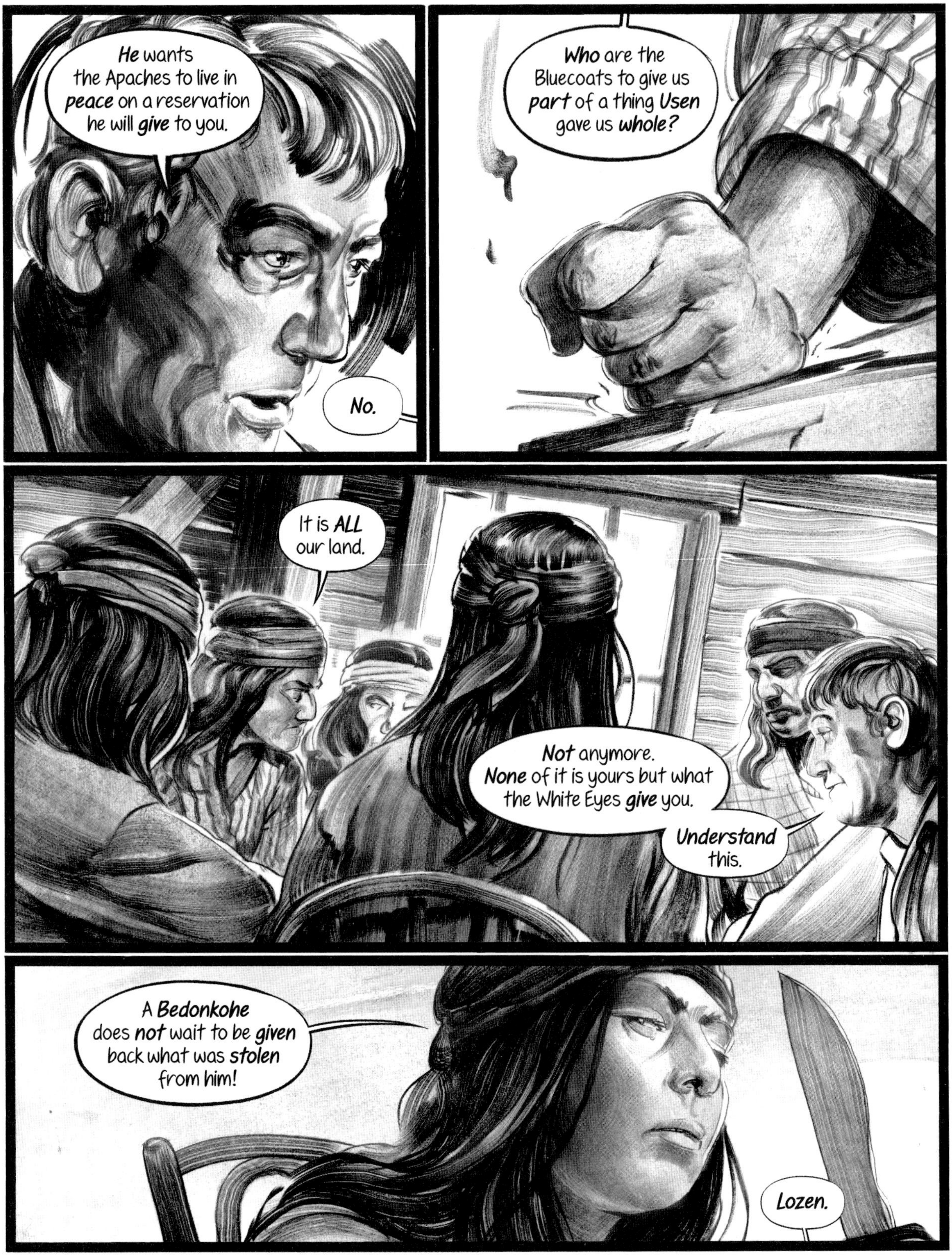
He wants the Apaches to live in peace on a reservation he will give to you.
No.
Who are the Bluecoats to give us part of a thing Usen gave us whole?
It is ALL our land.
Not anymore. None of it is yours but what the White Eyes give you.
Understand this.
A Bedonkohe does not wait to be given back what was stolen from him!
Lozen.

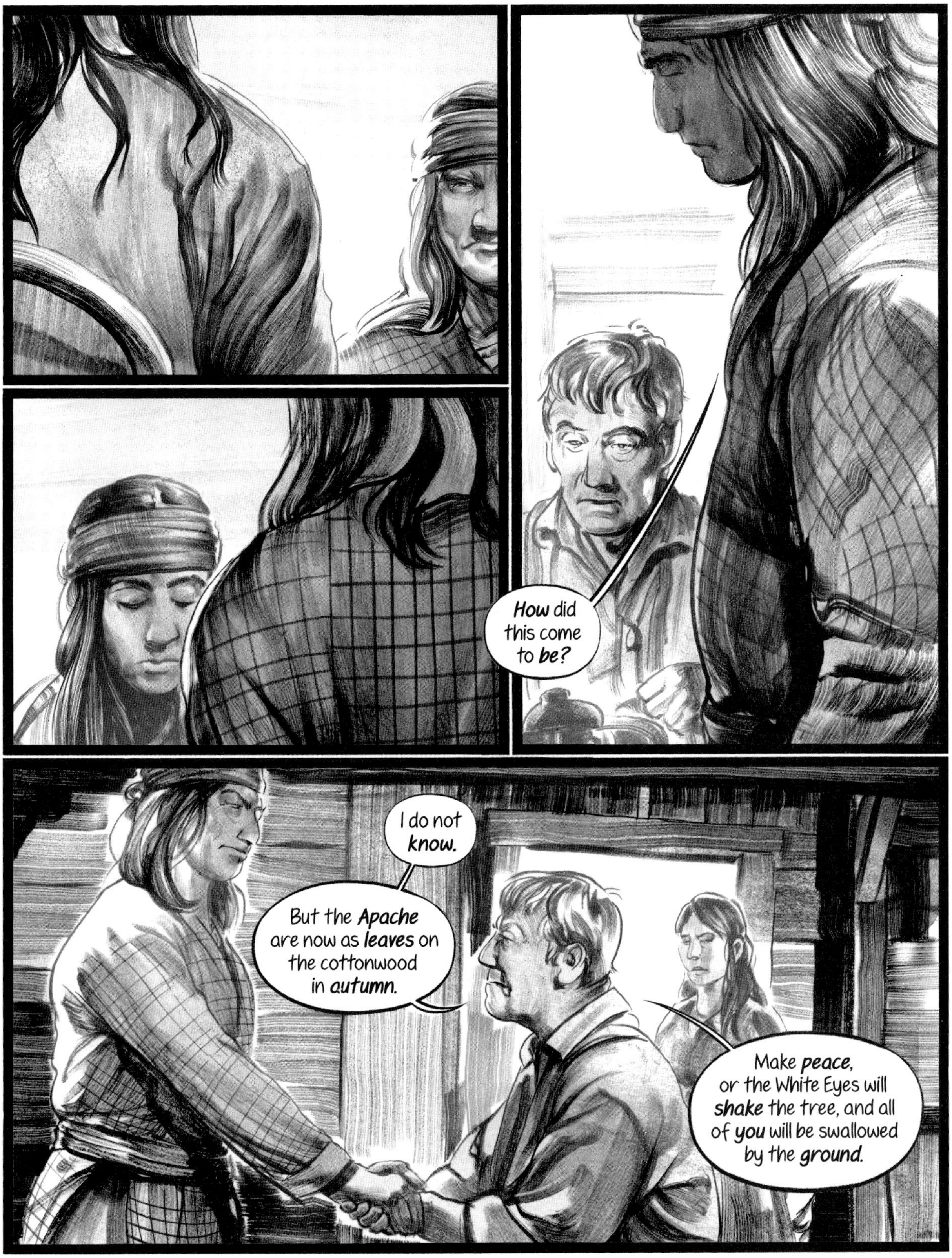
How did this come to be?
I do not know.
But the Apache are now as leaves on the cottonwood in autumn.
Make peace, or the White Eyes will shake the tree, and all of you will be swallowed by the ground.

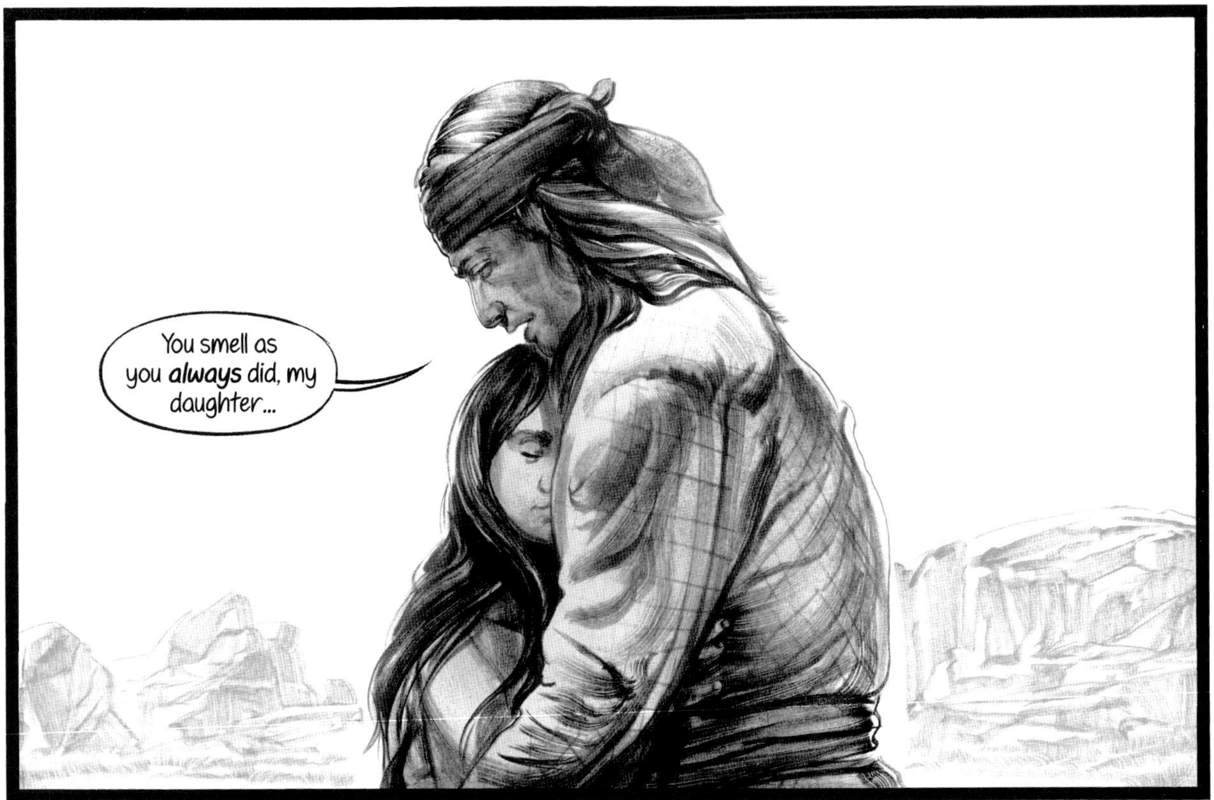
You smell as you **always** did, my daughter...

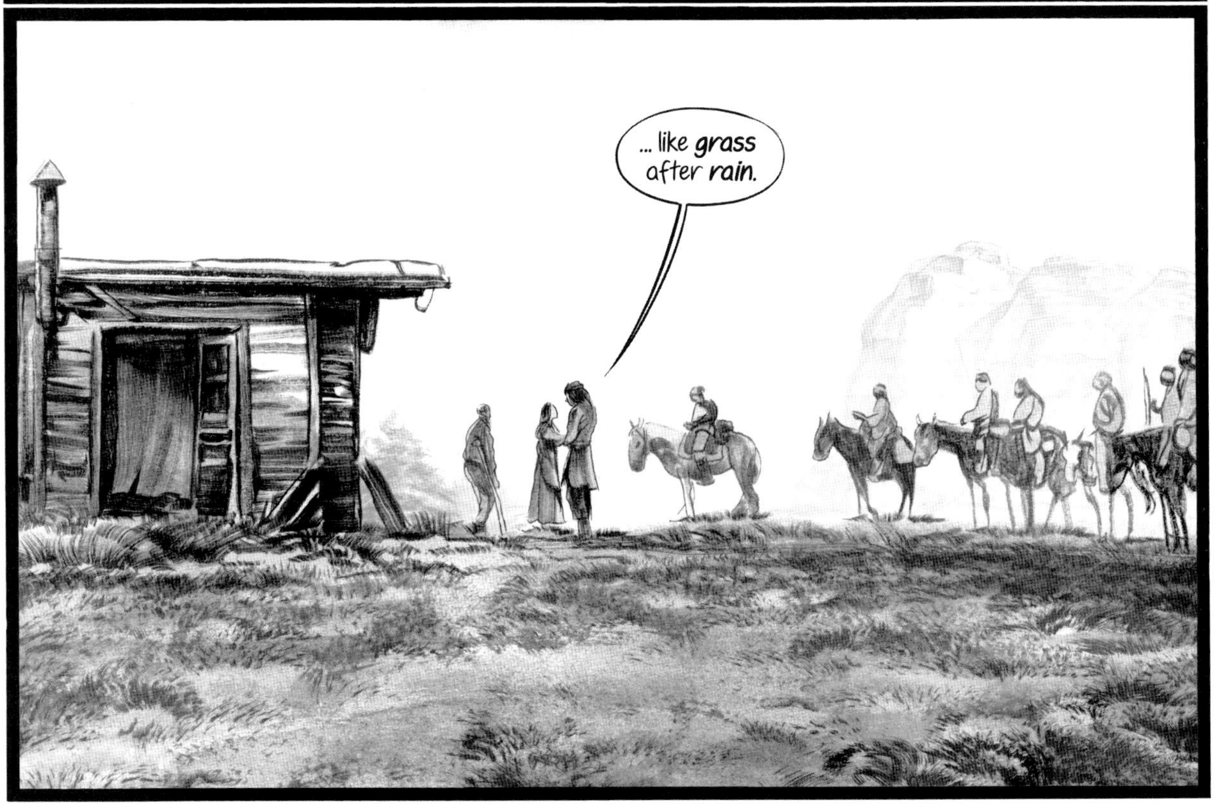
... like **grass** after **rain**.

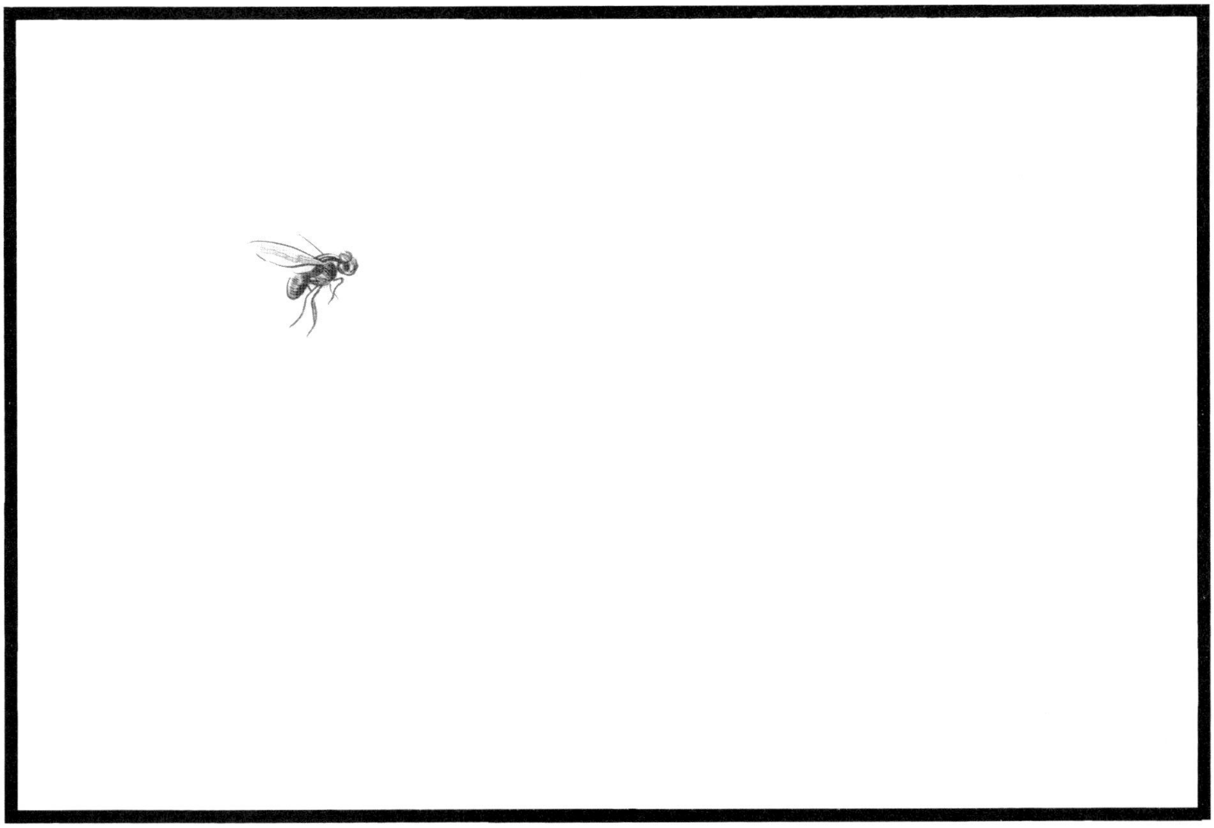

TWO MOONS BEFORE WINTER · FORT BOWIE

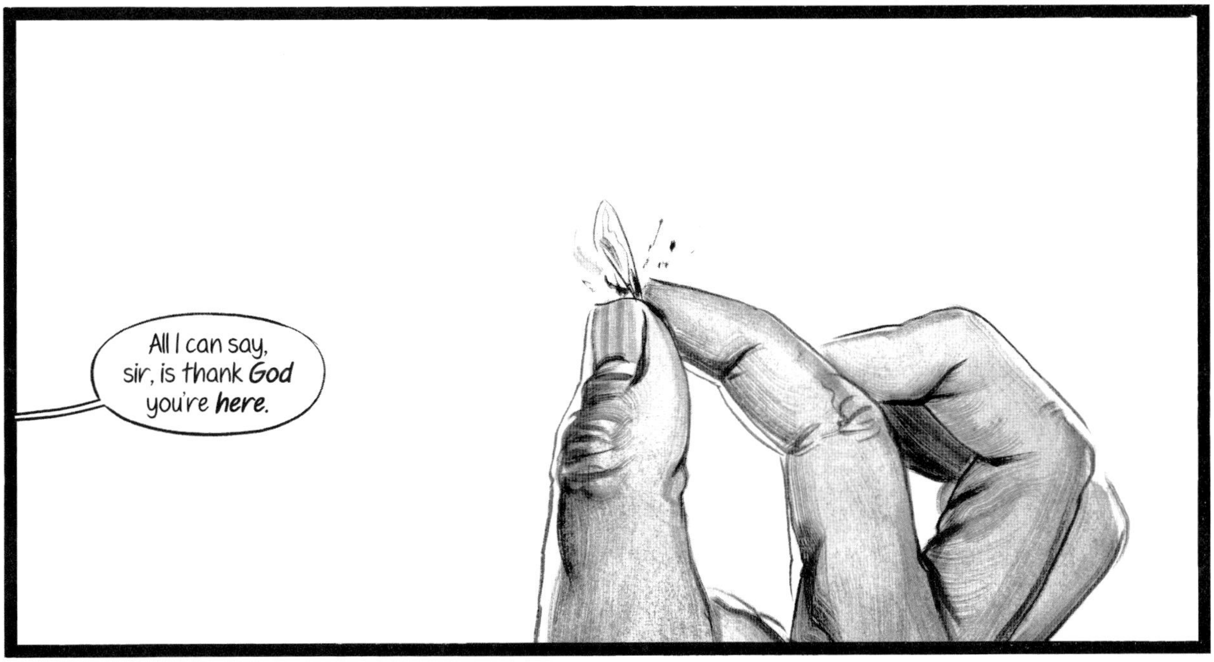
All I can say, sir, is thank God you're here.

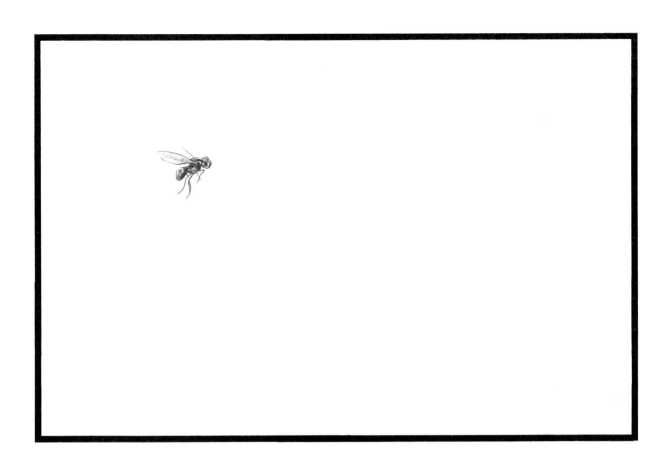

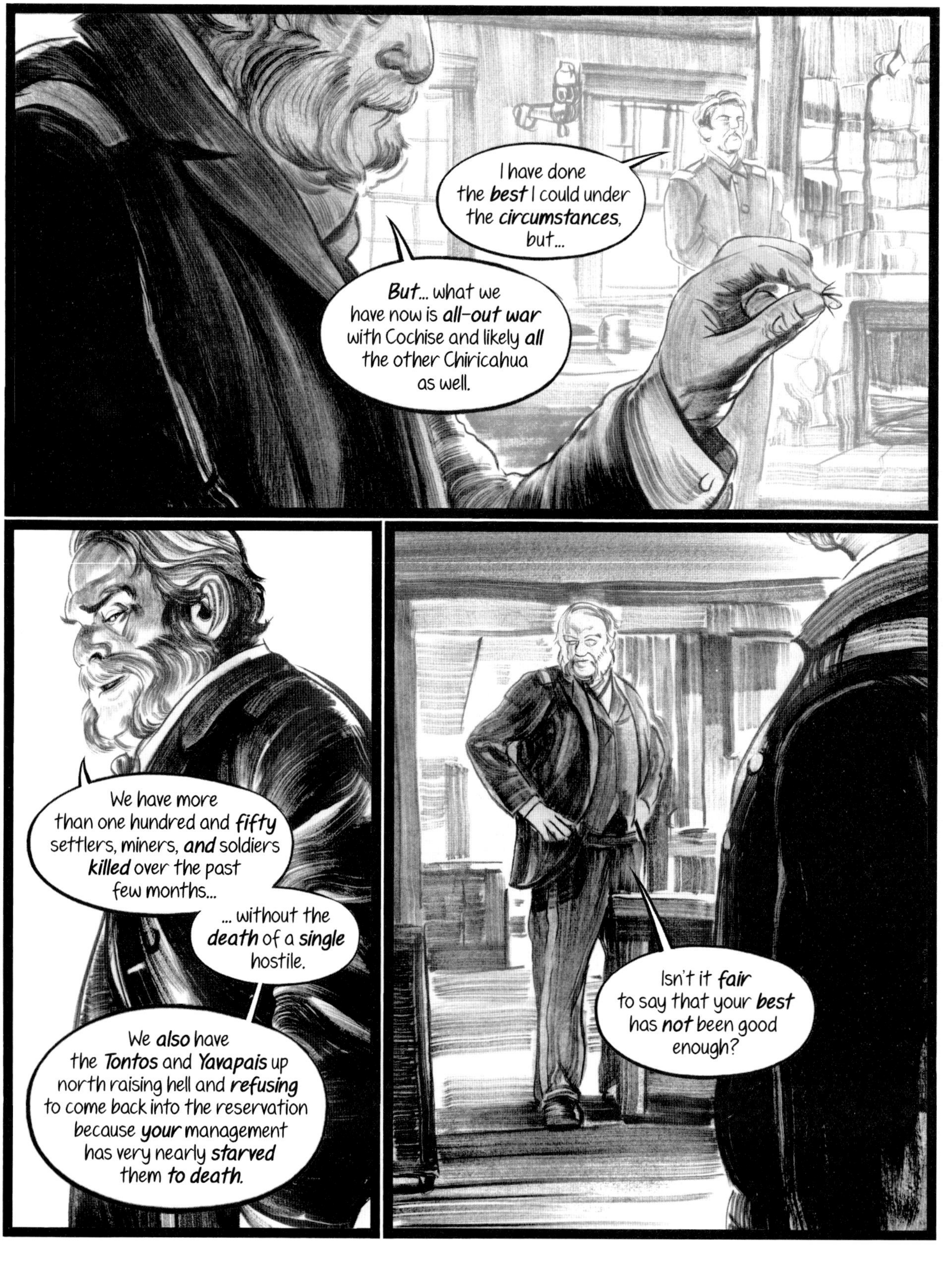
I have done the best I could under the circumstances, but...
But... what we have now is all-out war with Cochise and likely all the other Chiricahua as well.
We have more than one hundred and fifty settlers, miners, and soldiers killed over the past few months...
... without the death of a single hostile.
We also have the Tontos and Yavapais up north raising hell and refusing to come back into the reservation because your management has very nearly starved them to death.
Isn't it fair to say that your best has not been good enough?

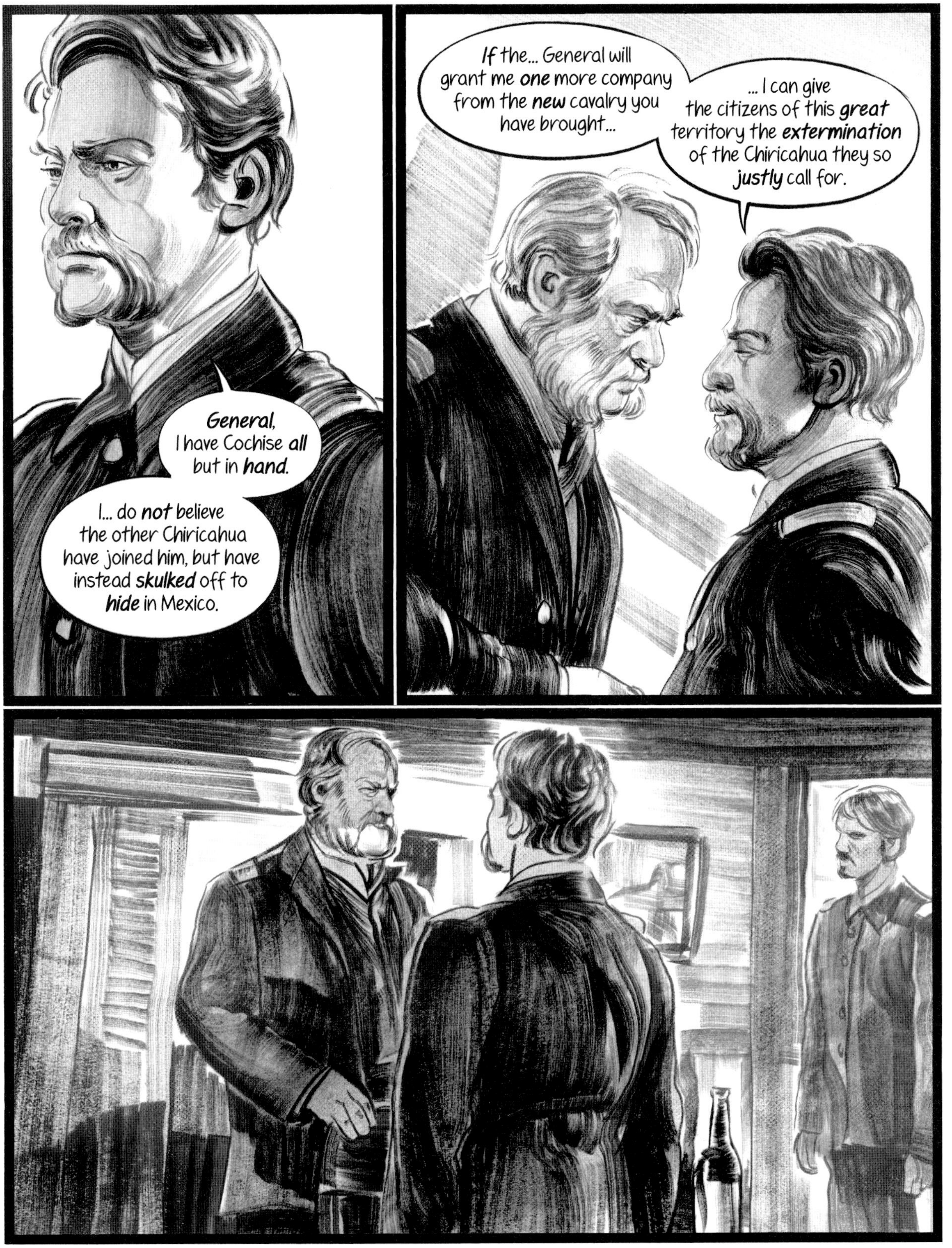
General, I have Cochise all but in hand.
I... do not believe the other Chiricahua have joined him, but have instead skulked off to hide in Mexico.
If the... General will grant me one more company from the new cavalry you have brought...
... I can give the citizens of this great territory the extermination of the Chiricahua they so justly call for.

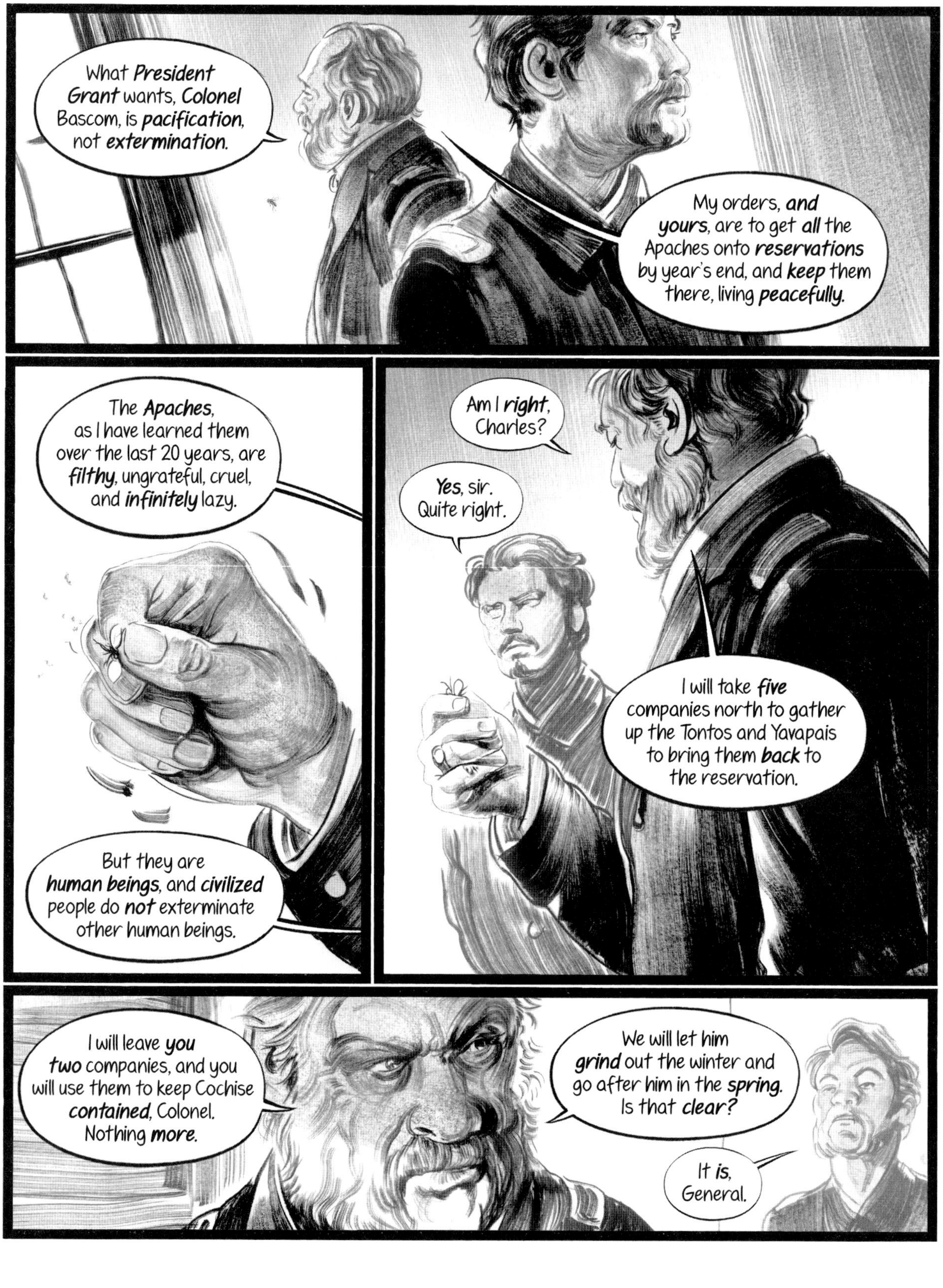
What President Grant wants, Colonel Bascom, is pacification, not extermination.
My orders, and yours, are to get all the Apaches onto reservations by year's end, and keep them there, living peacefully.
The Apaches, as I have learned them over the last 20 years, are filthy, ungrateful, cruel, and infinitely lazy.
But they are human beings, and civilized people do not exterminate other human beings.
Am I right, Charles?
Yes, sir. Quite right.
I will take five companies north to gather up the Tontos and Yavapais to bring them back to the reservation.
I will leave you two companies, and you will use them to keep Cochise contained, Colonel. Nothing more.
We will let him grind out the winter and go after him in the spring. Is that clear?
It is, General.

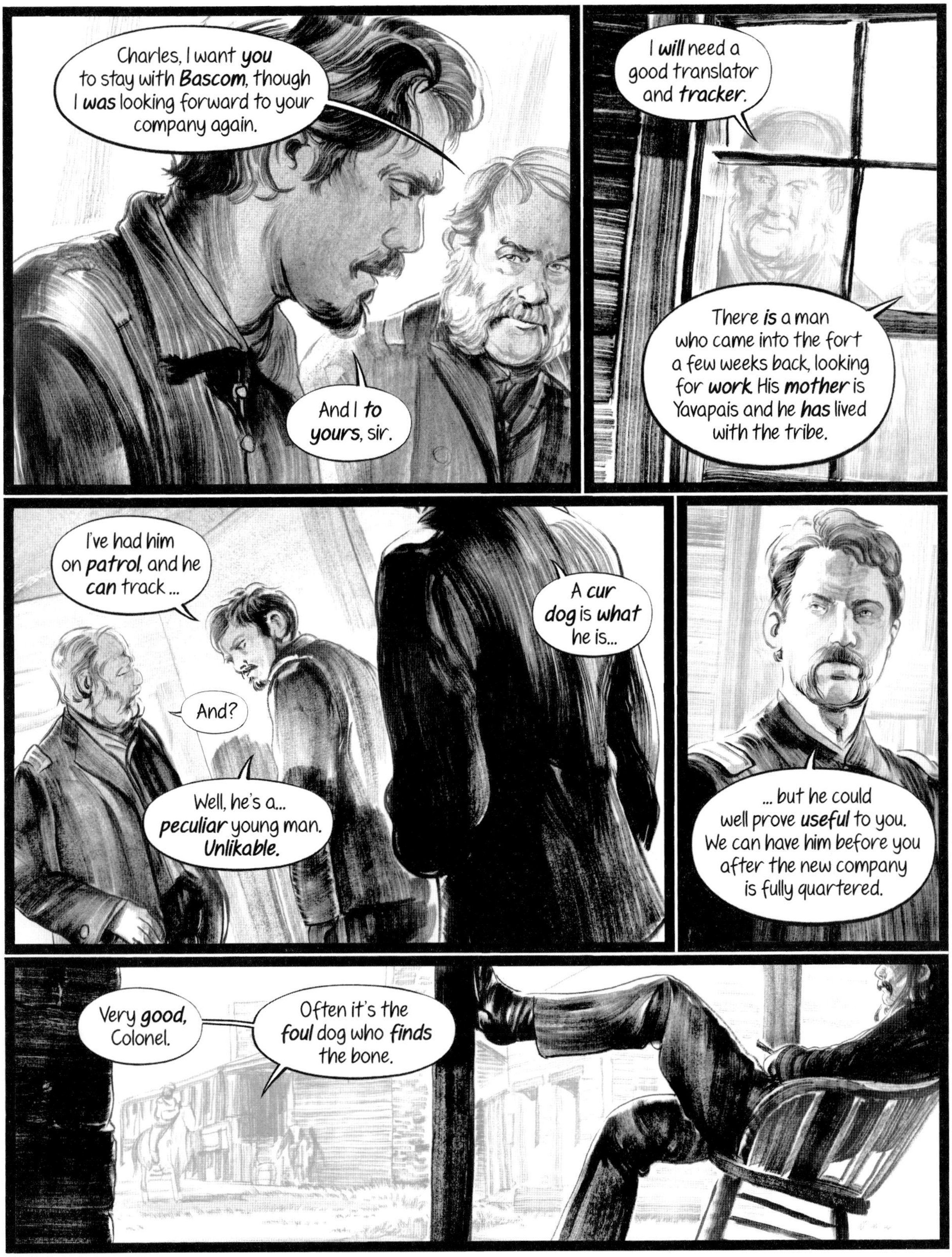
Charles, I want **you** to stay with **Bascom**, though I **was** looking forward to your company again.
And I **to yours**, sir.
I **will** need a good translator and **tracker**.
There **is** a man who came into the fort a few weeks back, looking for **work**. His **mother** is Yavapais and he **has** lived with the tribe.
I've had him on **patrol**, and he **can** track ...
And?
Well, he's a... **peculiar** young man. **Unlikable.**
A **cur dog** is **what** he is...
... but he could well prove **useful** to you. We can have him before you after the new company is fully quartered.
Very **good**, Colonel.
Often it's the **foul** dog who **finds** the bone.

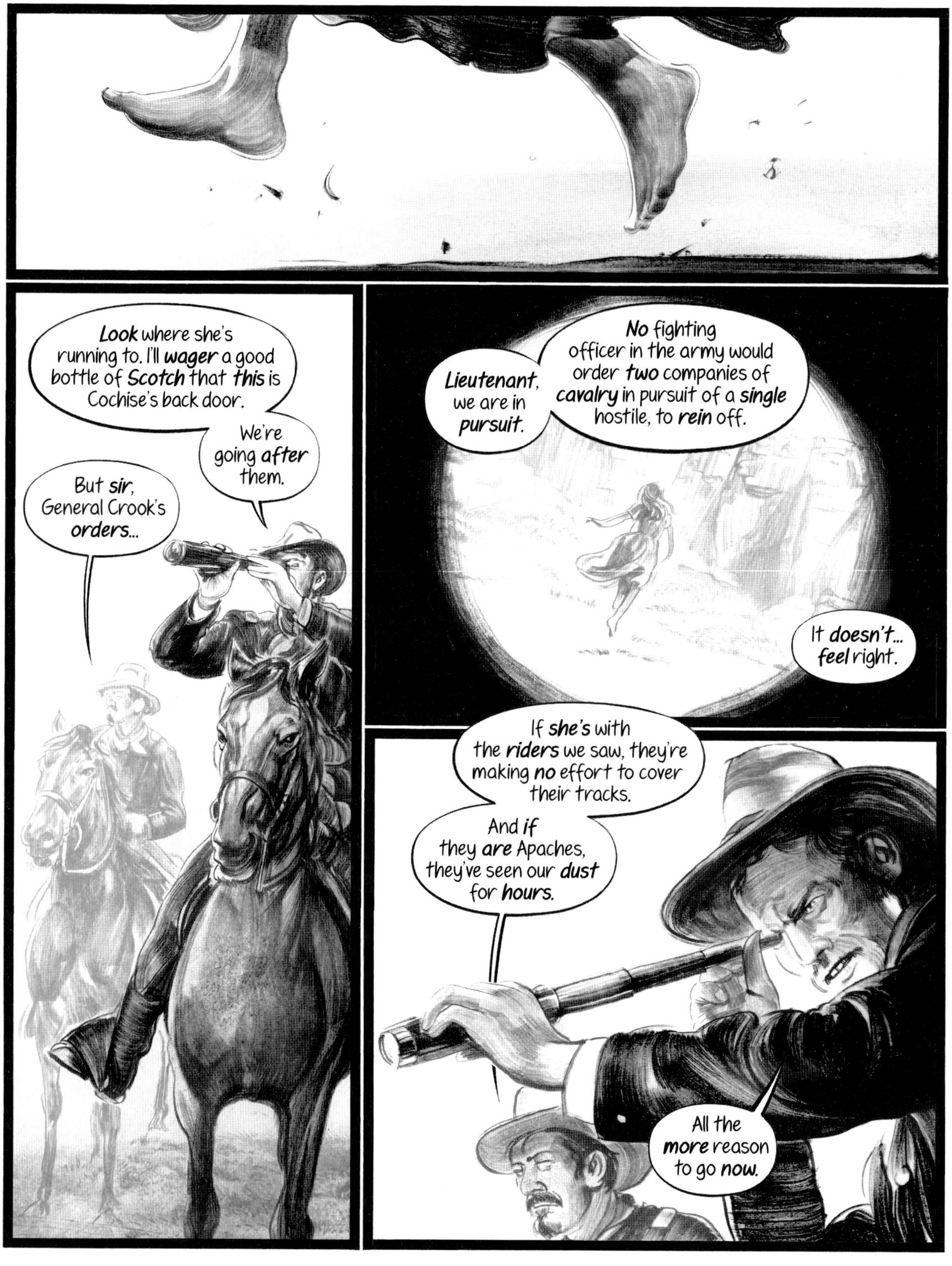

Look where she's running to. I'll wager a good bottle of Scotch that this is Cochise's back door.
We're going after them.
But sir, General Crook's orders...
Lieutenant, we are in pursuit.
No fighting officer in the army would order two companies of cavalry in pursuit of a single hostile, to rein off.
It doesn't... feel right.
If she's with the riders we saw, they're making no effort to cover their tracks.
And if they are Apaches, they've seen our dust for hours.
All the more reason to go now.

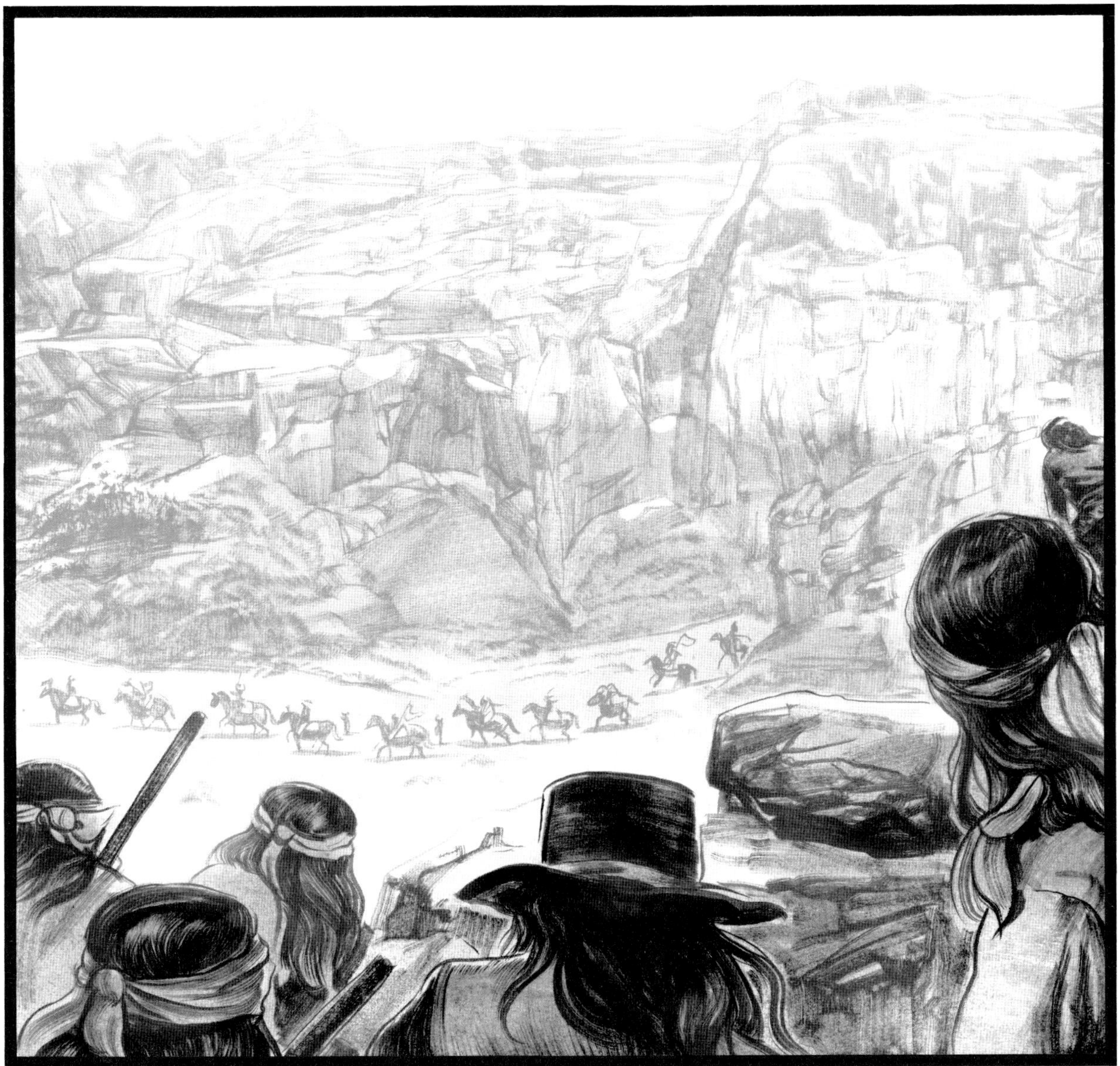

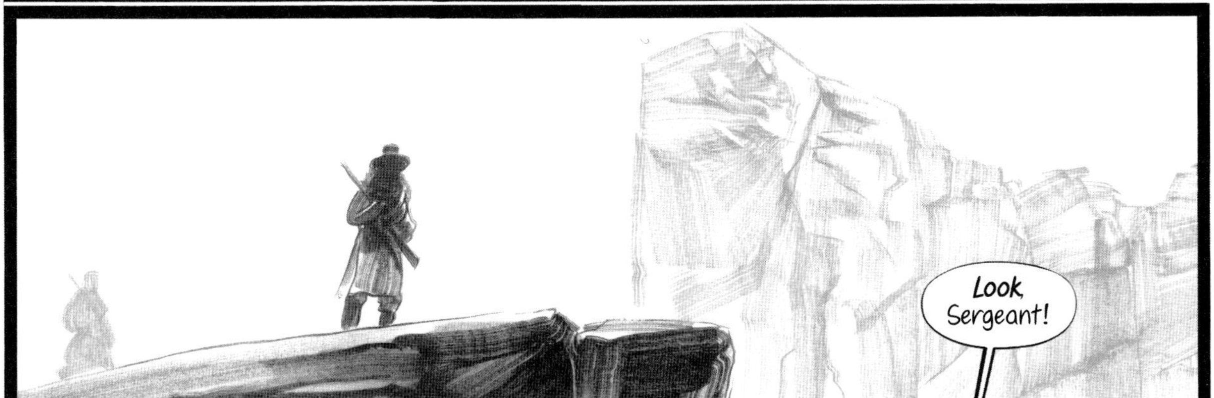
Look, Sergeant!

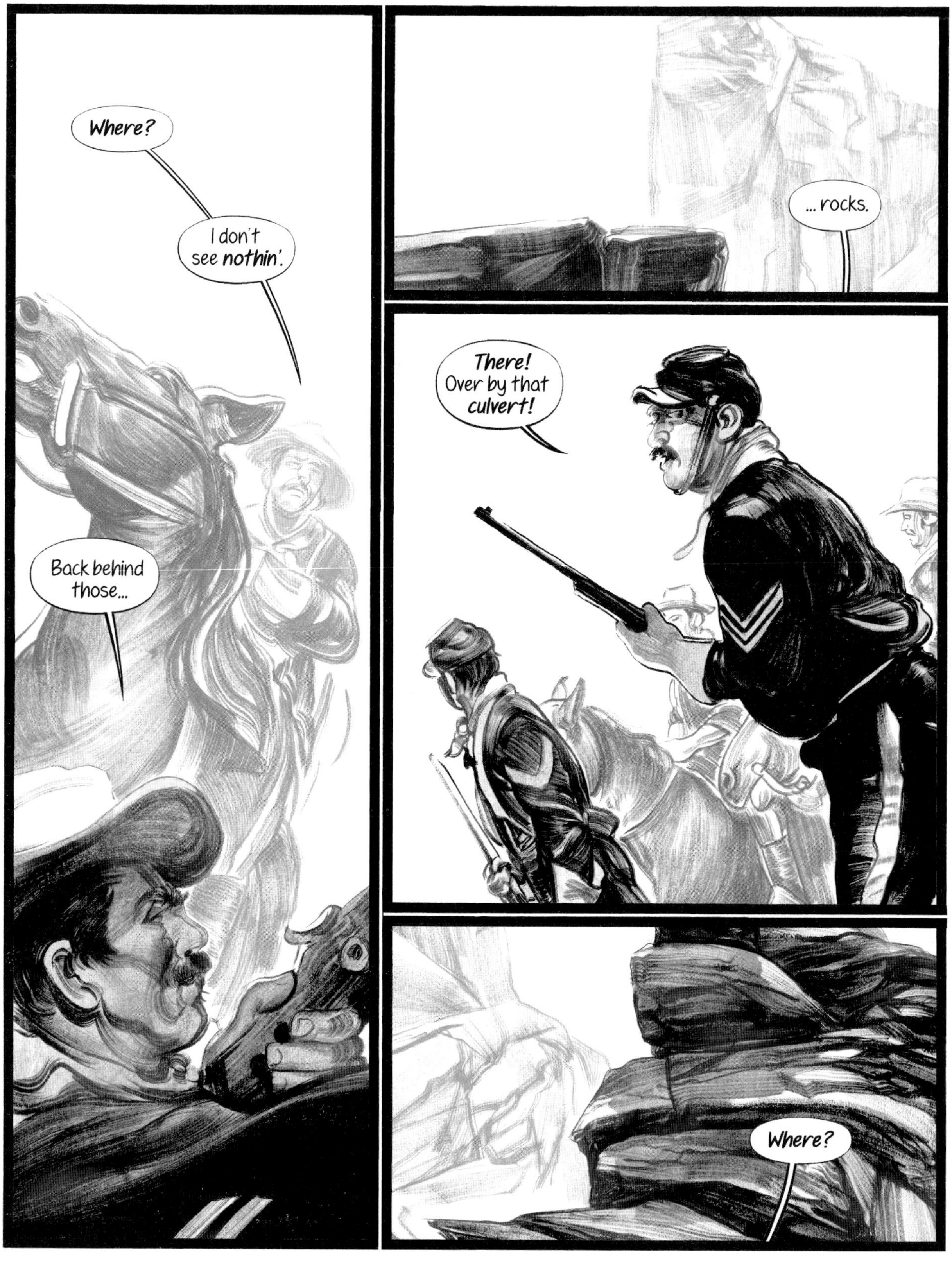
Where?
I don't see nothin'.
Back behind those...
... rocks.
There! Over by that culvert!
Where?

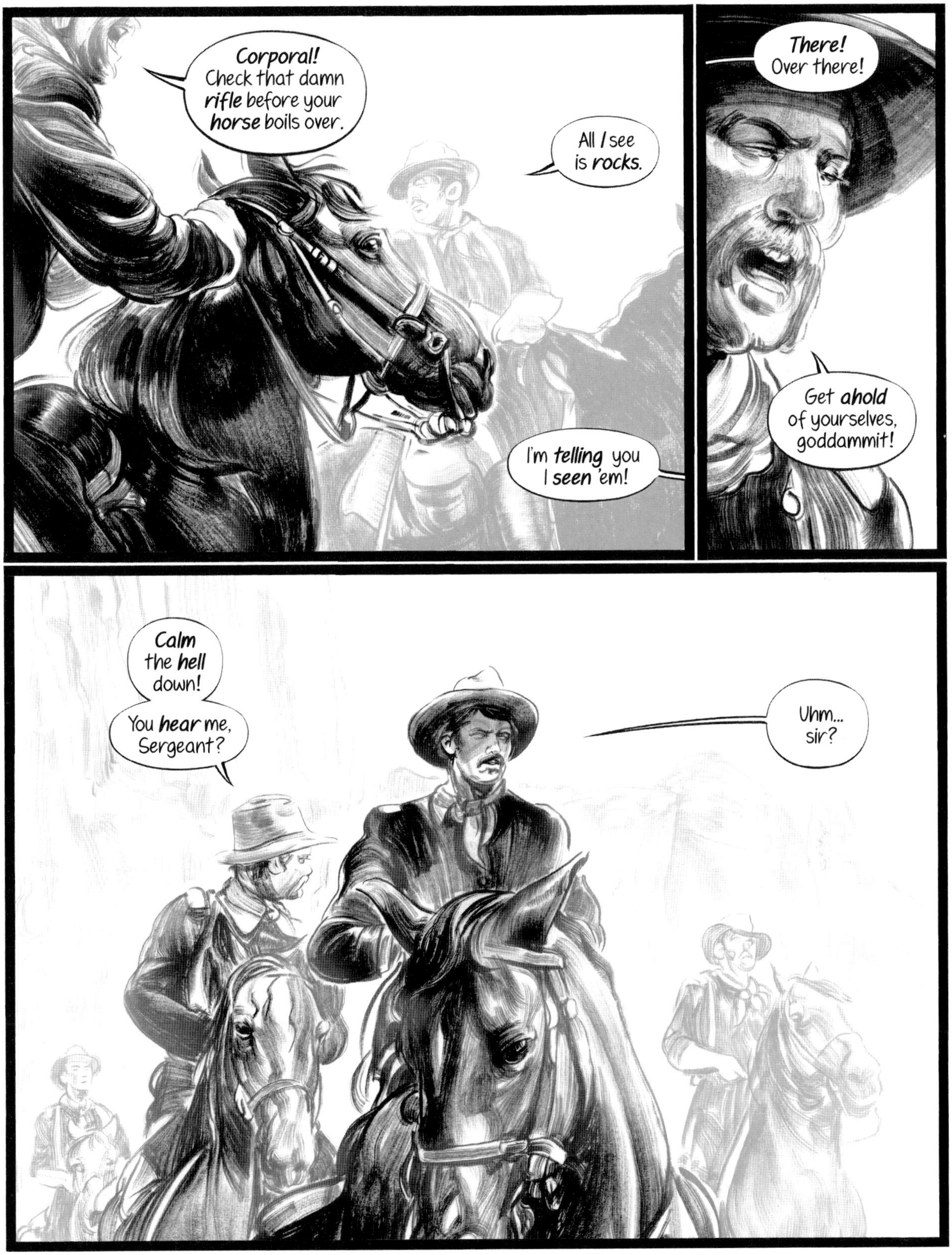
Corporal! Check that damn rifle before your horse boils over.
All I see is rocks.
I'm telling you I seen 'em!
There! Over there!
Get ahold of yourselves, goddammit!
Calm the hell down!
You hear me, Sergeant?
Uhm... sir?

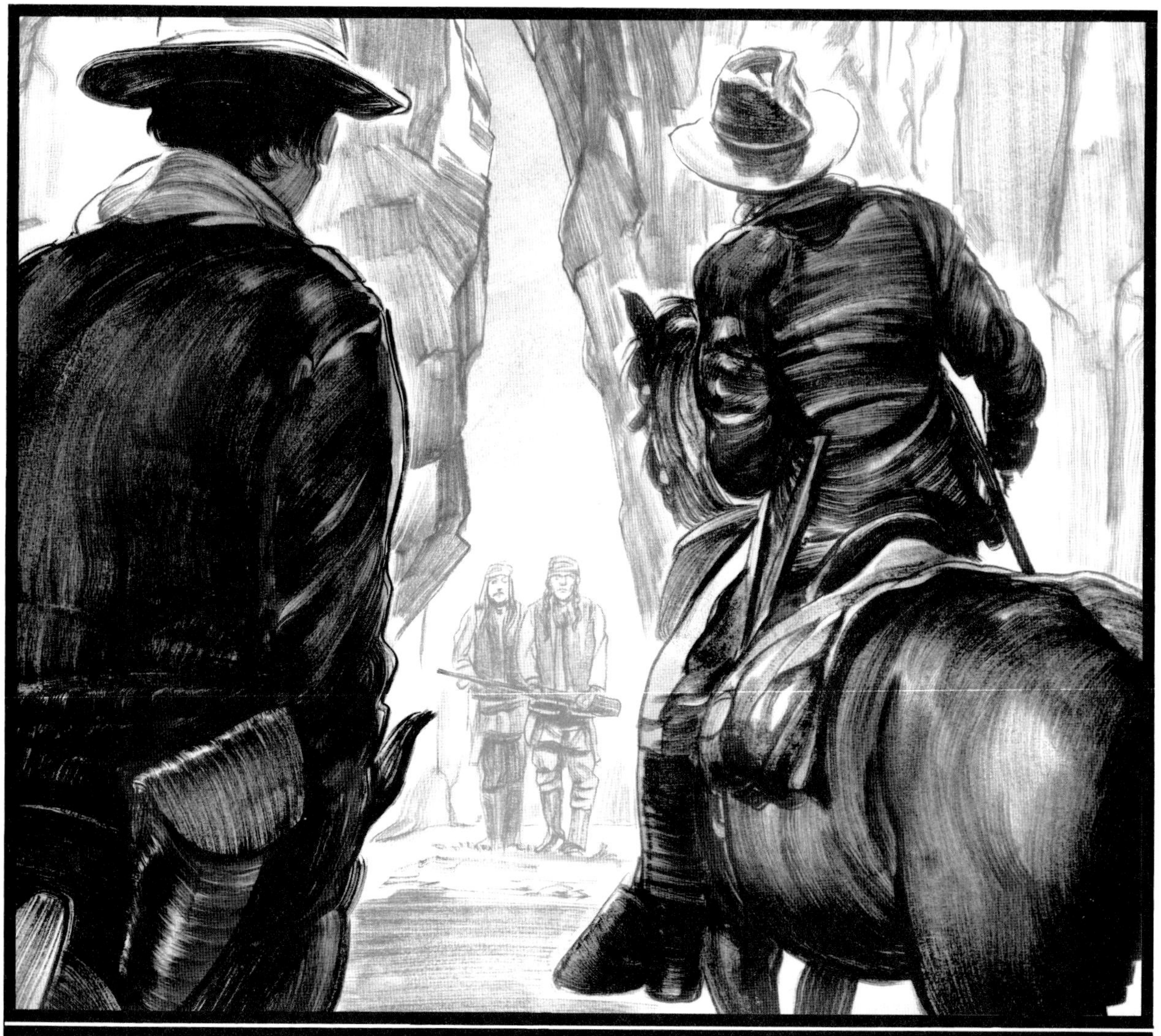

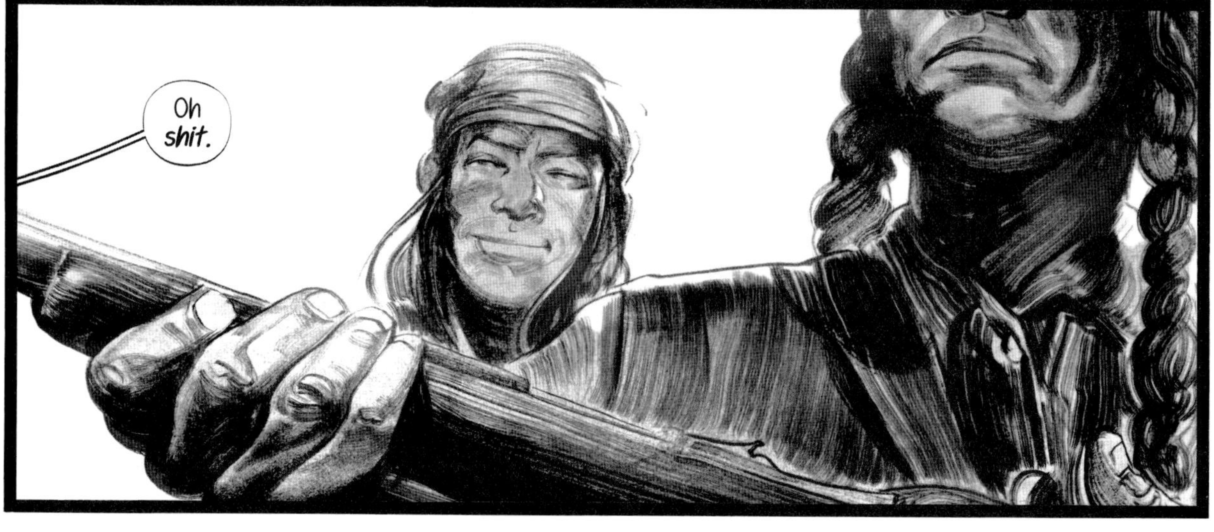
Oh shit.

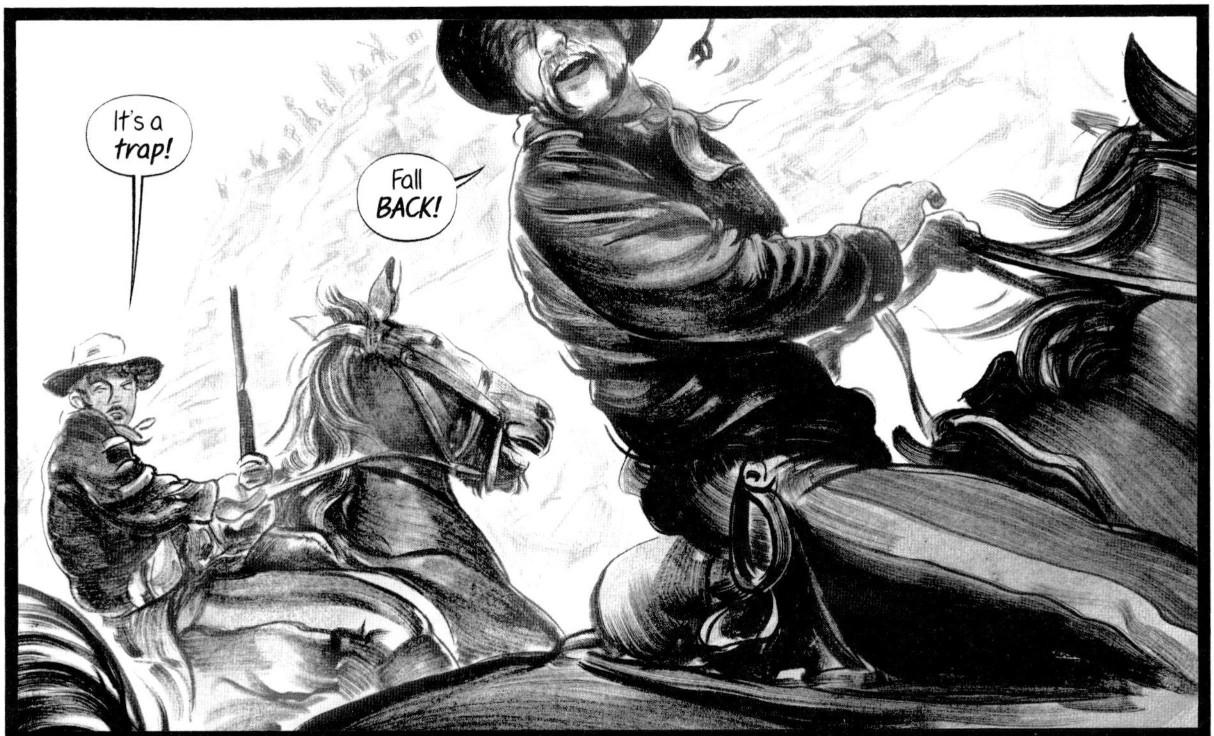
It's a trap!
Fall BACK!

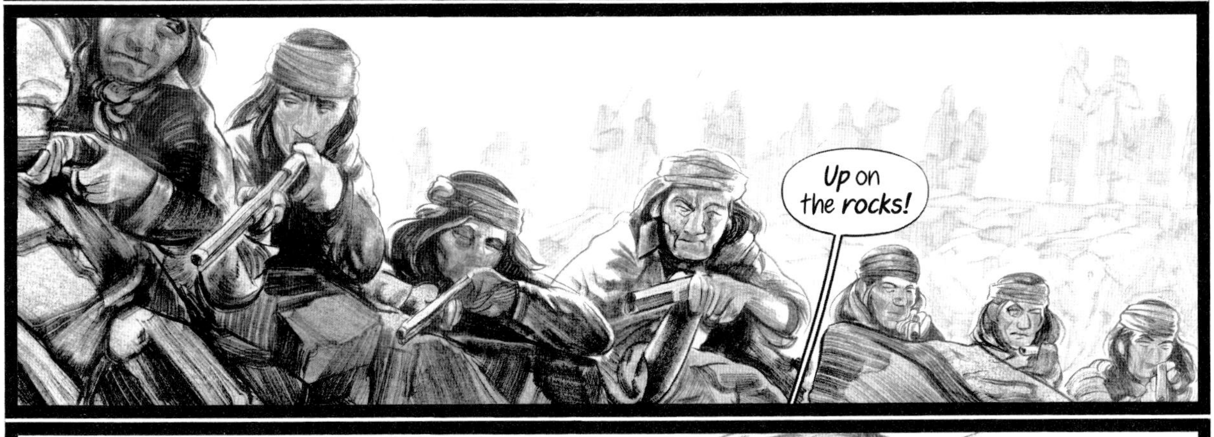
Up on the rocks!

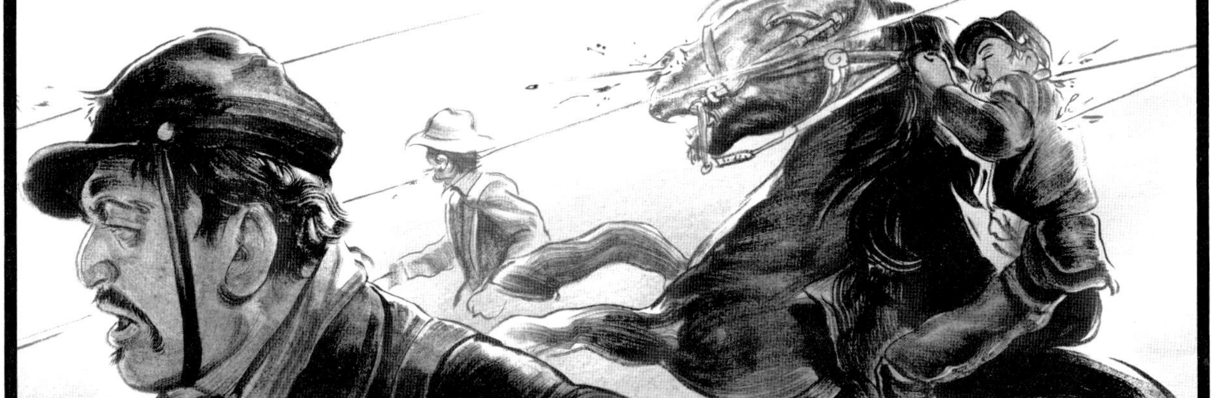

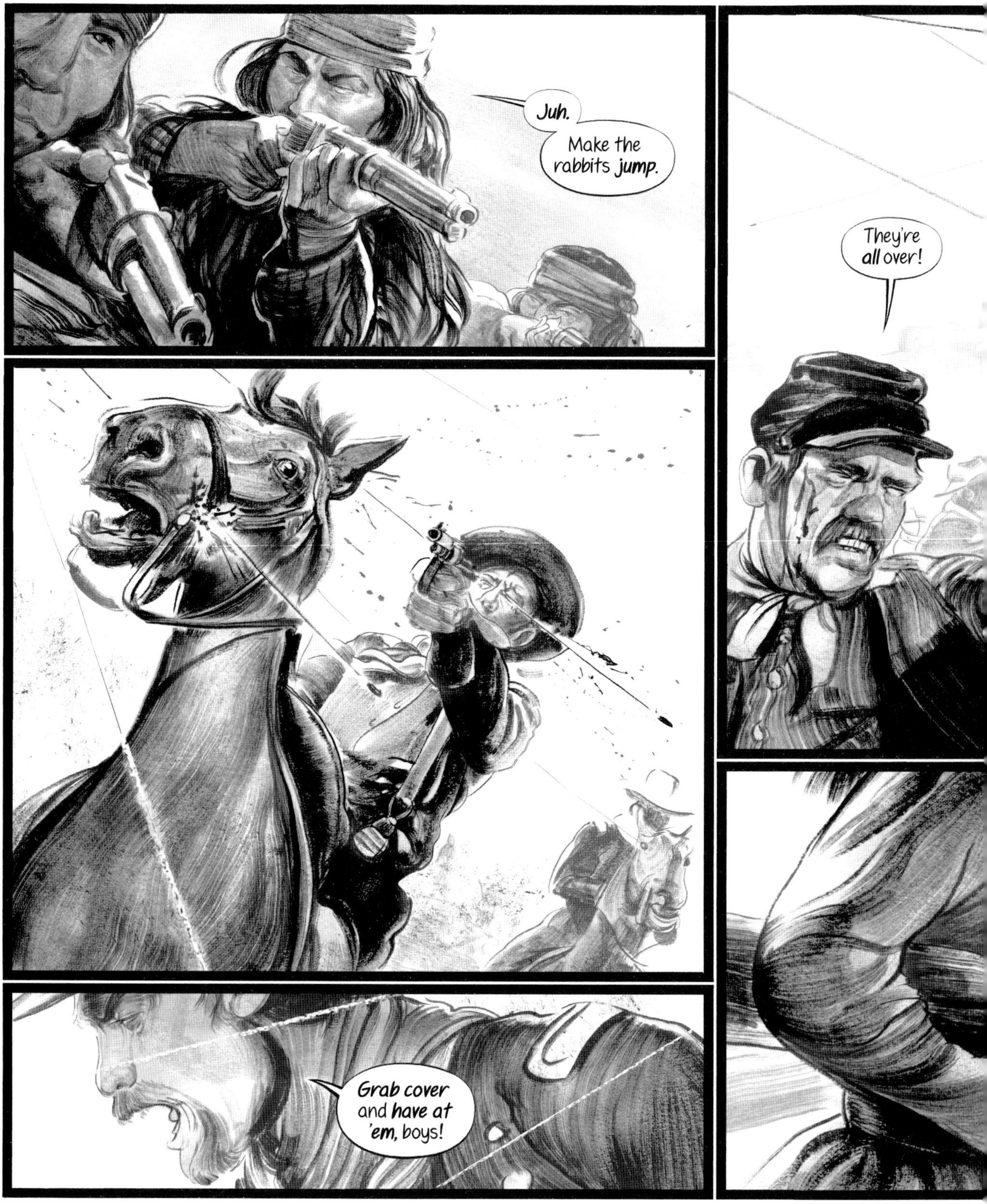
Juh.
Make the rabbits jump.
They're all over!
Grab cover and have at 'em, boys!

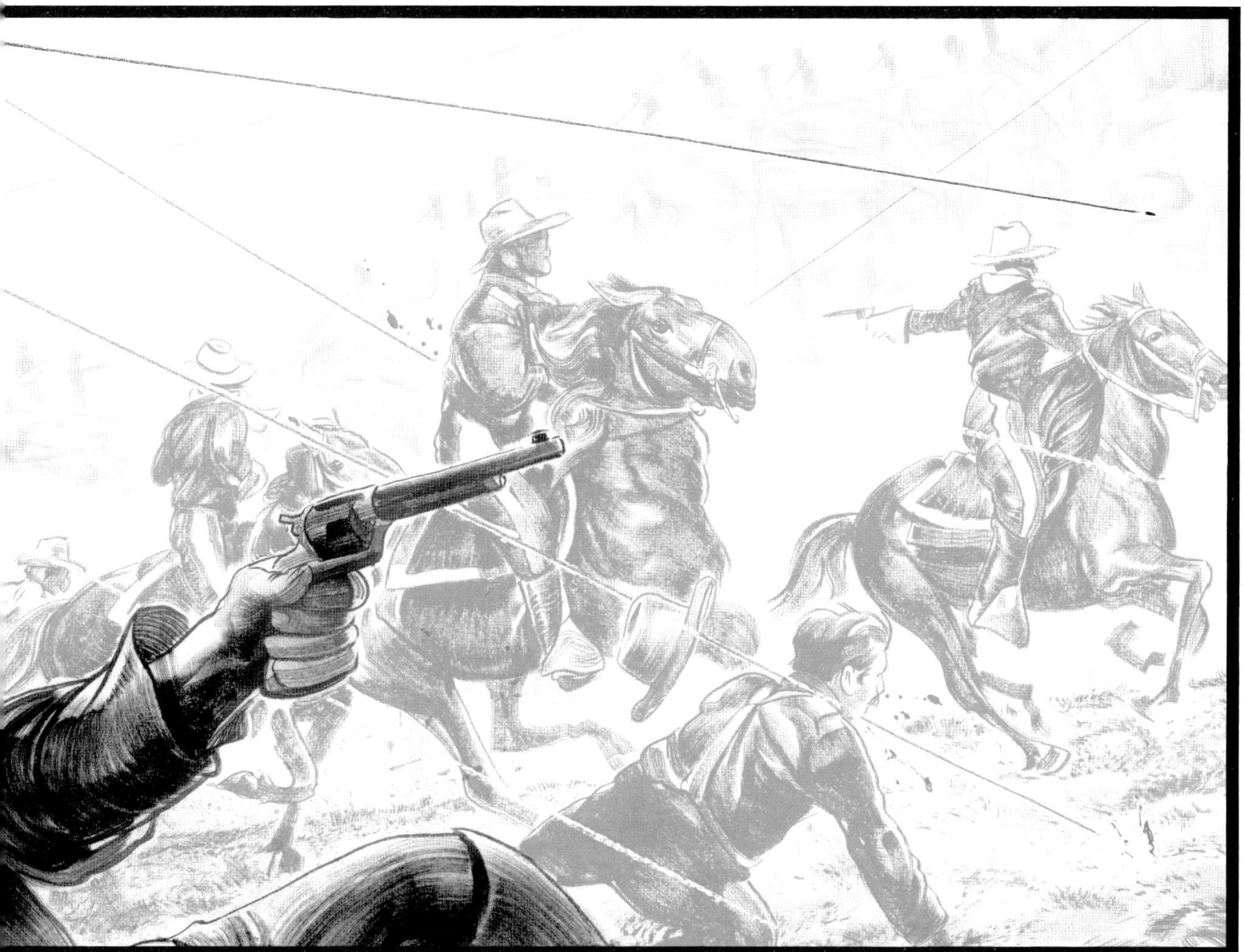

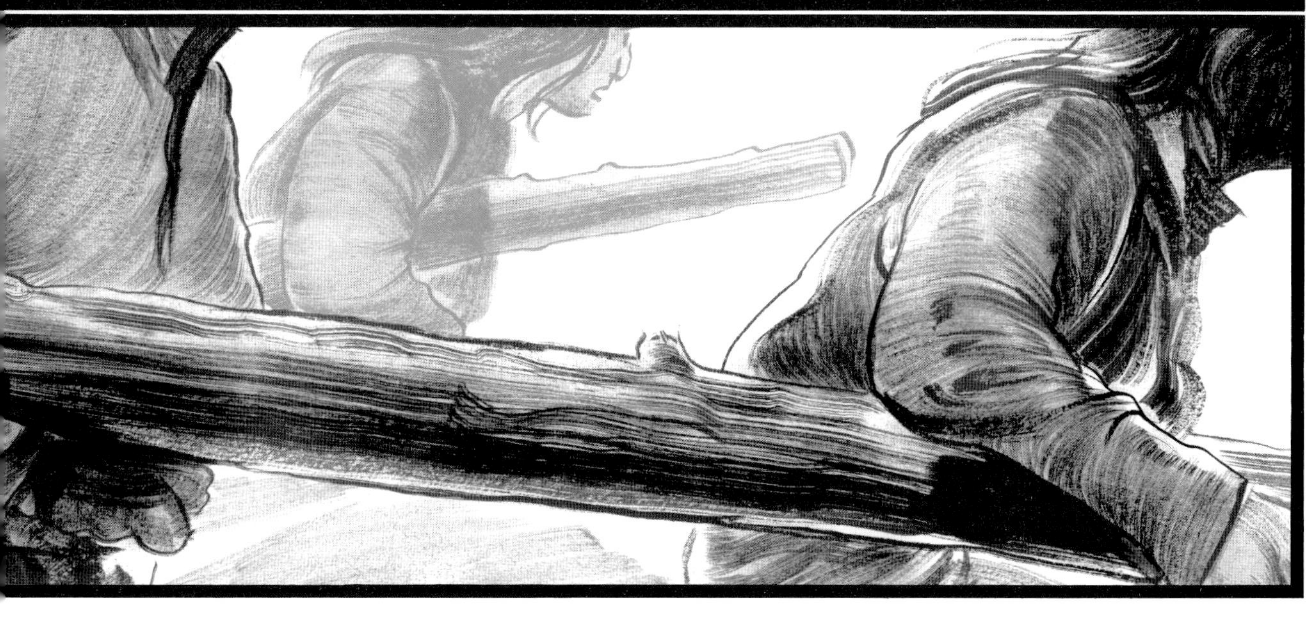

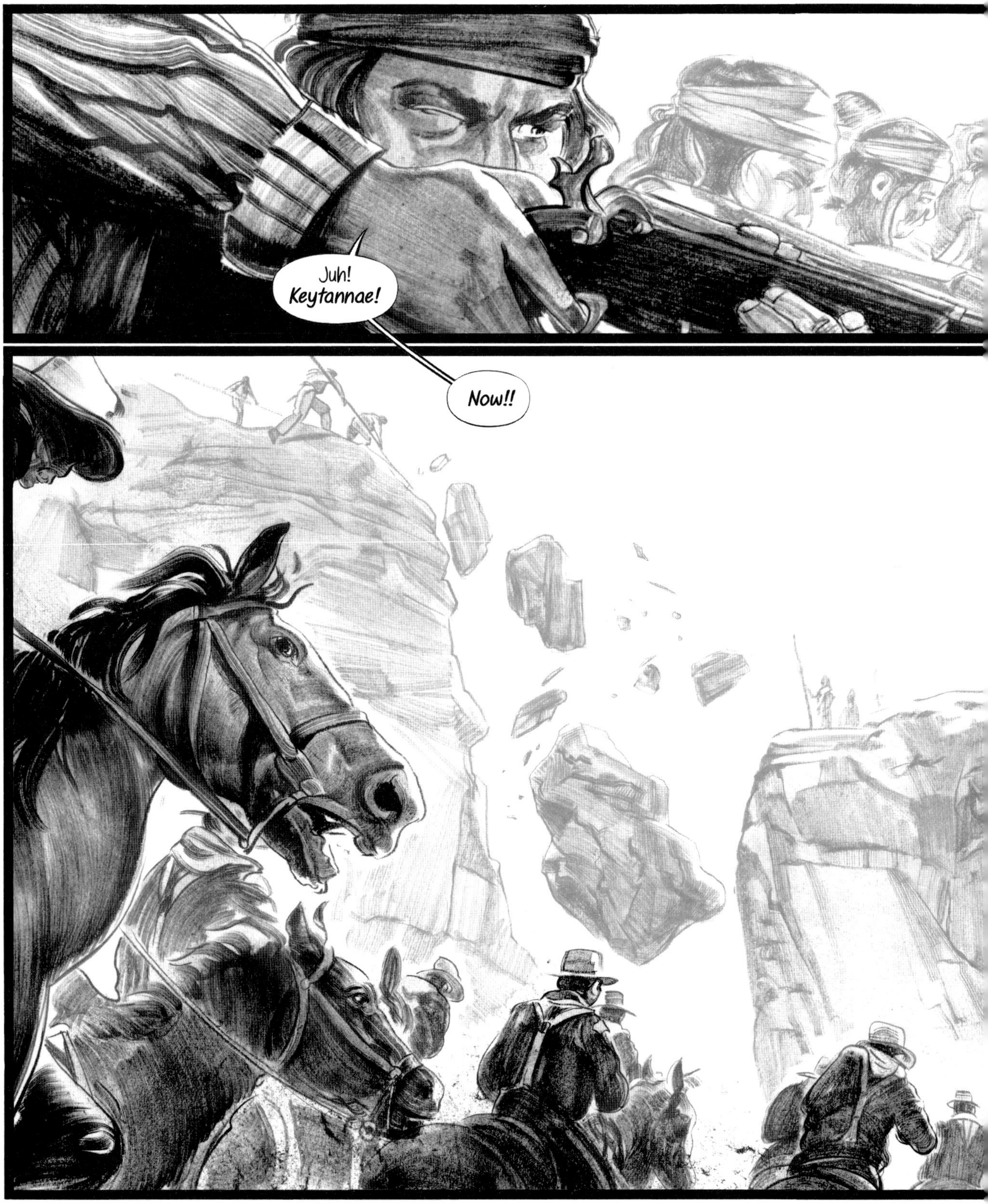
Juh! Keytannae!
Now!!

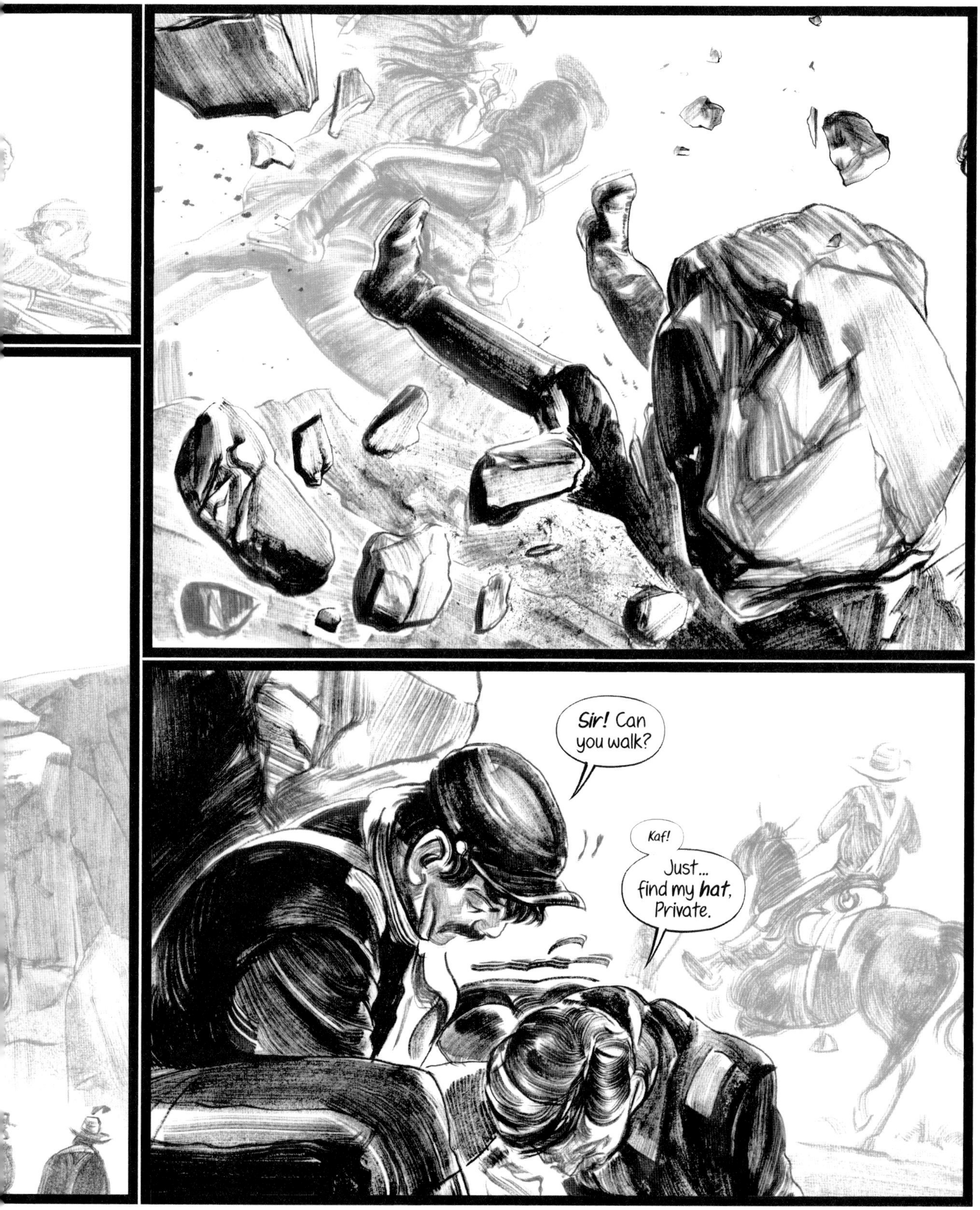
Sir! Can you walk?
Kaf!
Just... find my hat, Private.

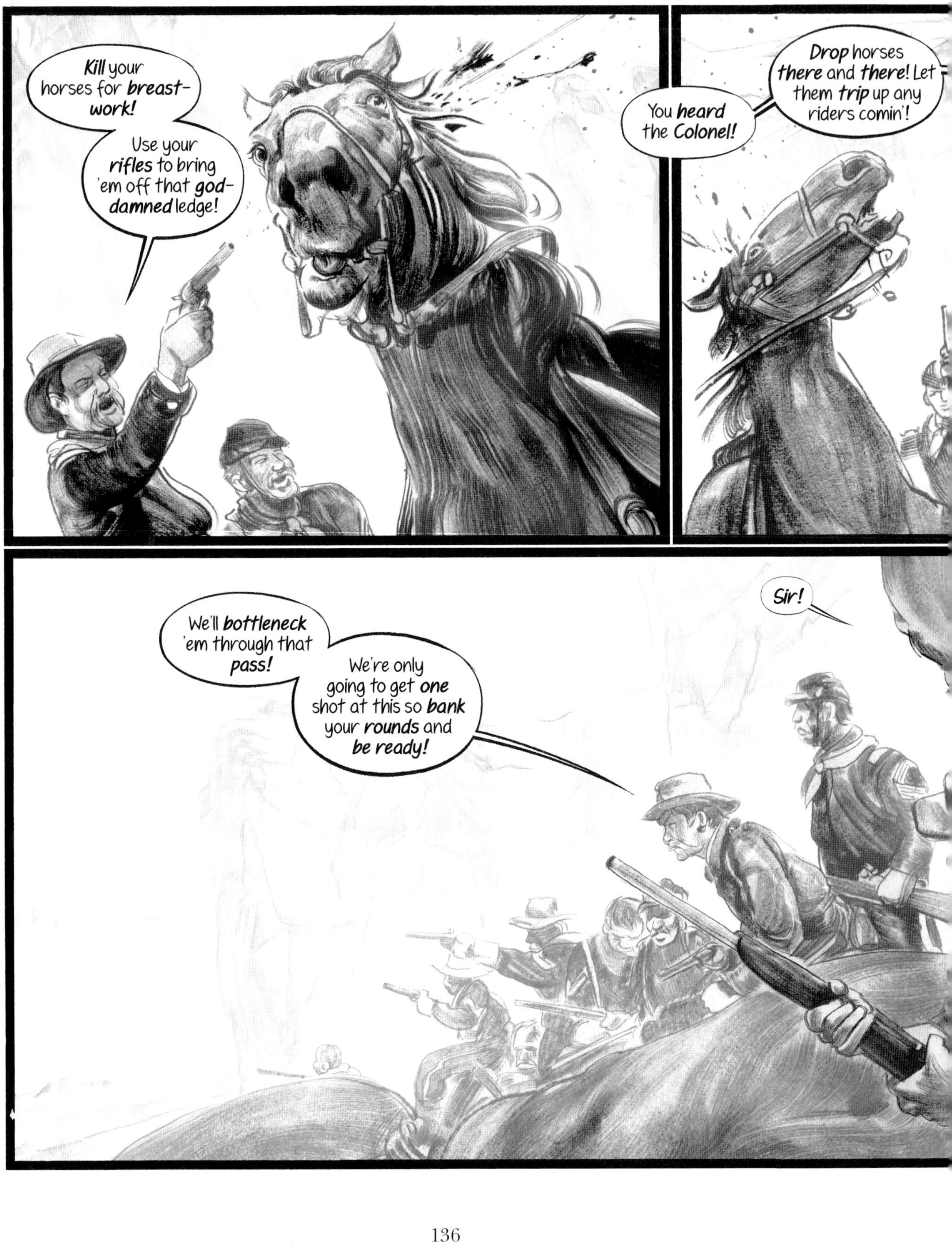
Kill your horses for breast-work!
Use your rifles to bring 'em off that god-damned ledge!
You heard the Colonel!
Drop horses there and there! Let them trip up any riders comin'!
Sir!
We'll bottleneck 'em through that pass!
We're only going to get one shot at this so bank your rounds and be ready!

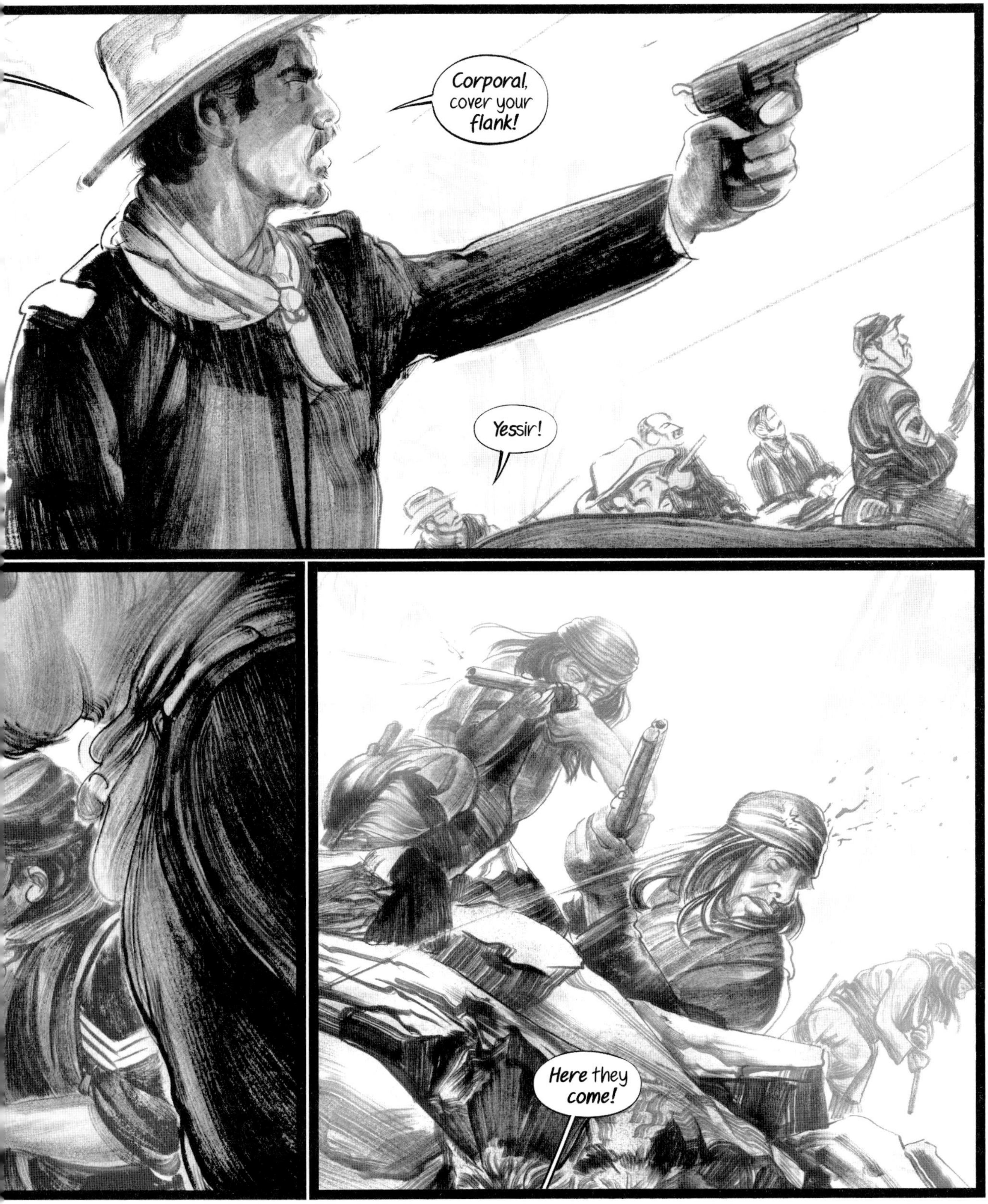
Corporal, cover your flank!
Yessir!
Here they come!

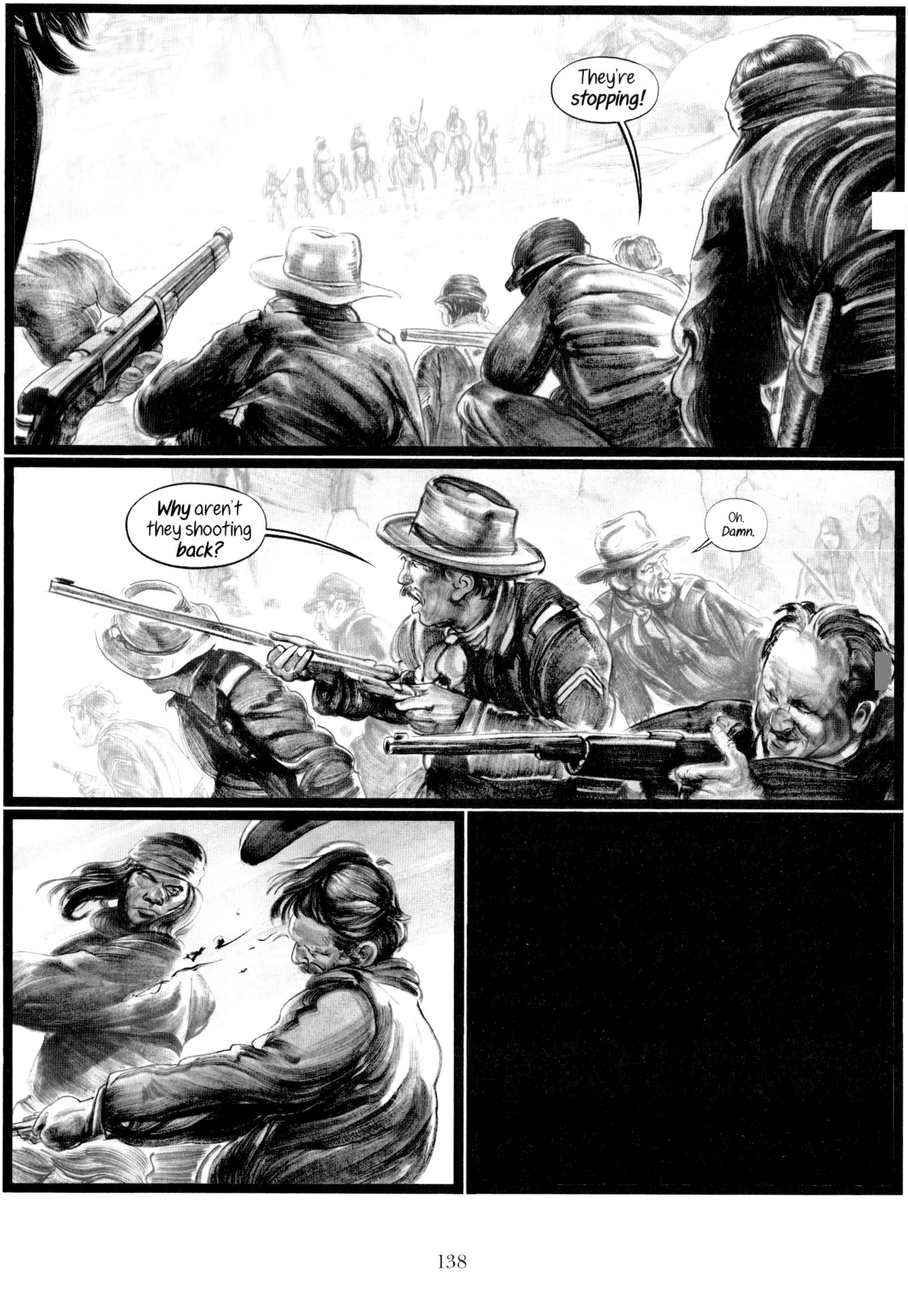
They're stopping!
Why aren't they shooting back?
Oh. Damn.

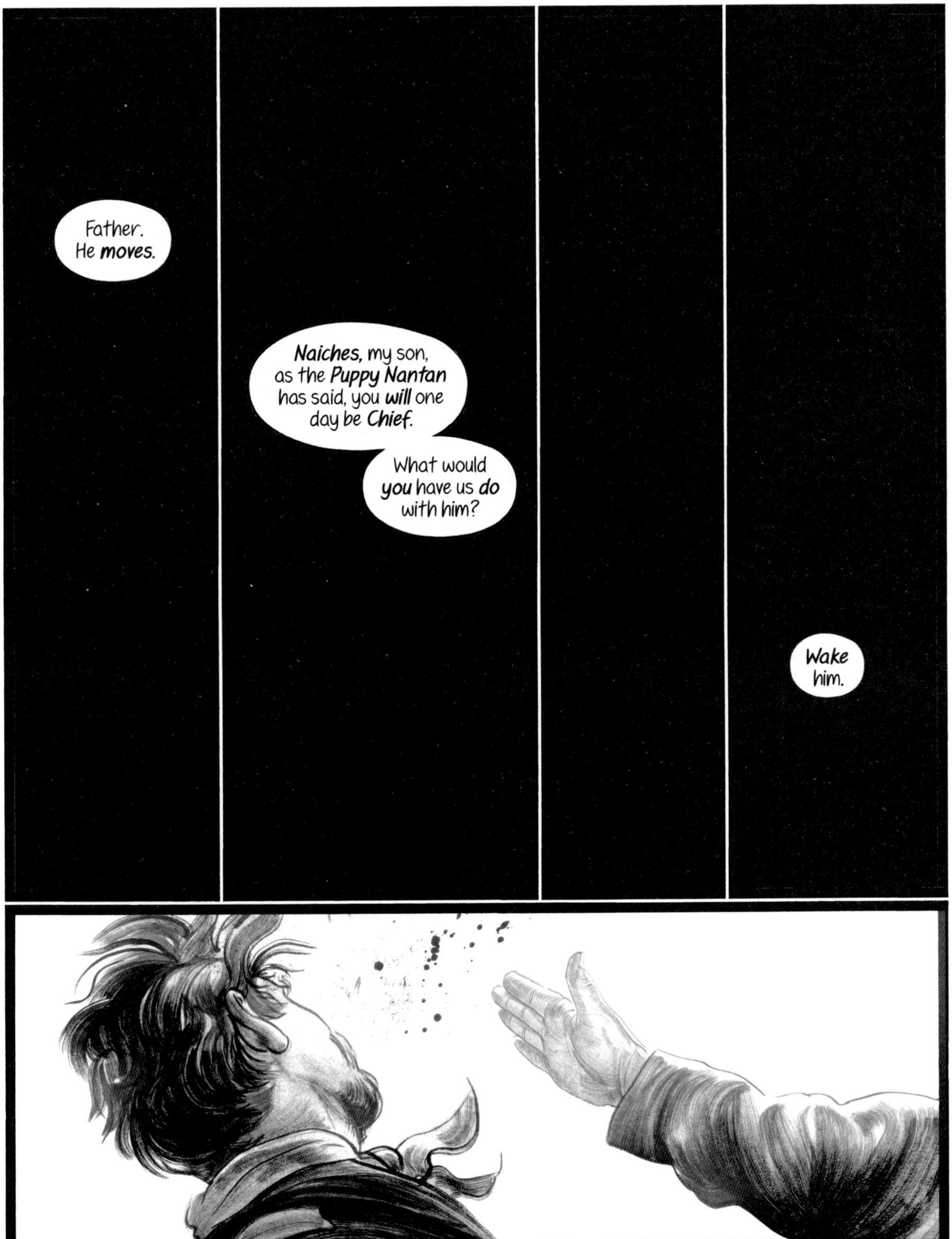
Father. He **moves.**
Naiches, my son, as the ***Puppy Nantan*** has said, you ***will*** one day be ***Chief.***
What would ***you*** have us ***do*** with him?
Wake him.

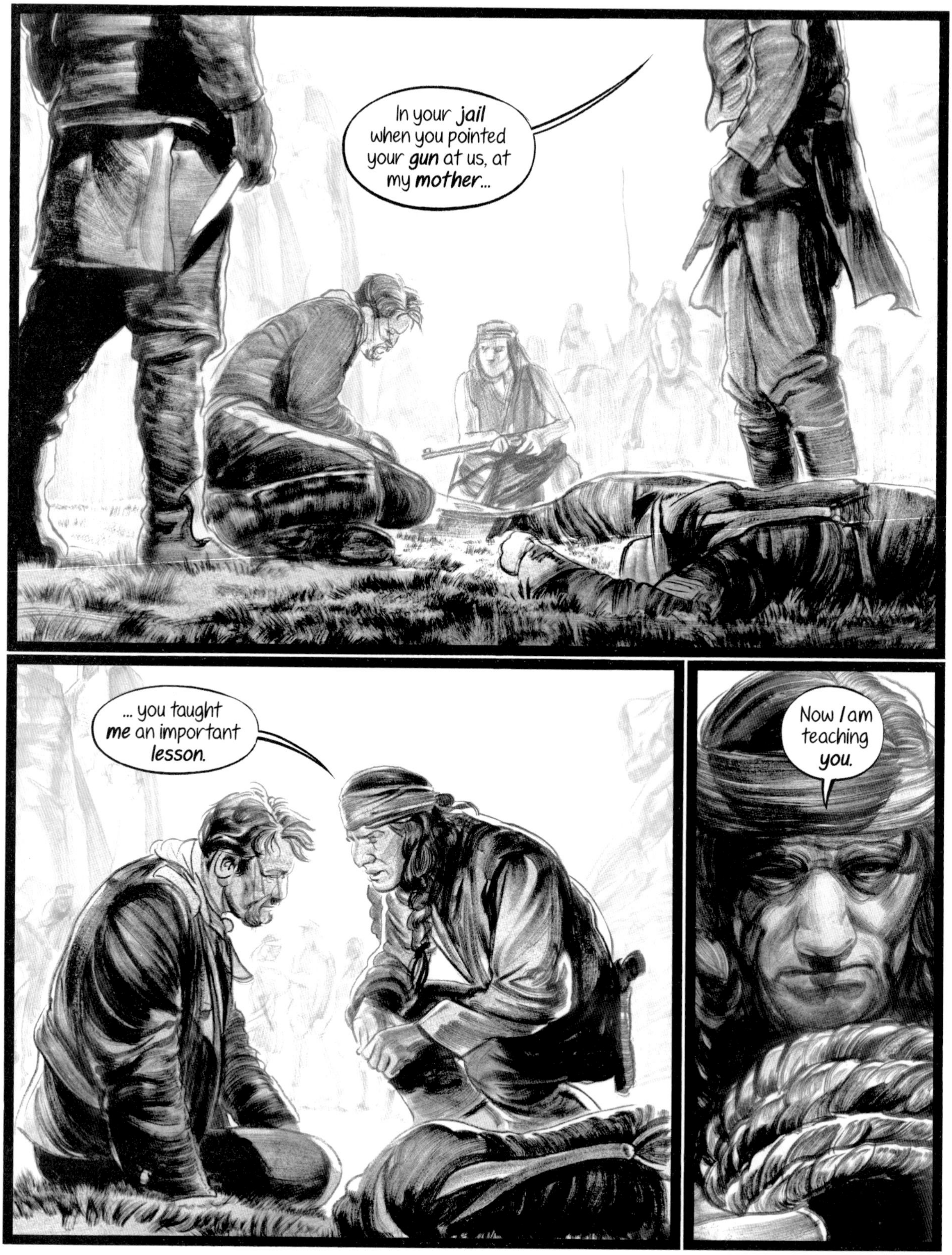

In your jail when you pointed your gun at us, at my mother...
... you taught me an important lesson.
Now I am teaching you.

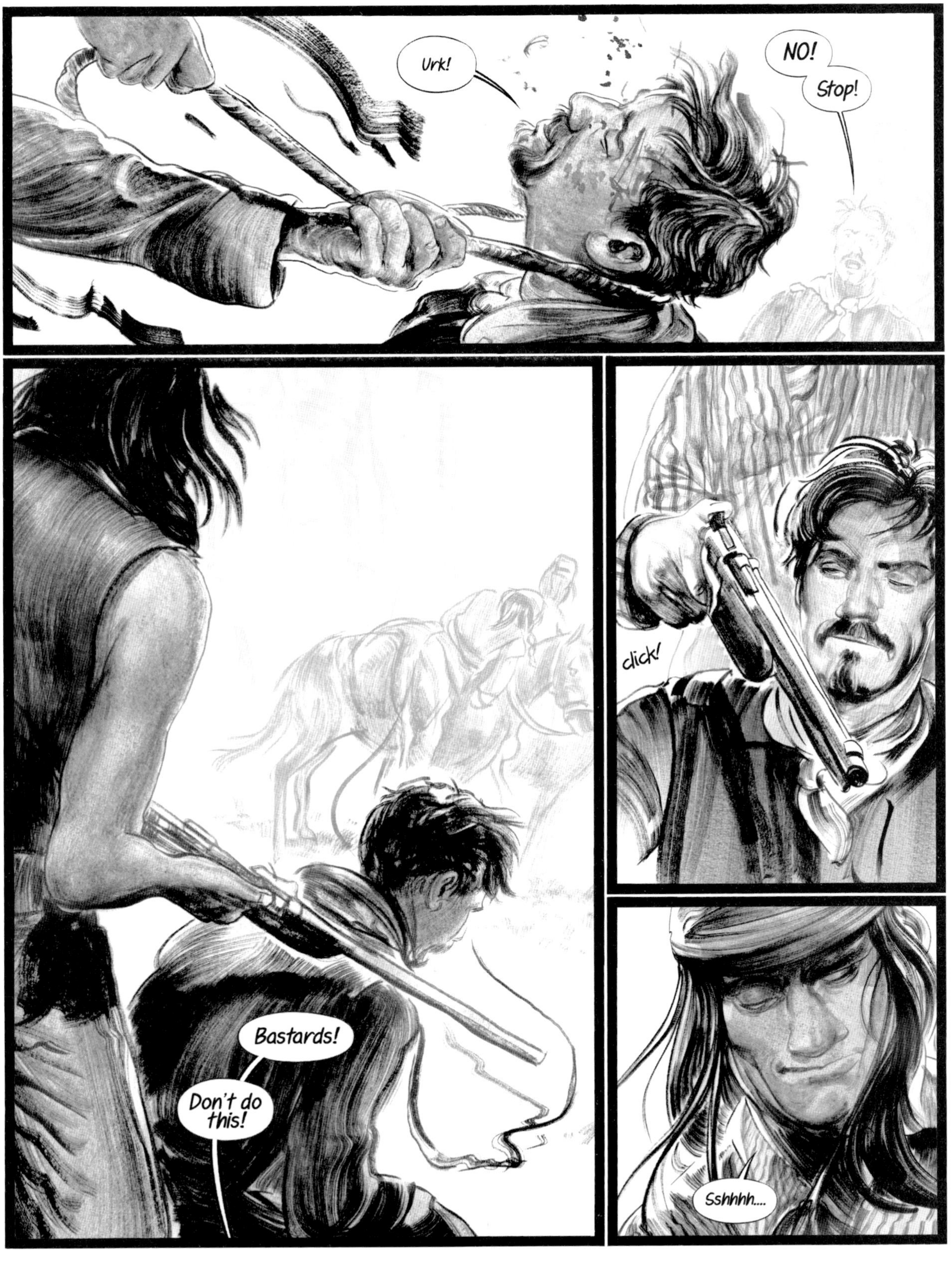
Urk!
NO!
Stop!
Bastards!
Don't do this!
click!
Sshhhh....

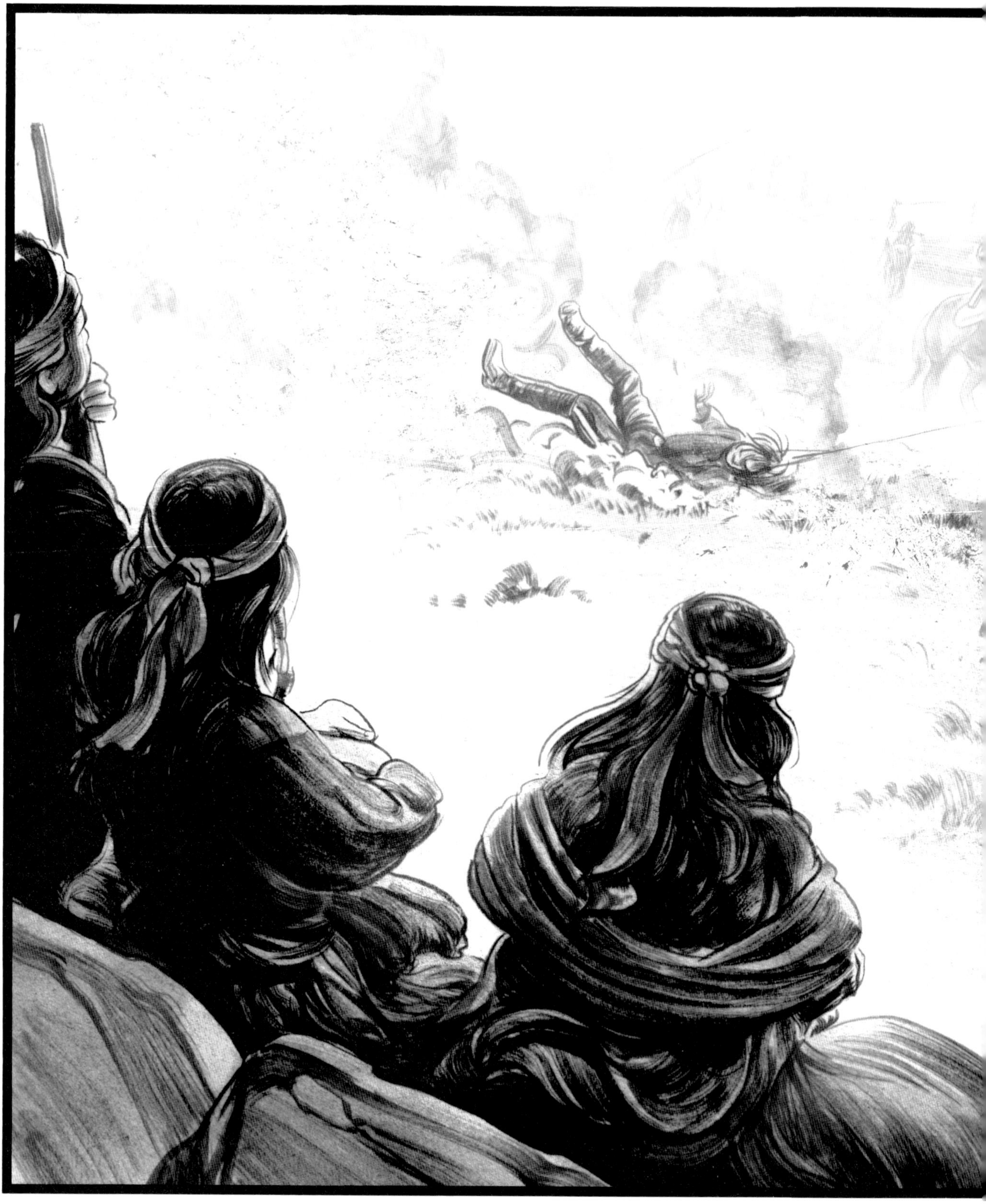

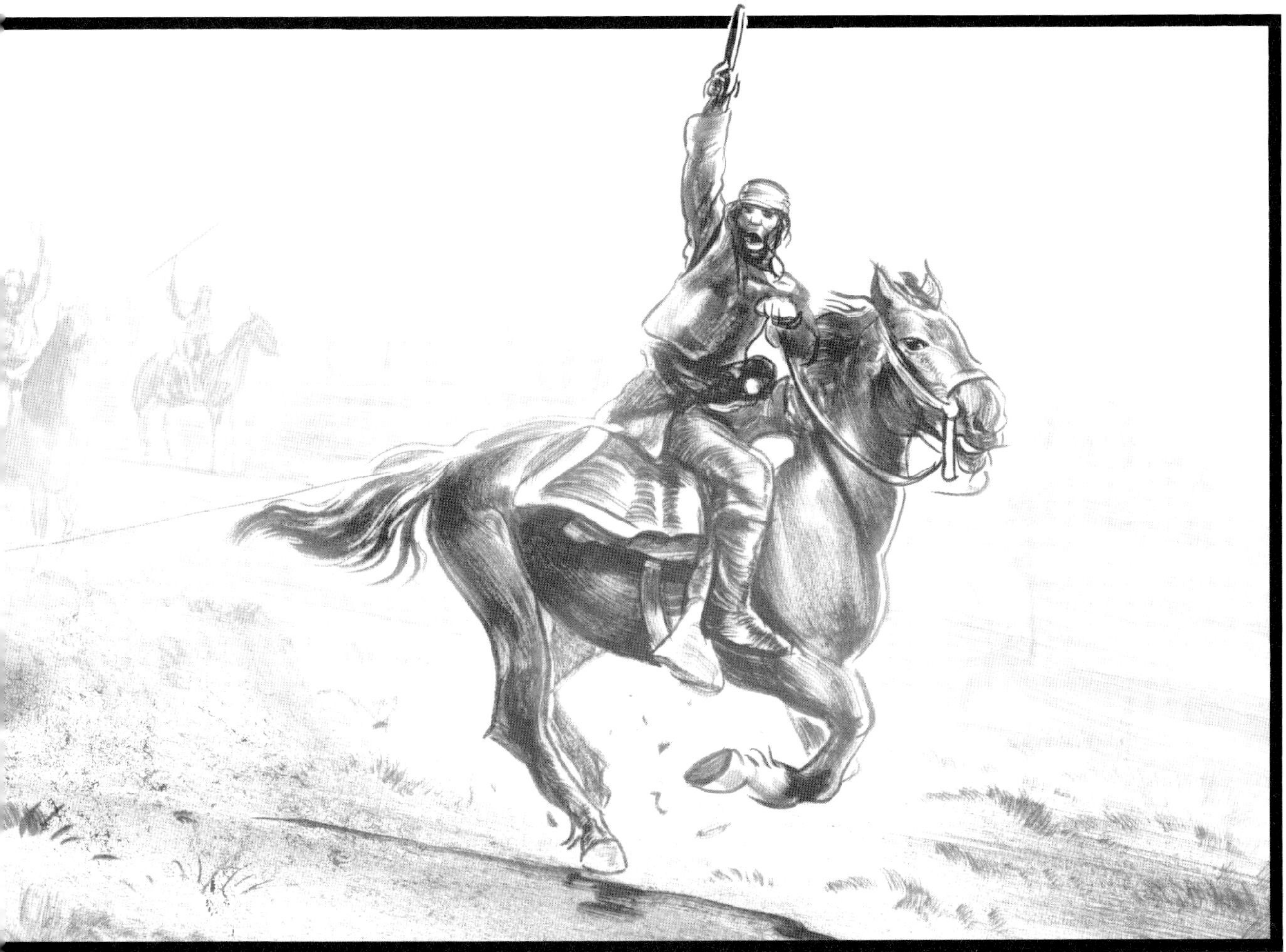

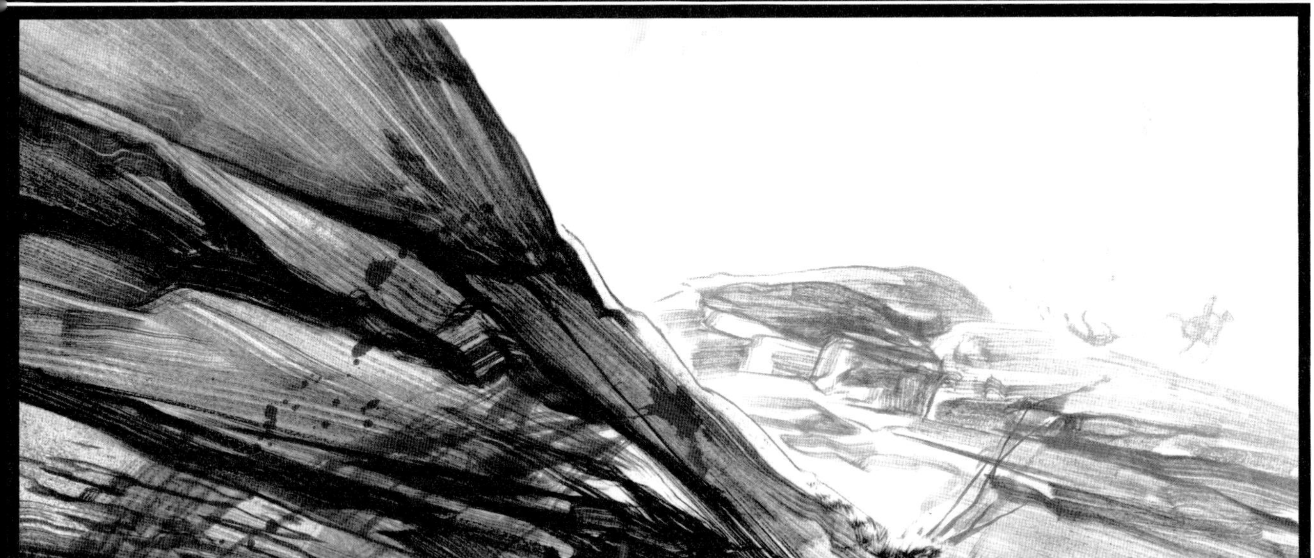

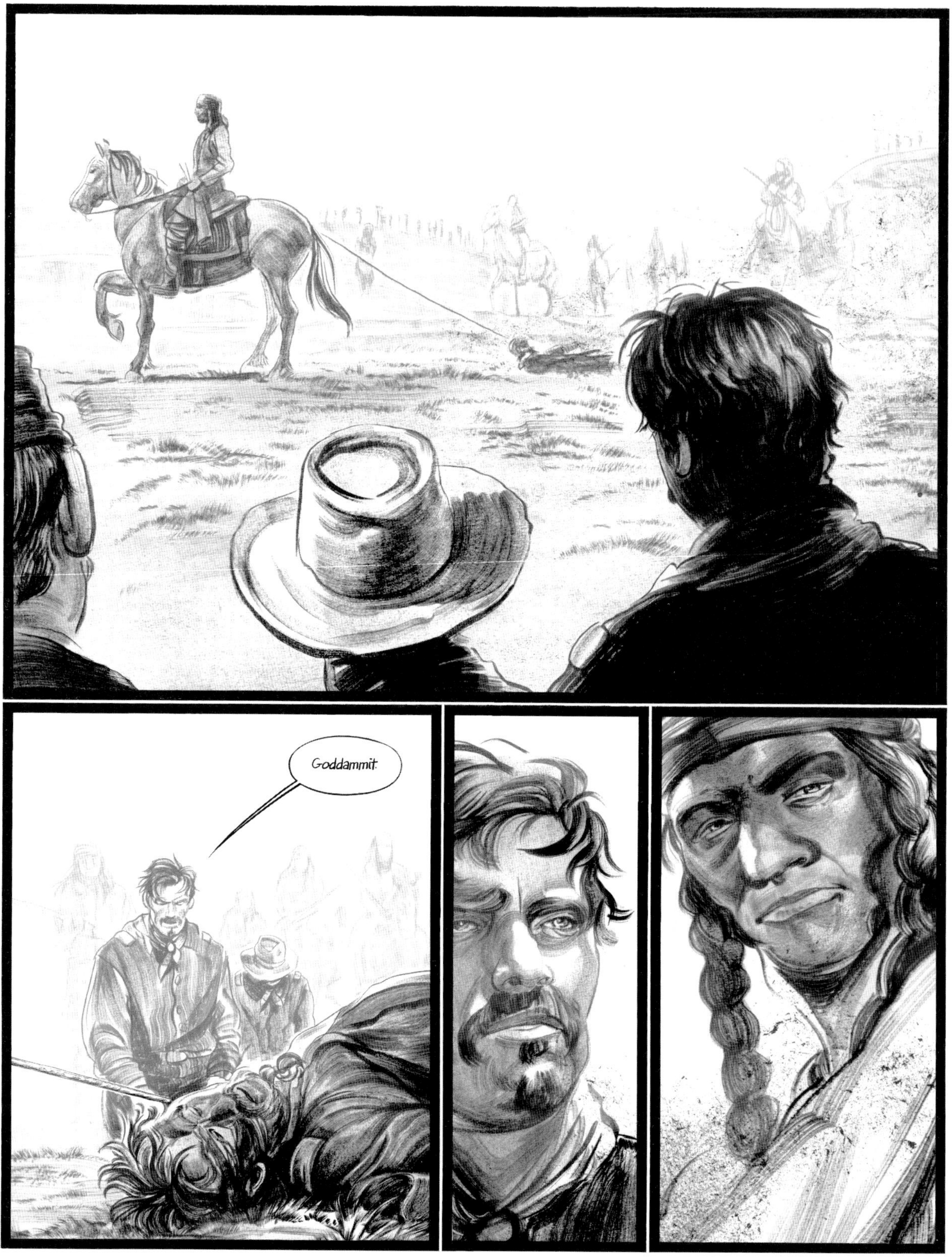
Goddammit.

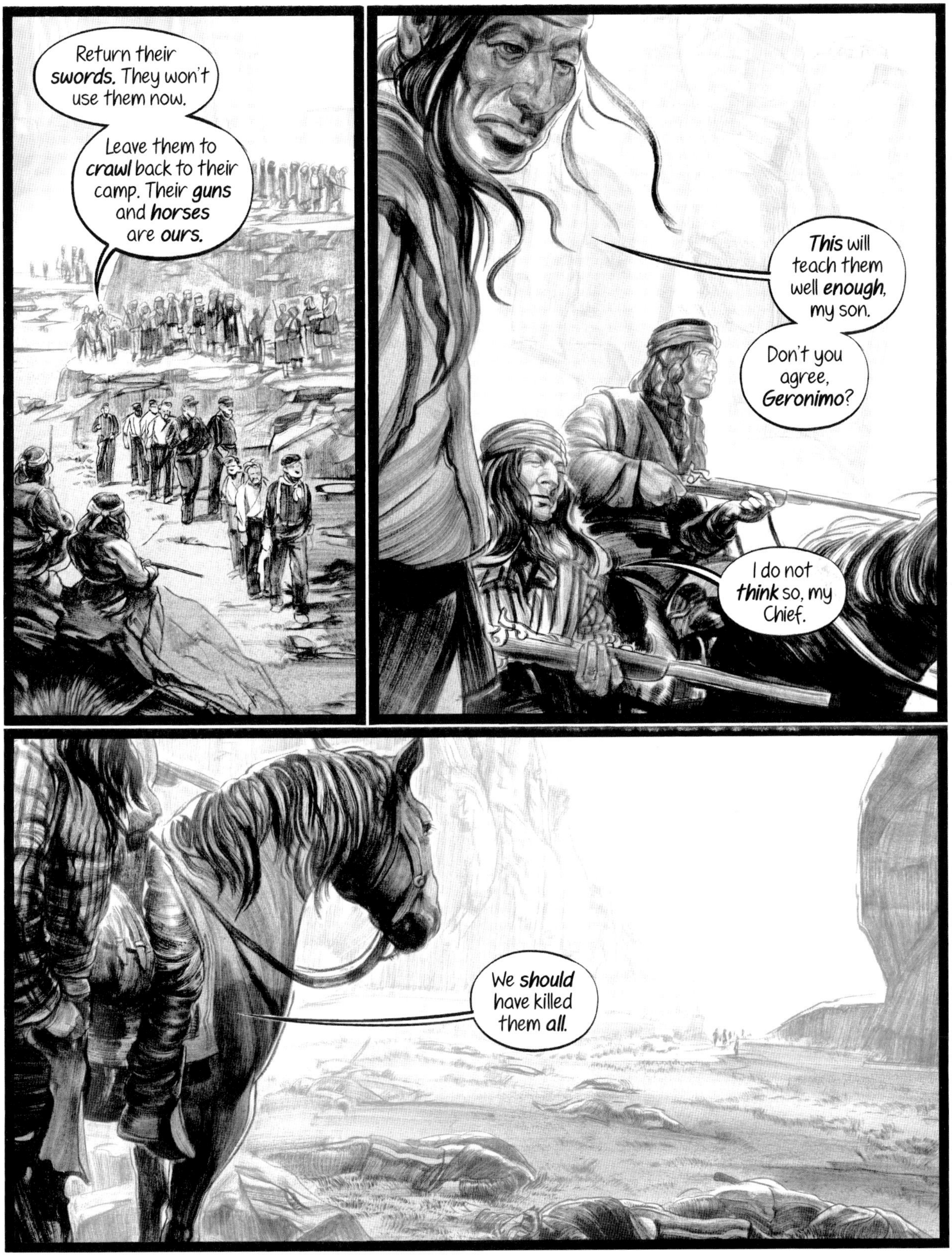
Return their swords. They won't use them now.
Leave them to crawl back to their camp. Their guns and horses are ours.
This will teach them well enough, my son.
Don't you agree, Geronimo?
I do not think so, my Chief.
We should have killed them all.

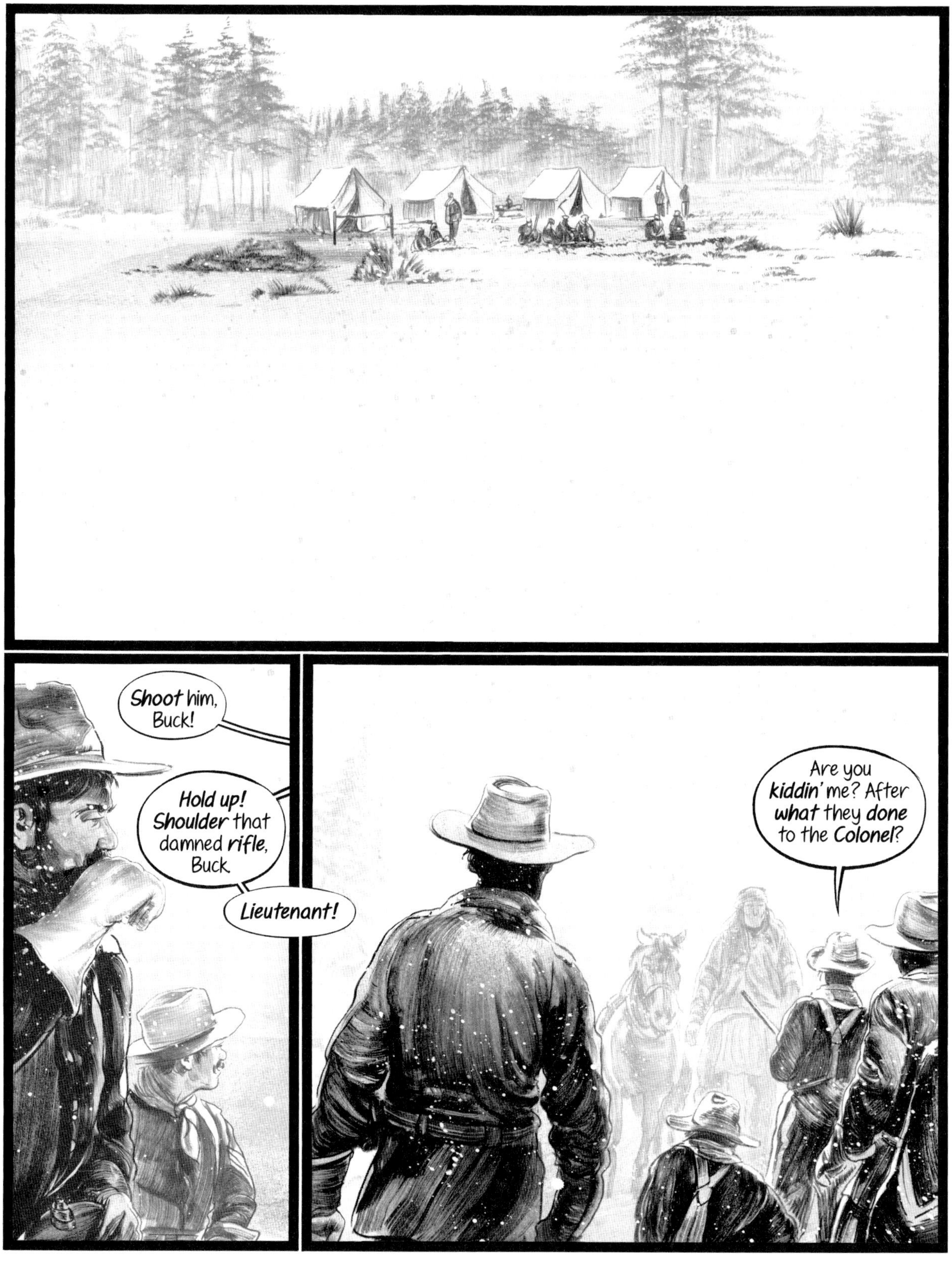
Shoot him, Buck!
Hold up! Shoulder that damned rifle, Buck.
Lieutenant!
Are you kiddin' me? After what they done to the Colonel?

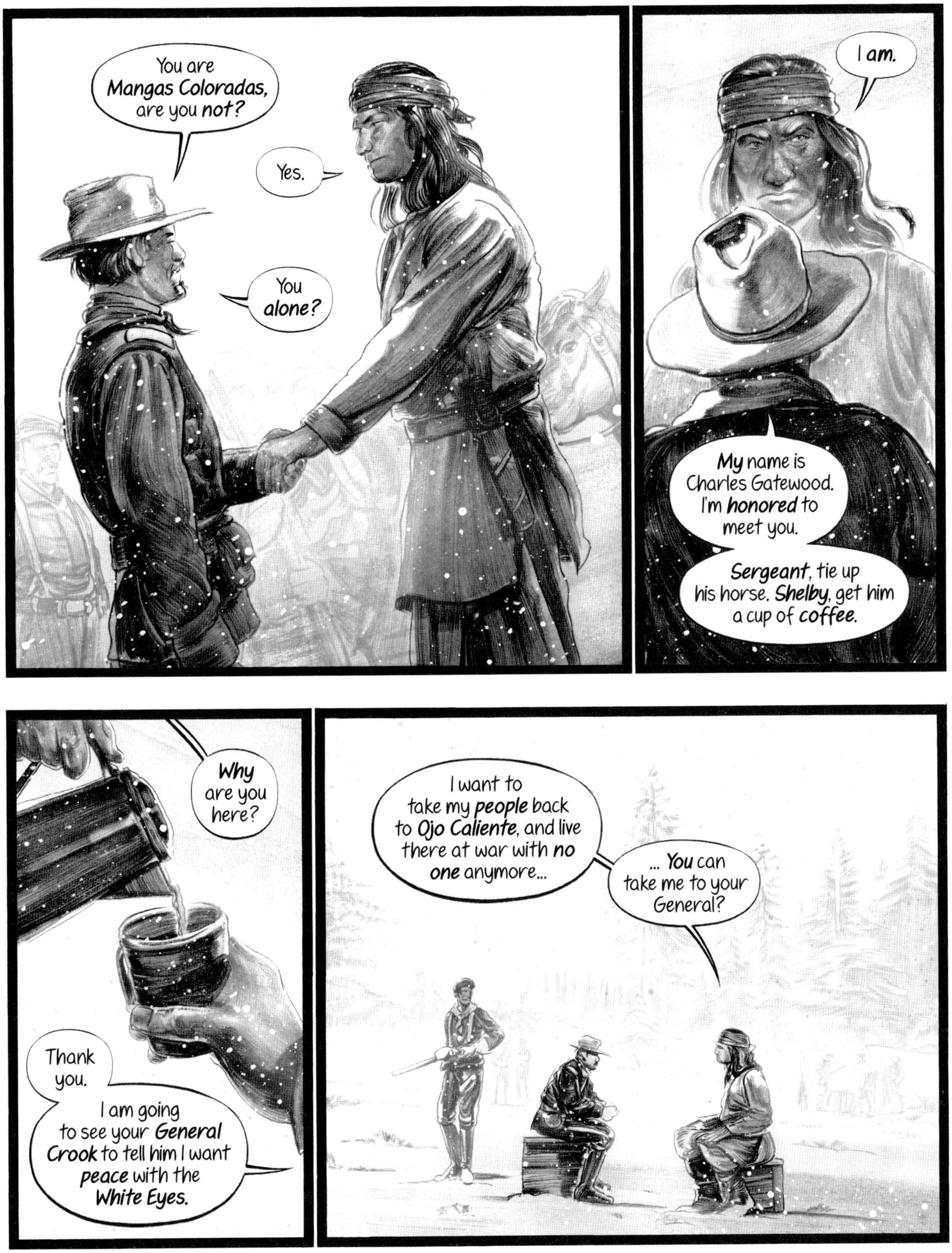
You are Mangas Coloradas, are you not?
Yes.
You alone?
I am.
My name is Charles Gatewood. I'm honored to meet you.
Sergeant, tie up his horse. Shelby, get him a cup of coffee.
Why are you here?
Thank you.
I am going to see your General Crook to tell him I want peace with the White Eyes.
I want to take my people back to Ojo Caliente, and live there at war with no one anymore...
... You can take me to your General?

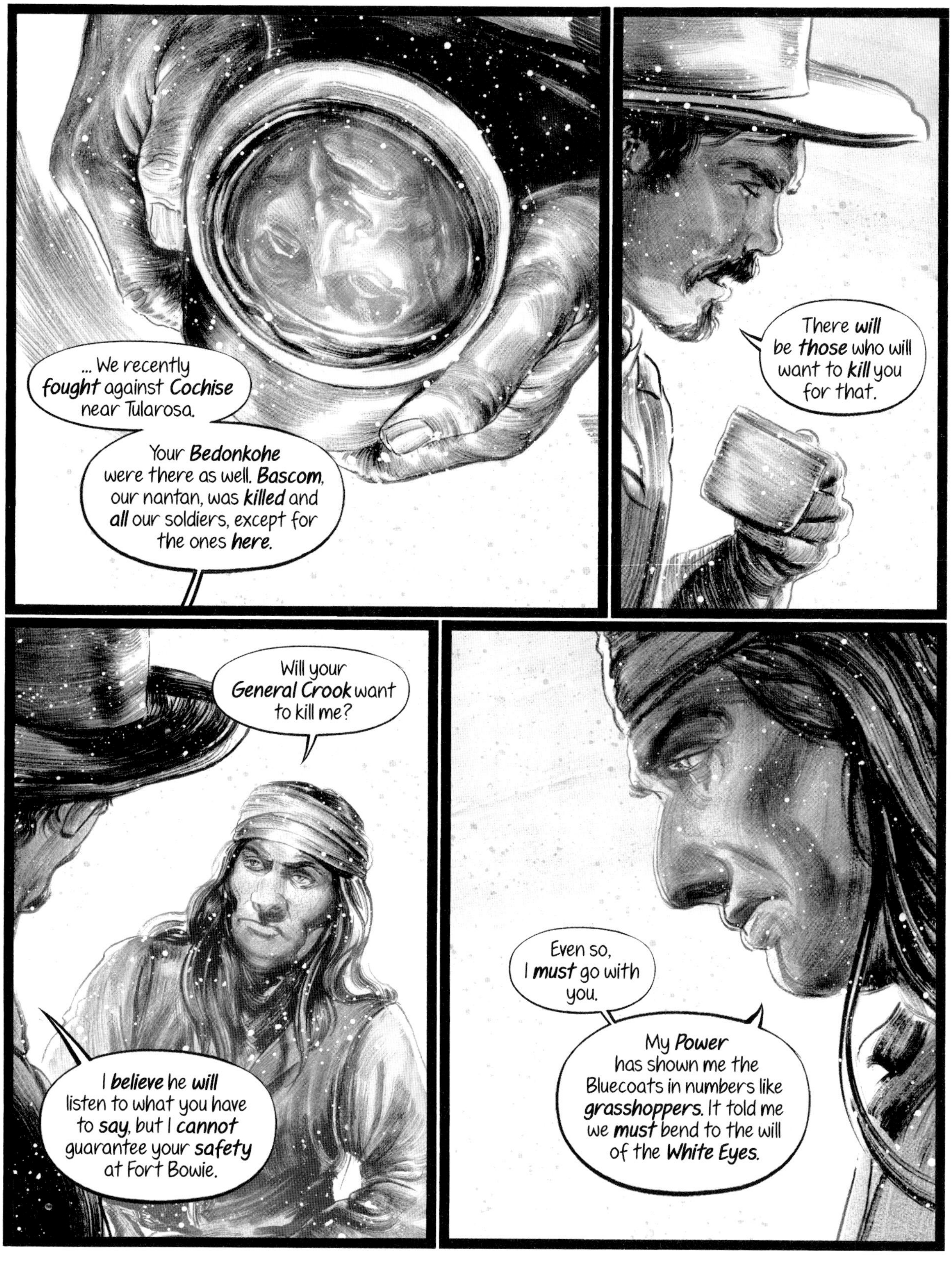
... We recently fought against Cochise near Tularosa.
Your Bedonkohe were there as well. Bascom, our nantan, was killed and all our soldiers, except for the ones here.
There will be those who will want to kill you for that.
Will your General Crook want to kill me?
I believe he will listen to what you have to say, but I cannot guarantee your safety at Fort Bowie.
Even so, I must go with you.
My Power has shown me the Bluecoats in numbers like grasshoppers. It told me we must bend to the will of the White Eyes.

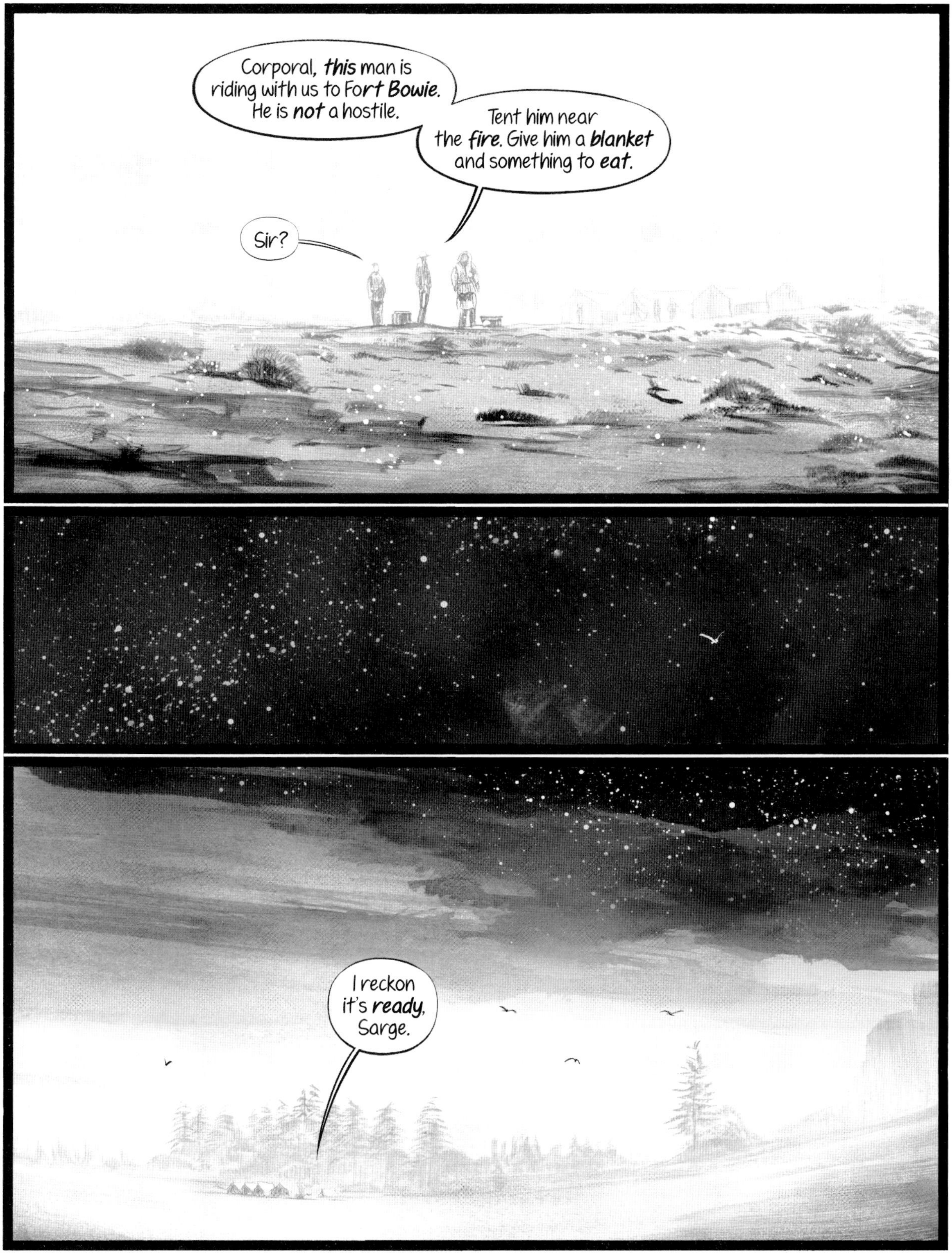
Corporal, this man is riding with us to Fort Bowie. He is not a hostile.
Tent him near the fire. Give him a blanket and something to eat.
Sir?
I reckon it's ready, Sarge.

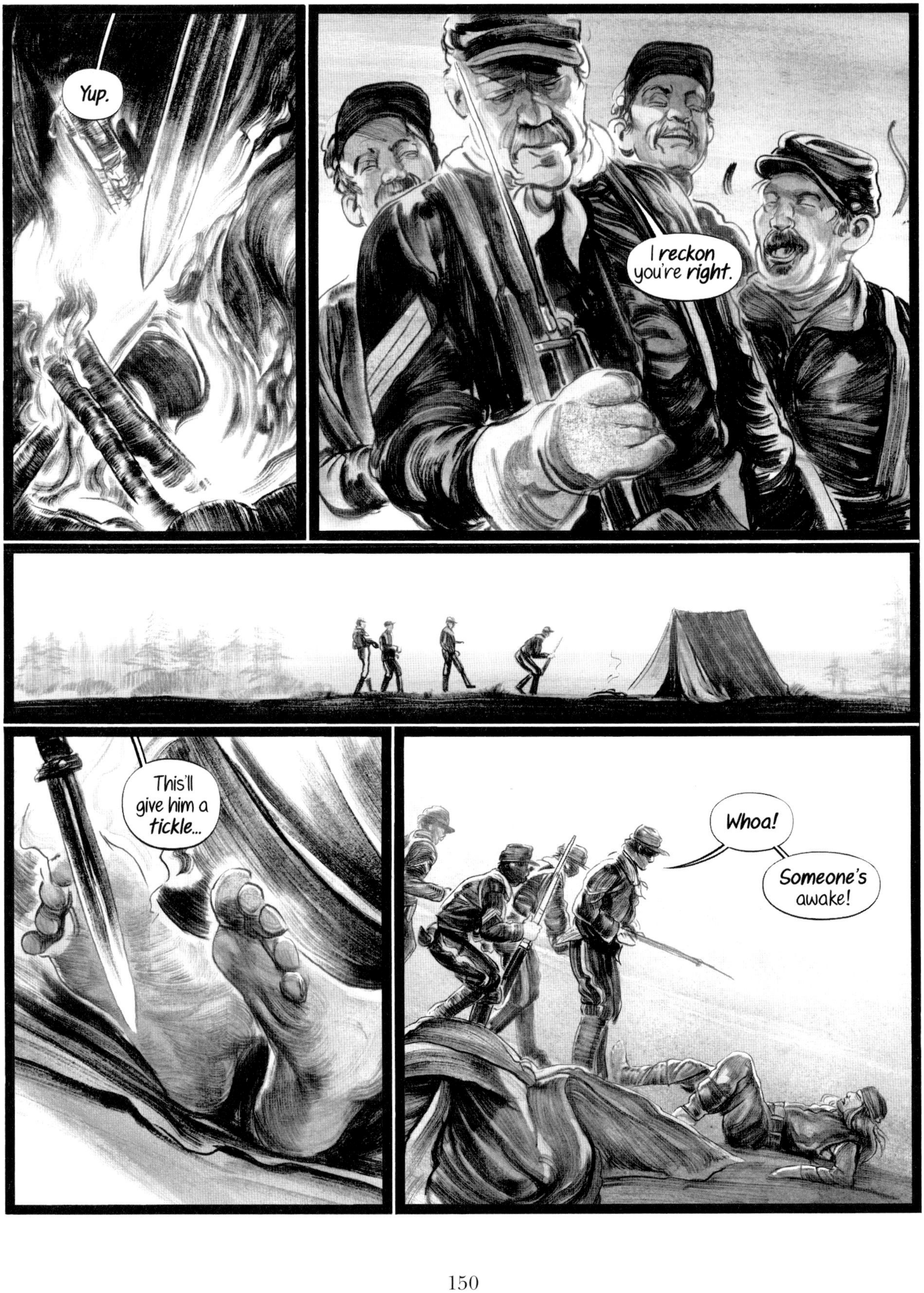
Yup.
I reckon you're right.
This'll give him a tickle...
Whoa!
Someone's awake!

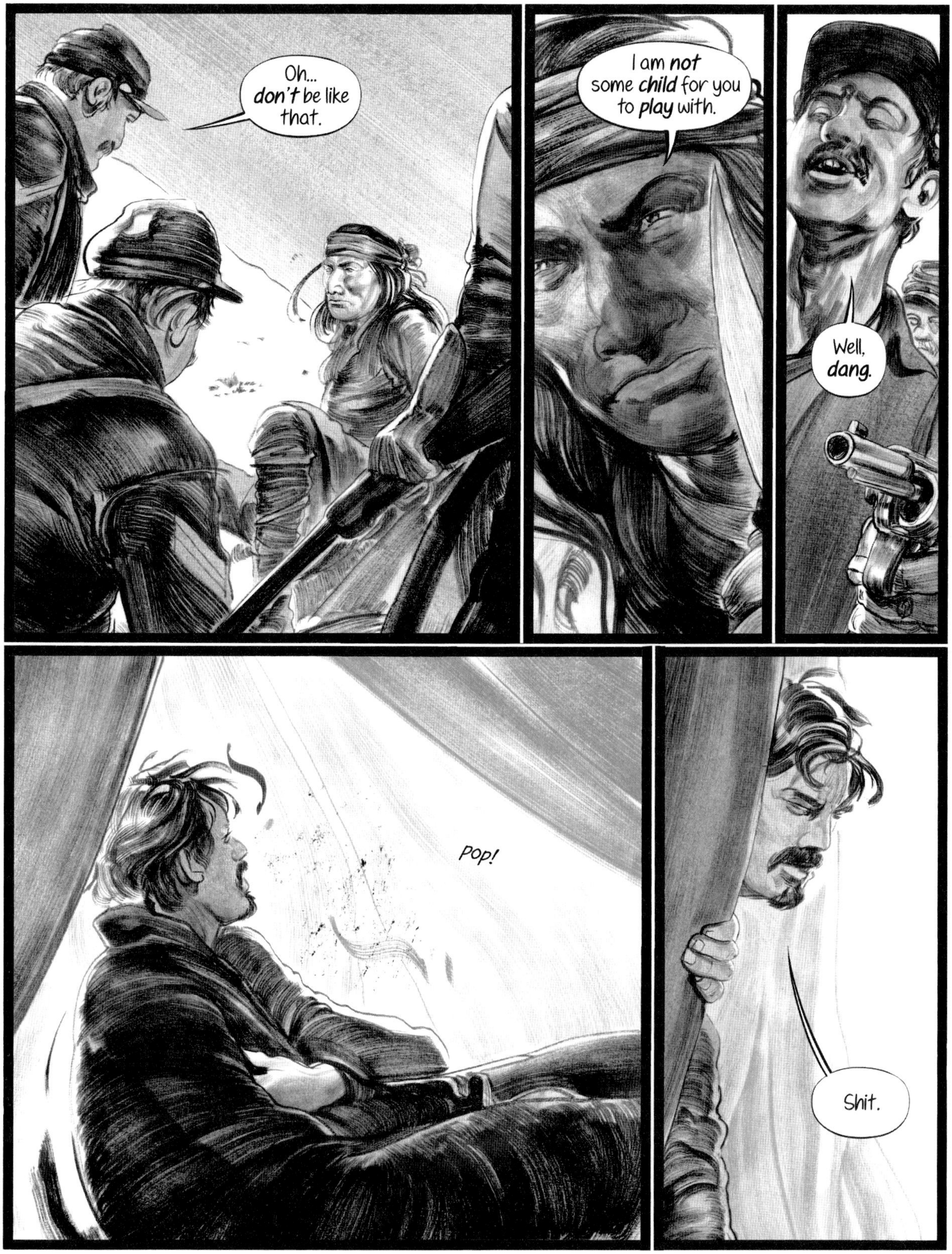
Oh... don't be like that.
I am not some child for you to play with.
Well, dang.
Pop!
Shit.

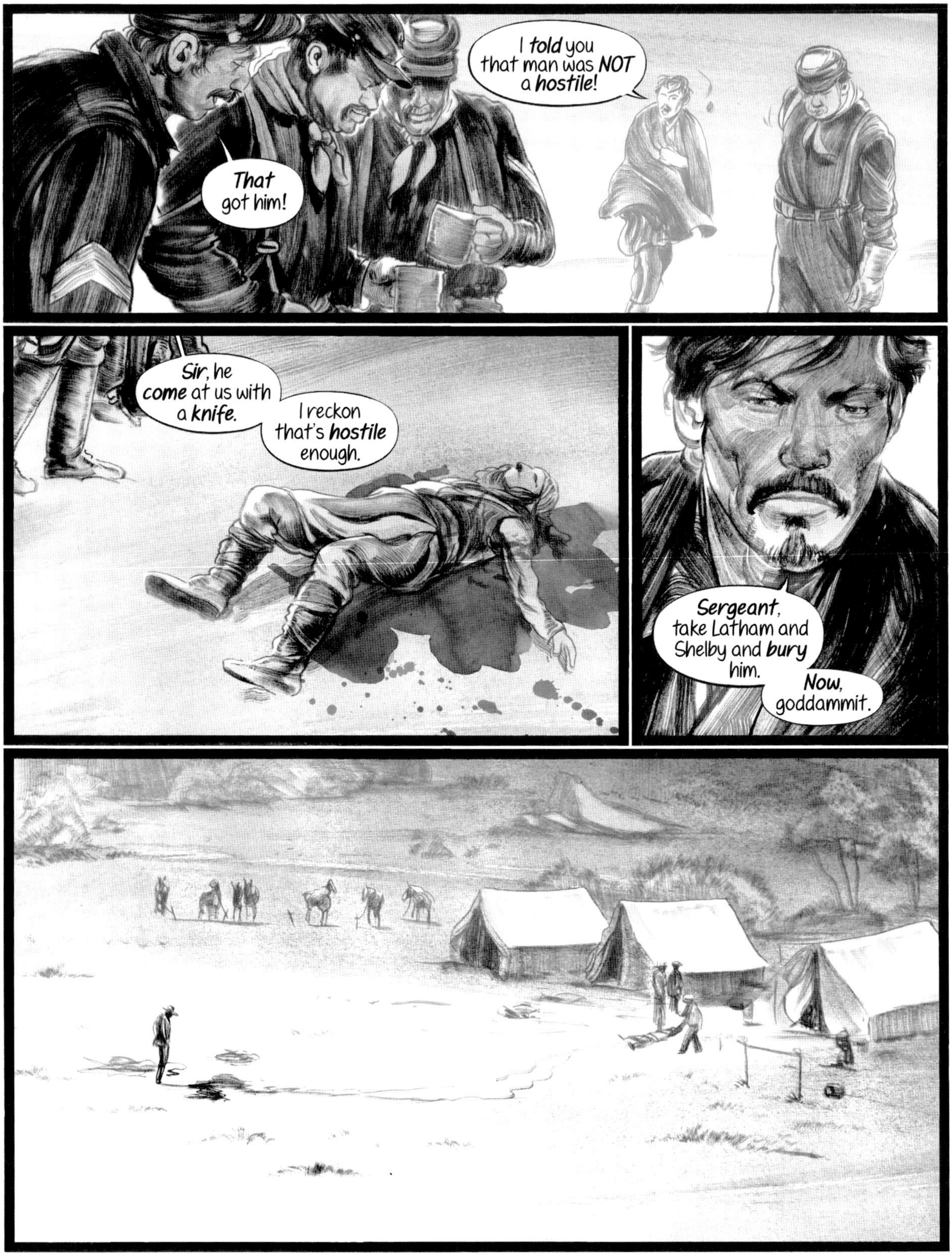
That got him!
I told you that man was NOT a hostile!
Sir, he come at us with a knife.
I reckon that's hostile enough.
Sergeant, take Latham and Shelby and bury him.
Now, goddammit.

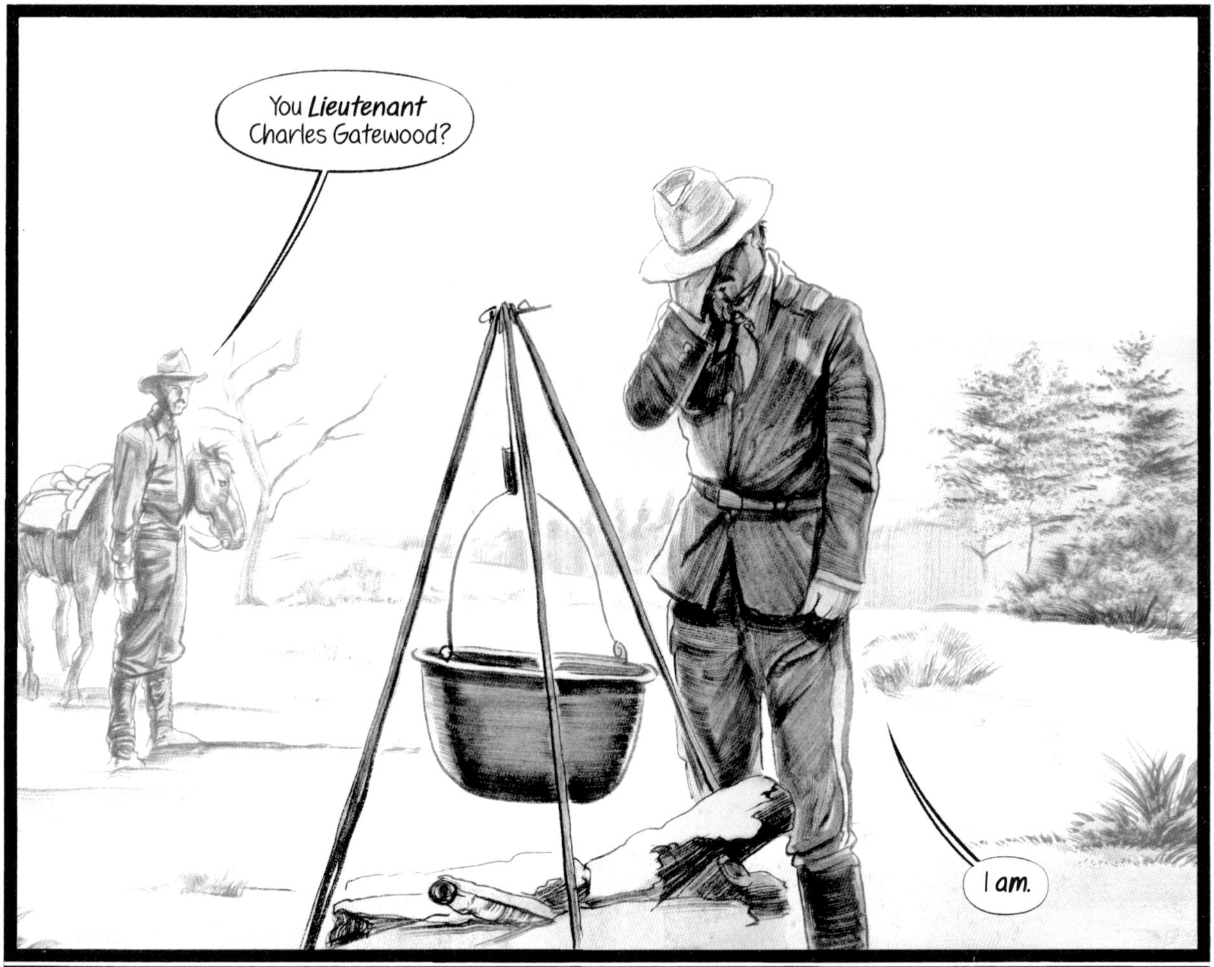
You **Lieutenant** Charles Gatewood?
I **am**.

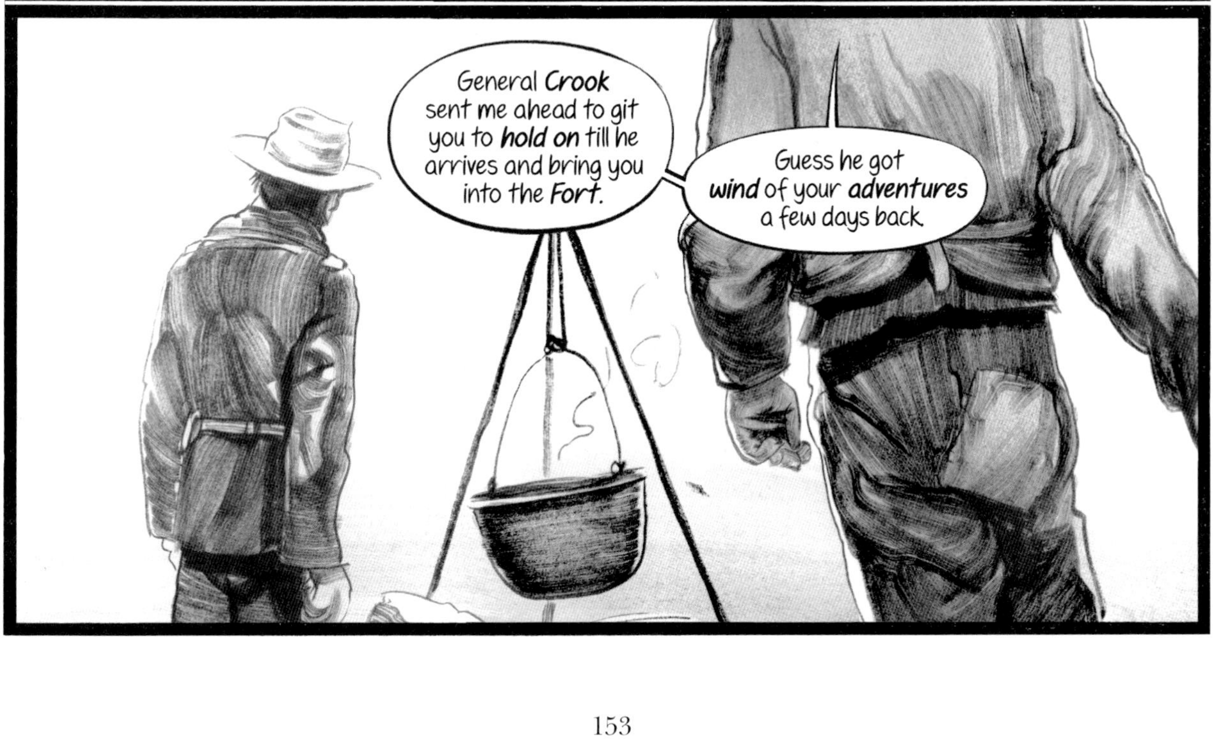
General **Crook** sent me ahead to git you to **hold on** till he arrives and bring you into the **Fort**.
Guess he got **wind** of your **adventures** a few days back.

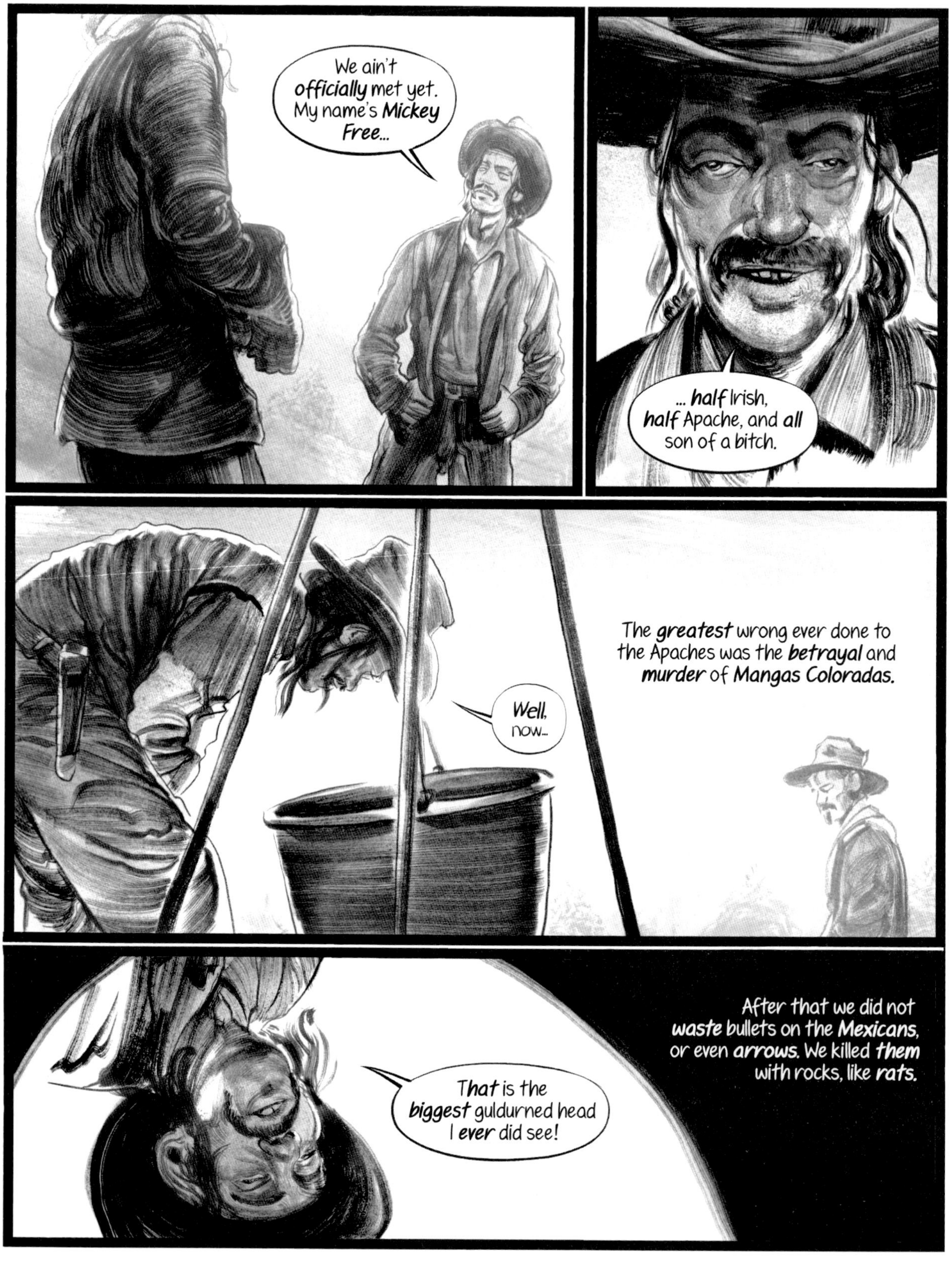
We ain't officially met yet. My name's Mickey Free...
... half Irish, half Apache, and all son of a bitch.
The greatest wrong ever done to the Apaches was the betrayal and murder of Mangas Coloradas.
Well, now...
After that we did not waste bullets on the Mexicans, or even arrows. We killed them with rocks, like rats.
That is the biggest guldurned head I ever did see!

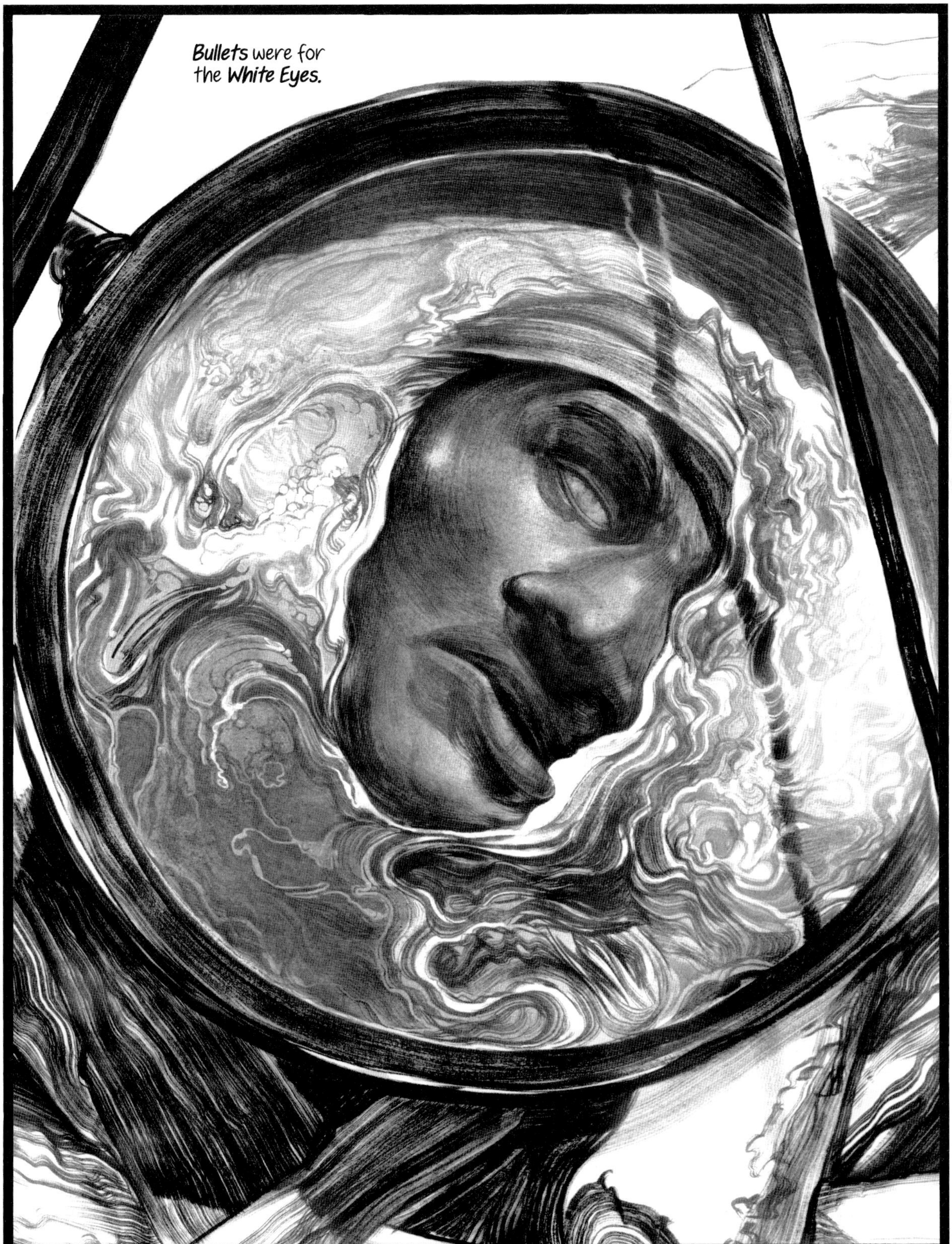
Bullets were for the **White Eyes.**

· PART THREE ·

A THREE-HEADED GOD

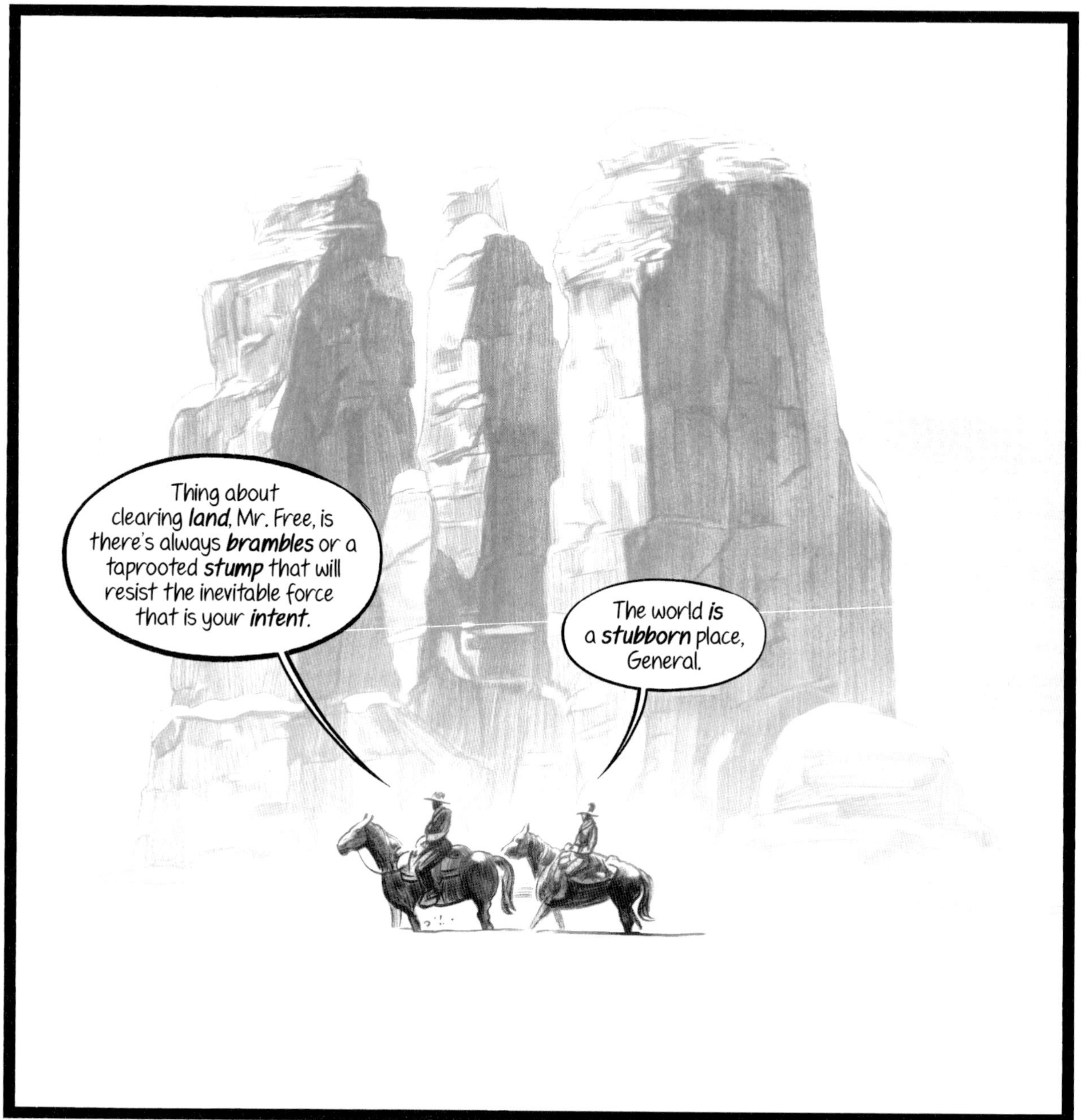
Thing about clearing **land**, Mr. Free, is there's always **brambles** or a taprooted **stump** that will resist the inevitable force that is your **intent**.
The world **is** a **stubborn** place, General.

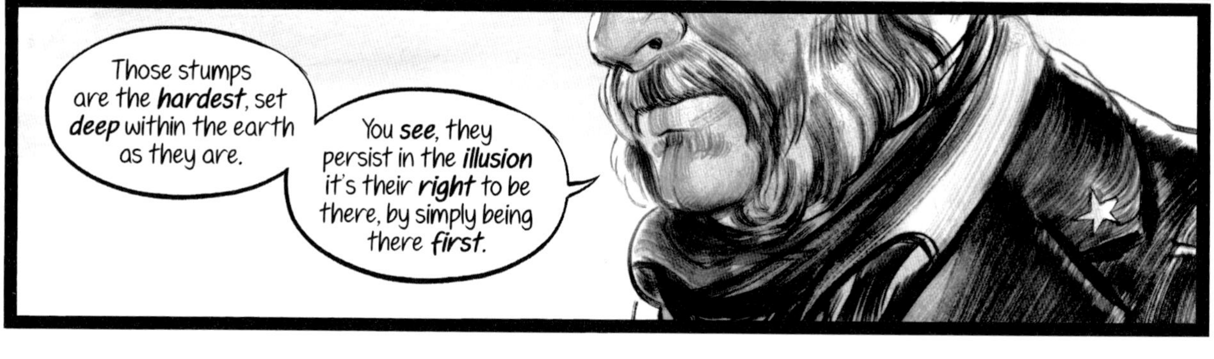
Those stumps are the **hardest**, set **deep** within the earth as they are.
You **see**, they persist in the **illusion** it's their **right** to be there, by simply being there **first**.

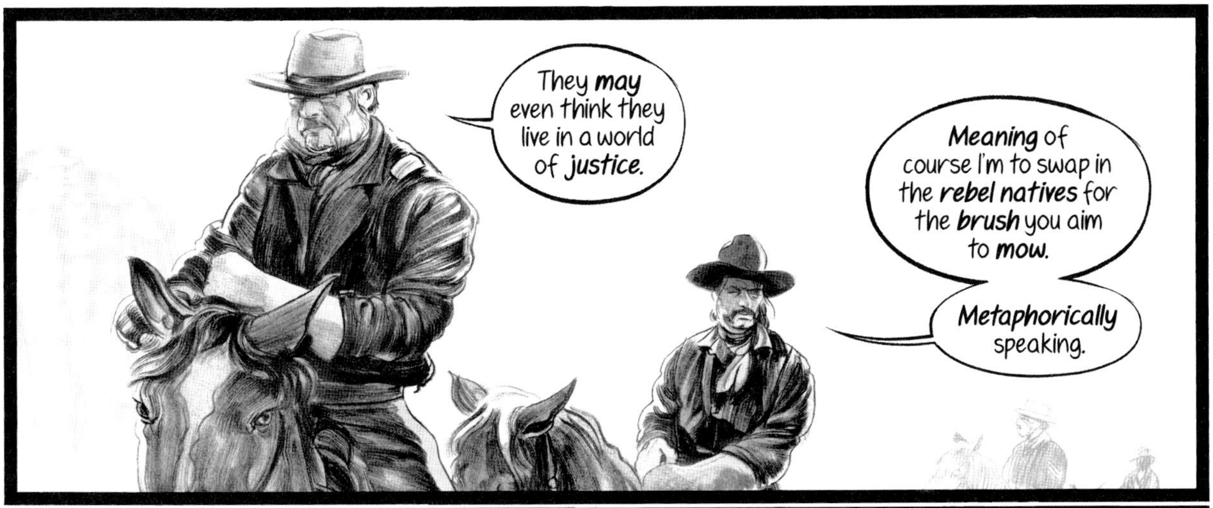
They **may** even think they live in a world of **justice.**
Meaning of course I'm to swap in the ***rebel natives*** for the ***brush*** you aim to ***mow.***
Metaphorically speaking.

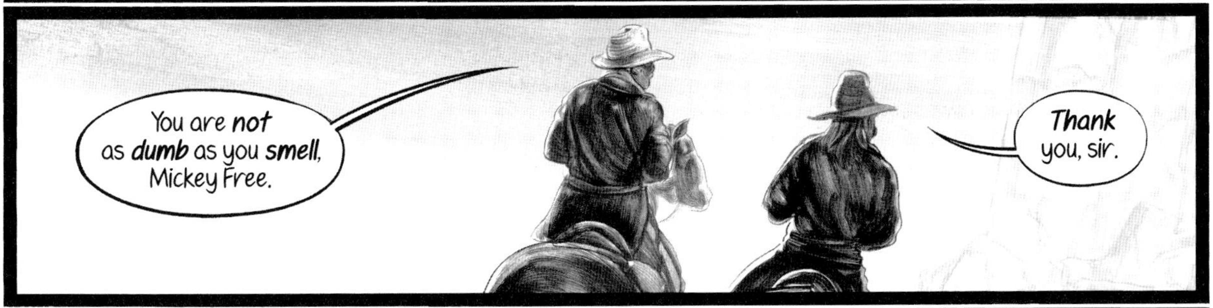
You are **not** as ***dumb*** as you **smell,** Mickey Free.
Thank you, sir.

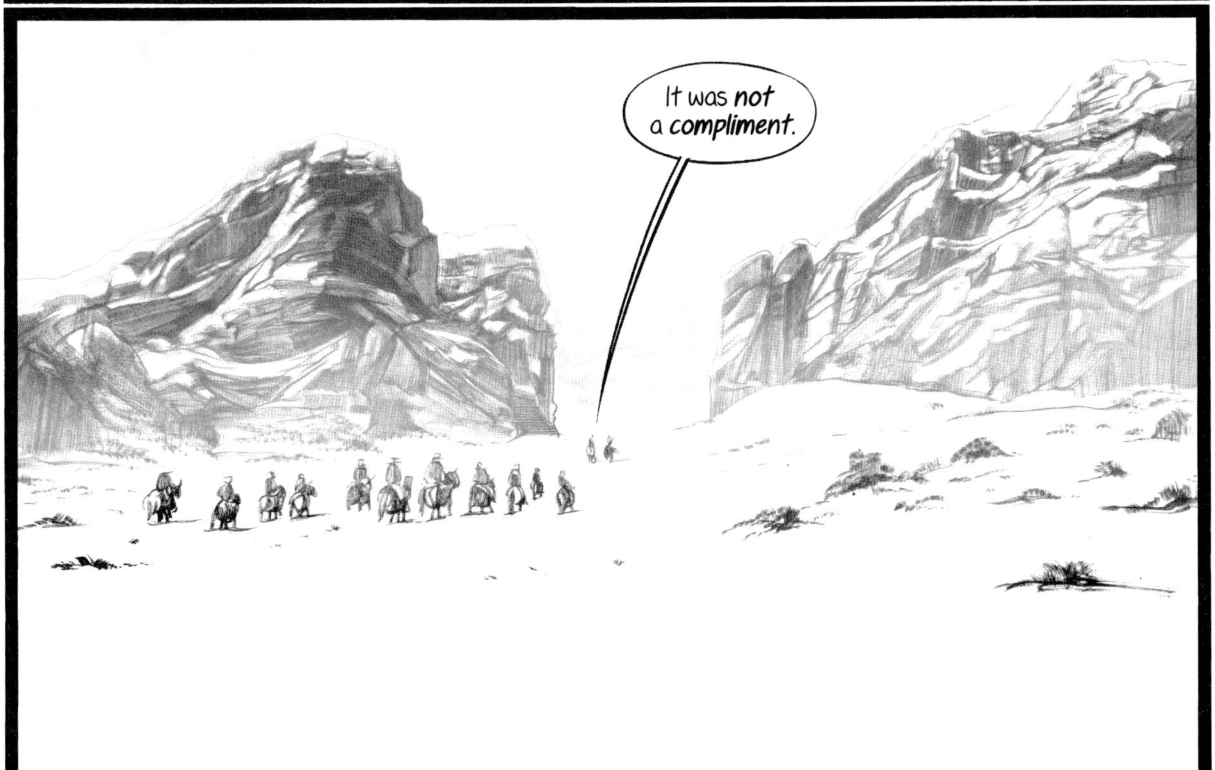
It was ***not*** a ***compliment.***

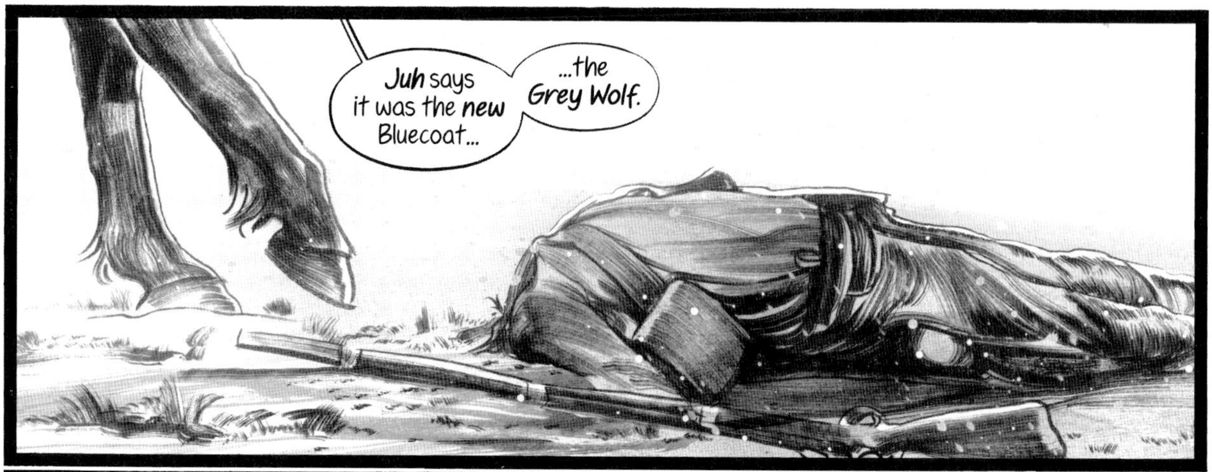
Juh says it was the new Bluecoat...
...the Grey Wolf.

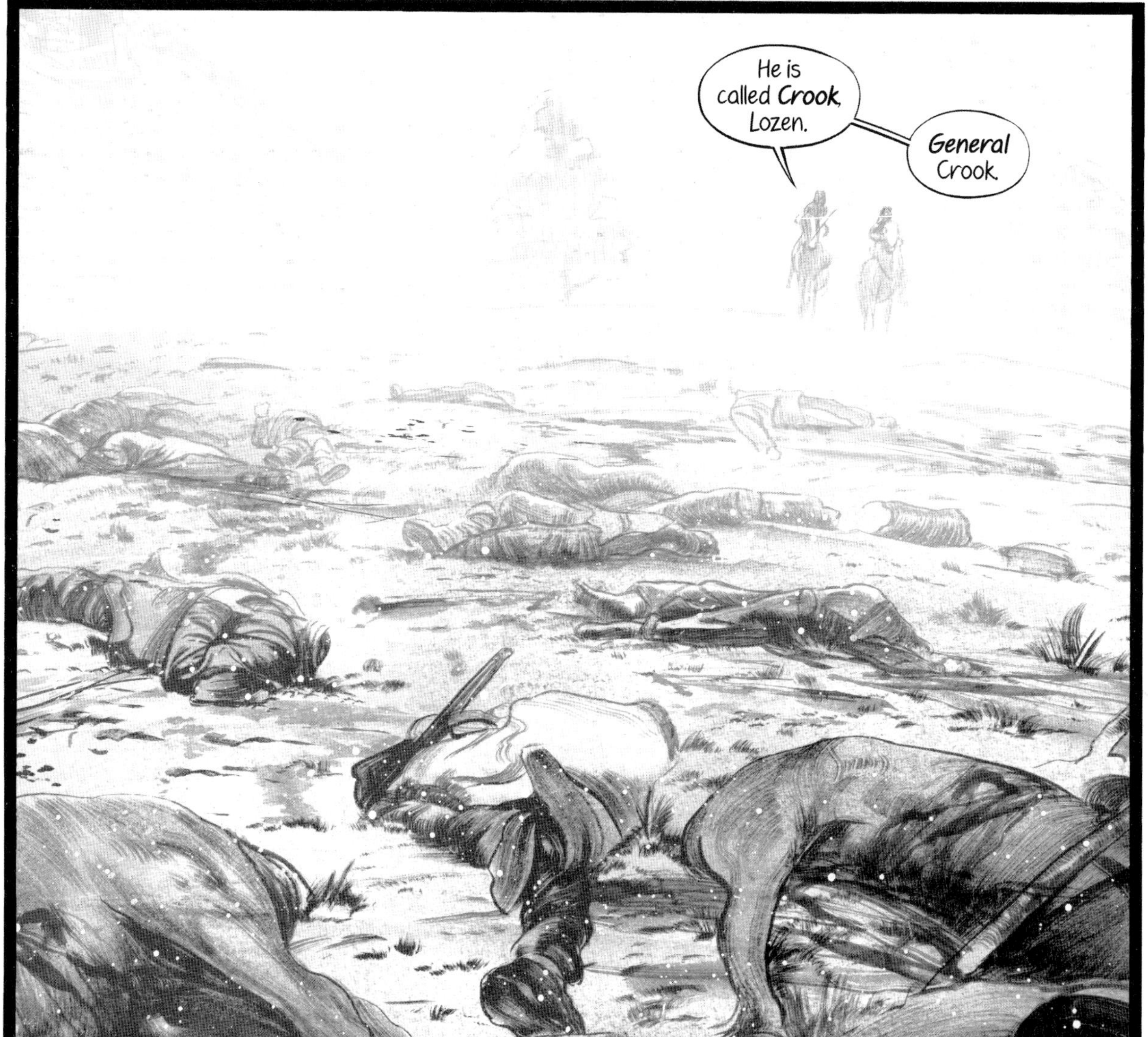
He is called Crook, Lozen.
General Crook.

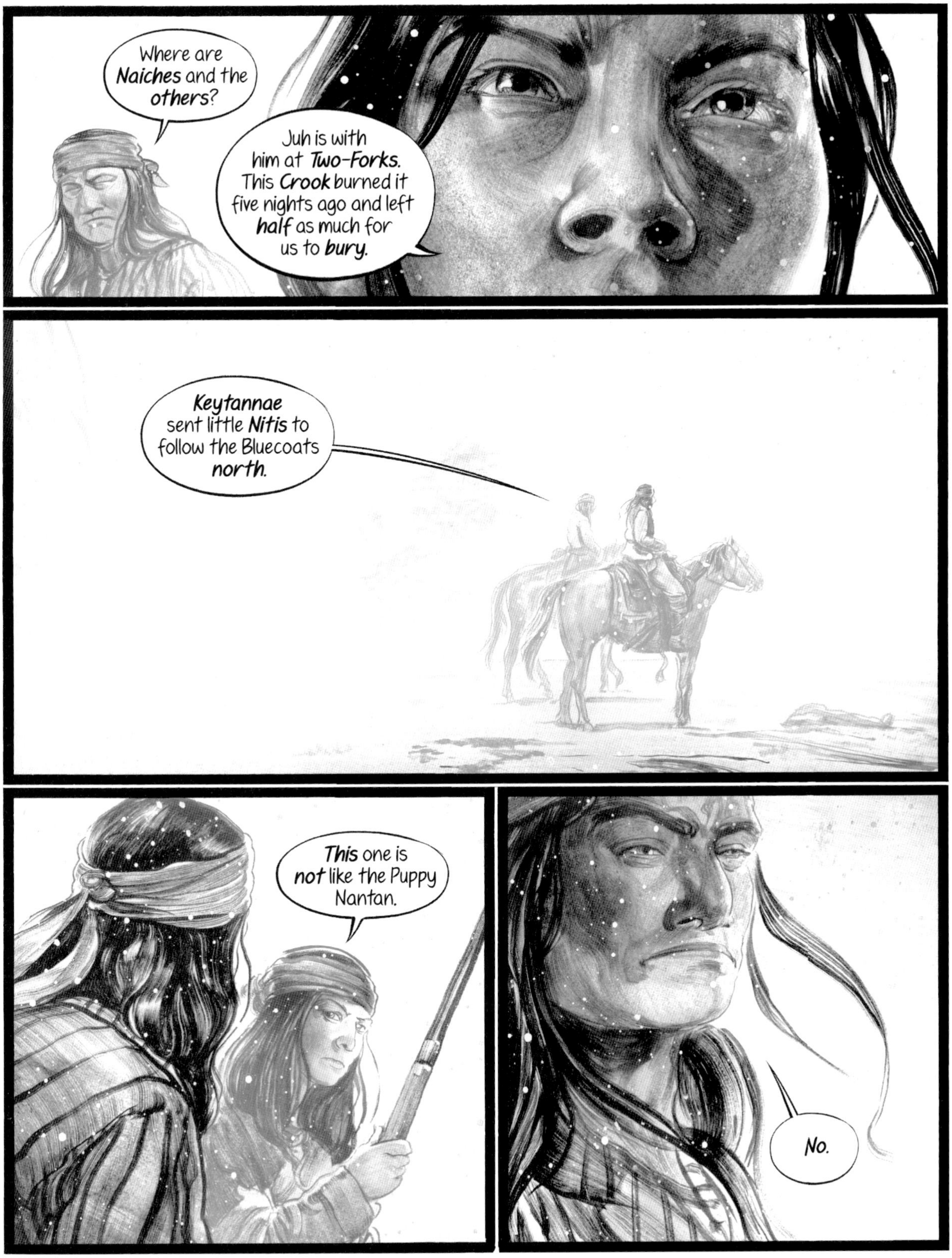
Where are Naiches and the others?
Juh is with him at Two-Forks. This Crook burned it five nights ago and left half as much for us to bury.
Keytannae sent little Nitis to follow the Bluecoats north.
This one is not like the Puppy Nantan.
No.

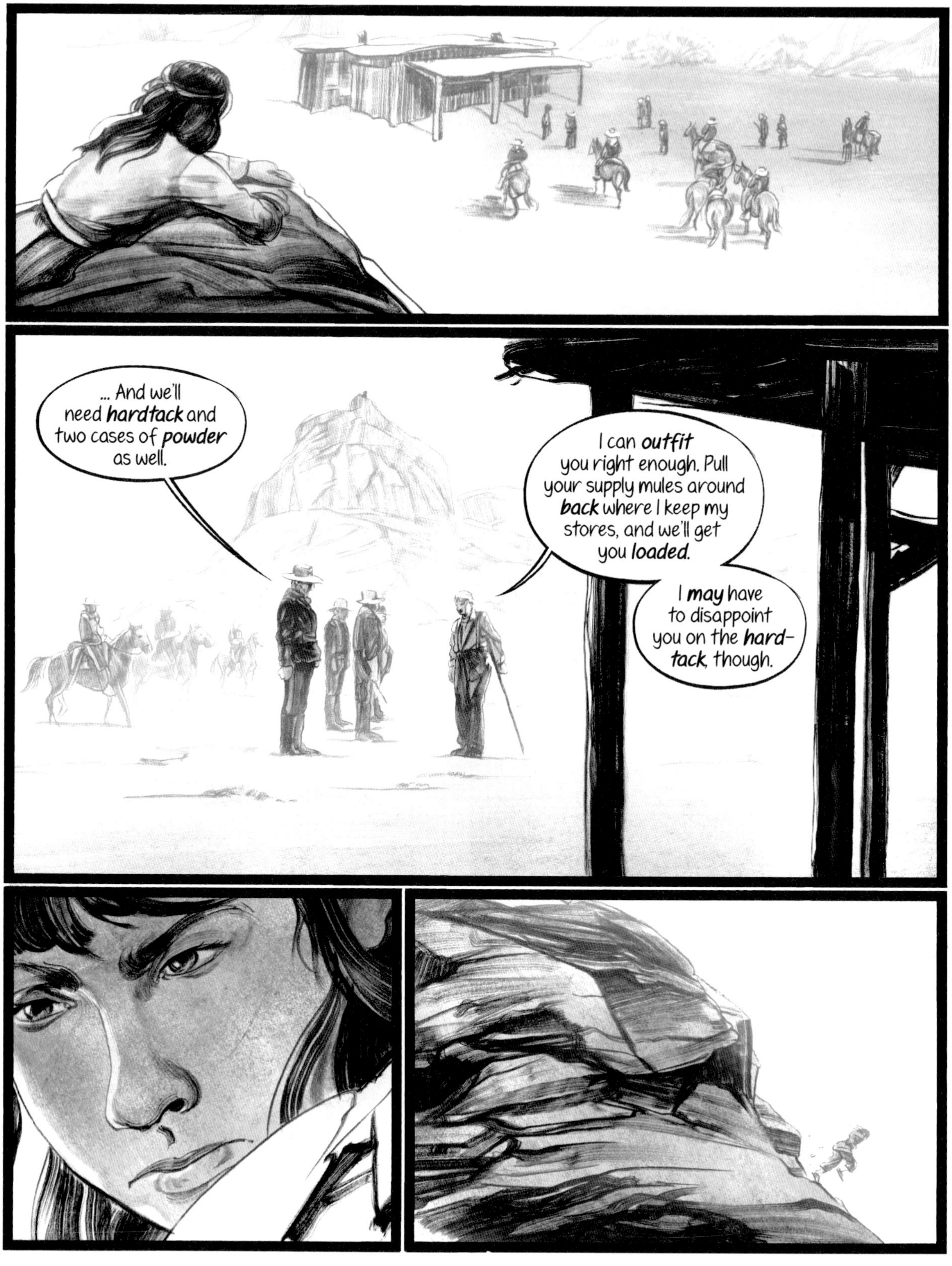
... And we'll need **hardtack** and two cases of **powder** as well.
I can **outfit** you right enough. Pull your supply **mules** around **back** where I keep my stores, and we'll get you **loaded**.
I **may** have to disappoint you on the **hard-tack**, though.

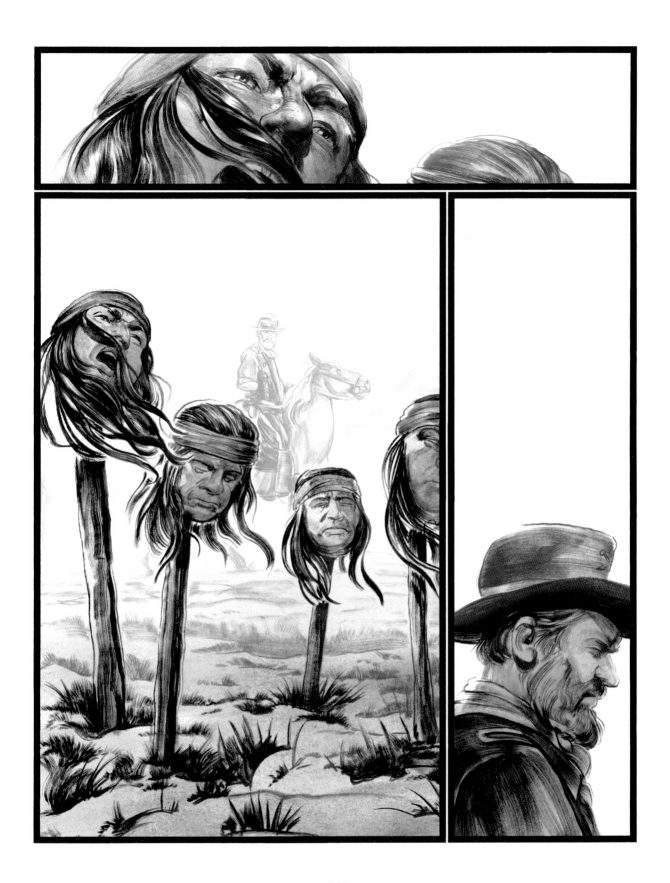

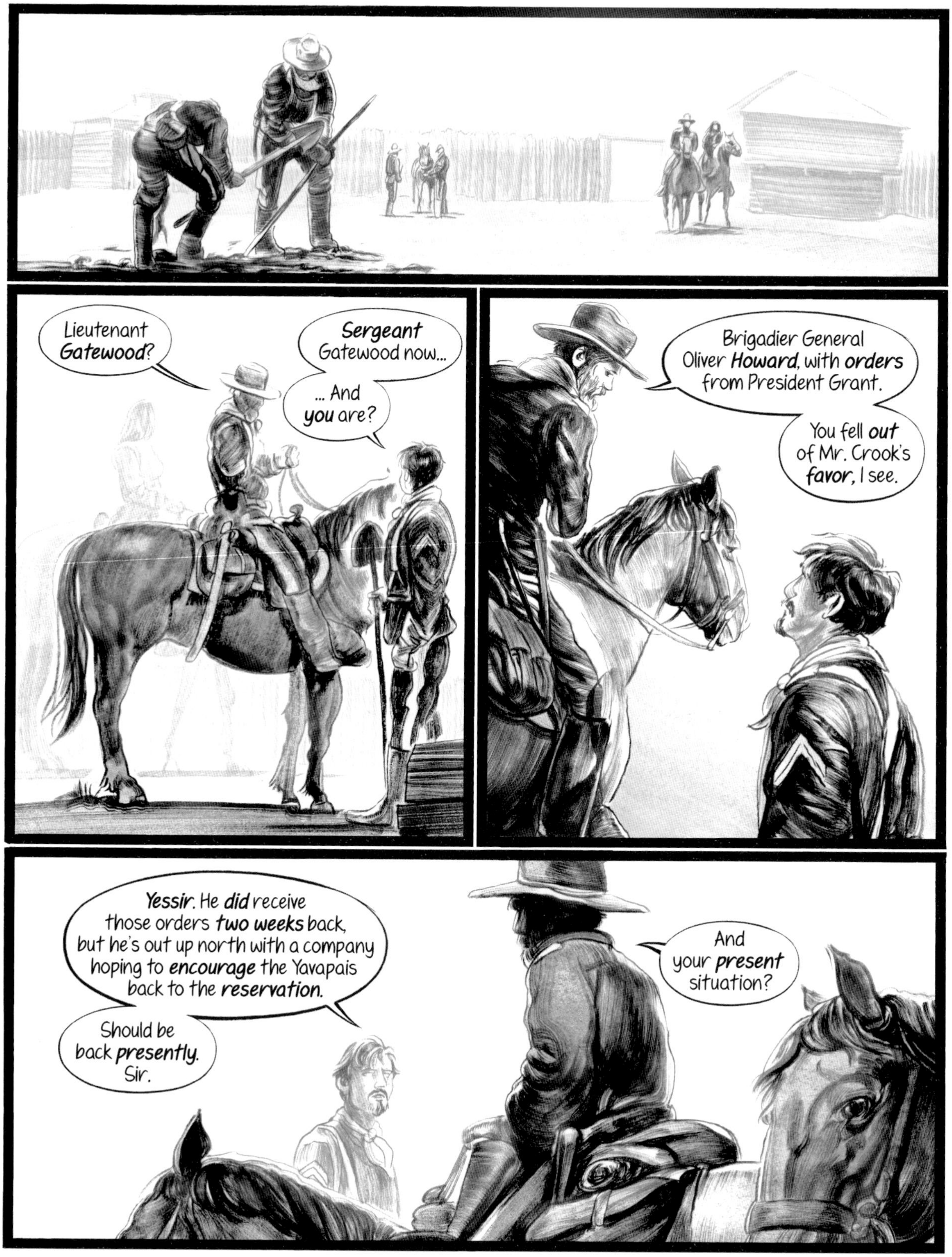
Lieutenant Gatewood?
Sergeant Gatewood now...
... And you are?
Brigadier General Oliver Howard, with orders from President Grant.
You fell out of Mr. Crook's favor, I see.
Yessir. He did receive those orders two weeks back, but he's out up north with a company hoping to encourage the Yavapais back to the reservation.
Should be back presently. Sir.
And your present situation?

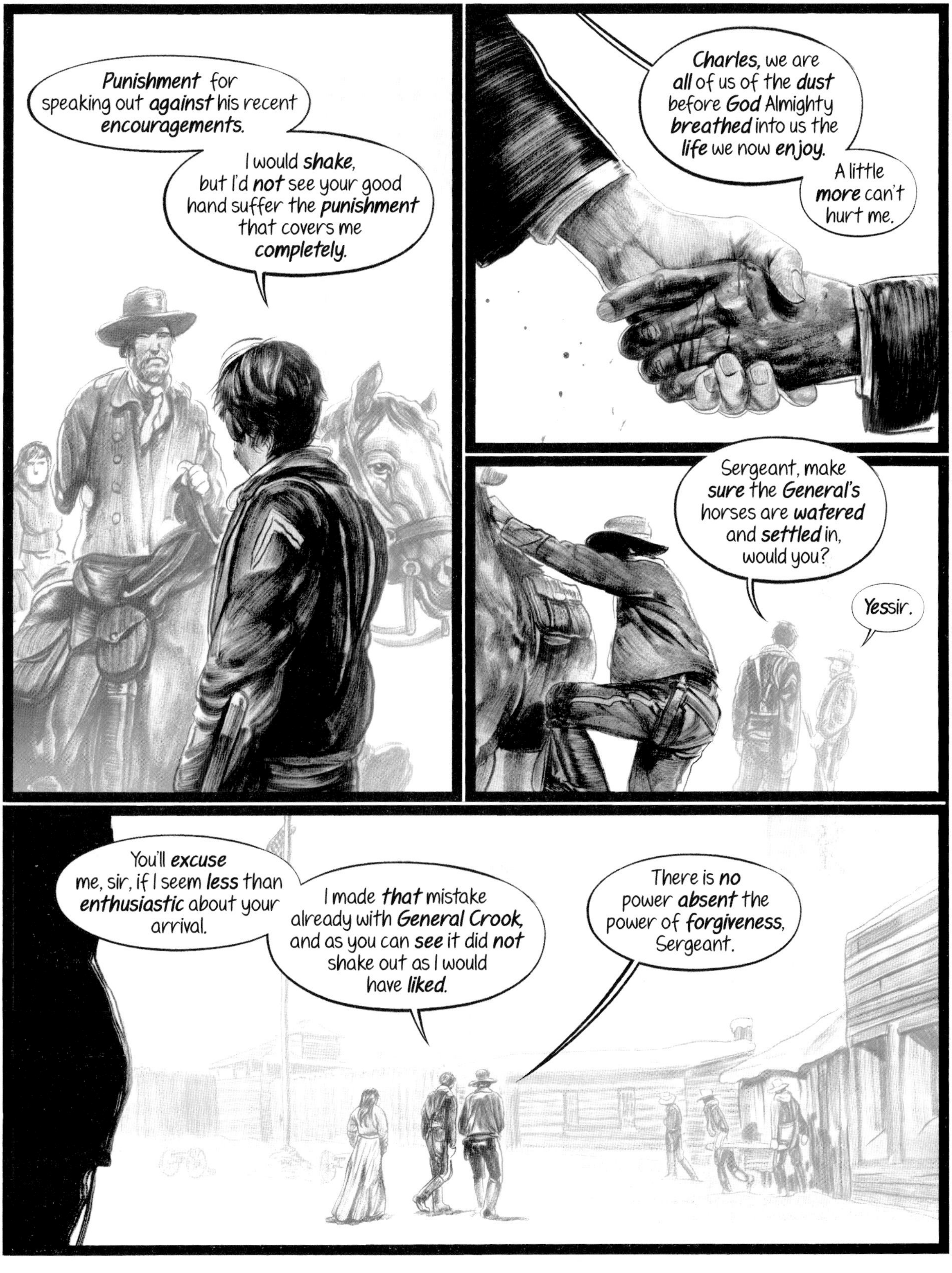
Punishment for speaking out against his recent encouragements.
I would shake, but I'd not see your good hand suffer the punishment that covers me completely.
Charles, we are all of us of the dust before God Almighty breathed into us the life we now enjoy.
A little more can't hurt me.
Sergeant, make sure the General's horses are watered and settled in, would you?
Yessir.
You'll excuse me, sir, if I seem less than enthusiastic about your arrival.
I made that mistake already with General Crook, and as you can see it did not shake out as I would have liked.
There is no power absent the power of forgiveness, Sergeant.

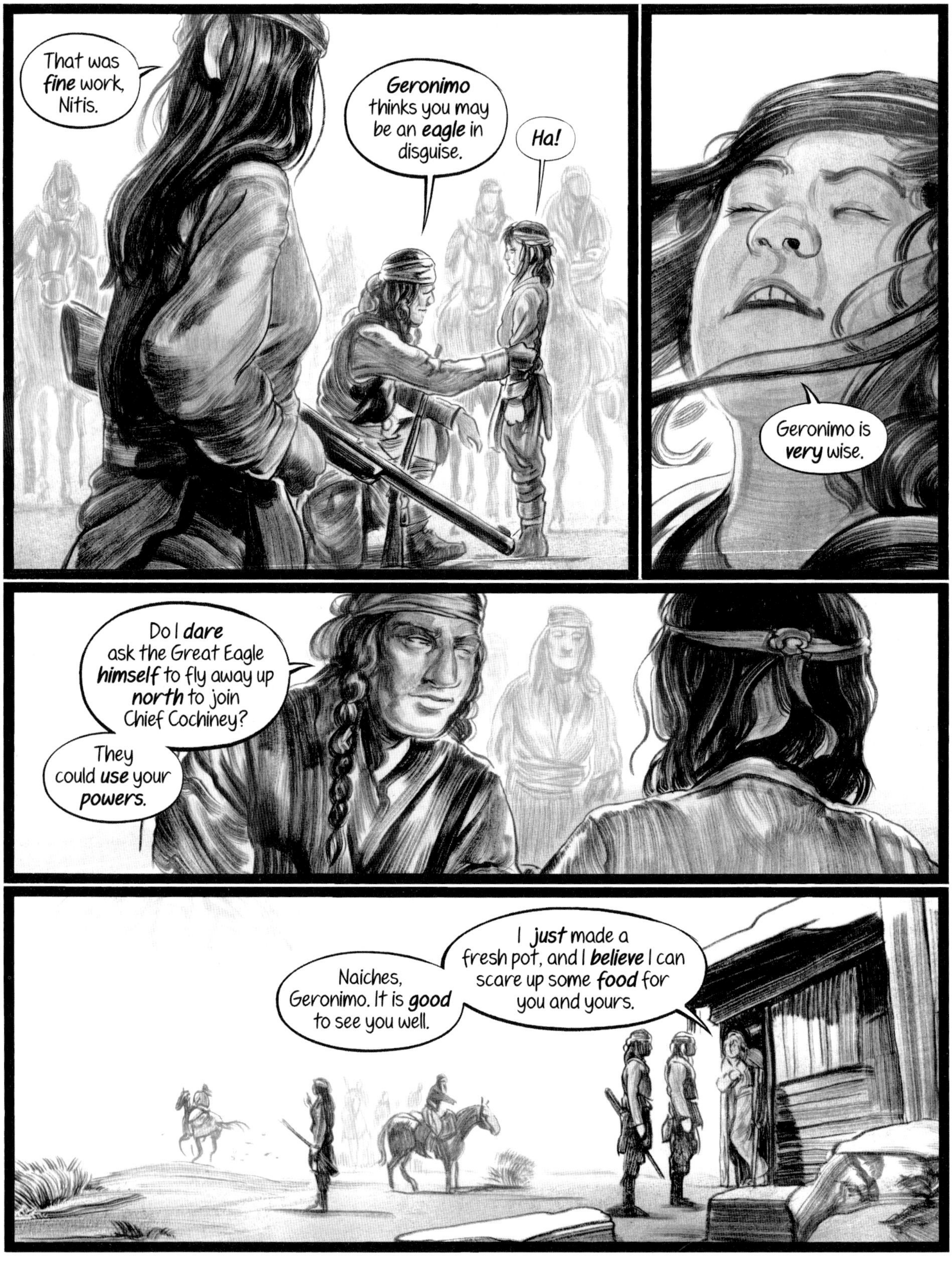
That was fine work, Nitis.
Geronimo thinks you may be an eagle in disguise.
Ha!
Geronimo is very wise.
Do I dare ask the Great Eagle himself to fly away up north to join Chief Cochiney?
They could use your powers.
Naiches, Geronimo. It is good to see you well.
I just made a fresh pot, and I believe I can scare up some food for you and yours.

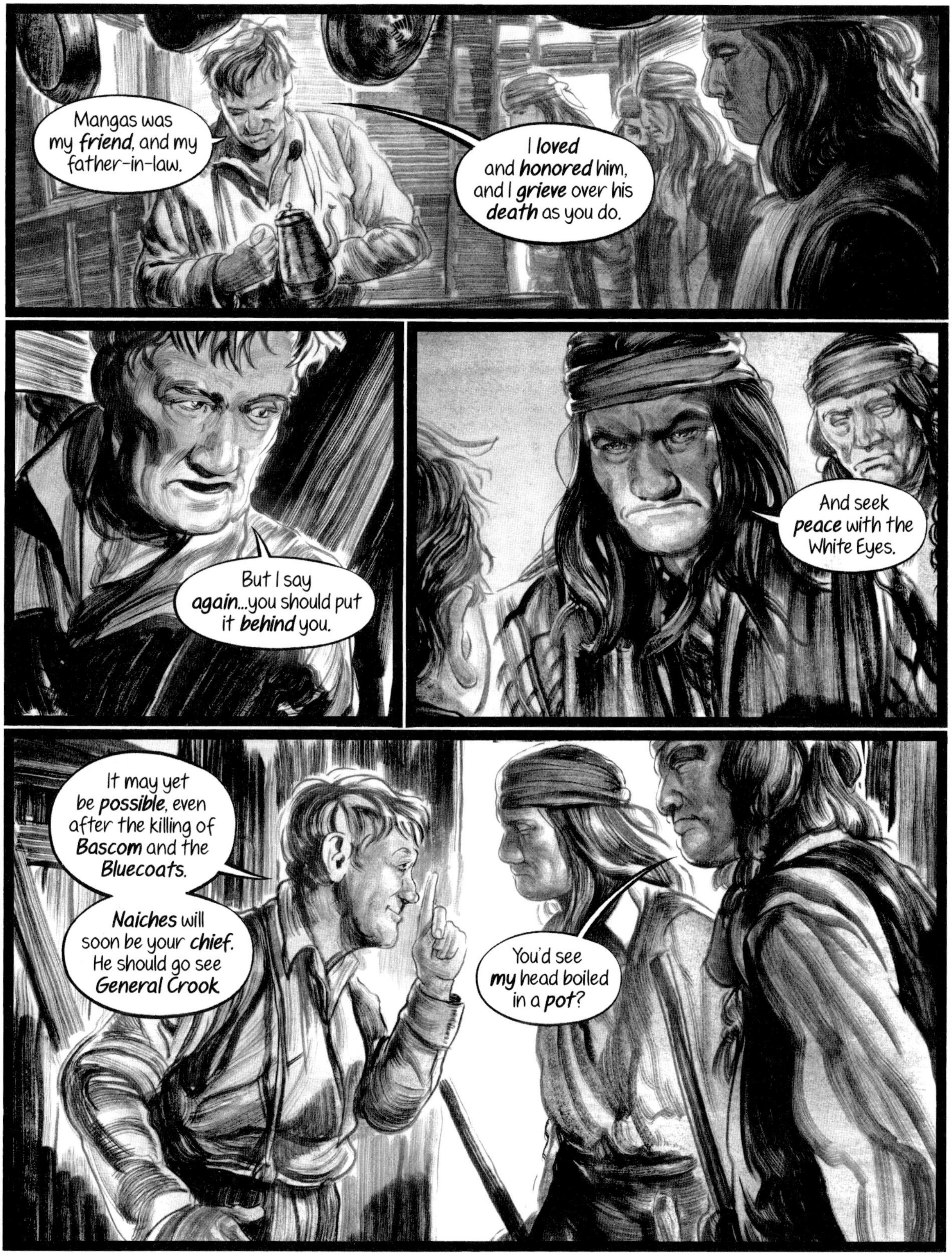
Mangas was my *friend*, and my father-in-law.
I *loved* and *honored* him, and I *grieve* over his *death* as you do.
But I say *again*...you should put it *behind* you.
And seek *peace* with the White Eyes.
It may yet be *possible*, even after the killing of *Bascom* and the *Bluecoats*.
Naiches will soon be your *chief*. He should go see *General Crook*
You'd see *my* head boiled in a *pot*?

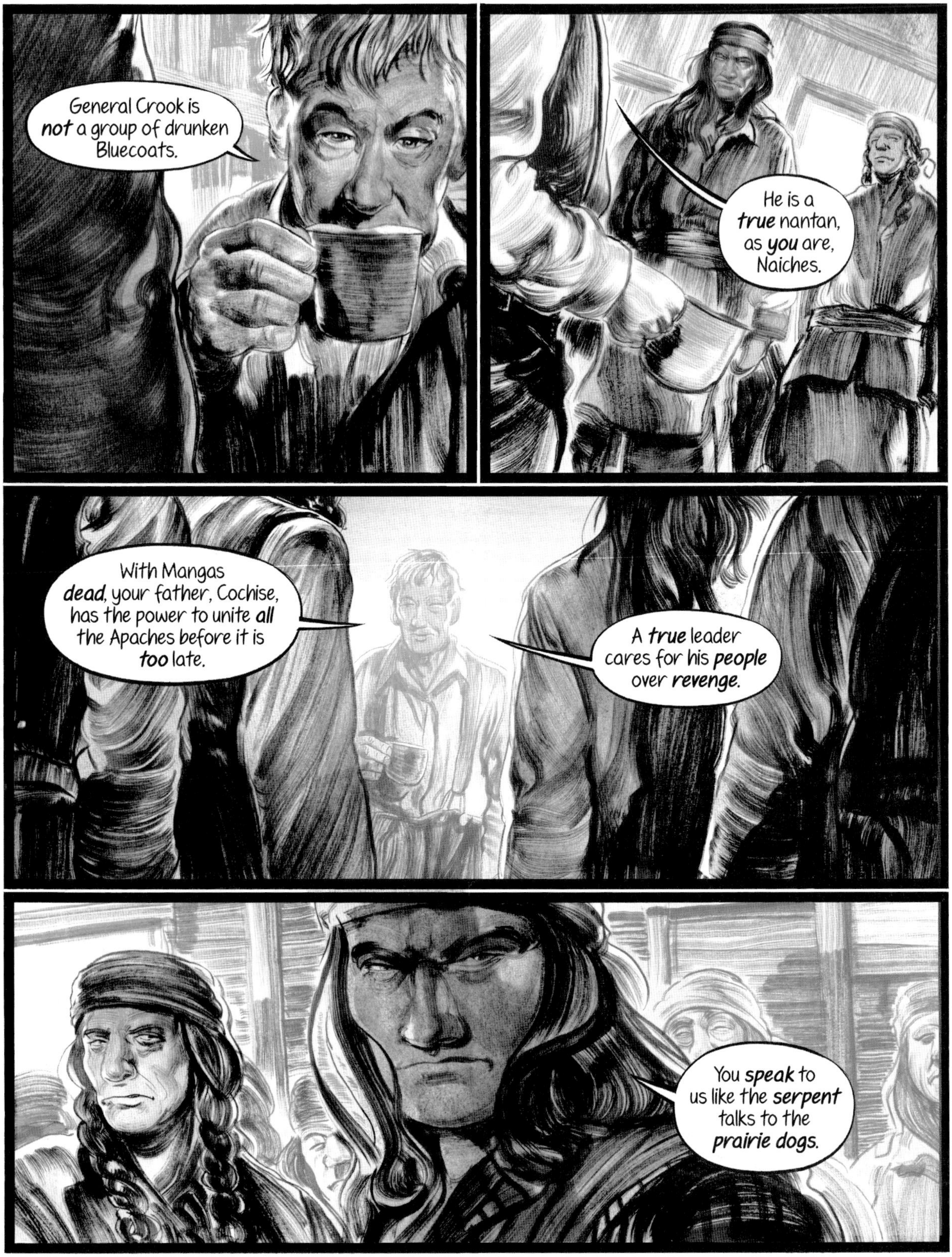
General Crook is **not** a group of drunken Bluecoats.
He is a **true** nantan, as **you** are, Naiches.
With Mangas **dead**, your father, Cochise, has the power to unite **all** the Apaches before it is **too** late.
A **true** leader cares for his **people** over **revenge**.
You **speak** to us like the **serpent** talks to the **prairie dogs**.

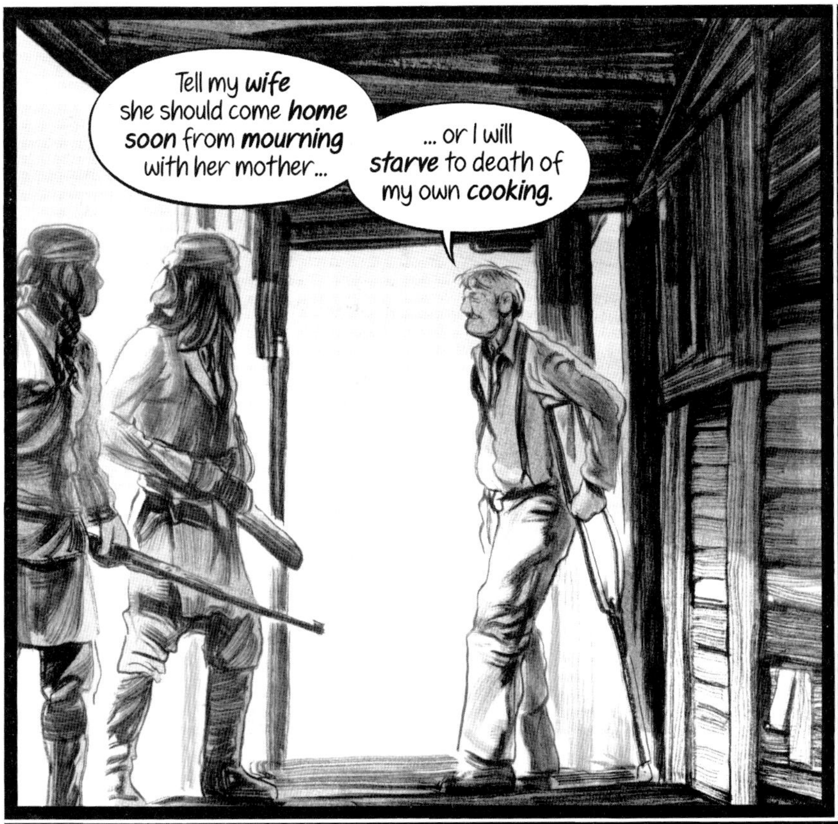
Tell my **wife** she should come **home soon** from **mourning** with her mother...
... or I will **starve** to death of my own **cooking**.

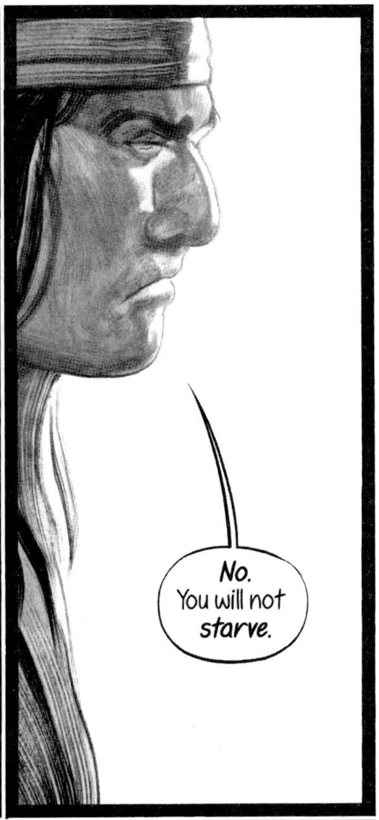
No. You will not **starve**.

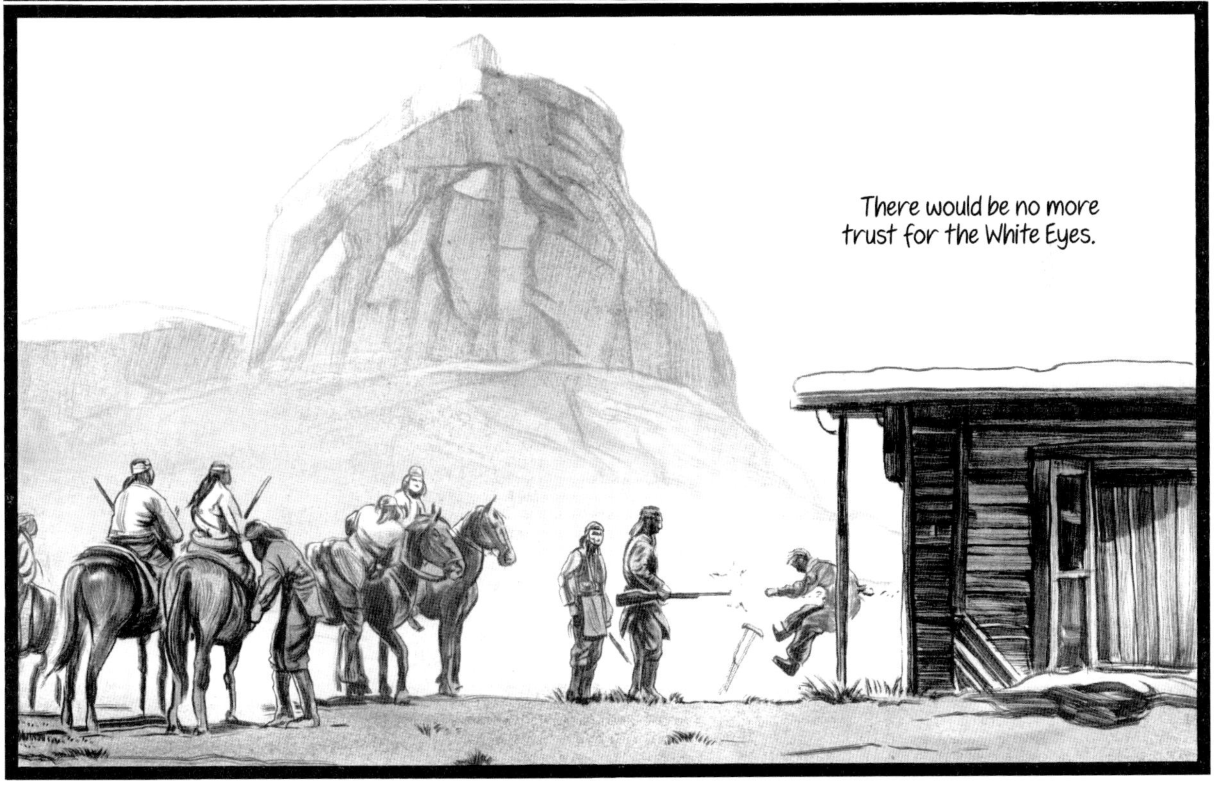
There would be no more trust for the White Eyes.

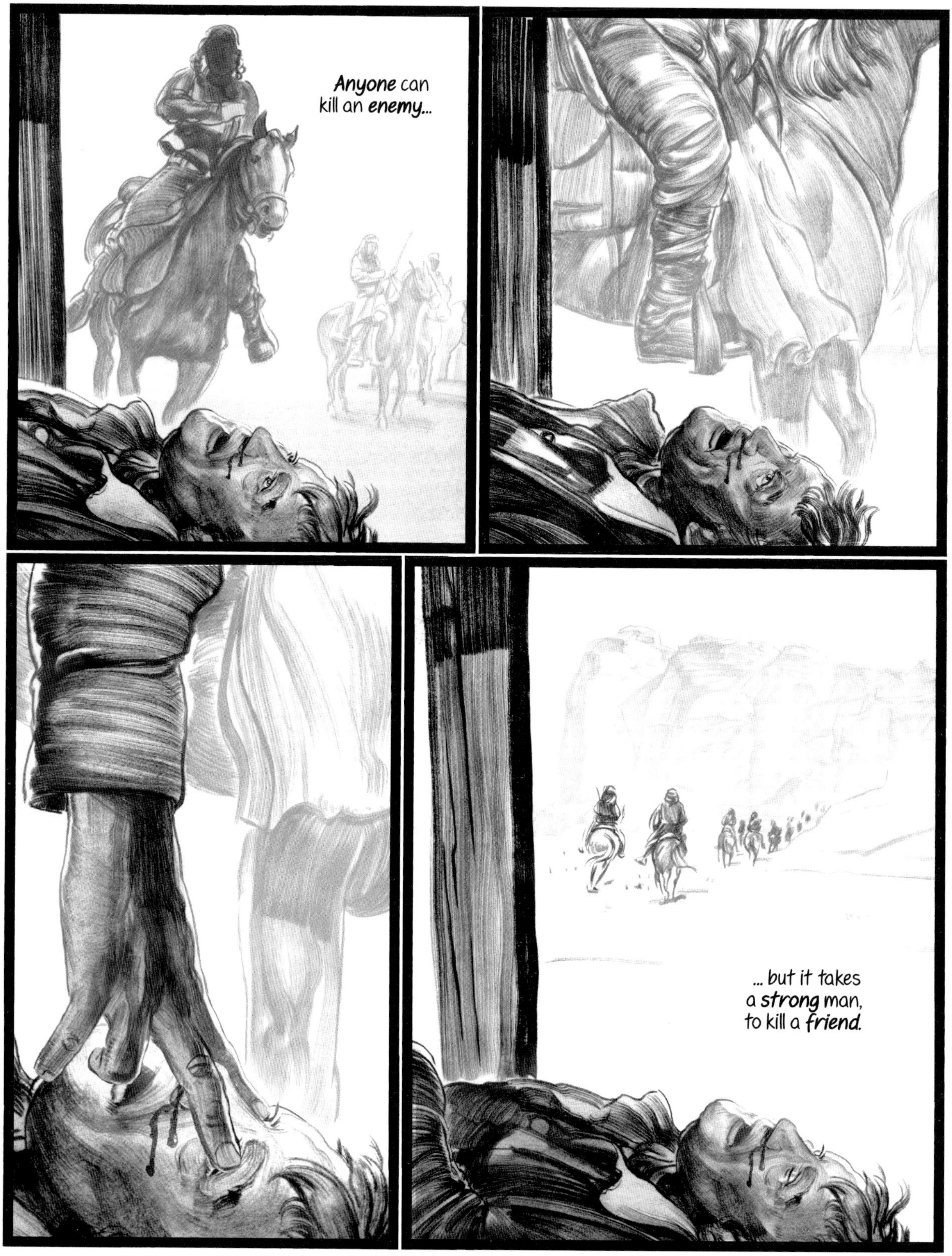
Anyone can kill an enemy...
... but it takes a strong man, to kill a friend.

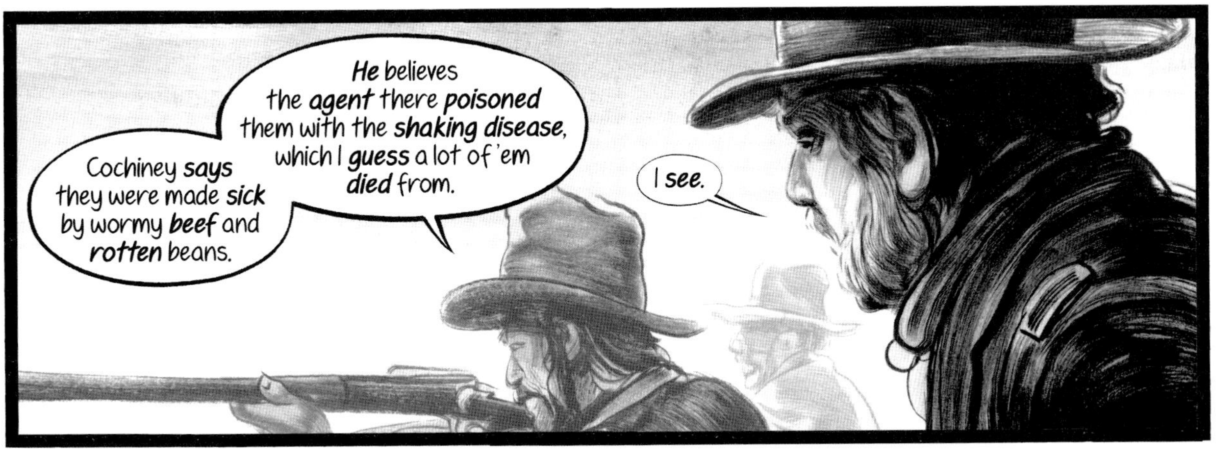
Cochiney says they were made sick by wormy beef and rotten beans.
He believes the agent there poisoned them with the shaking disease, which I guess a lot of 'em died from.
I see.

SKELETON CAVE • ARIZONA

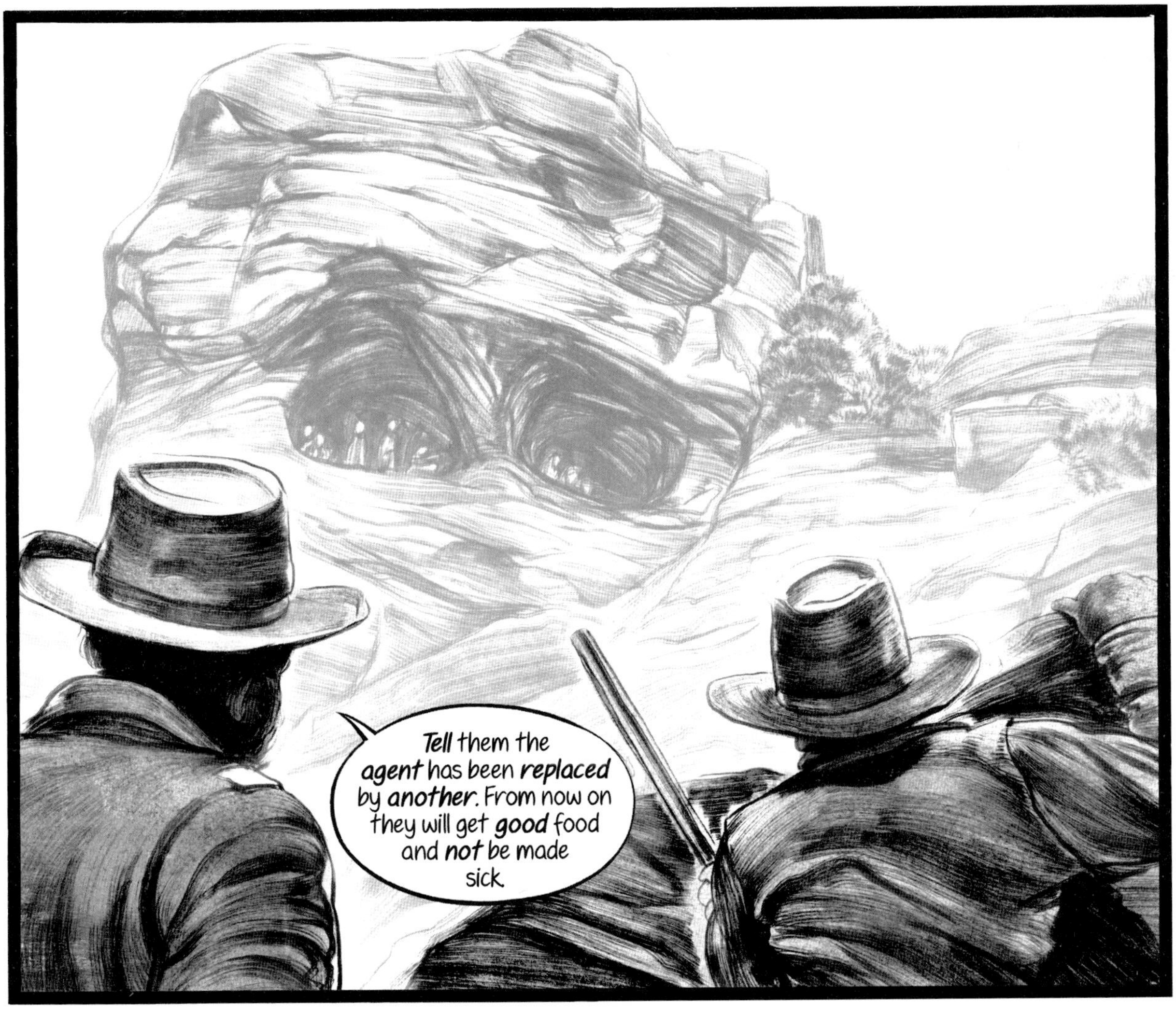
Tell them the agent has been replaced by another. From now on they will get good food and not be made sick.

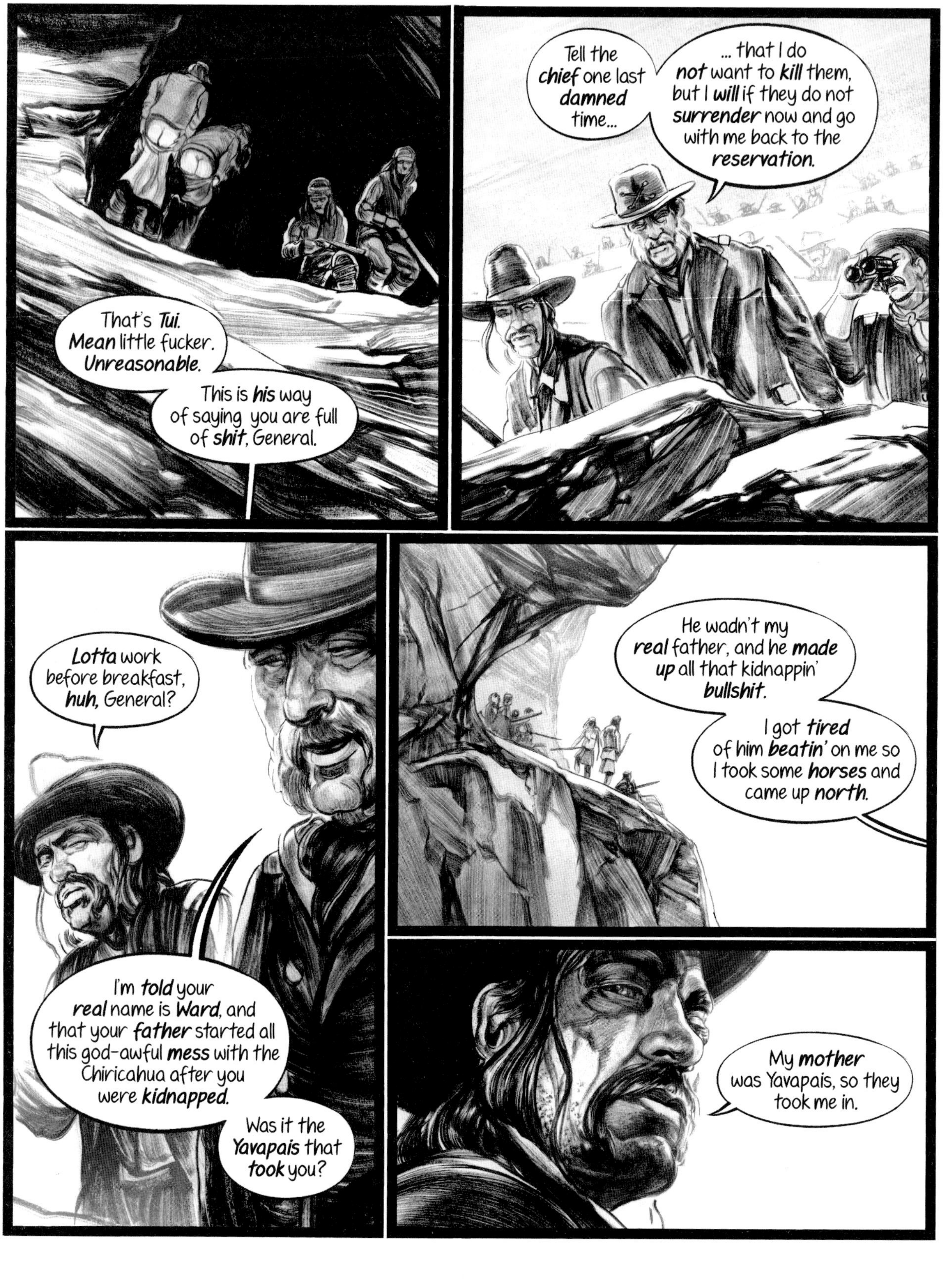
That's Tui. Mean little fucker. Unreasonable.
This is his way of saying you are full of shit, General.
Tell the chief one last damned time...
... that I do not want to kill them, but I will if they do not surrender now and go with me back to the reservation.
Lotta work before breakfast, huh, General?
I'm told your real name is Ward, and that your father started all this god-awful mess with the Chiricahua after you were kidnapped.
Was it the Yavapais that took you?
He wadn't my real father, and he made up all that kidnappin' bullshit.
I got tired of him beatin' on me so I took some horses and came up north.
My mother was Yavapais, so they took me in.

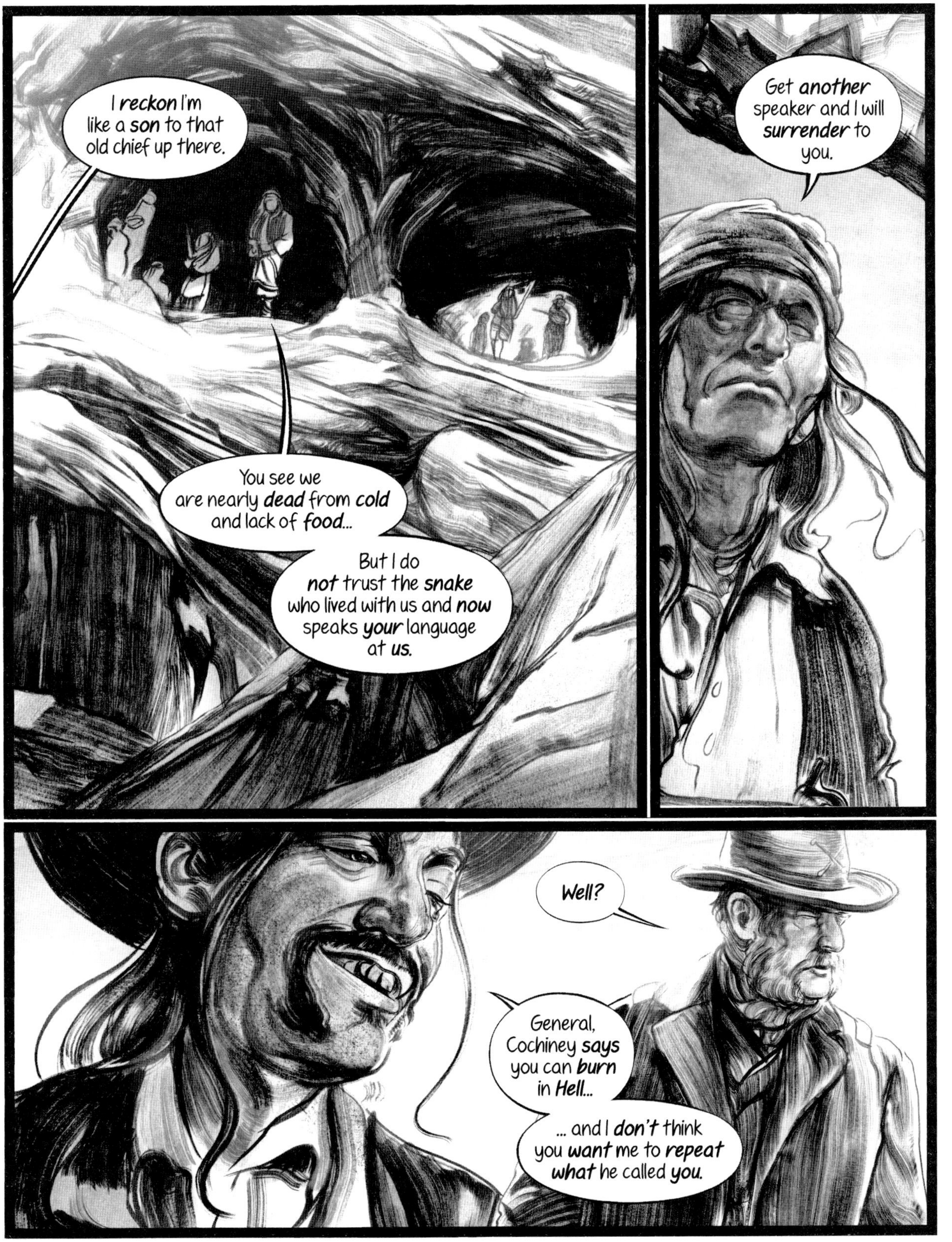

I reckon I'm like a son to that old chief up there.
You see we are nearly dead from cold and lack of food...
But I do not trust the snake who lived with us and now speaks your language at us.
Get another speaker and I will surrender to you.
Well?
General, Cochiney says you can burn in Hell...
... and I don't think you want me to repeat what he called you.

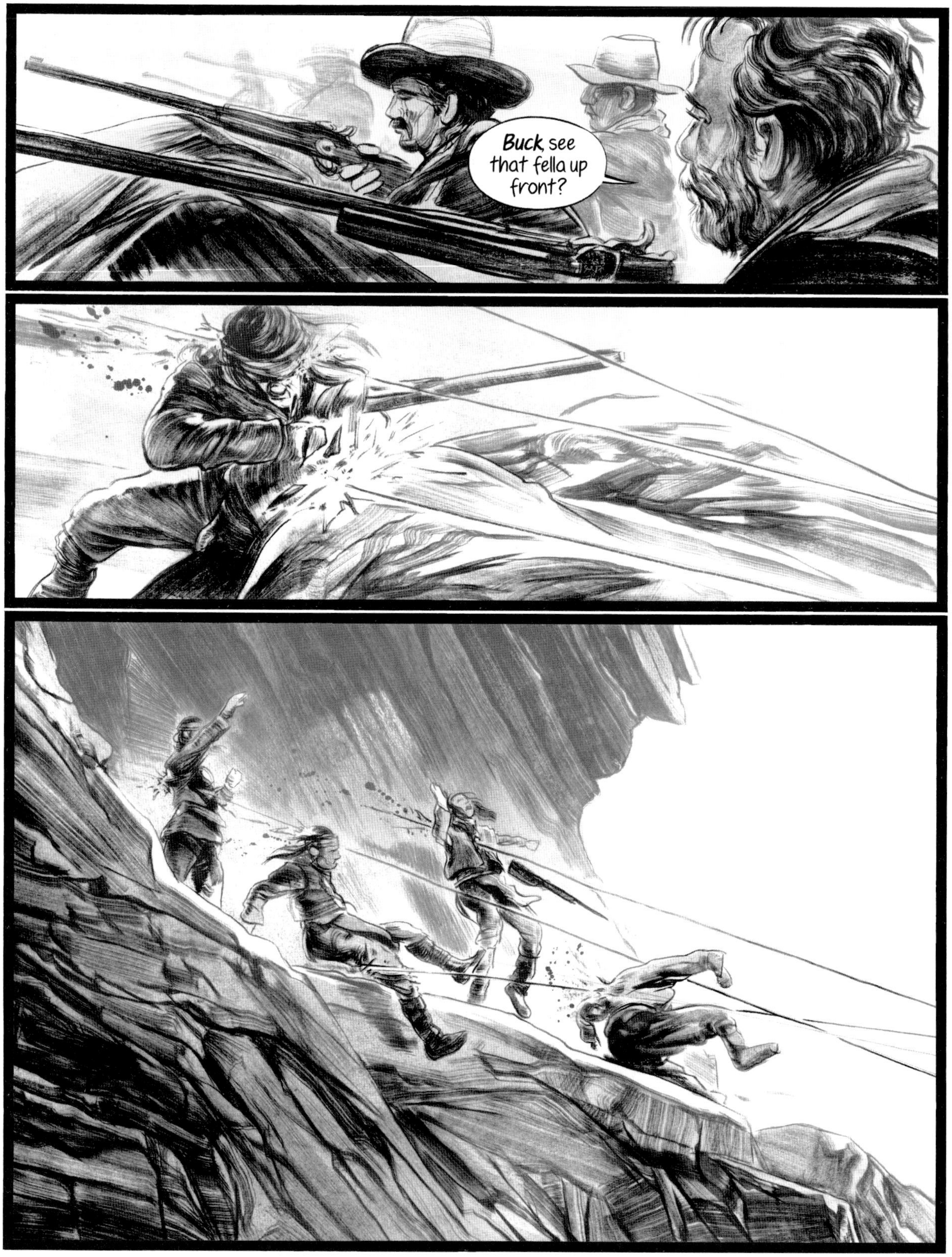
Buck, see that fella up front?

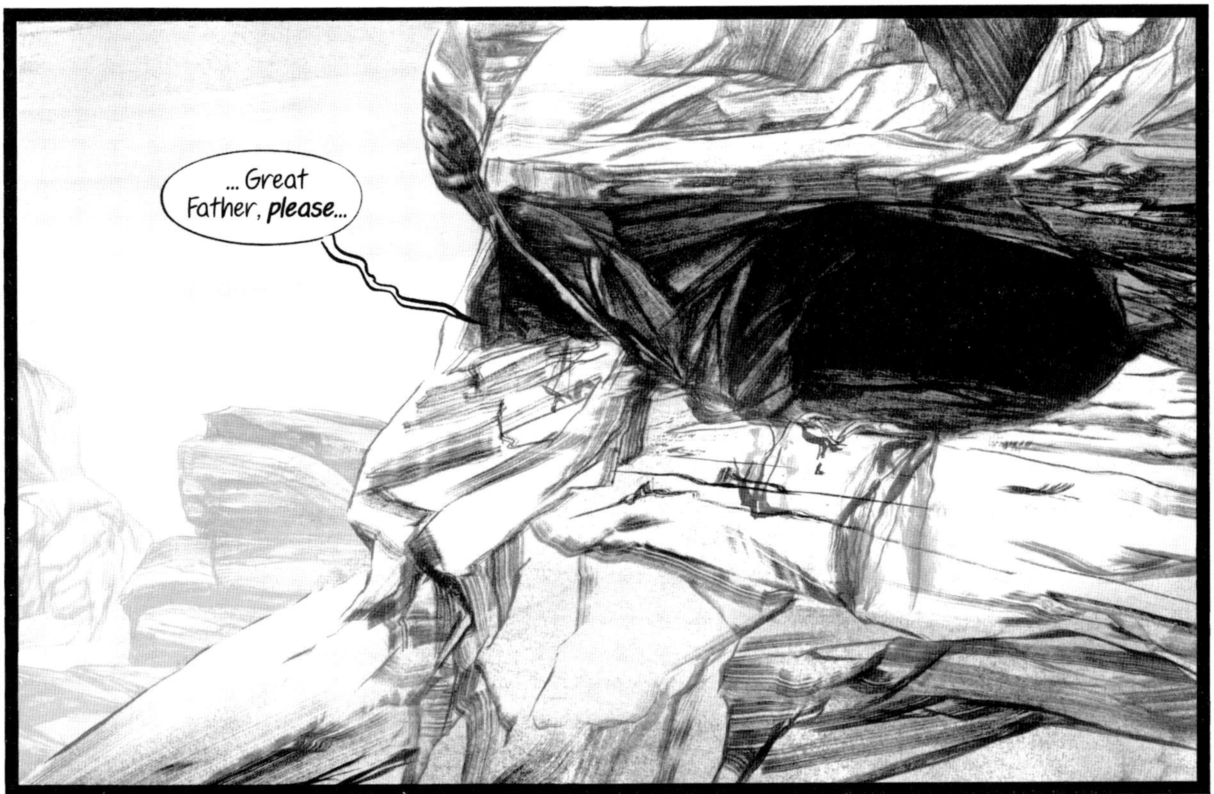
... Great Father, please...

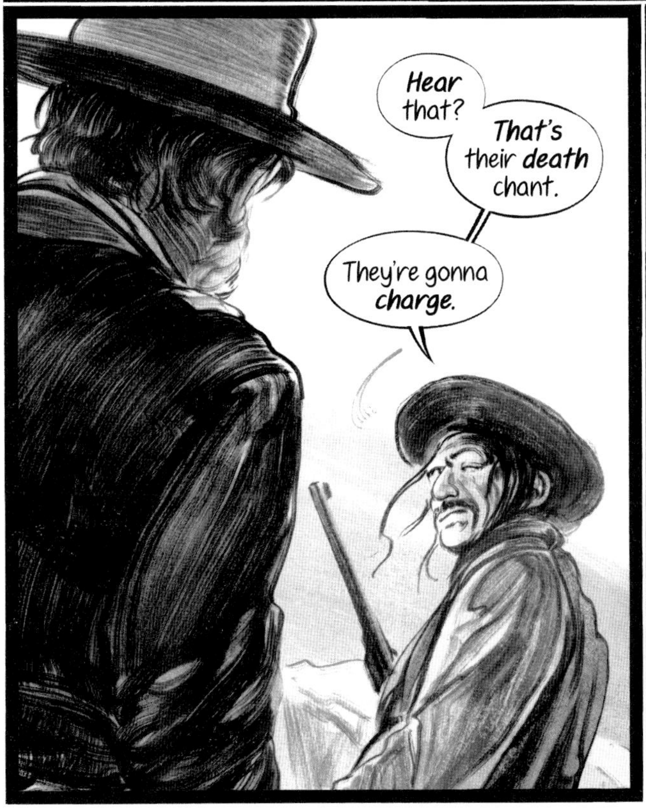
Hear that?
That's their death chant.
They're gonna charge.

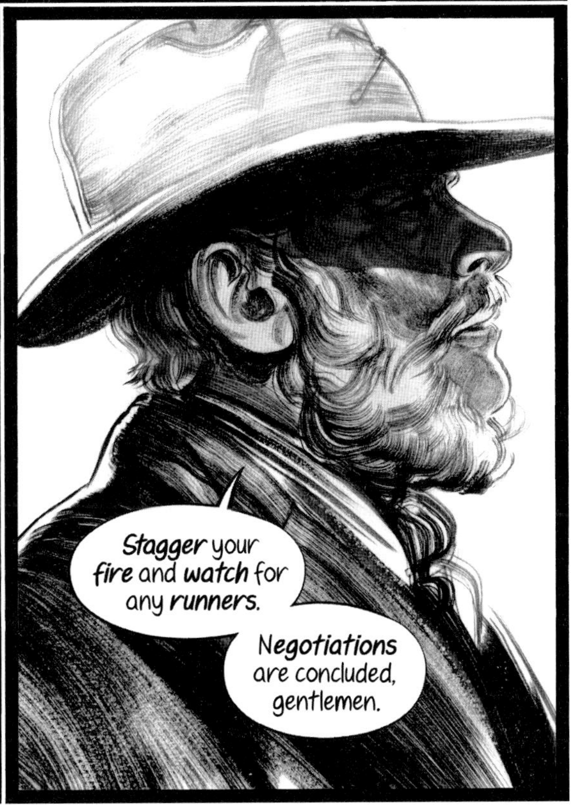
Stagger your fire and watch for any runners.
Negotiations are concluded, gentlemen.

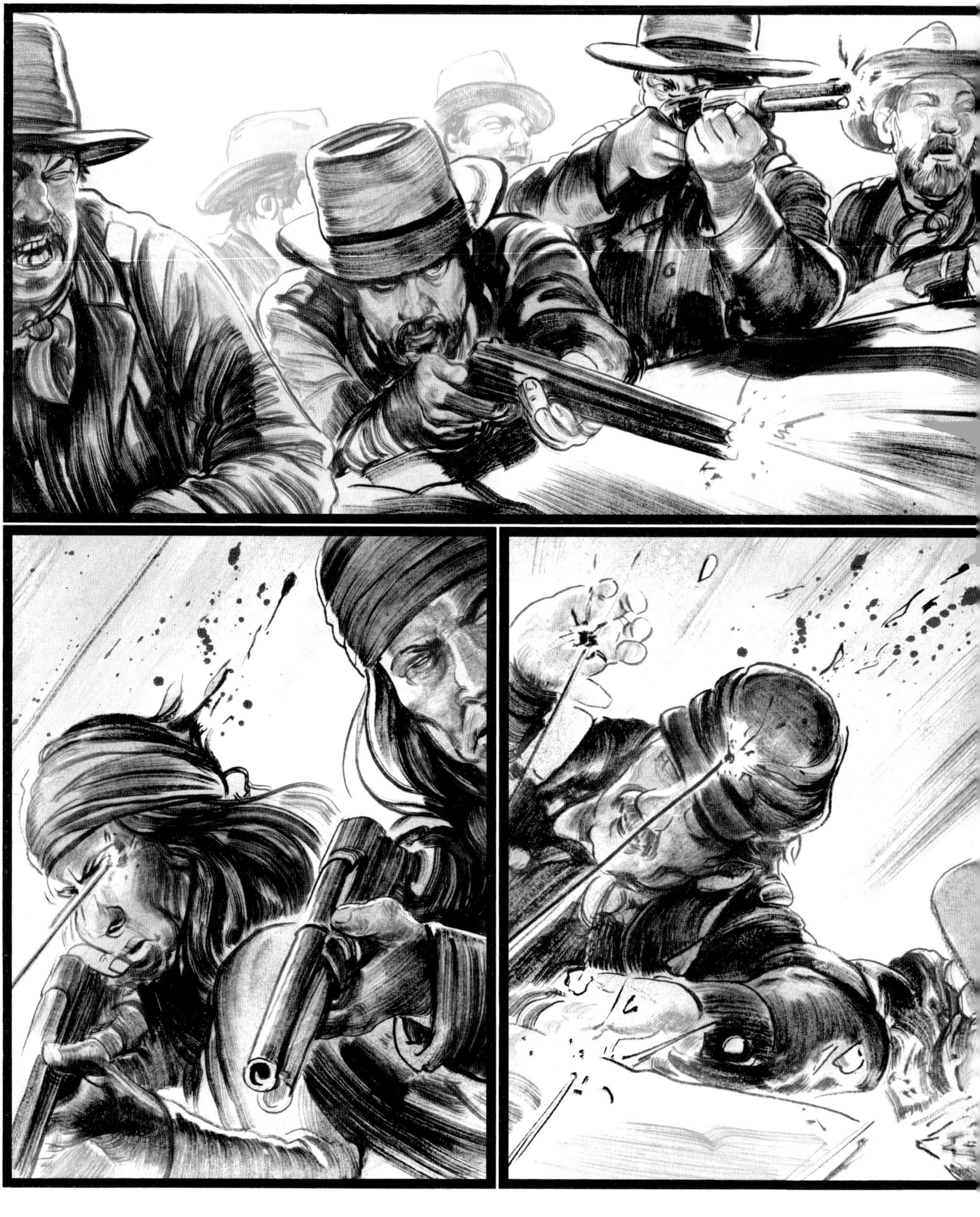

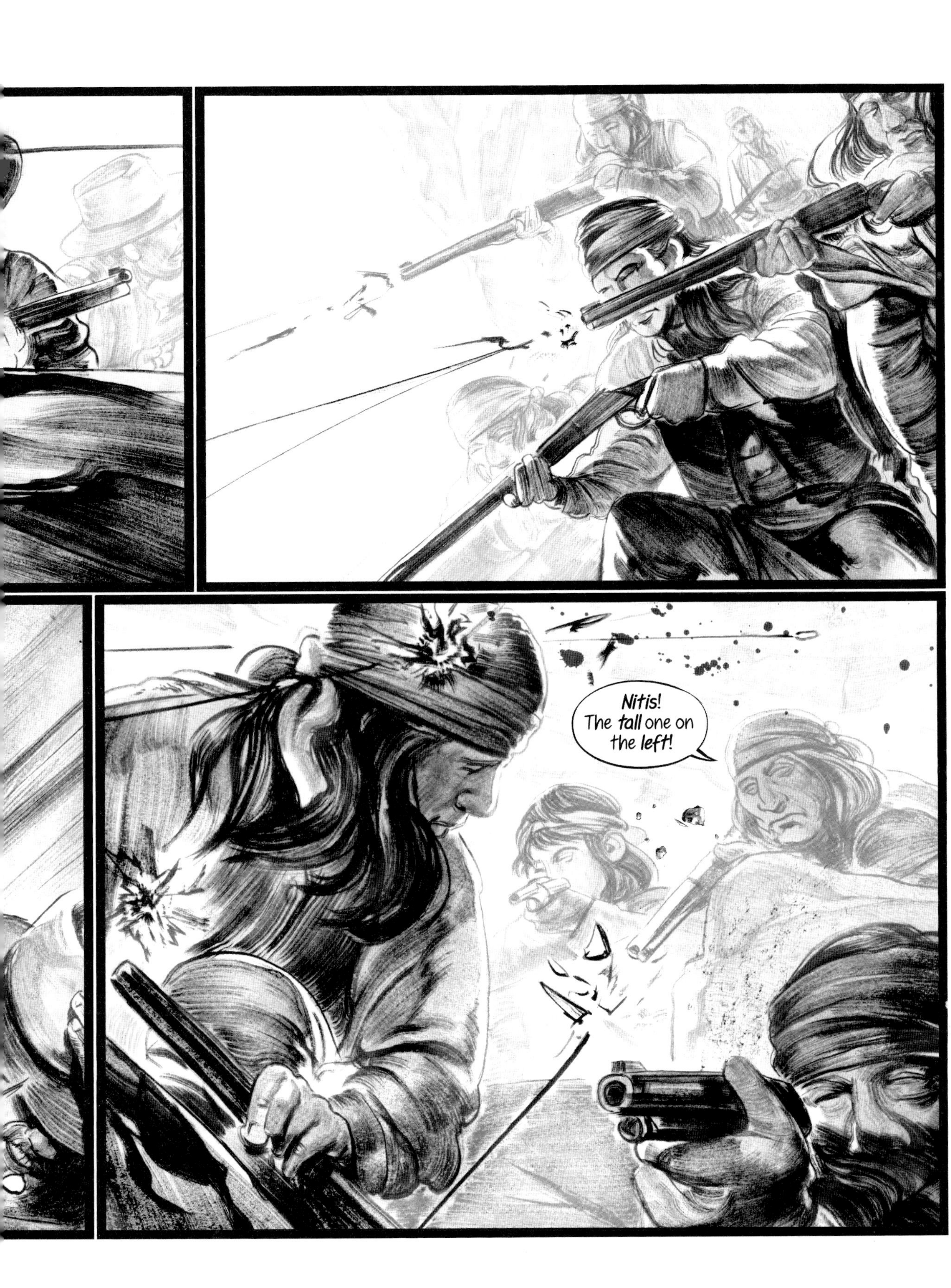
Nitis! The tall one on the left!

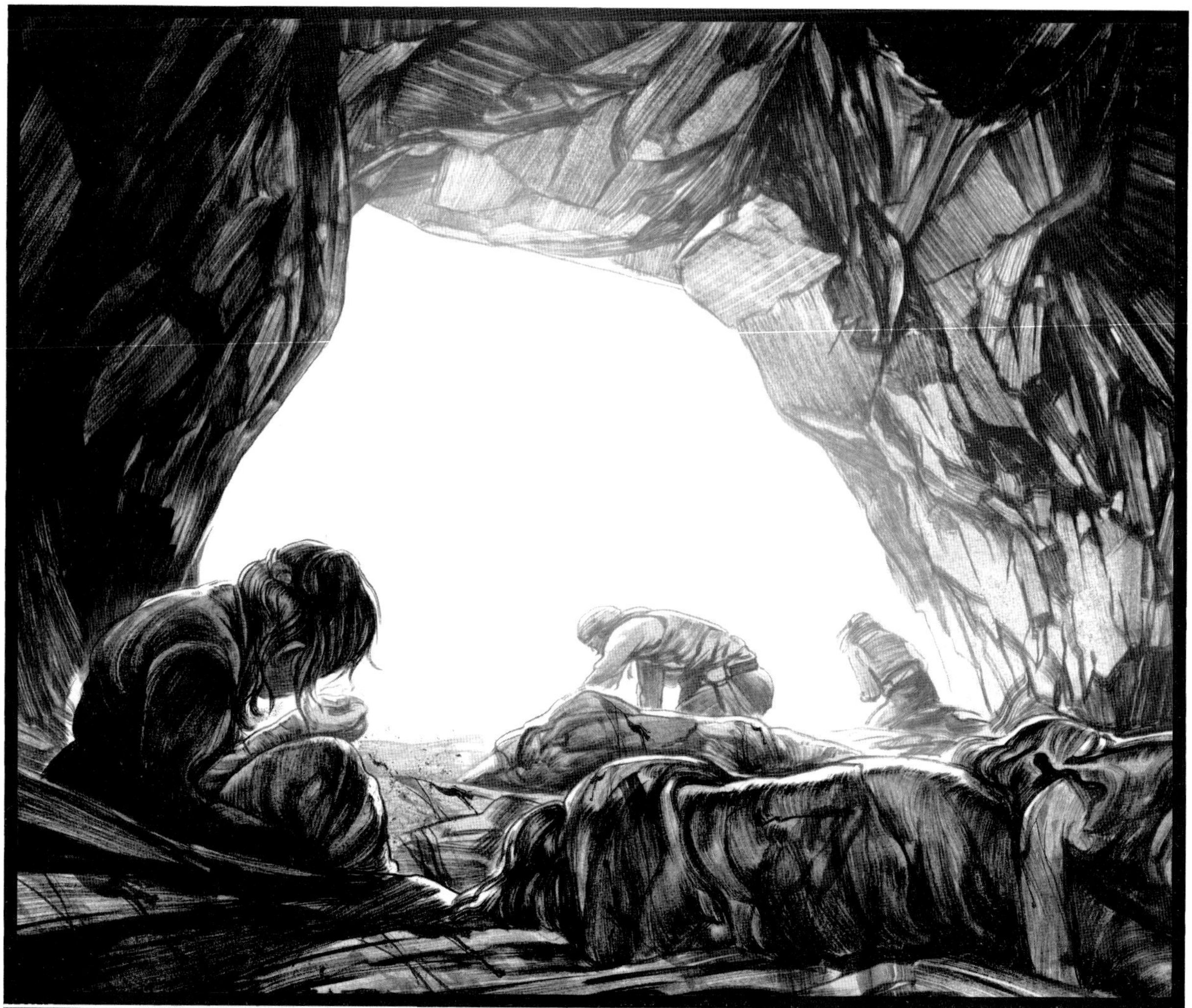

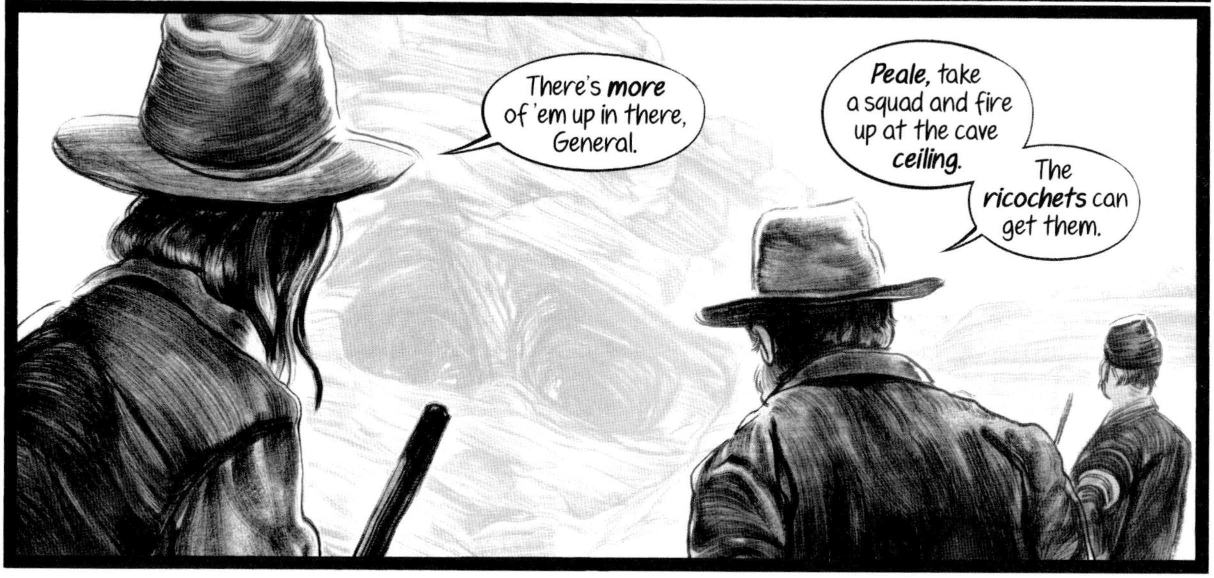
There's **more** of 'em up in there, General.
Peale, take a squad and fire up at the cave **ceiling.**
The **ricochets** can get them.

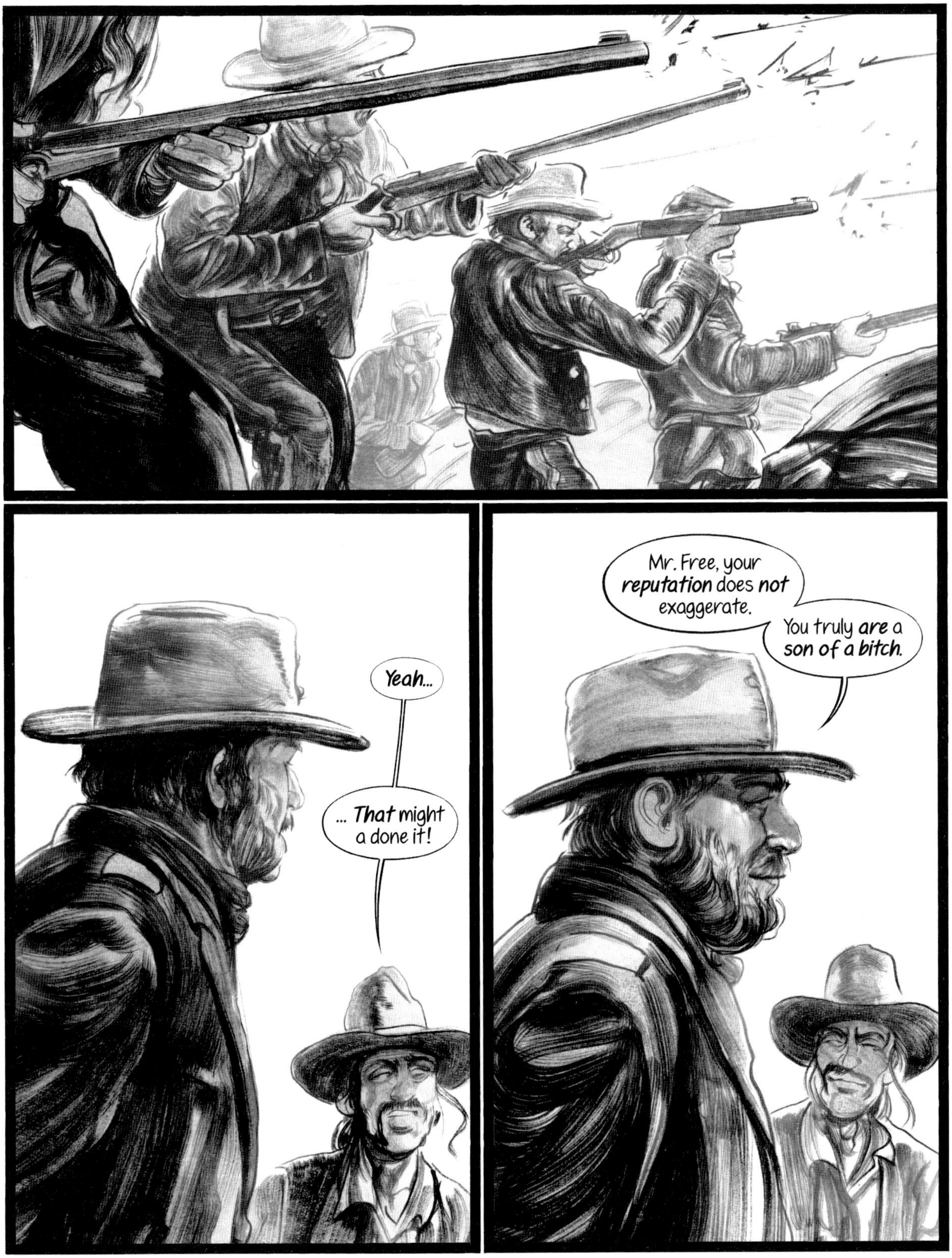
Yeah...
... That might a done it!
Mr. Free, your reputation does not exaggerate.
You truly are a son of a bitch.

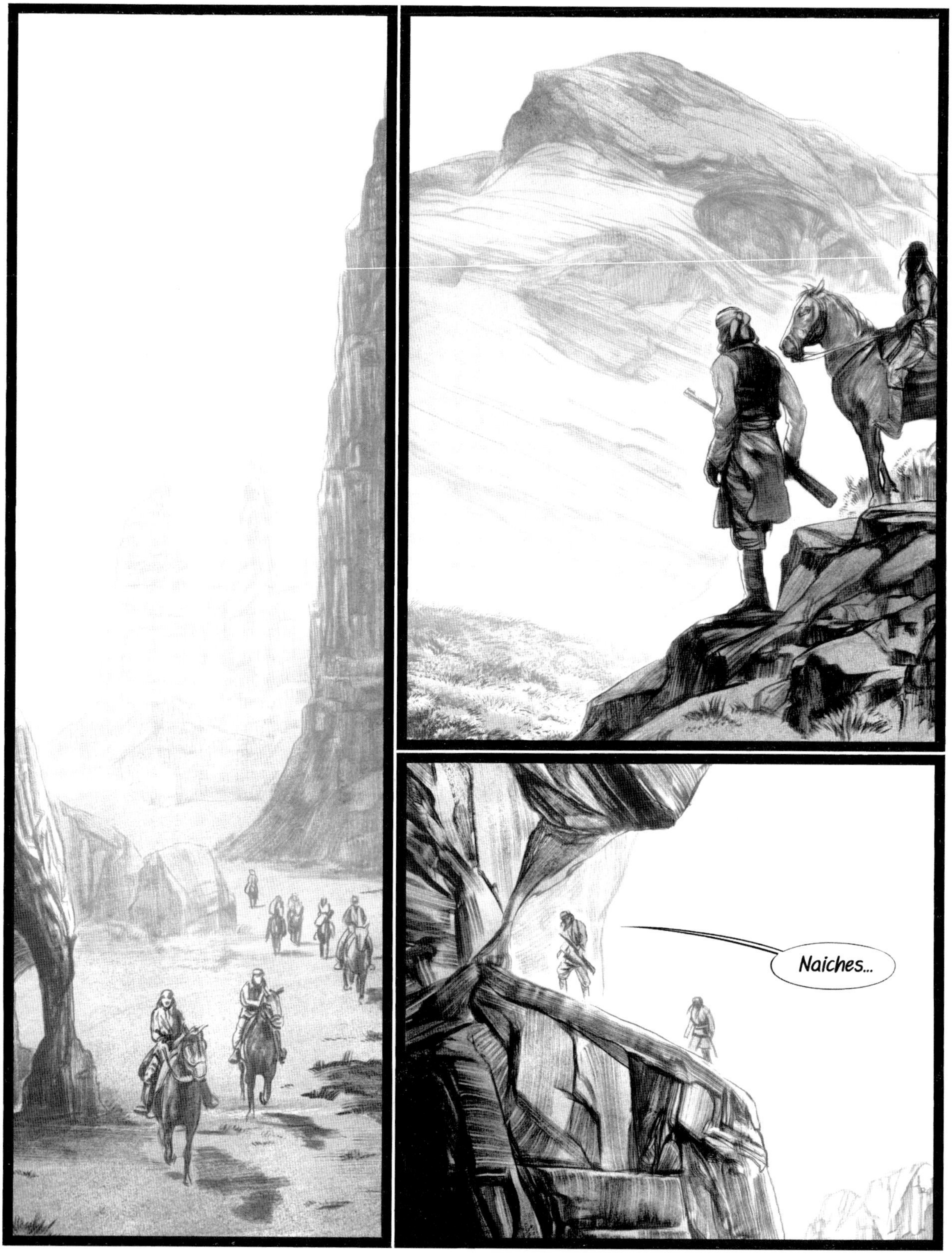
Naiches...

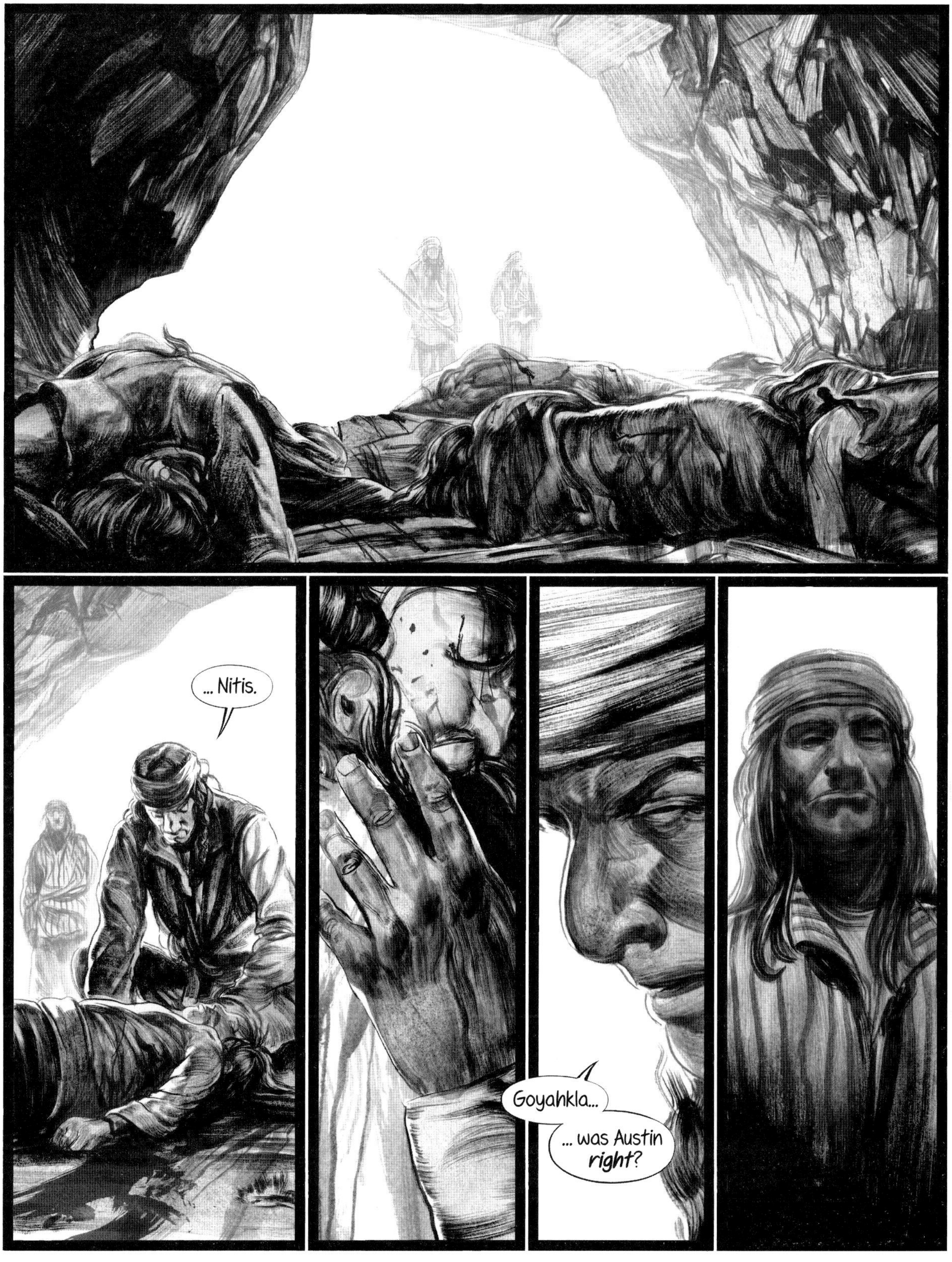
... Nitis.
Goyahkla...
... was Austin *right*?

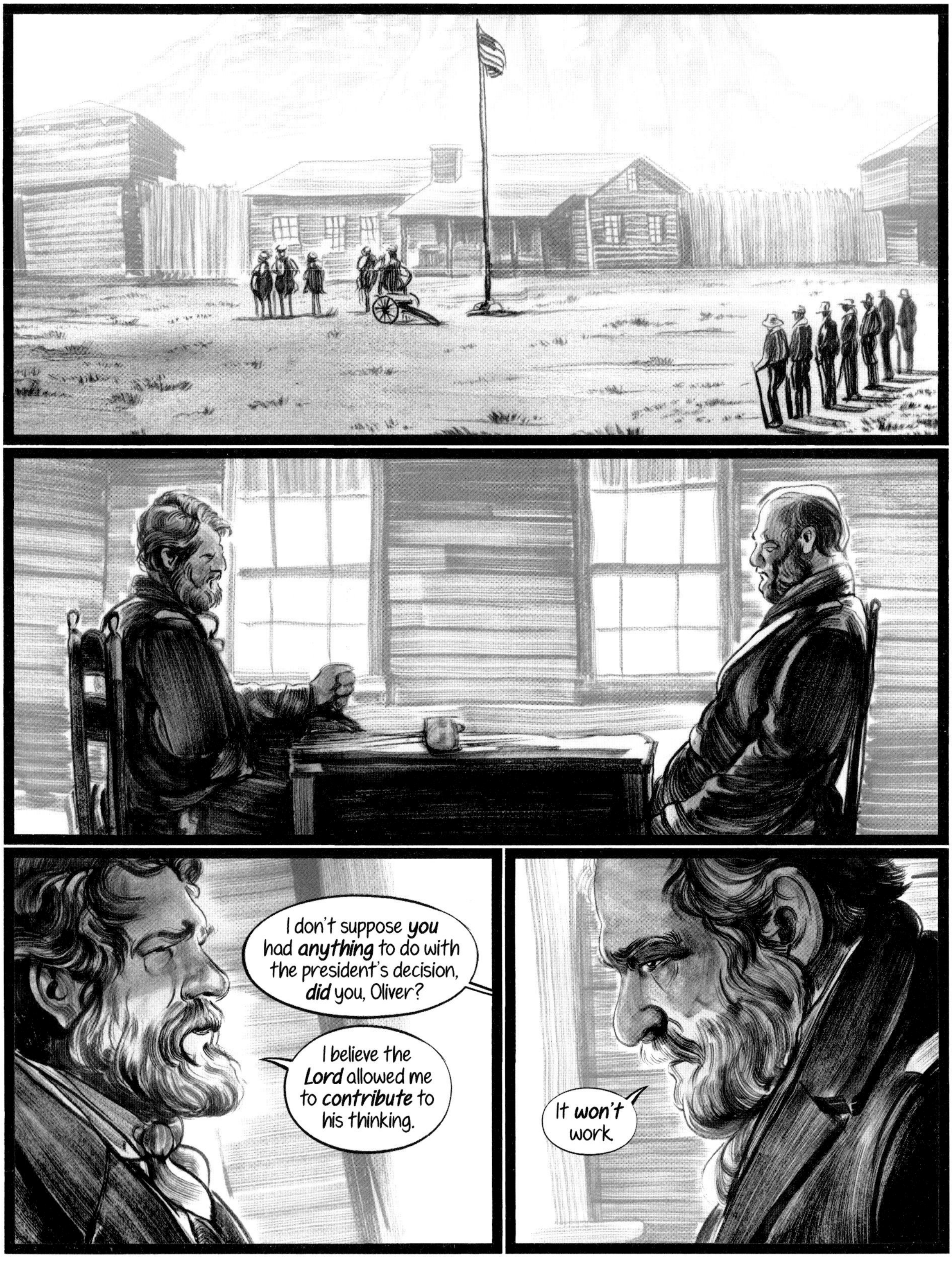
I don't suppose you had anything to do with the president's decision, did you, Oliver?
I believe the Lord allowed me to contribute to his thinking.
It won't work.

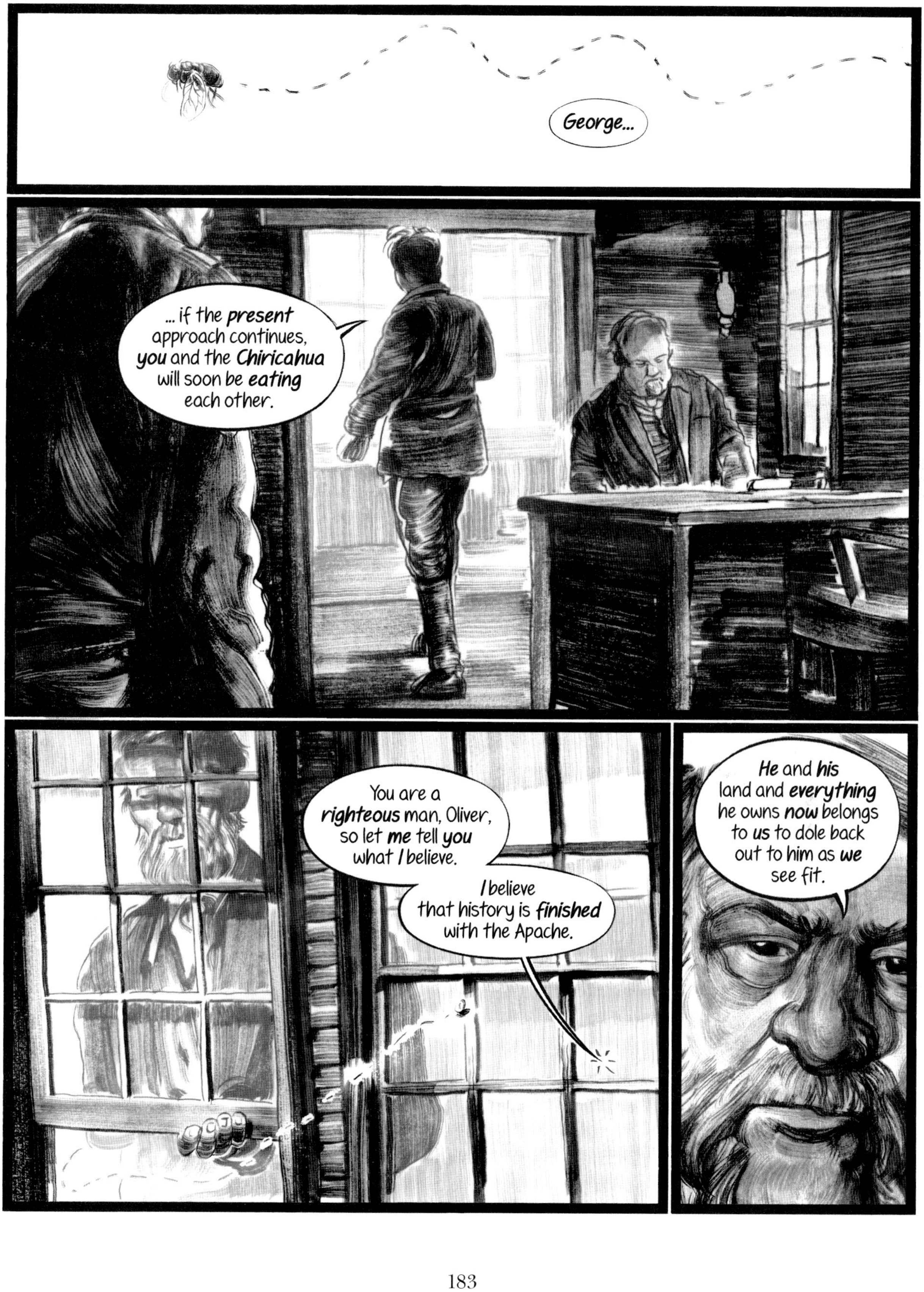
George...
... if the present approach continues, you and the Chiricahua will soon be eating each other.
You are a righteous man, Oliver, so let me tell you what I believe.
I believe that history is finished with the Apache.
He and his land and everything he owns now belongs to us to dole back out to him as we see fit.

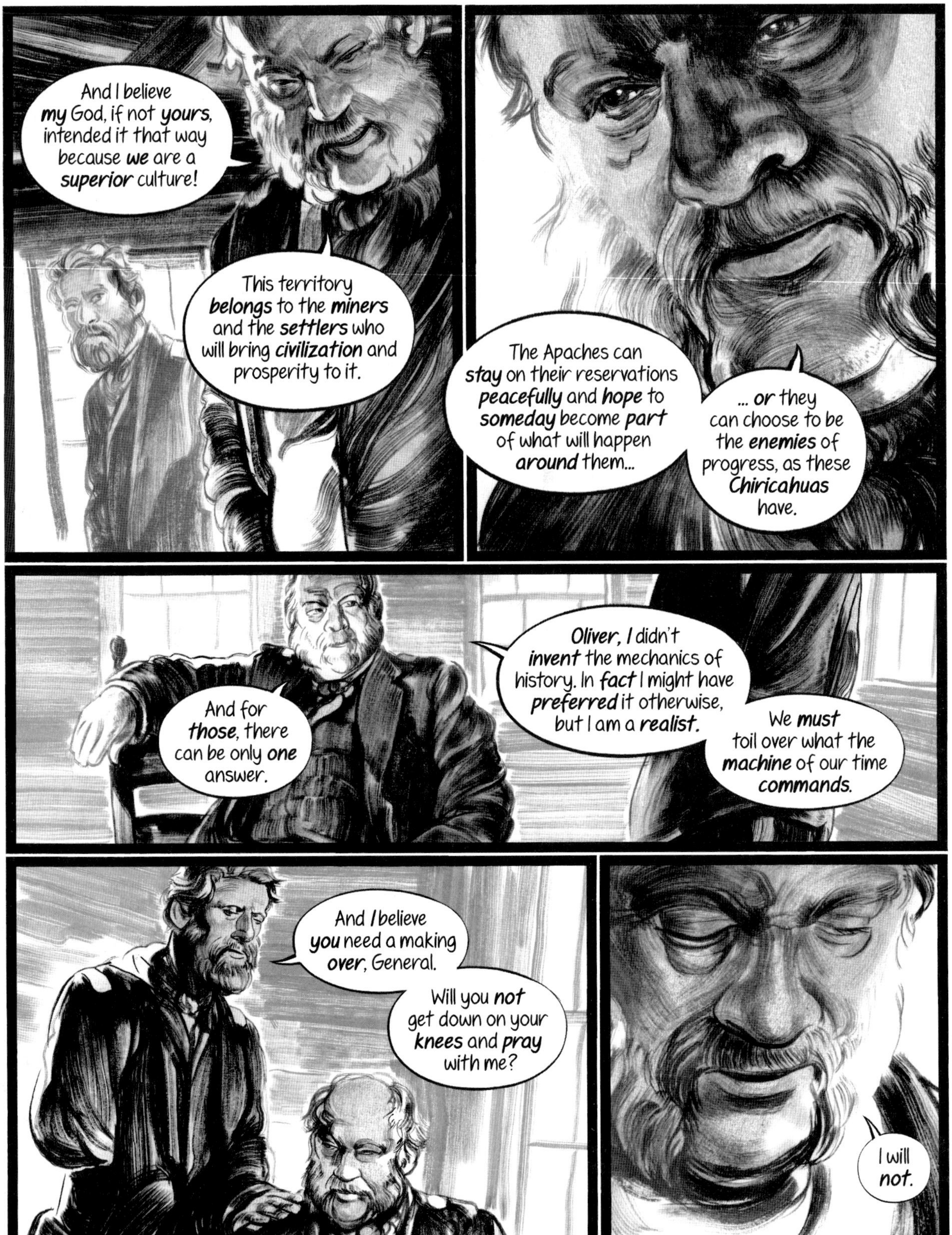

And I believe my God, if not yours, intended it that way because we are a superior culture!
This territory belongs to the miners and the settlers who will bring civilization and prosperity to it.
The Apaches can stay on their reservations peacefully and hope to someday become part of what will happen around them...
... or they can choose to be the enemies of progress, as these Chiricahuas have.
And for those, there can be only one answer.
Oliver, I didn't invent the mechanics of history. In fact I might have preferred it otherwise, but I am a realist.
We must toil over what the machine of our time commands.
And I believe you need a making over, General.
Will you not get down on your knees and pray with me?
I will not.

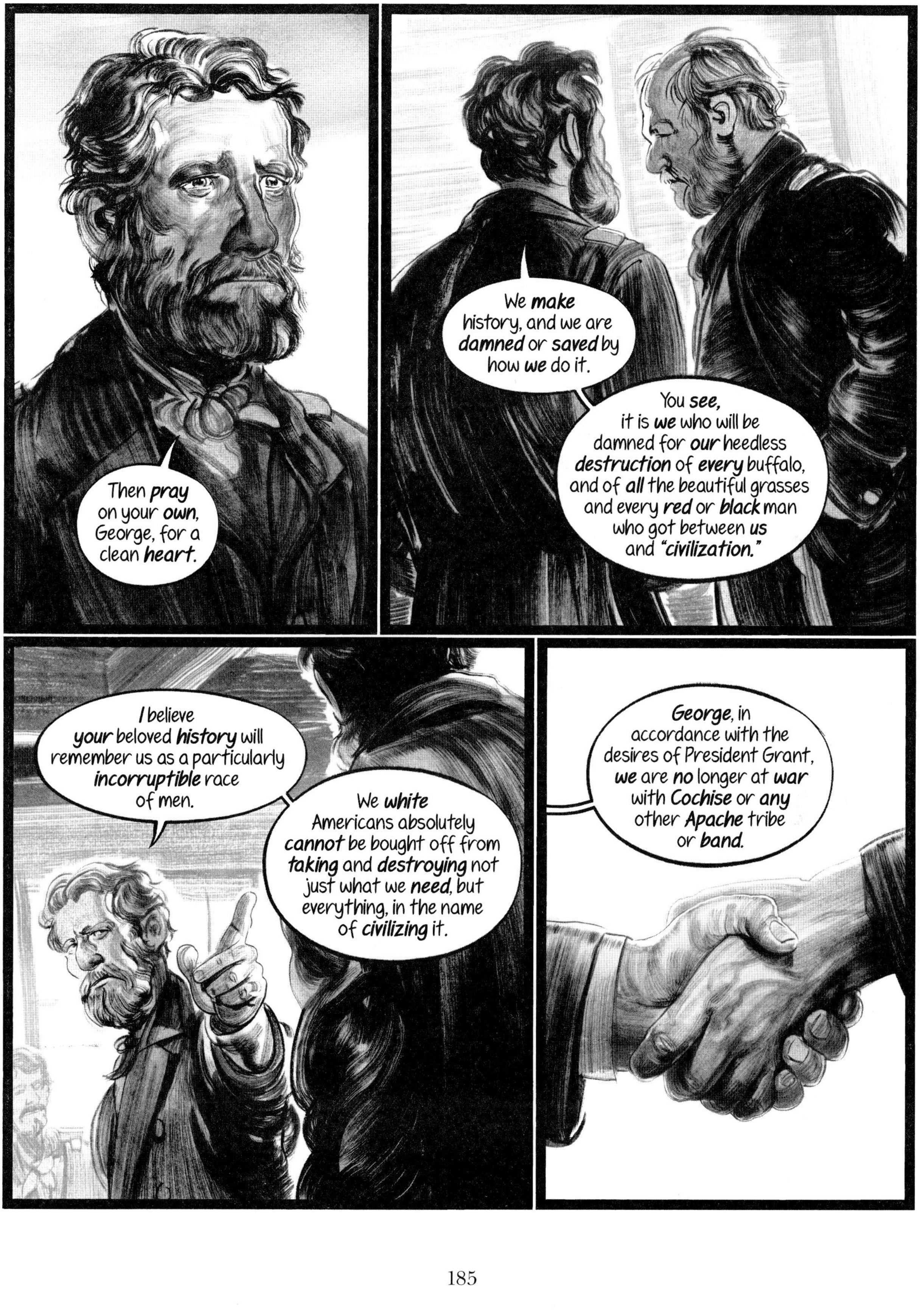
Then pray on your own, George, for a clean heart.
We make history, and we are damned or saved by how we do it.
You see, it is we who will be damned for our heedless destruction of every buffalo, and of all the beautiful grasses and every red or black man who got between us and "civilization."
I believe your beloved history will remember us as a particularly incorruptible race of men.
We white Americans absolutely cannot be bought off from taking and destroying not just what we need, but everything, in the name of civilizing it.
George, in accordance with the desires of President Grant, we are no longer at war with Cochise or any other Apache tribe or band.

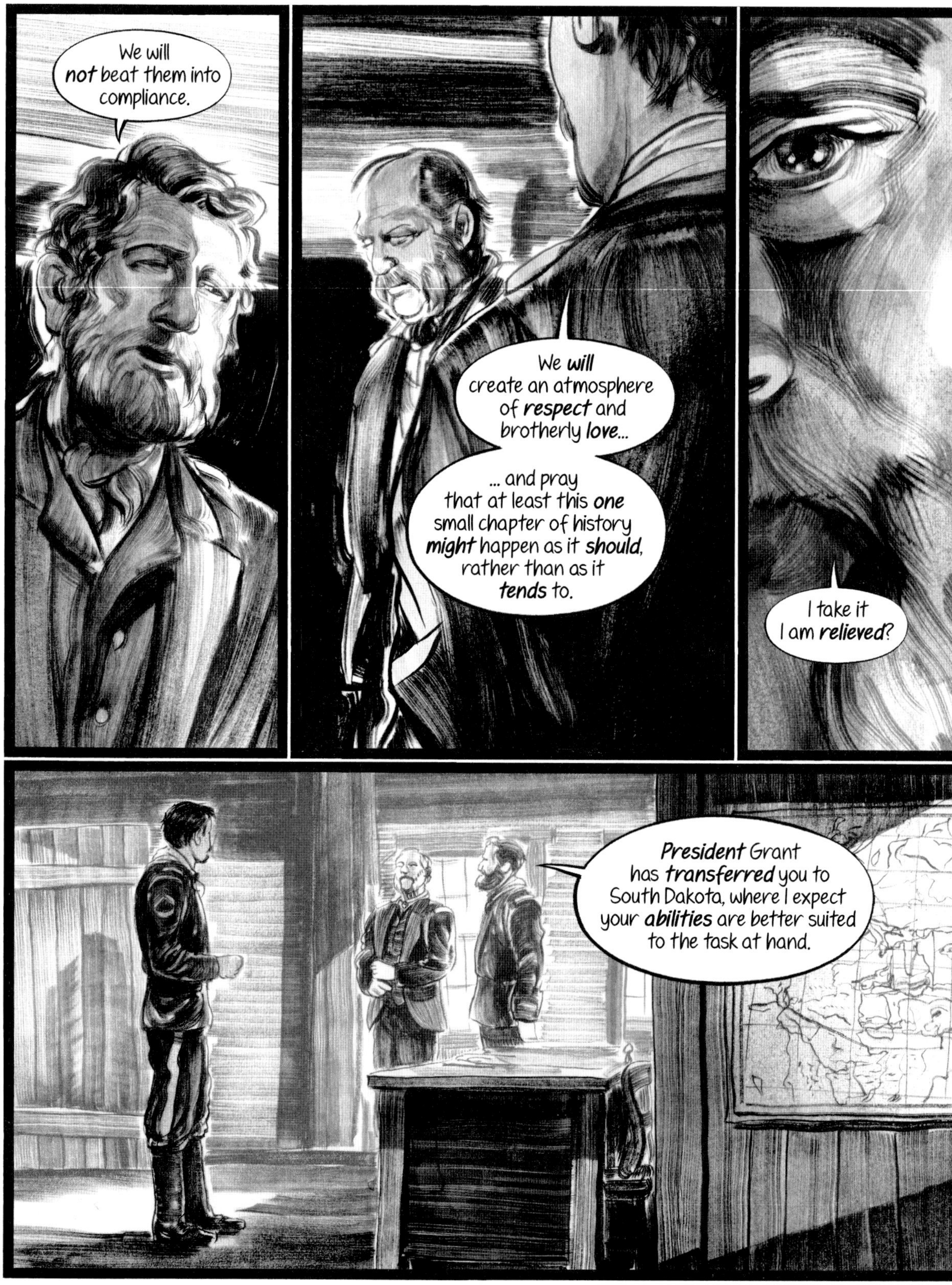
We will not beat them into compliance.
We will create an atmosphere of respect and brotherly love...
... and pray that at least this one small chapter of history might happen as it should, rather than as it tends to.
I take it I am relieved?
President Grant has transferred you to South Dakota, where I expect your abilities are better suited to the task at hand.

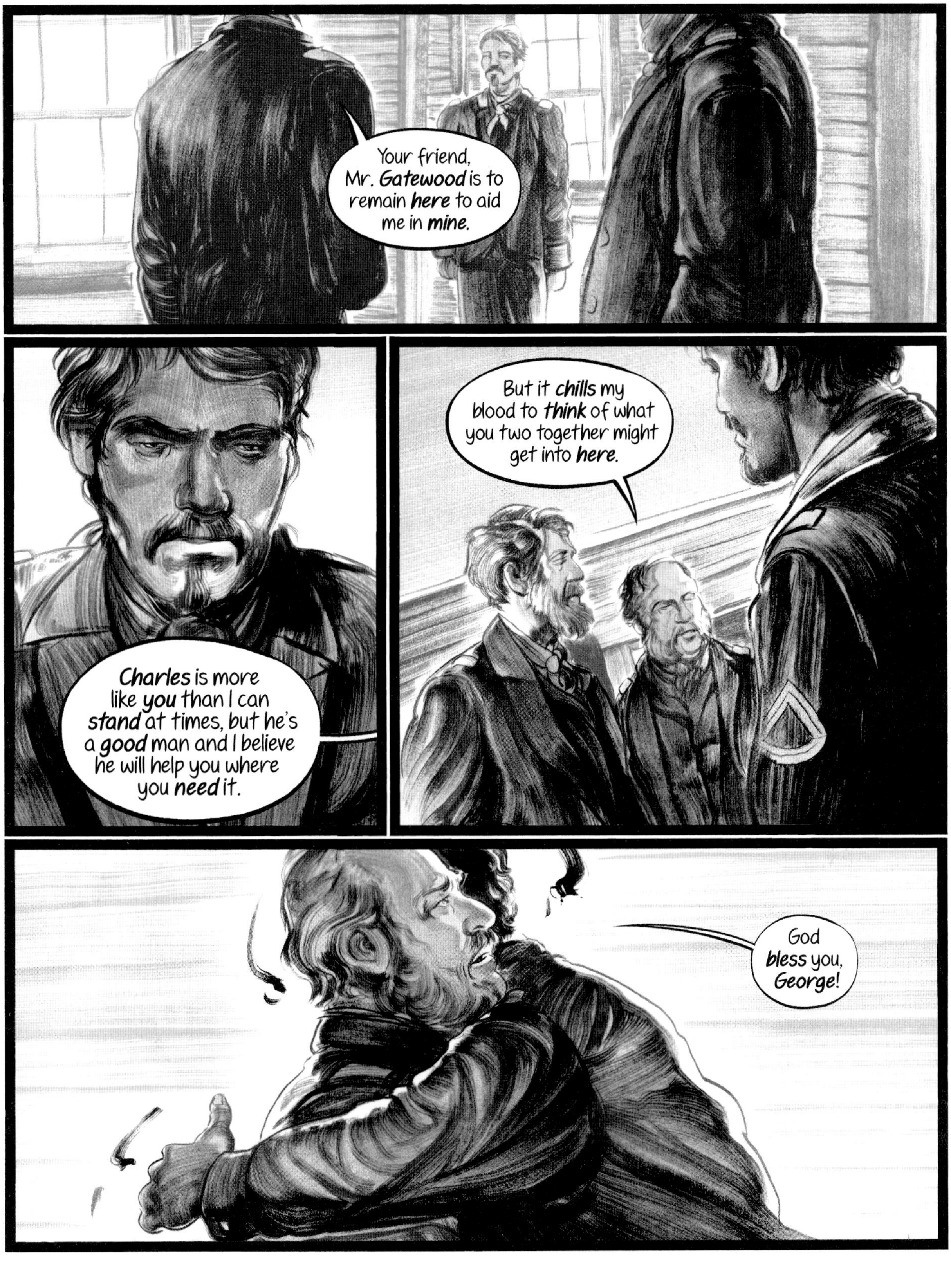
Your friend, Mr. Gatewood is to remain here to aid me in mine.
Charles is more like you than I can stand at times, but he's a good man and I believe he will help you where you need it.
But it chills my blood to think of what you two together might get into here.
God bless you, George!

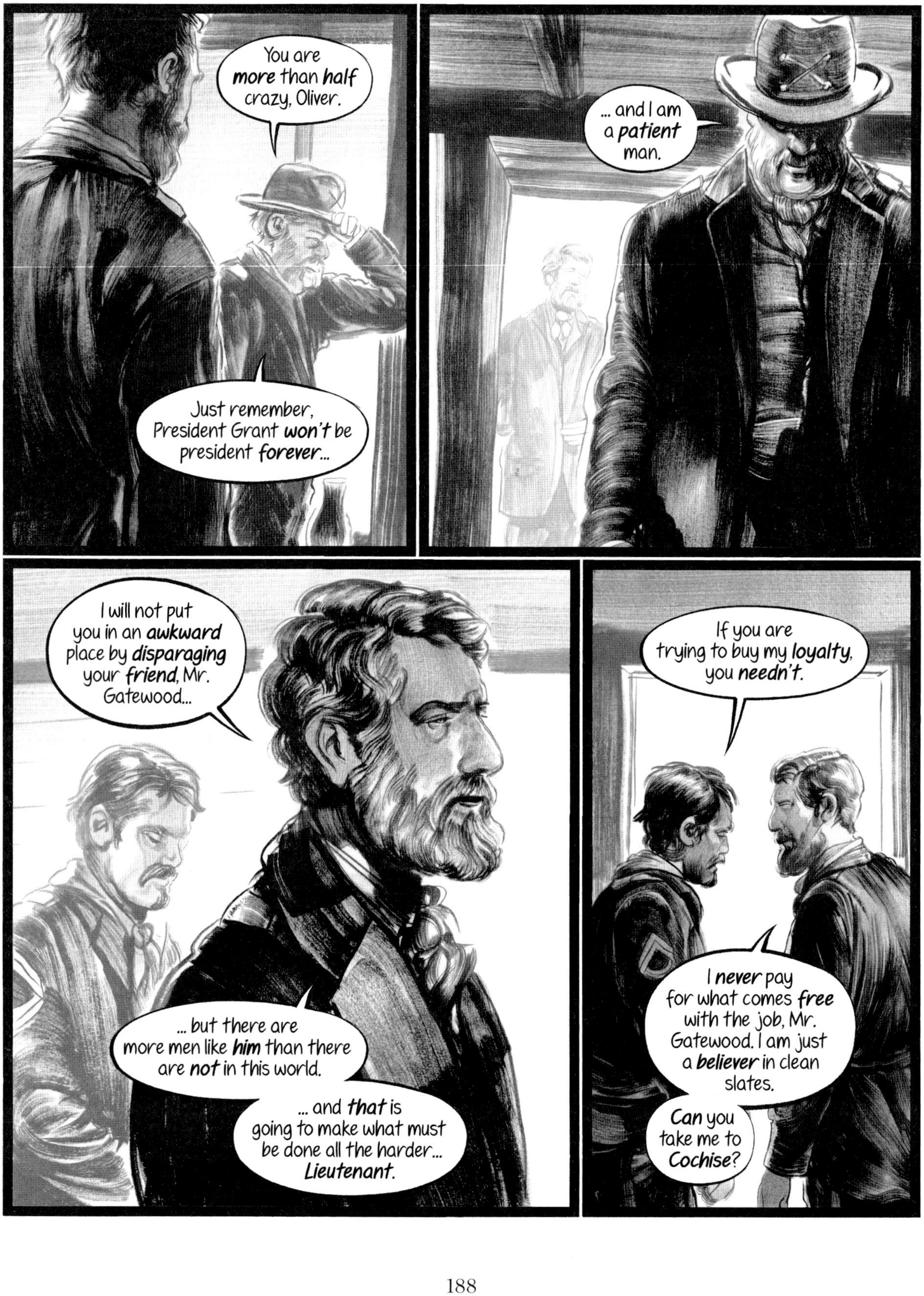
You are more than half crazy, Oliver.
Just remember, President Grant won't be president forever...
... and I am a patient man.
I will not put you in an awkward place by disparaging your friend, Mr. Gatewood...
... but there are more men like him than there are not in this world.
... and that is going to make what must be done all the harder... Lieutenant.
If you are trying to buy my loyalty, you needn't.
I never pay for what comes free with the job, Mr. Gatewood. I am just a believer in clean slates.
Can you take me to Cochise?

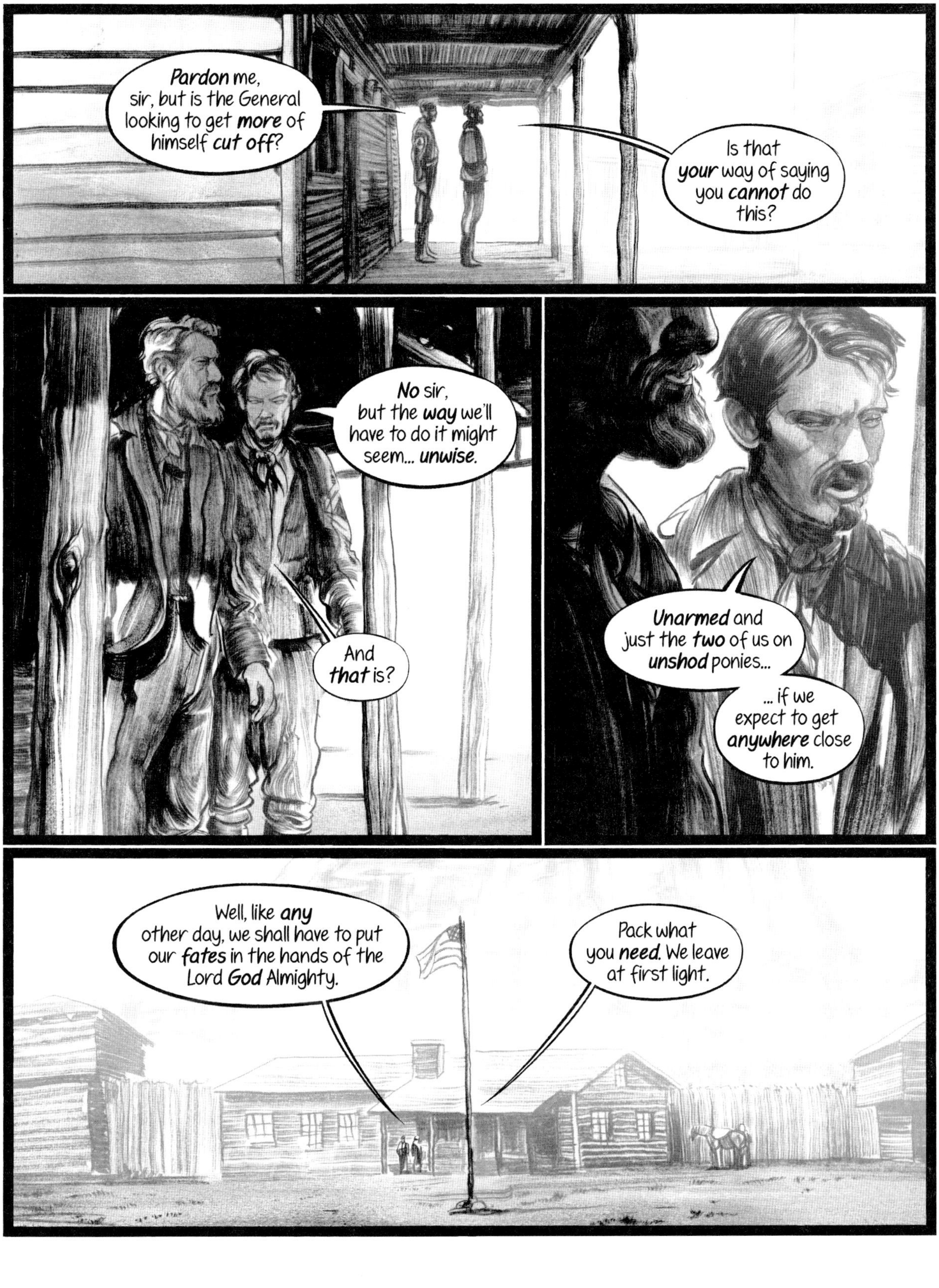

Pardon me, sir, but is the General looking to get more of himself cut off?
Is that your way of saying you cannot do this?
No sir, but the way we'll have to do it might seem... unwise.
And that is?
Unarmed and just the two of us on unshod ponies...
... if we expect to get anywhere close to him.
Well, like any other day, we shall have to put our fates in the hands of the Lord God Almighty.
Pack what you need. We leave at first light.

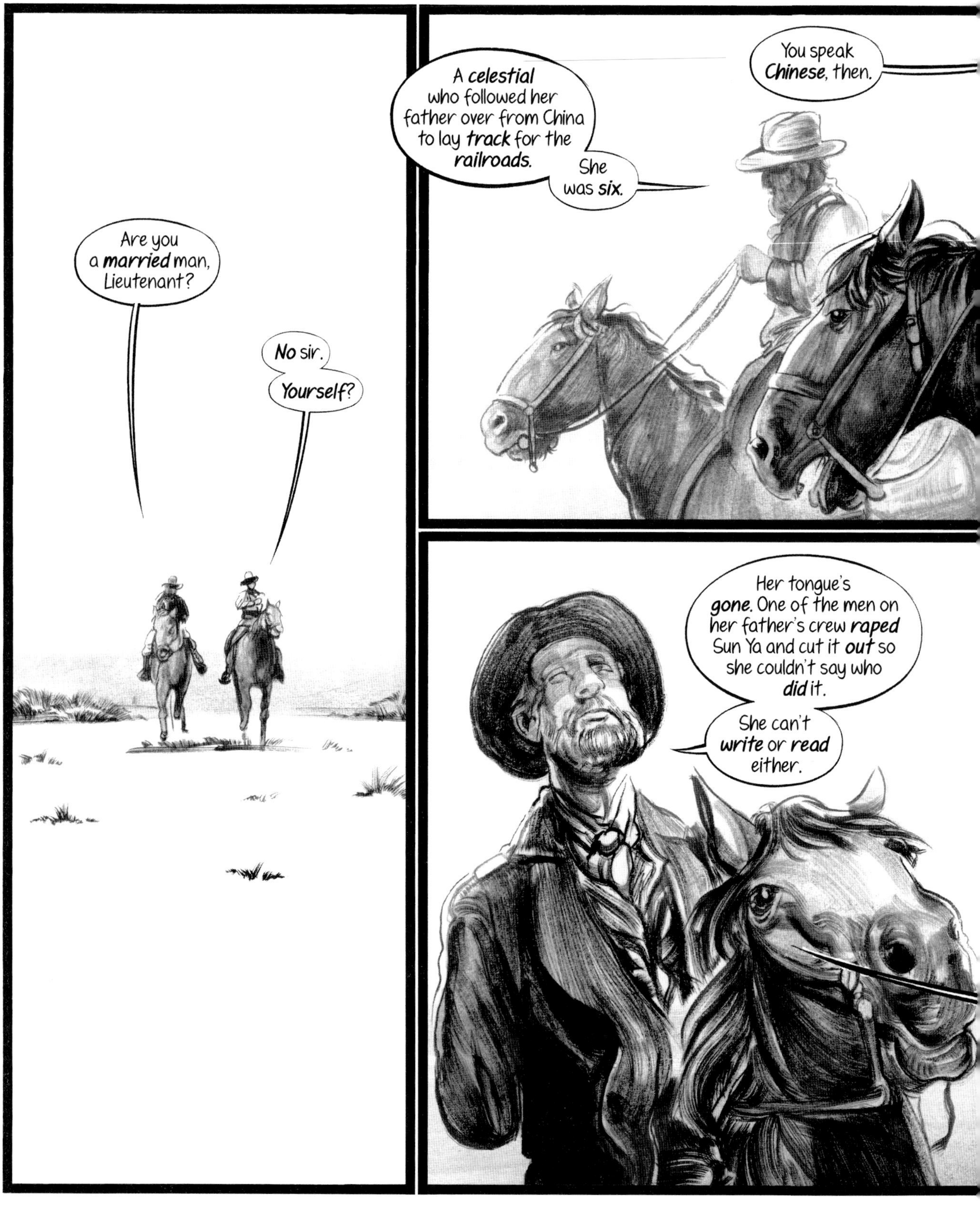
Are you a married man, Lieutenant?
No sir.
Yourself?
A celestial who followed her father over from China to lay track for the railroads.
She was six.
You speak Chinese, then.
Her tongue's gone. One of the men on her father's crew raped Sun Ya and cut it out so she couldn't say who did it.
She can't write or read either.

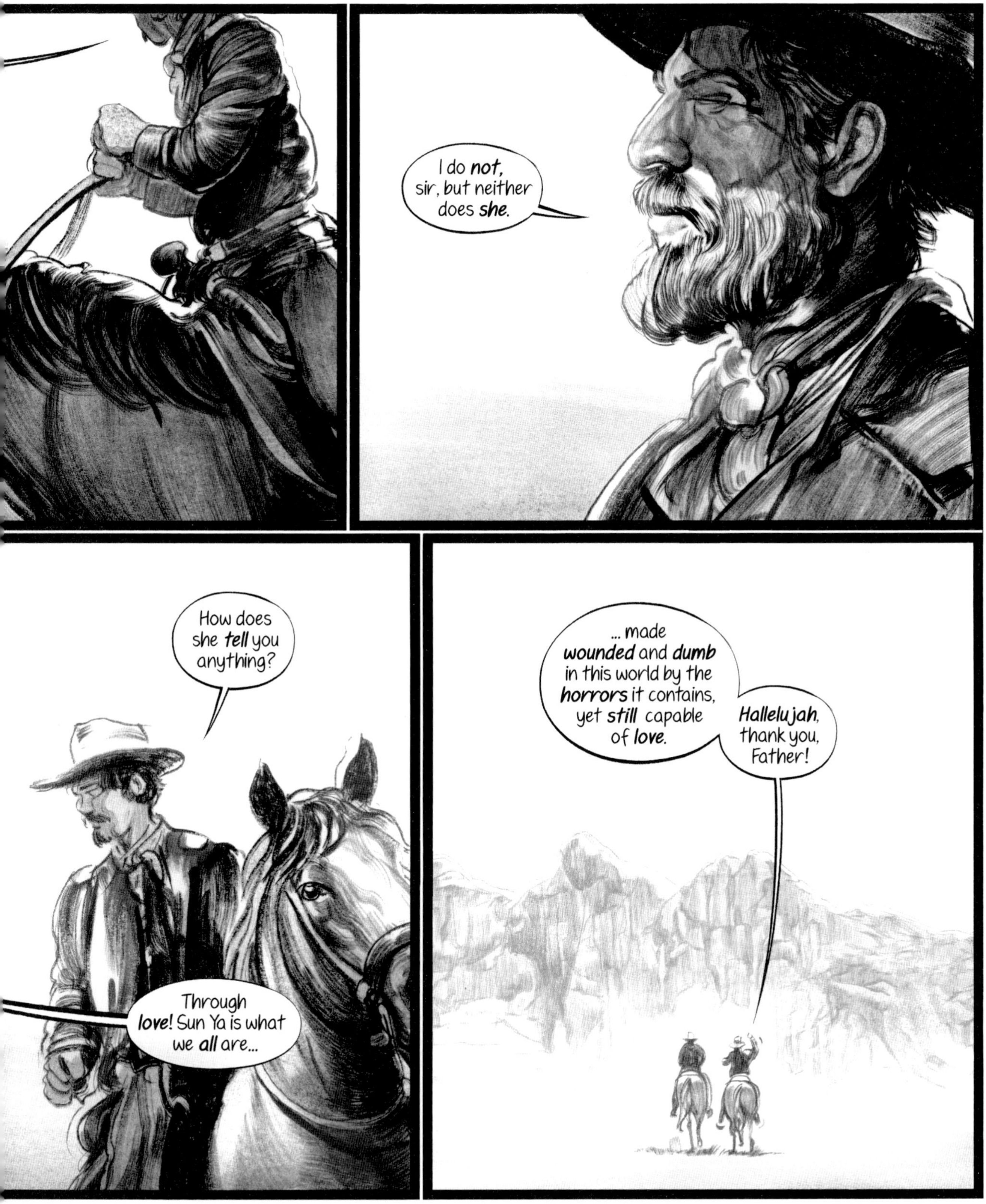
I do not, sir, but neither does she.
How does she tell you anything?
Through love! Sun Ya is what we all are...
... made wounded and dumb in this world by the horrors it contains, yet still capable of love.
Hallelujah, thank you, Father!

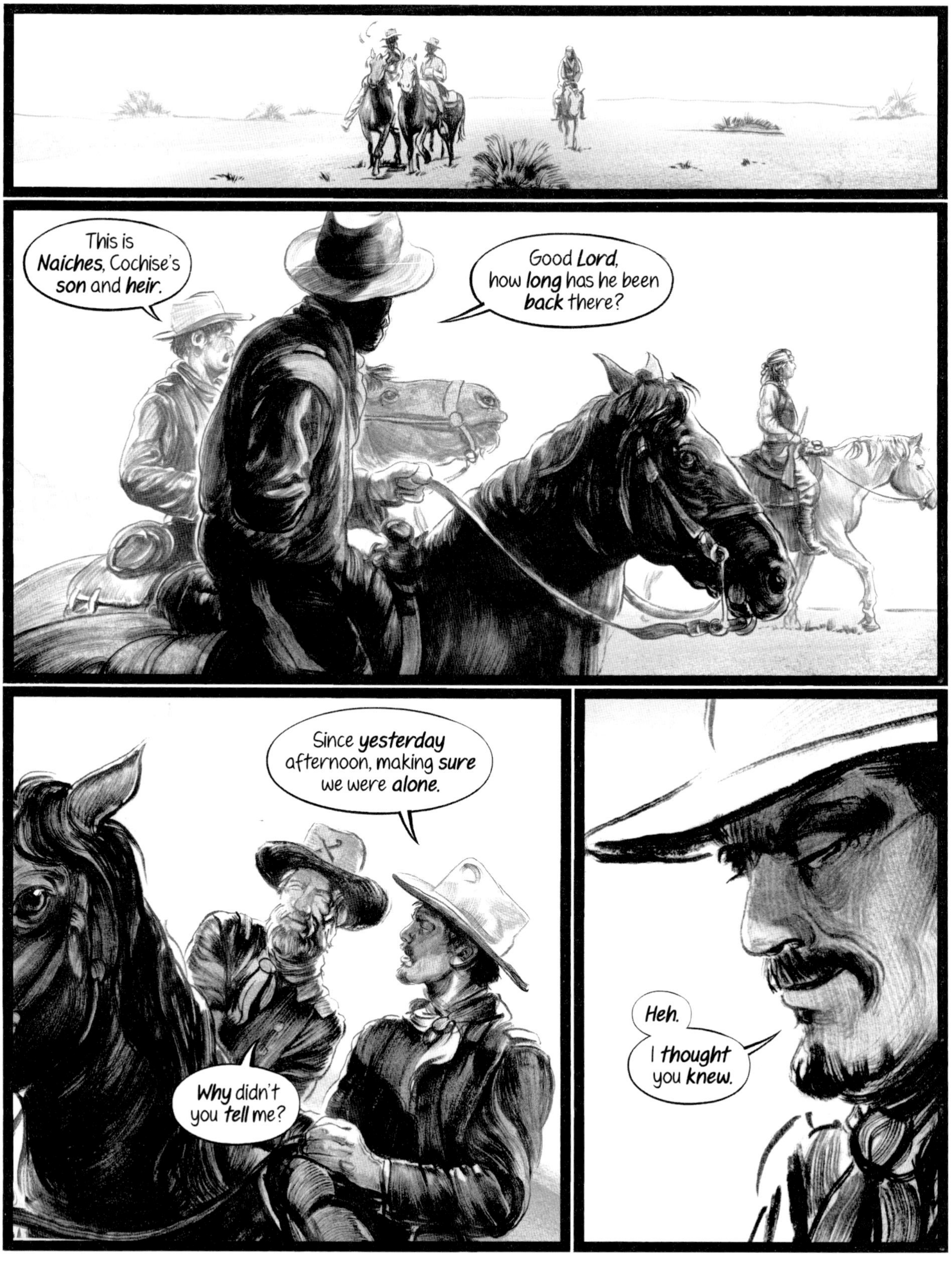
This is Naiches, Cochise's son and heir.
Good Lord, how long has he been back there?
Since yesterday afternoon, making sure we were alone.
Why didn't you tell me?
Heh. I thought you knew.

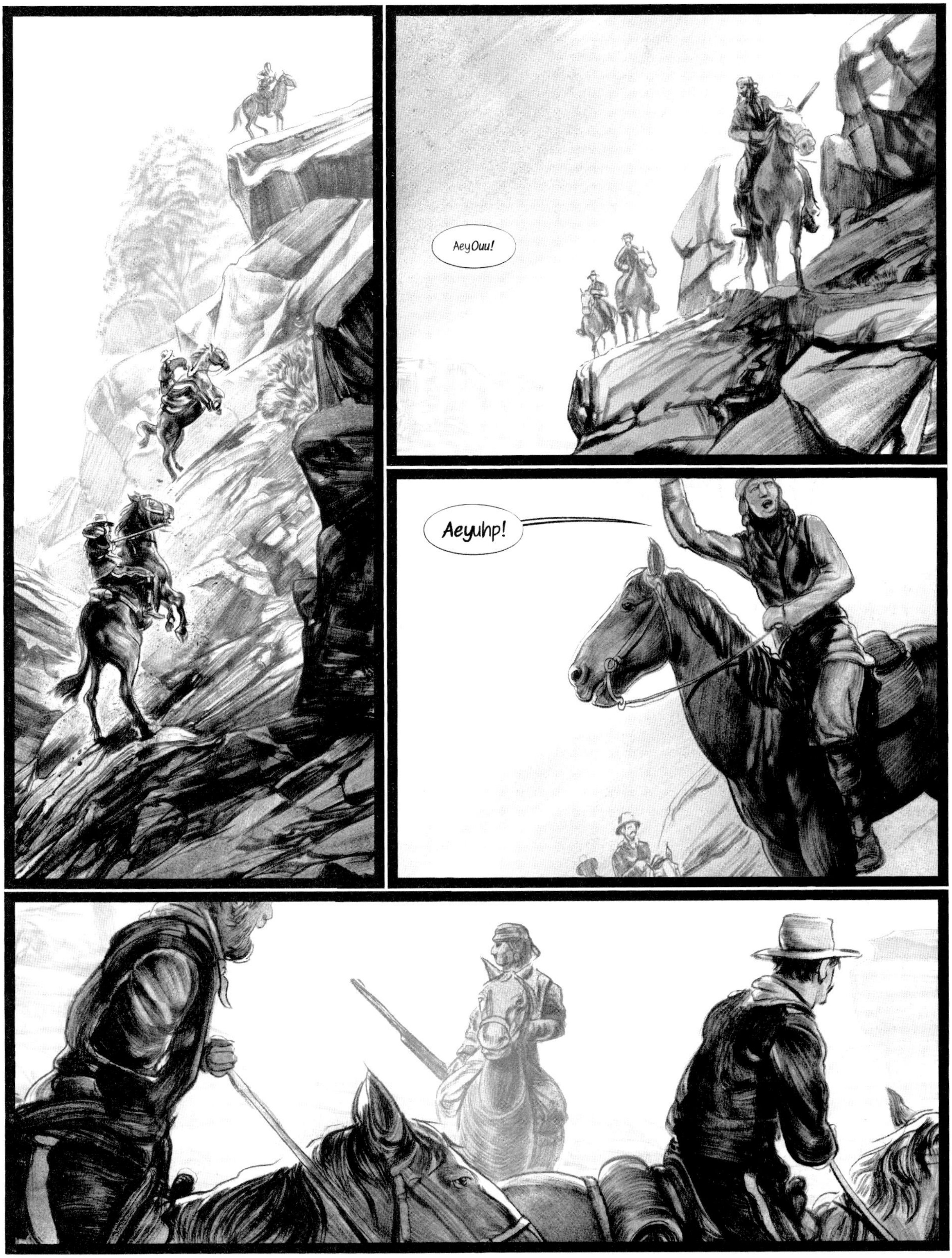
AeyOuu!
Aeyuhp!

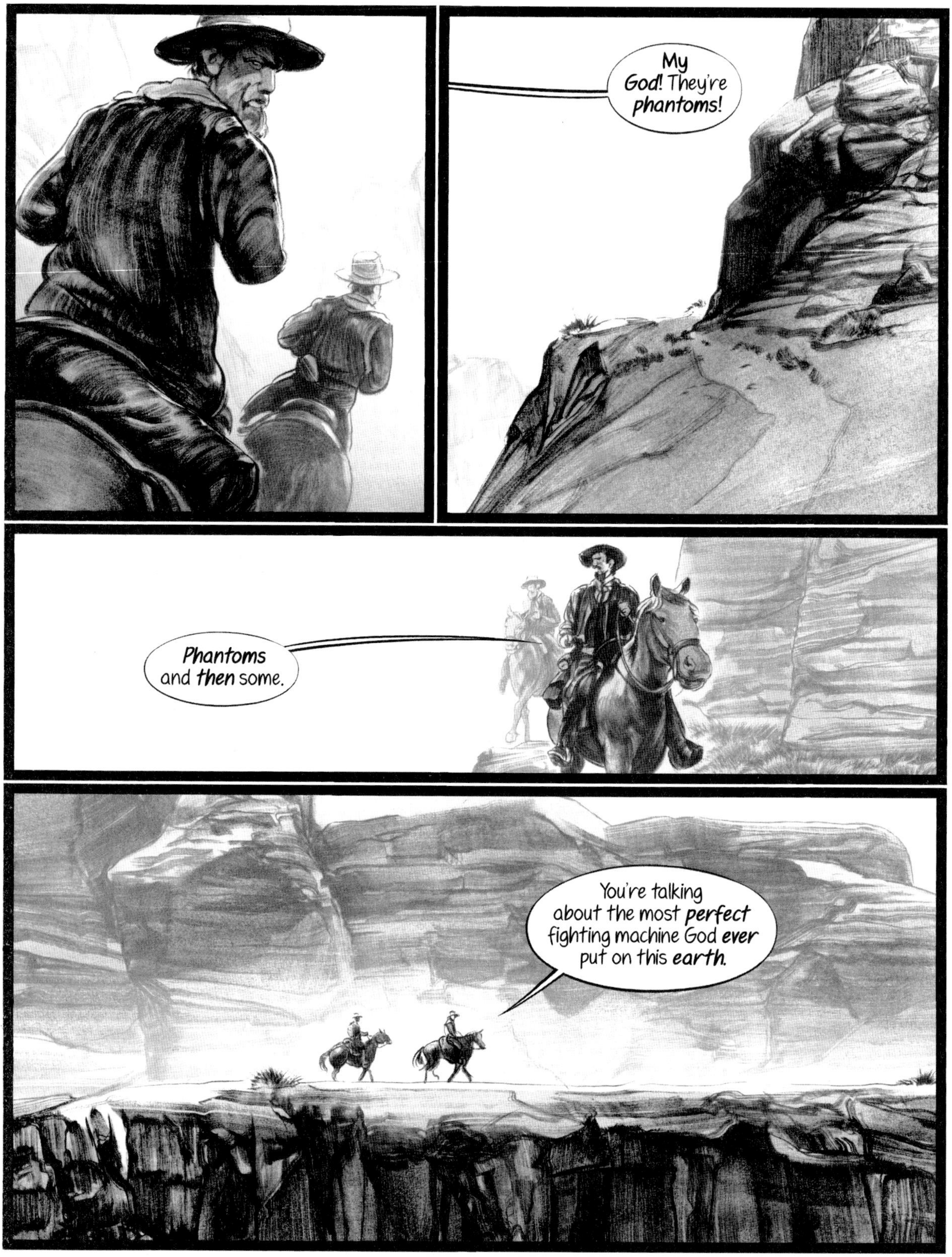
My God! They're phantoms!
Phantoms and then some.
You're talking about the most perfect fighting machine God ever put on this earth.

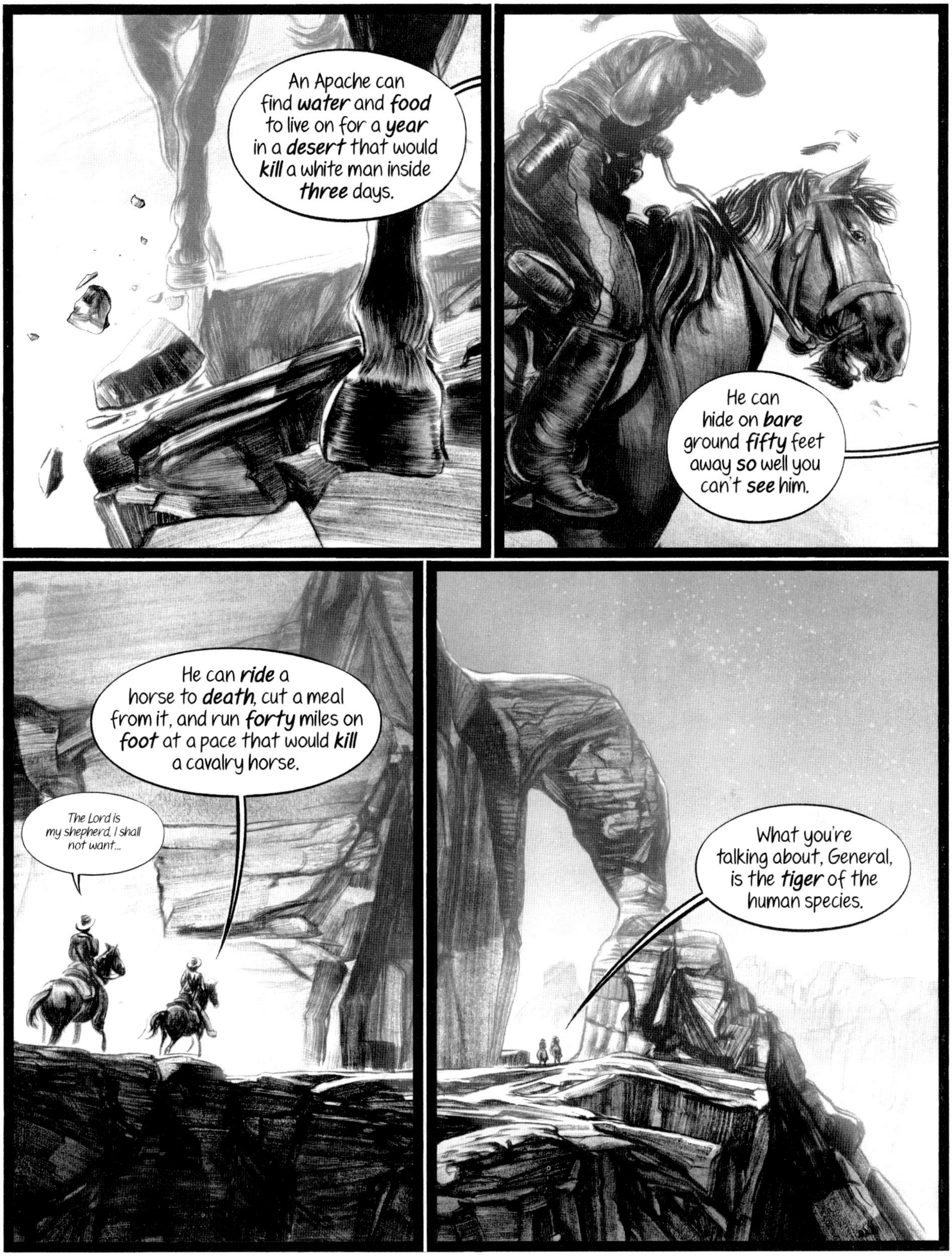
An Apache can find water and food to live on for a year in a desert that would kill a white man inside three days.
He can hide on bare ground fifty feet away so well you can't see him.
He can ride a horse to death, cut a meal from it, and run forty miles on foot at a pace that would kill a cavalry horse.
The Lord is my shepherd, I shall not want...
What you're talking about, General, is the tiger of the human species.

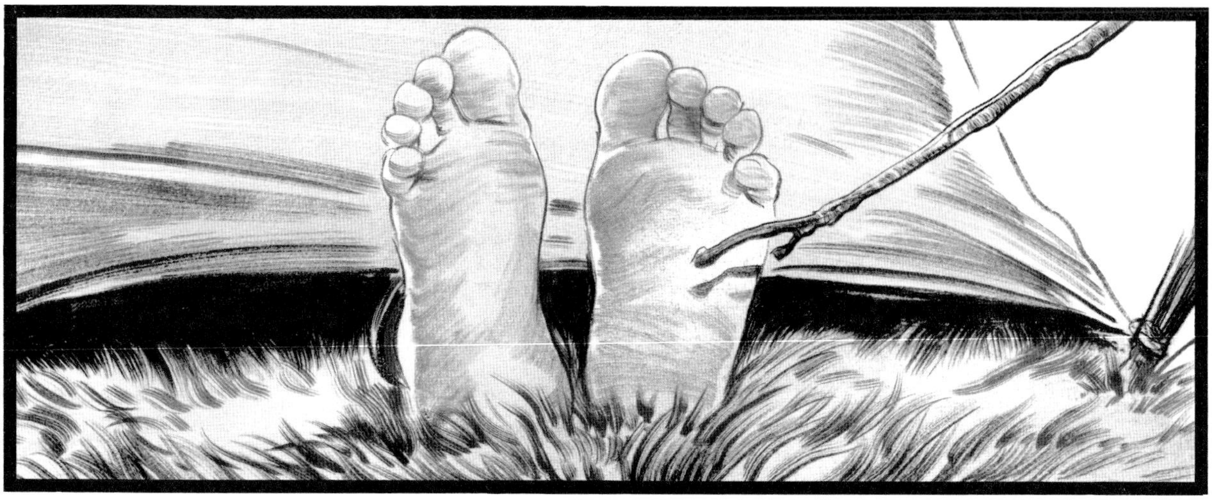

COCHISE · THE DRAGOON MOUNTAINS

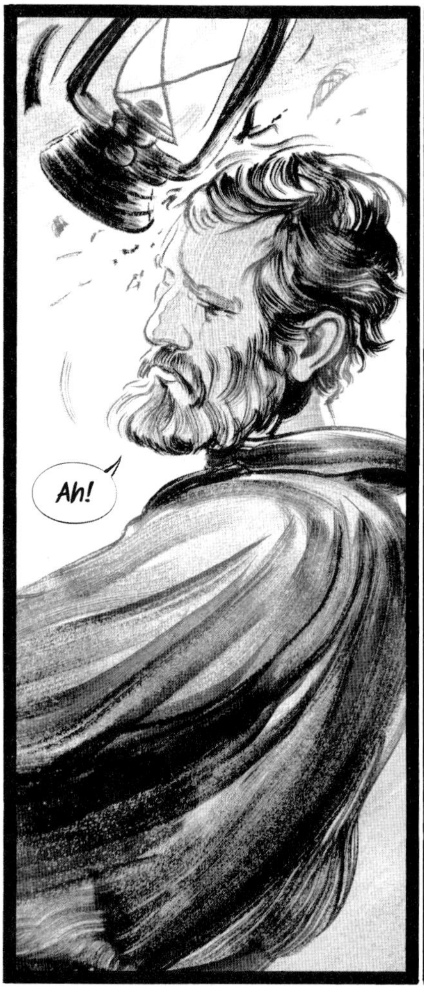
Ah!

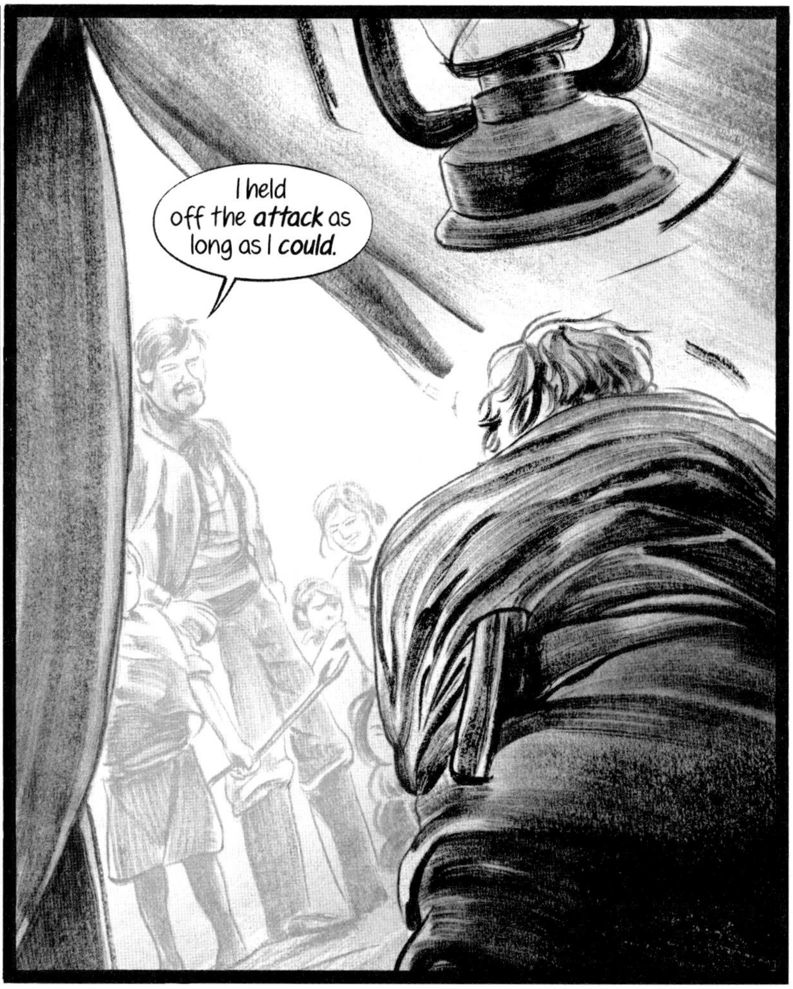
I held off the *attack* as long as I **could.**

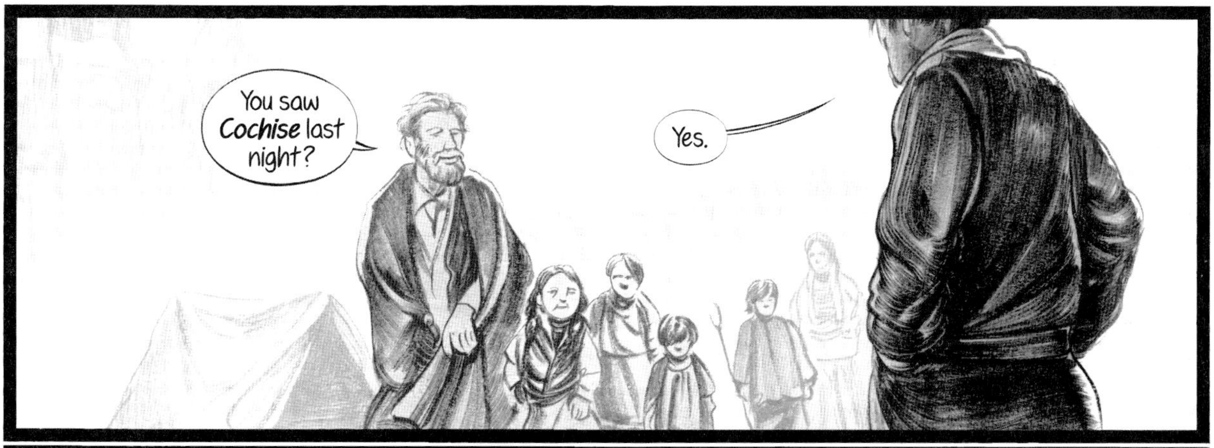
You saw Cochise last night?
Yes.
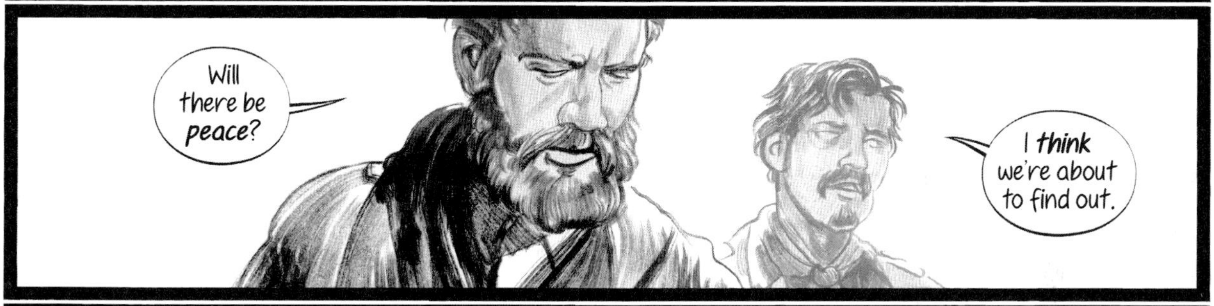
Will there be peace?
I think we're about to find out.
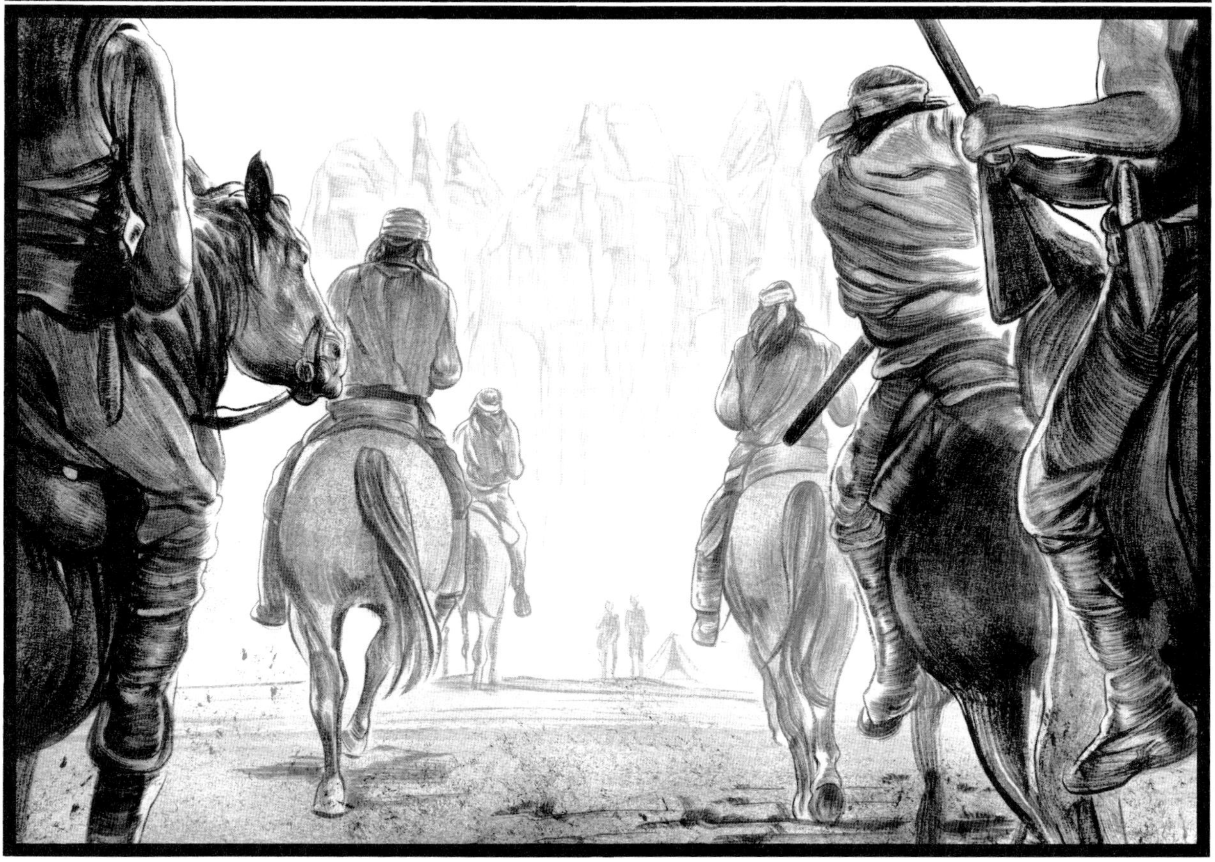

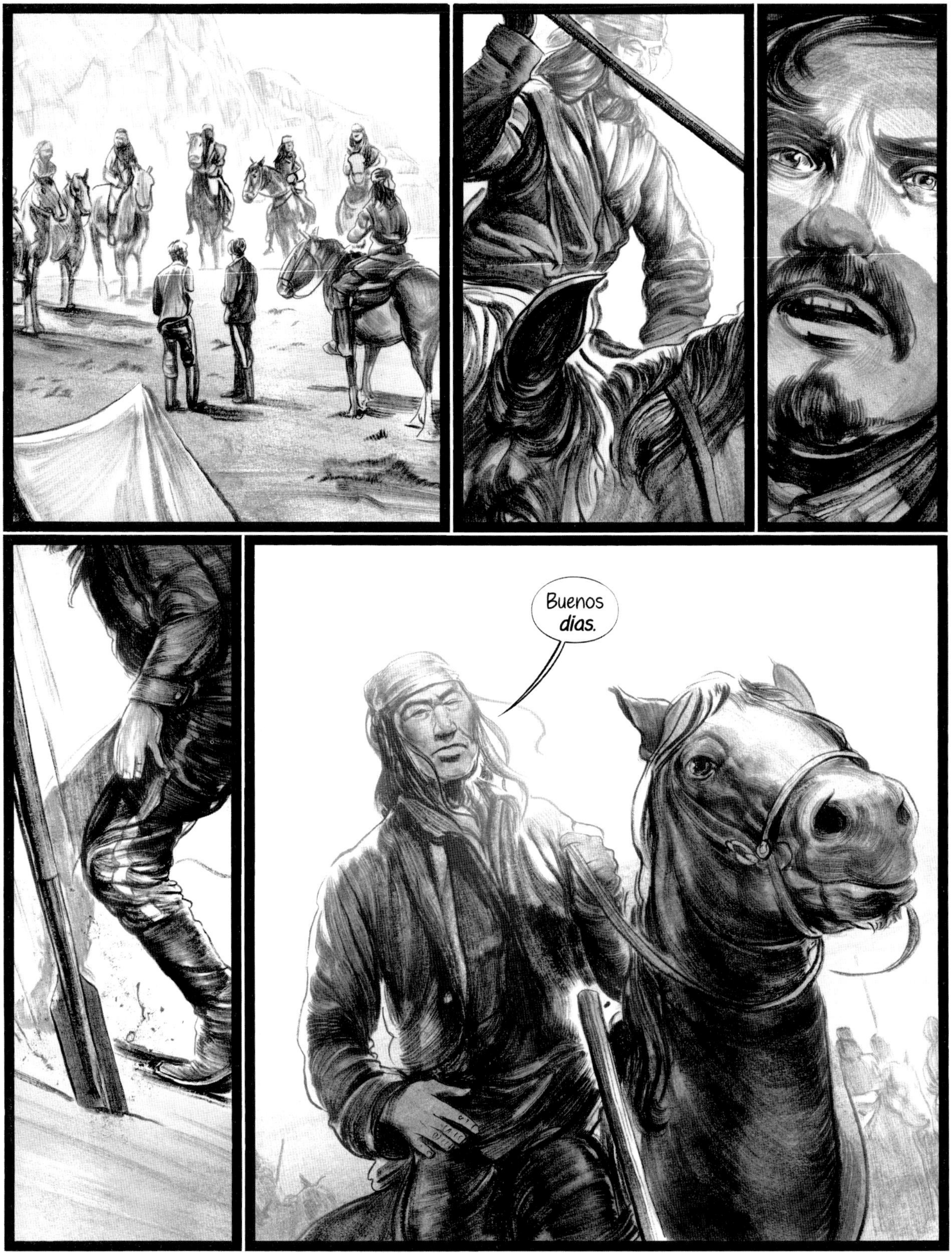
Buenos dias.

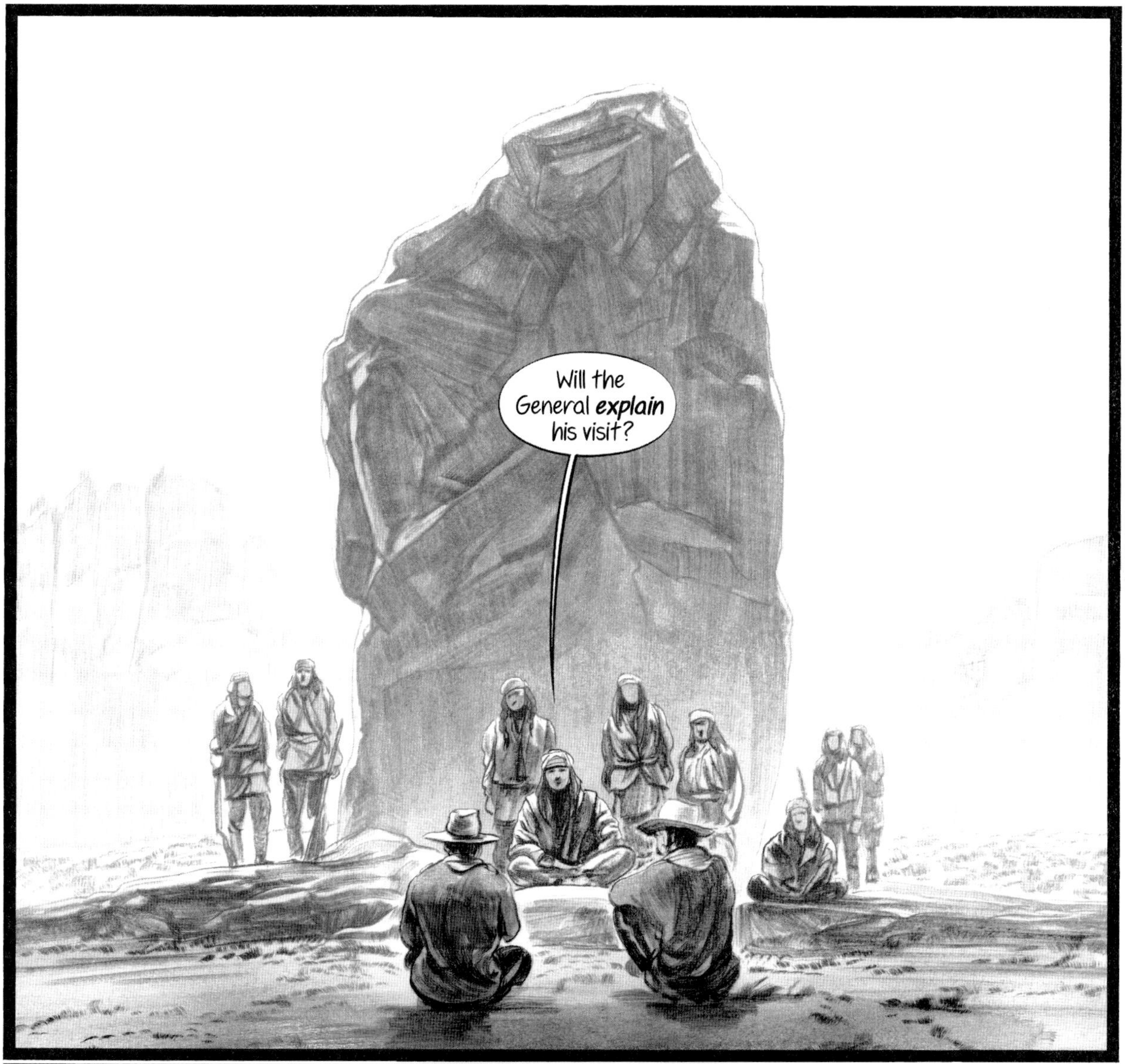
Will the General **explain** his visit?

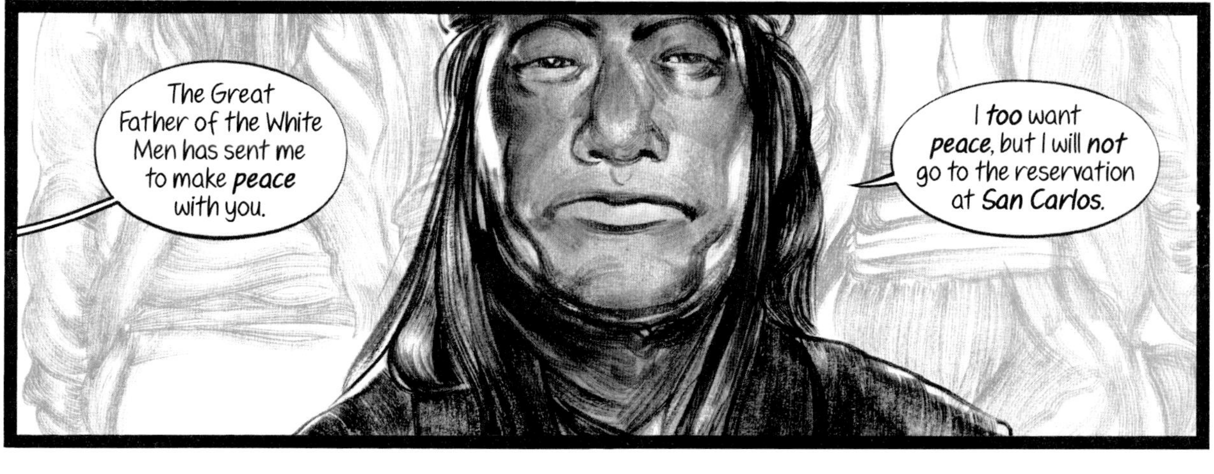
The Great Father of the White Men has sent me to make **peace** with you.
I **too** want **peace**, but I will **not** go to the reservation at **San Carlos**.

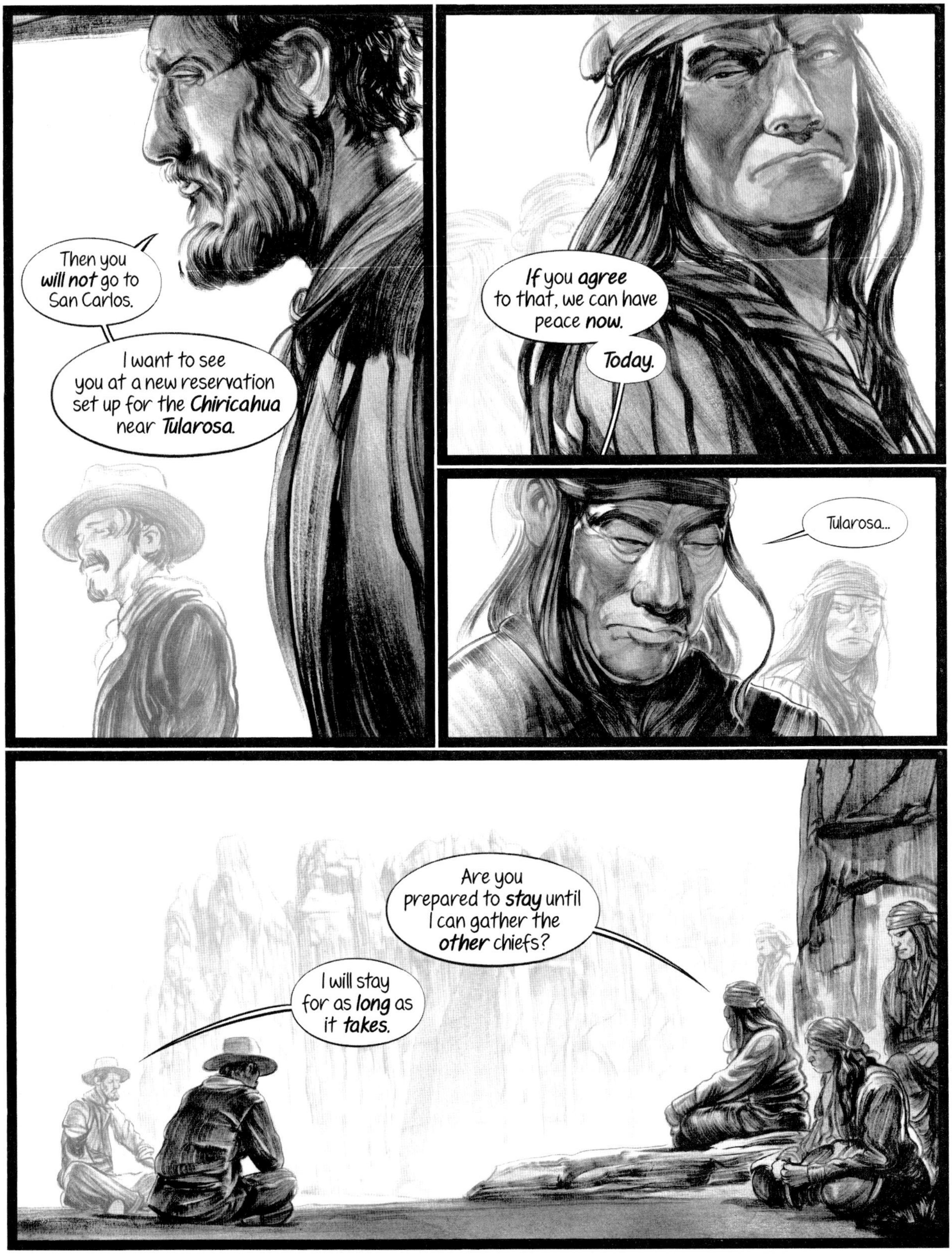
Then you will not go to San Carlos.
I want to see you at a new reservation set up for the Chiricahua near Tularosa.
If you agree to that, we can have peace now.
Today.
Tularosa...
Are you prepared to stay until I can gather the other chiefs?
I will stay for as long as it takes.

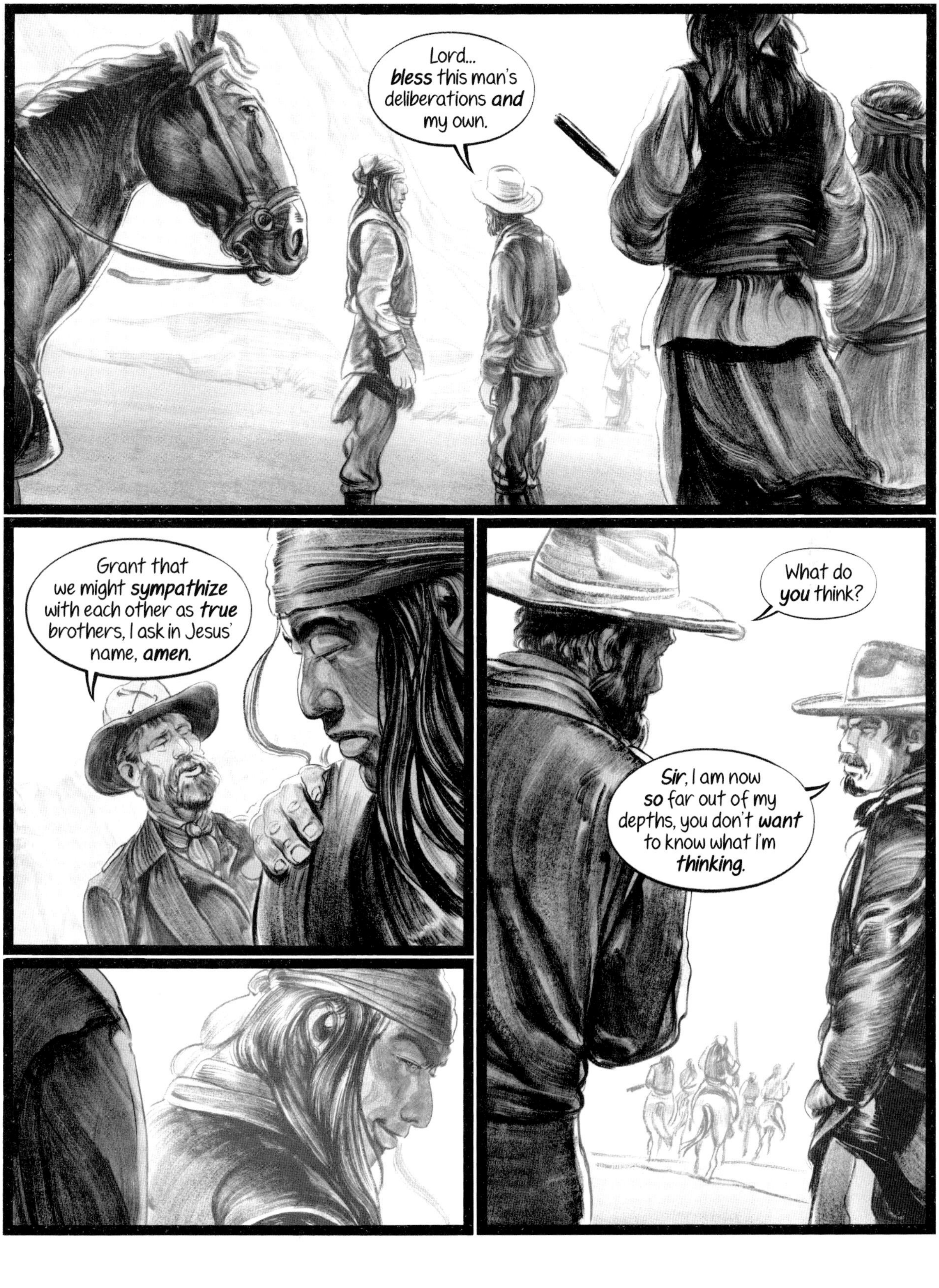
Lord... bless this man's deliberations and my own.
Grant that we might sympathize with each other as true brothers, I ask in Jesus' name, amen.
What do you think?
Sir, I am now so far out of my depths, you don't want to know what I'm thinking.

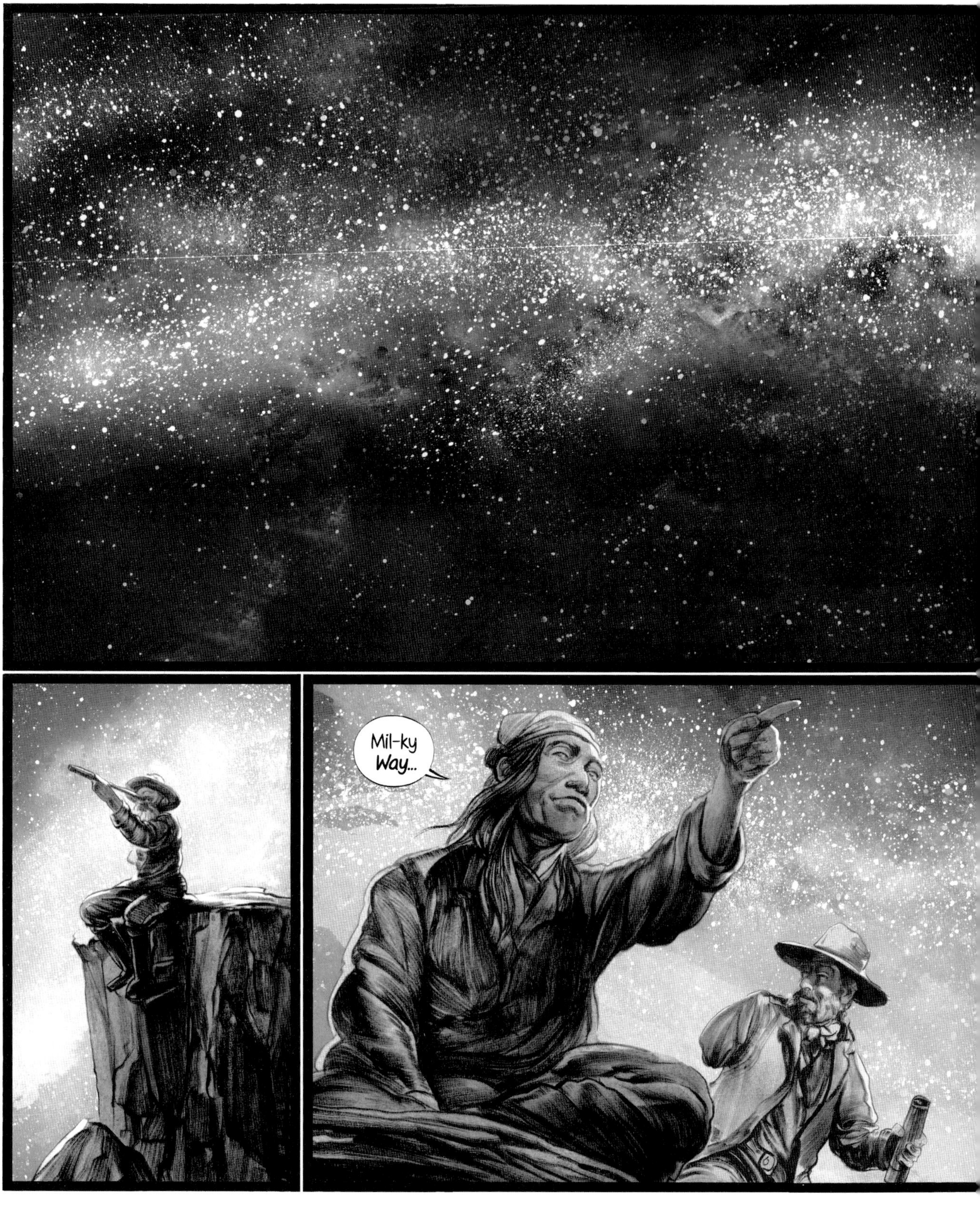
Mil-ky Way...

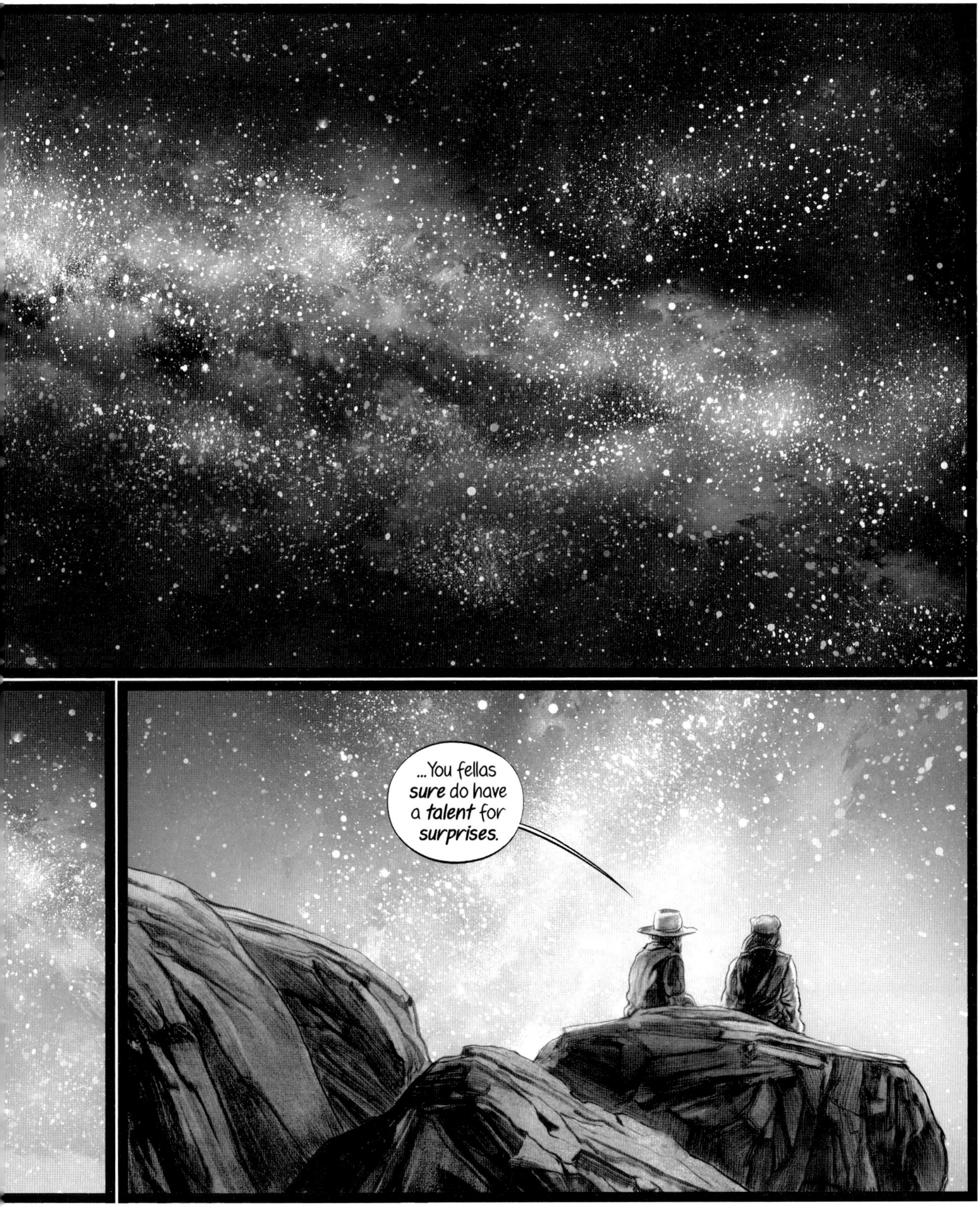
...You fellas sure do have a talent for surprises.

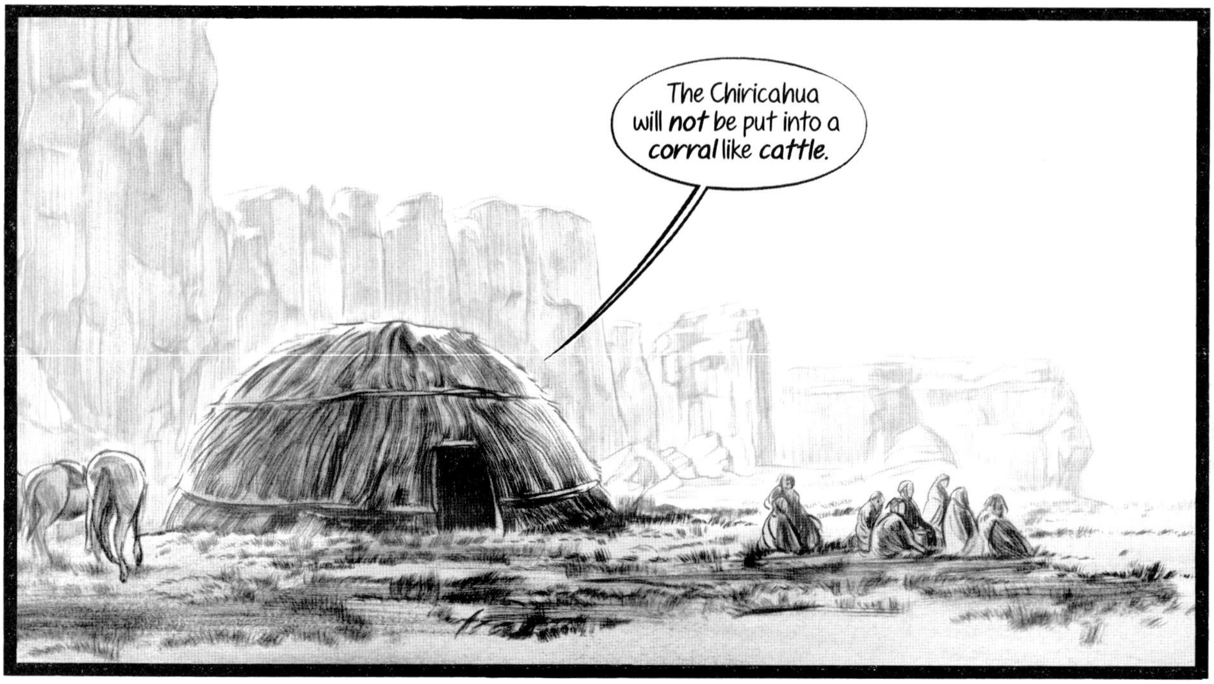
The Chiricahua will not be put into a corral like cattle.

FORTY MOONS AFTER THE MASSACRE AT SKELETON CAVE

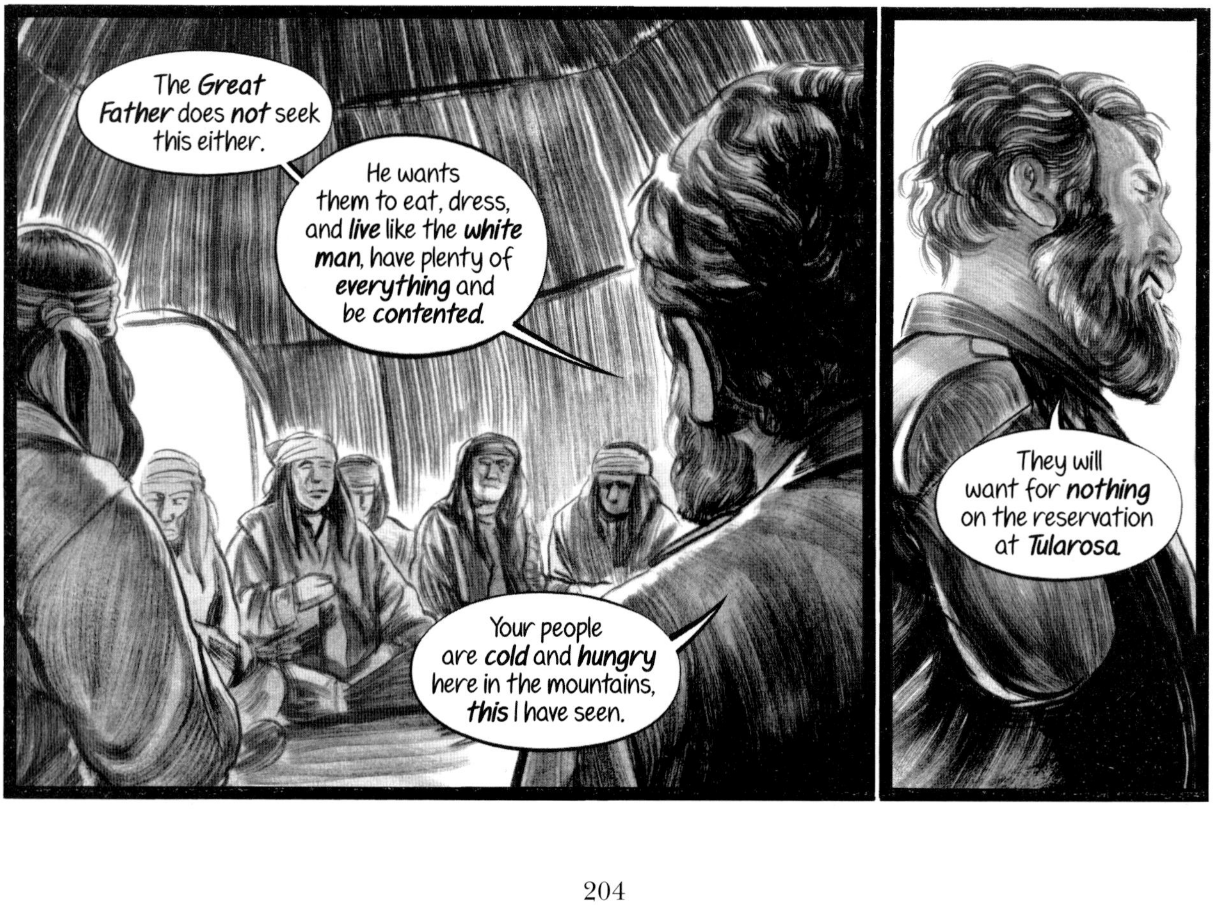
The Great Father does not seek this either.
He wants them to eat, dress, and live like the white man, have plenty of everything and be contented.
Your people are cold and hungry here in the mountains, this I have seen.
They will want for nothing on the reservation at Tularosa.

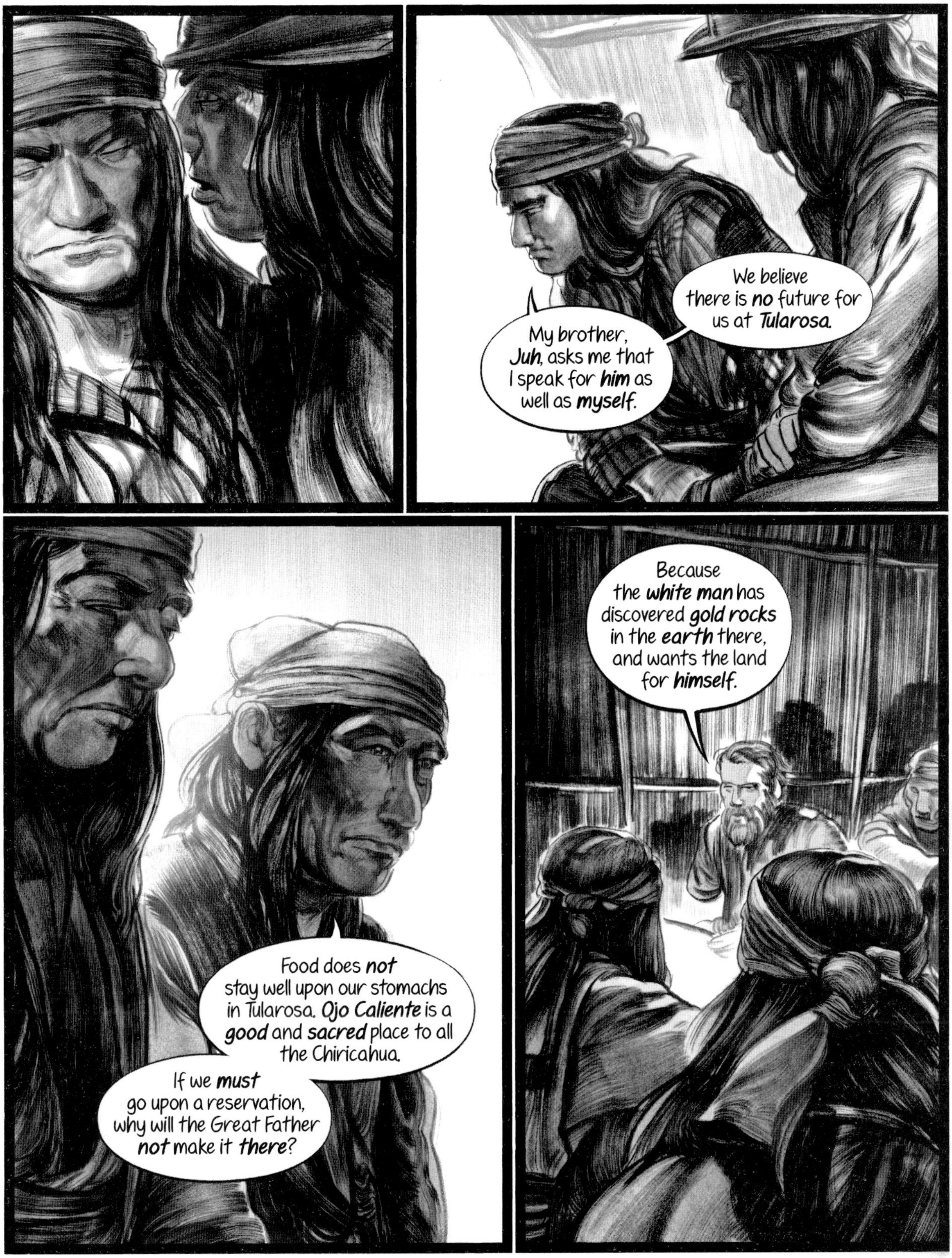
My brother, Juh, asks me that I speak for him as well as myself.
We believe there is no future for us at Tularosa.
Food does not stay well upon our stomachs in Tularosa. Ojo Caliente is a good and sacred place to all the Chiricahua.
If we must go upon a reservation, why will the Great Father not make it there?
Because the white man has discovered gold rocks in the earth there, and wants the land for himself.

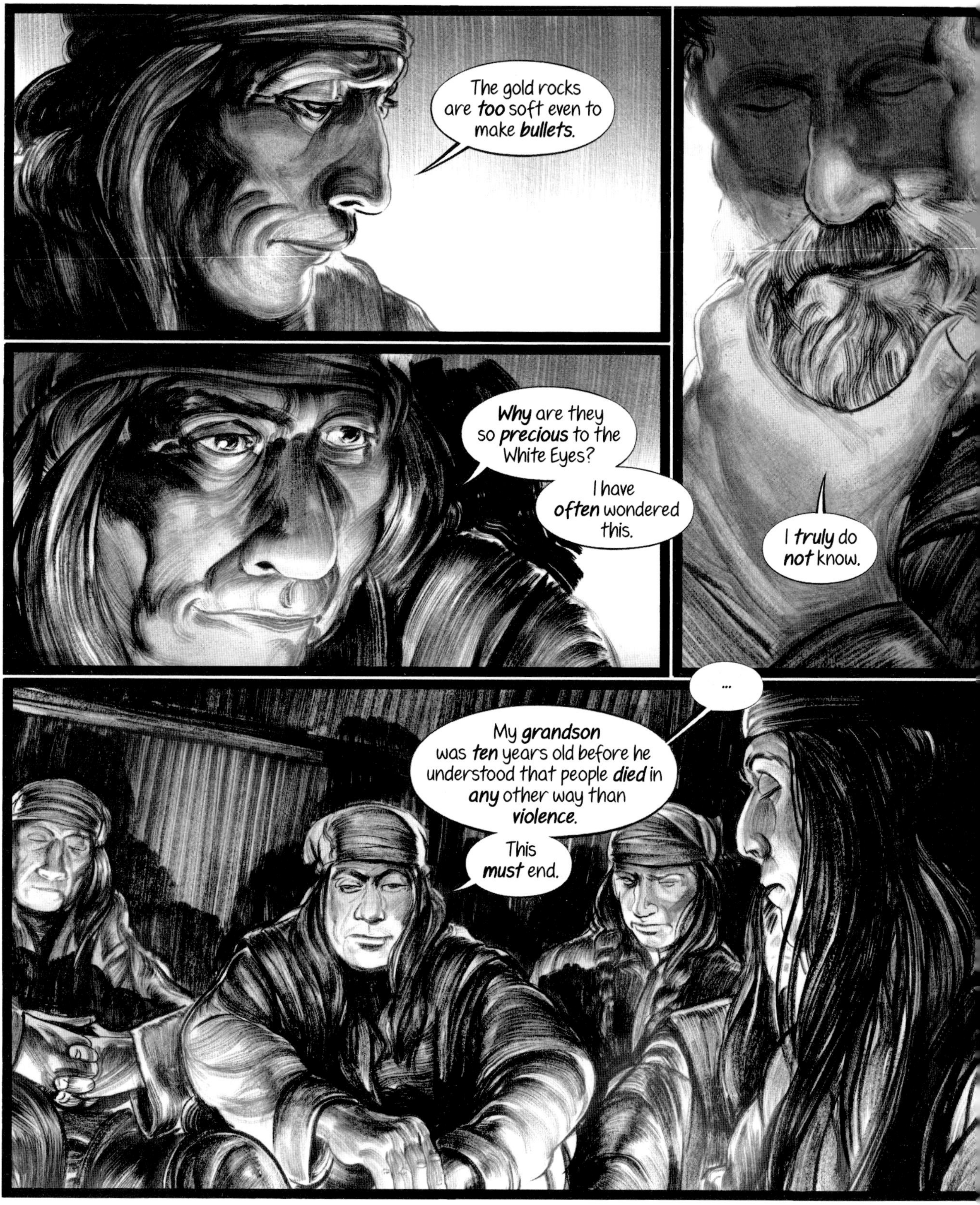
The gold rocks are too soft even to make bullets.
Why are they so precious to the White Eyes?
I have often wondered this.
I truly do not know.
...
My grandson was ten years old before he understood that people died in any other way than violence.
This must end.

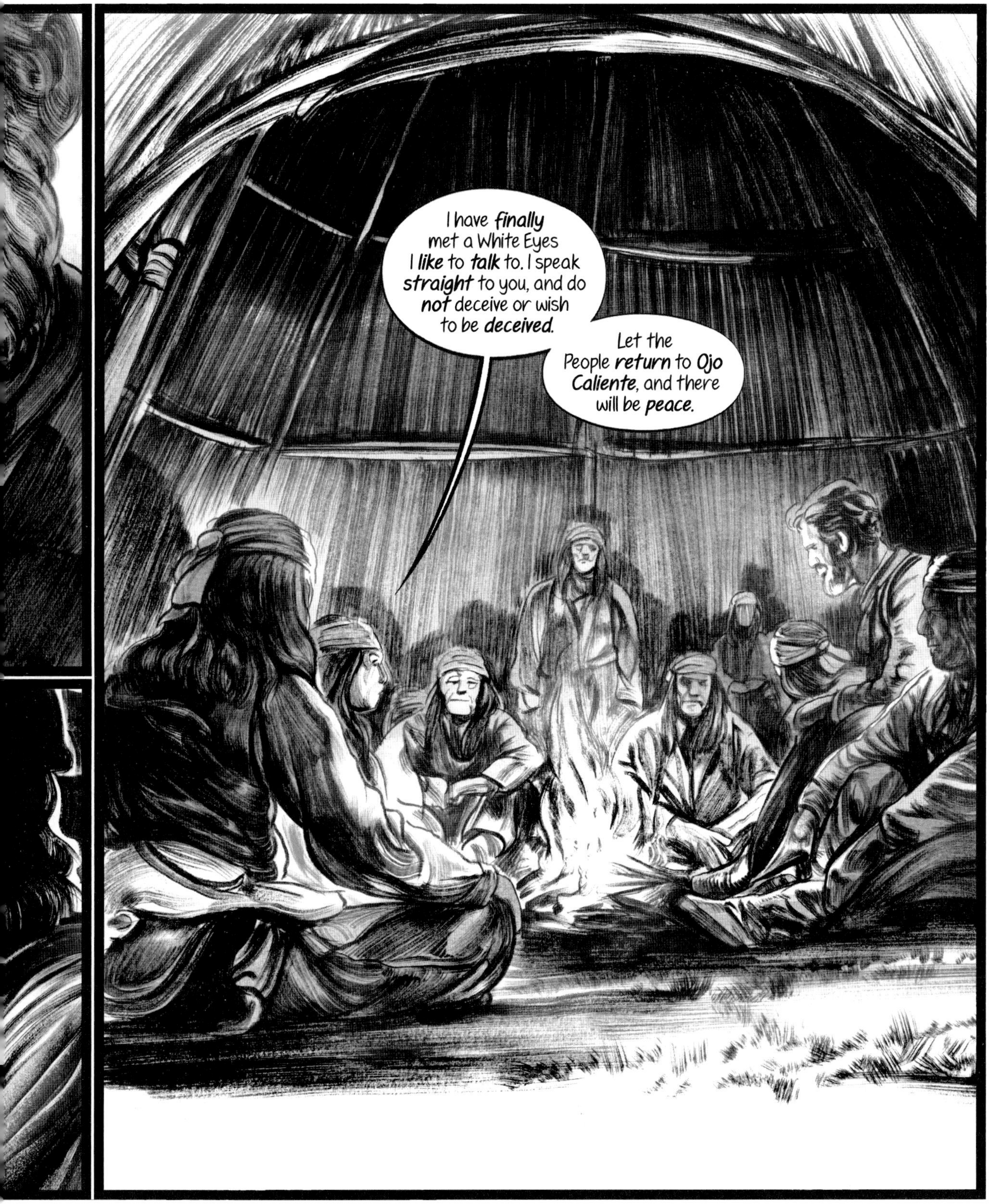
I have finally met a White Eyes I like to talk to. I speak straight to you, and do not deceive or wish to be deceived.
Let the People return to Ojo Caliente, and there will be peace.

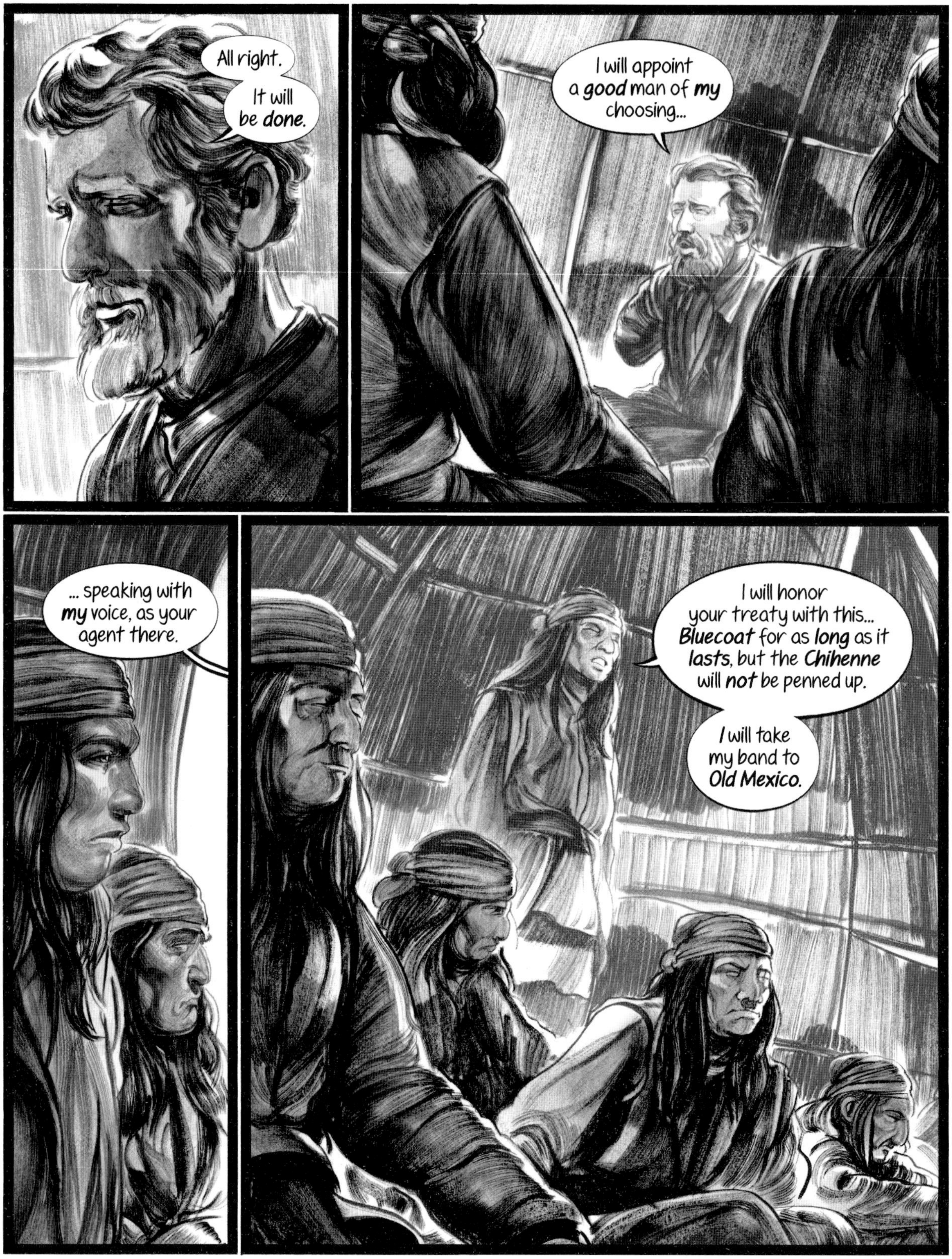
All right.
It will be *done*.
I will appoint a **good** man of **my** choosing...
... speaking with **my** voice, as your agent there.
I will honor your treaty with this... ***Bluecoat*** for as ***long*** as it ***lasts***, but the ***Chihenne*** will ***not*** be penned up.
I will take my band to **Old Mexico**.

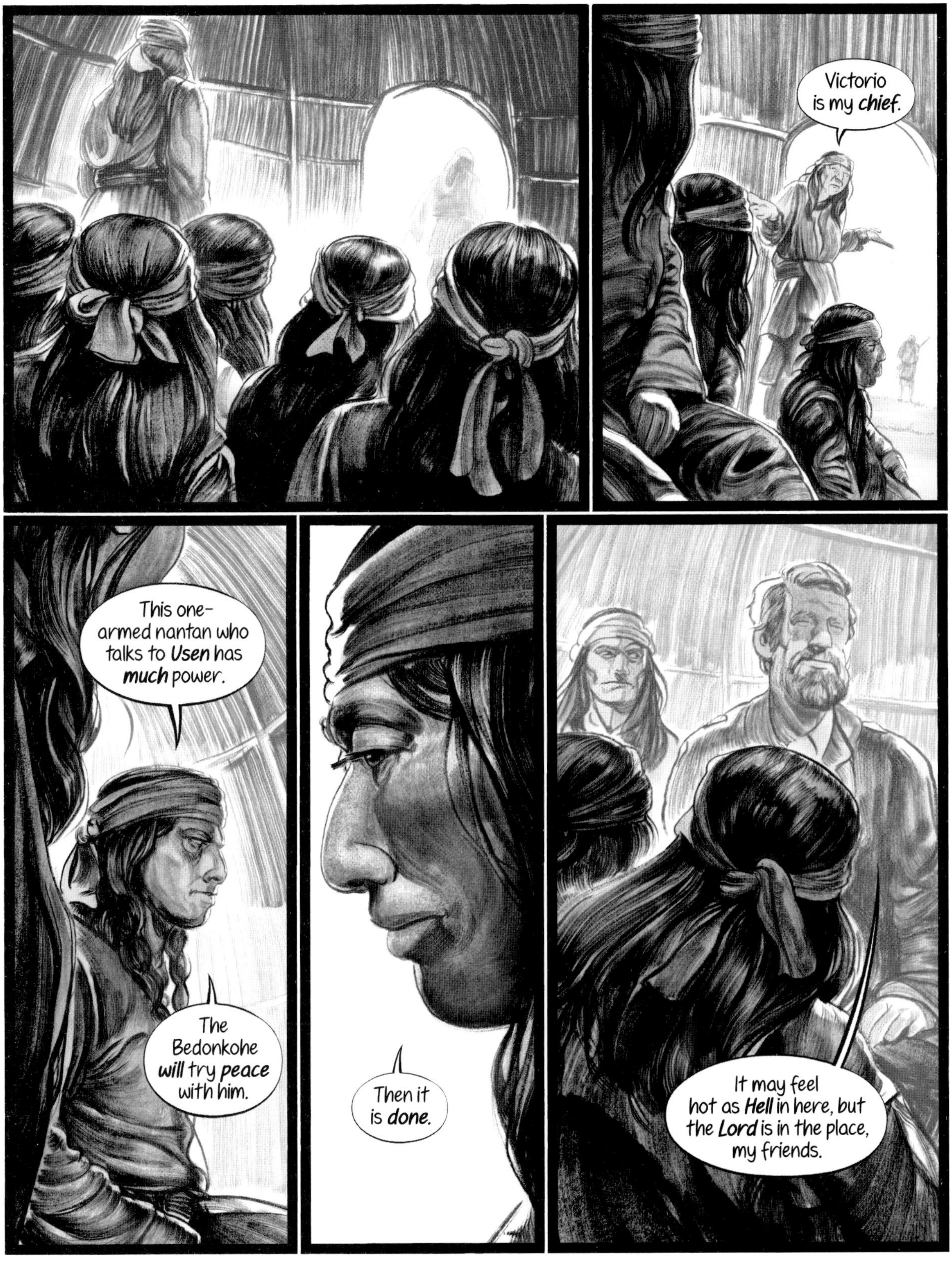
Victorio is my *chief*.
This one-armed nantan who talks to *Usen* has *much* power.
The Bedonkohe *will* try *peace* with him.
Then it is *done*.
It may feel hot as *Hell* in here, but the *Lord* is in the place, my friends.

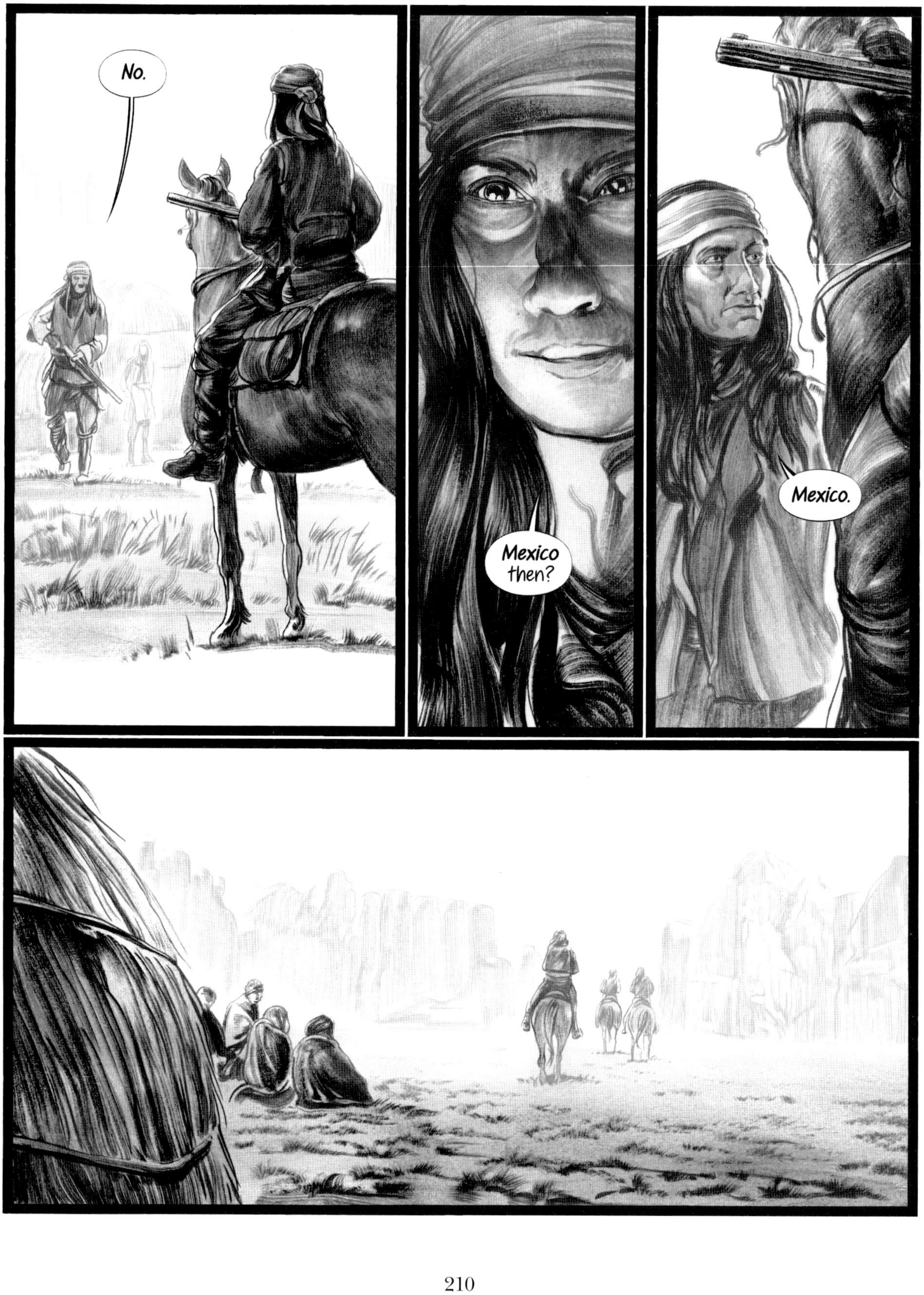
No.
Mexico then?
Mexico.

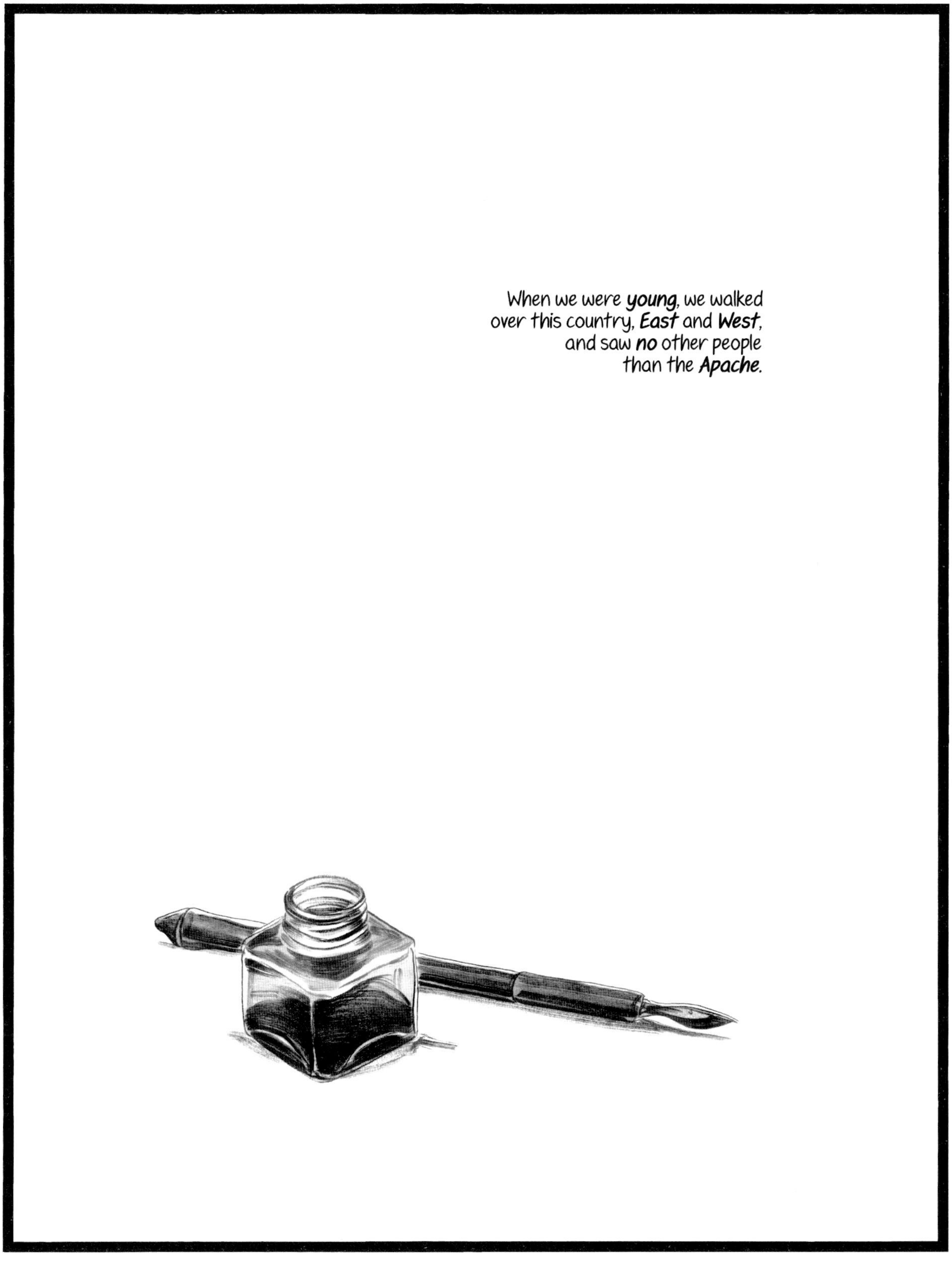
When we were young, we walked over this country, East and West, and saw no other people than the Apache.

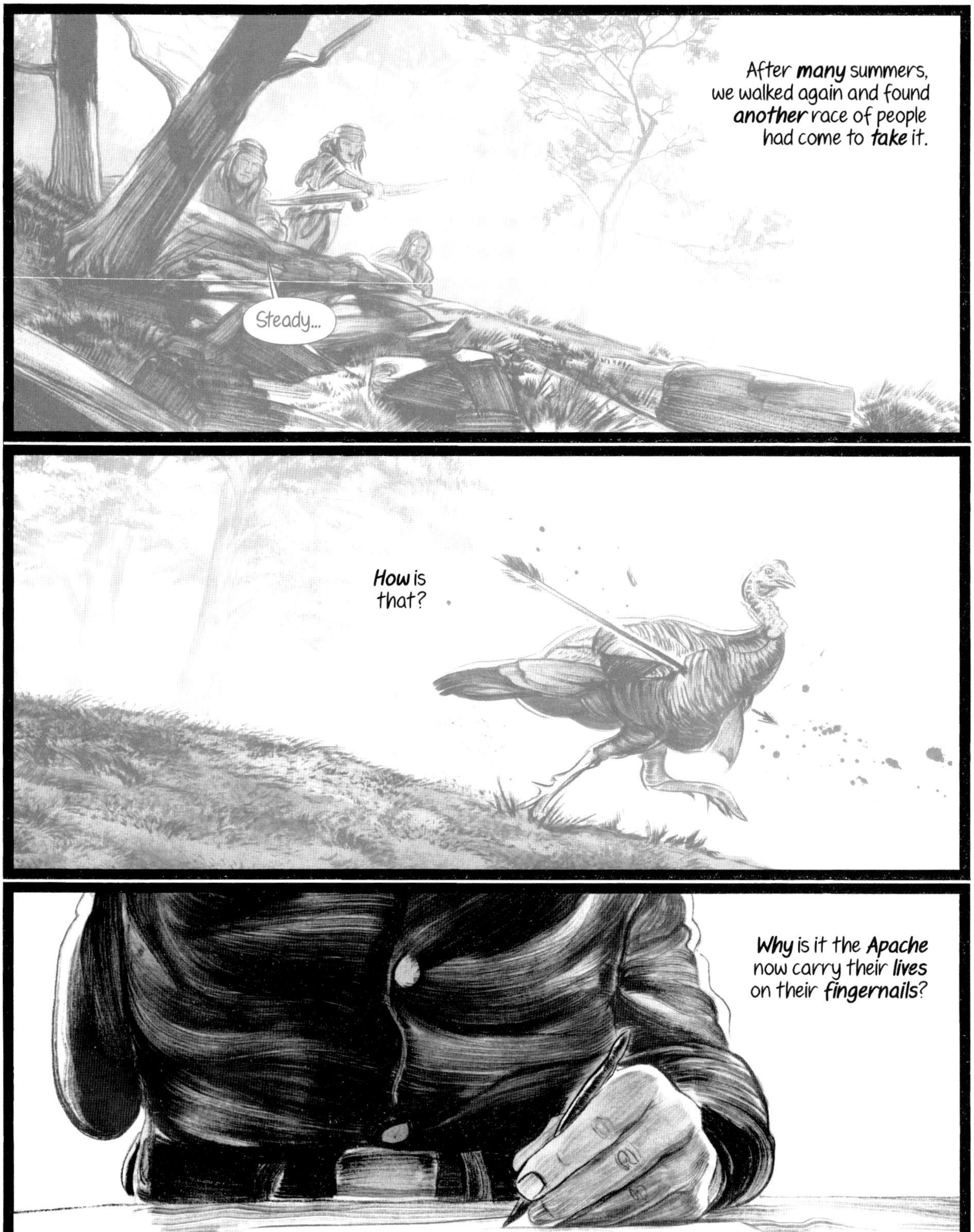
After many summers, we walked again and found another race of people had come to take it.
Steady...
How is that?
Why is it the Apache now carry their lives on their fingernails?

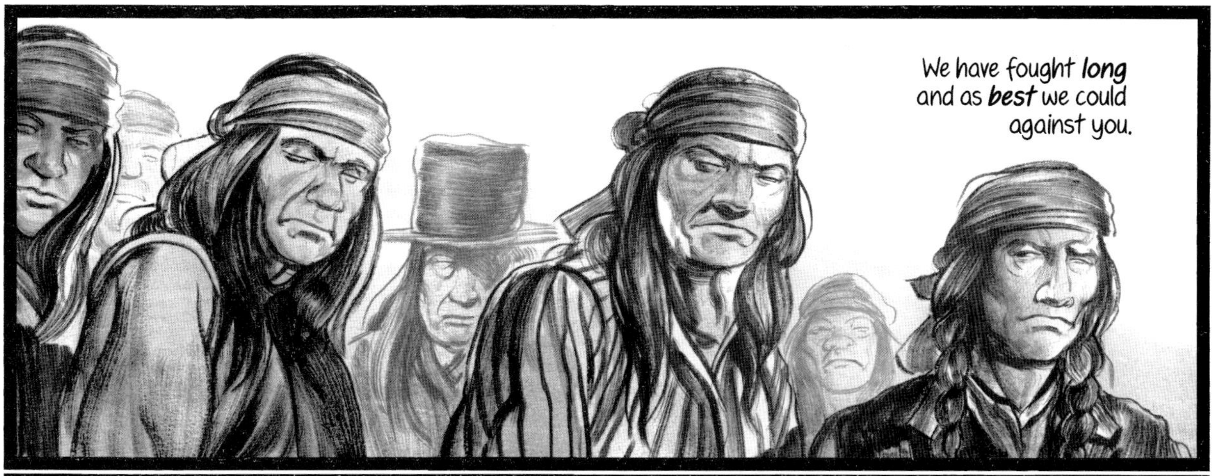
We have fought **long** and as **best** we could against you.

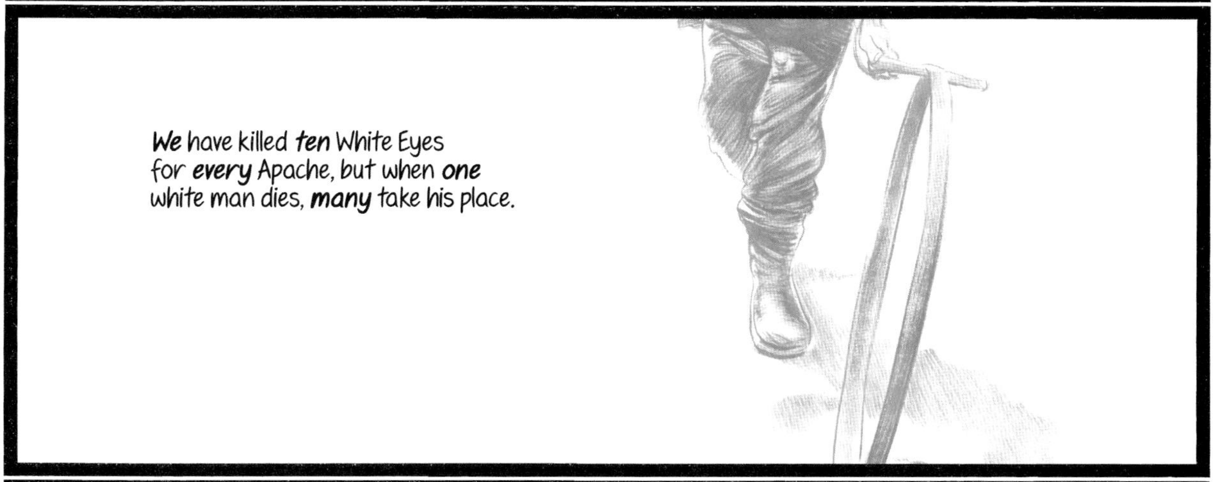
We have killed **ten** White Eyes for **every** Apache, but when **one** white man dies, **many** take his place.

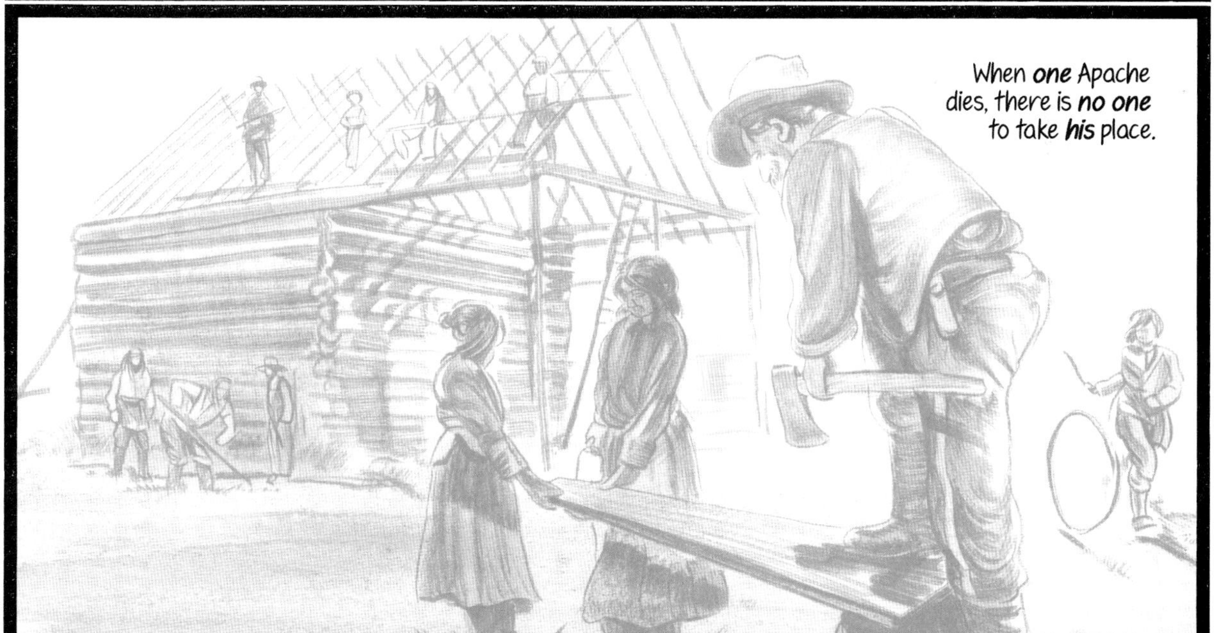
When **one** Apache dies, there is **no one** to take **his** place.

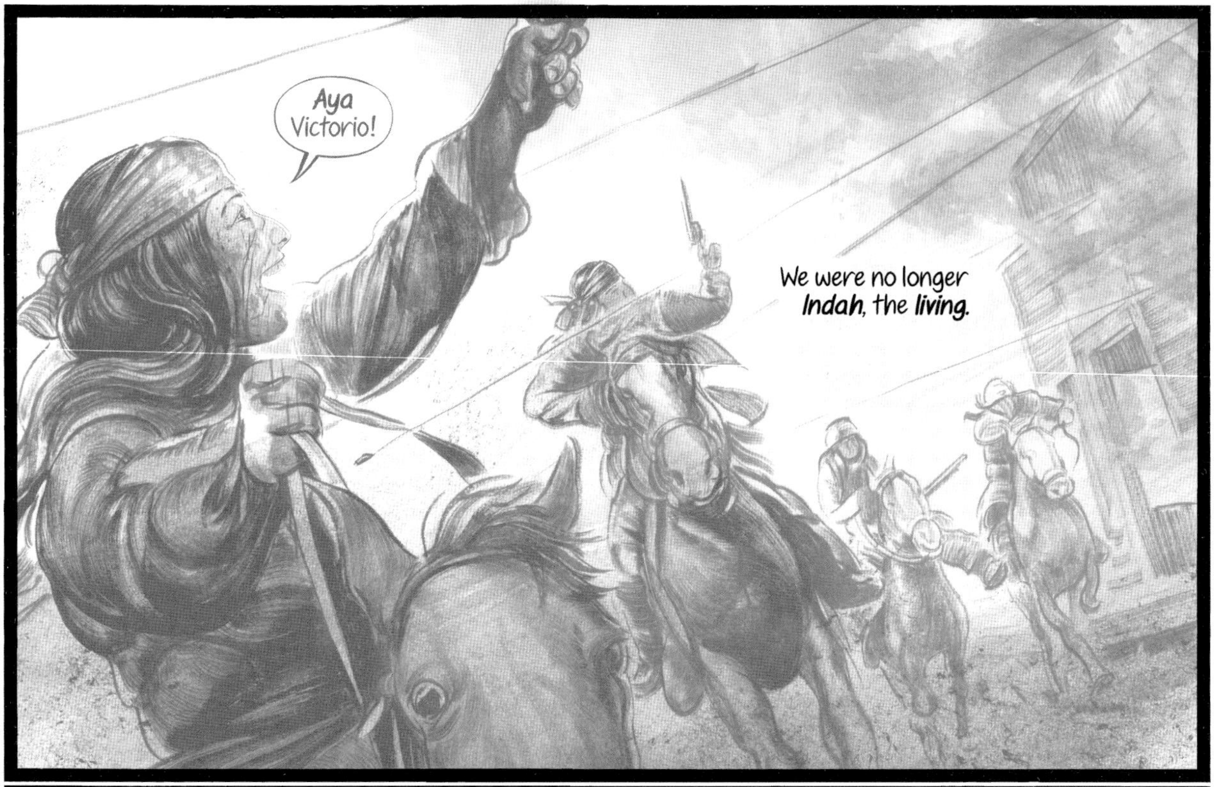
Aya Victorio!
We were no longer **Indah**, the **living**.

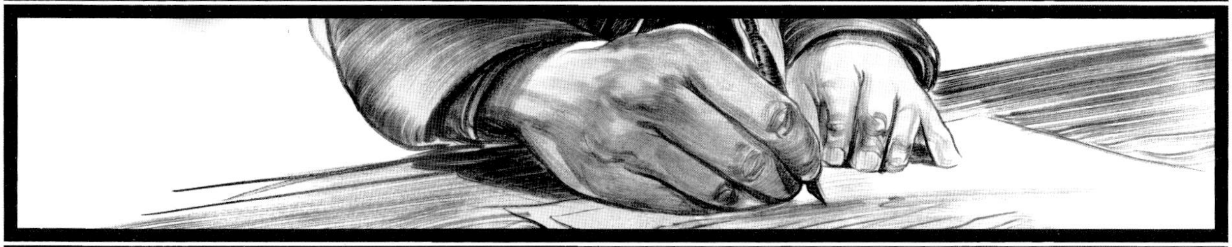

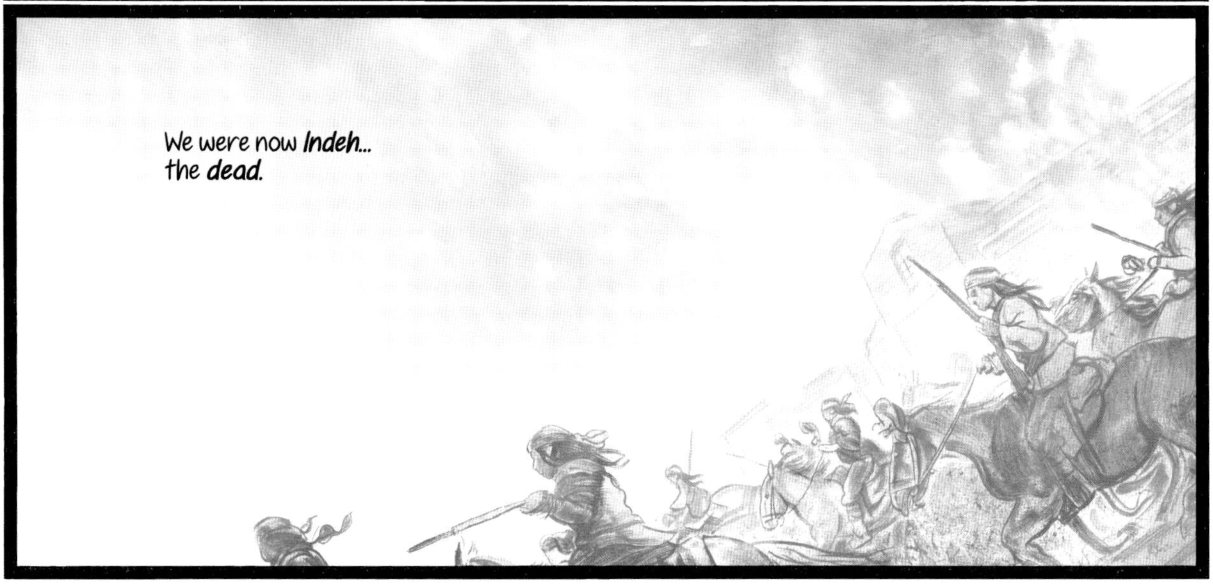
We were now **Indeh**... the **dead**.

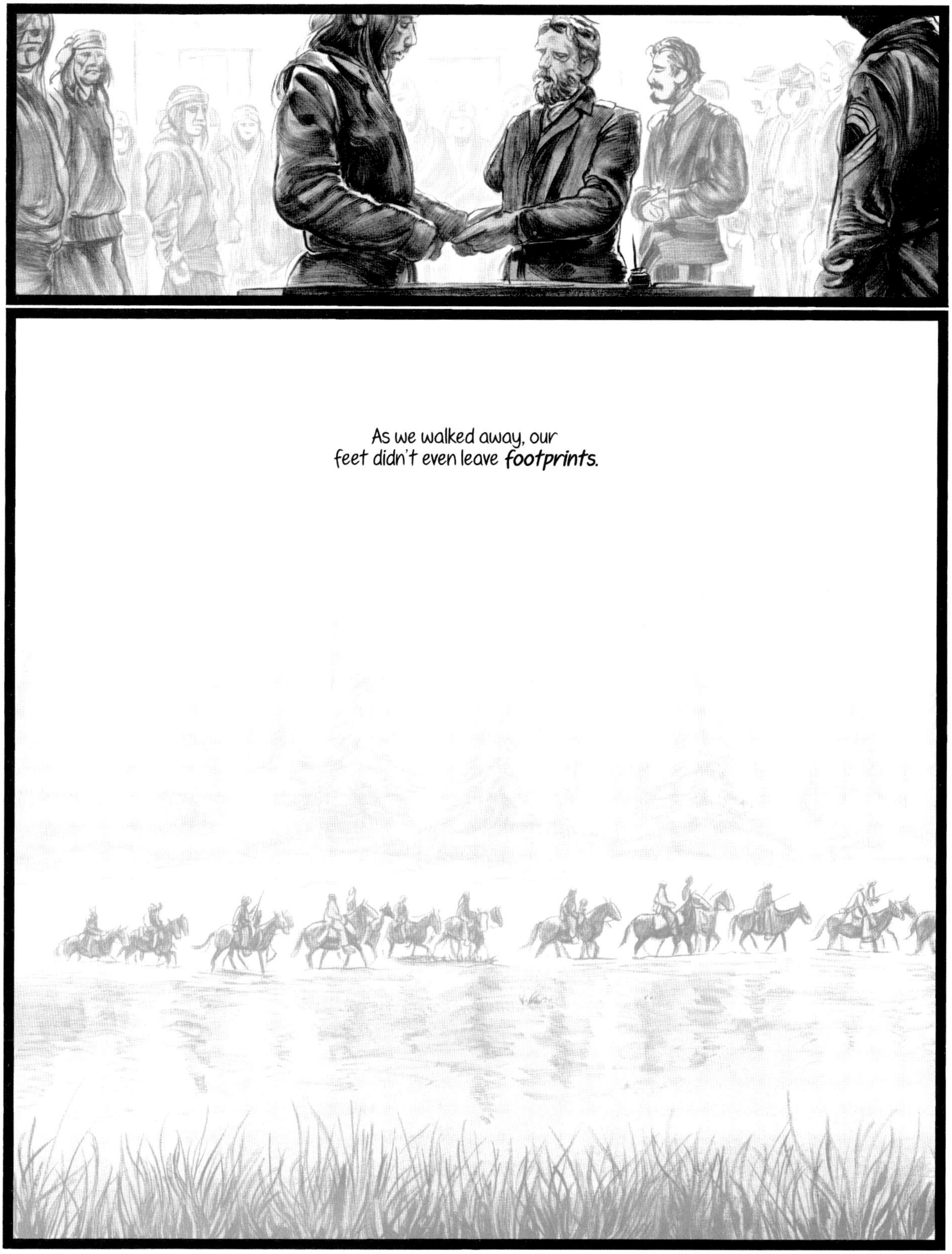
As we walked away, our feet didn't even leave *footprints*.

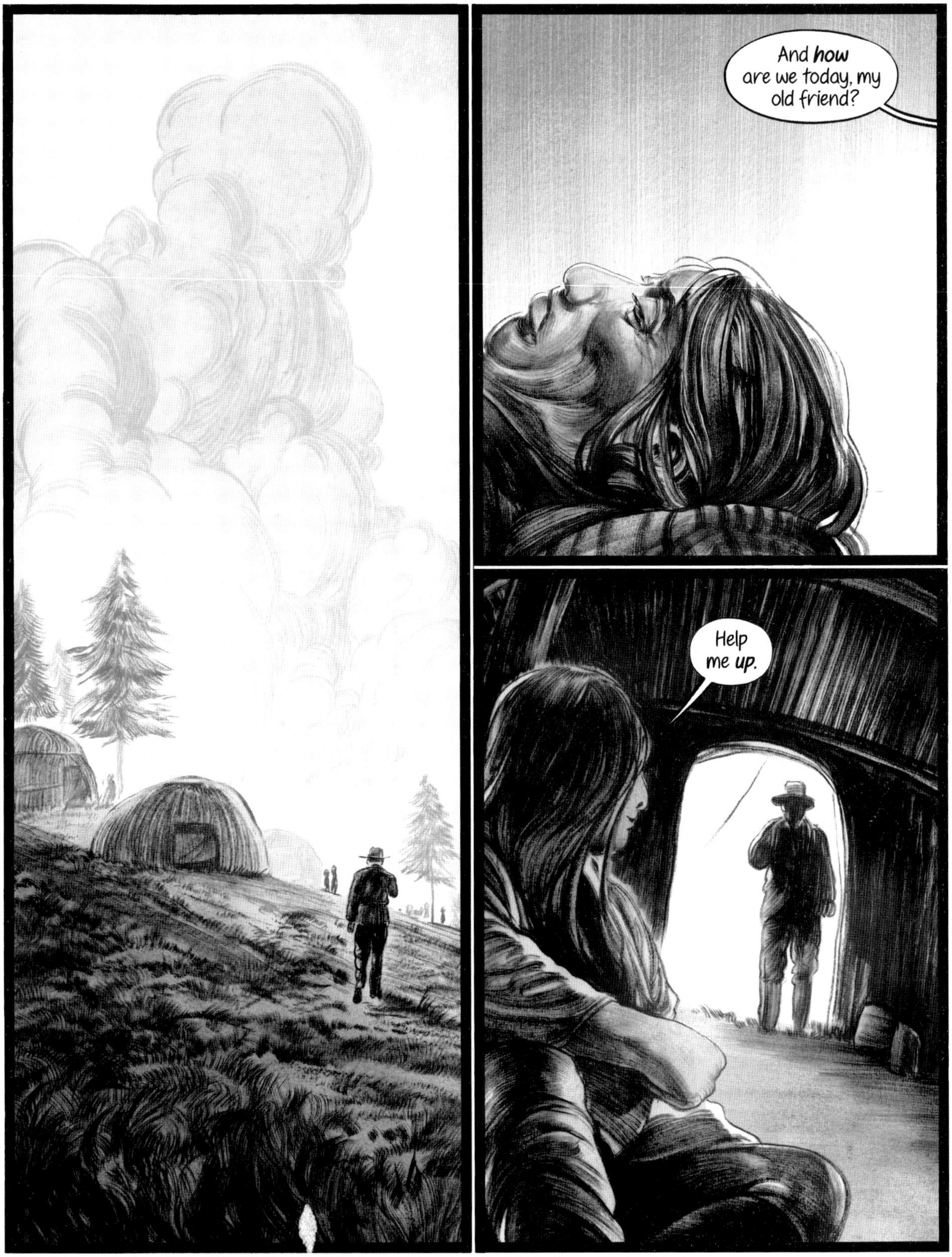
And **how** are we today, my old friend?
Help me **up**.

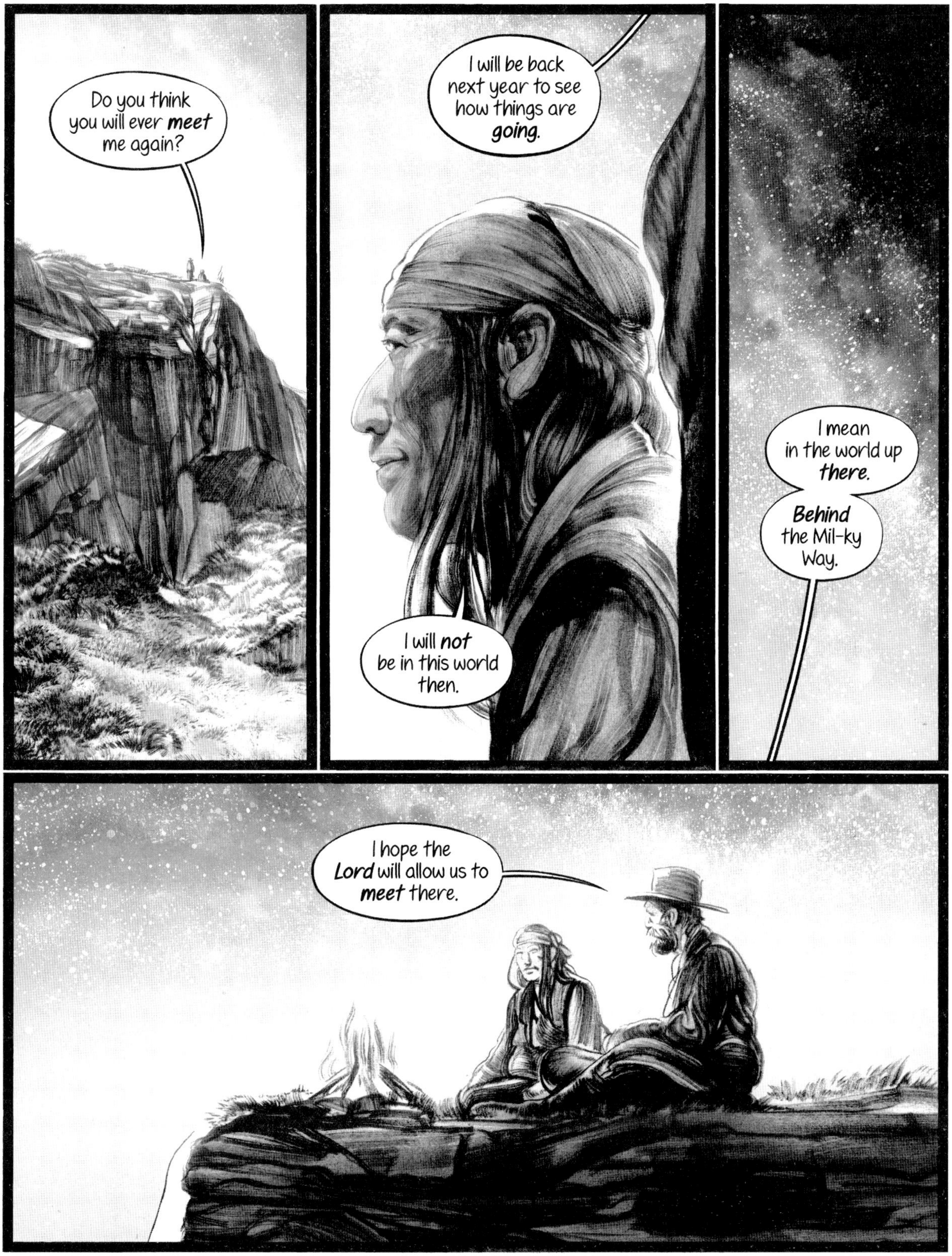
Do you think you will ever **meet** me again?
I will be back next year to see how things are **going**.
I will **not** be in this world then.
I mean in the world up **there**.
Behind the Mil-ky Way.
I hope the **Lord** will allow us to **meet** there.

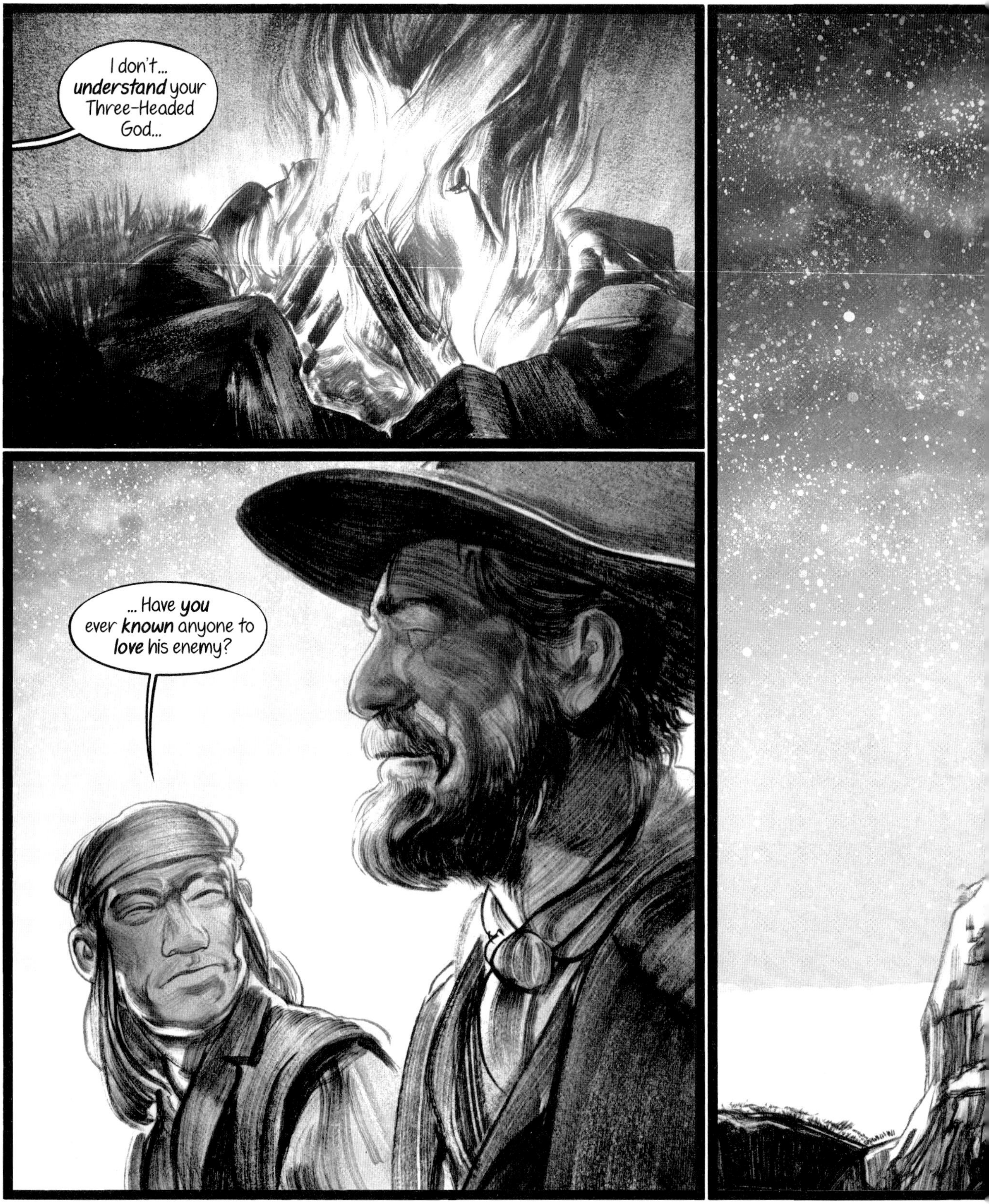
I don't... understand your Three-Headed God...
... Have you ever known anyone to love his enemy?

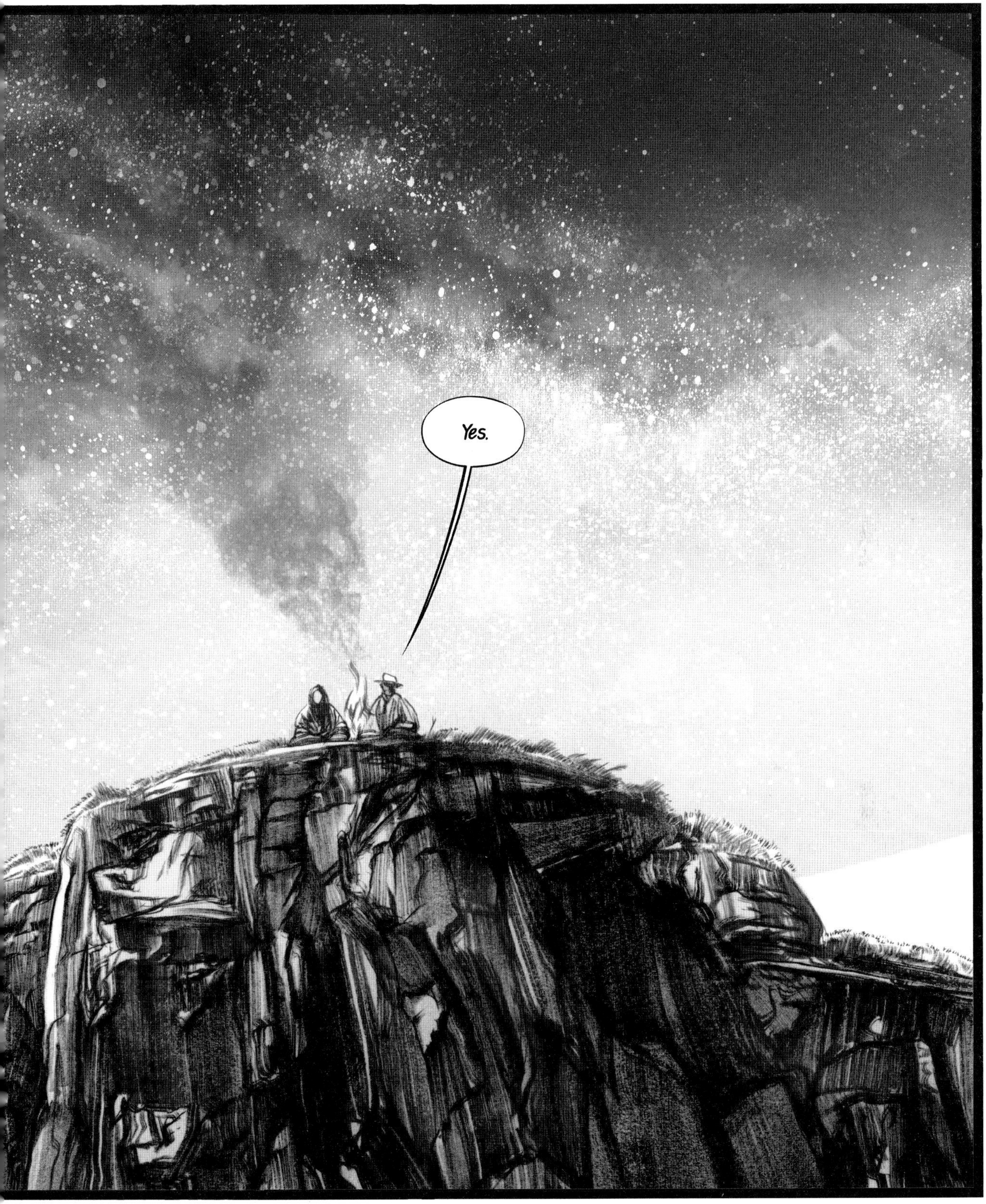
Yes.

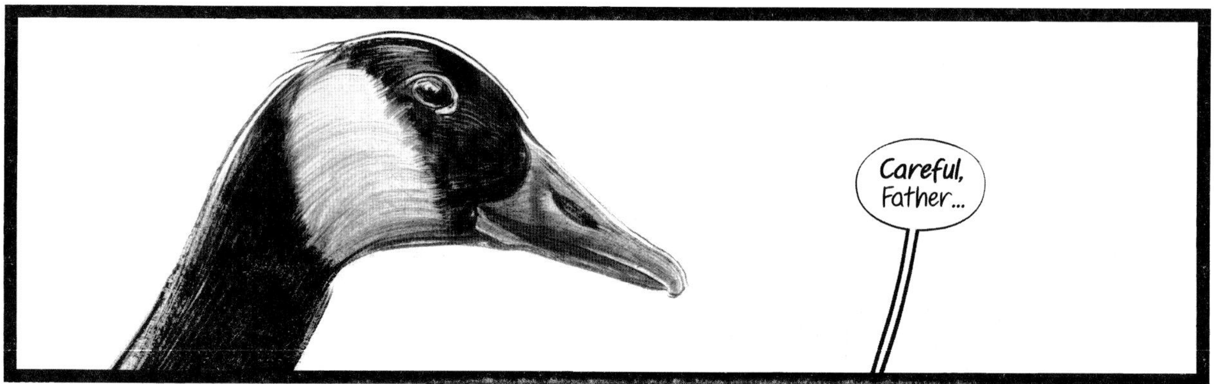
Careful, Father...

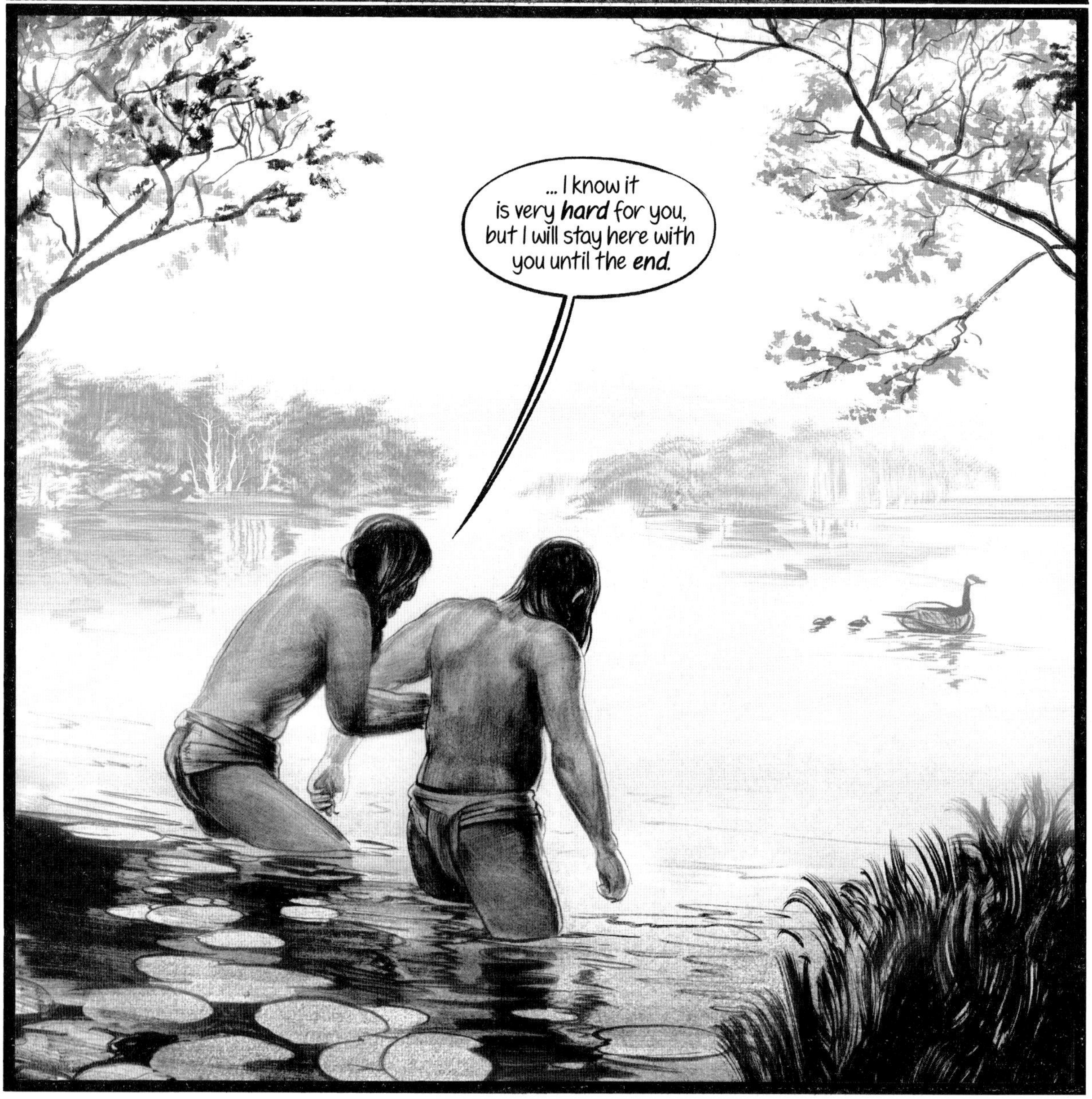
... I know it is very **hard** for you, but I will stay here with you until the **end**.

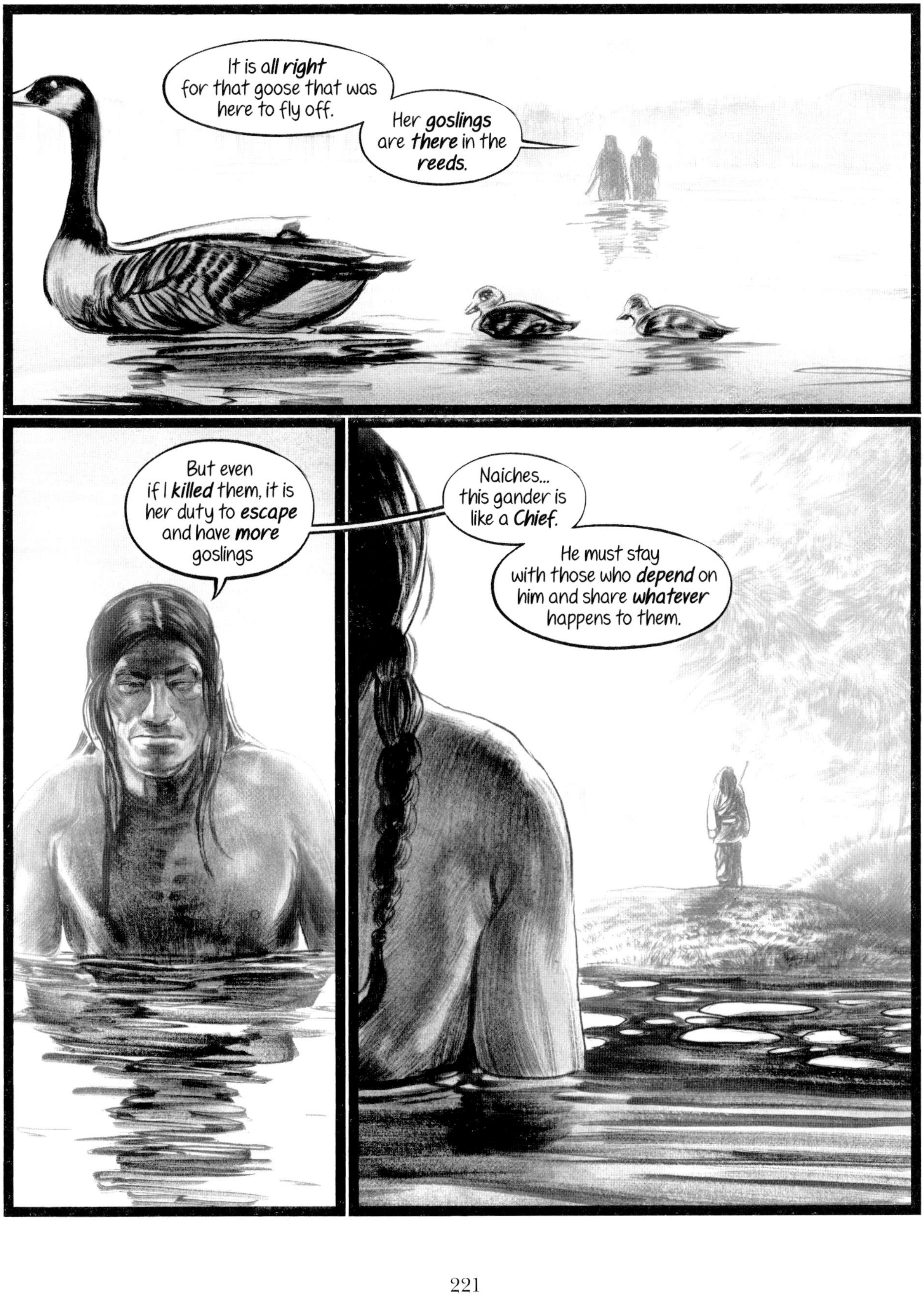
It is all **right** for that goose that was here to fly off.
Her **goslings** are **there** in the **reeds**.
But even if I **killed** them, it is her duty to **escape** and have **more** goslings
Naiches... this gander is like a **Chief**.
He must stay with those who **depend** on him and share **whatever** happens to them.

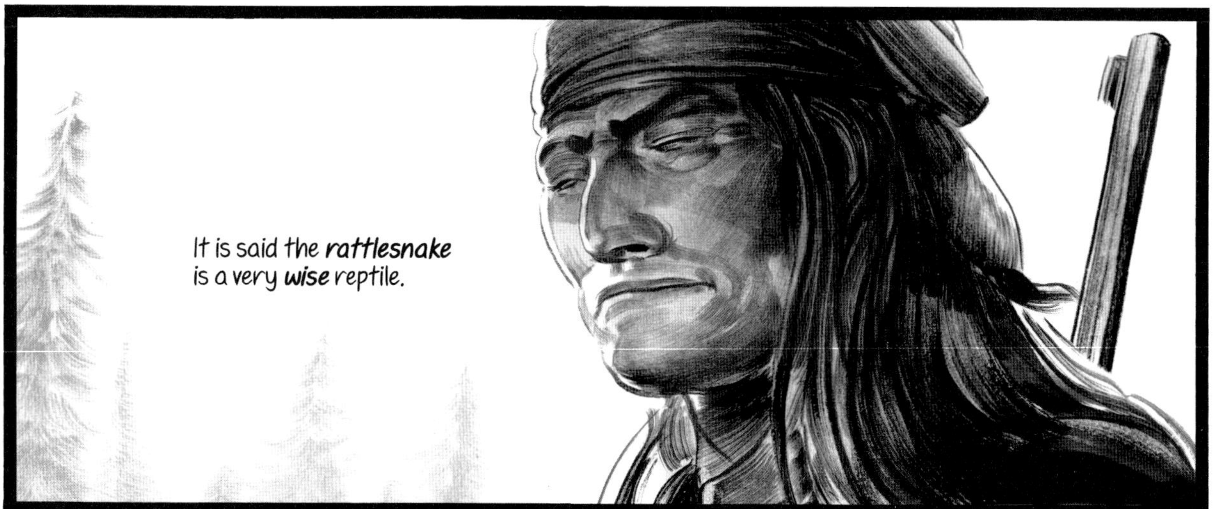
It is said the ***rattlesnake*** is a very ***wise*** reptile.

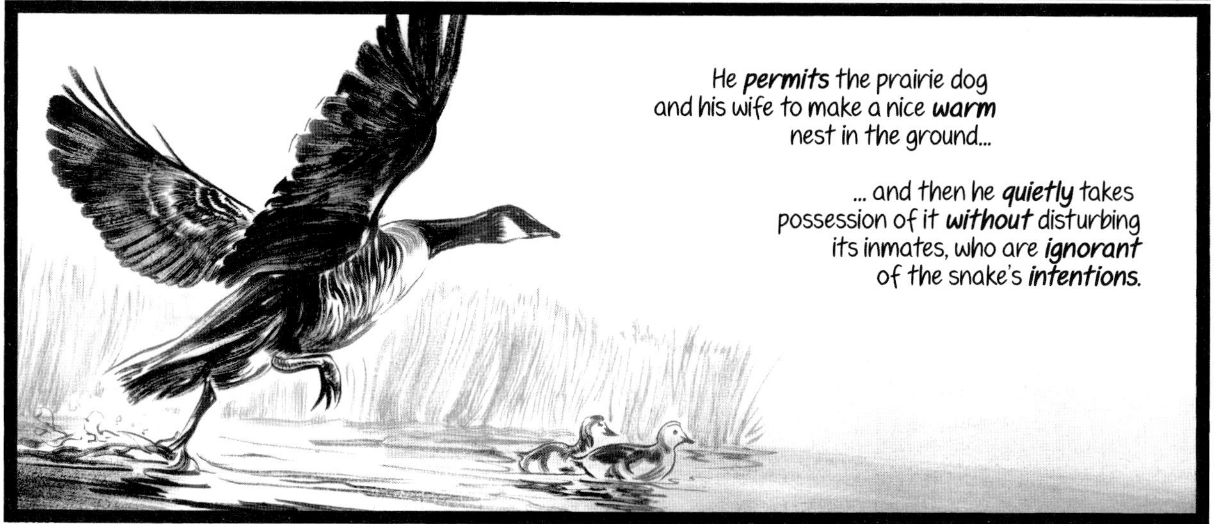
He ***permits*** the prairie dog and his wife to make a nice ***warm*** nest in the ground...
... and then he ***quietly*** takes possession of it ***without*** disturbing its inmates, who are ***ignorant*** of the snake's ***intentions.***

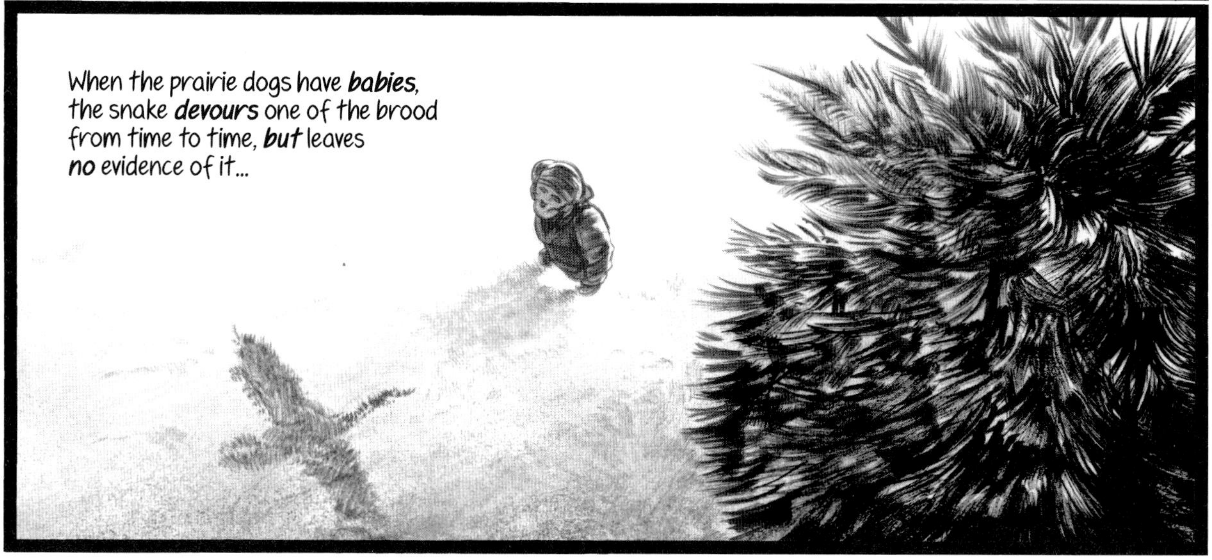
When the prairie dogs have ***babies***, the snake ***devours*** one of the brood from time to time, ***but*** leaves ***no*** evidence of it...

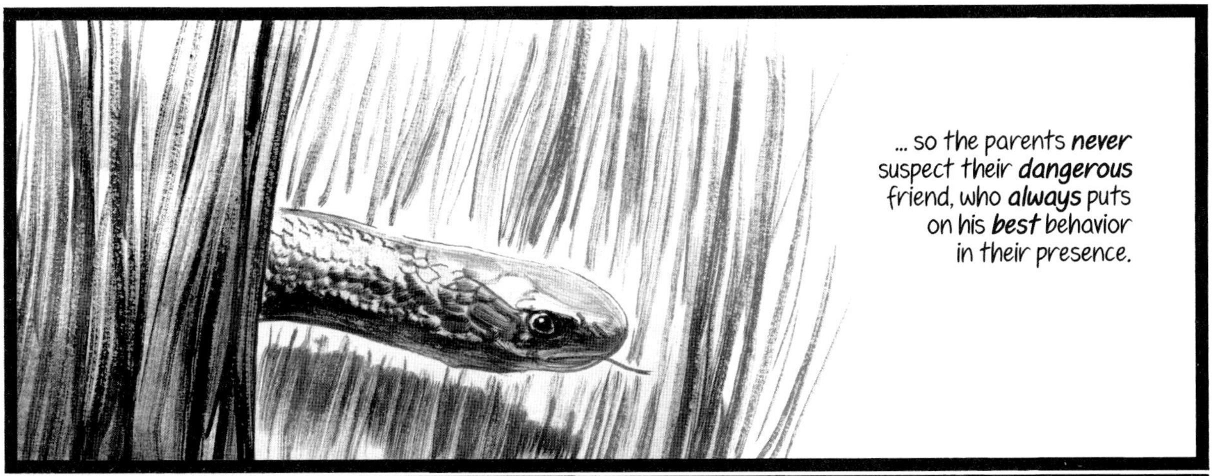
... so the parents never suspect their dangerous friend, who always puts on his best behavior in their presence.

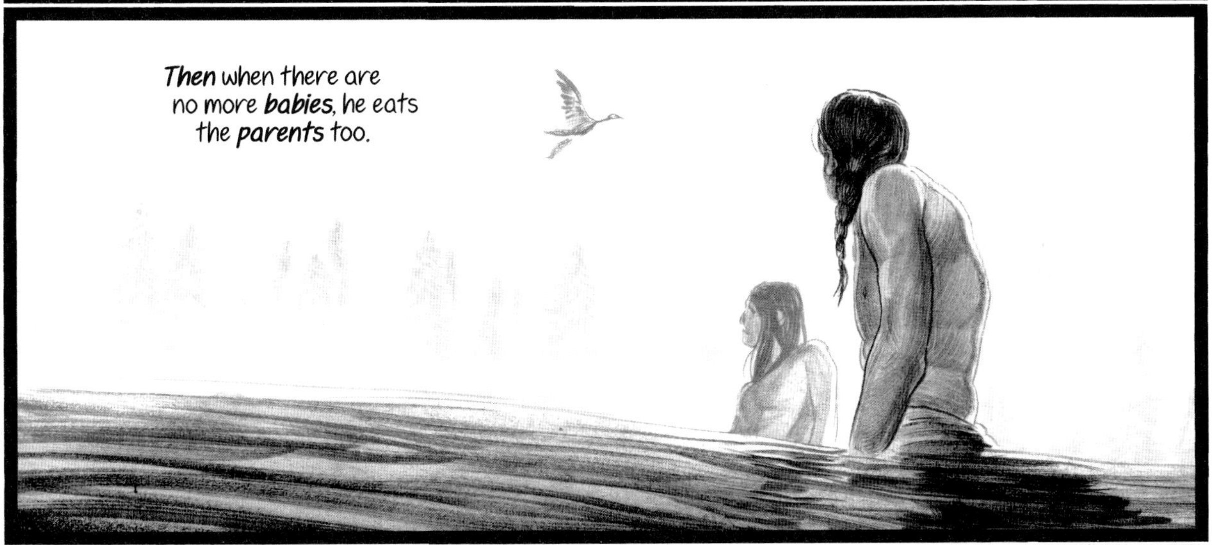
Then when there are no more babies, he eats the parents too.

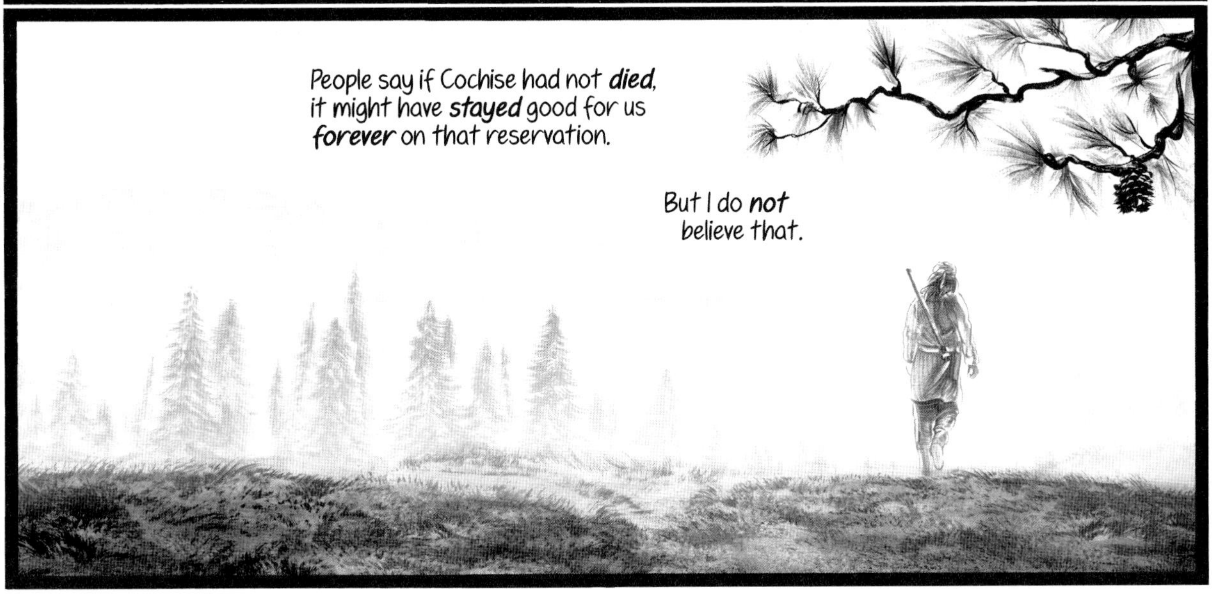
People say if Cochise had not died, it might have stayed good for us forever on that reservation.
But I do not believe that.

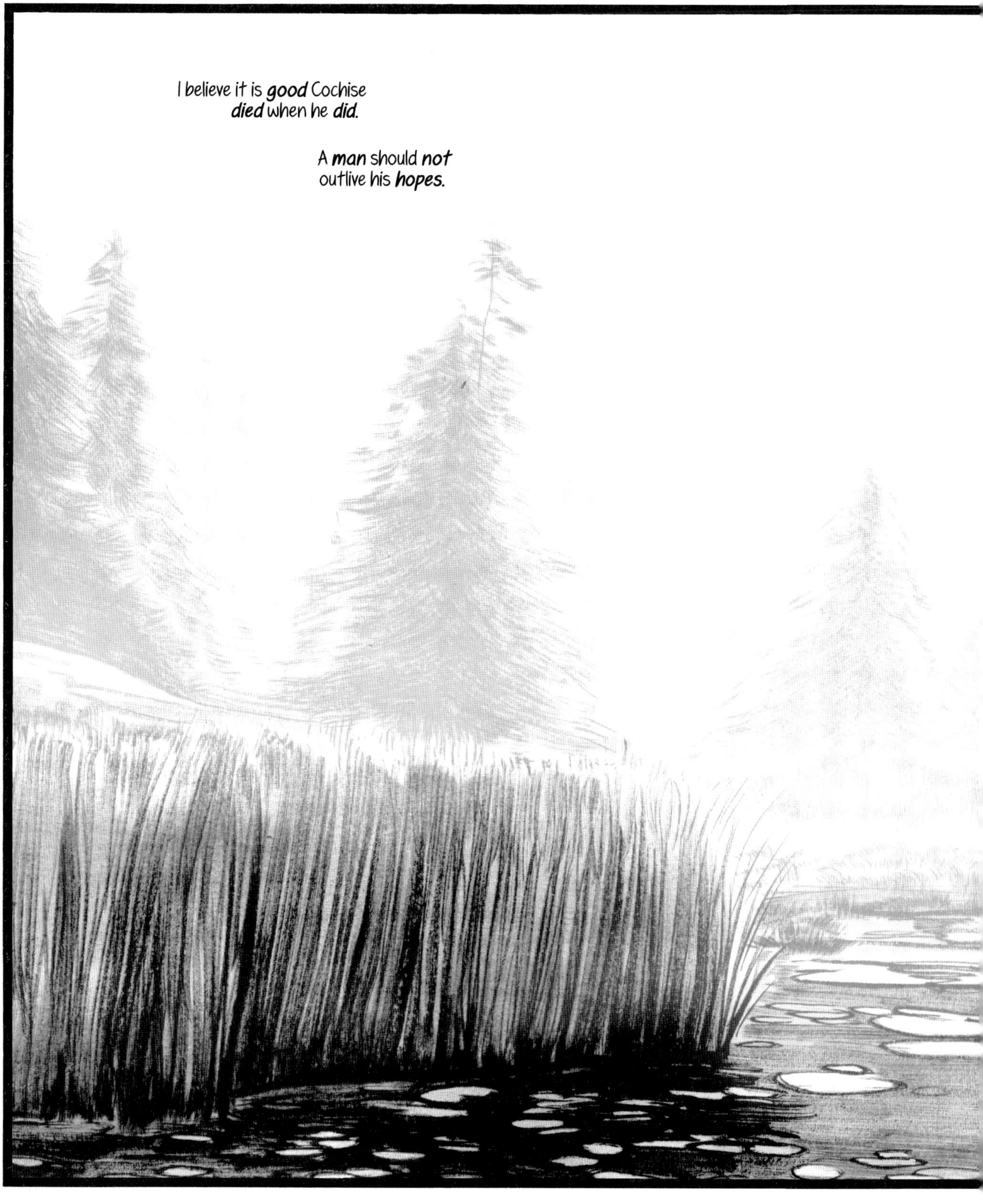
I believe it is **good** Cochise **died** when he **did.**
A **man** should **not** outlive his **hopes.**

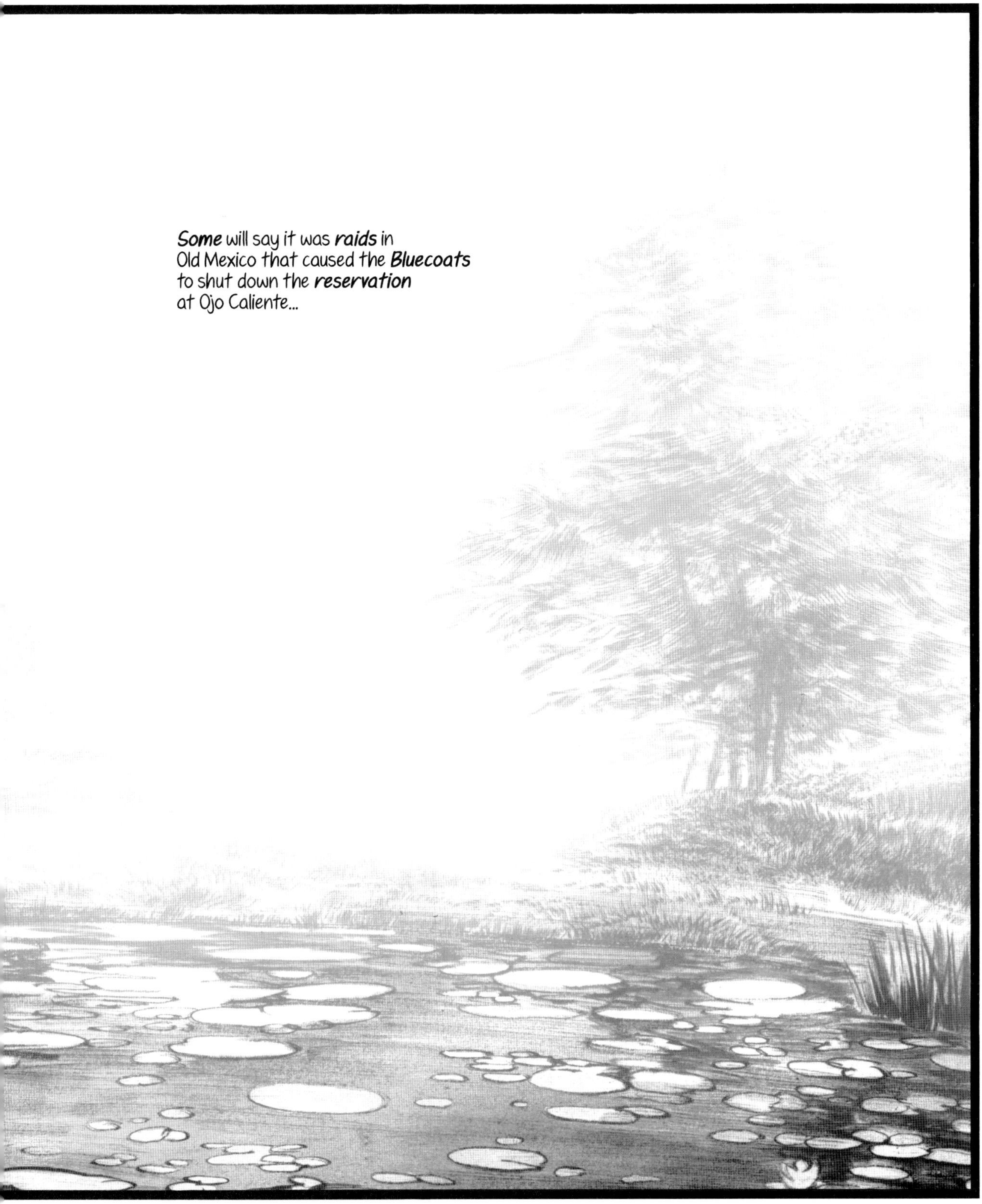
Some will say it was **raids** in Old Mexico that caused the **Bluecoats** to shut down the **reservation** at Ojo Caliente...

... but *that* is just
what the *rattlesnake*
told the *prairie dogs*.

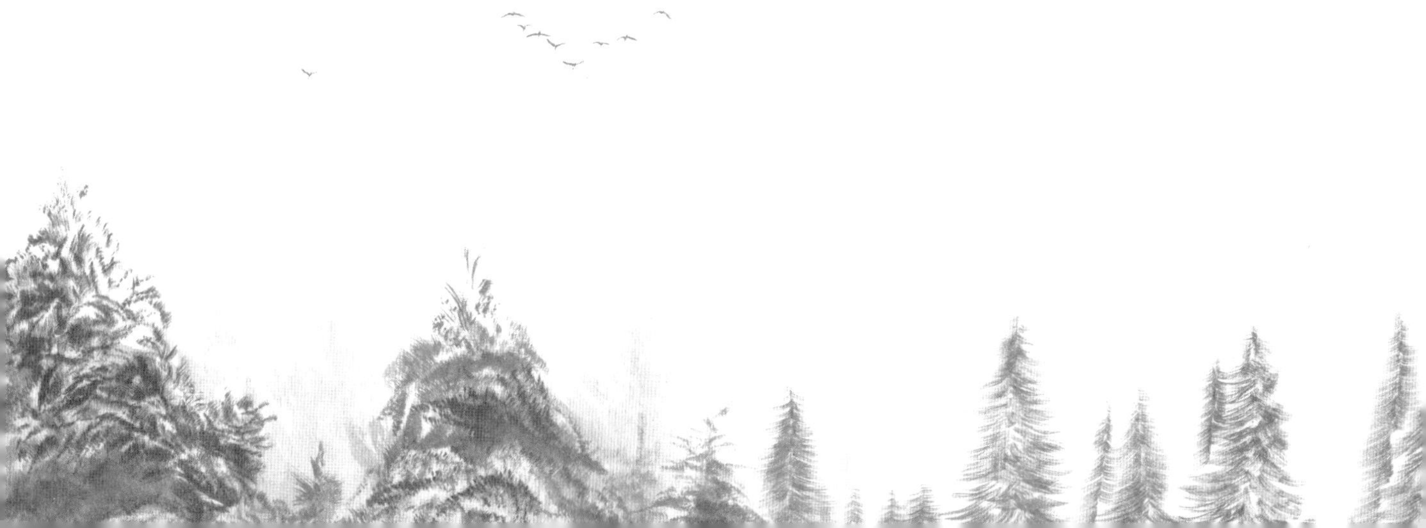

AFTERWORD

Eight years old and sitting in the back of my dad's baby blue Plymouth Barracuda, I engaged my *Star Trek* figures in battle on the armrest. My dad was heartbroken, trying to heal from his divorce by taking me camping in the most remote places he could find. Out in the red dirt along the Arizona–New Mexico border one day, I felt the atmosphere of the car shift. My dad, my real-life Captain Kirk, was suddenly nervous. An old man waved us down from the center of the two-lane road—the only living thing as far as my eyes could see. I heard him say in an unfamiliar cadence, "You are not supposed to be here."

My father apologized. The man came to the window and peered in at me. He was wearing a blue jean tuxedo and had the sort of ancient eyes you'd imagine might belong to a tree.

"You're lucky it's me who found you," he said, looking directly at me.

"What happened?" I asked once we had turned around and were heading away.

My father explained what an Indian reservation was, what an Apache was, how we really shouldn't have been there at all, and how lucky he was not to have gotten his ass kicked. Why were we lucky it was the old man who found us? What did he mean?

My father told me, "Many of the Indians are very angry. And they damn well should be."

"At me?" I asked.

The Barracuda drove on, but the old man's eyes stayed with me. At the roadside shops I started buying books about Geronimo, about Cochise and Victorio and Lozen—anything I could find. Some were mindless, some boring, others full of mystery and power. Abruptly the cowboy movies I'd always loved took on a different hue. They were full of lies. Those gunfights weren't cool, heroic frays—they were slaughters.

Growing up with my mother—back in Vermont, New York, New Jersey—the West held its grip on my imagination. I'd forage libraries for books on

227

Geronimo as if maybe I could find my dad and me camping in one of them, as if maybe the answer to why the world was so full of treachery might be found somewhere in the Apache story.

Late in my youth and early in my acting career I made a movie in Alaska alongside Native American actors who helped me develop a less juvenile and romanticized view of their history. Eventually I ran across a few films that rang true—*Smoke Signals, Powwow Highway*—and I discovered Sherman Alexie's *The Lone Ranger and Tonto Fistfight in Heaven*, but authentic Native American perspectives were mostly absent from the dominant historical narrative of the Old West.

Years later, by a twist of fate, or because history is prone to repeat itself, I found myself on a canoe trip out west, attempting to recover from my own failed marriage. It was then that I became friends with my guide, the prodigious writer Charles Gaines. He too had a passion for Native American history, and he introduced me to David Roberts's *Once They Moved Like the Wind*, a beautifully crafted account of the Apache Wars. Inspired by the book, we set about writing a film—and my education began in earnest.

Soon I was the divorced dad taking my own kids camping in New Mexico and Arizona. As I researched for our script I was shocked at how much of this pivotal piece of American history remains unknown even to the people who live there. The horrors of genocide sit differently in the mind when you're no longer in the backseat playing with *Star Trek* figures—when it's your turn to drive the car. The more I read about the history of this country and its original human inhabitants, the more I yearned to make the film. The Apache Wars are a vital part of our American history that needs to be told in a way that honestly appreciates and integrates, rather than appropriates, Native American history. The story needs to be told again and again until the names of Geronimo and Cochise are as familiar to young American ears as Washington and Lincoln. I knew that it was not really my story to tell, but my heart felt compelled to tell it.

Geronimo made the perfect protagonist for an epic tale. He was complex—part villain, part victor—a real Shakespearean hero. The script, however, with all Native American leads, was a difficult sell in the star-driven Hollywood marketplace. It would also be extremely costly to shoot. After a few years without any progress in getting the film made, an idea occurred to me one afternoon as my son and I wandered the aisles of Forbidden Planet in New York City: this story might be served better by another medium.

I asked renowned graphic novelist Greg Ruth to read the script. I had been moved by his art, by its powerfully emotional qualities. He liked the script but made it clear that if I was looking for someone to simply storyboard my film script, I had picked the wrong guy—he had too much respect for the form and possibilities of the graphic novel. But if I wanted to dig in and work hard to use this material to build something unique to the medium, he would dig in with me. The writing, poetry, passion, and research of Charles Gaines are also woven throughout the work you hold in your hands now, and Greg and I are both indebted to him.

It has taken a long time for the two of us to complete this project—one of the most mysterious, surprising, and soul-enriching endeavors of my life. I have come across a handful of radical and brilliant artistic minds in my thirty-plus years of acting but no one shines brighter than Greg Ruth. I have learned much about storytelling from him. For the last several years, every few weeks Greg would send me a handful of images and we would write, rewrite, and write again. We have worked on it backstage at my plays, in his studio in Massachusetts, over the phone as we picked up our kids from school, in Albuquerque, and even at the scene of one of the crimes—the original El Rancho Motel, where the cast and crew of the old-time Westerns stayed while they were making their Hollywood fables.

The little boy who scoured roadside souvenir shops so many years ago wanted to know the whole story, and I hope through this book young people like my own son and daughters will gain a deeper understanding of the Apache Wars. It's an important strand in the fabric of our American history.

> In the last analysis, we must all, Indian and non-Indian, come together. This earth is our mother, this land is our shared heritage. Our histories and fates are intertwined, no matter where our ancestors were born and how they interacted with each other.
> —*Kent Nerburn, Neither Wolf nor Dog*

Ethan Hawke
September 2015

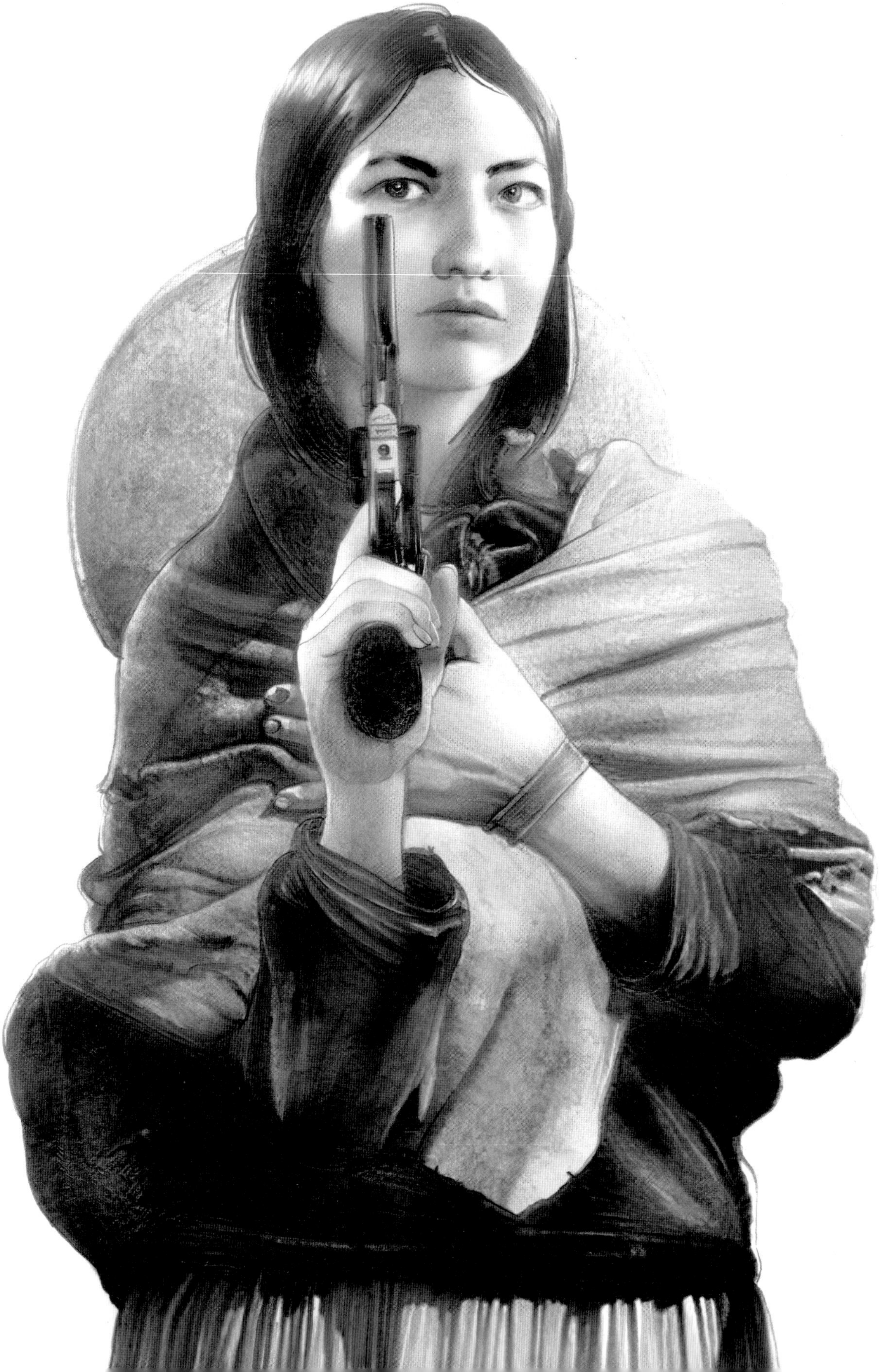

FURTHER READING

Ball, Eve. *In the Days of Victorio*. Tucson: The University of Arizona Press, 2008.

—. *Indeh: An Apache Odyssey*. Norman: University of Oklahoma Press, 1988.

Barrett, S. M. *Geronimo's Story of His Life*. Williamstown: Corner House Publishers, 1989.

Betzinez, Jason. *I Fought with Geronimo*. New York: Bonanza Books, 1959.

Bourke, John G. *An Apache Campaign in the Sierra Madre*. Lincoln: University of Nebraska Press, 1987.

Cremony, John C. *Life Among the Apaches*. Lincoln: University of Nebraska Press, 1983.

Debo, Angie. *Geronimo: The Man, His Time, His Place*. Norman: University of Oklahoma Press, 1976.

Gulbrandsen, Don. *Edward S. Curtis: Visions of the First Americans*, Edison: Chartwell Books, 2006.

Howard, Oliver Otis. *Autobiography of Oliver Otis Howard, Major General, United States Army*. Lexington: Bibliolife, 2010.

Jackson, Clarence S. *William Henry Jackson: Picture Maker of the Old West*, New York: Charles Scribner's Sons, 1947.

Machula, Paul R. *Tale of the Apache Kid*. Globe: 2006.

Marquis, Arnold. *A Guide to America's Indians: Ceremonials, Reservations, and Museums*. Norman: University of Oklahoma Press, 1975.

Miles, Dale Curtis, and Paul R. Machula. *History of the San Carlos Apache*. San Carlos: San Carlos Apache Historic and Cultural Preservation Office, 1997.

Moody, Ralph. *Geronimo: Wolf of the Warpath*. New York: Sterling Publishing Co., 2006.

Nerburn, Kent. *Neither Wolf nor Dog: On Forgotten Roads with an Indian Elder*. Novato: New World Library, 2002.

Opler, Morris Edward. *Myths and Tales of the Chiricahua Apache Indians*. Lincoln: University of Nebraska Press, 1994.

Roberts, David. *Once They Moved Like the Wind: Cochise, Geronimo, and the Apache Wars*. New York: Simon and Schuster, 1994.

Rowe, Jeremy. *Photographers in Arizona 1850–1920: A History and Directory*. Nevada City: Carl Mautz Publishing, 1997.

Scherer, Joanna Cohan. *Indians: The Great Photographs That Reveal North American Indian Life, 1847–1929, From the Unique Collection of the Smithsonian Institution*. New York: Bonanza Books, 1973.

Soens, A.L., ed. *I, the Song: Classical Poetry of Native North America*. Salt Lake City: The University of Utah Press, 1999.

Sonnichsen, C. L. *Geronimo and the End of the Apache Wars*. Lincoln: University of Nebraska Press, 1990.

Sweeney, Edwin R. *From Cochise to Geronimo: The Chiricahua Apaches 1974–1886*. Norman: University of Oklahoma Press, 2012.

Utley, Robert M. *A Clash of Cultures: Fort Bowie and the Chiricahua Apaches*. D.C.: National Park Service Division of Publications, 1977.

—. *Geronimo*. New Haven: Yale University Press, 2012.

Worcester, Donald E. *The Apaches: Eagles of the Southwest*. Norman: University of Oklahoma Press, 1979.

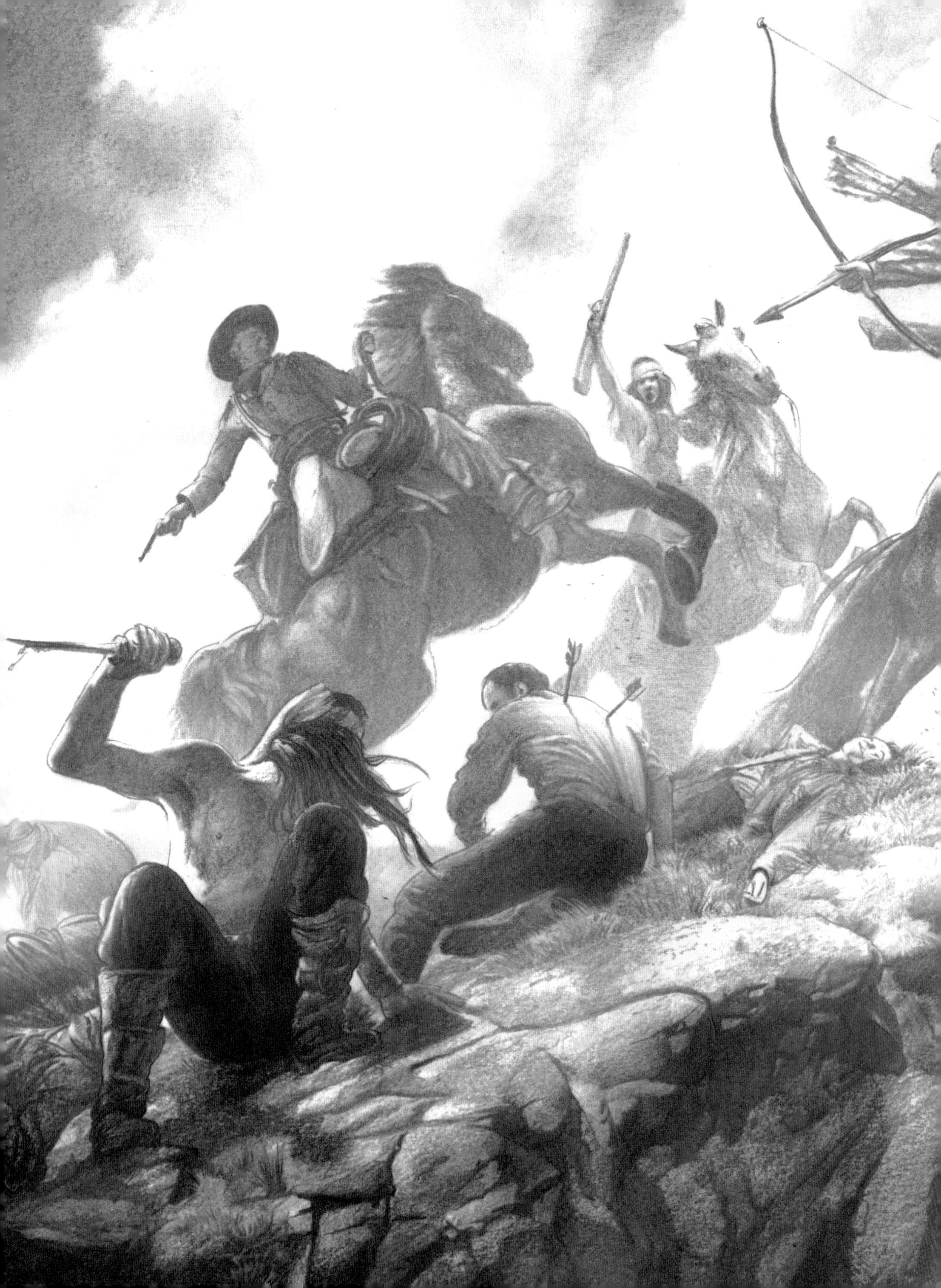